"ONE OF THE BEST BOOKS I'VE EVER READ . . .

Expertise, pace, compassion, terrific writing, a beautifully intricate plot and a hero to applaud."
—Carol Brener, Murder Ink

"A stylish thriller that is as complex as it is timely. . . . Kellerman writes with the decisive style of an expert but also with a gritty intensity, sensitivity, and even humor."
—*Richmond Times-Dispatch*

"SUSPENSEFUL, NEATLY SPUN, FASCINATING. . . . One helluva good, spooky book."
—*Philadelphia Daily News*

"A slick and polished cop drama with haunting credibility. . . . Sparkling characterizations and plenty of suspense."
—*Library Journal*

"A potent, suspenseful novel of violence, victimization and detection. . . . I hated to see it come to an end."
—*Wichita Eagle-Beacon*

"AN ENGROSSING THRILLER...This knockout of an entertainment is the kind of book which establishes a career in one stroke."
—NEWSDAY

"GRAB YOURSELF A COPY SOON!"
—LOS ANGELES TIMES

WHEN THE BOUGH BREAKS

Jonathan Kellerman

A SIGNET BOOK

NEW AMERICAN LIBRARY

To Faye, Jesse and Rachel

NAL BOOKS ARE AVAILABLE AT QUANTITY DISCOUNTS WHEN USED TO PROMOTE PRODUCTS OR SERVICES. FOR INFORMATION PLEASE WRITE TO PREMIUM MARKETING DIVISION, NEW AMERICAN LIBRARY, 1633 BROADWAY, NEW YORK, NEW YORK 10019.

Copyright © 1985 by Jonathan Kellerman

All rights reserved. For information address Atheneum Publishers, Inc., 115 Fifth Avenue, New York, New York 10003.

This is an authorized reprint of a hardcover edition published by Atheneum Publishers, Inc. The hardcover edition was published simultaneously in Canada by McClelland and Stewart Ltd.

SIGNET TRADEMARK REG. U.S. PAT. OFF. AND FOREIGN COUNTRIES
REGISTERED TRADEMARK—MARCA REGISTRADA
HECHO EN CHICAGO, U.S.A.

SIGNET, SIGNET CLASSIC, MENTOR, ONYX, PLUME, MERIDIAN and NAL BOOKS are published by NAL PENGUIN INC., 1633 Broadway, New York, New York 10019

First Signet Printing, May, 1986

9   10   11   12   13   14   15   16

PRINTED IN THE UNITED STATES OF AMERICA

1

It was shaping up as a beautiful morning. The last thing I wanted to hear about was murder.

A cool Pacific current had swept its way across the coastline for two days running, propelling the pollution to Pasadena. My house is nestled in the foothills just north of Bel Air, situated atop an old bridle path that snakes its way around Beverly Glen, where opulence gives way to self-conscious funk. It's a neighborhood of Porsches and coyotes, bad sewers and sequestered streams.

The place itself is eighteen hundred square feet of silvered redwood, weathered shingles and tinted glass. In the suburbs it might be a shack; up here in the hills it's a rural retreat—nothing fancy, but lots of terraces, decks, pleasing angles and visual surprises. The house had been designed by and for a Hungarian artist who went broke trying to peddle oversized polychromatic triangles to the galleries on La Cienega. Art's loss had been my gain by way of L.A. probate court. On a good day—like today—the place came with an ocean view, a cerulean patch that peeked timidly above the Palisades.

I had slept alone with the windows open—burglars and neoMansonites be damned—and awoke at ten, naked, covers thrown to the floor in the midst of some forgotten dream. Feeling lazy and sated, I propped myself on my elbows, drew up the covers and stared at the caramel layers of sunlight streaming through French doors. What finally got me up was the invasion of a housefly who alternated between searching my sheets for carrion and dive-bombing my head.

I shuffled to the bathroom and began filling a tub, then

made my way to the kitchen to scavenge, taking the fly with me. I put up coffee, and the fly and I shared an onion bagel. Ten-twenty on a Monday morning with nowhere to go and nothing to do. Oh, blessed decadence.

It had been almost half a year since my premature retirement and I was still amazed at how easy it was to make the transition from compulsive overachiever to self-indulgent bum. Obviously I'd had it in me from the beginning.

I returned to the bathroom, sat on the rim of the tub munching and drew up a vague plan for the day: a leisurely soak, a cursory scan of the morning paper, perhaps a jog down the canyon and back, a shower, a visit to—

The doorbell jarred me out of my reverie.

I tied a towel around my waist and walked to the front entry in time to see Milo let himself in.

"It was unlocked," he said, closing the door hard and tossing the *Times* on the sofa. He stared at me and I drew the towel tighter.

"Good morning, nature boy."

I motioned him in.

"You really should lock the door, my friend. I've got files at the station that illustrate nicely what happens to people who don't."

"Good morning, Milo."

I padded into the kitchen and poured two cups of coffee. Milo followed me like a lumbering shadow, opened the refrigerator and took out a plate of cold pizza that I had no recollection of ever owning. He tailed me back to the living room, collapsed on my old leather sofa—an artifact of the abandoned office on Wilshire—balanced the plate on his thigh and stretched out his legs.

I turned off the bathwater and settled opposite him on a camelskin ottoman.

Milo is a big man—six-two, two-twenty—with a big man's way of going loose and dangly when he gets off his feet. This morning he looked like an oversized rag doll slumped against the cushions—a doll with a broad, pleasant face, almost boyish except for the acne pits that peppered the skin, and the tired eyes. The eyes were startlingly green and rimmed with red, topped by shaggy dark brows and a Kennedyesque shock of thick black hair. His nose was large and high-bridged, his lips full, childishly soft. Sideburns five years out of date trailed down the scarred cheeks.

As usual he wore ersatz Brooks Brothers: olive-green gabardine suit, yellow button-down, mint and gold rep stripe tie, oxblood wing tips. The total effect was as preppy as W. C. Fields in red skivvies.

He ignored me and concentrated on the pizza.

"So glad you could make it for breakfast."

When his plate was empty he asked, "So, how are you doing, pal?"

"I *was* doing great. What can I do for you, Milo?"

"Who says I want you to do anything?" He brushed crumbs from his lap to the rug. "Maybe this is a social call."

"You waltzing in, unannounced, with that bloodhound look all over your face isn't a social call."

"Such intuitive powers." He ran his hands over his face, as if washing without water. "I need a favor," he said.

"Take the car. I won't be needing it until late afternoon."

"No, it's not that this time. I need your professional services."

That gave me pause.

"You're out of my age range," I said. "Besides, I'm out of the profession."

"I'm not kidding, Alex. I've got one of your colleagues lying on a slab at the morgue. Fellow by the name of Morton Handler."

I knew the name, not the face.

"Handler's a psychiatrist."

"Psychiatrist, psychologist. Minor semantic distinction at this point. What he is, is dead. Throat slashed, a little bit of evisceration tossed in. Along with a lady friend— same treatment for her but worse—sexual mutilation, nose sliced off. The place where it happened—his place—was an abattoir."

Abattoir. Milo's master's degree in American Lit asserting itself.

I put down my coffee cup.

"Okay, Milo. I've lost my appetite. Now tell me what all of that has to do with me."

He went on as if he hadn't heard me.

"I got called on it at five A.M. I've been knee-deep in blood and crud since then. It stunk in there—people smell bad when they die. I'm not talking decay, this is the stench that sets in before decay. I thought I was used to it. Every so often I catch another whiff and it gets me right here." He poked himself in the belly. "Five in the morning. I left an irritated lover in bed. My head feels ready to implode. Gobs of flesh at five in the morning. Jesus."

He stood and looked out the window, gazing out over the tops of pines and eucalyptus. From where I sat I could see smoke rising in indolent swirls from a distant fireplace.

"It's really nice up here, Alex. Does it ever bore you, being in paradise with nothing to do?"

"Not a hint of ennui."

"Yeah. I guess not. You don't want to hear any more about Handler and the girl."

"Stop playing passive-aggressive, Milo, and spit it out."

He turned and looked down at me. The big, ugly face showed new signs of fatigue.

"I'm depressed, Alex." He held out his empty cup like some overgrown, slack-jawed Oliver Twist. "Which is why I'll tolerate more of this disgusting swill."

I took the cup and got him a refill. He gulped it audibly.

"We've got a possible witness. A kid who lives in the same building. She's pretty confused, not sure what she saw. I took one look at her and thought of you. You could talk to her, maybe try a little hypnosis to enhance her memory."

"Don't you have Behavioral Sciences for that?"

He reached into his coat pocket and took out a handful of Polaroids. "Look at these beauties."

I gave the pictures a second's glance. What I saw turned my stomach. I returned them quickly.

"For God's sake, don't show me stuff like that!"

"Some mess, huh? Blood and crud." He drained his cup, lifting it high to catch every last drop. "Behavioral Science is cut down to one guy who's kept busy weeding weirdos out of the department. Next priority is counseling the weirdos who slip through. If I put in an application for this kind of thing I'll get a request to fill out another application form. They don't want to do it. On top of that, they don't know anything about kids. You do."

"I don't know anything about homicide."

"Forget homicide. That's my problem. Talk to a seven-year-old."

I hesitated. He held out his hands. The palms were white, well-scrubbed.

"Hey, I'm not expecting a total freebie. I'll buy you lunch. There's a fair-to-middling Italian place with surprisingly good gnocchi not far from the . . ."

"Not far from the abattoir?" I grimaced. "No thanks. Anyway, I can't be bought for noodles."

"So what can I offer you by way of a bribe—you've got everything—the house in the hills, the fancy car, the Ralph Lauren gear with jogging shoes to match. Christ, you've got retirement at thirty-three and a goddamn perpetual tan. Just talking about it is getting me pissed."

"Yes, but am I happy?"

"I suspect so."

"You're right." I thought of the grisly photos. "And I'm certainly not in need of a free pass to the Grand Guignol."

"You know," he said, "I'll bet underneath all of that mellow is a bored young man."

"Crap."

"Crap nothing. How long has it been, six months?"

"Five and a half."

"Five and a half, then. When I met you—correct that, soon *after* I met you, you were a vibrant guy, high energy, lots of opinions. Your *mind* was working. Now all I hear about is hot tubs, how fast you run your goddamned mile, the different kinds of sunset you can see from your deck—to use your jargon, it's *regression*. Cutesy-poo short pants, roller-skating, water play. Like half the people in this city, you're functioning on a six-year-old level."

I laughed.

"And you're making me this offer—to get involved in blood and crud—as a form of occupational therapy."

"Alex, you can break your ass trying to achieve Nirvana Through Inertia, but it won't work. It's like that

Woody Allen line—you mellow too much, you ripen and rot.''

I slapped my bare chest.

"No signs of decay yet."

"It's internal, comes from within, breaks through when you're least expecting it."

"Thank you, Doctor Sturgis."

He gave me a disgusted look, went into the kitchen and returned with his mouth buried in a pear.

"S'good."

"You're welcome."

"All right, Alex, forget it. I've got this dead, psychiatrist and this Gutierrez girl hacked up. I've got a seven-year-old who thinks she might have seen or heard something except she's too damned scared to make any sense of it. I ask you for two hours of your time—and time is one thing you've got plenty of—and I get bullshit."

"Hold on. I didn't say I wouldn't do it. You have to give me time to assimilate this. I just woke up and you barge in and drop double homicide on me."

He shot his wrist out from under his shirt cuff and peered at his Timex. "Ten thirty-seven. Poor baby." He glared at me and chomped into the pear, getting juice on his chin.

"Anyway, you might recall that the last time I had anything to do with police business it was traumatic."

"Hickle was a fluke. And you were a victim—of sorts. I'm not interested in getting you involved in this. Just an hour or two talking to a little kid. Like I said, some hypnosis if it looks right. Then we eat gnocchi. I return to my place and try to reclaim my amour, you're free to go back to Spaceout Castle here. Finis. In a week we get together for a pure social time—a little sashimi down in Japtown. Okay?"

"What did the kid actually see?" I asked and watched my relaxing day fly out the window.

"Shadows, voices, two guys, maybe three. But who really knows? She's a little kid, she's totally traumatized. The mother's just as scared and she impresses me as a lady who was no nuclear physicist in the first place. I didn't know how to approach her, Alex. I tried to be nice, go easy. It would have been helpful to have a juvie officer there, but there aren't too many of those any more. The department would rather keep three dozen pencil-pushing deputy chiefs around."

He gnawed the pear down to the core.

"Shadows, voices. That's it. You're the *language specialist*, right? You know how to communicate with the little ones. If you can get her to open up, great. If she comes forth with anything resembling an I.D., fantastic. If not, them's the breaks and at least we tried."

Language specialist. It had been a while since I'd used the phrase—back in the aftermath of the Hickle affair, when I'd found myself suddenly spinning out of control, the faces of Stuart Hickle and all the kids he'd harmed marching through my head. Milo had taken me drinking. At about two in the morning he had wondered out loud why the kids had let it go on for so long.

"They didn't talk because nobody knew how to listen," I'd said. "They thought it was their fault, anyway."

"Yeah?" He looked up, bleary-eyed, gripping his stein with both hands. "I hear stuff like that from the juvie gals."

"That's the way they think when they're little, egocentric. Like they're the center of the world. Mommy slips, breaks a leg, they blame themselves."

"How long does it last?"

"In some people it never goes away. For the rest of us it's a gradual process. By eight or nine we see things more clearly—but at any age an adult can manipulate kids, convince them it's their fault."

"Assholes," muttered Milo. "So how do you get their heads straight?"

"You have to know how kids think at different ages. Developmental stages. You talk their language—you become a language specialist."

"That's what you do?"

"That's what I do."

A few minutes later he asked: "You think guilt is bad?"

"Not necessarily. It's part of what holds us together. Too much, though, can cripple."

He nodded. "Yeah, I like that. Shrinks always seem to

be saying guilt is a no-no. Your approach I can buy. I tell you, we could use a lot more guilt—the world's full of fucked-up savages."

At that moment he got no argument from me.

We talked a bit more. The alcohol tugged at our consciousness and we started to laugh, then cry. The bartender stopped polishing his glasses and stared.

It had been a low—a seriously low—period in my life and I remembered who'd been there to help me through it.

I watched Milo nibble at the last specks of pear with curiously small, sharp teeth.

"Two hours?" I asked.

"At the most."

"Give me an hour or so to get ready, clear up some business."

Having convinced me to help him didn't seem to cheer him up. He nodded and exhaled wearily.

"All right. I'll give a run down to the station and do my business." Another consultation of the Timex. "Noon?"

"Fine."

He walked to the door, opened it, stepped out on the balcony and tossed the pear core over the railing and into the greenery below. Starting down the stairs he stopped mid-landing and looked up at me. The sun's glare hit his ravaged face and turned it into a pale mask. For a moment I was afraid he was going to get sentimental.

I needn't have worried.

"Listen, Alex, as long as you're staying here can I borrow the Caddy? That," he pointed accusingly at the ancient Fiat, "is giving out. Now it's the starter."

"Bull, you just love my car." I went into the house, got the spare keys and threw them at him.

He fielded them like Dusty Baker, unlocked the Seville and squirmed in, adjusting the seat to accommodate his long legs. The engine started immediately, purring with vigor. Looking like a sixteen-year-old going to his first prom in Daddy's wheels, he cruised down the hill.

2

MY LIFE had been frantic ever since adolescence. A straight-A student, I started college at sixteen, worked my way through school free-lancing as a guitarist, and churned through the doctoral program in clinical psychology at UCLA, earning a Ph.D. at twenty-four. I accepted an internship up north at the Langley Porter Institute, then returned to L.A. to complete a postdoctoral fellowship at Western Pediatric Medical Center. Once out of training I took a staff position at the hospital and a simultaneous professorship at the medical school affiliated with Western Peds. I saw lots of patients and published lots of papers.

By twenty-eight I was an associate professor of pediatrics and psychology and director of a support program for medically ill youngsters. I had a title too long for my secretaries to memorize and I kept publishing, constructing a paper tower within which I dwelled: case studies, controlled experiments, surveys, monographs, textbook chapters and an esoteric volume of my own on the psychological effects of chronic disease in children.

The status was great, the pay less so. I began to moonlight, seeing private patients in an office rented from a Beverly Hills analyst. My patient load increased until I was putting in seventy hours a week and running between hospital and office like a deranged worker ant.

I entered the world of tax avoidance after discovering that without write-offs and shelters I'd be paying out to the IRS more than I used to consider a healthy yearly income. I hired and fired accountants, bought California real estate before the boom, sold at scandalous profits, bought more. I became an apartment-house manager—another five to ten hours a week. I supported a battalion of service personnel—gardeners, plumbers, painters and electricians. I received lots of calendars at Christmas.

By the age of thirty-two, I had a non-stop regimen of working to the point of exhaustion, grabbing a few hours of fitful sleep and getting up to work some more. I grew a beard to save five minutes shaving time in the morning. When I remembered to eat, the food came out of hospital vending machines and I stuffed my mouth while zipping down the corridors, white coat flapping, notepad in hand, like some impassioned speed freak. I was a man with a mission, albeit a mindless one.

I was successful.

There was little time for romance in such a life. I engaged in occasional carnal liaisons, frenzied and meaningless, with nurses, female interns, graduate students and social workers. Not to forget the fortyish, leggy blond secretary—not my type at all had I taken the time to think—who captivated me for twenty minutes of thrashing behind the chart-stuffed shelves of the medical records room.

By day it was committee meetings, paperwork, trying to quell petty staff bickering and more paperwork. By night it was facing the tide of parental complaints that the child therapist grows accustomed to, and providing comfort and support to the young ones caught in the crossfire.

In my spare time I received tenants' gripes, scanned the *Wall Street Journal* to measure my gains and losses, and sorted through mountains of mail, most of it, it seemed, from white-collared, white-toothed smoothies who had ways of making me instantly rich. I was nominated as an Outstanding Young Man by an outfit hoping to sell me their hundred-dollar, leather-bound directory of similarly-honored individuals. In the middle of the day, there were times, suddenly, when I found it hard to breathe, but I brushed it off, too busy for introspection.

Into this maelstrom stepped Stuart Hickle.

Hickle was a quiet man, a retired lab technician. He looked the part of the kindly neighbor on a situation comedy—tall, stooped, fiftyish, fond of cardigans and old briar pipes. His tortoise-shell horn-rims perched atop a thin, pinched nose shielding kindly eyes the color of dish-water. He had a benign smile and avuncular mannerisms.

He also had an unhealthy appetite for fondling little children's privates.

When the police finally got him, they confiscated over five hundred color photographs of Hickle having his way with scores of two-, three-, four- and five-year-olds—boys and girls, white, black, Hispanic. In matters of gender and race he wasn't picky. Only age and helplessness concerned him.

When I saw the photos it wasn't the graphic starkness that got to me, though that was repulsive in its own right. It was the look in the kids' eyes—a terrified yet knowing vulnerability. It was a look that said *I know this is wrong. Why is this happening to me?* The look was in every snapshot, on the face of the youngest victim.

It personified violation.

It gave me nightmares.

Hickle had unique access to little children. His wife, a Korean orphan whom he'd met as a GI in Seoul, ran a successful day-care center in affluent Brentwood.

Kim's Korner had a solid reputation as one of the best places to leave your children when you had to work or play or just be alone. It had been in business for a decade when the scandal broke, and despite the evidence there were plenty of people who refused to believe that the school had served as a haven for one man's pedophilic rituals.

The school had been a cheerful-looking place, occupying a large, two-story house on a quiet residential street not far from UCLA. In its last year, it had cared for over forty children, most of them from affluent families. A large proportion of Kim Hickle's charges had been very young because she was one of the few day-care operators to accept children not yet toilet-trained.

The house had a basement—a rarity in earthquake country—and the police spent a considerable amount of time in that damp, cavernous room. They found an old army cot, a refrigerator, a rusty sink and five thousand dollars' worth of photographic equipment. Particular scrutiny was given to the cot, for it served up a host of fascinating forensic details—hair, blood, sweat and semen.

The media latched on to the Hickle case with predictable vigor. This was a juicy one that played on everyone's primal fears, evoking memories of the Cosmic Bogeyman. The evening news featured Kim Hickle fleeing a mob of reporters, hands over face. She protested her ignorance. There was no evidence of her complicity so they closed the school down, took away her license and left it at that. She filed for divorce and departed for parts unknown.

I had my doubts about her innocence. I'd seen enough of these cases to know that the wives of child molesters often played a role, explicit or covert, in setting up the dirty deed. Usually these were women who found sex and physical intimacy abhorrent, and in order to get out of conjugal chores, they helped find substitute partners for their men. It could be a cold, cruel parody of a harem joke—I'd seen one case where the father had been bedding three of his daughters on a scheduled basis, with mom drawing up the schedule.

It was also hard to believe that Kim Hickle had been playing Legos with the kids while downstairs Stuart was molesting them. Nevertheless, they let her go.

Hickle himself was thrown to the wolves. The TV cameras didn't miss a shot. There were lots of instant minispecials, filled with interviews with the more vocal of my colleagues, and several editorials about the rights of children.

The hoopla lasted two weeks, then the story lost its appeal and was replaced by reports of other atrocities. For there was no lack of nasty stories in L.A. The city spawned ugliness like a predatory insect spewing out blood-hungry larvae.

I was consulted on the case three weeks after the arrest. It was a back-page story now and someone got to thinking about the victims.

The victims were going through hell.

The children woke up screaming in the middle of the night. Toddlers who'd been toilet-trained started to wet and soil themselves. Formerly quiet, well-behaved kids began to hit, kick and bite without provocation. There were lots of stomach aches and ambiguous physical symptoms reported, as well as the classic signs of depression—

loss of appetite, listlessness, withdrawal, feelings of worthlessness.

The parents were racked with guilt and shame, seeing or imagining the accusing glances of family and friends. Husbands and wives turned on each other. Some of them spoiled the victimized children, increasing the youngsters' insecurity and infuriating the siblings. Later, several brothers and sisters were able to admit that they'd wished they'd been molested in order to be eligible for special treatment. Then they'd felt guilty about those thoughts.

Entire families were coming apart, much of their suffering obscured by the public blood lust for Hickle's head. The families might have been permanently shunted to obscurity, saddled with their confusion, guilt and fear but for the fact that the great aunt of one of the victims was a philanthropic member of the board of Western Pediatric Medical Center. She wondered out loud why the hell the hospital wasn't doing anything, and where was the institution's sense of public service, anyway. The chairman of the board salaamed and simultaneously saw the chance to grab some good press. The last story about Western Peds had exposed salmonella in the cafeteria's cole slaw, so positive P.R. was mighty welcome.

The medical director issued a press release announcing a psychological rehabilitation program for the victims of Stuart Hickle, with me as therapist. My first inkling of being appointed was reading about it in the *Times*.

When I got to his office the next morning I was ushered in immediately. The director, a pediatric surgeon who hadn't operated in twenty years and had acquired the smugness of a well-fed bureaucrat, sat behind a gleaming desk the size of a hockey field and smiled.

"What's going on, Henry?" I held up the newspaper.

"Sit down, Alex. I was just about to call you. The board decided you'd be perfect—pluperfect—for the job. Some urgency was called for."

"I'm flattered."

"The board remembered the beautiful work you did with the Brownings."

"Brownells."

"Yes, whatever."

The five Brownell youngsters had survived a light plane

crash in the Sierras that had killed their parents. They'd been physically and psychologically traumatized—over-exposed, half-starved, amnesiac, mute. I'd worked with them for two months and the papers had picked up on it.

"You know, Alex," the director was saying, "sometimes in the midst of trying to synthesize the high technology and heroics that comprise so much of modern medicine, one loses sight of the human factor."

It was a great little speech. I hoped he'd remember it when budget time rolled around next year.

He went on stroking me, talking about the need for the hospital to be in the "forefront of humanitarian endeavors," then smiled and leaned forward.

"Also, I imagine there'd be significant research potential in all of this—at least two or three publications by June."

June was when I came up for full professorship. The director was on the tenure committee at the medical school.

"Henry, I believe you're appealing to my baser instincts."

"Perish the thought." He winkled slyly. "Our main interest is helping those poor, poor children." He shook his head. "A truly repugnant affair. The man should be castrated."

A surgeon's justice.

I threw myself, with customary monomania, into designing the treatment program. I received permission to run the therapy sessions in my private office after promising that Western Peds would get all the credit.

My goals were to help the families express the feelings that had been locked inside since Hickle's subterranean rites had been exposed, and to help them share those feelings with each other in order to see that they weren't alone. The therapy was designed as an intensive, six-week program, using groups—the kids, parents, siblings and multiple families—as well as individual sessions as needed. Eighty percent of the families signed up and no one dropped out. We met at night in my suite on Wilshire, when the building was quiet and empty.

There were nights when I left the sessions physically and emotionally drained after hearing the anguish pour out like blood from a gaping wound. Don't let anyone ever tell you different: Psychotherapy is one of the most taxing endeavors known to mankind. I've done all sorts of work, from picking carrots in the scorching sun to sitting on national committees in paneled boardrooms, and there's nothing that compares to confronting human misery, hour after hour, and bearing the responsibility for easing that misery using only one's mind and mouth. At its best it's tremendously uplifting, as you watch the patient open up, breathe, let go of the pain. At its worst it's like surfing in a cesspool, struggling for balance while being slapped with wave after putrid wave.

The treatment worked. Sparkle returned to the kids' eyes. The families reached out and helped each other. Gradually, my role diminished to that of silent observer.

A few days before the last session I received a call from a reporter for *National Medical News*—a throwaway for physicians. His name was Bill Roberts, he was in town and wanted to interview me. The piece would be for practicing pediatricians, to alert them to the issue of child molestation. It sounded like a worthy project and I agreed to meet him.

It was seven-thirty in the evening when I nosed my car out of the hospital parking lot and headed westward. Traffic was light and I reached the black-granite-and-glass tower that housed my office by eight. I parked in the subterranean garage, walked through double glass doors into a lobby that was silent save for Muzak and rode the elevator to the sixth floor. The doors slid open, I made my way down the corridor, turned a corner and stopped.

There was nobody waiting for me, which was unusual because I'd always found reporters to be punctual.

I approached my office door and saw a stiletto of light slashed diagonally across the floor. The door was ajar, perhaps an inch. I wondered if the night cleaning crew had let Roberts in. If so I'd have a talk with the building manager over that breach of security.

When I reached the door I knew something was wrong. There were scratch marks around the knob, metal filings in the rug. Yet, as if working from a script, I entered.

"Mr. Roberts?"

The waiting room was empty. I went into the consultation office. The man on my sofa wasn't Bill Roberts. I'd never met him but I knew him very well.

Stuart Hickle slumped in the soft cotton cushions. His head—what was left of it—was propped against the wall, the eyes staring vacantly at the ceiling. His legs splayed out spastically. One hand rested near a wet spot on his groin. He had an erection. The veins in his neck stood out in bas relief. His other hand lay limply across his chest. One finger hooked around the trigger of an ugly little blue steel pistol. The gun dangled, butt downward, the muzzle an inch from Hickle's open mouth. There were bits of brain, blood and bone on the wall behind the head. A crimson splotch decorated the soft-green print of the wallpaper like a child's fingerpainting. More crimson ran out of the nose, the ears and the mouth. The room smelled of firecrackers and human waste.

I dialed the phone.

The coroner's verdict was death by suicide. The final version went something like this: Hickle had been profoundly depressed since his arrest and, unable to bear the public humiliation of a trial, he'd taken the Samurai way out. It was he, as Bill Roberts, who'd set up the appointment with me, he who'd picked the lock and blown his brains out. When the police played me tapes of his confession the voice did sound similar to that of ''Roberts''—at least similar enough to prevent my saying it wasn't a match.

As for why he'd chosen my office for his swan song, the supporting cast of shrinks had an easy answer: Because of my role as the victims' therapist, I was a symbolic father figure, undoing the damage he'd perpetrated. His death was an equally symbolic gesture of repentance.

Finis.

But even suicides—especially those connected with felonies—must be investigated, the loose ends tied up, and there began a buck-passing contest between the Beverly Hills Police Department and L.A.P.D. Beverly Hills acknowledged the suicide had taken place on their turf but claimed that it was an extension of the original crimes—which had occurred in West L.A. Division territory. Punt. West L.A. would have liked to kick it back but the case

was still in the papers and the last thing the department
wanted was a dereliction-of-duties story.

So West L.A. got stuck with it. Specifically, Homicide
Detective Milo Bernard Sturgis got stuck with it.

I didn't start to have problems until a week after finding
Hickle's body, a normal delay, because I was denying the
whole thing and was more than a little numb. Since, as a
psychologist, I was presumed able to handle such things,
no one thought to inquire after my welfare.

I held myself in check when facing the children and
their families, creating a façade that was calm, knowledge-
able and accepting. I looked *in control.* In therapy we
talked about Hickle's death, with an emphasis upon *them,*
upon how *they* were coping.

The last session was a party during which the families
thanked me, hugged me and gave me a framed print of
Braggs' *The Psychologist.* It was a good party, lots of
laughter and mess on the carpet, as they rejoiced at getting
better, and, in part, at the death of their tormentor.

I got home close to midnight and crawled between the
covers feeling hollow, cold and helpless, like an orphaned
child on an empty road. The next morning the symptoms
began.

I grew fidgety and had trouble concentrating. The epi-
sodes of labored breathing increased and intensified. I
became unaccountably anxious, had a constantly queasy
feeling in my gut, and suffered from premonitions of
death.

Patients began asking me if I was all right. At that point
I must have been noticeably troubled because it takes a lot
to shift a patient's focus away from himself.

I had enough education to know what was going on but
not enough insight to make sense of it.

It wasn't finding the body, for I was used to shocking
events, but the discovery of Hickle's corpse was a catalyst
that plunged me into a full-fledged crisis. Looking back
now I can see that treating his victims had allowed me to
step off the treadmill for six weeks, and that the end of
treatment had left me with time to engage in the dangerous
pastime of self-evaluation. I didn't like what I learned.

I was alone, isolated, without a single real friend in the

world. For almost a decade the only humans I'd related to had been patients, and patients by definition were takers, not givers.

The feelings of loneliness grew painful. I turned further inward and became profoundly depressed. I called in sick to the hospital, canceled my private patients and spent days in bed watching soap operas.

The sound and lights of the TV washed over me like some vile paralytic drug, deadening but not healing.

I ate little and slept too much, felt heavy, weak and useless. I kept the phone off the hook and never left the house except to shove the junk mail inside the door and retreat to solitude.

On the eighth day of this funereal existence Milo appeared at the door wanting to ask me questions. He held a notepad in his hands, just like an analyst. Only he didn't look like an analyst: a big, droopy, shaggy-haired fellow in slept-in clothes.

"Dr. Alex Delaware?" He held up his badge.

"Yes."

He introduced himself and stared at me. I was dressed in a ratty yellow bathrobe. My untrimmed beard had reached rabbinic proportions and my hair looked like electrified Brillo. Despite thirteen hours of sleep I looked and felt drowsy.

"I hope I'm not disturbing you, Doctor. Your office referred me to your home number, which was out of order."

I let him in and he sat down, scanning the place. Foot-high stacks of unopened mail littered the dining-room table. The house was dark, drapes drawn, and smelled stale. "Days of Our Lives" flickered on the tube.

He rested his notepad on one knee and told me the interview was a formality for the coroner's inquest. Then he had me rehash the night I'd found the body, interrupting to clarify a point, scratching and jotting and staring. It was tediously procedural and my mind wandered often, so that he had to repeat his questions. Sometimes I talked so softly he asked me to repeat my answers.

After twenty minutes he asked:

"Doctor, are you all right?"

"I'm fine." Unconvincingly.

"Oka-ay." He shook his head, asked a few more questions, then put his pencil down and laughed nervously.

"You know I feel kind of funny asking a doctor how he feels."

"Don't worry about it."

He resumed questioning me and, even through the haze, I could see he had a curious technique. He'd skip from topic to topic with no apparent line of inquiry. It threw me off balance and made me more alert.

"You're an assistant professor at the medical school?"

"Associate."

"Pretty young to be an associate professor, aren't you."

"I'm thirty-two. I started young."

"Uh-huh. How many kids in the treatment program?"

"About thirty."

"Parents?"

"Maybe ten, eleven couples, half a dozen single parents."

"Any talk about Mr. Hickle in treatment?"

"That's confidential."

"Of course, sir."

"You ran the treatment as part of your job at—" he consulted his notes—"Western Pediatric Hospital."

"It was volunteer work associated with the hospital."

"You didn't get paid for it?"

"I continued to receive my salary and the hospital relieved me of other duties."

"There were fathers in the treatment groups, too."

"Yes." I thought I'd mentioned couples.

"Some of those guys were pretty mad at Mr. Hickle, I guess."

Mr. Hickle. Only a policeman could be so artificially polite as to call a dead pervert *sir*. Between themselves they used other terms, I supposed. Insufferable etiquette was a way of keeping the barrier between cop and civilian.

"That's confidential, Detective."

He grinned as if to say *Can't blame a fella for trying*, and scribbled in his notepad.

"Why so many questions about a suicide?"

"Just routine." He answered automatically without looking up. "I like to be thorough."

He stared at me absently, then asked:

"Did you have any help running the groups?"

"I encouraged the families to participate—to help themselves. I was the only professional."

"Peer counseling?"

"Exactly."

"We've got it in the department now." Noncommittal. "So they kind of took over."

"Gradually. I was always there."

"Did any of them have a key to your office?"

Aha.

"Absolutely not. You're thinking one of those people killed Hickle and faked it to look like suicide?" Of course he was. The same suspicion had occurred to me.

"I'm not drawing conclusions. Just investigating." This guy was elusive enough to *be* an analyst.

"I see."

Abruptly he stood, closed his pad and put his pencil away.

I rose to walk him to the door, teetered and blacked out.

The first thing I saw when things came back into focus was his big ugly face looming over me. I felt damp and cold. He was holding a washcloth that dripped water on to my face.

"You fainted. How do you feel?"

"Fine." The last thing I felt was *fine*.

"You don't look wonderful. Maybe I should call a doctor, Doctor."

"No."

"You sure?"

"No. It's nothing. I've had the flu for a few days. I just need to get something in my stomach."

He went into the kitchen and came back with a glass of orange juice. I sipped slowly and started to feel stronger.

I sat up and held the glass myself.

"Thank you," I said.

"To protect and serve."

"I'm really fine now. If you don't have any more questions . . ."

"No. Nothing more at this time." He got up and opened some windows; the light hurt my eyes. He turned off the TV.

"Want something to eat before I go?"

What a strange, motherly man.

"I'll be fine."

"Okay, Doctor. You take care now."

I was eager to see him go. But when the sound of his car engine was no longer audible I felt disoriented. Not depressed, like before, but agitated, restless, without peace. I tried watching "As the World Turns" but couldn't concentrate. Now the inane dialogue annoyed me. I picked up a book but the words wouldn't come into focus. I took a swallow of orange juice and it left a bad taste in my mouth and a stabbing pain in my throat.

I went out on the patio and looked up at the sky until luminescent discs danced in front of my eyes. My skin itched. Bird songs irritated me. I couldn't sit still.

It went on that way the entire afternoon. Miserable.

At four-thirty he called.

"Dr. Delaware? This is Milo Sturgis. Detective Sturgis."

"What can I do for you, Detective?"

"How are you feeling?"

"Much better, thank you."

"That's good."

There was silence.

"Uh, Doctor, I'm kind of on shaky ground here . . ."

"What's on your mind?"

"You know, I was in the Medical Corps in Viet Nam. We used to see a lot of something called acute stress reaction. I was wondering if . . ."

"You think that's what I've got?"

"Well . . ."

"What was the prescribed treatment in Viet Nam?"

"We got them back into action as quickly as possible. The more they avoided combat the worse they got."

"Do you think that's what I should do? Jump back into the swing of things?"

"I can't say, Doctor. I'm no psychologist."

"You'll diagnose but you won't treat."

"Okay, Doctor. Just wanted to see if—"

"No. Wait. I'm sorry. I appreciate your calling." I was confused, wondering what ulterior motive he could possibly have.

"Yeah, sure. No problem."

"Thanks, really. You'd make a hell of a shrink, Detective."

He laughed.

"That's sometimes part of the job, sir."

After he hung up I felt better than I'd felt in days. The next morning I called him at the West L.A. Division headquarters and offered to buy him a drink.

We met at Angela's, across from the West L.A. station on Santa Monica Boulevard. It was a coffee shop with a smoky cocktail lounge in the back populated by several groupings of large, solemn men. I noticed that few of them acknowledged Milo, which seemed unusual. I had always thought cops did a lot of backslapping and good-natured cussing after hours. These men took their drinking seriously. And quietly.

He had great potential as a therapist. He sipped Chivas, sat back, and let me talk. No more interrogation now. He listened and I spilled my guts.

By the end of the evening, though, he was talking too.

Over the next couple of weeks Milo and I found out that we had a lot in common. We were about the same age—he was ten months older—and had been born into working-class families in medium-sized towns. His father had been a steelworker, mine an electrical assembler. He too had been a good student, graduating with honors from Purdue and with an M.A. in literature from Indiana U., Bloomington. He'd planned to be a teacher when he was drafted. Two years in Viet Nam had somehow turned him into a policeman.

Not that he considered his job at odds with his intellectual pursuits. Homicide detectives, he informed me, were the intellectuals of any police department. Investigating murder requires little physical activity and lots of brainwork. Veteran homicide men sometimes violate regulations and don't carry a weapon. Just lots of pens and pencils. Milo packed his .38 but confessed that he really didn't need it.

"It's very white collar, Alex, with lots of paperwork, decision-making, attention to detail."

He liked being a cop, enjoyed catching bad guys. Sometimes he thought he might like to try something else, but exactly what that something else was, wasn't clear.

We had other interests in common. We'd both done some martial arts training. Milo had taken a mixed bag of self-defense courses while in the army. I'd learned fencing and karate while in graduate school. We were miserably out of shape but deluded ourselves that it would all come back if we needed it. Both of us appreciated good food, good music and the virtues of solitude.

The rapport between us developed quickly.

About three weeks after we'd known each other he told me he was homosexual. I was taken by surprise and had nothing to say.

"I'm telling you now because I don't want you to think I've been trying to put the make on you."

Suddenly I was ashamed, because that had been my initial thought, exactly.

It was hard to accept, at first, his being gay, despite all my supposed psychological sophistication. I know all the facts. That *they* make up 5 to 10 percent of virtually any human grouping. That most of *them* look just like me and you. That *they* could be anybody—the butcher, the baker, the local homicide dick. That most of *them* are reasonably well-adjusted.

And yet the stereotypes adhere to the brain. You expect them to be mincing, screaming, nelly fairies; leather-armored shaven-skull demons; oh-so-preppy mustachioed young things in Izod shirts and khaki trousers; or hiking-booted bulldykes.

Milo didn't look homosexual.

But he was and had been comfortable with it for several years. He wasn't in the closet, neither did he flaunt it.

I asked him if the department knew about it.

"Uh-huh. Not in the sense of filing an official report. It's just something that's known."

"How do they treat you?"

"Disapproval from a distance—cold looks. But basically it's live and let live. They're short-staffed and I'm good. What do they want? To drag in the ACLU and lose a good detective in the bargain? Ed Davis was a homophobe. He's gone and it's not so bad."

"What about the other detectives?"

He shrugged.

"They leave me alone. We talk business. We don't double-date."

Now the lack of recognition by the men at Angela's made sense.

Some of Milo's initial altruism, his reaching out to help me, was a little more understandable, too. He knew what it was like to be alone. A gay cop was a person in limbo. You could never be one of the gang back at the station, no matter how well you did your job. And the homosexual community was bound to be suspicious of someone who looked, acted like and *was* a cop.

"I figured I should tell you, since we seem to be getting friendly."

"It's no big deal, Milo."

"No?"

"No." I wasn't really all that comfortable with it. But I was damn well going to work on it.

A month after Stuart Hickle stuck a .22 in his mouth and blasted his brains all over my wallpaper, I made some major changes in my life.

I resigned my job at Western Pediatric and closed down my practice. I referred all my patients to a former student, a first rate therapist who was starting out in practice and needed the business. I had taken very few new referrals since starting the groups for the Kim's Korner families, so there was less separation anxiety than would normally be expected.

I sold an apartment building in Malibu, forty units that I'd purchased seven years before, for a large profit. I also let go of a duplex in Santa Monica. Part of the money—the portion that would eventually go to taxes—I put in a high-yield money market. The rest went into tax-free municipals. It wasn't the kind of investing that would make me richer, but it would provide financial stability. I figured I could live off the interest for two or three years as long as I didn't get too extravagant.

I sold my old Chevy Two and bought a Seville, a seventy-nine, the last year they looked good. It was forest-green with a saddle-colored leather interior that was cushy and quiet. With the amount of driving I'd be doing, the lousy mileage wouldn't make much difference. I threw away most of my old clothes and got new stuff—mostly soft fabrics—knits, cords, rubber-soled shoes, cashmere sweaters, robes, shorts, and pullovers.

I had the pipes cleaned out on the hot tub that I'd never used since I bought the house. I started to buy food and drink milk. I pulled my old Martin out of its case and strummed it on the balcony. I listened to records. I read for pleasure for the first time since high school. I got a tan. I shaved off my beard and discovered I had a face, and not a bad one at that.

I dated good women. I met Robin and things really started to get better.

Be-kind-to-Alex time. Early retirement six months before my thirty-third birthday.

It was fun while it lasted.

MORTON HANDLER'S last residence—if you didn't count the morgue—had been a luxury apartment complex off Sunset Boulevard in Pacific Palisades. It had been built into a hillside and designed to give a honeycomb effect: a loosely connected chain of individual units linked by corridors that had been placed at seemingly random locations, the apartments staggered to give each one a full view of the ocean. The motif was bastard Spanish: blindingly white textured stucco walls, red tile roofs, window accents of black wrought iron. Plantings of azalea and hibiscus filled in occasional patches of earth. There were lots of potted plants sunk in large terra-cotta containers: coconut palms, rubber plants, sun ferns, temporary-looking, as if someone planned on moving them all out in the middle of the night.

Handler's unit was on an intermediate level. The front door was sealed, with an L.A.P.D. sticker taped across it. Lots of footprints dirtied the terrazzo walkway near the entrance.

Milo led me across a terrace filled with polished stones and succulents to a unit cater-cornered from the murder scene. Adhesive letters spelling out the word MAN GER were affixed to the door. Bad jokes about Baby Jesus flashed through my mind.

Milo knocked.

I realized then that the place was amazingly silent. There must have been at least fifty units but there wasn't a soul in sight. No evidence of human habitation.

We waited a few minutes. He raised his fist to knock again just before the door opened.

"Sorry. I was washin' my hair."

The woman could have been anywhere from twenty-five to forty. She had pale skin with the kind of texture that looked as if a pinch would crumble it. Large brown eyes topped by plucked brows. Thin lips. A slight underbite. Her hair was wrapped in an orange towel and the little that peeked out was medium brown. She wore a faded cotton shirt of ochre-and-orange print over rust-colored stretch pants. Dark blue tennis shoes on her feet. Her eyes darted from Milo to me. She looked like someone who'd been knocked around plenty and refused to believe that it wasn't going to happen again at any moment.

"Mrs. Quinn? This is Dr. Alex Delaware. He's the psychologist I told you about."

"Please to meet you, Doctor."

Her hand was thin and cold and moist and she pulled away as quickly as she could.

"Melody's watchin' TV in her room. Out of school, with all that's been goin' on. I let her watch to keep her mind off it."

We followed her into the apartment.

Apartment was a charitable word. What it was, really, was a couple of oversized closets stuck together. An architect's postscript. Hey, Ed, we've got an extra four hundred square feet of corner in back of terrace number 142. Why don't we throw a roof over it, nail up some drywall and call it a manager's unit? Get some poor soul to do scutwork for the privilege of living in Pacific Palisades . . .

The living room was filled with one floral sofa, a masonite end table and a television. A framed painting of Mount Rainier that looked as if it came from a Savings and Loan calendar and a few yellowed photographs hung on the wall. The photos were of hardened, unhappy-looking people and appeared to date from the Gold Rush.

"My grandparents," she said.

A cubicle of a kitchen was visible and from it came the smell of frying bacon. A large bag of sour-cream-and-onion-flavored potato chips and a six pack of Dr Pepper sat on the counter.

"Very nice."

"They came here in 1902. From Oklahoma." She made it sound like an apology.

There was an unfinished wooden door and from behind

it came the sound of sudden laughter and applause, bells and buzzers. A game show.

"She's watchin' back there."

"That's just fine, Mrs. Quinn. We'll let her be until we're ready for her."

The woman nodded her head in assent.

"She don't get much chance to watch the daytime shows, bein' in school. So she's watchin' 'em now."

"May we sit down, ma'am?"

"Oh yes, yes." She flitted around the room like a mayfly, tugging at the towel on her head. She brought in an ashtray and set it down on the end table. Milo and I sat on the sofa and she dragged in a tubular aluminum-and-Naugahyde chair from the kitchen for herself. Despite the fact that she was thin her haunches settled and spread. She took out a pack of cigarettes, lit one up and sucked in the smoke until her cheeks hollowed. Milo spoke.

"How old is your daughter, Mrs. Quinn?"

"Bonita. Call me Bonita. Melody's the girl. She's just seven this past month." Talking about her daughter seemed to make her especially nervous. She inhaled greedily on her cigarette and blew little smoke out. Her free hand clenched and unclenched in rapid cadence.

"Melody may be our only witness to what happened here last night." Milo looked at me with a disgusted frown.

I knew what he was thinking. An apartment complex with seventy to one hundred residents and the only possible witness a child.

"I'm scared for her, Detective Sturgis, if someone else finds out." Bonita Quinn stared at the floor as if doing it long enough would reveal the mystic secret of the Orient.

"I assure you, Mrs. Quinn, that no one will find out. Dr. Delaware has served as a special consultant to the police many times." He lied shamelessly and glibly. "He understands the importance of keeping things secret. Besides—" he reached over to pat her shoulder reassuringly. I thought she'd go through the ceiling "—all psychologists demand confidentiality when working with their patients. Isn't that so, Dr. Delaware?"

"Absolutely." We wouldn't get into the whole muddy issue of children's rights to privacy.

Bonita Quinn made a strange, squeaking noise that was impossible to interpret. The closest thing to it that I could remember was the noise laboratory frogs used to make in Physiological Psych right before we pithed them by plunging a needle down into the tops of their skulls.

"What's all this hypnotism gonna do to her?"

I lapsed into my shrink's voice—the calm, soothing tones that had become so natural over the years that they switched on automatically. I explained to her that hypnosis wasn't magic, simply a combination of focused concentration and deep relaxation, that people tended to remember things more clearly when they were relaxed and that was why the police used it for witnesses. That children were better at going into hypnosis than were adults because they were less inhibited and enjoyed fantasy. That it didn't hurt, and was actually pleasant for most youngsters and that you couldn't get stuck in it or do anything against your will while hypnotized.

"All hypnosis," I ended, "is self-hypnosis. My role is simply to help your daughter do something that comes natural to her."

She probably understood about 10 percent of it, but it seemed to calm her down.

"You can say that again, natural. She daydreams all the time."

"Exactly. Hypnosis is like that."

"Teachers complain all the time, say she's driftin' off, not doing her work."

She was talking as if she expected me to do something about it.

Milo broke in.

"Has Melody told you anything more about what she saw, Mrs. Quinn?"

"No, no." An emphatic shake of the head. "We haven't been talkin' about it."

Milo pulled out his notepad and flipped through a few pages.

"What I have on record is that Melody couldn't sleep and was sitting in the living room—in this room at around one in the morning."

"Must've been. I go in by eleven-thirty and I got up once for a cigarette at twenty after twelve. She was asleep then and I didn't hear her for the while it took me to fall off. I'd 'a' heard her. We share the room.''

"Uh-huh. And she saw two men—here it says 'I saw big men.' The officer's question was 'How many, Melody?' And she answered, 'Two, maybe three.' When he asked her what did they look like, all she could say was that they were dark.'' He was talking to me now. ''We asked her black, Latino. Nothing. Only *dark*.''

"That could mean shadows. Could mean anything to a seven-year-old,'' I said.

"I know.''

"Which could mean two men, or one guy with a shadow, or—''

"Don't say it.''

Or nothing at all.

"She don't always tell the truth about everything.''

We both turned to look at Bonita Quinn who had used the few seconds we had ignored her to put out her cigarette and light a new one.

"I'm not sayin' she's a bad kid. But she don't always tell the truth. I don't know why you want to depend on her.''

I asked, "Do you have problems with her chronically lying—about things that don't make much sense—or does she do it to avoid getting in trouble?''

"The second. When she don't want me to paddle her and I know somethin's broken, it's got to be her. She tells me no, mama, not me. And I paddle her double.'' She looked to me for disapproval. ''For not tellin' the truth.''

"Do you have other problems with her?'' I asked gently.

"She's a good girl, Doctor. Only the daydreams, and the concentration problems.''

"Oh?'' I needed to understand this child if I was going to be able to do hypnosis with her.

"The concentratin'—it's hard for her.''

No wonder, in this tiny, television-saturated cell. No doubt the apartments were Adults Only and Melody Quinn was required to keep a low profile. There's a large segment of the population of Southern California that views the sight of anyone too young or too old as offensive. It's as if nobody wants to be reminded from whence they came or to where they will certainly go. That kind of denial, coupled with face lifts and hair transplants and makeup, creates a comfortable little delusion of immortality. For a short while.

I was willing to bet that Melody Quinn spent most of her time indoors despite the fact that the complex boasted three swimming pools and a totally equipped gym. Not to mention the ocean a half-mile away. Those playthings were meant for the grownups.

"I took her to the doctor when the teachers kept sendin' home these notes sayin' she can't sit still, her mind wanders. He said she was overactive. Somethin' in the brain."

"Hyperactive?"

"That's right. Wouldn't surprise me. Her dad wasn't altogether right up there." She tapped her forehead. "Used the illegal drugs and the wine until he—" she stopped cold, looking at Milo with sudden fear.

"Don't worry, Mrs. Quinn, we're not interested in that kind of thing. We only want to find out who killed Dr. Handler and Ms. Gutierrez."

"Yeah, the headshrinker—" she stopped again, this time staring at me. "Can't seem to say anythin' right, today." She forced a weak smile.

I nodded reassurance, smiled understandingly.

"He was a nice guy, that doctor." Some of my best friends are psychotherapists. "Used to joke with me a lot and I'd kid him, ask him if he had any shrunken heads in there." She laughed, a strange giggle, and showed a mouthful of teeth badly in need of repair. By now I had narrowed her age to middle thirties. In ten years she'd look truly elderly. "Terrible about what happened to him."

"And Ms. Gutierrez."

"Yeah, her too. Only her I wasn't so crazy about. She was Mexican, you know, but uppity Mexican. Where I come from they did the stoop labor and the cleanup. This one had the fancy dresses and the little sports car. And her a teacher, too." It wasn't easy for Bonita Quinn, brought up to think of all Mexicans as beasts of burden, to see that in the big city, away from the lettuce fields, some of them looked just like real people. While she did the donkey work.

"She was always carryin' herself like she was too good

for you. You'd say hello to her and she'd be lookin' off into the distance, like she had no time for you."

She took another drag on her cigarette and smiled slyly.

"This time I'm okay," she said.

We both looked at her.

"Neither of you gents is a Mex. I didn't put my foot in it again."

She was extremely pleased with herself and I took advantage of her lifted spirits to ask her a few more questions.

"Mrs. Quinn, is your daughter on any sort of medication for her hyperactivity?"

"Oh yeah, sure. The doc gave me pills to give her."

"Do you have the prescription slip handy?"

"I got the bottle." She got up and returned with an amber vial half full of tablets.

I took it and red the label. Ritalin. Methylphenidate hydrochloride. A super-amphetamine that speeds up adults but slows down kids, it's one of the most commonly prescribed drugs for American youngsters. Ritalin is addictive and potent and has a host of side effects, one of the most common of which is insomnia. Which might explain why Melody Quinn was sitting, staring out the window of a dark room at one in the morning.

Ritalin is a sweetheart drug when it comes to controlling children. It improves concentration and reduces the frequency of problem-behaviors in hyperactive kids—which sounds great, except that the symptoms of hyperactivity are hard to differentiate from those of anxiety, depression, acute stress reaction, or simple boredom at school. I've seen kids who were too bright for their classroom look hyper. Ditto for little ones going through the horrors of divorce or any other significant trauma.

A doctor who's doing his job correctly will require comprehensive psychological and social evaluation of a child before prescribing Ritalin or any other behavior-modifying drug. And there are plenty of good doctors. But some physicians take the easy way out, using the pills as the first step. If it's not malpractice it's dangerously close.

I opened the vial and shook some pills onto my palm. They were amber, the 20-milligram kind. I examined the label. One tablet three times daily. Sixty mg was the maximum recommended dosage. Strong stuff for a seven-year-old.

"You give her these three times a day?"

"Uh-huh. That's what it says, don't it?"

"Yes, it does. Did your doctor start off with something smaller—white or blue pills?"

"Oh yeah. We had her takin' three of the blue ones at first. Worked pretty good but I still got the complaints from the school, so he said it was okay to try these."

"And this dosage works well for Melody?"

"Works real fine for me. If it's gonna be a rough day with lots of visitors comin' over—she don't do real good with lots of people, lots of commotion—I give her an extra one."

Now we were talking overdose.

Bonita Quinn must have seen the look of surprise and disapproval that I tried unsuccessfully to conceal, for she spoke up with indignation in her voice.

"The doc says it was okay. He's an important man. You know, this place don't allow kids and I get to stay here only on account as she's a quiet kid. M and M Properties—they own the place—told me any time there's complaints about kids, that's it."

No doubt that did wonders for Melody's social life. Chances are she had never had a friend over.

There was cruel irony to the idea of a seven-year-old imprisoned amidst single-swingle splendor, tucked away in a slum pocket on an aerie high above the high Pacific, and dosed up with Ritalin to appease the combined wishes of the Los Angeles school system, a dim-witted mother and M and M Properties.

I examined the label on the vial to find out the name of the prescribing physician. When I found it, things began to fall into place.

L.W. Towle. Lionel Willard Towle, M.D. One of the most established and respected pediatricians on the West Side. I had never met him but knew him by reputation. He was on the senior staff of Western Pediatric and a half dozen other Westside hospitals. A big shot in the Academy of Pediatrics. A guest speaker, highly in demand, at seminars on learning disabilities and behavior problems.

Dr. Towle was also a paid consultant to three major

pharmaceutical concerns. Translate: pusher. He had a reputation, especially among the younger doctors who were generally more conservative about drugs, as easy with the prescription pad. No one said it too loudly, because Towle had been around a long time and had lots of important patients and plenty of connections, but the whispered consensus was that he was a Dr. Feelgood for tots. I wondered how someone like Bonita Quinn had ended up in his practice. But there was no easy way to ask without appearing unduly nosy.

I handed the vial back to her and turned to Milo, who'd been sitting through the exchange in silence.

"Let me talk to you," I said.

"Just one moment, ma'am."

Outside the apartment I told him, "I can't hypnotize this kid. She's drugged to the gills. It would be a risk to work with her, and besides, there's little chance of getting anything worthwhile out of her."

Milo digested this.

"Shit." He scratched his head. "What if we take her off the pills for a few days?"

"That's a medical decision. We get into that and we're way out of bounds. We need the physician's permission. Which blows confidentiality."

"Who's the doc?"

I told him about Towle.

"Wonderful. But maybe he'll agree to let her off for a few days."

"Maybe, but there's no guarantee she'll give us anything. This kid's been on stimulants for a year. And what about Mrs. Q? She's scared plenty as is. Take her darling off the pills and first thing she'll do is lock the kid inside twelve hours a day. They like it quiet here."

The complex was still silent as a mausoleum. At one-forty-five in the afternoon.

"Can you at least look at the kid? Maybe she's not that doped."

Across the way the door to the Handler apartment was open. I caught a glimpse of elegance in disarray—oriental rugs, antiques, and severe acrylic furniture broken and upended, blood-spattered white walls. The police lab men worked silently, like moles.

"By now she's had her second dose, Milo."

"Shit." He punched his fist into his palm. "Just meet the kid. Give me your impression. Maybe she'll be alert."

She wasn't. Her mother led her into the living room and then left with Milo. She stared off into the distance, sucking her thumb. She was a small child. If I hadn't known her age I would have guessed it at five, maybe five-and-a-half. She had a long, grave face with oversized brown eyes. Her straight blond hair hung to her shoulders, held in place by twin plastic barettes. She wore blue jeans and a blue-green-and-white-striped T-shirt. Her feet were dirty and bare.

I led her to a chair and sat opposite her on the couch.

"Hello, Melody. I'm Dr. Delaware. I'm a psychologist. Do you know what that is?"

No response.

"I'm the kind of doctor who doesn't give shots. What I do is talk and draw and play with kids. I try to help kids who are sad, or angry, or scared."

At the word *scared* she looked up for a second. Then she resumed staring past me and sucked her thumb.

"Do you know why I'm talking to you?"

A shake of the head.

"It's not because you're sick or because you've done anything wrong. We know you're a good girl."

Her eyes moved around the room, avoiding me.

"I'm here because you may have seen something last night that's important. When you couldn't sleep and were looking out the window."

She didn't answer. I continued.

"Melody, what kind of things do you like to do?"

Nothing.

"Do you like to play?"

She nodded.

"I like to play too. And I like to skate. Do you skate?"

"Uh-uh." Of course not. Skates make noise.

"And I like to watch movies. Do you watch movies?"

She mumbled something. I bent closer.

"What's that, hon?"

"On TV." Her voice was thin and quivering, a trembling breathy sound like the breeze through dry leaves.

"Uh-huh. On TV. I watch TV, too. What shows do you like to watch?"

"Scooby-Doo."

"Scooby-Doo. That's a good show. Any other shows?"

"My mama watches the soap operas."

"Do you like the soap operas?"

She shook her head.

"Pretty boring, huh?"

A hint of a smile, around the thumb.

"Do you have toys, Melody?"

"In my room."

"Could you show them to me?"

The room she shared with her mother was neither adult nor childlike in character. It was no more than ten foot square, low-ceilinged with a solitary window set high in the wall, which gave it the ambience of a dungeon. Melody and Bonita shared one twin bed unadorned by a headboard. It was half unmade, the thin chenille spread folded back to reveal rumpled sheets. On one side of the bed was a nightstand filled with bottles and jars of cold cream, hand lotion, brushes, combs and a piece of cardboard onto which a score of bobby pins were clasped. On the other side was a huge, moth-eaten stuffed walrus, made of fuzzy material and colored an atrocious turquoise blue. A baby picture was the sole adornment on the wall. A sagging bureau made of unfinished pine and covered with a crocheted doily, and the TV, were the only other pieces of furniture in the room.

In one corner was a small pile of toys.

Melody led me over to it, hesitantly. She picked up a grimy, naked plastic baby doll.

"Amanda," she said.

"She's beautiful."

The child clutched the doll to her chest and rocked back and forth.

"You must really take good care of her."

"I do." It was said defensively. This was a child who was not used to praise.

"I know you do," I said gently. I looked over to the walrus. "Who's he?"

"Fatso. My daddy gave him to me."

"He's cute."

She walked over to the animal, which was as tall as she, and stroked it purposefully.

"Mama wants me to throw him out 'cause he's too big. But I won't let her."

"Fatso's really important to you."

"Uh-huh."

"Daddy gave him to you."

She nodded, emphatically, and smiled. I'd passed some kind of test.

For the next twenty-five minutes we sat on the floor and played.

When Milo and the mother returned, Melody and I were in fine spirits. We'd built and destroyed several worlds.

"Well, you're sure lookin' frisky," said Bonita.

"We're having a good time, Mrs. Quinn. Melody's been a very good girl."

"That's good." She went over to her daughter and placed a hand on her head. "That's good, hon."

There was unexpected tenderness in her eyes, then it was gone. She turned to me and asked:

"How'd it go with the hypnotism?"

She asked it the same way she might inquire, how's my kid doing in arithmetic.

"We haven't done any hypnosis yet. Melody and I are just getting to know each other."

I drew her aside.

"Mrs. Quinn, hypnosis requires trust on the part of the child. I usually spend a little time with children beforehand. Melody was very cooperative."

"She didn't tell you nothin'?" She reached into the breast pocket of her shirt and pulled out another cigarette. I lit it for her and the gesture surprised her.

"Nothing of importance. With your permission I'd like to come over some time tomorrow and spend a little more time with Melody."

She eyed me suspiciously, chewed on the cigarette, then shrugged.

"You're the doctor."

We rejoined Milo and the child. He was kneeling on one leg and showing her his detective's badge. Her eyes were wide.

"Melody, if it's okay with you, I'd like to come by tomorrow and play with you some more."

She looked up at her mother and began sucking her thumb again.

"It's fine with me," Bonita Quinn said curtly. "Now run along."

Melody sprang for her room. She stopped in the doorway and gave me a tentative look. I waved, she waved back and then she disappeared. A second later the TV began blaring.

"One more thing, Mrs. Quinn. I'll need to talk to Dr. Towle before I do any hypnosis with Melody."

"That's okay."

"I'll need your permission to talk with Dr. Towle about the case. You realize he's professionally bound to keep this confidential, just as I am."

"That's okay. I trust Dr. Towle."

"And I may ask him to take her off her medicine for a couple of days."

"Oh all right, all right." She waved her hand, exasperated.

"Thank you, Mrs. Quinn."

We left her standing in front of her apartment, smoking frantically, taking the towel off her head and shaking her hair loose in the midday sun.

I took the wheel of the Seville and drove slowly up toward Sunset.

"Stop smirking, Milo."

"What's that?" He was looking out the passenger window, his hair flapping like duck wings.

"You know you've got me hooked, don't you? A kid like that, those big eyes like something out of a Keene painting."

"If you want to quit right now, it wouldn't make me happy, Alex. But I wouldn't stop you. There's still time for gnocchi."

"The hell with gnocchi. Let's talk with Dr. Towle."

The Seville was consuming fuel with customary gluttony. I pulled into a Chevron self-serve at Bundy. While Milo pumped gas I got Towle's number from information

and dialed it. I used my title and got through to the doctor
in a half-minute. I gave him a brief explanation of why I
needed to talk with him and told him we could chat now
over the phone.

"No," he said. "I've got an office full of kids." His
voice was smooth and reassuring, the kind of voice a
parent would want to hear at two in the morning when the
baby was turning blue.

"When would be a good time to call you?"

He didn't answer. I could hear the bustle of activity in
the background, then muffled voices. He came back on the
line.

"How about dropping by at four-thirty? I've got a lull
around then."

"I appreciate your time, Doctor."

"No bother." And he hung up.

I left the phone booth. Milo was removing the nozzle
from the rear of the Seville, holding it at arm's length to
avoid getting gasoline on his suit.

I settled in the driver's seat and stuck my head out the
window.

"Catch the windshield for me, son."

He made a gargoyle face—not much of an effort—and
gave me the finger. Then he went to work with paper
towels.

It was two-forty and we were only fifteen minutes from
Towle's office. That left over an hour to kill. Neither of us
was in a good enough mood to want first-rate food, so we
drove back to West L.A. and went to Angela's.

Milo ordered something called a San Francisco Deluxe
Omelette. It turned out to be a bright yellow horror stuffed
with spinach, tomatoes, ground beef, chilies, onions and
marinated eggplant. He dug into it with relish while I
contented myself with a steak sandwich and a Coors. In
between bites he talked about the Handler murder.

"It's a puzzler, Alex. You've got all the signs of a
psychotic thrill killer—both of them trussed up in the
bedroom, like animals ready for the slaughter. And stuck
about five dozen times. The girl looked like she ran into
Jack the Ripper with her—"

"Spare me." I pointed to my food.

"Sorry. I forget when I'm talking to a civilian. You get

used to it after wading in it for a few years. You can't stop living, so you learn to eat and drink and fart through all of it." He wiped his face with his napkin and took a long, deep swallow of his beer. "Anyway, despite the craziness, there's no sign of forced entry. The front door was open. Normally that would be very puzzling. Except in this case with the victim being a psychiatrist, it might make sense, his knowing the bad guy and letting him in."

"You think it was one of his patients?"

"It's a good possibility. Psychiatrists have been known to deal with crazies."

"I'd be surprised if it turned out that way, Milo. Ten to one Handler had a typical West Side practice—depressed middle-aged women, disillusioned executives, and a few adolescent identity crises thrown in for good measure."

"Do I detect a note of cynicism?"

I shrugged.

"That's just the way it is in most cases. High-priced friendship—not that it's not valuable, mind you. But there's very little real mental illness in what most of us—psychiatrists, psychologists—see in practice. The real crazies, the really disturbed ones, are hospitalized."

"Handler worked at a hospital before he went out on his own. Encino Oaks."

"Maybe you'll dig up something there," I said doubtfully. I was tired of being the wet blanket so I didn't tell him that Encino Oaks Hospital was a repository for the suicidal progeny of the rich. Very little sexual psychopathy, there.

He pushed his empty plate away and motioned for the waitress.

"Bettijean, a nice slab of that green apple pie, please."

"À la mode, Milo?"

He patted his gut and pondered.

"What the hell, why not. Vanilla."

"And you, sir?"

"Just coffee, please."

When she had gone he continued, thinking out loud more than talking to me.

"Anyway, it appears as if Dr. Handler let someone in to his place sometime between midnight and one and got ripped up for his efforts."

"And the Gutierrez woman?"

"Your quintessential innocent bystander. Being in the wrong place at the wrong time."

"She was Handler's girlfriend?"

He nodded.

"For about six months. From the little we've learned she started out as a patient and ended up going from couch to bed."

A not uncommon story.

"The irony of it was that she was hacked up worse than he was. Handler got his throat slit and probably died relatively quickly. There were a few other holes in him but nothing lethal. It looks as if the killer took his time with her. Makes sense if it's a sexual crazy."

I could feel my digestive process come to a halt. I changed the subject.

"Who's your new love?"

The pie came. Milo smiled at the waitress and attacked the pastry. I noticed that the filling was indeed green, a bright, almost luminescent green. Someone in the kitchen was fooling around with food dyes. I shuddered to think what they could do with something really challenging, like a pizza. It would probably end up looking like a mad artist's palette.

"A doctor. A nice Jewish doctor." He looked heavenward. "Every mother's dream."

"What happened to Larry?"

"He's gone off to find his fortunes in San Francisco."

Larry was a black stage manager with whom Milo had conducted an on-again, off-again relationship for two years. Their last half-year had been grimly platonic.

"He's hooked up with some show sponsored by an anonymous corporation. Something racy for educational television, along the lines of 'Our Agricultural Heritage: Your Friend the Plough.' Hot stuff."

"Bitchy, bitchy."

"No, really, I do wish the boy well. Behind that neurotic exterior was genuine talent."

"How did you meet your doctor?"

"He works the Emergency Room at Cedars. A surgeon, no less. I was following up an assault that turned into manslaughter, he was commandeering the catheters, and our eyes locked. The rest is history.''

I laughed so hard the coffee almost went up my nose.

"He's been out of the closet for about two years. Marriage in medical school, messy divorce, excommunication by family. The whole bit. Fantastic guy, you'll have to meet him.''

"I'd like to.''

"Give me a few days to slog through Morton Handler's life history and we'll double.''

"It's a deal.''

It was five to four. I let the Los Angeles Police Department pay for my lunch. In the best tradition of policemen the world over, Milo left an enormous tip. He patted Bettijean's fanny on the way out and her laughter followed us out on to the street.

Santa Monica Boulevard was beginning to choke up with traffic and the air had started to foul. I closed the Seville's windows and turned on the air-conditioning. I slipped a tape of Joe Pass and Stephane Grappelli into the deck. The sound of "Only a Paper Moon," delivered hot forties style, filled the car. The music made me feel good. Milo took a cat nap, snoring deeply. I eased the Seville into the traffic and headed back to Brentwood.

TOWLE'S OFFICE was on a side street off San Vicente, not far from the Brentwood Country Mart—one of the few neighborhoods where movie stars could shop without being harassed. It was in a building designed during the early fifties, when tan brick, low-slung roofs and wall inserts of glass cubes were in vogue. Plantings of asparagus fern and climbing bougainvillaea did something to relieve the starkness, but it still looked pretty severe.

Towle was the building's sole occupant and his name was stenciled in gold leaf on the glass front door. The parking lot was a haven for wood-sided station wagons. We pulled in next to a blue Lincoln with a SPEAK UP FOR CHILDREN bumper sticker that I figured belonged to the good doctor himself.

Inside, the decor was something else. It was as if some interior decorator had tried to make up for the harshness of the building by cramming the waiting room full of mush. The furniture was colonial maple with nubby seat cushions. The walls were covered with needlepoint homilies and cutesy-poo prints of little boys fishing and little girls preening themselves in front of mirrors, wearing mommy's hat and shoes. The room was full of children and harried-looking mothers. Magazines, books and toys cluttered the floor. There was an odor of dirty diapers in the air. If this was Towle's lull I didn't want to be there during his busy period.

When we walked in, two childless males, we drew stares from the women. We had agreed beforehand that Towle would relate better doctor to doctor, so Milo found a seat sandwiched in between two five-year-olds and I walked to the reception window. The girl on the other side was a sweet young thing with Farah Fawcett hair and a face almost as pretty as that of her role model. She was dressed in white and her name tag proclaimed her to be Sandi.

"Hi. I'm Dr. Delaware. I've got an appointment with Dr. Towle."

I got a smile fronted by lots of nice, white teeth.

"Appointments don't mean much this afternoon. But come right in. He'll be with you in just a minute."

I walked through the door with several pairs of maternal eyes boring into my back. Some of them had probably been waiting for over an hour. I wondered why Towle didn't hire an associate.

Sandi showed me into the doctor's consultation office, a dark-paneled room about twelve by twelve.

"It's about the Quinn child, isn't it?"

"That's right."

"I'll pull the chart." She came back with a manila folder and placed it on Towle's desk. There was a red tag on the cover. She saw me looking at it.

"The reds are the hypers. We code them. Yellow for chronically ill ones. Blue for specialty consults."

"Very efficient."

"Oh, you have no idea!" She giggled and placed one hand on a shapely hip. "You know," she said, leaning a bit closer and letting me have a whiff of something fragrant, "between you and me that poor child has it rough growing up with a mother like that."

"I know what you mean." I nodded, not knowing what she meant at all but hoping she'd tell me. People usually do when you don't seem to care.

"I mean, she's such a scatterbrain—the mother. Everytime she comes here she forgets something, or loses something. One time it was her purse. The other time she locked her keys in the car. She really doesn't have it together."

I clucked sympathetically.

"Not that she hasn't had it rough, growing up doing farm work and then marrying that guy who ended up in pris—"

"Sandi."

We both turned to see a short, sixtyish woman with hair

cut in an iron-grey helmet, standing in the doorway, arms folded across her bosom. Her eyeglasses hung suspended from a chain around her neck. She, too, was dressed in white, but on her it looked like a uniform. *Her* name tag proclaimed her to be Edna.

I knew her right away. The doctor's right hand gal. She'd probably been working for him since he hung out his shingle and was making about the same amount of money she'd started out with. But no matter, lucre wasn't what she was after. She was secretly in love with the Great Man. I was willing to bet a handful of blue chip stocks that she called him *Doctor*. No name after it. Just Doctor. As if he were the only one in the world.

"There are some charts that need filing," she said.

"Okay, Edna." Sandi turned to me, gave a conspiratorial look that said Isn't this old witch a drag? and sashayed down the hall.

"Can I do anything for you?" Edna asked me, still keeping her arms crossed.

"No, thank you."

"Well, then, Doctor will be right with you."

"Thank you." Kill 'em with courtesy.

Her glance let me know that she didn't approve of my presence. No doubt anything that upset Doctor's routine was viewed as an intrusion upon Paradise. But she finally left me alone in the office.

I took a look around the room. The desk was mahogany and battered. It was piled high with charts, medical journals, books, mail, drug samples, and a jar full of paper clips. The desk chair and the easy chair in which I sat were once classy items—burnished leather—now both aged and cracked.

Two of the walls were covered with diplomas, many of which hung askew and at odds with one another. It looked like a room that had just been nudged by a minor earthquake—nothing broken, just shaken up a bit.

I casually examined the diplomas. Lionel W. Towle had amassed an impressive collection of paper over the years. Degrees, certificates of internship and residency, a walnut plaque with gavel commemorating his chairmanship of some medical task force, honorary membership in this and that, specialty board certification, commendations for public service on the Good Ship Hope, consultant to the California Senate subcommittee on child welfare. And on and on.

The other wall displayed photographs. Most were of Towle. Towle in fisherman's garb, knee-deep in some river holding aloft a clutch of steelhead. Towle with a marlin the size of a Buick. Towle with the mayor and some little squat guy with Peter Lorre eyes—everyone smiling, shaking hands.

There was one exception to this seeming self-obsession. In the center of the wall hung a color photograph of a young woman holding a small child. The colors were faded and from the styles of clothing worn by the subjects, the picture looked three decades old. There was some of the tell-tale fuzziness of an enlarged snapshot. The hues were misty, almost pastel.

The woman was pretty, fresh-faced, with a sprinkle of freckles across her nose, dark eyes and medium-length brown hair with a natural wave. She wore a filmy-looking, short-sleeved dress of dotted swiss cotton, and her arms were slender and graceful. They wrapped around the child—a boy—who looked around two or younger. He was beautiful. Rosy-cheeked, blond, with cupid's-bow lips and green eyes. He was dressed in a white sailor suit and sat beaming in his mother's embrace. The mountains and lake in the distance looked real.

"It's a lovely picture, isn't it?" said the voice I'd heard over the phone.

He was tall, at least six-three, and lean, with the kind of features bad novels label as chiseled. He was one of the most handsome middle-aged men I had ever seen. His face was noble—a strong chin bisected by a perfect cleft, the nose of a Roman senator, and twinkling eyes the color of a clear sky. His thick, snow-white hair hung down over his forehead, Carl Sandburg style. His eyebrows were twin white clouds.

He wore a short white coat over a blue oxford shirt, burgundy print tie, and dark gray trousers of a subtle check. His shoes were black calfskin loafers. Very proper, very tasteful. But clothes didn't make the man. He would have looked patrician in doubleknits.

"Dr. Delaware? Will Towle."

"Alex."

I stood and we shook hands. His grip was firm and dry. The fingers that clasped mine were enormous and I was conscious of abundant strength behind them.

"Please, sit."

He took his place behind the desk, swiveled back and threw his feet up on top, resting on a year's back issues of the *Journal of Pediatrics*.

I responded to his question.

"It is a beautiful shot. Somewhere in the Pacific Northwest?"

"Washington state. Olympic National Forest. We were vacationing there in fifty-one. I was a resident. That was my wife and son. I lost them a month later. In a car crash."

"I'm sorry."

"Yes." A distant, sleepy look came on his face; it was a moment before he shook himself out of it and came back into focus.

"I know you by reputation, Alex, so it's a pleasure to get to meet you."

"Same here."

"I've followed your work, because I have a strong interest in behavioral pediatrics. I was particularly interested in your work with those children who'd been victimized by Stuart Hickle. Several of them were in the practice. The parents spoke highly of your work."

"Thank you." I felt as if I was expected to say more but that was one subject that was closed. "I do remember sending consent forms to you."

"Yes, yes. Delighted to cooperate."

Neither of us spoke, then we both spoke at the same time.

"What I'd like to—" I said.

"What can I do for—" he said.

It came out a garbled mess. We laughed, good old boys at the University Club. I deferred to him. Despite the graciousness I sensed an enormous ego lurking behind that white forelock.

"You're here about the Quinn child. What can I do for you?"

I filled him in on as few details as possible, stressing the importance of Melody Quinn as a witness and the benign nature of the hypnotic intervention. I ended by requesting that he allow her to go off Ritalin for one week.

"You really think this child will be able to give you information of substance?"

"I don't know. I've asked the same question. But she's all the police have got."

"And your role in all of this?"

I thought up a quicky title.

"I'm a special consultant. They call me in sometimes when there are children involved."

"I see."

He played with his hands, constructing ten-legged spiders and killing them.

"I don't know, Alex. When we start to remove a patient from what has been determined to be an optimal dosage we sometimes upset the entire pattern of biochemical response."

"You think she needs to be on medication constantly."

"Of course I do. Why else would I prescribe it for her?" He wasn't angry or defensive. He smiled calmly and with great forbearance. The message was clear: Only an idiot would doubt him.

"There'd be no way to reduce the dosage?"

"Oh, that's certainly possible, but it creates the same type of problem. I don't like to tamper with a winning combination."

"I see." I hesitated, then continued. "She must have posed quite a problem to merit sixty mgs."

Towle placed a pair of reading glasses low on his nose, picked up the chart and flipped through it.

"Let me see. Ah, yes. Hmm. 'Mother complains of severe behavioral problems.' " After thumbing through a few more pages: " 'Teachers report failure to complete school assignments. Difficulty in maintaining attention span for more than brief periods.' Ah—here's a later notation— 'Child struck mother during argument about keeping room clean' And here's a note of mine: 'Poor peer relations, few friends.' "

I was certain that the argument had something to do with giving away the giant walrus, Fatso. The gift from

Daddy. And as for friends—it was easy to see that M and M Properties wouldn't truck with that kind of nonsense.

"That sounds pretty severe to me, don't you think?"

What I thought was that it was horseshit. There'd been nothing resembling a thorough psychological evaluation. Nothing beyond taking the mother at her word. I looked at Towle and saw a quack. A nice-looking, white-haired quack with lots of connections and the right pieces of paper on his wall. I longed to tell him so, but that would do nobody—Melody, Milo—any good.

So I hedged.

"I can't say. You're her doc." Faking the comradely grin was an exercise in moral self-control.

"That's right, Alex. I am." He leaned back in his chair and placed his hands behind his head. "I know what you're thinking. Will Towle is a pill pusher. Stimulants are just another form of child abuse."

"I wouldn't say that."

He waved away my objection.

"No, no, I know. And I don't hold it against you. Your training is behavioral and you see things behaviorally. We all do it, settle into professional tunnel vision. The surgeons want to cut everything out. We prescribe and you fellows like to analyze it to death."

It was starting to sound like a lecture.

"Granted, drugs have risks. But it's a matter of cost-risk analysis. Let's consider a child like the little Quinn girl. What does she start out with? Inferior genes—both parents somewhat *limited* intellectually." He made the word *limited* sound very cruel. "Lousy genes and poverty, and a broken marriage. Absent father—although in some of these cases the children are better off without the kind of role models the fathers provide. Bad genes, bad environment. The child's got two strikes against her before she leaves the womb.

"Is it any wonder then that soon we're seeing all the telltale signs—antisocial behavior, noncompliance, poor school performance, unsatisfactory impulse control?"

I felt a sudden urge to defend little Melody. Her genial doctor was describing her as some kind of total misfit. I kept silent.

"Now a child like this—" he took off his glasses and

put down the chart—"is going to have to do moderately well in school in order to achieve some semblance of a decent life for herself. Otherwise it's another generation of P.P.P."

Piss-poor protoplasm. One of the quaint expressions dreamed up by the medical profession to describe especially unfortunate patients.

Playing straight man to Towle wasn't my idea of a fun afternoon. But I had a hunch it was some kind of ritual, that if I held out and let him smilingly browbeat me he might give me what I came for.

"But there is no way a child like this *can* achieve with her genes and her environment working against her. Not without help. And that's where stimulant medication comes in. Those pills allow her to sit still long enough and pay attention long enough to be able to learn something. They control her behavior to the point where she no longer alienates everyone around her."

"I got the impression that the mother was using the medication in a haphazard way—giving her an extra pill on days when there were lots of visitors at the apartment complex."

"I'll have to check that." He didn't sound concerned. "You have to remember, Alex, that this child does not exist in a vacuum. There's a social context here. If there's nowhere for her mother and her to live, that isn't exactly therapeutic, is it?"

I listened, certain there was more. Sure enough: "Now you may ask, what about psychotherapy? What about behavior modification? My answer is: What about them? There is no chance of this particular mother developing the capacity for insight to successfully benefit from psychotherapy. And she lacks the ability to even comply with a stable system of rules and regulations necessary for behavior mod. What she *can* deal with is administering three pills a day to her child. Pills that work. And I don't mind telling you, I don't feel a damn bit guilty about prescribing them, because I think they're this child's only hope."

It was a great ending. No doubt it made a big hit at the Western Pediatric Ladies Auxiliary Tea. But basically it was all crap. Pseudoscientific gibberish mixed in with a lot of condescending fascism. Dope up the *Untermenschen* to make them good citizens.

He had worked himself up a bit. But now he was perfectly composed, as handsome and in control as ever.

"I haven't convinced you, have I?" He smiled.

"It's not a matter of that. You raise some interesting points. I'll have to think about it."

"That's always a good idea, thinking things over." He rubbed his hands together. "Now, back to what you came for—and please forgive my little diatribe. You really think that taking this child off stimulants will make her more susceptible to hypnosis."

"I do."

"Despite the fact that her concentration will be poorer?"

"Despite that. I've got inductions that are especially suited for children with short attention spans."

The snowy eyebrows rose.

"Oh, really? I'll have to find out about those. You know, I did some hypnosis, too. In the Army, for pain control. I know it works."

"I can send you some recent publications."

"Thank you, Alex." He rose and it was clear that my time was up.

"Pleasure to meet you Alex." Another handshake.

"The pleasure is mine, Will." This was getting sickening.

The unasked question hung in the air. Towle snagged it.

"I'll tell you what I'm going to do," he said, smiling ever faintly.

"Yes?"

"I'm going to *think* about it."

"I see."

"Yes, I'll think it over. Call me in a couple of days."

"I'll do that, Will." And may your hair and teeth fall out overnight, you sanctimonious bastard.

On the way out Edna glared and Sandi smiled at me. I ignored them both and rescued Milo from the trio of munchkins that was climbing over him as if he were playground equipment. We made our way through the now-boiling mob of children and mothers and reached the car safely.

5

I TOLD Milo about the encounter with Towle as we drove back to my place.

"Power play." His forehead creased and cherry-sized lumps appeared just above his jawline.

"That and something else that I can't quite figure. He's a strange guy. Comes across very courtly—almost obsequious—then you realize he's playing games."

"Why'd he have you come all the way out there for something like that?"

"I don't know." It was a puzzle, his taking time out from a frantic afternoon to deliver a leisurely lecture. Our entire conversation could have been handled in a five-minute phone call. "Maybe it's his idea of recreation. One-upping another professional."

"Hell of a hobby for a busy man."

"Yeah, but the ego comes first. I've met guys like Towle before, obsessed with being in control, with being the boss. Lots of them end up as department heads, deans and chairmen of committees."

"And captains and inspectors and police chiefs."

" Right . . ."

"You going to call him like he said?" He sounded defeated.

"Sure, for what it's worth."

"Yeah."

Milo reclaimed his Fiat and after a few moments of prayer and pumping it started up. He leaned out of the window and looked at me wearily.

"Thanks, Alex. I'm going to go home and crash. This no-sleep routine is catching up with me . . ."

"You want to take a nap here and then head out?"

"No thanks. I'll make it if this pile of junk will." He slapped the dented door. "Thanks anyway."

"I'll follow up with Melody."

"Great. I'll call you tomorrow." He drove a way until I stopped him with my shout. He backed up.

"What?"

"It's probably not important, but I thought I'd mention it. The nurse in Towle's office told me Melody's dad's in prison."

He nodded somnambulantly.

"So's half the county. It's that way when the economy goes bad. Thanks."

Then he was off.

It was six-fifteen and already dark. I lay down on my bed for a few minutes and when I awoke it was after nine. I got up, washed my face, and called Robin. No one answered.

I took a quick shave, threw on a windbreaker and drove down to Hakata, in Santa Monica. I drank sake and ate sushi for an hour, and bantered with the chef, who, as it turned out had a master's degree in psychology from the University of Tokyo.

I got home, stripped naked, and took a hot bath, trying to erase all thoughts of Morton Handler, Melody Quinn and L.W. Towle, M.D., from my mind. I used self-hypnosis, imagining Robin and myself making love on top of a mountain in the middle of a rain forest. Flushed with passion I got out of the tub and called her again. After ten rings, she answered, mumbling and confused and half-asleep.

I apologized for waking her, told her I loved her and hung up.

Half a minute later she called back.

"Was that you, Alex?" She sounded as if she was dreaming.

"Yes, hon. I'm sorry to wake you."

"No, that's okay—what time is it?"

"Eleven-thirty."

"Oh, I must have conked out. How are you, sweetie?"

"Fine. I called you around nine."

"I was out all day buying wood. There's an old violin-maker out in Simi Valley who's retiring. I spent six hours choosing tools and picking out maple and ebony. I'm sorry I missed you."

She sounded exhausted.

"I'm sorry too, but go back to bed. Get some sleep and I'll call you tomorrow."

"If you want to come over, you can."

I thought about it. But I was too restless to be good company.

"No, doll. You rest. How about dinner tomorrow? You pick the place."

"Okay, darling." She yawned—a soft, sweet sound. "I love you."

"Love you too."

It took me a while to fall asleep and when I finally did, it was restless slumber, punctuated by black-and-white dreams with lots of frantic movement in them. I don't remember what they were about, but the dialogue was sluggish and labored, as if everyone were talking with paralyzed lips and mouths filled with wet sand.

In the middle of the night I got up to check that the doors and windows were locked.

6

I WOKE UP at six the next morning, filled with random energy. I hadn't felt that way for over five months. The tension wasn't all bad, for with it came a sense of purpose, but by seven it had built up some, so that I paced around the house like a jaguar on the prowl.

At seven-thirty I decided it was late enough. I dialed Bonita Quinn's number. She was wide-awake and she sounded as if she'd been expecting my call.

"Morning, Doctor."

"Good morning. I thought I'd drop by and spend a few hours with Melody."

"Why not? She's not doin' anything. You know—" she lowered her voice—"I think she liked you. She talked about how you played with her."

"That's good. We'll do some more today. I'll be there in half an hour."

When I arrived she was all dressed and ready to go. Her mother had put her in a pale yellow sundress that exposed bony white shoulders and pipe-stem arms. Her hair was tied back in a ponytail, fastened by a yellow ribbon. She clutched a tiny patent-leather purse. I had thought we'd spend some time in her room and then perhaps go out for lunch, but it was clear she was primed for an outing.

"Hi, Melody."

She averted her gaze and sucked her thumb.

"You look very pretty this morning."

She smiled shyly.

"I thought we'd take a drive, go to a park. How does that sound?"

"Okay." The shaky voice.

"Great." I peeked my head in the apartment. Bonita Quinn was pushing around a vacuum cleaner as if it were a wagonload of sins. She wore a blue bandana on her head and a cigarette dangled from her lips. The television was tuned in to a gospel show, but snow obscured the picture and the choir was drowned out by the sound of the vacuum.

I touched her shoulder. She jumped.

"I'm taking her now, okay?" I yelled over the din.

"Sure." When she spoke the cigarette bobbled like a trout lure in a rushing brook.

She resumed her chore, stooping over the roaring machine and plowing it forward.

I rejoined Melody.

"Let's go."

She walked alongside me. Midway to the parking lot a small hand slipped into mine.

Through a series of hilltop turns and lucky detours, I connected to Ocean Avenue. I drove south, toward Santa Monica, until we reached the park at the top of the cliff overlooking Pacific Coast Highway. It was eight-thirty in the morning. The sky was clear, pebbled only with a handful of clouds that might have been as distant as Hawaii. I found a parking space on the street, directly in front of the Camera Obscura and the Senior Citizens' Recreation Center.

Even that early in the morning the place was bustling. Old people packed the benches and the shuffleboard court. Some of them jabbered nonstop to each other, or themselves. Other stared out at the boulevard in mute trance. Leggy girls in skimpy tops and satin shorts that covered a tenth of their gluteal regions skated by, transforming the walkways between the palms into fleshy freeways. Some of them wore stereo headsets—speeding spacewomen, with glazed, beatific expressions on their California-perfect faces.

Japanese tourists snapped pictures, nudged each other, pointed and laughed. Shabby bums loitered against the guardrail that separated the crumbling bluff from sheer space. They smoked behind cupped hands and regarded the world with distrust and fear. A surprising number of them were young men. They all looked as if they'd crawled out of some deep, dark, unproductive mine.

There were students reading, couples sprawled on the grass, small boys darting between the trees and a few furtive encounters that looked suspiciously like dope deals.

Melody and I walked along the outer rim of the park, hand in hand, talking little. I offered to buy her a hot pretzel from a street vendor, but she said she wasn't hungry. I remembered that loss of appetite was another side effect of Ritalin. Or maybe she'd just had a big breakfast.

We came to the walkway that led to the pier.

"Have you ever been on a merry-go-round?" I asked her.

"Once. We went on a school trip to Magic Mountain. The fast rides scared me but I liked the merry-go-round."

"C,mon." I pointed out toward the pier. "There's one here. We'll take a ride."

In contrast to the park, the pier was nearly deserted. There were a few men fishing here and there, mostly older blacks and Asians, but their expressions were pessimistic, their buckets empty. Dried fish scales were embedded in the aged wooden planks of the walkway, giving it a sequined effect in the morning sun. There were cracks in several of the weathered boards, and as we walked I caught glimpses of the water below slapping against the pilings and retreating with a hissed warning. In the shadow of the pier's underbelly the water looked greenish black. There was a strong smell of creosote and salt in the air, a ripe, raw fragrance of loneliness and wasted hours.

The pool hall where I used to hide while playing hookey had been closed down. In its place was an arcade full of electric video games. A solitary Mexican boy intently pulled the joystick on one of the garishly painted robots. Computer noise emerged in blips and dreeps.

The merry-go-round was housed in a cavernous barn of a building that looked as if it would collapse with the next high tide. The operator was a tiny man with a potbelly the size of a cantaloupe and flaky skin around his ears. He was sitting on a stool reading a racing form and trying to pretend we weren't there.

"We'd like to ride the merry-go-round."

He looked up, gave us the once-over. Melody was

staring at the ancient posters on the wall. Buffalo Bill.
Victorian Love.

"Quarter a spin."

I handed him a couple of bills.

"Keep it going for a while."

"Sure."

I lifted her up onto a large white-and-gilded horse with a
pink plume for a tail. The brass rod upon which it was
impaled had diagonal stripes running across it. A sure bet
to go up and down. I stood next to her.

The tiny man was buried in his reading. He reached out
a hand, pushed a button on a rusty console, pulled a lever
and a rheumy rendition of the "Blue Danube Waltz"
piped out of a dozen hidden speakers. The carousel started
off slowly, and then it began to turn; horses, monkeys,
chariots coming to life, moving in vertical counterpoint to
the revolution of the machine.

Melody's hands tightened around the neck of her steed;
she stared straight ahead. Gradually, she relaxed her grip
and allowed herself to look around. By the twentieth revolution, she was swaying with the music, eyes closed,
mouth open in silent laughter.

When the music finally stopped I helped her down and
she stepped dizzily onto the dirty concrete floor. She was
giggling and swinging her purse in joyful rhythm, in time
with the now dissipated waltz.

We left the barn and ventured to the end of the pier. She
was fascinated by the enormous bait tanks teeming with
squirming anchovies, amazed at the bin of fresh rockfish
that was being brought up by a trio of muscled, bearded
fishermen. The reddish fish lay dead in a heap. The quick
ascent from the bottom of the ocean had caused the air
bladders on several of them to explode and extrude from
their open mouths. Crabs the size of bees crawled in and
around the motionless bodies. Gulls swooped down to
plunder and were waved off by the horned brown hands of
the fishermen.

One of the fishermen, a boy of no more than eighteen,
saw her staring.

"Pretty gross, huh?"

"Yeah."

"Tell your daddy to take you to prettier places on his day off." He laughed.

Melody smiled. She didn't try to correct him.

Someone was deep-frying shrimp. I saw her nose wrinkle.

"You hungry?"

"Kind of." She looked uneasy.

"Anything wrong?"

"Mama told me not to be too grabby."

"Don't you worry. I'm going to tell your mom what a good girl you've been. Have you had breakfast?"

"Kind of."

"What'd you have?"

"Some juice. A piece of donut. The white powdery kind."

"That's it?"

"Uh-huh." She looked up at me as if expecting to be punished. I softened my tone.

"I guess you weren't hungry at breakfast time."

"Uh-huh." So much for the big-breakfast theory.

"Well, *I'm* pretty hungry." It was true. All I'd had was coffee. "What do you say we both get something?"

"Thank you, Doctor Del—" she stumbled over my name.

"Call me Alex."

"Thank you, Alex."

We located the source of the cooking smells at a shabby dinerette sandwiched between a souvenir shop and a bait and tackle stand. The woman behind the counter was pasty white and obese. Steam and smoke rose in billows around her moon face, creating a shimmering halo. Deep fryers crackled in the background.

I bought a large greasy bag full of goodies: foil-wrapped servings of shrimp and fried cod, a basket of french fries the size of billy clubs, plastic covered tubs of tartar sauce and ketchup, fluted paper tubes of salt, two cans of an off-brand of cola.

"Don't forget these, sir."

The fat woman held out a handful of napkins.

"Thanks."

"You know kids." She looked down at Melody. "You enjoy yourself now, hon."

We carried the food off the pier and found a quiet spot

on the beach, not far from the Pritikin Longevity Center. We ate our greasy fare watching middle-aged men attempt to jog around the block, fueled by whatever heartless menu the center was serving nowadays.

She ate like a trucker. It was getting close to noon, which meant that normally she'd be ready for her second dose of amphetamine. Her mother hadn't offered the medication to me, and I hadn't thought—or wanted—to ask.

The change in her behavior became evident halfway through lunch, and grew more obvious each minute.

She began to move more. She was more alert. Her face became more animated. She fidgeted, as if waking from a long, confusing sleep. She looked around, newly in touch with her environment.

"Look at them." She pointed to a covey of wet-suited surfers riding waves in the distance.

"They look like seals, don't they?"

She giggled.

"Could I go in the water, Alex?"

"Take your shoes off and wade near the shoreline—where the water touches the sand. Try not to get your dress wet."

I popped shrimp in my mouth, leaned back and watched her run along the tideline, skinny legs kicking up the water. Once she turned in my direction and waved.

I watched her play that way for twenty minutes or so, and then I rolled up my pants legs, took off my shoes and socks and joined her.

We ran together. Her legs worked better with every passing moment; soon she was a gazelle. She whooped and splashed and kept going until we were both out of breath. We walked back to our picnic site and collapsed on the sand. Her hair was a mess so I loosened the barettes and re-fastened them for her. Her small chest heaved. Her feet were crusted with grit from the ankle down. When she finally caught her breath she asked me:

"I—I've been a good girl, haven't I?"

"You've been great."

She looked unsure.

"Don't you think so, Melody?"

"I don't know. Sometimes I think I am and Mama gets mad or Mrs. Brookhouse says I'm bad."

"You're always a good girl. Even if someone thinks you've done something wrong. Do you understand that?"

"I guess so."

"Not sure, huh?"

"I—I get mixed up."

"Everyone gets mixed up. Kids and moms and dads. And doctors."

"Dr. Towle, too?"

"Even Dr. Towle."

She digested that for a while. The large, dark eyes darted around, moving from the water, to my face, to the sky, and back to me.

"Mama said you were going to hypnotize me." She pronounced it hip-mo-tize.

"Only if you want me to. Do you understand why we think it might be helpful?"

"Sort of. To make me think better?"

"No. You think just fine. This—" I patted her head—"works fine. We want to try hypnosis—hypnotizing—so that you can do us a favor. So that you can remember something."

"About when the other doctor was hurt."

I hesitated. My habit was to be honest with children, but if she hadn't been told about Handler and Gutierrez being dead I wasn't going to be the one to break the news. Not without the chance to be around to help pick up the pieces.

"Yes. About that."

"I told the policeman I didn't remember anything. It was all dark and everything."

"Sometimes people remember better after being hypnotized."

She looked at me, frightened.

"Are you scared of being hypnotized?"

"Uh-huh."

"That's okay. It's okay to be scared of new things. But there really isn't anything scary about hypnotizing. It's really kind of fun. Have you ever seen anyone hypnotized before?"

"Nope."

"Never? Even in a cartoon?"

She lit up. "Yeah, when the guy in the pointy hat hypnotized Popeye and the waves came out his hands and

Popeye walked out of the window into the air and he didn't fall.''

"Right. I've seen that one too. The guy in the pointy hat made Popeye do all sorts of weird things."

"Yeah."

"Well that's great for cartoons, but real hypnotizing isn't anything like that." I gave her a child's version of the lecture I'd delivered to her mother. She seemed to believe me, because fascination took the place of fear.

"Can we do it now?"

I hesitated. The beach was empty; there was plenty of privacy. And the moment was right. To hell with Towle . . .

"I don't see why not. First, let's get real comfortable."

I had her fix her eyes upon a smooth shiny pebble as she held it in her hand. Within moments she was blinking in response to suggestion. Her breathing slowed and became regular. I told her to close her eyes and listen to the sound of the waves slapping against the shore. Then I instructed her to imagine herself descending a flight of stairs and passing through a beautiful door to a favorite place.

"I don't know where it is, or what's in it, but it's a special place for you. You can tell me or keep it secret, but being there makes you feel so comfortable, so happy, so in control . . ."

A bit more of that and she was in a deep hypnotic state.

"Now you can hear the sound of my voice without having to listen. Just continue to enjoy your favorite place, and have a real good time."

I let her go for five more minutes. There was a peaceful, angelic expression on her thin little face. A soft wind rustled the loose strands of her hair. She looked tiny, sitting in the sand, hands resting in her lap.

I gave her a suggestion to go back in time, brought her back to the night of the murder. She tensed momentarily, then resumed the deep, regular breathing.

"You're still feeling totally relaxed, Melody. So comfortable and in control. But now you can watch yourself, just as if you were a star on TV. You see yourself getting out of bed . . ."

Her lips parted, she ran the tip of her tongue over them.

"And you go to the window and sit there, just looking out. What do you see?"

"Dark." The word was barely audible.

"Yes, it's dark. And is there anything else."

"No."

"Okay. Let's sit there a while longer."

A few minutes later:

"Can you see anything else in the dark, Melody?"

"Uh-uh. Dark."

I tried a few more times, and then gave up. Either she had seen nothing, and the talk of two or three dark men had been confabulation, or she was blocking. In either event I wasn't going to get anything from her.

I let her enjoy her favorite place, gave her suggestions for mastery, control, and feeling refreshed and happy, and brought her gently out of hypnosis. She came out smiling.

"That was fun!"

"I'm glad you liked it. You seemed to have a real good favorite place."

"You said I don't have to tell you!"

"That's true. You don't."

"Well what if I want to?" she pouted.

"Then you can."

"Hmm." She savored her power for a moment. "I want to tell you. It was riding around on the merry-go-round. Going round and round, faster and faster."

"That's a great choice."

"Each time I went around I felt happier and happier. Can we go again some time?"

"Sure." Now you've done it, Alex. Gotten yourself into something that won't be easy to pull out of. Instant daddy, just add guilt.

Back in the car she turned to me.

"Alex, you said hypnotizing makes you remember better?"

"It can."

"Could I use it to remember my daddy?"

"When's the last time you saw him?"

"Never. He left when I was a little baby. He and Mama don't live together any more."

"Does he visit?"

"No. He lives far away. Once he called me, before

Christmas, but I was sleeping, so Mama didn't wake me up. That made me mad.''

"I can understand that.''

"I hit her.''

"You must have been really mad.''

"Yeah.'' She bit her lip. "Sometimes he sends me stuff.''

"Like Fatso?''

"Yeah, and other stuff.'' She dug in her purse and pulled out what looked to be a large dried pit, or seed. It had been carved to resemble a face—a snarling face—with rhinestone eyes, and strands of black acrylic hair glued to the top. A head, a shrunken head. The kind of hideous trash you can pick up at any Tijuana tourist stall. From the way she held it, it could have been the Crown Jewel of Kwarshiorkor.

"Very nice.'' I handled the knobby thing and gave it back to her.

"I'd like to see him but Mama says she doesn't know where he is. Can hypnotizing help remember him?''

"It would be hard, Melody, because you haven't seen him in a long time. But we could try. Do you have anything to remember him by—any picture of him?''

"Yeah.'' She searched in her purse again and came up with a spindled and mutilated snapshot. It had probably been fingered like a rosary. I thought of the photograph on Towle's wall. This was the week for celluloid memories. Mr. Eastman, if you only knew how your little black box can be used to preserve the past like a stillborn fetus in a jar of formalin.

It was a faded color photograph of a man and woman. The woman was Bonita Quinn in younger, but not much prettier, days. Even in her twenties she had possessed a sad mask of a face that foreshadowed a merciless future. She wore a dress that exposed too much undernourished thigh. Her hair was long and straight and parted in the middle. She and her companion were in front of what looked like a rural bar, the kind of watering place you find peeking out around sudden highway curves. The walls of the building were rough-hewn logs. There was a Budweiser sign in the window.

Her arm was around the waist of the man, who had

placed his arm around her shoulder. He wore a T-shirt, jeans and Wellington boots. The rump of a motorcycle was visible next to him.

He was a strange-looking bird. One side of him—the left—sagged and there was more than a hint of atrophy running all the way down from face to foot. He looked crooked, like a piece of fruit that had been sliced and then put back together with less than full precision. When you got past the asymmetry he wasn't bad-looking—tall, slender, with shoulder-length shaggy blond hair and a thick mustache.

He had a wise-guy expression on his face that contrasted with Bonita's solemnity. It was the kind of look you see on the face of the local yokels when you walk into a small-town tavern in a strange place, just wanting a cold drink and some solitude. The kind of look you go out of your way to avoid, because it means trouble, and nothing else.

I wasn't surprised its owner had ended up behind bars.

"Here you go." I handed the photo back to her and she carefully put it back in her purse.

"Want to take another run?"

"Naw. I'm kinda tired."

"Want to go home?"

"Yeah."

During the ride back to the apartment complex she was very quiet, as if she'd been doped up again. I had the uneasy feeling that I hadn't done right by this child, that I had overstimulated her, only to return her to a dreary routine.

Was I prepared to play the rescuing good guy on a regular basis?

I thought of the parting lecture one of the senior professors in graduate school had given our graduating class of aspiring psychotherapists.

"When you choose to earn your living by helping people who are in emotional pain, you're also making a choice to carry them on your back for a while. To hell with all that talk of taking responsibility, assertiveness. That's crap. You're going to be coming up against helplessness every day of your lives. Your patients will imprint you, like goslings who latch on to the first creature they see when they stick their heads out of the egg shell. If you can't handle it, become an accountant.''

Right now a ledger book full of numbers would have been a welcome sight.

7

I DROVE OUT to Robin's studio at half-past seven. It had been several days since I'd seen her and I missed her. When she opened the door she was wearing a gauzy white dress that accentuated the olive tint of her skin. Her hair hung loose and she wore gold hoops in her ears

She held out her arms to me and we embraced for a long while. We walked inside, still clinging together.

Her place is an old store on Pacific Avenue in Venice. Like lots of other studios nearby, it's unmarked, the windows painted over in opaque white.

She led me past the front part, the work area full of power tools—table saw, band saw, drill press—piles of wood, instrument molds, chisels, gauges and templates. As usual the room smelled of sawdust and glue. The floor was covered with shavings.

She pushed open swinging double doors and we were in her living quarters: sitting room, kitchen, sleeping loft with bath, small office. Unlike the shop, her personal space was uncluttered. She had made most of the furniture herself, and it was solid hardwood, simple and elegant.

She sat me down on a soft cotton couch. There was coffee and pie set out on a ceramic tray, napkins, plates and forks.

She sidled next to me. I took her face in my hands and kissed her.

"Hello, darling." She put her arms around me. I could feel the firmness of her back through the thin fabric, firmness couched in yielding, curving softness. She worked with her hands and it always amazed me to find in her that special combination of muscles and distinctly female lush-

71

ness. When she moved, whether manipulating a hunk of
rosewood around the rapacious jaws of a band saw or
simply walking, it was with confidence and grace. Meeting her was the best thing that had ever happened to me. It
alone had been worth dropping out for.

I'd been browsing at McCabe's, the guitar shop in Santa
Monica, looking through the old sheet music, trying out
the instruments that hung on the walls. I'd spied one
particularly attractive guitar, like my Martin but even better made. I admired the craftsmanship—it was a hand-
made instrument—and ran my fingers over the strings,
which vibrated with perfect balance and sustain. Taking it
off the wall I played it and it sounded as good as it looked,
ringing like a bell.

"Like it?"

The voice was feminine and belonged to a gorgeous
creature in her mid-twenties. She stood close to me—how
long she'd been there I wasn't sure; I'd been lost in the
music. She had a heart-shaped face topped by a luxuriant
mop of auburn curls. Her eyes were almond-shaped, wide-
set, the color of antique mahogany. She was small, not
more than five-two, with slender wrists leading to delicate
hands and long, tapering fingers. When she smiled, her
upper two incisors, larger than the rest of her teeth, flashed
ivory.

"Yes. I think it's terrific."

"It's not that good." She put her hands on her hips—
very definite hips. She had the kind of figure, small-
waisted, busty and gently concave, that couldn't be
camouflaged by the overalls she'd thrown on over her
turtleneck.

"Oh, really?"

"Oh, really." She took the guitar from me. "There's a
spot right here—" she tapped the soundboard "—where
it's been sanded too thin. And the balance between head-
stock and box could be better." She strummed a few
chords. "All in all I'd give it an eight on a scale of one to
ten."

"You seem to be quite an expert on it."

"I should be. I made it."

She took me to her shop that afternoon and showed me

the instrument she was working on. "This one's going to be a ten. The other was one of my first. You learn as you go along."

Some weeks later she admitted it had been her way of picking me up, her version of *come up and see my etchings*.

"I liked the way you played. Such sensitivity."

We saw each other regularly after that. I learned that she had been an only child, the special daughter of a skilled cabinetmaker who had taught her everything he knew about how to transform raw wood into objects of beauty. She had tried college, majoring in design, but the regimentation had angered her, as had the fact that her dad had known more about form and function intuitively than all the teachers and books combined. After he died, she dropped out, took the money he left her and invested in a shop in San Luis Obispo. She got to know some local musicians, who brought her their instruments to fix. At first it was a sideline, for she was trying to make a living designing and manufacturing custom furniture. Then she began to take a greater interest in the guitars, banjos and mandolins that found their way to her workbench. She read a few books on instrument-making, found she had all the requisite skills and made her first guitar. It sounded great and she sold it for five hundred dollars. She was hooked. Two weeks later she moved to L.A., where the musicians were, and set up shop.

When I met her she was making two instruments a month as well as handling repairs. She'd been written up in trade magazines and was back-ordered for four months. She was starting to make a living.

I probably loved her the first day I met her but it took me a couple of weeks to realize it.

After three months we started to talk about living together, but it didn't happen. There was no philosophical objection on either side, but her place was too small for two people and my house couldn't accommodate her shop. It sounds unromantic, letting mundane matters like space and comfort get in the way, but we were having such a good time with each other while maintaining our privacy, that the incentive to make a change wasn't there. Often she would spend the night with me, other times I'd collapse in her loft. Some evenings we'd go our separate ways.

It wasn't a bad arrangement.

I sipped coffee and eyed the pie.

"Have some, babe."

"I don't want to pork out before dinner."

"Maybe we won't go out for dinner." She stroked the back of my neck. "Ooh, such tension." She began to knead the muscles of my upper back. "You haven't felt this way in a long time."

"There's a good reason for it." And I told her about Milo's morning visit, the murder, Melody, Towle.

When I was through she placed her hands on my shoulders.

"Alex, do you really want to get into something like this?"

"Do I have a choice? I see that kid's eyes in my sleep. I was a fool for getting sucked in, but now I'm stuck."

She looked at me. The corners of her mouth lifted in a smile.

"You are such a pushover. And so sweet."

She nuzzled me under my chin. I held her to me and buried my face in her hair. It smelled of lemon and honey and rosewood.

"I really love you."

"I love you, too, Alex."

We undressed each other and when we were totally naked, I lifted her in my arms and carried her up the stairs to the loft. Not wanting to be apart from her for one second I kept my mouth fastened upon hers while I maneuvered myself on top of her. She clung to me, her arms and legs like tendrils. We connected, and I was home.

8

WE SLEPT until 10 P.M., then awoke famished. I went down to the kitchen and made sandwiches of Italian salami and Swiss cheese on rye, found a jug of burgundy and toted it all back upstairs for a late supper in bed. We shared garlicky kisses, got crumbs in the bed, hugged each other and fell back asleep.

We were jolted awake by the telephone.

Robin answered it.

"Yes, Milo, he's here. No, that's all right. Here he is."

She handed me the receiver and buried herself under the covers.

"Hello, Milo. What time is it?"

"Three A.M."

I sat up and rubbed my eyes. Through the skylight the heavens were black.

"What's going on."

"It's the kid—Melody Quinn. She's freaked out—woke up screaming. Bonita called Towle who called me. Demanded you get over there. He sounds pissed."

"Screw him. I'm not his errand boy."

"You want me to tell him that? He's right here."

"You're over there now? At her place?"

"Certainly. Neither rain nor hail nor darkness stays this trusted civil servant and all that shit. We're having a little party. The doctor, Bonita, me. The kid's sleeping. Towle gave her a shot of something."

"Figures."

"The kid spilled to her mom about the hypnosis. He wants you there if she wakes up again—to rehypnotize or something."

"That asshole. The hypnosis didn't cause this. The kid's got sleep problems because of all the dope he's been shoving into her system."

But I was far from certain of that. She *had* been troubled after the session on the beach.

"I'm sure you're right, Alex. I just wanted to give you the option to come down here, to know what was going on. If you want me to tell Towle to forget it, I will."

"Hold on a minute." I shook my head, trying to clear it. "Did she say anything when she woke up—anything coherent?"

"I just caught the tail end of it. They said it was the fourth time tonight. She was screaming for her daddy: 'Oh Daddy. Daddy, Daddy'—like that, but very loud. It looked and sounded pretty bad, Alex."

"I'll be down there as soon as I can."

I gave the sleeping mummy next to me a kiss on the fanny, got up, and threw on my clothes.

I sped along Pacific, heading north. The streets were empty and slick with marine mist. The guide lights at the end of the pier were distant pinpoints. A few trawlers sat on the horizon. At this hour the sharks and other nocturnal predators would be prowling the bottom of the ocean floor. I wondered how much carnage was hidden by the glossy black outer skin of the water; and how many of the night-hunters lurked on dry land, hiding in alleys, behind trash bins, concealed among the leaves and twigs of suburban shrubbery, wild-eyed, breathing hard.

As I drove I developed a new theory of evolution. Evil had its own metamorphic intelligence: The sharks and the razor-toothed serpents, the slimy, venomous things that hid in the silt, hadn't given way in an orderly progression to amphibian, reptile, bird and mammal. A single quantum leap had taken evil from water to land. From shark to rapist, eel to throat-slasher, poison slug to skull-crusher, with bloodlust at the core of the helix.

The darkness seemed to press against me, insistent, fetid. I pushed down harder on the accelerator and forced my way through it.

When I got to the apartment complex, Milo met me at the door.

"She's just started again."

I could hear it before I got to the bedroom.

The light was dim. Melody sat upright in her bed, her body rigid, eyes wide open but unfocused. Bonita sat next to her. Towle, in sports clothes, stood on the other side.

The child was sobbing, a wounded animal sound. She wailed and moaned and rocked back and forth. Then the moan picked up volume, gradually, like a siren, until she was screaming, her thin voice a piercing, shrieking assault upon the silence.

"Daddy! Daddy! Daddy!"

Her hair was plastered against her face, slick with sweat. Bonita tried to hold her but she flailed and struck out. The mother was helpless.

The screaming continued for what seemed like forever, then it stopped and she began moaning again.

"Oh, Doctor," Bonita pleaded, "she's going at it again. Do something."

Towle spotted me.

"Maybe Dr. Delaware can help." His tone of voice was nasty.

"No, no, I don't want *him* near her! He caused all of this!"

Towle didn't argue with her. I could have sworn he looked smug.

"Mrs. Quinn—" I began.

"No. You stay away! Get out!"

Her screaming set Melody off, and she began calling for her father again.

"Stop it!"

Bonita went for her, putting her hand over the child's mouth. Shaking her.

Towle and I moved at the same time. We pulled her off. He took her aside and said something that quieted her down.

I moved next to Melody. She was breathing hard. Her pupils were dilated. I touched her. She stiffened.

"Melody," I whispered, "It's Alex. You're okay. You're safe."

As I talked she calmed down. I blabbed on, knowing that what I said was less important than how I said it. I maintained a low, rhythmic pattern of speech, easy-going, reassuring. Hypnotic.

Soon she had slipped lower in the bed. I helped her lie down. Her hands unfolded. I kept talking to her soothingly. Her muscles began to relax and her breathing became slow and regular. I told her to close her eyes and she did. I stroked her shoulder, continued to talk to her, to tell her everything was all right, that she was safe.

She snuggled into a fetal position, drew the covers over her, and placed her thumb in her mouth.

"Turn off the light," I said. The room became dark. "Let's leave her alone." The three of them left.

"Now you're going to continue sleeping, Melody, and you'll have a very peaceful, restful night, with good dreams. When you wake up in the morning you'll feel very good, very rested."

I could hear her snoring ever so slightly.

"Goodnight, Melody." I leaned over and gave her a light kiss on the cheek.

She mumbled one word.

"Da-da."

I closed the door to her room. Bonita was in the kitchen, wringing her hands. She wore a frayed man's terrycloth robe. Her hair had been pulled back in a bun and covered with a scarf. She looked paler than I remembered as she busied herself cleaning up.

Towle bent over his black bag. He clicked it shut, stood and ran his fingers through his hair. Seeing me he raised himself up to his full height and glared down, ready to give another lecture.

"I hope you're happy," he said.

"Don't start," I warned him. "No I-told-you-so's."

"You can see why I was reluctant to tamper with this child's mind."

"Nobody tampered with anything." I could feel tension rising in my gut. He was every hypocritical authority figure I'd detested.

He shook his head condescendingly.

"Obviously your memory needs some polishing."

"Obviously you're a sanctimonious prick."

The blue eyes flashed. He tightened his lips.

"What if I bring you up before the ethics committee of the State Medical Board?"

"You do that, Doctor."

"I'm seriously considering it." He looked like a Calvinist preacher, all stern and tight and self-righteous.

"You do it and we'll get into a little discussion on the proper use of stimulant medication with children."

He smiled.

"It will take more than you to tarnish my reputation."

"I'm sure it will." My fists were clenched. "You've got legions of loyal followers. Like that woman in there." I pointed toward the kitchen. "They bring their kids to you, human jalopies, and you tinker with them, give 'em a quick tune-up and a pill; you fix them to their specifications. Make them nice and quiet, compliant, and obedient. Drowsy little zombies. You're a goddamn hero."

"I don't have to listen to this." He moved forward.

"No you don't, hero. But why don't you go in there and tell her what you really think of her? Piss-poor protoplasm, and let's see—bad genes, no insight."

He stopped in his tracks.

"Easy, Alex." Milo spoke from the corner, cautiously.

Bonita came in from the kitchen.

"What's going on?" she wanted to know. Towle and I were facing each other like boxers after the bell.

He changed his manner and smiled at her charmingly. "Nothing, my dear. Just a professional discussion. Doctor Delaware and I were trying to decide what was best for Melody."

"What's best is no more hypnotizing. You told me that."

"Yes." Towle tapped his foot, tried not to look uncomfortable. "That was my professional opinion." He loved that word, professional. "And it still is."

"Well, you tell *him* that." She pointed at me.

"That's what we were discussing, dear."

He must have been just a little too smooth, because her face got tight and her voice lowered suspiciously.

"What's to discuss? I don't want him or him—" the second jab was at Milo "—around here no more." She turned to us. "You try and be a good Samaritan and help the cops and you get the shaft! Now my baby's got the seizures and she's screamin' and I'm gonna lose my place. I know I'm gonna lose it!''

Her face crumpled. She buried it in her hands and began to cry. Towle moved in like a Beverly Hills gigolo, putting his arms around her, consoling her, saying now, now.

He guided her to the couch and sat her down, standing over her, patting her shoulder.

''I'm gonna lose my place,'' she said into her hands. ''They don't like noise here.'' She uncovered her face and looked wet-eyed up at Towle.

''Now, now, it's going to be all right. I'll see to that.''

''But what about the seizures!?''

''I'll see to that, too.'' He gave me a sharp look, full of hostility and, I was sure, a bit of fear.

She sniffled and wiped her nose on her sleeve.

''I don't understand why she has to wake up screaming Daddy Daddy! That bastard's never been around to lift a finger or give me a cent of child support! He has no love for her! Why does she cry out for *him*, Doctor Towle?'' She looked up at him, a novitiate beseeching the pope.

''Now, now.''

''He's a crazy man, that Ronnie Lee is. Look at this!'' She tore the scarf from her head, shook her hair loose and lowered her head exposing the top of it. Giving a whimper she parted the strands at the center of her crown. ''Look at this!''

It was ugly. A thick, raw red scar the size of a fat worm. A worm that had burrowed under her scalp and settled there. The skin around it was livid and lumpy, showing the results of bad surgery, devoid of hair.

''Now you know why I cover it!'' she cried. ''*He* did that to me! With a *chain!* Ronnie Lee Quinn.'' She spat out the name. ''A crazy, evil bastard. That's the Daddy Daddy she's cryin' out for! That scum!''

''Now, now,'' said Towle. He turned to us. ''Do you gentlemen have anything more to discuss with Mrs. Quinn?''

''No, Doctor,'' said Milo and turned to leave. He took hold of my arm to guide me out. But I had something to say.

''Tell her, Doctor. Tell her those were not seizures. They were night terrors and they'll go away by themselves

if you keep her calm. Tell her there'll be no need for
phenobarbitol or Dilantin or Tofranil.''

Towle continued to pat her shoulder.

"Thank you for your professional opinion, Doctor. I'll
manage this case as I see fit.''

I stood there rooted.

"Come on, Alex." Milo eased me out the door.

The parking lot of the apartment complex was crammed
full of Mercedes, Porsches, Alfa Romeo's and Datsun Z's.
Milo's Fiat, parked in front of a hydrant, looked sadly out
of place, like a cripple at a track meet. We sat in it, glum.

"What a mess," he said.

"The bastard.''

"For a minute I thought you were going to hit him." He
chuckled.

"It was tempting. The bastard.''

"It looked like he was baiting you. I thought you guys
got along.''

"On his terms. On an intellectual level we were good
old boys. When things fell apart he had to find a scape-
goat. He's an egomaniac. *Doctor* is omnipotent. *Doctor*
can fix anything. Did you see how she worshipped him,
the goddamned Great White Father? Probably slit the kid's
wrists if he told her to.''

"You're worried about the kid, aren't you?"

"You're damn right I am. You know exactly what he's
going to do, don't you—more dope. She'll be a total space
cadet in two days.''

Milo chewed on his lip. After a few minutes he said:

"Well, there's nothing we can do about it. I'm sorry I
pulled you into it in the first place.''

"Forget it. It wasn't your fault.''

"Nah, it was. I've been lazy, trying for an instant
miracle on this Handler mess. Been avoiding the old wear-
down-the-shoe-leather routine. Question Handler's associ-
ates, get the list of known bad guys with razor-happy
fingers from the computer and plod through it. Go through
Handler's files. The whole thing was iffy in the first place,
a seven-year-old kid.''

"She could have turned out to be a good witness.''

"Is it ever that easy?" He started up the engine, after three attempts. "Sorry for ruining your night."

"You didn't. He did."

"Forget him, Alex. Assholes are like weeds—a bitch to get rid of and when you do, another one grows back in the same place. That's what I've been doing for eight years—pouring weed-killer and watching them grow back faster than I can clear them away."

He sounded weary and looked old.

I got out of the car and leaned in through the window.

"See you tomorrow."

"What?"

"The files. We have to go through Handler's files. I'll be able to tell faster than you will which ones were dangerous."

"You're kidding."

"Nope. I'm carrying around a huge Zeigarnik."

"A what?"

"Zeigarnik. She was a Russian psychologist who discovered that people develop tension for unfinished business. They named it after her. The Zeigarnik effect. Like most overachievers I've got a big one."

He looked at me like I was talking nonsense.

"Uh-huh. Right. And this Zeigarnik is big enough for you to let it intrude upon the mellow life?"

"What the hell, life was getting boring." I slapped him on the back.

"Suit yourself." He shrugged. "Regards to Robin."

"You give regards to your doctor."

"If he's still there when I get back. This middle-of-the-night stuff is testing that relationship." He scratched at the corner of his eye and scowled.

"I'm sure he'll put up with it, Milo."

"Oh yeah? Why's that?"

"If he's crazy enough to go for you in the first place, he's crazy enough to stick with you."

"That's very reassuring, pal." He ground the Fiat into first and sped away.

9

AT THE TIME of his murder, Morton Handler had been in practice as a psychiatrist for a little under fifteen years. During that period he had consulted on or treated over two thousand patients. The records of these individuals were stored in manila folders and packed, one hundred and fifty to a box, in cardboard cartons that were taped shut and stamped with the L.A.P.D. seal.

Milo brought these boxes to my house, assisted by a slight, balding, black detective named Delano Hardy. Huffing and wheezing, they loaded the cartons in my dining room. Soon it looked as if I was either moving in or moving out.

"It's not as bad as it seems," Milo assured me. "You won't have to go through all of them. Right, Del?"

Hardy lit a cigarette and nodded assent.

"We've done some preliminary screening," he said. "We eliminated anyone known to be deceased. We figured they'd be low probability suspects."

The two of them laughed. Dark detective laughs.

"And the coroner's report," he continued, "says Handler and the girl were cut by someone with a lot of muscle. The throat wound on him went clear back to the spine on the first try."

"Which means," I interrupted, "a man."

"Could be one hell of a tough lady," laughed Hardy, "but we're betting on a male."

"There are six hundred male patients," added Milo. "Those four boxes over there."

"Also," said Hardy, "we brought you a little present." He gave me a small package wrapped in green and red

83

Christmas paper with a bugle and holly wreath pattern on it. It was tied with red ribbon.

"Couldn't find any other paper," Hardy explained.

"We hope you like it," added Milo. I began to feel as if I were the audience for a salt-and-pepper comedy team. A curious transformation had come over Milo. In the presence of another detective he had distanced himself from me and adopted the tough-wiseacre banter of the veteran cop.

I unwrapped the box and opened it. Inside, on a bed of cotton, was a plastic-coated L.A.P.D. identification badge. It bore a picture of me like the one on my driver's license, with that strange, frozen look that all official photos seem to have. Under the picture was my signature, also from my license, my name printed out, my degree and the title "Special Consultant." Life imitates art . . .

"I'm touched."

"Put it on," said Milo. "Make it official."

The badge wasn't unlike the one I had worn at Western Pediatric. It came with a clasp. I affixed it to my shirt collar.

"Very attractive," said Hardy. "That and ten cents might get you a local phone call." He reached into his jacket and drew out a folded piece of paper. "Now, if you'll just read and sign this." He held out a pen.

I read it, all small print.

"This says you don't have to pay me."

"Right," said Hardy with mock sadness. "And if you get a paper cut looking over the files you can't sue the department."

"It makes the brass happy, Alex," said Milo.

I shrugged and signed.

"Now," said Hardy, "you're an official consultant to the Los Angeles Police Department." He folded the paper and slipped it back in his pocket. "Just like the rooster who was jumping the bones of all the hens in the henhouse. So they castrated him and turned him into a consultant."

"That's very flattering, Del."

"Any friend of Milo and all that."

Milo, meanwhile, was opening the sealed cartons with a Swiss Army knife. He took out files in dozens and made neat little piles that covered the dining-room table.

"These are alphabetized, Alex. You can go through them and pull out the weird ones."

He finished setting things up and he and Hardy got ready to go.

"Del and I will be talking to bad guys off the NCIC printout."

"We've got our work cut out for us," said Hardy. He cracked his knuckles and looked for a place to put out his cigarette, which was smoked down to the filter.

"Toss it in the sink."

He left to do so.

When we were alone Milo said: "I really appreciate this, Alex. Don't drive yourself—don't try to get it all done today."

"I'll do as many as I can before the eyes start to blur."

"Right. We'll call you a couple of times today. To see if you've got anything we can pick up while we're on the road."

Hardy came back straightening his tie. He was dapper in a three-piece navy worsted suit, white shirt, blood-red tie, shiny black calfskin loafers. Next to him Milo looked more shopworn than ever in his sagging trousers and lifeless tweed sport coat.

"You ready, my man?" Hardy asked.

"Ready."

"Onward."

When they were gone I put a Linda Ronstadt record on the turntable. To the accompaniment of "Poor, Poor Pitiful Me," I started to consult.

Eighty percent of the male patients in the files fell into two categories: affluent executive types referred by their internists due to a variety of stress-related symptoms— angina, impotence, abdominal pain, chronic headaches, insomnia, skin rashes of unknown origins—and depressed men of all ages. I reviewed these and put aside the remaining 20 percent for more detailed perusal.

I knew nothing about what kind of psychiatrist Morton Handler had been when I started, but after several hours of reviewing his charts I began to build an image of him— one that was far from saintly.

His therapy session notes were sketchy, careless, and so

ambiguous as to be meaningless. It was impossible to
know from reading them what he had done during those
countless forty-five-minute hours. There was scant mention of treatment plans, prognoses, stress histories—anything
that could be considered medically or psychologically relevant. This shoddiness was most evident in notes taken
during the last five or six years of his life.

His financial records, on the other hand, were meticu-
lous and detailed. His fees were high, his form letters to
debtors strongly worded.

Though during the last few years he had done less
talking and more prescribing, the rate at which he ordered
medication wasn't unusual. Unlike Towle, he didn't appear to be a pusher. But he wasn't much of a therapist,
either.

What really bothered me was his tendency, again more
common during later years, to inject snide comments into
the notes. These, which he didn't even bother to couch in
jargon, were nothing more than sarcastic put-downs of his
patients. "Likes to alternately whimper and simper" was
the description of one older man with a mood disorder.
"Unlikely to be capable of anything constructive" was his
pronouncement on another. "Wants therapy as camouflage
for a boring, meaningless life." "A real washout." And
so on.

By late afternoon my psychological autopsy of Handler
was complete. He was a burnout, one of the legions of
worker ants who had grown to hate his chosen profession.
He might have cared at one time—the early files were
decent, if not inspired—but he hadn't by the end. Nevertheless, he had kept it up, day after day, session after
session, unwilling to give up the six-figure income and the
perquisites of prosperity.

I wondered how he had occupied his time as his patients
poured out their inner turmoil. Did he daydream? Engage
in fantasies (sexual? financial? sadistic?)? Plan the evening's dinner menu? Do mental arithmetic? Count sheep?
Compute how many manic depressives could dance on the
head of a pin?

Whatever it had been, it hadn't included really listening
to the human beings who sat before him believing he
cared.

It made me think of the old joke, the one about the two shrinks who meet on the elevator at the end of the day. One of them is young, a novice, and he is clearly bedraggled—tie askew, hair messed, fraught with fatigue. He turns and notices that the other, a seasoned veteran, is totally composed—tan, fit, every hair in place, a fresh carnation stuck jauntily in his lapel.

"Doctor," beseeches the young one, "please tell me how you do it?"

"Do what, my son?"

"Sit, hour after hour, day after day, listening to people's problems without letting it get to you."

"Who listens?" replies the guru.

Funny. Unless you were shelling out ninety bucks a session to Morton Handler and getting a covert assessment as a simpering whimperer for your money.

Had one of the subjects of his nasty prose somehow discovered the sham and murdered him? It was difficult to imagine someone engaging in the kind of butchery that had been visited upon Handler and his girlfriend in order to avenge a peeve of that kind. But you never knew. Rage was a tricky thing; sometimes it lay dormant for years, only to be triggered by a seemingly trivial stimulus. People had been ripped apart over a nudged car bumper.

Still I found it hard to believe that the depressives and psychosomaticizers whose files I had reviewed were the stuff of which midnight skulkers were fashioned. What I really didn't want to believe was that there were two thousand potential suspects to deal with.

It was close to five. I pulled a Coors out of the refrigerator, took it out to the balcony and lay down on a lounge, my feet propped up on the guardrail. I drank and watched the sun dip beneath the tops of the trees. Someone in the neighborhood was playing punk rock. Strangely enough it didn't seem discordant.

At five-thirty Robin called.

"Hi, hon. You want to come over? *Key Largo*'s on tonight."

"Sure," I said. "Should I pick up anything to eat?"

She thought a moment.

"How about chili dogs? And beer."

"I've got a head start on the beer." Three squashed Coors empties sat on the kitchen counter.

"Give me time to catch up, love. See you around seven."

I hadn't heard from Milo since one-thirty. He'd called in from Bellflower, just about to interrogate a guy who'd assaulted seven women with a screwdriver. Very little similarity to the Handler case but you had to work with what you had.

I phoned West L.A. Division and left the message for him that I'd be out for the evening.

Then I called Bonita Quinn's number. I waited for five rings and when nobody answered, hung up.

Humphrey and Lauren were great, as usual. The chili dogs left us belching, but satisfied. We held each other and listened to Tal Farlow and Wes Montgomery for a while. Then I picked up one of the guitars she had lying around the studio and played for her. She listened, eyes closed, a faint smile on her lips, then gently removed my hands from the instrument and pulled me to her.

I had planned to stay the night but at eleven I grew restless.

"Is anything the matter, Alex?"

"No." Just my Zeigarnik tugging at me.

"It's the case, isn't it?"

I said nothing.

"I'm starting to worry about you, sweetie." She put her head on my chest, a welcome burden. "You've been so edgy since Milo got you into all of this. I never knew you before, but from what you told me it sounds like the old days."

"The old Alex wasn't such a bad guy," I reacted defensively.

She was wisely silent.

"No," I corrected myself. "The old Alex was a bore. I promise not to bring him back, okay?"

"Okay." She kissed the tip of my chin.

"Just give me a little time to get through this."

"All right."

But as I dressed she looked at me with a combination of

worry, hurt, and confusion. When I started to say something, she turned away. I sat down on the edge of the bed and took her in my arms. I rocked her until her arms slid around my neck.

"I love you," I said. "Give me a little time."

She made a warm sound and held me tighter.

When I left her she was sleeping, her eyelids fluttering in the throes of the first dream of the night.

I tore into the one hundred and twenty files I had set aside, working until the early morning hours. Most of these turned out also to be rather mundane documents. Ninety-one of the patients were physically ill men whom Handler had seen as a consultant when he was still working at Cedars-Sinai as part of the liaison psychiatry team. Another twenty had been diagnosed schizophrenic, but they turned out to be senile (median age, seventy-six) patients at a convalescent hospital where he'd worked for a year.

The remaining nine men were of interest. Handler had diagnosed them all as psychopathic character disorders. Of course those diagnoses were suspect, as I had little faith in his judgment. Nevertheless the files were worth examining more closely.

They were all between the ages of sixteen and thirty-two. Most had been referred by agencies—the Probation Department, the California Youth Authority, local churches. A couple had experienced several scrapes with the law. At least three were judged violent. Of these, one had beaten up his father, another had stabbed a fellow high school student, and the third had used an automobile to run down someone with whom he'd exchanged angry words.

A bunch of real sweethearts.

None of them had been involved in therapy for very long, which was not surprising. Psychotherapy hasn't much to offer the person with no conscience, no morals, and, quite often, no desire to change. In fact, the psychopath by his very nature is an affront to modern psychology, with its egalitarian and optimistic philosophical underpinnings.

Therapists become therapists because down deep they feel that people are really good and have the capacity to change for the better. The notion that there exist individuals who are simply evil—bad people—and that such evil cannot be explained by any existing combination of nature or nurture is an assault upon a therapist's sensitivities. The psychopath is to the psychologist and the psychiatrist what the terminal cancer patient is to the physician: walking, breathing evidence of hopelessness and failure.

I knew such evil people existed. I had seen a mercifully small number of them, mostly adolescents, but some children. I remember one boy, in particular, not yet twelve years old, but possessed of a cynical, hardened, cruelly grinning face that would have done a San Quentin lifer proud. He'd handed me his business card—a bright rectangle of shocking pink paper with his name on it, followed by the single word *Enterprises*.

And an enterprising young man he had been. Buttressed by my assurances of confidentiality, he had told me proudly, of the dozens of bicycles he had stolen, of the burglaries he had pulled off, of the teenage girls he had seduced. He was so pleased with himself.

He had lost his parents in a plane crash at the age of four and had been brought up by a baffled grandmother who tried to assure everyone—and herself—that down deep he was a good boy. But he wasn't. He was a *bad* boy. When I asked him if he remembered his mother, he leered and told me she looked like a real piece of ass in the pictures he had seen. It wasn't defensive posturing. It was really him.

The more time I spent with him, the more discouraged I grew. It was like peeling an onion and finding each inner layer more rotten than the last. He was a bad boy, irredeemably so. Most likely, he would get worse.

And there was nothing I could do. There was little doubt he would end up establishing an anti-social career. If society was lucky, it would be limited to con games. If not, a lot of blood would be shed. Logic dictated that he should be locked up, kept out of harm's way, incarcerated for the protection of the rest of us. But democracy said otherwise, and, on balance, I had to admit it shouldn't be any other way.

Still, there were nights when I thought of that eleven-year-old and wondered if I'd be seeing his name in the papers one day.

I set the nine files aside.

Milo would have more of his work cut out for him.

10

THREE DAYS of the old wear-down-the-shoe-leather routine had worn Milo down.

"The computer was a total bust," he lamented, flopping down on my leather sofa. "All of those bastards are either back in the joint, dead, or alibied. The coroner's report has no forensic magic for us. Just six and a half pages of gory details telling us what we knew the first time we saw the bodies: Handler and Gutierrez were hacked up like sausage filler."

I brought him a beer, which he drained in two long gulps. I brought him another.

"What about Handler? Anything on him?" I asked.

"Oh yeah, you were definitely right in your initial impression. The guy was no Mr. Ethical. But it doesn't lead anywhere."

"What do you mean?"

"Six years ago, when he was doing hospital consultations, there was a bit of a stink—insurance fraud. Handler and some others were running a little scam. They'd peek their heads in for a second, say hello to a patient, and bill it as a full visit, which I take it is supposed to be forty-five or fifty minutes long. Then they'd make a note in the chart, bill for another visit, talk to the nurse, another visit, talk to the doctor, etc., etc. It was big bucks—one guy could put in for thirty, forty visits a day, at seventy, eighty bucks a visit. Figure it out."

"No surprise. It's done all the time."

"I'm sure. Anyway, it blew wide open because one of the patients had a son who was a doctor, and he started to get suspicious, reading the chart, seeing all these psychiat-

ric visits. Especially 'cause the old man had been unconscious for three months. He griped to the medical director,
who called Handler and the others in on the carpet. They
kept it quiet, on the condition that the crooked shrinks
leave.''

Six years ago. Just before Handler's notes had started to
get slipshod and sarcastic. It must have been hard going
from four hundred grand a year to a measly one hundred.
And having to actually work for it. A man could get
bitter . . .

"And you don't see an angle in that?"

"What? Revenge? From whom? It was insurance companies that were getting bilked. That's how they kept it
going so long. They never billed the patients, just billed
insurance." He took a swig of beer. "I've heard bad
things about insurance companies, pal, but I can't see
them sending around Jack the Ripper to avenge their honor."

"I see what you mean."

He got up and paced the room.

"This goddamn case sucks. It's been a week and I've
got absolutely zilch. The captain sees it as a dead end.
He's pulled Del off and left me with the whole stinking
mess. Tough breaks for the faggot."

"Another beer?" I held one out to him.

"Yeah, goddammit, why not? Drown it all in suds." He
wheeled around. "I tell you, Alex, I should have been a
schoolteacher. Viet Nam left me with this big psychic
hole, you know? All that death for nothing. I thought
becoming a cop would help me fill that hole, catch bad
guys, make some sense out of it all. Jesus, was I wrong!"

He grabbed the Coors out of my hand, tilted it over his
mouth, and let some of the foam dribble down his chin.

"The things that I see—the monstrous things that we
supposed humans do to each other. The shit I've become
inured to. Sometimes it makes me want to puke."

He drank silently for a few minutes.

"You're a goddamn good listener, Alex. All that training wasn't for naught."

"One good turn, my friend."

"Yeah, right. Now that you mention it, Hickle was
another shitty case. I never convinced myself that was
suicide. It stunk to high heaven."

"You never told me."

"What's to tell? I've no evidence. Just a gut feeling. I've got lots of gut feelings. Some of them gnaw at me and keep me up at night. To paraphrase Del, my gut feelings and ten cents."

He crushed the empty can between his thumb and forefinger, with the ease of someone pulverizing a gnat.

"Hickle stunk to high heaven, but I had no evidence. So I wrote it off. Like a bad debt. No one argued, no one gave a shit, just like no one'll give a shit when we write off Handler and the Gutierrez girl. Keep the records tidy, wrap it up, seal it, and kiss it good-bye."

Seven more beers, another half-hour of ranting and punishing himself, and he was stoned drunk. He crashed on the leather sofa, going down like a B-52 with a bellyful of shrapnel.

I slipped his shoes off and placed them on the floor beside him. I was about just to leave him that way, when I realized it had turned dark.

I called his home number. A deep, rich male voice answered.

"Hello."

"Hello, this is Alex Delaware, Milo's friend."

"Yes?" Wariness.

"The psychologist."

"Yes. Milo's spoken of you. I'm Rick Silverman."

The doctor, the mother's dream, now had a name.

"I just called to let you know that Milo stopped by here after work to discuss a case and he got kind of—intoxicated."

"I see."

I felt an absurd urge to explain to the man at the other end that there was really nothing going on between Milo and me, that we were just good friends. I suppressed it.

"Actually, he got stoned. Had eleven beers. He's sleeping it off now. I just wanted you to know."

"That's very considerate of you," Silverman said, acidly.

"I'll wake him, if you'd like."

"No, that's quite all right. Milo's a big boy. He's free to do as he pleases. No need to check in."

I wanted to tell him, listen you insecure, spoiled brat, I just called to do you a favor, to set your mind at ease.

Don't hand me any of your delicate indignation. Instead, I tried flattery.

"Okay, just thought I'd call you to let you know, Rick. I know how important you are to Milo, and I thought he'd want me to."

"Uh, thanks. I really appreciate it." Bingo. "Please excuse me. I've just come off a twenty-four-hour shift myself."

"No problem." I'd probably woken the poor devil. "Listen, how about if we get something some time—you and Milo and my girlfriend and myself?"

"I'd like that, Alex. Sure. Send the big slob home when he sobers up and we'll work out the details."

"Will do. Good talking to you."

"Likewise." He sighed. "Goodnight."

At nine thirty Milo awoke with a wretched look on his face. He started to moan, turning his head from side to side. I mixed tomato juice, a raw egg, black pepper, and Tabasco in a tall glass, propped him up and poured it down his throat. He gagged, sputtered, and opened his eyes suddenly, as if a bolt of lightning had zapped him in the tailbone.

Forty minutes later he looked every bit as wretched but he was painfully sober.

I got him to the door and stuck the files of the nine psychopaths under his arm.

"Bedtime reading, Milo."

He tripped down the stairs, swearing, made his way to the Fiat, groped at its door handle and threw himself in with a single lurching movement. With the aid of a rolling start, he got it ignited.

Alone at last, I got into bed, read the *Times*, watched TV—but damned if I could tell you what I saw, other than that it had lots of flat punch lines and jiggling boobs and cops who looked like male models. I enjoyed the solitude for a couple of hours, only pausing to think of murder and greed and twisted evil minds a few times before drifting off to sleep.

"ALL RIGHT," said Milo. We were sitting in an interrogation room at West L.A. Division. The walls were pea-green paint and one-way mirrors. A microphone hung from the ceiling. The furniture consisted of a gray metal table and three metal folding chairs. There was a stale odor of sweat and falsehood and fear in the air, the stink of diminished human dignity.

He had fanned out the folders on the table and picked up the first one with a flourish.

"Here's the way your nine bad guys shape up. Number one, Rex Allen Camblin, incarcerated at Soledad, assault and battery." He let the folder drop.

"Number two, Peter Lewis Jefferson, working on a ranch in Wyoming. Presence verified."

"Pity the poor cattle."

"That's a fact—he looked like a likely one. Number three, Darwin Ward—you'll never believe this—attending law school, Pennsylvania State University."

"A psychopathic attorney—not all that amazing, really."

Milo chuckled and picked up the next folder.

"Número cuatro—uh—Leonard Jay Helsinger, working construction on the Alaska pipeline. Location likewise confirmed by Juneau P.D. Five, Michael Penn, student at Cal State Northridge. Him we talk to." He put Penn's file aside. "Six, Lance Arthur Shattuck, short-order cook on the Cunard Line luxury cruiser *Helena*, verified by the Coast Guard to have been floating around in the middle of the Aegean Sea somewhere for the past six weeks. Seven, Maurice Bruno, sales representative for Presto Instant Print in Burbank—another interviewee.'' Bruno's file went on top of Penn's.

"Eight, Roy Longstreth, pharmacist for Thrifty's Drug chain, Beverly Hills branch. Another one. And—last but not least—Gerard Paul Mendenhall, Corporal, United States Army, Tyler, Texas, presence verified.''

Beverly Hills was closer than either Northride or Burbank, so we headed for Thrifty's. The Beverly Hills branch turned out to be a brick-and-glass cube on Canon Drive just north of Wilshire. It shared a block with trendy boutiques and a Häagen Dazs ice-cream parlor.

Milo showed his badge surreptitiously to the girl behind the liquor counter and got the manager, a light-skinned middle-aged black, in seconds flat. The manager got nervous and wanted to know if Longstreth had done anything wrong. In classic cop style, Milo hedged.

"We just want to ask him a few questions.''

I had trouble keeping a straight face through that one, but the cliché seemed to satisfy the manager.

"He's not here now. He comes on at two-thirty, works the night shift.''

"We'll be back. Please don't tell him we were here.''

Milo gave him his card. When we left he was studying it like a map to buried treasure.

The ride to Northridge was a half-hour cruise on the Ventura Freeway West. When we got to the Cal State campus, we headed straight for the registrar's office. Milo obtained a copy of Michael Penn's class schedule. Armed with that and his mug shot, we located him in twenty minutes, walking across a wide, grassy triangle accompanied by a girl.

"Mr. Penn?''

"Yes?'' He was a good-looking fellow, medium height, with broad shoulders and long legs. His light brown hair was cut preppy short. He wore a light blue Izod shirt and blue jeans, penny loafers with no socks. I knew from his file that he was twenty-six but he looked five years younger. He had a pleasant, unlined face, a real All-American type. He didn't look like the kind of guy who'd try to run someone down with a Pontiac Firebird.

"Police.'' Again, the badge. "We'd like to talk to you for a few moments.''

"What about?" The hazel eyes narrowed and the mouth got tight.

"We'd prefer to talk to you in private."

Penn looked at the girl. She was young, no more than nineteen, short, dark, with a Dorothy Hamill wedge cut.

"Give me a minute, Julie." He chucked her under the chin.

"Mike . . .?"

"Just a minute."

We left her standing there and walked to a concrete area furnished with stone tables and benches. Students moved by as if on a treadmill. There was little standing around. This was a commuter campus. Many of the students worked part-time jobs and squeezed classes in during their spare time. It was a good place to get your B.A. in computer science or business, a teaching credential or a master's in accounting. If you wanted fun or leisurely intellectual debates in the shade of an ivy-encrusted oak, forget it.

Michael Penn looked furious but he was working hard at concealing it.

"What do you want?"

"When's the last time you saw Dr. Morton Handler?"

Penn threw back his head and laughed. It was a disturbingly hollow sound.

"That asshole? I read about his death. No loss."

"When did you see him last?"

Penn was smirking now.

"Years ago, *officer.*" He made the title sound like an insult. "When I was in *therapy.*"

"I take it you didn't think much of him."

"Handler? He was a shrink." As if that explained it.

"You don't think much of psychiatrists."

Penn held out his hands, palms up.

"Hey listen. That whole thing was a big mistake. I lost control of my car and some paranoid idiot claimed I tried to kill him with it. They busted me, railroaded me and then they offered me probation if I saw a shrink. Gave me all those garbage tests."

Those garbage tests included the Minnesota Multiphasic Personality Inventory and a handful of projectives. Though far from perfect, they were reliable enough when it came to someone like Penn. I had read his MMPI profile and psychopathy oozed from every index.

"You didn't like Dr. Handler?"

"Don't put words in my mouth." Penn lowered his voice. He moved his eyes back and forth, restless, jumpy. Behind the handsome face was something dark and dangerous. Handler hadn't misdiagnosed this one.

"You did like him." Milo played with him like a gaffed stingray.

"I didn't like him or dislike him. I had no use for him. I'm not crazy. And I didn't kill him."

"You can account for your whereabouts the night he was murdered?"

"When was that?"

Milo gave him the date and time.

Penn cracked his knuckles and looked through us as if zeroing in on a distant target.

"Sure. That entire night I was with my girl."

"Julie?"

Penn laughed.

"Her? No I've got a mature woman, officer. A woman of means." His brow creased and his expression changed from smug to sour. "You're going to have to talk to her, aren't you?"

Milo nodded his head.

"That'll screw things up for me."

"Gee, Mike, that's really too bad."

Penn threw him a hateful look, then changed it to bland innocence. He could play his face like a deck of cards, shuffling, palming from the bottom, coming up with a new number every second.

"Listen, officer, that whole incident is behind me. I'm holding down a job, going to school—I'm getting my degree in six months. I don't want to get messed up because my name's in Handler's files."

He sounded like Wally on "Leave It to Beaver"—all earnest innocence. Gosh, Beave . . .

"We'll have to verify your alibi, Mike."

"Okay, okay, do it. Just don't tell her too much, okay? Keep it general."

Keep it general so I can fabricate something. You could see the gears spinning behind the high, tan forehead.

"Sure, Mike." Milo took his pencil out and tapped it on his lips.

"Sonya Magary. She owns the Puff 'n' Stuff Children's Boutique in the Plaza de Oro in Encino."

"Have you got the number handy?" Milo asked pleasantly.

Penn clenched his jaws and gave it to him.

"We'll call her, Mike. Don't you call her first, okay? We treasure spontaneity." Milo put away his pencil and closed his notepad. "Have a nice day, now."

Penn looked from me to Milo, then back to me, as if seeking an ally. Then he got up and walked away in long, muscular strides.

"Oh, Mike!" Milo called.

Penn turned around.

"What are you getting your degree in?"

"Marketing."

As we left the campus we could see him walking with Julie. Her head was on his shoulder, his arm around her waist. He was smiling down on her and talking very fast.

"What do you think?" Milo asked as he settled behind the wheel.

"I think he's innocent as far as this case goes, but I'll bet you he's got some kind of dirty deal going on. He was really relieved when he found out what we were there for."

Milo nodded.

"I agree. But what the hell—that's someone else's headache."

We got back on the freeway, heading east. We exited in Sherman Oaks, found a little French place on Ventura near Woodman and had lunch. Milo used the pay phone to call Sonya Magary. He came back to the table, shaking his head.

"She loves him. 'That dear boy, that sweet boy, I hope he's not in trouble.' " He imitated a thick Hungarian accent. "She verifies he was with her on the fateful night. Sounds proud of it. I expected her to tell me about their sex life—in Technicolor."

He shook his head and buried his face in a plate of steamed mussels.

*   *   *

We caught up with Roy Longstreth as he got out of his Toyota in the Thrifty's parking lot. He was short and frail-looking, with watery blue eyes and an undernourished chin. Prematurely bald, what little hair he did have was on the sides; he had left it long, hanging down over his ears, so that the general effect was of a friar who'd been meditating too long and had neglected his personal grooming. A mousy brown mustache snuck across his upper lip. He had none of Penn's bravado but there was that same jumpiness in the eyes.

"Yes, what do you want?" He piped up in a squeaky voice after Milo gave him the badge routine. He looked at his watch.

When Milo told him, he looked as if he were going to cry. Uncharacteristic anxiety for a supposed psychopath. Unless the whole thing was an act. You never knew the tricks those types could come up with when they had to.

"When I read about it I just knew you'd come after me." The insignificant mustache trembled like a twig in a storm.

"Why's that, Roy?"

"Because of the things he said about me. He told my mother I was a psychopath. Told her not to trust me. I'm probably on some whacko list, right?"

"Can you account for your whereabouts the night he was killed?"

"Yes. That's the first thing I thought of when I read about it—they're going to come and ask me questions about it. I made sure I knew. I even wrote it down. Wrote a note to myself. Roy, you were at church that night. So when they come and ask you, you'll know where you were—"

He could have gone on that way for a couple of days but Milo cut him off.

"Church? You're a religious man, Roy?"

Longstreth gave a laugh that was choked with panic.

"No, no. Not praying. The Westside Singles group at Bel Air Presbyterian—it's the same place Ronald Reagan used to go to."

"The singles group?"

"No, no, no. The church. He used to worship there before he was elected and—"

"Okay, Ron. You were at the Westside Singles group from when to when?"

The sight of Milo taking notes made him even more nervous. He began bouncing up and down, a marionette at the hands of a palsied puppeteer.

"From nine to one-thirty—I stayed to the end. I helped clean up. I can tell you what they served. It was guacamole and nachos and there was Gallo jug wine and shrimp dip and—"

"Of course there'll be lots of people who saw you there."

"Sure," he said, then stopped. "I—I didn't really mingle much. I helped out, tending bar. I saw lots of people but I don't know if any of them will—remember me." His voice had quieted to a whisper.

"That could be a problem, Roy."

"Unless—no—yes—Mrs. Heatherington. She's an older woman. She volunteers at church functions. She was cleaning up, too. And serving. I spent a lot of time talking to her—I can even tell you what we talked about, It was about collectables—she collects Norman Rockwells and I collect Icarts."

"Icarts?"

"You know, the Art Deco prints."

The works of Louis Icart went for high prices these days. I wondered how a pharmacist could afford them.

"Mother gave me one when I was sixteen and they—" he searched for the right word—"captivated me. She gives them to me on my birthday and I pick up a few myself. Dr. Handler collected them, too, you know. That—" he let his words trail off.

"Oh, really? Did he show you his collection?"

Longstreth shook his head energetically.

"No. He had one in his office. I noticed it and we started talking. But he used it against me later on."

"How's that?"

"After the evaluation—you know I was sent to him by the court after I was caught—" he looked nervously at the Thrifty's building—"shoplifting." Tears filled his eyes. "For God's sake, I took a tube of rubber cement at Sears and they caught me! I thought Mother would die from the shame. And I worried the School of Pharmacy would find out—it was horrible!''

"How did he use the fact that you collected Icarts against you?" asked Milo patiently.

"He kind of implied, never came out and said it, but phrased it so you knew what he meant but he couldn't be pinned down.''

"Implied what, Roy?"

"That he could be bought off. That if I bribed him with an Icart or two—he even mentioned the ones he liked—he would write a favorable report.''

"Did you?"

"What? Bribe him? Not on your life. That would be dishonest!''

"And did he press the issue?"

Longstreth picked at his fingernails.

"Like I said, not so you could pin him down. He just said that I was a borderline case—psychopathic personality, or something less stigmatizing—anxiety reaction or something like that—that I could go either way. In the end he told Mother I was a psychopath.''

The wan face screwed up with rage.

"I'm glad he's dead! There, I've said it! It's what I thought the first time I read about it in the paper.''

"But you didn't do it.''

"Of course not. I couldn't. I run from evil, I don't embrace it!''

"We'll talk to Mrs. Heatherington, Roy.''

"Yes. Ask her about the nachos and the wine—I believe it was Gallo Hearty Burgundy. And there was fruit punch with slices of orange floating in it, too. In a cut glass bowl. And one of the women got sick on the floor at the end. I helped mop it up—''

"Thanks, Roy. You can go now.''

"Yes. I will.''

He turned around like a robot, a thin figure in a short blue druggist's smock, and walked into Thrifty's.

"He's dispensing drugs?" I asked, incredulous.

"If he's not in some whacko file he should be.'' Milo pocketed his notepad and we walked to the car. "He look like a psychopath to you?"

"Not unless he's the best actor on the face of the earth. Schizoid, withdrawn. Pre-schizophrenic, if anything."

"Dangerous?"

"Who knows? Put him up against enough stress and he might blow. But I'd judge him more likely to go the hermit route—curl up in bed, play with himself, wither, stay that way for a decade or two while Mommy propped his pillows."

"If that story about the Icarts is true it sheds some light on our beloved victim."

"Handler? A real Dr. Schweitzer."

"Yeah," said Milo. "The kind of guy someone might want dead."

We got on Coldwater Canyon before it clogged with the cars of commuters returning to their homes in the Valley, and made it to Burbank by half past four.

Presto Instant Print was one of scores of gray concrete edifices that filled the industrial park near the Burbank airport like so many oversized tombstones. The air smelled toxic and the flatulent roar of jets shattered the sky at regular intervals. I wondered about the life expectancy of those who spent their daylight hours here.

Maurice Bruno had come up in the world since his file had been compiled. He was now a vice-president, in charge of sales. He was also unavailable, we were told by his secretary, a lissome brunette with arched eyebrows and a mouth meant for saying no.

"Then give me his boss," barked Milo. He shoved his badge under her nose. We were both hot and tired and discouraged. The last place we wanted to be stalled was Burbank.

"That would be Mr. Gershman," she said as if discovering some new insight.

"Then that would be who I want to talk to."

"Just one second."

She wiggled off and came back with her clone in a blond wig.

"I'm Mr. Gershman's secretary," the clone announced.

It must be the poison in the air, I decided. It caused brain damage, eroded the cerebral cortex to the point where simple facts took on an aura of profundity.

Milo took a deep breath.

"We'd like to talk with Mr. Gershman."

"May I inquire what it's about?"

"No, you may not. Bring us to Gershman now."

"Yes, sir." The two secretaries looked at each other. Then the brunette pushed a buzzer and the blonde led us through double glass doors into an enormous production area filled with machines that chomped, stamped, bit, snarled, and smeared. A few people hung around the periphery of the rabid steel monsters, dull-eyed, loose-jawed, breathing in fumes that reeked of alcohol and acetone. The noise, alone, was enough to kill you.

She made a sudden left, probably hoping to lose us to the maws of one of the behemoths, but we hung on, following the movement of her swaying butt until we came to another set of double doors. These she pushed and let go, forcing Milo to fall forward to catch them. A short corridor, another set of doors, and we were confronted by silence so complete as to be overwhelming.

The executive suite at Presto Instant Print might have been on another planet. Plush, plum-colored carpets that you had to bargain with in order to reclaim your ankles, walls paneled in real walnut. Large doors of walnut burl with names made of brass letters tastefully centered on the wood. And silence.

The blonde stopped at the end of the hall, in front of an especially large door with especially tasteful gold letters that said Arthur M. Gershman, President. She let us into a waiting room the size of an average house, motioned us to sit in chairs that looked and felt like unbaked bread dough. Settling behind her desk, a contraption of plexiglass and rosewood that afforded the world a perfect view of her legs, she pushed a button on a console that belonged at NASA Control Center, moved her lips a bit, nodded, and stood up again.

"Mr. Gershman will see you, now."

The inner sanctum was as expected—the size of a cathedral, decorated like something conceived in the pages of *Architectural Digest*, softly lit and comfortable but hard-edged enough to keep you awake—but the man behind the desk was a complete surprise.

He wore khaki pants and a short sleeved white shirt that

needed ironing. His feet were clad in Hush Puppies and since they were on the desk the holes in their soles were obvious. He was in his mid-seventies, bald, bespectacled, with one of the sidepieces of his glasses held together with masking tape, and potbellied.

He was talking on the phone when we came in.

"Hold the wire, Lenny." He looked up. "Thanks, Denise." The blonde disappeared. To us: "One second. Sit down, fix something." He pointed to a fully stocked bar that covered half of one wall.

"Okay, Lenny, I got cops here, gotta go. Yeah, cops. I don't know, you wanna ask em? Ha ha. Yeah, I'll tell em that for sure, you *momzer*. I'll tell em what *you* did in Palm Springs the last time we were there. Yeah. Okay, the Sahara job in lots of three hundred thousand with coasters and matchbooks—not boxes, books. I got it. I give you delivery in two weeks. What? Forget it." He winked at us. "Go ahead, go to someone local, see if I care. I got maybe one, two more months before I drop dead from this business—you think I care if an order drops dead? It's all gonna go to Uncle Sam and Shirley and my prince of a son who drives a German car. Nah, nah. A BMW. With my money. Yeah. What can you do, it's out of control. Ten days?" He made a masturbating motion with his free hand and beamed at us. "You're jerking off, Lenny. At least close the door, no one will see. Twelve days, tops. Okay? Twelve it is. Right. Gotta go, these cossacks are going to drag me away any minute. Good-bye."

The phone slammed down, the man shot up like an uncoiled spring.

"Artie Gershman."

He held out an ink-stained hand. Milo shook it, then I did. It was as hard as granite and horned with callus.

He sat down again, threw his feet back up on the desk.

"Sorry for the delay." He had the joviality of someone who was surrounded by enough automatons like Denise to ensure his privacy. "You deal with casinos they think they got a right to instant everything. That's the mob, you know—but what the hell am I telling you that, you're cops, you know that, right? Now, what can I do for you, officers? The parking situation I know is a problem. If it's that bastard at Chemco next door complaining, all I want to say is he can go straight to hell in a handbasket, because his Mexican ladies park in my lot all the time—you should also check how many of them are legal—if he wants to get really nasty, I can play that game too.''

He paused to catch his breath.

"It's not about parking.''

"No? What then?''

"We want to talk to Maurice Bruno.''

"Morry? Morry's in Vegas. We do a lot of our business there, with the casinos, the motels and hotels. Here.'' He opened a drawer of the desk and tossed a handful of matchbooks at us. Most of the big names were represented.

Milo pocketed a few.

"When will he be back?''

"In a few days. He went on a selling trip two weeks ago, first to Tahoe, then Reno, end up in Vegas—probably playing around a bit on company time, not to mention the expense account—but who cares, he's a terrific salesman.''

"I thought he was a vice-president.''

"Vice-president in charge of sales. It's a salesman with a fancy title, a bigger salary, a nicer office—what do you think of this place—looks like some fag fixed it up, right?''

I searched Milo's face for a reaction, found none.

"My wife. She did this herself. This place used to be nice. There was papers all over the place, a couple of chairs, white walls—normal walls so you could hear the noise from the plant, know something was going on. This feels like death, you know. That's what I get for taking a second wife. A first wife leaves you alone, a second one wants to make you into a new person.''

"Are you sure Mr. Bruno's in Las Vegas?''

"Why shouldn't I be sure? Where else would he go?''

"How long has Mr. Bruno been working for you, Mr. Gershman?''

"Hey, what's this—this isn't child support or something like that?''

"No. We just want to talk to him about a homicide investigation we're conducting.''

"Homicide?'' Gershman shot out of _his_ chair. "Murder? Morry Bruno? You got to be kidding. He's a gem of a guy!''

A gem who had been excellent at passing rubber checks.

"How long has he been working for you, sir?"

"Let me see—a year and a half, maybe two."

"And you've had no problem with him?"

"Problem? I tell you he's a gem. Knew nothing about the business, but I hired him on hunch. Hell of a salesman. Outsold all the other guys—even the old-timers—by the fourth month. Reliable, friendly, never a problem."

"You mentioned child support. Mr. Bruno's divorced?"

"Divorced," said Gershman sadly. "Like everyone. Including my son. They give up too easily nowadays."

"Does he have family here in Los Angeles?"

"Nah. The wife, kids—three of em, I think—they moved back east. Pittsburgh, or Cleveland, some place with no ocean. He missed 'em, talked about it. That's why he volunteered at the Casa."

"Casa?"

"That kids' place, up in Malibu. Morry used to spend his weekends there, volunteering with the kids. He got a certificate. C'mon I'll show you."

Bruno's office was a quarter the size of Gershman's, but decked out in the same eclectically elegant style. The place was neat as a pin, not surprising, since Bruno spent most of his time on the road. Gershman pointed to a framed plaque that shared wall space with a half-dozen Number One Salesman commendations.

"You see—'awarded to Maurice Bruno in recognition of voluntary service to the homeless children of La Casa de los Niños' blah blah blah. I told you he was a gem."

The certificate was signed by the Mayor, as honorary witness, and by the director of the children's home, a Reverend Augustus J. McCaffrey. It was all calligraphy and floral intaglio. Very impressive.

"Very nice," said Milo. "Do you know what hotel Mr. Bruno was staying at?"

"He used to stay at the MGM, but after the fire, I don't know. Let's go back to the office and find out."

Back in Office Beautiful, Gershman picked up the telephone, punched the intercom and barked into the receiver.

"Denise, where's Morry staying in Vegas? Do that."

A half-minute later the intercom buzzed.

"Yeah? Good. Thanks, darling." He turned to us. "The Palace."

"Caesar's Palace?"

"Yeah. You want me to call there, you can talk to him?"

"If you don't mind, sir. We'll charge it to the Police Department."

"Nah!" Gershman waved his hand. "On me. Denise, call Caesar's Palace, get Morry on the phone. He's not there, leave him a message to call—"

"Detective Sturgis. West L.A. Division."

Gershman completed the instructions.

"You're not thinking about Morry as a suspect, are you?" he asked when he got off the phone. "This is a witness thing, right?"

"We really can't say anything about it, Mr. Gershman." Milo paid lip service to discretion.

"I can't believe it!" Gershman slapped his head with his hand. "You think Morry's a murderer! A guy who works with kids on the weekend—a guy who never had a cross word with anybody here—go ask around, I give you permission. You find someone who has a bad word to say about Morry Bruno, I'll eat this desk!"

He was interrupted by the intercom buzzer.

"Yes, Denise. What's that? You're sure? Maybe it was a mistake. Check again. And then call the Aladdin, the Sands, maybe he changed his mind."

The old man's face was solemn when he hung up.

"He's not at the Palace." He said it with the sadness and fear of someone about to be torn from the comforting warmth of his preconceptions.

Maurice Bruno wasn't at the Aladdin or the Sands or any other major hotel in Las Vegas. Additional calls from Gershman's office revealed the fact that none of the airlines had a record of him flying from L.A. to Vegas.

"I'd like his home address and phone number, please."

"Denise will give it to you," said Gershman. We left him sitting alone in his big office, grizzled chin resting in his hands, frowning like a battered old bison who'd spent too many years at the zoo.

Bruno lived in Glendale, normally a ten-minute drive from the Presto plant, but it was 6 P.M., there had been an accident just west of the Hollywood—Golden State interchange, and the freeway was stagnant all the way from Burbank to Pasadena. By the time we exited on Brand, it was dark and both of us were in foul moods.

Milo turned north and headed toward the mountains. Bruno's house was on Armelita, a side street half a mile from where the boulevard ended. It was situated at the end of a cul-de-sac, a small, one-story mock Tudor fronted by a neat, square lawn, yew hedges and sprigs of juniper stuffed in the empty spaces. Two large arborvitae bushes guarded the entrance. It wasn't the kind of place I would have imagined for a Vegas-haunting bachelor. Then I remembered what Gershman had said about the divorce. No doubt this was the homestead left behind by the fleeing wife and children.

Milo rang the doorbell a couple of times, then he knocked hard. When no one answered he went to the car and called the Glendale police. Ten minutes later a squad car pulled up and two uniformed officers got out. Both were tall, beefy and sandy-haired and wore bushy, bristly, strawlike mustaches under their noses. They came over with that swagger unique to cops and drunks trying hard to look sober, and conferred with Milo. Then they got on their radio.

The street was quiet and devoid of visible human habitation. It stayed that way as the three additional squad cars and the unmarked Dodge drove up and parked. There was a brief conference that resembled a football huddle and then guns were drawn. Milo rang the bell again, waited a minute and then kicked the door in. The assault was on.

I stayed outside, watching, waiting. Soon the sound of gagging and retching could be heard. Then cops began running out of the house, spilling out on the lawn, their hands to their noses, an action sequence in reverse. One particularly stalwart patrolman busied himself puking into the junipers. When it appeared that they'd all retreated, Milo came to the door, a handkerchief held over his nose and mouth. His eyes were visible and they made contact with me. They gave me a choice.

Against my better judgment I pulled out my own handkerchief, masked the lower part of my face and went in.

The thin cotton was scant defense against the hot stench that rose up against me as I stepped across the threshold. It was as if raw sewage and swamp gas had blended into a bubbling, swirling soup, then vaporized and sprayed into the air.

My eyes watering, I fought the urge to vomit, and followed Milo's advancing silhouette into the kitchen.

He was sitting there at a Formica table. The bottom part of him, the part in clothing, still looked human. The sky-blue salesman's suit, the maize-colored button-down shirt with blue silk foulard. The dandy's touches—the breast pocket hankie, the shoes with tiny tassles, the gold bracelet that hung around a wrist teeming with maggots.

From the neck up he was something the pathologists threw out. It looked as if he'd been worked over with a crowbar—the entire front part of what used to be his face was caved in—but it was really impossible to know what the swollen bloody lump attached to his shoulders had been subjected to, so advanced was the state of decay.

Milo began throwing open windows and I realized that the house felt as hot as a blast furnace, fueled by the hydrocarbons emitted by decomposing organic matter. A quick answer to the energy crisis: Save kilowatts, kill a friend . . .

I couldn't take any more. I ran for the door, gasping, and flung away the handkerchief when I reached the outdoors. I gulped hungrily at the cool night air. My hands shook.

There was lots of excitement on the block now. Neighbors—men, women and children—had come out of their castles, pausing in the middle of the evening news, interrupting their defrosted feasts to gawk at the blinking crimson lights and listen to the stuttering radio static of the squad car, staring at the coroner's van that had pulled up to the curb with the cold authority of a parading despot. A few kids rode their bikes up and down the street. Mumbling voices took on the sound of ravaging locusts. A dog barked. Welcome to suburbia.

I wondered where they'd all been when someone had gotten into Bruno's house, battered him into jelly, closed all the windows and left him to rot.

Milo finally came out, looking green. He sat on the front steps and hung his head between his knees. Then he got up and called the attendants from the coroner's office over. They had come prepared, with gas masks and rubber gloves. They went in with an empty stretcher and came out carrying something wrapped in a black plastic sheath.

"Ugh. Gross," said a teenage girl to her friend.

It was as eloquent a way to put it as any.

12

THREE MORNINGS after we discovered the butchery of Bruno, Milo wanted to come over to review the salesman's psychiatric file in detail. I postponed it until the afternoon. Motivated by instincts that were unclear to me, I called André Jaroslav at his studio in West Hollywood and asked him if he had time to help me refresh my karate skills.

"Doctor," he said, the accent as thick as goulash, "such a long time since I see you."

"I know, André. Too long. I've let myself go. But I hope you can help me."

He laughed.

"Tsk, tsk. I have intermediate group at eleven and private lessons at twelve. Then I am going to Hawaii, Doctor. To choreograph fight scenes for new television pilot. Girl policeperson who knows judo and catches rapists. What do you think?"

"Very original."

"Ya. I get to work with the redheaded chickie—this Shandra Layne. To teach her how to throw around large men. Like Wonder Woman, ya?"

"Ya. Do you have any time before eleven?"

"For you, Doctor—certainly. We get you in shape. Come at nine and I give you two hours."

The Institute of Martial Arts was located on Santa Monica at Doheny, next to the Troubador nightclub. It was an L.A. institution, predating the Kung Fu craze by fifteen years. Jaroslav was a bandy-legged Czech Jew who'd escaped during the fifties. He had a high, squeaky voice that he attributed to having been shot in the throat by the

Nazis. The truth was that he'd been born with the vocal register of a hysterical capon. It hadn't been easy, being a squeaky-voiced Jew in postwar Prague. Jaroslav had developed his own way of coping. Starting as a boy he taught himself physical culture, weight-lifting and the arts of self-defense. By the time he was in his twenties he had total command of every martial arts doctrine from saber-fencing to hopkaido, and a lot of bullies received painful surprises.

He greeted me at the door, naked from the waist up, a spray of daffodils in his hand. The sidewalk was filled with anorectic individuals of ambiguous gender, hugging guitar cases as if they were life preservers, dragging deeply on cigarettes and regarding the passing traffic with spaced-out apprehension.

"Audition," he squeaked, pointing a finger at the door to the Troubador and glancing at them scornfully. "The artisans of a new age, Doctor."

We went into the studio, which was empty. He placed the flowers in a vase. The practice room was an expanse of polished oak floor bordered by whitewashed walls. Autographed photographs of stars and near-stars hung in clusters. I went into a dressing room with the set of stiff white garments he gave me and emerged looking like an extra in a Bruce Lee movie.

Jaroslav was silent, letting his body and his hands talk. He positioned me in the center of the studio and stood facing me. He smiled faintly, we bowed to each other and he led me through a series of warm-up exercises that made my joints creak. It had been a long time.

When the introductory *katas* were through, we bowed again. He smiled, then proceeded to wipe the floor with me. At the end of one hour I felt as if I'd been stuffed down a garbage disposal. Every muscle fiber ached, every synapse quivered in exquisite agony.

He kept it up, smiling and bowing, sometimes letting out a perfectly controlled, high-pitched scream, tossing me around like a bean bag. By the end of the second hour, pain had ceased to be obtrusive—it had become a way of life, a state of consciousness. But when we stopped I was starting to feel in command of my body once again. I was breathing hard, stretching, blinking. My eyes burned as the perspiration dripped into them. Jaroslav looked as if he'd just finished reading the morning paper.

"You take a hot bath, Doctor, get some chickie to massage you, use a little witch hazel. And remember: practice, practice, practice."

"I will, André."

"You call me when I get back, in a week. I tell you about Shandra Layne and check if you've been practicing." He poked a finger in my gut, playfully.

"It's a deal."

He held out his hand. I reached out to take it, then tensed, wondering if he was going to throw me again.

"Ya, good," he said. Then he laughed and let me go.

The throbbing agony made me feel righteous and ascetic. I had lunch at a restaurant run by one of the dozens of quasi-Hindu cults that seem to prefer Los Angeles to Calcutta. A vacant-eyed, perpetually smiling girl swaddled in white robes and burnoose took my order. She had a rich kid's face coupled with the mannerisms of a nun and managed to smile while she talked, smile as she wrote, smile as she walked away. I wondered if it hurt.

I finished a plate heaped with chopped lettuce, sprouts, refried soya beans and melted goat cheese on *chapati* bread—a sacred tostada—and washed it down with two glasses of pineapple-coconut-guava nectar imported from the holy desert of Mojave. The bill came to ten dollars and thirty-nine cents. That explained the smiles.

I made it back to the house just as Milo pulled up in an unmarked bronze Matador.

"The Fiat finally died," he explained. "I'm having it cremated and scattering the ashes over the offshore rigs in Long Beach."

"My condolences." I picked up Bruno's file.

"Contributions to the down payment on my next lemon will be accepted in lieu of flowers."

"Get Dr. Silverman to buy you one."

"I'm working on it."

He let me read for a few minutes then asked, "So what do you think?"

"No profound insights. Bruno was referred to Handler by the Probation Department after the bad-check bust.

Handler saw him a dozen times over a four-month period. When the probationary period was over so was the treatment. One thing I did notice was that Handler's notes on him are relatively benign. Bruno was one of the more recently acquired patients. At the time he started therapy, Handler was at his nastiest, yet there are no vicious comments about him. Here, in the beginning Handler calls him a 'slick con man.' '' I flipped some pages. "A couple of weeks later he makes a crack about Bruno's 'Cheshire grin.' But after that, nothing.''

"As if they became buddies?''

"Why do you say that?''

Milo handed me a piece of paper. "Here,'' he said, "look at this.''

It was a printout from the phone company.

"This,'' he pointed to a circled seven-digit code, "is Handler's number—his home number, not the office. And this one is Bruno's.''

Lines had been drawn between the two, like lacing on a high-topped shoe. There'd been lots of connections over the last six months.

"Interesting, huh?''

"Very.''

"Here's something else. Officially the coroner says it's impossible to fix a time of death for Bruno. The heat inside the house screwed up the decomposition tables—with the flack they've been getting they're not willing to go out on a limb and take the chance of being wrong. But I got one of the young guys to give me an off-the-record guess and he came up with ten to twelve days.''

"Right around the time Handler and Gutierrez were murdered.''

"Either right before or right after.''

"But what about the differing m.o.'s?''

"Who says people are consistent, Alex? Frankly there are other differences between the two cases besides m.o. In Bruno's case it looks like forced entry. We found broken bushes under a rear window and chisel marks on the pane—used to be a kid's room. Glendale P.D. also thinks they've got two sets of heelprints.''

"Two? Maybe Melody really saw something.'' *Dark men. Two or three.*

"Maybe. But I've abandoned that line of attack. The kid will never be a reliable witness. In any event, despite the discrepancies, it looks like we might be on to something—what, I don't know. Patient and doctor, concrete proof that they maintained some kind of contact after treatment was over, both ripped off around the same time. It's too cute for coincidence."

He studied his notes, looking scholarly. I thought about Handler and Bruno and then it hit me.

"Milo, we've been held back in our thinking by social roles."

"What the hell are you talking about?"

"Roles. Social roles—prescribed sets of behaviors. Like doctor and patient. Psychiatrist and psychopath. What are the characteristics of a psychopath?"

"Lack of conscience."

"Right. And an inability to relate to other people except by exploiting them. The good ones have a glib, smooth façade, often they're goodlooking. Usually above-average intelligence. Sexually manipulative. A predilection to engage in cons, blackmail, frauds."

Milo's eyes opened wide.

"Handler."

"Of course. We've been thinking of him as the doctor in the case and assuming psychological normalcy—he's been protected, in our eyes, by his role. But take a closer look. What do we know about him? He was involved in insurance fraud. He tried to blackmail Roy Longstreth, using his power as a psychiatrist. He seduced at least one patient—Elaine Gutierrez—and who knows how many more? And those putdowns in the margins of his notes—at first I thought they were evidence of burnout, but now I don't know. That was cold, pretending to listen to people, taking their money, insulting them. His notes were confidential—he never expected anyone else to read them. He could hang it all out, show his true colors. Milo, I tell you the guy comes across like your classic psychopath."

"The evil doctor."

"Not exactly a *rara avis*, is it? If there can be a Mengele, why not scores of Morton Handlers? What better façade for an intelligent psychopath than the title of Doctor—it yields instant prestige and credibility."

"Psychopathic doctor and psychopathic patient." He mulled it over. "Not buddies, but partners in crime."

"Sure. Psychopaths don't have buddies. Only victims and accomplices. Bruno must have been Handler's dream come true if he was plotting something and needed one of his own kind for help. I'll bet you those first sessions were incredible, the two of them hungry hyenas, checking each other out, looking over their shoulders, sniffing the ground."

"Why Bruno, in particular? Handler treated other psychopaths."

"They were too crude. Short-order cooks, cowboys, construction workers. Handler needed a smooth type. Besides, how do we know how many of those guys were deliberately misdiagnosed like Longstreth?"

"Just to play devil's advocate for one second—one of those jokers was in law school."

I thought about it for a minute.

"Too young. In Handler's eyes a callow punk. In a few years, with degree in hand and a veneer of sophistication, maybe. Handler needed a businessman type for what he wanted to pull off. Someone really slick. And Bruno appears to have fit that bill. He fooled Gershman, who's no idiot."

Milo got up and paced the room, running his fingers through his hair, creating a bird's nest.

"It's definitely appealing. Shrinker and shrinkee pulling off a scam." He seemed amused.

"It's not the first time, Milo. There was a guy back East a few years ago—very good credentials. Married into a rich family and started a clinic for juvenile delinquents—back when they still called them that. He used his in-laws' social connections to organize fund-raising soirées for the clinic. While the champagne flowed, the j.d.'s were busy burglarizing the partygoers' townhouses. They finally caught him with a warehouse full of silver and crystal, furs and rugs. He didn't even need the stuff. He was doing it for the challenge. They sent him away to one of those discreet institutions in the rolling hills of southern Maryland—for all I know he's running the place by now. It never hit the papers. I found out about it through the professional grapevine. Convention gossip."

Milo pulled out his pencil. He started writing, thinking out loud.

"To the marble corridors of high finance. Bank records, brokerage statements, businesses filed under fictitious names. See what's left in the safe-deposit boxes after the IRS has done its dirty work. County assessor for info on property ventures. Insurance claims out of Handler's office." He stopped. "I hope this gets me somewhere, Alex. This goddamn case hasn't helped my status in the department. The captain is aiming for promotion and he wants to show more arrests. Handler and Gutierrez weren't ghetto types he can afford to let fade away. And he's running scared that Glendale will solve Bruno first and make us look like shmucks. You remember Bianchi."

I nodded. A small-town police chief in Bellingham, Washington, had caught the Hillside Strangler—something the L.A.P.D. war machine hadn't been able to do.

He got up, went into the kitchen and ate half of a cold chicken standing over the sink. He washed it down with a quart of orange juice and came back wiping his mouth.

"I don't know why I'm fighting not to laugh, up to my ass in dead bodies and no apparent progress, but it seems so funny, Handler and Bruno. You send a guy to a shrink to get his head straight and the doc is as fucked-up as the patient and *systematically* puts the warp on him."

Put that way it didn't *sound* funny. He laughed anyway.

"What about the girl?" he asked.

"Gutierrez? What about her."

"Well, I was thinking about those social roles. We've been looking at her as the innocent bystander. If Handler could connive with one patient, why not with two?"

"It's not impossible. But we know Bruno was psychopathic. Any of that kind of evidence about her?"

"No," he admitted. "We looked for Handler's file on her and couldn't find it. Maybe he shredded it when their relationship changed. Do you guys do that?"

"I wouldn't know. I never slept with my patients—or their mothers."

"Don't be touchy. I tried to interview her family. The old, plump *mamacita,* two brothers one of 'em with those angry, macho eyes. There's no father—he died ten years ago. The three of them live in a tiny place in Echo Park.

When I got there they were in the middle of mourning. The place was full of the girl's pictures, in shrines. Lots of candles, baskets of food, weeping neighbors. The brothers were sullen. Mama barely spoke English. I made a serious attempt to be sensitive, culturally aware and all that. I borrowed Sanchez from Ramparts Division to translate. We brought food, kept a low profile. I got *nada*. Hear no evil, speak no evil. I honestly don't think they knew much about Elena's life. To them West L.A.'s as distant as Atlantis. But even if they did they sure as hell weren't going to tell me."

"Even," I asked, "if it would help find her murderer?"

He looked at me wearily.

"Alex, people like that don't think the police can help them. To them *la policía* are the bastards who roust their *cholos* and insult their home girls and are never around when the low riders cruise the neighborhood at night with their lights off and pop shotgun shells through bedroom windows. Which reminds me—I interviewed a friend of the girl. Her roommate, also a teacher. This one was outwardly hostile. Made it clear she wanted nothing to do with me. Her brother had been killed five years ago in a gang shootout and the police did nothing for her and her family then, so to hell with me now."

He got up and padded around the room like a tired lion.

"In summation, Elaine Gutierrez is a cipher. But there's nothing to indicate she wasn't as pure as the freshly driven snow."

He looked miserable, plagued with self-doubt.

"It's a tough case, Milo. Don't be so hard on yourself."

"It's funny you should say that. That's what my mother used to tell me. Go easy, Milo Bernard. Don't be such a *profectionist*—that was the way she pronounced it. The whole family had a tradition of low personal expectations. Drop out of school in tenth grade, go to work at the foundry, lay out a life for yourself of plastic dishes, TV, church picnics, and steel splinters that stuck in your skin. After thirty years enough pension and disability to give you a weekend in the Ozarks once in a while, if you're lucky. My Dad did it, his dad, and both of my brothers. The Sturgis game plan. But not the *profectionist*. For one, the game plan worked best if you got married and I'd been liking boys since I was nine. And second—this was more important—I figured I was too smart to do what the rest of those peasants were doing. So I broke the mold, shocked them all. And the hotshot who everyone thought was going to become a lawyer or a professor or at least some kind of accountant goes and ends up as a member of *la policia*. Ain't that something for a guy who wrote a goddamn thesis on transcendentalism in the poetry of Walt Whitman?''

He turned away from me and stared at the wall. He had worked himself into a funk. I had seen it before. The most therapeutic thing to say was nothing. I ignored him and did some calisthenics.

"Goddamn Jack La Lanne," he muttered.

It took him ten minutes to come out of it, ten minutes of clenching and unclenching his big fists. Then came the tentative raising of the eyes, the inevitable sheepish grin.

"How much for the therapy, Doctor?''

I thought a minute.

"Dinner. At a good place. No crap.''

He stood up and stretched, growled like a bear.

"How about sushi? I'm goddamn barbaric tonight. I'll eat those fish alive.''

We drove to Oomasa, in Little Tokyo. The restaurant was crowded, mostly with Japanese. This was no trendy hotspot decked out in shojiscreen elegance and waxed pine counters. The decor was red Naugahyde, stiff-backed chairs and plain white walls decorated only by a few Nikon calendars. The solitary concession to style was a large aquarium, in full view of the sushi bar, in which fancy goldfish struggled to propel themselves through bubbling, icy clear water. They gasped and bobbed, mutations ill-suited for survival in any but the most rarefied captivity, the products of hundreds of years of careful Oriental tinkering with nature—lionheads with faces obscured by glossy, raspberry growths, bug-eyed black moors, celestials with eyes forced perpetually heavenward, *ryukins* so overloaded with finnage that they could barely move. We stared at them and drank Chivas.

"That girl," Milo said, "the roommate. I felt she could help me. That she knew something about Elaine's lifestyle, maybe something about her and Handler. She was nailed tight, goddamn her.''

He finished his drink and motioned for another. It came and he gulped down half.

A waitress skittered over on geisha feet and handed us hot towels. We wiped our hands and face. I felt my pores open, hungry for air.

"You should be pretty good at talking to teachers, right? Probably did a lot of it back in the days when you were earning an honest living."

"Sometimes teachers hate psychologists, Milo. They see us as dilettantes dropping theoretical pearls of wisdom on them while they do the dirty work."

"Hmm." The rest of the Scotch disappeared.

"But no matter. I'll talk to her for you. Where can I find her?"

"Same school Gutierrez taught at. In West L.A., not far from you." He wrote the address on a napkin and gave it to me. "Her name's Raquel Ochoa." He spelled it, his voice thickening, slurring the words. "Use your badge." He slapped me on the back.

There was a grating sound above our heads. We looked up to find the sushi chef smiling and sharpening his knives.

We ordered. The fish was fresh, the rice just slightly sweet. The *wasabe* horseradish cleared my sinuses. We ate in silence, against a backdrop of *samisen* music and foreign chatter.

13

I AWOKE as stiff as if I'd been spray-starched; a full-fledged charley horse had taken hold of my muscles, a souvenir of my dance with Jaroslav. I fought it by taking a two-mile run down the canyon and back. Then I practiced karate moves out on the rear deck, to the amused comments of a pair of mockingbirds who interrupted their domestic quarrel long enough to look me over, then delivered what had to be the avian equivalent of a raspberry.

"Fly down here, you little bastards," I grunted, "and I'll show you who's tough." They responded with hilarious screeching.

The day was shaping up as a lung-buster, grimy fingers of pollution reaching over the mountains to strangle the sky. The ocean was obscured by a sulfurous sheath of airborne garbage. My chest ached in harmony with the stiffness in my joints, and by ten I was ready to quit.

I planned to time my visit to the school where Raquel Ochoa taught for the noon break, hoping to find her free. That left enough time for a long, hot bath, a cold shower, and a carefully assembled breakfast of eggs with mushrooms, sourdough toast, grilled tomatoes and coffee.

I dressed casually in dark brown slacks, tan corduroy sport coat, checked shirt and brown knit tie. Before I left I dialed a now-familiar number. Bonita Quinn answered.

"Yes?"

"Mrs. Quinn, Dr. Delaware. I just wanted to call to find out how Melody's been doing."

"She's fine." Her tone would have frosted a beer mug. "Fine."

Before I could say more she hung up.

* * *

The school was in a middle-class part of town, but it could have been anywhere. It was the old familiar layout of citadels of learning throughout the city: flesh-colored buildings arranged in classic penitentiary style, surrounded by a desert of black asphalt and secured by ten-foot-high chain link fencing. Someone had tried to brighten it up by painting a mural of children playing along the side of one of the buildings but it was scant redemption. What helped a bit more were the sight and sound of real children playing—running, jumping, tumbling, chasing each other, screaming like banshees, throwing balls, crying out with the fervor of the truly persecuted ("Teacher, he *hit* me!"), sitting in circles, reaching for the sky. A small group of bored-looking teachers watched from the sidelines.

I climbed the front stairs and found the main office with little trouble. The internal floor plan of schools was as predictable as the drab exterior.

I used to wonder why all the schools I knew were so hopelessly ugly, so predictably oppressive, then I dated a nurse whose father was one of the chief architects for the firm that had been building schools for the state for the past fifty years. She had unresolved feelings about him, and talked a lot about him: a drunken, melancholic man who hated his wife and despised his children more, who saw the world in terms of minimally varying shades of disappointment. A real Frank Lloyd Wright.

The office reeked of mimeographing fluid. Its sole occupant was a stern, black woman in her forties, ensconced in a fortress of scarred golden oak. I showed her my badge, which didn't interest her, and asked for Raquel Ochoa. The name didn't seem to interest her either.

"She's a teacher here. Fourth grade," I added.

"It's lunchtime. Try the teachers' dining room."

The dining room turned out to be an airless place, twenty feet by fifteen, into which folding tables and chairs had been crammed. A dozen men and women sat hunched over sack lunches and coffee, laughing, smoking, chewing. When I entered the room all activity ceased.

"I'm looking for Ms. Ochoa."

"You won't find her here, honey," said a stout woman with platinum hair.

Several of the teachers laughed. They let me stand there for a while and then a fellow with a young face and old eyes said:

"Room 304. Probably."

"Thanks."

I left. I was halfway down the hall before they started talking again.

The door to 304 was half-open. I went in. Rows of unoccupied school desks filled every square inch of space, with the exception of a few feet at the front that had been cleared for the teacher's desk, a boxy metal rectangle behind which sat a woman busy at work. If she had heard me enter she gave no indication, as she continued to read, make checkmarks, cross out errors. An unopened brown bag sat at her elbow. Light streamed in through dusty windows in beams that were suffused with dancing, suspended particles. The Vermeer softness was at odds with the utilitarian severity of the room: stark white walls, a blackboard veneered with chalky residue, a soiled American flag.

"Ms. Ochoa?"

The face that looked up was out of a mural by Rivera. Reddish-brown skin stretched tightly over sharply defined but delicately constructed bones; liquid lips and melting black eyes gabled by full, dark brows. Her hair was long and sleek, parted in the middle, hanging down her back. Part Aztec, part Spanish, part unknown.

"Yes?" Her voice was soft in volume but the timbre was defensively hard. Some of the hostility Milo had described was immediately apparent. I wondered if she was one of those people who had turned psychological vigilance into a fine art.

I walked over to her, introduced myself and showed her the badge. She inspected it.

"Ph.D. in what?"

"Psychology."

She looked at me with disdain.

"The police don't get satisfaction, so they send in the shrinks?"

"It's not that simple."

"Spare me the details." She returned her eyes to her paperwork.

"I just want to talk to you for a few minutes. About your friend."

"I told that big detective everything I know."

"This is just a double-check."

"How thorough." She picked up her red pencil and began slashing at the paper. I felt sorry for the students whose work was coming under scrutiny at this particular moment.

"This isn't a psychological interview, if that's what you're worried about. It's—"

"I'm not worried about anything. I told him everything."

"He doesn't think so."

She slammed the pencil down. The point broke.

"Are you calling me a liar, Mr. Ph.D?" Her speech was crisp and articulate but it still bore a Latin tinge.

I shrugged.

"Labels aren't important. What is, is finding out as much as possible about Elaine Gutierrez."

"*Elena,*" she snapped. "There's nothing to tell. Let the police do their job and stop sending their scientific snoopers around harassing people who are busy."

"Too busy to help find the murderer of your best friend?"

The head shot up. She brushed furiously at a loose strand of hair.

"Please leave," she said between clenched jaws. "I have work to do."

"Yes, I know. You don't even eat lunch with the rest of the teachers. You're very dedicated and serious—that's what it took to get out of the *barrio*—and that puts you above the laws of common courtesy."

She stood up, all five feet of her. For a moment I thought she was going to slap me, as she drew her hand back. But she stopped herself, and stared.

I could feel the acid heat coming my way but I held my gaze. Jaroslav would have been proud.

"I'm busy," she finally said, but there was a pleading quality to the statement, as if she was trying to convince herself.

"I don't want to take you on a cruise. I just want to ask a few questions about Elena."

She sat down.

"What kind of psychologist are you? You don't talk like one."

I gave her a capsulized, deliberately vague history of my involvement in the case. She listened and I thought I saw her soften.

"A child psychologist. We could use you around here."

I looked around the classroom, counted forty-six desks in a space meant for twenty-eight.

"I don't know what I could do—help you tie them down?"

She laughed, then realized what she was doing and cut it off, like a bad connection.

"It's no use talking about Elena," she said. "She only got—into trouble because of being involved with that . . ." She trailed off.

"I know Handler was a creep. Detective Sturgis—the big guy—knows. And you're probably right. She was an innocent victim. But let's make sure, okay?"

"You do this a lot? Work for the police?" She evaded me.

"No. I'm retired."

She looked at me with disbelief "At your age?"

"Post-burnout."

That hit home. She dropped her mask a notch and a bit of humanity peeked through.

"I wish I could afford it. Retirement."

"I know what you mean. It must be crazy working with this kind of bureaucracy." I threw out the lure of empathy—administrators were the object of every teacher's ire. If she didn't go for it I wasn't sure what I'd do to gain rapport.

She looked at me suspiciously, searching for a sign that I was patronizing her.

"You don't work at all?" she asked.

"I do some free-lance investing. It keeps me busy enough."

We chatted for a while about the vagaries of the school system. She carefully avoided mention of anything personal, keeping it all in the realm of pop sociology—how rotten things were when parents weren't willing to get emotionally and intellectually involved with their children, how difficult it was to teach when half the kids came from broken homes and were so upset they could barely concentrate, the frustration of dealing with administrators who'd given up on life and stuck around only for their pensions, anger at the fact that a teacher's starting salary was less than that of a trash collector. She was twenty-nine and she'd lost any shred of idealism that had survived the transition from East L.A. to the world of Anglo bourgeoisie.

She could really talk when she got going, the dark eyes flashing, the hands gesticulating—flying through the air like two brown sparrows.

I sat like the teacher's pet and listened, giving her what everyone wants when they're unloading—empathy, an understanding gesture. Part of it was calculated—I wanted to break through to her in order to find out more about Elena Gutierrez—but some of it was my old therapeutic persona, thoroughly genuine.

I was starting to think I'd gotten through when the bell rang. She became a teacher again, the arbiter of right and wrong.

"You must go now. The children will be coming back."

I stood up and leaned on her desk.

"Can we talk later? About Elena?"

She hesitated, biting her lip. The sound of a stampede began as a faint rumble and grew thunderous. High-pitched voices wailed their way closer.

"All right. I'm off at two-thirty."

An offer to buy her a drink would have been a mistake. Keep it businesslike, Alex.

"Thank you. I'll meet you at the gate."

"No. Meet me in the teachers' parking lot. At the south side of the building." Away from prying eyes.

Her car was a dusty white Vega. She walked toward it carrying a stack of books and papers that reached up to her chin.

"Can I help you?"

She gave me the load, which must have weighed at least twenty pounds, and took a minute to find her keys. I noticed that she'd put on makeup—eye shadow that accentuated the depth of her orbs. She looked around eighteen.

"I haven't eaten yet," she said. It was less an angling for an invitation than a complaint.

"No brown bag?"

"I threw it out. I make a lousy lunch. On a day like today it's too lousy to take. There's a chop house on Wilshire."

"Can I drive you?"

She looked at the Vega.

"Sure, why not? I'm low on gas, anyway. Toss those on the front seat." I put the books down and she locked the car. "But I'll pay for my own lunch."

We left the school grounds. I led her to the Seville. When she saw it her eyebrows rose.

"You must be a good investor."

"I get lucky from time to time."

She sank back in the soft leather and let out a breath. I got behind the wheel and started up the engine.

"I've changed my mind," she said. "You pay for the lunch."

She ate meticulously, cutting her steak into tiny pieces, spearing each morsel individually and slipping it into her mouth, and wiping her mouth with her napkin every third bite. I was willing to bet she was a tough grader.

"She was my best friend," she said, putting down her fork and picking up her water glass. "We grew up to-gether in East L.A. Rafael and Andy—her brothers—played with Miguel." At the mention of her dead brother her eyes misted then grew hard as obsidian. She pushed her plate away. She'd eaten a quarter of her food. "When we moved to Echo Park the Gutierrezes moved with us. The boys were always getting into trouble—minor mischief, pranks. Elena and I were good girls. Goody-goodies, actu-ally. The nuns loved us." She smiled.

"We were as close as sisters. And like sisters there was a lot of competition between us. She was always better-looking."

She read the doubt in my face.

"Really. I was a scrawny kid. I developed late. Elena was—voluptuous, soft. The boys followed her around with their tongues hanging out. Even when she was eleven and twelve. Here." She reached into her purse and took out a snapshot. More photographic memories.

"This is Elena and me. In high school."

Two girls leaned against a graffiti-filled wall. They wore Catholic school uniforms—short-sleeved white blouses, gray skirts, white socks and saddle shoes. One was tiny, thin and dark. The other a head taller, had curves the uniform couldn't conceal and a complexion that was surprisingly fair.

"Was she a blonde?"

"Surprising, isn't it? Some German rapist way back, no doubt. Later she lightened it even more, to be really all-American. She got sophisticated, changed her name to Elaine, spent lots of money on clothes, her car." She realized she was criticizing the dead girl and quickly changed her tune. "But she was a person of substance underneath all of that. She was a truly gifted teacher—there aren't many like that. She taught EH, you know."

Educationally Handicapped classes were for children who weren't retarded but still had difficulties learning. The category could include everything from bright kids with specific perceptual problems to youngsters whose emotional conflicts got in the way of their learning to read and write. Teaching EH was tough. It could be constant frustration or a stimulating challenge, depending on a teacher's motivation, energy and talent.

"Elena had a real gift for drawing them out—the kids no one else could work with. She had patience. You wouldn't have thought it to look at her. She was—flashy. She used lots of makeup, dressed to show herself off. Sometimes she looked like a party girl. But she wasn't afraid to get down on the floor with the children, didn't mind getting her hands dirty. She got into their heads—she dedicated herself to them. The children loved her. Look."

Another photograph. Elena Gutierrez surrounded by a group of smiling children. She was kneeling and the kids were climbing on her, tugging at the hem of her skirt, putting their heads in her lap. A tall, well-built young woman, pretty rather than beautiful, with an earthy, open look, the yellow hair a styled, thick shag framing an oval face, and contrasting dramatically with the Hispanic features. Except for those features she was the classic California girl. The kind who should have been lying face down in the Malibu sand, bikini top undone, smooth brown back exposed to the sun. A girl for cola commercials and custom van shows and running down to the market in halter and shorts for a six-pack. She shouldn't have ended up as savaged, lifeless flesh in a refrigerated drawer downtown.

Raquel Ochoa took the picture out of my hands and I thought I saw jealousy in her face.

"She's dead," she said, putting it back in her purse, frowning, as if I'd committed some kind of heresy.

"It looked like they adored her," I said.

"They did. Now they've brought in some old bag who doesn't give a damn about teaching. Now that Elena's—gone."

She started to cry, using her napkin to shield her face from my eyes. Her thin shoulders shook. She sank lower in the booth, trying to disappear, sobbing.

I got up, moved to her side and put my arms around her. She felt as frail as a cobweb.

"No, no. I'm all right." But she moved closer to me, burying herself in the folds of my jacket, burrowing in for the long, cold winter.

As I held her I realized that she felt good. She smelled good. This was a surprisingly soft, feminine person in my arms. I fantasized swooping her up, featherweight and vulnerable, carrying her to bed where I'd still her painful cries with that ultimate panacea: orgasm. A stupid fantasy because it would take more than a fuck and a hug to solve her problems. Stupid because that wasn't what this encounter was all about. I felt an annoying heat and tension in my groin. Tumescence rearing its ugly head when least appropriate. Still, I held her until her sobbing slowed and her breathing became regular. Thinking of Robin, I finally let her go and moved back to my side.

She avoided my eyes, took out her compact and fixed her face.

"That was really dumb."

"No it wasn't. That's what eulogies are for."

She thought for a moment then managed a faint smile.

"Yes, I suppose you're right." She reached across the table and placed a small hand on mine. "Thank you. I miss her so much."

"I understand."

"Do you?" She drew her hand away, suddenly cross.

"No, I guess not. I've never lost anyone to whom I was that close. Will you accept a serious attempt at empathy?"

"I'm sorry. I've been rude—from the moment you walked in. It's been so hard. All of these feelings—sadness, and emptiness and anger at the monster who did it—it had to be a monster, didn't it?"

"Yes."

"Will you catch him? Will that big detective catch him?"

"He's a very capable guy, Raquel. In his own way, quite gifted. But he's got little to go on."

"Yes. I suppose I should help you, shouldn't I?"

"It would be nice."

She found a cigarette in her purse and lit it with trembling hands. She took a deep drag and let it out.

"What do you want to know?"

"For starts, how about the old cliché—did she have any enemies?"

"The clichéd answer: No. She was popular, well-liked. And besides, whoever did this to her was no acquaintance —we didn't know anyone like that." She shuddered, confronting her own vulnerability.

"Did she go out with a lot of men?"

"The same questions." She sighed. "She dated a few guys before she met *him*. Then it was the two of them all the way."

"When did she begin seeing him?"

"She started as a patient almost a year ago. It's hard to know when she began sleeping with him. She didn't talk to me about that kind of thing."

I could imagine sexuality being a taboo topic for the two best friends. With their upbringing there was bound to be lots of conflict. And given what I had seen of Raquel and heard about Elena it was almost certain they had gone about resolving those conflicts in different ways: one, the party girl, a man's woman; the other, attractive but perceiving herself in pitched battle with the world. I looked across the table at the dark, serious face and knew her bed would be ringed with thorns.

"Did she tell you they were having an affair?"

"An affair? That sounds so light and breezy. He violated his professional ethics and she fell for it." She puffed on her cigarette. "She giggled about it for a week or so then came out and told me what a wonderful guy he was. I put two and two together. A month later he picked her up at our place. It was out in the open."

"What was he like?"

"Like you said before—a creep. Too well-dressed—velvet jackets, tailored pants, sunlamp tan, shirt unbuttoned to show lots of chest hair—curly gray chest hair. He smiled a lot and got familiar with me. Shook my hand and held on too long. Lingered with a good-bye kiss—nothing you could pin him on." The words were almost identical to Roy Longstreth's.

"Slick?"

"Exactly. Slippery. She'd gone for that type before. I couldn't understand it—she was such a good person, so real. I figured it had something to do with losing her dad at a young age. She had no good male role model. Does that sound plausible?"

"Sure." Life was never as simple as the psych texts but it made people feel good to find solutions.

"He was a bad influence on her. When she started going with him was when she dyed her hair and changed her name and bought all those clothes. She even went out and bought a new car—one of those Datsun-Z turbos."

"How did she afford it?" The car cost more than most teachers made in a year.

"If you're thinking he paid for it, forget it. She bought it on payments. That was another thing about Elena. She had no conception of money. Just let it pass through her fingers. She always joked how she was going to have to marry a rich guy to accommodate her tastes."

"How often did they see each other?"

"At first once or twice a week. By the end she might as well have moved in with him. I rarely saw her. She'd drop in to pick up a few things, invite me to go out with them."

"Did you?"

She was surprised at the question.

"Are you kidding? I couldn't stand to be around him. And I have a life of my own. I had no need to be the odd one out."

A life, I suspected, of grading papers until ten and then retiring, nightgown buttoned high, with a gothic novel and a cup of hot cocoa.

"Did they have friends, other couples with whom they associated?"

"I have no idea. I'm trying to tell you—I kept out of it." An edge crept into her voice and I retreated.

"She started out as his patient. Do you have any idea why she went to a psychiatrist in the first place?"

"She said she was depressed."

"You don't think she was?"

"It's hard to tell with some people. When I get depressed everyone knows about it. I withdraw, don't want anything to do with anybody. It's like I shrink, crawl into myself. With Elena, who knows? It's not like she had trouble eating or sleeping. She would just get a little quiet."

"But she said she was depressed?"

"Not until after she told me she was seeing Handler— after I asked her why. She said she was feeling down, the work was getting to her. I tried to help but she said she needed more. I was never a big fan of psychiatrists and psychologists." She smiled apologetically. "If you have friends and family you should be able to work it out."

"If that's enough, great. Sometimes it's like she said, Raquel. You need more."

She put out her cigarette.

"Well, I suppose it's fortunate for you that many people agree with that."

"I suppose so."

There was an awkward silence. I broke it.

"Did he prescribe any medication for her?"

"Not as far as I know. Just talked to her. She went to see him weekly, and then twice a week after one of her students died. Then she was obviously depressed—cried for days."

"When was this?"

"Let me see, it was pretty soon after she started going to Handler, maybe after they were already dating—I don't know. About eight months ago."

"How did it happen?"

"Accident. Hit-and-run. The kid was walking along a dark road at night and a car hit him. It destroyed her. She'd been working with him for months. He was one of her miracles. Everyone thought he was mute. Elena got him to talk." She shook her head. "A miracle. And then to have it all go down the drain like that. So meaningless."

"The parents must have been shattered."

"No. There were no parents. He was an orphan. He came from La Casa."

"La Casa de los Niños? In Malibu Canyon?"

"Sure. Why the surprise? They contract with us to provide special education to some of their kids. They do it with several of the local schools. It's part of a state-funded project or something. To mainstream children without families into the community."

"No surprise," I lied. "It just seems so sad for something like that to happen to an orphan."

"Yes. Life is unfair." The declaration seemed to give her satisfaction.

She looked at her watch.

"Anything more? I've got to get back."

"Just one. Do you recall the name of the child who died?"

"Nemeth. Cary or Corey. Something like that."

"Thanks for your time. You've been helpful."

"Have I? I don't see how. But I'm glad if it brings you closer to that monster."

She had a concrete vision of the murderer that Milo would have envied.

We drove back to the school and I walked her to her car.

"Okay," she said.

"Thanks again."

"You're welcome. If you have more questions you can come back." It was as forward as she was going to get—for her the equivalent of asking me over to her place. It made me sad, knowing there was nothing I could do for her.

"I will."

She smiled and held out her hand. I took it, careful not to hold on for too long.

14

I'VE NEVER BEEN a big believer in coincidence. I suppose it's because the notion of life being governed by the random collision of molecules in space cuts at the heart of my professional identity. After all, why spend all those years learning how to help people change when deliberate change is just an illusion? But even if I had been willing to give the Fates their due, it would have been hard to see as coincidence the fact that Cary or Corey Nemeth (deceased), a student of Elena Gutierrez (deceased), had been a resident of the same institution where Maurice Bruno (deceased) had volunteered.

It was time to learn more about La Casa de los Niños.

I went home and searched through the cardboard boxes I had stored in the garage since dropping out, until I found my old office Rolodex. I located Olivia Brickerman's number at the Department of Social Services and dialed it. A social worker for thirty years, Olivia knew more about agencies than anyone in the city.

A recording answered the phone and told me D.P.S.S.'s number had been changed. I dialed the new number and another recording told me to wait. A tape of Barry Manilow came on the line. I wondered if the city paid him royalties. Music to wait for your caseworker by.

"D.P.S.S."

"Mrs. Brickerman, please."

"One moment, sir." Two more minutes of Manilow. Then: "She's no longer with this office."

"Can you please tell me where I can locate her?"

"One moment." I was informed, once again, who wrote the music that made the whole world sing. "Mrs. Brickerman is now at the Santa Monica Psychiatric Medical Group.''

So Olivia had finally left the public domain.

''Do you have that number?''

''One moment, sir.''

''Thanks anyway.'' I hung up and consulted the Yellow Pages under Mental Health Services. The number belonged to an address on Broadway where Santa Monica approached Venice, not far from Robin's studio. I called it.

''S.M.P.M.G.''

''Mrs. Olivia Brickerman, please.''

''Who shall I say is calling?''

''Dr. Delaware.''

''One moment.'' The line was silent. Apparently the utility of phonehold Muzak hadn't become apparent to S.M.P.M.G.

''Alex! How are you?''

''Fine, Olivia, and you?''

''Wonderful, wonderful. I thought you were somewhere in the Himalayas.''

''Why's that?''

''Isn't that where people go when they want to find themselves—somewhere cold with no oxygen and a little old man with a beard sitting on top of a mountain munching on twigs and reading *People* magazine?''

''That was the sixties, Olivia. In the eighties you stay home and soak in hot water.''

''Ha!''

''How's Al?''

''His usual extroverted self. He was hunched over the board when I left this morning, muttering something about the Pakistani defense or some such *naarishkeit.*''

Her husband, Albert D. Brickerman, was the chess editor for the *Times*. In the five years I'd known him I hadn't heard him utter a dozen words in a row. It was difficult to imagine what he and Olivia, Miss Sociability of 1930 through '80, had in common. But they'd been married thirty-seven years, had raised four children, and seemed content with each other.

''So you finally left D.P.S.S.''

''Yes, can you believe it? Even barnacles can be dislodged!''

"What led to such an impulsive move?"

"I tell you, Alex, I would have stayed. Sure the system stank—what system doesn't? But I was used to it, like a wart. I like to think I was still doing a good job—though I tell you, the stories got sadder and longer. Such misery. And with cuts in funding the people would get less and less—and madder and madder. They took it out on the caseworkers. We had a girl stabbed in the downtown office. Now there're armed guards in every office. But what the hell, I was brought up in New York. Then my nephew, my sister's boy, Steve, he finished medical school and decided to become a psychiatrist—can you believe that, another mental health person in the family? His father's a surgeon and that was the safest way for him to rebel. Anyway, he's always been very close to me and it's been a running joke that when he goes into practice he was going to rescue Aunt Livvy from D.P.S.S. and take her into his office. And would you believe he took me up on it? Writes me a letter, tells me he's coming out to California and joining a group, and they need a social worker for intakes and short-term counseling, would I like to do it? So here I am, with a view of the beach, working for little Stevie—of course I don't call him that in front of other people."

"That's great, Olivia. You sound happy."

"I am. I go down to the beach for lunch, read a book, get tan. After twenty-two years I finally feel like I'm living in California. Maybe I'll take up roller-skating, huh?"

The image of Olivia, who was built somewhat like Alfred Hitchcock, whizzing by on skates, made me laugh.

"Ah, you scoff now. Just wait!" She chuckled. "Now, enough autobiography. What can I do for you?"

"I need some information on a place called La Casa de los Niños, in Malibu."

"McCaffrey's place? You thinking of sending someone there?"

"No. It's a long story."

"Listen, if it's that long why don't you give me a chance to dig in my files? Come over to the house tonight and I'll give it to you in person. I'll be baking and Albert will be meditating over the board. We haven't seen you in a long time."

"What are you baking?"

"Strudel, pirogis, fudge brownies."

"I'll be over. What time?"

"Eightish. You remember the place?"

"It hasn't been that long, Olivia."

"It's been twice as long. Listen, I don't want to be a yenta, but if you don't have a girlfriend there's a young lady—also a psychologist—who just came to work here. Very cute. The two of you would have brilliant children."

"Thanks, but I've got someone."

"Terrific. Bring her along."

The Brickermans lived on Hayworth, not far from the Fairfax district, in a small beige stucco house with Spanish tile roof. Olivia's mammoth Chrysler was parked in the driveway.

"What am I doing here, Alex?" Robin asked as we approached the front door.

"Do you like chess?"

"Don't know how to play."

"Don't worry about it. This is one house where you don't have to be concerned about what to say. You'll be lucky if you get a chance to talk. Eat brownies. Enjoy yourself."

I gave her a kiss and rang the doorbell.

Olivia answered it. She looked the same—maybe a few pounds heavier—her hair a hennaed frizz, her face rosy-cheeked and open. She was wearing a shift, a Hawaiian print, and ripples went through it as she laughed. She spread her hands and hugged me to a bosom the size and consistency of a small sofa.

"Alex!" She released me and held me at arm's length. "No more beard—you used to resemble D.H. Lawrence. Now you look like a graduate student." She turned and smiled at Robin. I introduced them.

"Pleased to meet you. You're very lucky, he's a darling boy."

Robin blushed.

"Come in."

The house was redolent with good, sweet baking smells.

Al Brickerman, a prophet with white hair and beard, sat hunched over an ebony-and-maple chessboard in the living room. He was surrounded by clutter—books in shelves and on the floor, bric-a-brac, photographs of children and grand-children, menorahs, souvenirs, overstuffed furniture, an old robe and slippers.

"Al, Alex and his friend are here."

"Hmm." He grunted and raised his hand, never avert-ing his eyes from the pieces on the board.

"Nice to see you again, Al."

"Hmm."

"He's a real schizoid," Olivia confided to Robin, "but he's dynamite in bed."

She ushered us into the kitchen. The room was the same as it had been when the house had been built forty years ago: yellow tile with maroon borders, narrow porcelain sink, window sills filled with potted plants. The refrigera-tor and stove were vintage Kenmore. A ceramic sign hung over the doorway leading out to the service porch: *How Can You Soar Like An Eagle When You're Surrounded by Turkeys?*

Olivia saw me looking at it.

"My going-away present when I left D.P.S.S. To my-self from myself." She brought over a plate of brownies, still warm.

"Here, have some before I eat them. Look at this—I'm growing obese." She patted her rear.

"More to love," I told her and she pinched my cheek.

"Mmm. These are great," Robin said.

"A woman with taste. Here, sit down."

We pulled up chairs around the kitchen table, the plate set down before us. Olivia checked the oven and then she joined us. "In about ten minutes you'll have strudel. Apples, raisins and figs. The latter an improvisation for Albert." She crooked a thumb toward the living room. "The system gets clogged, from time to time. Now then you want to know about Casa de los Niños. Not that it's any of my business, but could you tell me why?"

"It has to do with some work I'm doing for the police department."

"The police? You?"

I told her about the case, leaving out the gory details.

She had met Milo before—they'd hit it off marvelously—but hadn't been aware of the extent of our friendship.

"He's a nice boy. You should find him a nice woman like you found for yourself." She smiled at Robin and handed her another brownie.

"I don't think that would work, Olivia. He's gay."

It didn't stop her, only slowed her down. "So? Find him a nice young man."

"He's got one."

"Good. Forgive me, Robin, I tend to run off at the mouth. It's all those hours I spend with clients listening and nodding and saying uh-huh. Then I get home and you can imagine the depth of conversational interplay I get with Prince Albert. Anyway, Alex, these questions about La Casa, Milo asked you to ask them?"

"Not exactly. I'm following my own leads."

She looked at Robin.

"Philip Marlowe here?"

Robin gave her a helpless look.

"Is this dangerous, Alex?"

"No. I just want to look into a few things."

"You be careful, you understand?" She squeezed my bicep. She had a grip like a bouncer. "Make sure he's careful, darling."

"I try, Olivia. I can't control him."

"I know. These psychologists, they get so used to being in a position of authority they can't take advice. Let me tell you about this handsome fellow. I first met him when he was an intern assigned for three weeks to D.P.S.S. to teach him what life was like for people without money. He started out as a wise guy but I could tell he was special. He was the smartest thing on two feet. And he had compassion. His big problem was he was too hard on himself, he drove himself. He was doing twice as much work as anyone else and he thought he was doing nothing. I wasn't surprised when he took off like a missile, the fancy title and the books and all that. But I was worried he was going to burn himself out."

"You were right, Olivia," I admitted.

"I thought he went to the Himalayas, or something," she laughed, continuing to address Robin. "To get frozen so he could come back and appreciate California. Have more, both of you."

"I'm stuffed." Robin touched her flat tummy.

"You're probably right—keep the figure, if you have it. Me, I started out like a barrel, nothing to maintain. Tell me darling, do you love him?"

Robin looked at me. She put her arm around my neck. "I do."

"Fine, I pronounce you husband and wife. Who cares what he says?"

She got up and went to the oven, peering through the glass window.

"Still a few more minutes. I think the figs take longer to bake."

"Olivia, about La Casa de los Niños?"

She sighed and her bosom sighed along with her. "Okay. You're obviously serious about playing policeman." She sat down. "After you called I went into my old files and pulled out what I could find. You want coffee?"

"Please," said Robin.

"I'll have some too."

She came back with three steaming mugs, cream and sugar on a porcelain tray upon which had been silkscreened a panorama of Yellowstone Park.

"This is delicious, Olivia," Robin said, sipping.

"Kona. From Hawaii. This dress is from there, too. My younger son, Gabriel, he's there. He's in import-export. Does very well."

"Olivia—"

"Yes, yes, okay. La Casa de los Niños. The Children's Home. Started in 1974 by the Reverend Augustus McCaffrey, as a place of refuge for children with no home. That's right off the brochure."

"Do you have the brochure with you?"

"No, it's at the office. You want me to mail you a copy?"

"Don't bother. What kind of kids stay there?"

"Abused and neglected children, orphans, some status offenders—you know runaways. They used to put them in jail or the CYA but those places got too crowded with fourteen-year-old murderers and rapists and robbers, so now they try to find foster placement for them or a place

like La Casa. In general these institutions get the kids
nobody wants, the ones they can't find foster placement or
adoptive homes for. Lots of them have physical and psychological problems—spastic, blind, deaf, retarded. Or
they're too old to be attractive adoptees. There are also the
children of women in prison—mostly junkies and alco-
holics. We tried to place them with individual families, but
often nobody wanted them. To sum up, dear: chronic
wards of the Dependency Court.''

"How's a place like that funded?"

"Alex, the way the state and federal systems are set up,
an operator can pull in over a thousand dollars a month per
child if he knows how to bill it right. Kids with disabilities
bring in more—you get paid for all the special services.
On top of that I hear McCaffrey's terrific at bringing in
private donations. He's got connections—the land the place
is on is an example. Twenty acres in Malibu, used to
belong to the government. They interned the Japanese
there during World War II. Then it was used as a labor
camp for first offenders—embezzlers, politicians, that type.
He got the county to give it to him on long-term lease.
Ninety-nine years with token rent.''

"He must be a good talker."

"He is. A good old boy. Used to be a missionary down
in Mexico. I hear he ran a similar place there.''

"Why'd he move back up?"

"Who knows? Maybe he got tired of not drinking the
water? Maybe he longed for Kentucky Fried Chicken—
although I hear they've got it down there now.''

"What about the place? Is it a good one?"

"None of those places is utopia, Alex. The ideal would
be a little house in suburbia with a picket fence around it,
gingham curtains and a green lawn, Mommy and Daddy
and Rover the Dog. The reality is that there are over
seventeen thousand kids on the Dependency Court docket
in L.A. county alone. Seventeen thousand unwanted children! And they're piling into the system faster than they
can be—here's a terrible word—processed.''

"That's unbelievable," said Robin. She had a troubled
look on her face.

"We've turned into a society of child-haters, darling.
More and more abuse and neglect. People have kids and

then change their minds. Parents don't want to take responsibility for them so they shunt them over to the government—how's that from an old Socialist, Alex? And abortion—I hope this doesn't offend you, because I'm for liberation as much if not more than the next woman. I was screaming for equal pay before Gloria Steinem went through puberty. But let's face it, this wholesale abortion we've got is just another form of birth control, another way out for people to avoid their responsibility. And it's killing kids, at least in some sense, isn't it? Maybe it's better than having them and then trying to get rid of them—I don't know.'' She wiped the sweat from her forehead and dabbed at her upper lip with a paper napkin. ''Excuse me, that was a tedious polemic.''

She stood up and smoothed down her dress.

''Let me check the strudel.''

She came back with a steaming platter. ''Blow on it, it's hot.''

Robin and I looked at each other.

''You look so serious, I ruined your appetite with my polemic, didn't I?''

''No, Olivia.'' I took a slab of strudel and ate a bite. ''It's delicious and I agree with you.''

Robin looked grave. We'd discussed the abortion issue many times, never resolving anything.

''In answer to your question, is it a good place, I can only say that we had no complaints when I was with D.P.S.S. They offer the basics, it looked clean, the area is certainly nice—most of those kids never saw a mountain except on TV. They bus the kids to the public schools when they have special needs. Otherwise they've got in-house teaching. I doubt if anyone helps them with their homework—it's certainly not ''Father Knows Best'' over there, but McCaffrey keeps the place up, pushes for lots of community involvement. That means public exposure. Why do you want to know so much about it, you think that kid's death was suspicious?''

''No. There's no reason to suspect anything.'' I thought about her question. ''I guess I'm just fishing.''

''Well don't go fishing for minnows and come up with a shark, darling.''

We nibbled at the strudel. Olivia called into the living room:

"Al, you want some strudel—with the figs?"

There was no answer I could hear, but she put some pastry on a plate nonetheless and brought it into him.

"She's a nice lady," said Robin.

"One in a million. And very tough."

"And smart. You should listen to her when she says to be careful. Alex, please leave the detecting to Milo."

"I'll take care of myself, don't worry." I took her hand but she pulled away. I was about to say something but Olivia returned to the kitchen.

"The dead man—the salesman, you said he volunteered at La Casa?"

"Yes. He had a certificate in his office."

"He was probably a member of the Gentleman's Brigade. It's something dreamed up by McCaffrey to get the business community involved with the place. He gets corporations to get their executives to volunteer weekend time with the kids. How much of it is voluntary on the part of the 'Gentlemen' and how much is the result of pressure from the boss I don't know. McCaffrey gives them blazers and lapel pins and certificates signed by the mayor. They also get brownie points with their bosses. Hopefully the kids get something out of it too."

I thought of Bruno, the psychopath, working with homeless children.

"Is there any sort of screening?"

"The usual. Interviews, some paper-and-pencil tests. You know, dear boy, what that kind of thing is worth."

I nodded.

"Still, like I said, we never got any complaints. I'd have to give the place a B-minus, Alex. The major problem is that it's too big of an operation for the kids to get any personalized attention. A good foster home would definitely be preferable to having four to five hundred kids in one place at the same time—that's how many he's got. Aside from that, La Casa is as good as any."

"That's good to hear." But in some perverse way I was disappointed. It would have been nice to find out that the place was a hellhole. Anything to connect it with the three murders. Of course that meant misery for four hundred children. Was I becoming just another member of the child-hating society Olivia had described? Suddenly the strudel tasted like sugar-coated paper and the kitchen seemed oppressively hot.

"So, is there anything else you want to know?"

"No. Thanks."

"Now, darling." She turned to Robin. "Tell about yourself and how you met this impetuous fellow . . ."

We left an hour later. I put my arm around Robin. She let it lay there but was unresponsive. We walked to the car in silence as uncomfortable as a stranger's shoes.

Inside, I asked her:

"What's wrong?"

"Why did you bring me here tonight?"

"I just thought it would be nice . . ."

"Nice talking about murder and child abuse? Alex, that was no social call."

I had nothing to say so I started the car and pulled away from the curb.

"I'm worried sick about you," she said. "The things you were describing in there were hideous. What she said about sharks is true. You're like a little boy adrift on a raft in the middle of the ocean. Oblivious to what's going on around you."

"I know what I'm doing."

"Right." She looked out the window.

"What's wrong with my wanting to get involved in something other than hot tubs and jogging?"

"Nothing. But why can't it be something a little less hazardous than playing Sherlock Holmes? Something you know something about?"

"I'm a fast learner."

She ignored me. We cruised through darkened empty streets. A light drizzle speckled the windshield.

"I don't enjoy hearing about people getting their faces bashed in. Or children run down by hit-run drivers," she said.

"That's part of what's out there." I motioned toward the blackness of the night.

"Well, I don't want any part of it!"

"What you're saying is you'll go along for the ride as long as it's pretty."

"Oh, Alex! Stop being so damned melodramatic—that's right out of a soap opera."

"It's true, though, isn't it?"

"No, it's not—and don't try to put me on the defensive. I want the man I first met—someone who was satisfied with himself and not so full of insecurity that he had to run around trying to prove himself. That was what attracted me to you. Now you're like a—a man possessed. Since you've gotten involved in your little intrigues you haven't been there for me. I talk and your mind is somewhere else. It's like I told you before—you're going back to the bad old days."

There was something to that. The last few mornings had found me waking up early with a taut sense of urgency in my gut, the old obsessive drive to take care of business. Funny thing was, I didn't want to let go of it.

"I promise you," I told her, "I'll be careful."

She shook her head in frustration, leaned forward and switched on the radio. Loud.

When we got to her door she gave me a chaste peck on the cheek.

"Can I come in?"

She stared at me for a long moment and gave a resigned smile.

"Oh, hell, why not?"

Upstairs in the loft I watched her undress in the meager share of moonbeam admitted by the skylight. She stood on one foot, undoing her sandal, and her breasts swung low. A diagonal stroke of illumination turned her white, then gray as she pivoted, then invisible as she slipped under the covers. I reached out for her, aroused, and pulled her hand down toward me. She touched me for a second, then removed her fingers, moved them upward, let them settle around my neck. I buried myself in the sanctuary between her shoulder and the arching sweetness under her chin.

We fell asleep that way.

In the morning her side of the bed was empty. I heard rumbling and grinding and knew she was downstairs in the shop.

I got dressed, descended the narrow stairs and joined

her. She was wearing bib overalls and a man's work shirt.
Her mouth was covered with a bandana, her eyes goggled.

The air was full of wood dust.

"I'll call you later," I shouted over the din of the table
saw.

She stopped for a moment, waved, then resumed working. I left her surrounded by her tools, her machines, her
art.

15

I CALLED MILO at the station and gave him a full report of my interview with Raquel Ochoa and the Casa de los Niños connection, including the information given to me by Olivia.

"I'm impressed," he said. "You missed your calling."

"So what do you think? Shouldn't this McCaffrey be looked into?"

"What a minute, friend. The man takes care of four hundred kids and one of them is killed in an accident. That's not evidence of major mayhem."

"But that kid happened to be a student of Elena Gutierrez. Which means she probably discussed him with Handler. Not long after his death Bruno began volunteering at the place. A coincidence?"

"Probably not. But you don't understand the way things work around here. I am in the toilet with this case. So far those bank records are showing nothing—everything in both their accounts looks kosher. I've got more work to do on it, but singlehanded it takes time. Every day the captain looks me up and down with that *no-progress, Sturgis?* stare. I feel like a kid who hasn't done his homework. I expect him to pull me off the case any day and stick me on some garbage detail."

"If things are so screwed up I'd expect you to jump for joy at the prospect of a new lead."

"That's right. A lead. Not conjecture or a string of flimsy associations."

"They don't look that damned flimsy to me."

"Look at it this way—I start snooping around about McCaffrey, who's got connections from Downtown all the way to Malibu. He places a few strategic phone calls—no one can accuse him of obstructing justice because I've got no legitimate reason to be investigating him—and I'm yanked off the case faster than you can spit."

"All right," I conceded, "but what about the Mexican thing? The guy was down there for years. Then all of a sudden he leaves, surfaces in L.A., and becomes a hotshot."

"Upward mobility is no felony, and sometimes a cigar is a cigar, Dr. Freud."

"Shit. I can't stand it when you get overly cute."

"Alex, please. My life is far from rosy. I don't need crap from you on top of it all."

I seemed to be developing a talent for alienating those close to me. I had yet to call Robin, to find out where last night's dreams had led her.

"I'm sorry. I guess I'm over-involved."

He didn't argue.

"You've done good work. Been a big help. Sometimes things don't fall into place just because you do a good job."

"So what are you going to do? Drop it?"

"No. I'll look into McCaffrey's background—quietly. Especially the Mexican bit. I'm going to continue sifting through Handler and Bruno's financial records and I'll add Gutierrez's to that. I'm even going to call the Malibu Sheriff Station and get copies of the accident report on that kid. What did you say his name was?"

"Nemeth."

"Fine. That should be easy enough."

"Is there anything else you want from me?"

"What? Oh. No, nothing. You've done a great job, Alex. I want you to know I really mean that. I'll take it from here. Why don't you take it easy for a while?"

"Okay," I said without enthusiasm. "But keep me posted."

"I will," he promised. "Bye."

The voice on the other end was female and very professional. It greeted me with the sing-song lilt of a detergent jingle, an isn't-life-wonderful buoyancy that bordered on the obscene.

"Good morning! La Casa!"

"Good morning. I'd like to speak to someone about becoming a member of the Gentleman's Brigade."

"Just one moment, sir!"

In twenty seconds a male voice came on the line.

"Tim Kruger. Can I help you?"

"I'd like to talk about joining the Gentleman's Brigade."

"Yes, sir. And what corporation do you represent?"

"None. I'm inquiring as an individual."

"Oh. I see." The voice lost a touch of its friendliness. Disruption of routine did that to some people—threw them off, made them wary. "And your name, please."

"Dr. Alexander Delaware."

It must have been the title that did it because he shifted gears again, immediately.

"Good morning, Doctor. How are you today?"

"Just fine, thank you."

"Terrific. And what kind of doctor are you, if I might ask."

You might.

"Child psychologist. Retired."

"Excellent. We don't get many mental health professionals volunteering. I'm an M.F.C.C. myself, in charge of screening and counseling at La Casa."

"I'd imagine most of them would consider it too much like work," I said. "Being away from the field for a while, the idea of working with children again appeals to me."

"Wonderful. And what led you to La Casa?"

"Your reputation. I've heard you do good work. And you're well organized."

"Well, thank you, Doctor. We *do* try to do well by our kids!"

"I'm sure you do."

"We give group tours for prospective Gentlemen. The next one is scheduled a week from this Friday."

"Let me check my calendar." I left the phone, looked out the window, did a half-dozen knee bends, and came back. "I'm sorry, Mr. Kruger. That's a bad day for me. When's the next one?"

"Three weeks later."

"That's such a long way off. I was hoping to get going sooner." I tried to sound wistful and just a little impatient.

"Hmm. Well, Doctor, if you don't mind something a bit more impromptu than the group orientation, I can give you a personalized tour. There'll be no way to assemble the video show in time, but as a psychologist you know a lot of that stuff, anyway."

"That sounds just fine."

"In fact, if you're free this afternoon, I could arrange it for then. Reverend Gus is here today—he likes to meet all potential Gentlemen—and that's not always the case, what with his travel schedule. He's taping Merv Griffin this week, then flying to New York for an 'A.M. America.' "

He imparted the news of McCaffrey's television activities with the solemnity of a crusader unveiling the Holy Grail.

"Today would be perfect."

"Excellent. Around three?"

"Three it is."

"Do you know where we are?"

"Not exactly. In Malibu?"

"In Malibu Canyon." He gave me directions, then added: "While you're there you can fill out our screening questionnaires. It would be a formality in a case such as yours, Doctor, but we do have to go through the motions. Though I don't imagine psychological tests would be very valid for screening a psychologist, would they?"

"I don't imagine so. We write 'em, we can subvert 'em."

He laughed, straining to be collegial.

"Any other questions?"

"I don't think so."

"Terrific. I'll see you at three."

Malibu is as much an image as it is a place. The image is beamed into the living rooms of America on TV, splashed across the movie screen, etched into the grooves of LP's and emblazoned on the covers of trashy paperbacks. The image is one of endless stretches of sand; oiled, naked brown bodies; volleyball on the beach; sun-bleached hair; making love under a blanket with coital cadence timed to match the in-and-out of the tide; million-dollar shacks that teeter on pilings sunken into terra that isn't firma and, in fact, does the hula after a hard rain; Corvettes, seaweed and cocaine.

All of that is valid. But limited.

There's another Malibu, a Malibu that encompasses the canyons and dirt roads that struggle through the Santa Monica mountain range. This Malibu has no ocean. What little water it does possess comes in the form of streams that trickle through shaded gullies and disappear when the temperature rises. There are some houses in this Malibu, situated near the main canyon road, but there remain miles of wilderness. There are still mountain lions roaming the more remote regions of this Malibu, and packs of coyotes that prowl at night, making off with a chicken, a possum, a fat toad. There are shady groves where the tree frogs breed so abundantly that you step into them thinking your foot is resting on soft, gray earth. Until it moves. There are lots of snakes—kings, garters and rattlers—in this Malibu. And secluded ranches where people live under the illusion that the latter half of the twentieth century never occurred. Bridle trails punctuated by steaming mounds of horse droppings. Goats. Tarantulas.

There are also lots of rumors surrounding the second, beachless Malibu. Of ritual murders carried out by Satanic cults. Of bodies that will never—can never be found. Of people lost while hiking and never heard from again. Horror stories, but perhaps just as valid as Beach Blanket Bingo.

I turned off Pacific Coast Highway, up Rambla Pacifica, and traversed the boundary from one Malibu to the other. The Seville climbed the steep grade with ease. I had Django Reinhardt on the tape deck and the music of the Gypsy was in synch with the emptiness that unfolded before my windshield—the serpentine ribbon of highway, assaulted by the relentless Pacific sun one moment and shaded by giant eucalyptus the next. A dehydrated ravine to one side, a sheer drop into space on the other. A road that urged the weary traveler to keep going, that offered promises it could never keep.

I had slept fitfully the night before, thinking of Robin and myself, seeing the faces of children—Melody Quinn, the countless patients I had treated over the last ten years, the remains of a boy named Nemeth, who had died just a few miles up this same road. What had been his last vision, I wondered, what impulse had crossed a crucial synapse at the last possible moment before a giant machine-monster roared down on him from nowhere . . . And what had led him to walk this lonesome stretch of road in the dead of night?

Now, fatigue, nursed by the monotony of the journey, was tracing a slow but inexorable passage along my spine, so that I had to fight to remain alert. I turned the music louder and opened all the windows in the car. The air smelled clean, but tinged with the odor of something burning—a distant bridge?

So occupied was I in the struggle for clarity of consciousness that I almost missed the sign the county had erected announcing the exit for La Casa de los Niños in two miles.

The turnoff itself was easy to miss, only a few hundred yards past a hairpin bend in the road. The road was narrow, barely wide enough for two vehicles to pass in opposite directions, and heavily shadowed by trees. It rose a half-mile at an unrelenting incline, steep enough to discourage any but the most purposeful foot traveler. Clearly the site had never been meant to attract the walk-in trade. Perfect for a labor camp, work farm, detention center, or any nexus of activity not meant for the prying eyes of strangers.

The access road ended at a twelve-foot-high-barrier of chain link. Four-foot-high letters spelled out La Casa de los Niños in polished aluminum. A hand-painted sign of two huge hands holding four children—white, black, brown and yellow—rose to the right. A guardhouse was ten feet on the other side of the fence. The uniformed man inside took note of me, then spoke to me through a squawk box attached to the gate.

"Can I help you?" The voice came out steely and mechanical, like human utterance pureed into bytes, fed into a computer and regurgitated.

"Dr. Delaware. Here for a three o'clock appointment with Mr. Kruger."

The gate slid open.

The Seville was allowed a brief roll until it was stopped by an orange and white striped mechanical arm.

"Good afternoon, Doctor."

The guard was young, mustachioed, solemn. His uni-

form was dark gray, matching his stare. The sudden smile
didn't fool me. He was looking me over.

"You'll be meeting Tim at the administration building.
That's straight up this way and take the road to the left.
You can park in the visitors' lot."

"Thank you."

"You're quite welcome, Doctor."

He pushed a button and the striped arm rose in salute.

The administration building looked like it had once
served a similar purpose during the days of Japanese internment. It had the low-slung, angry look of military
architecture, but there was no doubt that the paint job—a
mural of a baby blue sky filled with cotton candy clouds—
was a contemporary creation.

The front office was paneled in cheap imitation oak and
occupied by a grandmotherly type in a colorless cotton
smock.

I announced myself and receivd a grandmotherly smile
for my efforts.

"Tim will be right with you. Won't you please sit down
and make yourself comfortable."

There was little of interest to look at. The prints on the
walls looked as if they'd been purloined from a motel.
There was a window but it afforded a view of the parking
lot. In the distance was a thick growth of forest—eucalyptus,
cypress, and cedar—but from where I sat only the bottoms
of the trees were visible, an uninterrupted stretch of gray-
brown. I tried to busy myself with a two-year-old copy of
California Highways.

It wasn't much of a wait.

A minute after I'd sat down the door opened and a
young man came out.

"Dr. Delaware?"

I stood.

"Tim Kruger." We shook hands.

He was short, mid-to-late twenties, and built like a
wrestler, all hard and knobby and endowed with just that
extra bit of muscle in all the strategic places. He had a face
that was well-formed, but overly stolid, like a Ken doll
that hadn't been allowed to bake sufficiently. Strong chin,
small ears, prominent straight nose of a shape that fore-

shadowed bulbousness in middle age, an outdoorsman's tan, yellowish-brown eyes under heavy brows, a low forehead almost totally hidden by a thick wave of sandy hair. He wore wheat-colored slacks, a light blue short-sleeved shirt and a blue-and-brown tie. Clipped to the corner of his collar was a badge that said T. Kruger, M.A., M.F.C.C., Director, Counseling.

"I was expecting someone quite a bit older, Doctor. You told me you were retired."

"I am. I believe in taking it early, when I can enjoy it."

He laughed heartily.

"There's something to be said for that. I trust you had no trouble finding us?"

"No. Your directions were excellent."

"Great. We can begin the tour, if you'd like. Reverend Gus is on the grounds somewhere. He should be back to meet you by four."

He held the door for me.

We crossed the parking lot and stepped onto a walkway of crushed gravel.

"La Casa," he began, "is situated on twenty-seven acres. If we stop right here, we can get a pretty good view of the entire layout."

We were at the top of a rise, looking down on buildings, a playground, spiraling trails, a curtain of mountains in the background.

"Out of those twenty-seven, only five are actually fully developed. The rest is wide-open space, which we believe is great for the kids, many of whom come from the inner city." I could make out the shapes of children, walking in groups, playing ball, sitting alone on the grass. "To the north"—he pointed to an expanse of open fields—"is what we call the Meadow. It's mostly alfalfa and weeds right now, but there are plans to begin a vegetable garden this summer. To the south is the Grove." He indicated the forest I'd seen from the office. "It's protected timberland, perfect for nature hikes. There's a surprising abundance of wildlife out there. I'm from the Northwest, myself, and before I got here I used to think the wildest life in L.A. was all on the Sunset Strip."

I smiled.

"Those buildings over there are the dorms."

He swiveled around and pointed to a group of ten large quonset huts. Like the administration building, they'd been gone at with the freewheeling paint brush, the corrugated iron sides festooned with rainbow-hued patterns, the effect bizarrely optimistic.

He turned again and I let my gaze follow his arm.

"That's our Olympic-sized pool. Donated by Majestic Oil." The pool shimmered green, a hole in the earth filled with lime jello. A solitary swimmer sliced through the water, cutting a foamy pathway. "And over there are the infirmary and the school."

I noticed a grouping of cinder-block buildings at the far end of the campus where the perimeter of the central hub met the edge of the "Grove." He didn't say what they were.

"Let's take a look at the dorms."

I followed him down the hill, taking in the idyllic panorama. The grounds were well-tended, the place bustling with activity but seemingly well-organized.

Kruger walked with long, muscular strides, chin to the wind, rattling off facts and figures, describing the philosophy of the institution as one that combined "structure and the reassurance of routine with a creative environment that encourages healthy development." He was resolutely positive—about La Casa, his job, the Reverend Gus, and the children. The sole exception was a grave lament about the difficulties of coordinating "optimal care" with running the financial affairs of the institution on a day-to-day basis. Even this was followed, however, by a statement stressing his understanding of economic realities in the eighties and a few upbeat paeans to the free-enterprise system.

He was well-trained.

The interior of the bright pink quonset hut was cold, flat white over a dark plank floor. The dorm was empty and our footsteps echoed. There was a metallic smell in the air. The children's beds were iron double bunks arranged barracks style, perpendicular to the walls, accompanied by foot lockers and bracket shelves bolted to the metal siding. There was an attempt at decoration—some of the children had hung up pictures of comic book superheroes, athletes, Sesame Street characters—but the absence of family pictures or other evidence of recent, intimate human connection was striking.

I counted sleeping space for fifty children.

"How do you keep that many kids organized?"

"It's a challenge," he admitted, "but we've been pretty successful. We use volunteer counselors from UCLA, Northridge, and other colleges. They get intro psych credit, we get free help. We'd love a full time professional staff but it's fiscally impossible. We've got it staffed two counselors to a dorm, and we train them to use behavior mod—I hope you're not opposed to that."

"Not if it's used properly."

"Oh, very definitely. I couldn't agree with you more. We minimize heavy aversives, use token economies, lots of positive reinforcement. It requires supervision—that's where I come in."

"You seem to have a good handle on things."

"I try." He gave an aw, shucks grin. "I wanted to go for a doctorate but I didn't have the bucks."

"Where were you studying?"

"U. of Oregon. I got an M.A. there—in counseling ed. Before that, a B.A. in psych from Jedson College."

"I thought everyone at Jedson was rich." The small college outside of Seattle had a reputation as a haven for the offspring of the wealthy.

"That's almost true," he grinned. "The place was a country club. I got in on an athletic scholarship. Track and baseball. In my junior year I tore a ligament and suddenly I was *persona non grata*." His eyes darkened momentarily, smoldering with the memory of almost-buried injustice. "Anyway, I like what I'm doing—plenty of responsibility and decision-making."

There was a rustling sound at the far end of the room. We both turned toward it and saw movement beneath the blankets of one of the lower bunks.

"Is that you, Rodney?"

Kruger walked to the bunk and tapped a wriggling lump. A boy sat up, holding the covers up to his chin. He was chubby, black and looked around twelve, but his exact age was impossible to gauge, for his face bore the telltale stigmata of Down's syndrome: elongated cranium, flattened features, deep-set eyes spaced close together, sloping brow, low-set ears, protruding tongue. And an expression of bafflement so typical of the retarded.

"Hello, Rodney." Kruger spoke softly. "What's the matter?"

I had followed him and the boy looked at me questioningly.

"It's all right, Rodney. He's a friend. Now tell me what's the matter."

"Rodney sick." The words were slurred.

"What kind of sickness?"

"Tummy hurt."

"Hmm. We'll have to have the doctor look at you when he makes his visit."

"No!" the boy screamed. "No docka!"

"Now, Rodney!" Kruger was patient. "If you're sick you're going to have to get a checkup."

"No docka!"

"All right, Rodney, all right." Kruger spoke soothingly. He reached out and touched the boy softly on the top of the head. Rodney went hysterical. His eyes popped out and his chin trembled. He cried out and lurched backward so quickly that he hit the rear of his head on the metal bedpost. He yanked the covers over his face, uttering an unintelligible wail of protest.

Kruger turned to me and sighed. He waited until the boy calmed down and then spoke to him again.

"We'll discuss the doctor later, Rodney. Now where are you supposed to be? Where's your group right now?"

"Snack."

"Aren't you hungry?"

The boy shook his head.

"Tummy hurts."

"Well you can't just lie here by yourself. Either come to the infirmary and we'll call someone to have a look at you or get up and join your group for snack."

"No docka."

"Okay. No doctor. Now get up."

The boy crawled out of bed, away from us. I could see now that he was older than I'd thought. Sixteen at least, with the beginning of beard growth dotting his chin. He stared at me, eyes wide in fright.

"This is a friend, Rodney. Mr. Delaware."

"Hello, Rodney." I held out my hand. He looked at it and shook his head.

"Be friendly, Rodney. That's how we earn our goodie points, remember?"

A shake of the head.

"Come on, Rodney, shake hands."

But the retarded boy was resolute. When Kruger took a step forward he retreated, holding his hands in front of his face.

It went on that way for several moments, a flat-out contest of wills. Finally Kruger gave in.

"Okay, Rodney," he said softly, "we'll forget social skills for today because you're ill. Now run along and join your group."

The boy backed away from us, circling the bed in a wide arc. Still shaking his head and holding his arms in front of him like a punchy fighter, he moved away. When he was close to the door he turned, bolted and half-ran, half-waddled out, disappearing into the sun's glare.

Kruger turned to me and smiled weakly.

"He's one of our more difficult ones. Seventeen and functioning like a three-year-old."

"He seems to be really afraid of doctors."

"He's afraid of lots of things. Like most Down's kids he's had plenty of medical problems—cardiac, infections, dental complications. Add that to the distorted thinking going on in that little head and it builds up. Have you had much experience with m.r.'s?"

"Some."

"I've worked with hundreds of them and I can't remember one who didn't have serious emotional problems. You know, the public thinks they're just like any other kids, but slower. It ain't so."

A trace of irritation had crept into his voice. I put it down to the humiliation of losing at psychic poker to the retarded boy.

"Rodney's come a long way," he said. "When he first got here he wasn't even toilet-trained. After thirteen foster homes." He shook his head. "It's really pathetic. Some of the people the county gives kids to aren't fit to raise dogs, let alone children."

He looked ready to launch into a speech, but stopped

and slipped his smile back on quickly. "Many of the kids we get are low-probability adoption cases—m.r., defective, mixed race, in and out of foster homes, or thrown on the trash heap by their families. When they come here they have no conception of socially appropriate behavior, hygiene, or basic day-to-day living skills. Quite often we're starting from ground zero. But we're pleased at our progress. One of the students is publishing a study on our results."

"That's a great way to collect data."

"Yes. And quite frankly, it helps us raise money, which is often the bottom line, Doctor, when you want to keep a great place like La Casa going. Come on." He took my arm. "Let's see the rest of the grounds."

We headed toward the pool.

"From what I hear," I said, "Reverend McCaffrey is an excellent fund-raiser."

Kruger gave me a sidelong glance, evaluating the intent of my words.

"He is. He's a marvelous person and it comes across. And it takes most of his time. But it's still difficult. You know, he ran another children's home in Mexico, but he had to close it down. There was no government support and the attitude of the private sector there was let the peasants starve."

We were poolside now. The water reflected the forest, green-black dappled with streaks of emerald. There was a strong odor of chlorine mixed with sweat. The lone swimmer was still in the water doing laps—using a butterfly stroke with a lot of muscle behind it.

"Hey, Jimbo!" Kruger called.

The swimmer reached the far end, raised his head out of the water and saw the counselor's wave. He glided effortlessly toward us and pulled himself waist-high out of the water. He was in his early forties, bearded and sinewy. His sun-baked body was covered with wet, matted hair.

"Hey, Tim."

"Dr. Delaware, this is Jim Halstead, our head coach. Jim, Dr. Alexander Delaware."

"Actually your only coach." Halstead spoke in a deep voice that emerged from his abdomen. "I'd shake your hand, but mine's kinda clammy."

"That's fine." I smiled.

"Dr. Delaware's a child psychologist, Jim. He's touring La Casa as a propective Gentleman."

"Great to meet you, Doc, and I hope you join us. It's beautiful out here, isn't it?" He extended a long, brown arm to the Malibu sky.

"Gorgeous."

"Jim used to work in the inner city," said Kruger. "At Manual Arts High. Then he got smart."

Halstead laughed.

"It took me too long. I'm an easy-going guy but when an ape with a knife threatened me after I asked him to do pushups, that was it."

"I'm sure you don't get that here." I said.

"No way," he rumbled. "The little guys are great."

"Which reminds me, Jim," interrupted Kruger, "I've got to talk to you about working out a program for Rodney Broussard. Something to build up his confidence."

"You bet."

"Check you later, Jim."

"Right on. Come back again, Doc."

The hirsute body entered the water, a sleek torpedo, and swam otterlike along the bottom of the pool.

We took a quarter-mile walk around the periphery of the institution. Kruger showed me the infirmary, a spotlessly white, smallish room with an examining table and a cot, sparkling of chrome and reeking of antiseptic. It was empty.

"We have a half-time R.N. who works mornings. For obvious reasons we can't afford a doctor."

I wondered why Majestic Oil or some other benefactor couldn't donate a part-time physician's salary.

"But we're lucky to have a roster of volunteer docs, some of the finest in the community, who rotate through."

As we walked, groups of youngsters and counselors passed us. Kruger waved, the counselors returned the greeting. More often than not the children were unresponsive. As Olivia had predicted and Kruger had confirmed, most had obvious physical or mental handicaps. Boys seemed to outnumber girls by about three to one and the majority of the kids were black or Hispanic.

Kruger ushered me into the cafeteria, which was highceilinged, stucco-walled and meticulously clean. Unspeaking Mexican women waited impassively behind a glass partition, serving tongs in hand. The food was typical institutional fare—stew, creative use of ground meat, Jello, overcooked vegetables in thick sauce.

We sat down at a picnic-type table and Kruger went behind the food counter to a back room. He emerged with a tray of Danish pastries and coffee. The baked goods looked high-quality. I hadn't seen anything like them behind the glass.

Across the room a group of children sat at a table eating and drinking under the watchful eyes of two student counselors. Actually, attempting to eat was more accurate. Even from a distance I could see that they suffered from cerebral palsy, some of them spastically rigid, others jerking in involuntary movements of head and limb, and had to struggle to get the food from table to mouth. The counselors watched and sometimes offered verbal encouragement. But they didn't help physically and lots of custard and Jello was ending up on the floor.

Kruger bit with gusto into a chocolate Danish. I took a cinammon roll and played with it. He poured us coffee and asked me if I had any questions.

"No. Everything looks very impressive."

"Great. Then let me tell you about the Gentleman's Brigade."

He gave me a canned history of the volunteer group, stressing the wisdom of the Reverend Gus in enlisting the participation of local corporations.

"The Gentlemen are mature, successful individuals. They represent the only chance most of these kids have of being exposed to a stable male role model. They're accomplished, the cream of our society and as such give the children a rare glimpse of success. It teaches them that it's indeed possible to be successful. They spend time with the kids here, at La Casa, and take them off-campus—to sporting events, movies, plays, Disneyland. And to their homes for family dinners. It gives the children access to a lifestyle they've never known. And it's fulfilling for the men, as well. We ask for a six-month commitment and sixty percent sign up for second and third hitches."

"Can't it be frustrating, for the kids," I asked, "to get a taste of the good life that's so far out of their grasp?"

He was ready for that one.

"Good question, Doctor. But we don't emphasize *anything* being out of our kids' reach. We want them to feel that the only thing limiting them is their own lack of motivation. That they must take responsibility for themselves. That they can reach the sky—that's the name of a book written for children by Reverend Gus. *Touch the Sky.* It's got cartoons, games, coloring pages. It teaches them a positive message."

It was Norman Vincent Peale spiced up with humanistic psychological jargon. I looked over and saw the palsied children battling with their food. No amount of exposure to the members of the privileged class was going to bring them membership in the Yacht Club, an invitation to the Blue Ribbon Upper Crust Debutante Ball of San Marino, or a Mercedes in the garage.

There were limits to the power of positive thinking.

But Kruger had his script and he stuck to it. He was damned good, I had to admit, had read all the right journals and could quote statistics like a Rand Corporation whiz kid. It was the kind of spiel designed to get you reaching for your wallet.

"Can I get you anything else?" he asked after finishing a second pastry. I hadn't touched my first.

"No thanks."

"Let's head back, then. It's almost four."

We passed through the rest of the place quickly. There was a chicken coop where two dozen hens pecked at the bars like Skinnerian pigeons, a goat at the end of a long leash eating trash, hamsters treading endlessly on plastic wheels and a basset hound who bayed half-heartedly at the darkening sky. The schoolroom had once been a barracks, the gym a World War II storage depot, I was informed. Both had been remodeled artfully and creatively on a budget, by someone with a good feel for camouflage. I complimented the designer.

"That's the work of Reverend Gus. His mark is on every square inch of this place. A remarkable man."

As we headed toward McCaffrey's office I saw, once again, the cinder-block buildings at the edge of the forest.

From up close I could see there were four structures, roofed in concrete, windowless, and half-submerged in the earth, like bunkers, with tunnel-like ramps sloping down to iron doors. Kruger showed no indication of explaining what they were, so I asked him.

He looked over his shoulder.

"Storage," he said casually. "Come on. Let's get back."

We'd come full circle, back to the cumulus-covered administration building. Kruger escorted me in, shook my hand, told me he hoped to hear from me again and that he'd be dropping off the screening materials while I talked to the Reverend. Then he handed me over to the good graces of Grandma, the receptionist, who tore herself away from her Olivetti and bade me sweetly to wait just a few moments for The Great Man.

I picked up a copy of *Fortune* and worked hard at building an interest in a feature on the future of microprocessors in the tool-and-die industry, but the words blurred and turned into gelatinous gray blobs. Futurespeak did that to me.

I'd barely had a chance to uncross my legs when the door opened. They were big on punctuality here. I'd started to feel like a hunk of raw material—what kind didn't really matter—being whisked along on an assembly line trough, melted, molded, tinkered with, tightened, and inspected.

"Reverend Gus will see you now," said Grandma.

The time had come, I supposed, for the final polishing.

16

IF WE'D been standing outdoors he would have blocked the sun.

He was six-and-a-half feet tall and weighed well over three hundred pounds, a pear-shaped mountain of pale flesh in a fawn-colored suit, white shirt, and black silk tie the breadth of a hotel hand towel. His tan oxfords were the size of small sailboats, his hands, twin sandbags. He filled the doorway. Black horn-rimmed glasses perched atop a meaty nose that bisected a face as lumpy as tapioca pudding. Wens, moles and enlarged pores trekked their way across the sagging cheeks. There was a hint of Africa in the flatness of his nose, the full lips as dark and moist as raw liver, and the tightly kinked hair the color of rusty pipes. His eyes were pale, almost without color. I'd seen eyes like that before. On mullet, packed in ice.

"Dr. Delaware, I'm Augustus McCaffrey."

His hand devoured mine then released it. His voice was strangely gentle. From the size of him I'd expected something along the lines of a tug horn. What came out was surprisingly lyrical, barely baritone, softened by the lazy cadence of the Deep South—Louisiana, I guessed.

"Come in, won't you?"

I followed him, a Hindu trailing an elephant, into his office. It was large and well-windowed but no more elegantly turned out than the waiting room. The walls were sheathed with the same false oak and were devoid of decoration save for a large wooden crucifix above the desk, a Formica-and-steel rectangle that looked like government surplus. The ceiling was low, perforated white squares suspended in a grid of aluminum. There was a door behind the desk.

I sat in one of a trio of vinyl upholstered chairs. He settled himself in a swivel chair that groaned in protest, laced his fingers together and leaned forward across the desk, which now looked like a child's miniature.

"I trust Tim has given you a comprehensive tour and has answered all of your questions."

"He was very helpful."

"Good," he drawled, giving the word three syllables. "He's a very capable young man. I handpick our staff." He squinted. "Just as I handpick all volunteers. We want only the best for our children."

He sat back and rested his hands on his belly.

"I'm extremely pleased that a man of your stature would consider joining us, Doctor. We've never had a child psychologist in the Gentleman's Brigade. Tim tells me you're retired."

He gazed at me jovially. It was clear I was expected to explain myself.

"Yes. That's true."

"Hmm." He scratched behind one ear, still smiling. Waiting. I smiled back.

"You know," he finally said, "when Tim mentioned your visit I thought your name was familiar. But I couldn't place it. Then it came to me, just a few moments ago. You ran that program for those children who were the victims of that day-care scandal, didn't you?"

"Yes."

"Wonderful work. How are they doing, the children?"

"Quite well."

"You—retired soon after the program was over, did you?"

"Yes."

The enormous head shook sadly.

"Tragic affair. The man killed himself, if I recall."

"He did."

"Doubly tragic. The little ones abused like that and a man's life wasted with no chance of salvation. Or," he smiled, "to use a more secular term, with no chance of rehabilitation. They're one and the same, salvation and rehabilitation, don't you think, Doctor?"

"I can see similiarity in the two concepts."

"Certainly. It depends upon one's perspective. I confess," he sighed, "that I find it difficult, at times, to divorce myself from my religious training when dealing with issues of human relations. I must struggle to do so, of course, in view of our society's abhorrence of even a minimal liaison between church and state."

He wasn't protesting. The broad face was suffused with calm, nourished by the sweet fruit of martyrdom. He looked at peace with himself, as content as a hippo sunning in a mudhole.

"Do you think the man—the one who killed himself— could have been rehabilitated?" he asked me.

"It's hard to say. I didn't know him. The statistics on treatment of lifelong pedophiles aren't encouraging."

"Statistics." He played with the word, letting it roll slowly off his tongue. He enjoyed the sound of his own voice. "Statistics are cold numbers, aren't they? With no consideration for the individual. And, Tim informs me, on a mathematical level, statistics have no relevance for an individual. Is that correct?"

"That's true."

"When folks quote statistics, it reminds me of the joke about the Okie—Okie jokes were fashionable before your time—woman who had borne ten children with relative equanimity but who became very agitated upon learning she was pregnant with the eleventh. Her doctor asked her why, after having gone through the travails of pregnancy, labor and delivery ten times she was suddenly so distraught. And she told him she had read that every eleventh child born in Oklahoma was an Indian, and durned if she was going to raise a redskin!"

He laughed, the belly heaving, the eyes black slits. His glasses slid down his nose and he righted them.

"That, Doctor, sums up my view of statistics. You know, most of the children at La Casa were statistics prior to their coming here—doctor numbers in the Dependency Court files, codes for the D.P.S.S. caseworkers to catalogue, scores on IQ tests. And those numbers said they were beyond hope. But we take them and we work strenuously to transform those numbers into little *individuals*. I don't care about a child's IQ score, I want to help him claim his birthright as a human being—opportunity, basic health and welfare, and, if you'll permit a clerical lapse, a *soul*. For there is a soul in every single one of those children, even the ones functioning at a vegetative level.''

"I agree that it's good not to be limited by numbers." His man, Kruger, had been pretty handy with statistics when they served his purpose and I was willing to bet La Casa made use of a computer or two to churn out the right numbers when the occasion called for it.

"Our work is effecting change. It's an alchemy of sorts. Which is why suicide—any suicide—saddens me deeply. For all men are capable of salvation. That man was a quitter, in the ultimate sense. But of course," he lowered his voice, "the quitter has become the archetype of modern man, hasn't he, Doctor? It has become fashionable to throw up one's hands after the merest travesty of effort. Everyone wants quick and easy solutions."

Including, no doubt, those who retired at thirty-two.

"There are miracles happening every day, right on these grounds. Children who've been given up on gain a new sense of themselves. A youngster who is incontinent learns to control his bowels." He paused, like a politician after an applause line. "So-called retarded children learn to read and write. Small miracles, perhaps, when measured against a man walking on the moon, or perhaps not." His eyebrows arched, the thick lips parted to reveal widely-spaced, horsey teeth. "Of course, Doctor, if you find the word miracle unduly sectarian, we can substitute *success*. That is a word the average American can relate to. Success."

Coming from someone else it could have been a cheap throwaway oration worthy of a Sunday morning Jesus-huckster. But McCaffrey was good and his words carried the conviction of one ordained to carry out a sacred mission.

"May I ask," he inquired pleasantly, "why you retired?"

"I wanted a change of pace, Reverend. Time to sort out my values."

"I understand. Reflection can be profoundly valuable. However I trust you won't absent yourself from your profession for too long. We need good people in your field."

He was still preaching, but now mixing it with an ego

massage. I understood why the corporate honchos loved him.

"In fact I have begun to miss working with children, which is why I called you."

"Excellent, excellent. Psychology's loss will be our gain. You worked at Western Pediatric, didn't you? I seem to remember that from the paper."

"There and in private practice."

"A first-rate hospital. We send many of our children there when the need for medical attention arises. I'm acquainted with several of the physicians on staff and many of them have been quite generous—giving of themselves."

"Those are busy men, Reverend; you must be quite persuasive."

"Not really. However, I do recognize the existence of a basic human need to *give*, an altruistic drive, if you will. I know this flies in the face of the modern psychologies which limit the notion of drive to self-gratification, but I'm convinced I'm right. Altruism is as basic as hunger and thirst. You, for example, satisfied your own altruistic need within the scope of your chosen profession. But when you stopped working, the hunger returned. And here," he spread his arms, "you are."

He opened a drawer of the desk, took out a brochure, and handed it to me. It was glossy and well-done, as polished as the quarterly report of an industrial conglomerate.

"On page six you'll see a partial list of our board."

I found it. For a partial list it was long, running the height of the page in small print. And impressive. It included two county supervisors, a member of the city council, the Mayor, judges, philanthropists, entertainment biggies, attorneys, businessmen, and plenty of M.D.'s, some of whose names I recognized. Like L. Willard Towle.

"Those are all busy men, Doctor. And yet they find the time for our children. Because we know how to tap that inner resource, that wellspring of altruism."

I flipped through the pages. There was a letter of endorsement from the governor, lots of photographs of children having fun, and even more pictures of McCaffrey. His looming bulk appeared pinstriped on the Donahue show, in tuxedo at a Music Center benefit, in a jogging suit with a group of his young charges at the victory line of the Special Olympics. McCaffrey with TV personalities, civil rights leaders, country singers and bank presidents.

Midway through the brochure I found a shot of McCaffrey in a room I recognized as the lecture hall at Western Pediatric. Next to him, white hair gleaming, was Towle. On the other side was a small man, froggy, squat, grim even as he smiled. The guy with Peter Lorre eyes whose photograph I'd seen in Towle's office. The caption beneath the photo identified him as the Honorable Edwin G. Hayden, supervising judge of the Dependency Court. The occasion was McCaffrey's address to the medical staff on "Child Welfare: Past, Present and Future."

"Is Dr. Towle very involved in La Casa?" I asked.

"He serves on our board and is one of our rotating physicians. Do you know him?"

"We've met. Casually. I know him by reputation."

"Yes, an authority on behavioral pediatrics. We find his services invaluable."

"I'm sure you do."

He spent the next quarter-hour showing me his book, a soft-covered, locally printed volume of saccharine clichés and first-rate graphics. I bought a copy, for fifteen bucks, after he gave me a more sophisticated version of the pitch for cash Kruger had thrown my way. The bargain basement ambience of the office lent credibility to the spiel. Besides, I was O.D'ed on positive thinking and it seemed a small price to pay for respite.

He took the three five-dollar bills, folded them and placed them conspicuously in a collection box atop the desk. The receptacle was papered with a drawing of a solemn-looking child with eyes that rivaled Melody Quinn's in size, luminosity and the ability to project a sense of inner hurt.

He stood, thanked me for coming, and took my hand in both of his. "I hope we see more of you, Doctor. Soon."

It was my turn to smile.

"Plan on it, Reverend."

Grandma was ready for me as I stepped into the waiting room, with a sheaf of stapled booklets and two sharpened number two pencils.

"You can fill these out right here, Doctor Delaware," she said sweetly.

I looked at my watch.

"Gee, it's much later than I thought. I'll have to take a raincheck."

"But—" She became flustered.

"How about you give them to me to take home? I'll fill them out and mail them back to you."

"Oh no, I couldn't do that! These are psychological tests!" She clutched the papers to her breast. "The rules are that you must fill them out here."

"Well, then, I'll just have to come back." I started to leave.

"Wait. Let me ask someone. I'll ask Reverend Gus if it's—"

"He told me he was going to retire for a period of meditation. I don't think he wants to be disturbed."

"Oh." She was disoriented. "I must ask someone. You wait right here, Doctor, and I'll find Tim."

"Sure."

When she was gone I slipped out the door, unnoticed.

The sun had almost set. It was that transitional time of day when the diurnal palette is slowly scraped dry, colors falling aside to reveal a wash of gray, that ambiguous segment of twilight when everything looks just a little bit fuzzy around the edges.

I walked toward my car unsettled. I'd spent three hours at La Casa and had learned little other than that the Reverend Augustus McCaffrey was a shrewd old boy with over-active charisma glands. He'd taken the time to check me out and wanted me to know it. But only a paranoiac could rightfully see anything ominous in that. He was showing off, displaying how well-informed and prepared he was. The same went for his advertising the abundance of friends in high places. It was psychological muscle-flexing. Power respected power, strength gravitated to strength. The more connections McCaffrey could show, the more he was going to get. And that was the way to big bucks. That, and collection boxes illustrated with sad-eyed waifs.

I had the key in the door of the Seville, facing the campus of the institution. It looked empty and still, like a well-run farm after the work's all done. Probably dinner time, with the kids in the cafeteria, the counselors watching, and the Reverend Gus delivering an eloquent benediction.

I felt foolish.

I was about to open the door when I caught a glimpse of a flurry of movement near the forestlike Grove, several hundred feet in the distance. It was hard to be certain, but I thought I saw a struggle, heard the sound of muffled cries.

I put the car keys back in my pocket and let the copy of McCaffrey's book drop to the gravel. There was no one else in sight, except for the guard in the booth at the entrance and his attention was focused in the opposite direction. I needed to get closer without being seen. Carefully I made my way down the hill upon which the parking lot sat, staying in the shadow of buildings whenever I could. The shapes in the distance were moving, but slowly.

I pressed myself against the flamingo-pink wall of the southernmost dormitory, as far as I could go without abandoning cover. The ground was moist and mushy, the air rotten with fumes given off by a nearby trash dumpster. Someone had tried to write FUCK in the pink paint, but the corrugated metal was a hostile surface and it came out chicken scratches.

The sounds were clearer and louder now, and they were definitely cries of distress—animal cries, bleating and plaintive.

I made out three silhouettes, two large, one much smaller. The small one seemed to be walking on air.

I inched closer, peering around the corner. The three figures passed before me, perhaps thirty feet away moving along the southern border of the institution. They walked across the concrete of the pool deck and came under the illumination of a yellow anti-bug light affixed to the eave of the poolhouse.

It was then that I saw them clearly, flash frozen in the lemon light.

The small figure was Rodney and he'd appeared suspended because he was being carried in the firm grip of Halstead, the coach, and Tim Kruger. They grasped him under the arms so that his feet dangled inches from the ground.

They were strong men but the boy was giving them a struggle. He squirmed and kicked like a ferret in a trap, opened his mouth and let out a wordless moan. Halstead clamped a hairy hand over the mouth but the child managed to wrench free and scream again. Halstead stifled him once more and it went on that way as they retreated out of the light and my line of vision, the alternating sounds of cries and muted grunts a crazy trumpet solo that grew faint then faded away.

Then it was silent and I was alone, back to the wall, bathed in sweat, clothes clammy and sticking to me. I wanted to perform some heroic act, to break out of the deadening inertia that had settled around my ankles like quick-drying cement.

But I couldn't save anybody. I was a man out of his element. If I followed them there'd be rational explanations for everything and a herd of guards to quickly turn me out, taking careful note of my face so that the gates of La Casa would never again open before it.

I couldn't afford that, just yet.

So I stood, up against the wall, rooted in the ghost-town stillness, feeling sick and helpless. I clenched my fists until they hurt and listened to the dry urgent sound of my own breathing like the scraping of boots against alley stones.

I forced the image of the struggling boy out of my mind.

When I was sure it was safe I sneaked back to my car.

17

THE FIRST TIME I called, at 8 A.M., nobody answered. A half-hour later the University of Oregon was open for business.

"Good morning, Education."

"Good morning. This is Dr. Gene Adler calling from Los Angeles. I'm with the Department of Psychiatry at Western Pediatric Medical Center in Los Angeles. We're currently recruiting for a counseling position. One of our applicants has listed on his resumé the fact that he received a master's degree in counseling education from your department. As part of our routine credentials check I was wondering if you could verify that for me."

"I'll switch you to Marianne, in transcripts."

Marianne had a warm, friendly voice but when I repeated my story for her she told me, firmly, that a written request would be necessary.

"That's fine with me," I said, "but that will take time. The job for which this individual has applied is being competitively sought by many people. We were planning to make a decision within twenty-four hours. It's just a formality—verification of records—but our liability insurance stipulates that we have to do it. If you'd like I can have the applicant call you to release the information. It's in his best interests."

"Well . . . I suppose it'll be all right. All you want to know is if this person received a degree, right? Nothing more personal than that?"

"That's correct."

"Who's the applicant?"

"A gentleman named Timothy Kruger. His records list an M.A. four years ago."

"One moment."

She was gone for ten minutes, and when she returned to the phone she sounded upset.

"Well, Doctor, your formality has turned out to be of some value. There is no record of a degree being granted to a person of that name in the last ten years. We do have record of a Timothy Jay Kruger attending one semester of graduate school four years ago, but his major wasn't in counseling, it was in secondary teaching, and he left after that single semester."

"I see. That's quite disturbing. Any indication of why he left?"

"None. Does that really matter now?"

"No, I suppose not—you're absolutely certain about this? I wouldn't want to jeopardize Mr. Kruger's career—"

"There's no doubt whatsoever." She sounded offended. "I checked and double-checked, Doctor, and then I asked the head of the department, Dr. Gowdy, and he was positive no Timothy Kruger graduated from here."

"Well, that settles it, doesn't it? And it certainly casts a new light on Mr. Kruger. Could you check one more thing?"

"What's that?"

"Mr. Kruger also listed a B.A. in psychology from Jedson College in Washington State. Would your records contain that kind of information as well?"

"It would be on his application to graduate school. We should have transcripts, but I don't see why you need to—"

"Marianne, I'm going to have to report this to the State Board of Behavioral Science examiners, because state licensure is involved. I want to know all the facts."

"I see. Let me check."

This time she was back in a moment.

"I've got his transcript from Jedson here, Doctor. He did receive a B.A. but it wasn't in psychology."

"What was it in?"

She laughed.

"Dramatic arts. Acting."

*　　*　　*

I called the school where Raquel Ochoa taught and had her pulled out of class. Despite that, she seemed pleased to hear from me.

"Hi. How's the investigation going?"

"We're getting closer," I lied. "That's what I called you about. Did Elena keep a diary or any kind of records around the apartment?"

"No. Neither of us were diary writers. Never had been."

"No notebooks, tapes, anything?"

"The only tapes I saw were music—she had a tape deck in her new car—and some cassettes Handler gave her to help her relax. For sleep. Why?"

I ignored the question.

"Where are her personal effects?"

"You should know that. The police had them. I suppose they gave them back to her mother. What's going on? Have you found out something?"

"Nothing definite. Nothing I can talk about. We're trying to fit things together."

"I don't care how you do it, just catch him and punish him. The monster."

I dredged up a rancid lump of false confidence and smeared it all over my voice. "We will."

"I know you will."

Her faith made me uneasy.

"Raquel, I'm away from the files. Do you have her mother's home address handy?"

"Sure." She gave it to me.

"Thanks."

"Are you planning on visiting Elena's family?"

"I thought it would be helpful to talk to them in person."

There was silence on the other end. Then she spoke.

"They're good people. But they may shut you out."

"It's happened before."

She laughed.

"I think you'd do better if I went with you. I'm like a member of the family."

"It's no hassle for you?"

"No. I want to help. When do you want to go?"

"This afternoon."

"Fine. I'll get off early. Tell them I'm not feeling well. Pick me up at two-thirty. Here's my address."

She lived in a modest West L.A. neighborhood not far from where the Santa Monica and San Diego Freeways merged in blissful union, an area of crackerbox apartment buildings populated by singles who couldn't afford the Marina.

She was visible a block away, waiting by the curb, dressed in a pigeon-blood crepe blouse, blue denim skirt and tooled western boots.

She got in the car, crossed a pair of unstockinged brown legs and smiled.

"Hi."

"Hi. Thanks for doing this."

"I told you, this is something I want to do. I want to feel useful."

I drove north, toward Sunset. There was jazz on the radio, something free form and atonal, with saxophone solos that sounded like police sirens and drums like a heart in arrest.

"Change it, if you'd like."

She pushed some buttons, fiddled with the dial, and found a mellow rock station. Someone was singing about lost love and old movies and tying it all together.

"What do you want to know from them?" she asked, settling back.

"If Elena told them anything about her work—specifically the child who died. Anything about Handler."

There were lots of questions in her eyes but she kept them there.

"Talking about Handler will be especially touchy. The family didn't like the idea of her going out with a man who was so much older. And" she hesitated, "an Anglo, to boot. In situations like that the tendency is to deny the whole thing, not even to acknowledge it. It's cultural."

"To some extent it's human."

"To some extent, maybe. We Hispanics do it more. Part of it is Catholicism. The rest is our Indian blood. How can you survive in some of the desolate regions we've lived in without denying reality? You smile, and pretend it's lush and fertile and there's plenty of water and food, and the desert doesn't seem so bad."

"Any suggestions how I might get around the denial?"

"I don't know." She sat with her hands folded in her

lap, a proper schoolgirl. "I think I'd better start the talking. Cruz—Elena's mom—always liked me. Maybe I can
get through. But don't expect miracles."

She had little to worry about on that account.

Echo Park is a chunk of Latin America transported to
the dusty, hilly streets that, buttressed by crumbling concrete embankments on either side of Sunset Boulevard,
rise between Hollywood and downtown. The streets have
names like Macbeth and Macduff, Bonnybrae and Laguna,
but are anything but poetic. They climb to the south and
dip down into the Union District ghetto. To the north they
climb, feeding into the tiny lake-centered park that gives
the area its name, continue through arid trails, get lost in
an incongruous wilderness that looks down upon Dodger
Stadium, and Elysian Park, home of the Los Angeles
Police Academy.

Sunset changes when it leaves Hollywood and enters
Echo Park. The porno theaters and by-the-hour motels
yield to *botánicas* and *bodegas*, outlets for Discos Latinos,
an infinite array of food stands—taco joints, Peruvian
seafood parlors, fast-food franchises—and first-rate Latino
restaurants, beauty shops with windows guarded by styro-
foam skulls wearing blond Dynel wigs, Cuban bakeries,
storefront medical and legal clinics, bars and social clubs.
Like many poor areas, the Echo Park part of Sunset is
continually clogged with foot traffic.

The Seville cut a slow swath through the afternoon mob.
There was a mood on the boulevard as urgent and sizzling
as the molten lard spitting forth from the fryers of the food
stands. There were homeboys sporting homemade tattoos,
fifteen-year-old mothers wheeling fat babies in rickety stroll-
ers that threatened to fall apart at every curb, rummies,
pushers, starched-collared immigration lawyers, cleaning
women on shore leave, grandmothers, flower vendors, a
never-ending stream of brown-eyed children.

"It's very weird," said Raquel, "coming back here. In
a fancy car."

"How long have you been gone?"

"A thousand years."

She didn't seem to want to say more so I dropped it. At
Fairbanks Place she told me to turn left. The Gutierrez
home was at the end of an alley-sized twister that peaked,

then turned into a dirt road just above the foothills. A quarter mile further and we'd have been the only humans in the world.

I'd noticed that she had a habit of biting herself—lips, fingers, knuckles—when she was nervous. And she was gnawing at her thumb right now. I wondered what kind of hunger it satisfied.

I drove cautiously—there was scarcely room for a single vehicle—passing young men in T-shirts working on old cars with the dedication of priests before a shrine, children sucking candy-coated fingers. Long ago, the street had been planted with elms that had grown huge. Their roots buckled the sidewalk and weeds grew in the cracks. Branches scraped the roof of the car. An old woman with inflamed legs wrapped in rags pushed a shopping cart full of memories up an incline worthy of San Francisco. Graffiti scarred every free inch of space, proclaiming the immortality of Little Willie Chacon, the Echo Parque Skulls, Los Conquistadores, the Lemoyne Boys and the tongue of Maria Paula Bonilla.

"There." She pointed to a cottagelike frame house painted light green and roofed with brown tarpaper. The front yard was dry and brown but rimmed with hopeful beds of red geraniums and clusters of orange and yellow poppies that looked like all-day suckers. There was rock trim at the base of the house and a portico over the entry that shadowed a sagging wooden porch upon which a man sat.

"That's Rafael, the older brother. On the porch."

I found a parking space next to a Chevy on blocks. I turned the wheels to the curb and locked them in place. We got out of the car, dust spiraling at our heels.

"Rafael!" she called and waved. The man on the porch took a moment to lift his gaze, then he raised his hand—feebly, it seemed.

"I used to live right around the corner," she said, making it sound like a confession. She led me up a dozen steps and through an open iron gate.

The man on the porch hadn't risen. He stared at us with apprehension and curiosity and something else that I couldn't identify. He was pale and thin to the point of being gaunt, with the same curious mixture of Hispanic features and fair

coloring as his dead sister. His lips were bloodless, his
eyes heavily lidded. He looked like the victim of some
systemic disease. He wore a long-sleeved white shirt with
the sleeves rolled up just below the elbows. It bloused out
around his waist, several sizes too large. His trousers were
black and looked as if they'd once belonged to a fat man's
suit. His shoes were bubble-toed oxfords, cracked at the
tips, worn unlaced with the tongues protruding and revealing thick white socks. His hair was short and combed
straight back.

He was in his mid-twenties but he had an old man's
face, a weary, wary mask.

Raquel went to him and kissed him lightly on the top of
his head. He looked up at her but was unmoved.

"H'lo, Rocky."

"Rafael, how are you?"

"O.K." He nodded his head and it looked for a moment
as if it would roll off his neck. He let his eyes settle on
me; he was having trouble focusing.

Raquel bit her lip.

"We came by to see you and Andy and your mom. This
is Alex Delaware. He works with the police. He's involved in investigating Elena's—case."

His face registered alarm, his hands tightened around
the arm of the chair. Then, as if responding to a stage
direction to relax, he grinned at me, slumped lower, winked.

"Yeah," he said.

I held out my hand. He looked at it, puzzled, recognized
it as a long-lost friend, and extended his own thin claw.

His arm was pitifully undernourished, a bundle of sticks
held together by a sallow paper wrapper. As our fingers
touched his sleeve rode up and I saw the track marks.
There were lots of them. Most looked old—lumpy charcoal smudges—but a few were freshly pink. One, in particular, was no antique, sporting a pinpoint of blood at its
center.

His handshake was moist and tenuous. I let go and the
arm fell limply to his side.

"Hey, man," he said, barely audible. "Good to meetja."
He turned away, lost in his own timeless dream-hell. For
the first time I heard the oldies music coming from a cheap
transistor radio on the floor beside his chair. The puny

plastic box crackled with static. The sound reproduction was atrocious, the music had the chalky quality of notes filtered through a mile of mud. Rafael had his head thrown back, enraptured. To him it was the Celestial Choir transmitting directly to his temporal lobes.

"Rafael," she smiled.

He looked at her, smiled, nodded off and was gone.

She stared at him, tears in her eyes. I moved toward her and she turned away in shame and rage.

"Goddammit."

"How long has he been shooting up?"

"Years. But I thought he'd quit. The last I'd heard he'd quit." She raised her hand to her mouth, swayed, as if ready to fall. I got in position to catch her but she righted herself. "He got hooked in Viet Nam. Came home with a heavy habit. Elena spent lots of time and money trying to help him get off. A dozen times he tried, and each time he slipped back. But he'd been off it for over a year. Elena was so happy about it. He got a job as a boxboy at the Lucky's on Alvarado."

She faced me, nostrils flaring, eyes floating like black lilies in a salty pond, lips quivering like harp-strings.

"Everything is falling apart."

She grasped the newel post on the porch rail for support. I came behind her.

"I'm sorry."

"He was always the sensitive one. Quiet, never dating, no friends. He got beat up a lot. When their dad died he tried to take over, to be the man of the house. Tradition says the oldest son should do that. But it didn't work. Nobody took him seriously. They laughed. We all did. So he gave up, as if he'd failed some final test. He dropped out of school, stayed home and read comic books and watched TV all day—just stared at the screen. When the army said they wanted him he seemed glad. Cruz cried to see him go, but he was happy . . ."

I looked at him, sitting so low he was almost parallel with the ground. Swallowed up by junkie-slumber. His mouth was open and he snored loudly. The radio played "Daddy's Home."

Raquel hazarded another look at him, then whipped her head away, disgusted. She wore an expression of noble suffering, an Aztec virgin steeling herself for the ultimate sacrifice.

I put my hands on her shoulders and she leaned back in my arms. She stayed there, tense and unyielding, allowing herself a miser's ration of tears.

"This is a hell of a start," she said. Inhaling deeply, she let out her breath in a breeze of wintergreen. She wiped her eyes and turned around. "You must think all I do is weep. Come on, let's go inside."

She pulled the screen door open and it slapped sharply against the wood siding of the house.

We stepped into a small front room furnished with old but cared-for relics. It was warm and dark, the windows shut tight and masked by yellowing parchment shades—a room unaccustomed to visitors. Faded lace curtains were tied back from the window frames and matching lace coverlets shielded the arms of the chairs—a sofa and loveseat set upholstered in dark green crushed velvet, the worn spots shiny and the color of jungle parrots, two wicker rockers. A painting of the two dead Kennedy brothers in black velvet hung over the mantel. Carvings in wood and Mexican onyx sat atop lace-covered end tables. There were two floor lamps with beaded shades, a plaster Jesus in agony hanging on the whitewashed wall next to a still life of a straw basket of oranges. Family portraits in ornate frames covered another wall and there was a large graduation picture of Elena suspended high above those. A spider crawled in the space where wall met ceiling.

A door to the right revealed a sliver of white tile. Raquel walked to the sliver and peeked in.

"Señora Cruz?"

The doorway widened and a small, heavy woman appeared, dishtowel in hand. She wore a blue print dress, unbelted, and her gray-black hair was tied back in a bun, held in place by a mock tortoiseshell comb. Silver earrings dangled from her ears and salmon spots of rouge punctuated her cheekbones. Her skin had the delicate, baby-soft look common in old women who had once been beautiful.

"Raquelita!"

She put her towel down, came out, and the two women embraced for a long moment.

When she saw me over Raquel's shoulder, she smiled.

But her face closed up as tight as a pawnbroker's safe. She pulled away and gave a small bow.

"Señor," she said, with too much deference, and looked at Raquel, arching one eyebrow.

"Señora Gutierrez."

Raquel spoke to her in rapid Spanish. I caught the words "Elena," "policía," and "doctor." She ended it with a question.

The older woman listened politely, then shook her head.

"No." Some things are the same in any language.

Raquel turned to me. "She says she knows nothing more than what she told the police the first time."

"Can you ask her about the Nemeth boy? They didn't ask her about that."

She turned to speak, then stopped.

"Why don't we take it slowly? It would help if we ate. Let her be a hostess, let her give to us."

I was genuinely hungry and told her so. She relayed the message to Mrs. Gutierrez, who nodded and returned to her kitchen.

"Let's sit down," Raquel said.

I took the loveseat. She tucked herself into a corner of the sofa.

The señora came back with cookies and fruit and hot coffee. She asked Raquel something.

"She'd like to know if this is substantial enough or would you like some homemade *chorizo?*"

"Please tell her this is wonderful. However if you think my accepting *chorizo* would help things along, I'll oblige."

Raquel spoke again. A few moments later I was facing a platter of the spicy sausage, rice, refried beans and salad with lemon-oil dressing.

"Muchas gracias, señora." I dug in.

I couldn't understand much of what they were saying, but it sounded and looked like small talk. The two women touched each other a lot, patting hands, stroking cheeks. They smiled, and seemed to forget my presence.

Then suddenly the wind shifted and the laughter turned to tears. Mrs. Gutierrez ran out of the room, seeking the refuge of her kitchen.

Raquel shook her head.

"We were talking about the old times, when Elena and I

were little girls. How we used to play secretary in the
bushes, pretend we had typewriters and desks out there. It
became difficult for her.''

I pushed my plate aside.

''Do you think we should go?'' I asked.

''Let's wait a while.'' She poured me more coffee and
filled a cup for herself. ''It would be more respectful.''

Through the screen door I could see the top of Rafael's
fair head above the rim of the chair. His arm had fallen, so
that the fingernails scraped the ground. He was beyond
pleasure or pain.

''Did she talk about him?'' I asked.

''No. As I told you, it's easier to deny.''

''But how can he sit there, shooting up, right in front of
her, with no pretense?''

''She used to cry a lot about it. After a while you accept
the fact that things aren't going to turn out the way you
want them to. She's had plenty of training in it, believe
me. If you asked her about him she'd say he was sick. Just
as if he had a cold, or the measles. It's just a matter of
finding the right cure. Have you heard of the *curanderos?*''

''The folk doctors? Yes. Lots of the Hispanic patients at
the hospital used them along with conventional medicine.''

''Do you know how they operate? By caring. In our
culture the cold, distant professional is regarded as someone who simply doesn't care, who is just as likely to
deliver the *mal ojo*—the evil eye—as he is to cure. The
curandero, on the other hand has little training or technology at his disposal—a few snake powders, maybe. But he
cares. He lives in the community, he is warm, and familiar, has tremendous rapport. In a way, he's a folk psychologist more than a folk doctor. That's why I suggested you
eat—to establish a personal link. I told her you were a
caring person. Otherwise she'd say nothing. She'd be
polite, ladylike—Cruz is from the old school—but she'd
shut you out just the same.'' She sipped at her coffee.

''That's why the police learned nothing when they came
here, why they seldom do in Echo Park, or East L.A., or
San Fernando. They're too professional. No matter how
well-meaning they may be, we see them as Anglo robots.
You do care, Alex, don't you?''

''I do.''

She touched my knee.

"Cruz took Rafael to a *curandero* years ago, when he first started dropping out. The man looked into his eyes and said they were empty. He told her it was an illness of the soul, not of the body. That the boy should be given to the church, as a priest or monk, so that he could find a useful role for himself."

"Not bad advice."

She sipped her coffee. "No. Some of them are very sophisticated. They live by their wits. Maybe it would have prevented the addiction if she'd followed through. Who knows? But she couldn't give him up. I wouldn't be surprised if she blames herself for what he's become. For everything."

The door to the kitchen opened. Mrs. Gutierrez came out wearing a black band around her arm and a new face that was more than just fresh makeup. A face hardened to withstand the acid bath of interrogation.

She sat down next to Raquel and whispered to her in Spanish.

"She says you may ask any questions you'd like."

I nodded with what I hoped was obvious gratitude.

"Please tell the señora that I express my sorrow at her tragic loss and also let her know that I greatly appreciate her taking the time during her period of grief to talk to me."

The older woman listened to the translation and acknowledged me with a quick movement of her head.

"Ask her, Raquel, if Elena ever talked about her work. Especially during the last year."

As Raquel spoke a nostalgic smile spread across the older woman's face.

"She says only to complain that teachers did not get paid enough. That the hours were long and the children could get difficult."

"Any particular children?"

A whispered conference.

'No child in particular. The señora reminds you that Elena was a special kind of teacher who helped children with problems in learning. All the children had difficulties."

I wondered to myself if there'd been a connection between growing up with a brother like Rafael and the dead girl's choice of specialty.

"Did she speak at all about the child who was killed. The Nemeth boy?"

Upon hearing the question Mrs. Gutierrez nodded, sadly, then spoke.

"She mentioned it once or twice. She said she was very sad about it. That it was a tragedy," Raquel translated.

"Nothing else?"

"It would be rude to pursue it, Alex."

"Okay. Try this. Did Elena seem to have more money than usual recently? Did she buy expensive gifts for anyone in the family?"

"No. She says Elena always complained about not having enough money. She was a girl who liked to have good things. Pretty things. One minute." She listened to the older woman, nodding affirmation. "This wasn't always possible, as the family was never rich. Even when her husband was alive. But Elena worked very hard. She bought herself things. Sometimes on credit, but she always made her payments. Nothing was repossessed. She was a girl to make a mother proud."

I prepared myself for more tears, but there were none. The grieving mother looked at me with a cold, dark expression of challenge. I dare you, she was saying, to besmirch the memory of my little girl.

I looked away.

"Do you think I can ask her about Handler now?"

Before Raquel could answer, Mrs. Gutierrez spit. She gesticulated with both hands, raised her voice and uttered what had to be a string of curses. She ended the diatribe by spitting again.

"Need I translate?" asked Raquel.

"Don't bother." I made a mental search for a new line of questioning. Normally, my approach would have been to start off with small talk, casual banter, and subtly switch to direct questions. I was dissatisfied with the crude way I was handling this interview, but working with a translator was like doing surgery wearing garden gloves.

"Ask her if there is anything else she can tell me that might help us find the man who—you phrase it."

The old woman listened and answered vehemently.

"She says there is nothing. That the world has become a crazy place, full of demons. That a demon must have done this to Elena."

"*Muchas gracias, señora.* Ask her if I might have a look at Elena's personal effects."

Raquel asked her and the mother deliberated. She looked me over from head to toe, sighed, and got up.

"*Venga,*" she said, and led me to the rear of the house.

The flotsam and jetsam of Elena Gutierrez's twenty-eight years had been stored in cardboard boxes and stuck in a corner of what passed, in the tiny house, as a service porch. There was a windowed door with a view of the backyard. An apricot tree grew there, gnarled and deformed, spreading its fruit-laden branches across the rotting roof of a single car garage.

Across the hall was a small bedroom with two beds, the domicile of the brothers. From where I knelt I could see a maple dresser and shelves constructed of unfinished planks resting on cinder blocks. The shelves held a cheap stereo and a modest record collection. A carton of Marlboros and a pile of paperbacks shared the top of the dresser. One of the beds was neatly made, the other a jumble of tangled sheets. Between them was a single pine end table holding a lamp with a plastic base, an ashtray, and a copy of a Spanish girlie magazine.

Feeling like a Peeping Tom, I pulled the first box close and began my excursion in pop archaeology.

By the time I'd gone through three boxes I'd succumbed to an indigo mood. My hands were filthy with dust, my mind filled with images of the dead girl. There'd been nothing of substance, just the broken shards that surface at any prolonged dig. Clothing smelling of girl, half-empty bottles of cosmetics—reminders that someone had once tried to make her eyelashes look thick and lush, to give her hair that Clairol shine, to cover her blemishes and gloss her lips and smell good in all the right places. Scraps of paper with reminders to pick up eggs at Vons and wine at Vendôme and other cryptograms, laundry receipts, gasoline credit-card stubs, books—lots of them, mostly biographies and poetry, souvenirs—a miniature ukulele from Hawaii, an ashtray from a hotel in Palm Springs, ski boots, an almost-full disc of birth control pills, old lesson plans, memos from the principal, children's drawings—none by a boy named Nemeth.

It was too much like graverobbing for my taste. I understood, more than ever, why Milo drank too much.

There were two boxes to go. I went at them, working faster, and was almost done when the roar of a motorcycle filled the air, then died. The back door opened, footsteps sounded in the foyer.

"What the fuck—"

He was nineteen or twenty, short and powerfully built, wearing a sweat-soaked brown tank top that showed every muscle, grease-stained khaki pants and work boots coated with grime. His hair was thick and shaggy. It hung to his shoulders and was held in place by a thonged leather headband. He had fine, almost delicate features that he'd tried to camouflage by growing a mustache and beard. The mustache was black and luxuriant. It dropped over his lips and glistened like sable fur. The beard was a skimpy triangle of down on his chin. He looked like a kid playing Pancho Villa in the school play.

There was a ring of keys hanging from his belt and the keys jingled when he came toward me. His hands were balled up into grimy fists and he smelled of motor oil.

I showed him my L.A.P.D. badge. He swore, but stopped.

"Listen man, you guys were here last week. We told you we had nothin'—" He stopped and looked down at the contents of the cardboard box strewn on the floor. "Shit, you went through all that stuff already. I just packed it up, man, gettin' it ready for the Goodwill."

"Just a recheck," I said amiably.

"Yeah, man, why don't you dudes learn to get it right in the first fuckin' place, okay?"

"I'll be through in a moment."

"You're through now, man. Out."

I stood.

"Give me a few minutes to wrap it up."

"Out, man." He crooked his thumb toward the back door.

"I'm trying to investigate the death of your sister, Andy. It wouldn't hurt you to cooperate."

He took a step closer. There were grease smudges on his forehead, and under his eyes.

"Don't 'Andy' me, dude. This is my place and it's *Mr.* Gutierrez. And don't give me that shit about investigating. You guys aren't never gonna catch the dude who did it to Elena 'cause you don't really give a fuck. Come bustin' into a home and going through personal stuff and treatin' us like peasants, man. You go out on the street and find the dude, man. This was Beverly Hills, he'd already 'a' been caught, he do this to some rich guy's daughter."

His voice broke and he shut up to hide it.

"Mr. Gutierrez," I said softly, "cooperation from family can be very helpful in these—"

"Hey, man, I told you, this family don't know nothing about this. You think we know what kind of crazy asshole do something like that? You think people around here act like that, man?"

He squinted at my badge, reading it with effort, moving his lips. He mouthed the word 'consultant' a couple of times before getting it.

"Aw, man, I don't believe it. You're not even a real cop. Fucking consultant, they send around here. What's Ph.D., man?"

"Doctorate in psychology."

"You a shrink, man—fuckin' headshrinker they send aroun' here, think someone's crazy here! You think someone in this family is crazy, man? Do you?"

He was breathing on me now. His eyes were soft and brown, longlashed and dreamy as a girl's. Eyes like that could make you doubt yourself, could lead a guy to get into some heavy macho posturing.

I thought the family had plenty of problems but I didn't answer his question.

"What the fuck you doin' here, psychin' us out, man?"

He sprayed me with spittle as he spoke. A balloon of anger expanded in my gut. Automatically my body assumed a defensive karate stance.

"It's not like that, I can explain. Or are you determined to be pigheaded?"

I regretted the words even as they left my mouth.

"Pig—goddammit man, you're the pig!" His voice rose an octave and he grabbed the lapel of my jacket.

I was ready but I didn't move. He's in mourning, I kept telling myself. He's not responsible.

I met his gaze and he backed off. Both of us would have welcomed an excuse to duke it out. So much for civilization.

"Get out, man. Now!"

"Antonio!"

Mrs. Gutierrez had come into the hallway. Raquel was visible behind her. Seeing her I felt suddenly ashamed. I'd done a great job of screwing up a sensitive situation. The brilliant psychologist . . .

"Mom, did you let this dude in?"

Mrs. Gutierrez apologized to me with her eyes and spoke to her son in Spanish. He seemed to wilt under mama's wagging finger and dark looks.

"Mom, I told you before, they don't give a—" He stopped, continued in Spanish. It sounded like he was defending himself, the machismo slowly rendered impotent.

They went back and forth for a while. Then he started in on Raquel. She gave it right back to him: "The man is trying to help you, Andy. Why don't you help him instead of chasing him away?"

"I don't need nobody's help. We're gonna take care of ourselves the way we always did."

She sighed.

"Shit!" He went into his room, came out with a pack of Marlboros and made a big deal out of lighting one and jamming it into his mouth. He disappeared, momentarily, behind a blue cloud, then the eyes flashed once again, moving from me to his mother, to Raquel, and back to me. He pulled his key ring from his belt and held the keys sandwiched between his fingers, impromptu brass knuckles.

"I'm leaving now, dude. But when I get back you fucking well better be gone."

He kicked the door open and jogged out. We heard the thunder of the motorcycle starting and the diminishing scream of the machine as it sped away.

Mrs. Gutierrez hung her head and said something to Raquel.

"She asks your forgiveness for Andy's rudeness. He's been very upset since Elena's death. He's working two jobs and under a lot of pressure."

I held a hand up to stop the apology.

"There's no need to explain. I only hope I haven't caused the señora needless troubles."

Translation was superfluous. The look on the mother's face was eloquent.

I rummaged through the last two boxes with little enthusiasm and came up with no new insights. The sour taste of the confrontation with Andy lingered. I experienced the kind of shame you feel upon digging too deep, seeing and hearing more than you need or want to. Like a child walking in on his parents lovemaking or a hiker kicking aside a rock only to catch a glimpse of something slimy on the underside.

I'd seen families like the Gutierrezes' before; I'd known scores of Rafaels and Andys. It was a pattern: the slob and the superkid, playing out their roles with depressing predictability. One unable to cope, the other trying to take charge of everything. The slob, getting others to take care of him, shirking his responsibilities, coasting through life but feeling like—a slob. The superkid, competent, compulsive, working two jobs, even three when the situation called for it, making up for the slob's lack of accomplishment, earning the admiration of the family, refusing to stoop under the weight of his burden, keeping his rage under wraps—but not always.

I wondered what role Elena had played when she was alive. Had she been the peacemaker, the go-between? Getting caught in the crossfire between slob and superkid could be hazardous to one's health.

I repacked her things as neatly as I could.

When we stepped onto the porch Rafael was still stuporous. The sound of the Seville starting up jolted him awake, and he blinked rapidly, as if coming out of a bad dream, stood with effort, and wiped his nose with his sleeve. He looked in our direction, puzzled. Raquel turned away from him, a tourist avoiding a leprous beggar. As I pulled away I saw a spark of recognition brighten his doped-up countenance, then more bewilderment.

The approaching darkness had dimmed the activity level on Sunset but there was still plenty of life on the streets. Car horns honked, raucous laughter rose above the exhaust fumes and mariachi music blared from the open doors of the bars. Traces of neon appeared and lights flickered in the foothills.

"I really blew it," I said.

"No, you can't blame yourself." In the mood she was in, boosting me took effort. I appreciated that effort and told her so.

"I mean it, Alex. You were very sensitive with Cruz—I can see why you were a successful psychologist. She liked you."

"It obviously doesn't run in the family."

She was silent for a few blocks.

"Andy's a nice boy—he never joined the gangs, took lots of punishment because of it. He expects a lot out of himself. Everything's on his shoulders, now."

"With all that weight why add a two-ton chip?"

"You're right. He makes more problems for himself—don't we all? He's only eighteen. Maybe he'll grow up."

"I keep wondering if there was some way I could have handled it better." I recounted the details of my exchange with the boy.

"The pigheaded crack didn't help things, but it didn't make a difference. He came in ready to fight. When Latin men get that way there's little you can do. Add alcohol to that and you can see why we pack the emergency rooms with knifing victims every Saturday night."

I thought of Elena Gutierrez and Morton Handler. They'd never made it to the emergency room. I allowed myself a short ride on that train of thought, then skidded to a stop and dumped the thoughts in a dark depot somewhere in the south of my subconscious.

I looked over at Raquel. She sat stiffly in the soft leather, refusing to give herself over to comfort. Her body was still but her hands played nervously with the fabric of her skirt.

"Are you hungry?" I asked. When in doubt, stick to basics.

"No. If you want you can stop for yourself."

"I can still taste the *chorizo*."

"You can take me home, then."

When I got to her apartment it was dark and the streets were empty.

"Thanks for coming with me."

"I hope it was helpful."

"Without you it would have been disastrous."

"Thank you." She smiled and leaned over. It started out as a kiss on the cheek but one or both of us moved and it turned into a kiss on the lips. Then a tentative nibble, nurtured with heat and want, that matured quickly into a gasping, ravenous adult bite. We moved closer simultaneously, her arms easing around my neck, my hands in her hair, on her face, at the small of her back. Our mouths opened and our tongues danced a slow waltz. We breathed heavily, squirming, struggling to get closer.

We necked like two teenagers for endless minutes. I undid a button of her blouse. She made a throaty sound, caught my lower lip between her teeth, licked my ear. My hand slithered around to the hot silk of her back, working with a mind of its own, undoing the clasp of her brassiere, cupping around her breast. The nipple, pebble-hard and moist, nestled against my palm. She lowered one hand, slender fingers tugging at my fly.

I was the one who stopped it.

"What's the matter?"

There's nothing you can say in a situation like that that doesn't sound like a cliché or totally idiotic, or both. I opted for both.

"I'm sorry. Don't take it personally."

She threw herself upright, busied herself with buttoning, fastening, smoothing her hair.

"How else should I take it?"

"You're very desirable."

"Very."

"I'm attracted to you, dammit. I'd love to make love to you."

"What is it, then?"

"A commitment."

"You're not married, are you? You don't act married."

"There are other commitments besides marriage."

"I see." She gathered up her purse and put her hand on the door handle. "The person you're committed to, it would matter to her?"

"Yes. More important, it would matter to me."

She burst out laughing, verging on hysteria.

"I'm sorry," she said, catching her breath. "It's so

damned ironic. You think I do this often? This is the first time I've been interested in a guy in a long time. The nun cuts loose and comes face to face with a saint.''

She giggled. It sounded feverish, fragile, made me uneasy. I was weary of being on the receiving end of someone's—anyone's—frustration but I supposed she was entitled to her moment of cathartic stardom.

"I'm no saint, believe me."

She touched my cheek with her fingers. It was like being raked with hot coals.

"No, you're just a nice guy, Delaware."

"I don't feel like that, either."

"I'm going to kiss you again," she said, "but it's going to stay chaste this time. The way it should have been in the first place."

And she did.

18

THERE WERE two surprises waiting for me when I got home.

The first was Robin, in my ratty yellow bathrobe, stretched out on the leather sofa, drinking hot tea. A fire burned in the hearth and the stereo played the Eagles' "Desperado."

She was wearing a magazine photograph of Lassie around her neck like a miniature sandwich sign.

"Hello, darling," she said.

I threw my jacket over a chair.

"Hi. What's with the dog?"

"Just my way of letting you know that I've been a bitch and I'm sorry."

"You have nothing to be sorry for." I removed the sign.

I sat beside her and took her hands in mine.

"I was rotten to you this morning, Alex, letting you leave like that. The moment the door closed I started missing you. You know how it is when you let your mind wander around—what if something happens to him, what if I never see him again—you go crazy. I couldn't work, couldn't be around machines in that state. The day was blown. I called you but I couldn't get through. So here I am."

"Virtue has its rewards," I muttered under my breath.

"What's that, sweetie?"

"Nothing." Any recounting of my minor-league indiscretion would suffer in the retelling, emerging as either a boorish bathroom scribble—'Yeah, I copped a fast feel from another broad, honey'—or, worse, a confession.

I lay down beside her. We held each other, said nice things, talked baby talk, stroked each other. I was pumped up from the waist down, some of it a residue of the curbside session with Raquel, most of it belonging to the moment.

"There are two giant porterhouses in the refrigerator and a Caesar salad and burgundy and sourdough." She whispered, tickling my nose with her pinkie.

"You're a very oral person," I laughed.

"Is that neurotic, Doctor?"

"No. It's wonderful."

"How about this? And this?"

The robe fell open. She kneeled above me, letting it slide down her shoulders. Backlit by the glow of the fire, she looked like a piece of glorious, golden statuary.

"Come on sweetie," she coaxed, "get out of those clothes." And she took the matter into her own hands.

"I do love you," she said later. "Even if you are catatonic."

I refused to budge, and lay spreadeagled on the floor.

"I'm cold."

She covered me, stood and stretched, and laughed with pleasure.

"How can you jump around afterwards?" I groaned.

"Women are stronger than men," she said gaily, and proceeded to dance around the room, humming, stretching more so that the muscles of her calves ascended in the slender columns of her legs like bubbles rising in a carpenter's level. Her eyes reflected orange Halloween light. When she moved a shudder went through me.

"Keep jiggling like that and I'll show you who's stronger."

"Later, big boy." She teased me with her foot and leaped away from my grabbing paws with fluid agility.

By the time the steaks were ready Mrs. Gutierrez's cuisine was a vague memory and I ate with gusto. We sat side by side in the breakfast nook, looking out through leaded glass as lights went on in the hills like the beacons of a distant search party. She rested her head on my shoulder. My arm went around her, my fingertips blindly traced the contours of her face. We took turns drinking from a single glass of wine.

"I love you," I said.

"I love you too." She kissed the underside of my chin. After several more sips:

"You were investigating those murders today, weren't you?"

"Yes."

She fortified herself with a large swallow and refilled the glass.

"Don't worry," she said. "I'm not going to hassle you about it. I can't pretend I like it, but I won't try to control you."

I hugged her by way of thanks.

"I mean, I wouldn't want you treating me that way, so I won't do it to you." She was giving liberation the old school try, but worry remained suspended in her voice like a fly in amber.

"I'm watching out for myself."

"I know you are," she said, too quickly. "You're a bright man. You can take care of yourself."

She handed me the wine.

"If you want to talk about it, Alex, I'll listen."

I hesitated.

"Tell me. I want to know what's going on."

I gave her a rehash of the last two days, ending it with the confrontation with Andy Gutierrez, leaving out the ten turbulent minutes with Raquel.

She listened, troubled and attentive, digested it, and told me, "I can see why you can't drop it. So many suspicious things, no connecting thread."

She was right. It was reverse Gestalt, the whole so much less than the sum of its parts. A random assortment of musicians, sawing, blowing, thumping, yearning for a conductor. But who the hell was I to play Ormandy?

"When are you going to tell Milo?"

"I'm not. I spoke to him this morning and he basically told me to mind my own business, stay out of it."

"But it's his job, Alex. He'll know what to do."

"Honey, Milo will get bent out of shape if I tell him I visited La Casa."

"But that poor child, the retarded one, isn't there something he could do about it?"

I shook my head.

"It's not enough. There'd be an explanation for it. Milo's got his suspicions—I'll bet they're stronger than he let on to me—but he's hemmed in by rules and procedures."

"And you're not," she said softly.

"Don't worry."

"Don't worry, yourself. I'm not going to try to stop you. I meant what I said."

I drank more wine. My throat had constricted and the cool liquid was astringently soothing.

She got up and stood behind me, putting her arms over my shoulders. It was a gesture of support not dissimilar from the one I'd offered Raquel just a few hours earlier. She reached down and played with the ridge of hair that vertically bisected my abdomen.

"I'm here for you, Alex, if you need me."

"I always need you. But not to get involved in crap like this."

"Whatever you need me for, I'm here."

I rose out of the chair and drew her to me, kissing her neck, her ears, her eyes. She threw bck her head and put my lips on the warm pulse at the base of her throat.

"Let's get into bed and snuggle," she said.

I turned on the radio and tuned it to KKGO. Sonny Rollins was extracting a liquid sonata from his horn. I switched on a dim light and drew back the covers.

The second surprise of the evening lay there, a plain white envelope, business-size, unmarked and partially covered by the pillow.

"Was this here when you arrived?"

She'd taken off her robe. Now she held it to her breasts, seeking cover, as if the envelope were a living, breathing intruder.

"Could have been. I didn't go in the bedroom."

I slit it open with my thumbnail and took out the single sheet of white paper folded inside. The page was devoid of date, address or any distinguishing logo. Just a white rectangle filled with lines of handwriting that slanted pessimistically downward. The penmanship, cramped and spidery, was familiar. I sat down on the edge of the bed and read.

Dear Doctor:

Here's hoping you sleep in your own bed in the near future so you have the opportunity to read this. I took the liberty of jimmying your rear door to get in and deliver this—you should get a better lock, by the way.

This afternoon I was relieved of my duties in the H-G case. El Capitán feels the case would benefit by the infusion of fresh blood—the tasteless choice of words was his, not mine. I have my doubts about his motivation, but I haven't exactly set any new detection records so I was in no position to debate it with him.

I must have looked pretty shattered by it, cause he got suddenly empathetic and suggested I take some R and R. In fact, he was very well-versed in the details of my personnel file, knew that I'd accrued lots of vacation time and strongly urged me to use some of it.

At first I wasn't overjoyed at the idea, but I've since come to view it as an excellent one. I've found my place in the sun. A quaint little watering hole named Ahuacatlan, just north of Guadalajara. Some preliminary checking via long distance reveals that said burg is extremely well-suited for someone of my recreational interests. Hunting and fishing, in particular.

I expect to be gone for two or three days. Phone contact is tenuous and undesirable—the natives cherish privacy. Will call when I get back. Regards to Stradivarius (Stradivariette?) and stay out of trouble.

> All the best,
> Milo

I gave it to Robin to read. She finished it and handed it back.

"What's he saying—that he was kicked off the case?"

"Yes. Probably because of outside pressure. But he's going to Mexico to look into McCaffrey's background. Apparently when he called down there he got enough over the phone to make him want to pursue it."

"He's going behind his captain's back."

"He must feel it's worth it." Milo was a brave man but

no martyr. He wanted his pension as much as the next guy.

"You were right then. About La Casa." She got under the covers and drew them up to her chin. She shivered, not from the cold.

"Yes." Never had being right seemed of such meager solace.

The music from the radio peeked around corners and took an unexpected pirouette. A drummer had joined Rollins, and he slapped out a tropical tattoo on his tom-toms . . . I could think only of cannibals and snake-encrusted vines. Shrunken heads . . .

"Hold me."

I got in beside her and kissed her and held her and tried to act calm. But all the while my mind was elsewhere, lost on some frozen piece of tundra, floating out to sea.

19

THE ENTRANCE LOBBY of Western Pediatric Medical Center
was walled with marble slabs engraved with the names of
long-dead benefactors. Inside, the lobby was filled with
the injured, the ill and the doomed, all simmering in the
endless wait that is as much a part of hospitals as are
intravenous needles and bad food.

Mothers clutched bundles to their breasts, wails escaping from within the layers of blanket. Fathers chewed their
nails, grappled with insurance forms and tried not to think
about the loss of masculinity resulting from encounters
with bureaucracy. Toddlers raced about, placing their hands
on the marble, withdrawing them quickly at the cold and
leaving behind grimy mementoes. A loudspeaker called
out names and the chosen plodded to the admissions desk.
A blue-haired lady in the green-and-white-striped uniform
of a hospital volunteer sat behind the information counter,
as baffled as those she was mandated to assist.

In a far corner of the lobby, children and grownups sat
on plastic chairs and watched television. The TV was
tuned to a serial that took place in a hospital. The doctors
and nurses on the screen wore spotless white, had coiffed
hair, perfect faces, and teeth that radiated a mucoid sparkle
as they conversed in slow, low, earnest tones about love,
hate, anguish and death. The doctors and nurses who
elbowed their way through the throng in the lobby were
altogether more human—rumpled, harried, sleepy-eyed.
Those entering rushed, responding to beepers and emergency phone calls. Those exiting did so with the alacrity of
escaping prisoners, fearing last-minute calls back to the
wards.

I wore my white coat and hospital badge and carried my briefcase as the automatic doors allowed me through and the sixtyish, red-nosed guard nodded as I passed:

"Morning, Doctor."

I rode the elevator to the basement along with a despondent black couple in their thirties and their son, a withered, gray-skinned nine-year-old in a wheelchair. At the mezzanine we were joined by a lab tech, a fat girl carrying a basket of syringes, needles, rubber tubing and glass cylinders full of the ruby syrup of life. The parents of the boy in the wheelchair looked longingly at the blood; the child turned his head to the wall.

The ride ended with a bump. We were disgorged into a dingy yellow corridor. The other passengers turned right, toward the lab. I went the other way, came to a door marked "Medical Records," opened it and went in.

Nothing had changed since I'd left. I had to turn sideways to get through the narrow aisle carved into the floor-to-ceiling stacks of charts. No computer here, no high tech attempt at organizing the tens of thousands of dog-eared manila files into a coherent system. Hospitals are conservative institutions, and Western Pediatric was the most stodgy of hospitals, welcoming progress the way a dog welcomes the mange.

At the end of the aisle was an unadorned gray wall. Just in front of it sat a sleepy-looking Filipino girl, reading a glamor magazine.

"May I help you?"

"Yes. I'm Dr. Delaware. I need to get hold of a chart of a patient of mine."

"You could have your secretary call us, Doctor, and we'd send it to you."

Sure. In two weeks.

"I appreciate that, but I need to look at it right now and my secretary's not here yet."

"What's the patient's name?"

"Adams. Brian Adams." The room was divided alphabetically. I picked a name that would take her to the far end of the A—K section.

"If you'll just fill out this form, I'll get it right for you."

I filled out the form, falsifying with ease. She didn't

bother to look at it and dropped it into a metal filebox. When she was gone, hidden between the stacks, I went to the L—Z side of the room, searched among the N's and found what I was looking for. I slipped it into my briefcase and returned.

She came back minutes later.

"I've got three Brian Adamses, here, Doctor. Which one is it?"

I scanned the three and picked one at random.

"This is it."

"If you sign this"—she held out a second form—"I can let you have it on twenty-four-hour loan."

"There'll be no need for that. I'll just examine it here."

I made a show of looking scholarly, leafed through the medical history of Brian Adams, age eleven, admitted for a routine tonsillectomy five years previously, clucked my tongue, shook my head, jotted down some meaningless notes, and gave it back to her.

"Thanks. You've been most helpful."

She didn't answer, having already returned to the world of cosmetic camouflage and clothing designed for the sado-intellectual set.

I found an empty conference room down the hall next to the morgue, locked the door from the inside and sat down to examine the final chronicles of Cary Nemeth.

The boy had spent the last twenty-two hours of his life in the Intensive Care Unit at Western Pediatric, not a second of it in a conscious state. From a medical point of view it was open and shut: hopeless. The admitting intern had kept his notes factual and objective, labeling it Auto versus Pedestrian, in the quaint lexicon of medicine that makes tragedy sound like a sporting event.

He'd been brought in by ambulance, battered, crushed, skull shredded, all but his most rudimentary bodily functions gone. Yet thousands of dollars had been spent delaying the inevitable, and enough pages had been filled to create a medical chart the size of a textbook. I leafed through them: nursing notes, with their compulsive accounting of intake and output, the child reduced to cubic centimeters of fluid and plumbing; ICU graphs, progress notes—that was a cruel joke—consultations from neurosurgeons, neurologists, nephrologists, radiologists, cardiologists; blood tests, X-rays, scans, shunts, sutures, intravenous feedings, parenteral nutritional supplements, respiratory therapy, and, finally, the autopsy.

Stapled to the back inside cover was the sheriff's report, another example of jargonistic reductionism. In this equally precious dialect, Cary Nemeth was V, for Victim.

V had been hit from behind while walking down Malibu Canyon Road just before midnight. He'd been barefoot, wearing pajamas—yellow, the report was careful to note. There were no skid marks, leading the reporting deputy to conclude that he'd been hit at full force. From the distance the body traveled, the estimated speed of the vehicle was between forty and fifty miles per hour.

The rest was paperwork, a cardboard snack for some downtown computer.

It was a depressing document. Nothing in it surprised me. Not even the fact that Cary Nemeth's private pediatrician of record, the physician who'd actually signed the death report, was Lionel Willard Towle, M.D.

I left the chart stuck under a stack of X-ray plates and walked toward the elevator. Two eleven-year-olds had escaped from the ward and were waging a wheelchair drag race. They whooped by, I.V. tubing looping like lariats, and I had to swerve to avoid them.

I reached for the elevator button and heard my name called.

"H'lo, Alex!"

It was the medical director, chatting with a pair of interns. He dismissed them and walked my way.

"Hello, Henry."

He'd put on a few pounds since I'd last seen him, jowls fighting the confines of his shirt collar. His complexion was unhealthily florid. Three cigars stuck out of his breast pocket.

"What a coincidence," he said, giving me a soft hand. "I was just about to call you."

"Really? What about?"

"Let's talk in the office."

He closed the door and scurried behind his desk.

"How've you been, son?"

"Just fine." Dad.

"Good, good." He took a cigar out of his pocket and made masturbatory motions up and down the cellophane wrapper. "I'm not going to beat around the bush, Alex. You know that's not my way—always come right out and say what's on your mind is my philosophy. Let people know where you stand."

"Please do."

"Yes. Hmm. I'll come out and say it." He leaned forward, either about to retch or preparing to impart some grave confidence. "I've—we've received a complaint about your professional conduct."

He sat back, pleasurably expectant, a boy waiting for a firecracker to explode.

"Will Towle?"

His eyebrows shot skyward. There were no fireworks up there, so they came back down again.

"You know?"

"Call it a good guess."

"Yes, well, you're correct. He's up in arms about some hypnotizing you've done or some such nonsense."

"He's full of shit, Henry."

His fingers fumbled with the cellophane. I wondered how long it had been since he'd done surgery. "I understand your point; however Will Towle is an important man, not to be taken lightly. He's demanding an investigation, some kind of—"

"Witch hunt?"

"You're not making this any easier, young man."

"I'm not beholden to Towle or anyone else. I'm retired, Henry, or have you forgotten that? Check the last time I received my salary."

"That's not the point—"

"The point is, Henry, if Towle has a gripe against me, let him bring it up before the State Board. I'm prepared to swap accusations. I guarantee it will be an educational experience for all concerned."

He smiled unctuously.

"I like you, Alex. I'm telling you this to warn you."

"Warn me of what?"

"Will Towle's family has donated hundreds of thousands of dollars to this hospital. They may very well have paid for the chair you're sitting on."

I stood up.

"Thanks for the warning."

His little eyes hardened. The cigar snapped between his fingers, showering the desk with shreds of tobacco. He looked down at his lost pacifier and for a moment I thought he'd break into tears. He'd be great fun on the analyst's couch.

"You're not as independent as you think you are. There's the matter of your staff privileges."

"Are you telling me that because Will Towle complained about me I'm in danger of losing my right to practice here?"

"I'm saying: Don't make waves. Call Will, make amends. He's not a bad fellow. In fact the two of you should have a lot in common. He's an expert in—"

"Behavioral Pediatrics. I know. Henry, I've heard his tune and we don't play in the same band."

"Remember this, Alex—the status of psychologists on the medical staff has always been tenuous."

An old speech came to mind. Something about the importance of the human factor and how it interfaced with modern medicine. I considered throwing it back in his face. Then I looked at his face and decided nothing could help it.

"Is that it?"

He had nothing to say. His type seldom does, when the conversation gets beyond platitudes, entendres, or threats.

"Good day, Doctor Delaware," he said.

I left quietly, closing the door behind me.

I was down in the lobby, which had cleared of patients and was now filled with a group of visitors from some ladies' volunteer group. The ladies had old money and good breeding written all over their handsome faces—sorority girls grown up. They listened raptly as an administration lackey gave them a prefabricated spiel about how the hospital was in the forefront of medical and humanitarian progress for children, nodding their heads, trying not to show their anxiety.

The lackey prattled on about children being the resources of the future. All that came to my mind was young bones ground up as grist for someone's mill.

I turned and walked back to the elevator.

The third floor of the hospital housed the bulk of the administrative offices, which were shaped in an inverted T, paneled in dark wood, and carpeted in something the color and consistency of moss. The medical staff office was situated at the bottom of the stem of the T, in a glass-walled suite with a view of the Hollywood Hills. The elegant blonde behind the desk was someone I hadn't counted upon seeing, but I straightened my tie and went in.

She looked up, contemplated not recognizing me, then thought better of it and gave me a regal smile. She extended her hand with the imperious manner of someone who'd been at the same job long enough to harbor illusions of irreplaceability.

"Good morning, Alex."

Her nails were long and thickly coated with mother-of-pearl polish, as if she'd plundered the depths of the ocean for the sake of vanity. I took the hand and handled it with the care it cried out for.

"Cora."

"How nice to see you again. It's been a long time."

"Yes it has."

"Are you returning to us—I'd heard you resigned."

"No, I'm not, and yes, I did."

"Enjoying your freedom?" She favored me with another smile. Her hair looked blonder, coarser, her figure fuller, but still first-rate, packed into a chartreuse knit that would have intimidated someone of less heroic proportions.

"I am. And you?"

"Doing the same old thing," she sighed.

"And doing it well, I'm sure."

For a moment I thought the flattery was a mistake. Her face hardened and grew a few new wrinkles.

"We know," I went on, "who really keeps things together around here."

"Oh, go on." She flexed her hand like an abalone-tipped fan.

"It sure ain't the doctors." I resisted calling her Ol' Buddy.

"Ain't that the truth. Amazing what twenty years of

education won't give you in the way of common sense. I'm just a wage slave but I know which end is up."

"I'm sure you could never be anyone's slave, Cora."

"Well, I don't know." Lashes as thick and dark as raven feathers lowered coquettishly.

She was in her early forties and under the merciless fluorescent lighting of the office every year showed. But she was well put together, with good features, one of those women who retain the form of youth but not the texture. Once, centuries ago, she'd seemed girlish, hearty and athletic, as we'd thrashed around the floor of the medical records office. It had been a one-shot deal, followed by mutual boycott. Now she was flirting, her memory cleansed by the passage of time.

"Have they been treating you okay?" I asked.

"As well as can be expected. You know how doctors are."

I grinned.

"I'm a fixture," she said. "If they ever move the office, they'll pick me up with the furniture."

I looked up and down her body.

"I don't think anyone could mistake you for furniture."

She laughed nervously and touched her hair self-consciously.

"Thanks." Self-scrutiny became too unsettling and she put me in the spotlight.

"What brings you down here?"

"Tying up loose ends—a few unfinished charts, paperwork. I've been careless about answering my mail. I thought I received a notice about overdue staff dues."

"I don't remember sending you one but it could have been one of the other girls. I was out for a month. Had surgery."

"I'm sorry to hear that, Cora. Is everything all right?"

"Female troubles." She smiled. "They say I'm fine." Her expression said that she thought "they" were abject liars.

"I'm glad."

We locked gazes. For just a moment she looked twenty, innocent and hopeful. She turned her back to me, as if wanting to preserve that image in my mind.

"Let me check your file."

She got up and slid open the drawer of a black-lacquered file cabinet, and came up with a blue folder.

"No," she said, "you're all paid up. You'll be getting a notice for next year in a couple of months."

"Thanks."

"Don't mention it."

She returned the folder.

"How about a cup of coffee?" I asked casually.

She looked at me, then at her watch.

"I'm not due for a break until ten, but what the hell, live it up, huh?"

"Right."

"Let me go to the little girls' room and freshen up." She fluffed her hair, picked up her purse and left the office to go into the lavatory across the hall.

When I saw the door shut after her I walked to the file cabinet. The drawer she'd opened was labeled "Staff A—G." Two drawers down I found what I wanted. Into the old briefcase it went.

I was waiting by the door when she came out, flushed, pink and pretty, and smelling of patchouli. I extended my arm and she took it.

Over hospital coffee I listened to her talk. About her divorce—a seven-year-old wound that wouldn't heal—the teenage daughter who was driving her crazy by doing exactly what she'd done as an adolescent, car troubles, the insensitivity of her superiors, the unfairness of life.

It was bizarre, getting to know for the first time a woman whose body I'd entered. In the scrambled word game of contemporary mating rituals, there was greater intimacy in her tales of woe than there had been in the opening of her thighs.

We parted friends.

"Come by again, Alex."

"I will."

I walked to the parking lot marveling at the ease with which I was able to slip on the cloak of duplicity. I'd always flattered myself with a self-assessment of integrity. But in the last three days I'd grown proficient at sneak-thievery, concealment of the truth, bald-faced lying and emotional whoring.

It must be the company I'd been keeping.

I drove to a cozy Italian place in West Hollywood. The estaurant had just opened and I was alone in my rear corner booth. I ordered veal in wine sauce, a side order of linguini with oil and garlic, and a Coors.

A shuffling waiter brought the beer. While I waited for the food I opened the briefcase and examined my plunder.

Towle's medical staff file was over forty pages long. Most of it consisted of Xeroxes of his diplomas, certificates and awards. His curriculum vitae was twenty pages of puffery, markedly devoid of scholarly publications—he'd coauthored one brief report while an intern, and nothing since—and filled with television and radio interviews, speeches to lay groups, volunteer service to La Casa and similar organizations. Yet he was a full clinical professor at the medical school. So much for academic rigor.

The waiter brought a salad and a basket of rolls. I picked up my napkin with one hand, started to return the file to the briefcase with the other, when something on the front page of the resumé caught my eye.

Under *college or university attended,* he'd listed Jedson College, Bellevue, Washington.

20

I GOT HOME, called the *L.A. Times*, and asked for Ned
Biondi at the Metro desk. Biondi was a senior writer for
the paper, a short, nervous character right out of *The Front
Page*. I'd treated his teenage daughter for anorexia nervosa
several years back. Biondi hadn't been able to come up
with the money for treatment on a journalist's salary—compounded with a penchant for playing the wrong horse at
Santa Anita—but the girl had been in trouble and I'd let it
go. It had taken him a year and a half to clear his debt. His
daughter had gotten straightened out after months of my
chipping away at layers of self-hatred that were surprisingly ossified in someone seventeen years old. I remembered her clearly, a tall, dark youngster who wore jogging
shorts and T-shirts that accentuated the skeletal condition
of her body; a girl ashen-faced and spindly legged who
alternated between deep, dark spells of brooding silence
and flights of hyperactivity during which she was ready to
enter every category of Olympic competition on three
hundred calories a day.

I'd gotten her admitted to Western Pediatric, where
she'd stayed for three weeks. That, followed by months of
psychotherapy, had finally gotten through to her, and allowed her to deal with the mother who was too beautiful,
the brother who was too athletic, and the father who was
too witty . . .

"Biondi."

"Ned, this is Alex Delaware."

It took a second for my name, minus title to register.

"Doctor! How are you."

"I'm fine. How's Anne Marie?"

"Very well. She's finishing up her second year at Wheaton—in Boston. She got A's and a few B's, but the B's didn't panic her. She's still too rough on herself, but she seems to be adjusting well to the peaks and troughs of life, as you called them. Her weight is stable at a hundred and two."

"Excellent. Give my regards when you speak to her."

"I certainly will. It's nice of you to call."

"Well actually there's more to this than professional follow-up."

' Oh?'' A foxy edge, the conditioned vigilance of one who pried open locked boxes for a living, came into his voice.

"I need a favor."

"Name it."

"I'm flying up north to Seattle tonight. I need to get into some transcripts at a small college near there. Jedson."

"Hey, that's not what I expected. I thought you wanted a blurb about a book in the Sunday edition or something. This sounds serious."

"It is."

"Jedson. I know it. Anne-Marie was going to apply there—we figured a small place would be less pressure for her—but it was fifty percent more expensive than Wheaton, Reed, and Oberlin—and they're no giveaways themselves. What do you want with their transcripts?"

"I can't say."

"Doctor." He laughed. "Pardon the expression, but you're prick-teasing. I'm a professional snoop. Dangle something weird in front of me I get a hard-on."

"What makes you think anything's weird?"

"Doctors running around trying to get into files is weird. Usually it's the shrinks who get broken into, if my memory serves me correctly."

"I can't go into it now, Ned."

"I'm good with a secret, Doc."

"No. Not yet. Trust me. You did before."

"Below the belt, Doc."

"I know. And I wouldn't gut-punch you if it wasn't important. I need your help. I may be onto something, maybe not. If I am you'll be the first to hear about it."

"Something big?"

I thought about it for a moment.

"Could be."

"Okay," he sighed, "what do you want me to do?"

"I'm giving your name as a reference. If anyone calls you, back up my story."

"What's the story?"

He listened.

"It seems harmless enough. Of course," he added cheerfully, "if you get found out I'll probably be out of a job."

"I'll be careful."

"Yeah. What the hell, I'm getting ready for the gold watch, anyway." There was a pause, as if he were fantasizing life after retirement. Apparently he didn't like what he saw, because when he came back on the line, there was verve in his voice and he offered a reporter's priapic lament.

"I'm gonna go nuts wondering about this. You sure you don't want to give me a hint about what you're up to?"

"I can't, Ned."

"Okay, okay. Go spin your yarn and keep me in mind if you knit a sweater."

"I will. Thanks."

"Oh, hell, don't thank me, I still feel crummy about taking all that time to pay you. I look at my baby now and I see a pink-cheeked, smiling young lady, a beauty. She's still a little too thin for my taste, but she's not a walking corpse like before. She's normal, at least as far as I can tell. She can smile now. I owe you, Doctor."

"Stay well, Ned."

"You too."

I hung up. Biondi's words of gratitude made me entertain a moment's doubt about my own retirement. Then I thought of bloody bodies and doubt got up and took a seat in the rear of the hearse.

It took several false starts and stops to reach the right person at Jedson College.

"Public relations, Ms. Dopplemeier."

"Ms. Dopplemeier, this is Alex Delaware. I'm a writer with the *Los Angeles Times*."

"What can I do for you, Mr. Delaware?"

"I'm doing a feature on the small colleges of the West,

concentrating on institutions that are not well-known but academically excellent nonetheless. Claremont, Occidental, Reed, etcetera. We'd like to include Jedson in the piece.''

"Oh, really?'' She sounded surprised, as if it was the first time anyone had labeled Jedson academically excellent. "That would be very nice, Mr. Delaware. I'd be happy to talk to you right now and answer any questions you might have."

"That wasn't exactly what I had in mind. I'm aiming for a more personal approach. My editor is less interested in statistics than in color. The tenor of the story is that small colleges offer a degree of personal contact and—intimacy—that is missing from the larger universities."

"How true.''

"I'm actually visiting the campuses, chatting with staff and students—it's an impression piece."

"I understand exactly what you mean. You want to come across with a voice that's human."

"Exactly. That's a marvelous way of putting it.''

"I did two years at a trade paper in New Jersey before coming to Jedson." Within the soul of every flack there lurks a journalistic homunculus, chafing to be released to proclaim "Scoop!" to the ears of the world.

"Ah, a kindred soul.''

"Well, I've left it, but I do think of going back from time to time."

"It's no way to get rich, but it does keep me hopping, Ms. Dopplemeier.''

"Margaret.''

"Margaret. I'm planning to fly up tonight and wondered if I might come by tomorrow and pay you a visit."

"Let me check.'' I heard paper rustling. "How about at eleven?''

"Fine.''

"Is there anything you'd like me to do by way of preparation?''

"One thing we're looking at is what happens to graduates of small colleges. I'd be interested in hearing about some of your notable alumni. Doctors, lawyers, that sort of thing.''

"I haven't had a chance to thoroughly acquaint myself

with the alumni roster—I've only been here for a few months. But I'll ask around and find out who can help you.''

"I'd appreciate that.''

"Where can I reach you if I need to?''

"I'll be in transit most of the time. You can leave any message with my colleague at the *Times*, Edward Biondi.'' I gave her Ned's number.

"Very good. It's all set for tomorrow at eleven. The college is in Bellevue, just outside of Seattle. Do you know where that is?''

"On the east shore of Lake Washington?'' Years back I'd been a guest lecturer at the University of Washington and had visited my host's home in Bellevue. I remembered it as an upper-middle-class bedroom community of aggressively contemporary homes, straight-edge lawns and low-rise shopping centers occupied by gourmet shops, antique galleries and high-priced haberdasheries.

"That's correct. If you're coming from downtown take I-5 to 520 which turns into the Evergreen Point Floating Bridge. Drive all the way across the bridge to the east shore, turn south at Fairweather and continue along the coastline. Jedson is on Meydenbauer Bay, right next to the yacht club. I'm on the first floor of Crespi Hall. Will you be staying for lunch?''

"I can't say for sure. It depends upon how my time is running.'' And what I find.

"I'll have something prepared for you, just in case.''

"That's very kind of you, Margaret.''

"Anything for a fellow journalist, Alex.''

My next call was to Robin. It took her nine rings to answer.

"Hi.'' She was out of breath. "I had the big saw going, didn't hear you. What's up?''

"I'm going out of town for a couple of days.''

"Tahiti, without me?''

"Nothing quite so romantic. Seattle.''

"Oh. Detective work?''

"Call it biographical research.'' I told her about Towle's having attended Jedson.

"You're really going after this guy.''

"He's going after me. When I was at W.P. this morning

Henry Bork grabbed me in the hall, trundled me off to his office and delivered a not-so-subtle version of the old arm twist. Seems Towle's been questioning my ethics in public. He keeps cropping up, like toadstools after a flood. He and Kruger share an alma mater and it makes me want to know more about the ivy-covered halls of Jedson.''

"Let me come up with you.''

"No. It's going to be all business. I'll take you on a real vacation, after this is all over.''

"The thought of you going up there all alone depresses me. It's dreary this time of year.''

"I'll be fine. You just take care of yourself and get some work done. I'll call you when I get settled.''

"You're sure you don't want me to come along?''

"You know I love your company, but there'll be no time for sightseeing. You'd be miserable.''

"All right," she said reluctantly. "I'll miss you.''

"I'll miss you too. I love you. Take care.''

"The same goes for you. Love you, sweetie. Bye bye.''

"Bye.''

I took a 9 p.m. flight out of LAX and landed at Sea-Tac Airport at 11:25. I picked up a rented Nova at a Hertz desk. It was no Seville but it did have an F.M. radio that someone had left on a classical station. A Bach organ fugue in a minor key unraveled out of the dash speaker and I didn't cut it off: the music matched my mood. I confirmed my reservation at the Westin, drove away from the airport, connected to the Interstate highway and headed north toward downtown Seattle.

The sky was as cold and hard as a handgun. Minutes after I hit the blacktop the gun proved to be loaded: it fired a blast of thunder and the water started coming down. Soon it was one of those angry Northwest torrents that transforms a highway into miles of drive-thru car wash.

"Welcome to the Pacific Northwest," I said out loud.

Pine, spruce and fir grew in opaque stands on both sides of the road. Starlit billboards advertised rustic motels and diners offering logger's breakfasts. Except for semis groaning under loads of timber I was the road's sole traveler. I thought to myself how nice it would be to be heading for a mountain cabin, Robin at my side, with a trunkload of fishing gear and provisions. I felt a sudden pang of loneliness and longed for human contact.

I reached downtown shortly after midnight. The Westin rose like a giant steel-and-glass test tube amid the darkened laboratory of the city. My seventh-floor room was decent, with a view of Puget Sound and the harbor to the west, Lake Washington and the islands to the east. I kicked off my shoes and stretched out on the bed, tired, but too jumpy for sleep.

I caught the sign-off edition of the news on a local station. The anchor man was wooden-jawed and shifty-eyed, and reported the day's events impersonally. He lent identical emphasis to an account of mass murder in Ohio and the hockey scores. I cut him off in midsentence, turned off the lights, stripped down in darkness and stared at the harbor lights until I fell asleep.

21

A THOUSAND YARDS of rain forest shielded the Jedson campus from the coastal road. The forest yielded to twin stone columns engraved with Roman numerals that marked the origin of a cobbled drive running through the center of the college. The drive terminated in a circular turn-around punctuated by a pockmarked sundial under a towering pine.

At first glance, Jedson resembled one of those small colleges back East that specialize in looking like dwarf Harvards. The buildings were fashioned of weathered brick and embellished with stone and marble cornices, slate and copper roofing—designed in an era when labor was cheap and intricate moldings, expansive arches, gargoyles and goddesses the order of the day. Even the ivy looked authentic, tumbling from slate peaks, sucking the brick, trimmed topiary-fashion to bypass recessed, leaded windows.

The campus was small, perhaps half a square mile, and filled with tree-shaded knolls, imposing stands of oak, pine, willow, elm and paper birch, and clearings inlaid with marble and bordered by stone benches and bronze monuments. All very traditional until you looked to the west and saw manicured lawns dipping down to the dock and the private harbor beyond. The slips were occupied by streamlined, teak-decked cruisers, fifty-foot craft and larger, topped with sonar and radar screens and clutches of antennae: clearly twentieth-century, obviously West Coast.

The rain had lifted and a triangle of light peeked out from under the charcoal folds of the sky. A few knots out of the harbor an armada of sailboats sliced through water that looked like tin foil. The boats were rehearsing some type of ceremony, for they each rounded the same buoy marker and unfurled outrageously colored spinnakers—oranges, purples, scarlets and greens, like the tailfeathers of a covey of tropical birds.

There was a lucite-encased map on a stand and I consulted it to locate Crespi Hall. The students passing by seemed a quiet lot. For the most part they were apple-cheeked and flaxen-haired, their eye color traversing the spectrum from light blue to dark blue. Their hairstyles were expensively executed but seemed to date from the Eisenhower age. Trousers were cuffed, pennies shined prettily from the tops of loafers and there were enough alligators on shirts to choke the Everglades. A eugenicist would have been proud to observe the straight backs, robust physiques and stiff-lipped self-assurance of those to the manor born. I felt as if I'd died and gone to Aryan Heaven.

Crespi was a three-story rhomboid fronted by Ionic columns of varicose-veined white marble. The public relations office was hidden behind a mahogany door labeled in gold stencil. When I opened it, the door creaked.

Margaret Dopplemeier was one of those tall, rawboned women predestined for spinsterhood. She'd tried to couch an ungainly body in a tentlike suit of brown tweed, but the angles and corners showed through. She had a big-jawed face, uncompromising lips, and reddish-brown hair cut in an incongruously girlish bob. Her office was hardly larger than the interior of my car—public relations was obviously not a prime concern for the elders of Jedson—and she had to squeeze between the edge of her desk and the wall to get up to greet me. It was a maneuver that would have looked clumsy performed by Pavlova and Margaret Dopplemeier turned it into a lurching stumble. I felt sorry for her but made sure not to show it: She was in her midthirties and by that age women like her have learned to cherish self-reliance. It's as good a way as any of coping with solitude.

"Hello, you must be Alex."

"I am. Pleased to meet you, Margaret." Her hand was thick, hard and chafed—from too much wringing or too much washing, I couldn't be sure.

"Please sit down."

I took a slat-backed chair and sat in it uncomfortably.

"Coffee?"

"Please. With cream."

There was a table with a hot plate in back of her desk. She poured coffee into a mug and gave it to me.

"Have you decided about lunch?"

The prospect of looking across the table at her for an extra hour didn't thrill me. It wasn't her plainness, nor her stern face. She looked ready to tell me her life story and I was in no mood to fill my head with extraneous material. I declined.

"How about a snack, then?"

She brought forth a tray of cheese and crackers, looking uncomfortable in the role of hostess. I wondered why she'd gravitated toward p.r. Library science would have seemed more fitting. Then the thought occurred to me that public relations at Jedson was probably akin to library work, a desk job involving lots of clipping and mailing and very little face-to-face contact.

"Thank you." I was hungry and the cheese was good.

"Well." She looked around her desk, found a pair of eyeglasses, and put them on. Behind the glass her eyes grew larger and somehow softer. "You want to get a feel for Jedson."

"That's right—the flavor of the place."

"It's quite a unique place. I'm from Wisconsin myself, went to school at Madison, with forty thousand students. There are only two thousand here. Everyone knows everyone else."

"Kind of like one big family." I took out a pen and notepad.

"Yes." At the word family her mouth pursed. "You might say that." She shuffled some papers and began reciting:

"Jedson College was founded by Josiah T. Jedson, a Scottish immigrant who made his fortune in mining and railroads in 1858. That's three years before the University of Washington was founded, so we're really the old school in town. Jedson's intention was to endow an institution of higher learning where traditional values coexisted side by side with education in the basic arts and sciences. To this day, primary funding for the college comes from an annuity from the Jedson Foundation, although other sources of income are existant."

"I've heard tuition is rather high."

"Tuition," she frowned, "is twelve thousand dollars a year, plus housing, registration and miscellaneous fees."

I whistled.

"Do you give scholarships?"

"A small number of scholarships for deserving students are given each year, but there is no extensive program of financial aid."

"Then there's no interest in attracting students from a wide socio-economic range."

"Not particularly, no."

She took off her glasses, put her prepared material aside and stared at me myopically.

"I would hope we don't get into that particular line of questioning."

"Why is that, Margaret?"

She moved her lips, trying on several unspoken words for size, rejecting them all. Finally she said: "I thought this was going to be an impression piece. Something positive."

"It will be. I was simply curious." I had touched a nerve—not that it did me any good, for upsetting my source of information was the last thing I needed. But something about the upper-class smugness of the place was irritating me and bringing out the bad boy.

"I see." She put her glasses back on and picked up her papers, scanned them and pursed her lips. "Alex," she said, "can I speak to you off the record—one writer to another?"

"Sure." I closed the notepad and put the pen in my jacket pocket.

"I don't know how to put this." She played with one tweed lapel, twisting the coarse cloth then smoothing it. "This story, your visit—neither are particularly welcomed by the administration. As you may be able to tell from the grandeur of our surroundings, public relations is not avidly sought by Jedson College. After I spoke to you yesterday I told my superiors about your coming, thinking they'd be more than pleased. In fact, just the opposite was true. I wasn't exactly given a pat on the back."

She pouted, as if recalling a particularly painful spanking.

"I didn't intend to get you in trouble, Margaret."

"There was no way to know. As I told you, I'm new here. They do things differently. It's another way of life—quiet, conservative. There's a timeless quality to the place."

"How," I asked, "does a college attract enrollment without attracting attention?"

She chewed her lip.

"I really don't want to get into it."

"Margaret, it's off the record. Don't stonewall me."

"It's not important," she insisted, but her bosom heaved and conflict showed in the flat, magnified eyes. I played on that conflict.

"Then what's the fuss? We writers need to be open with one another. There are enough censors out there."

She thought about that for a long time. The tug-of-war was evident on her face and I couldn't help but feel rotten.

"I don't want to leave here," she finally said. "I have a nice apartment with a view of the lake, my cats and my books. I don't want to lose—everything. I don't want to have to pack up and move back to the Midwest. To miles of flatland with no mountains, no way of establishing one's perspective. Do you understand?"

Her manner and tone were brittle—I knew that manner, for I'd seen it in countless therapy patients, just before the defenses came tumbling down. She wanted to let go and I was going to help her, manipulative bastard that I was . . .

"Do you understand what I'm saying?" she was asking.

And I heard myself answer, so smooth, so sweet:

"Of course I do."

"Anything I tell you has to be confidential. Not for print."

"I promise. I'm a feature writer. I have no aspirations of becoming Woodward or Bernstein."

A faint smile appeared on the large, bland features.

"You don't? I did, once upon a time. After four years on the Madison student paper I thought I was going to turn journalism on its ear. I went for one solid year with no writing job—I did waitressing. I hated it. Then I worked for a dog magazine, writing cutesy-poo press releases on poodles and schnauzers. They brought the little beasts into the office for photographs and they fouled the carpet. It stunk. When that folded I spent two years covering union meetings and polka parties in New Jersey and that finally squeezed all the illusions out of me. Now all I want is peace.''

Again the glasses came off. She closed her eyes and massaged her temples.

"When you get down to it, that's what all of us want," I said.

She opened her eyes and squinted in my direction. From the way she strained I must have been a blur. I tried to look like a trustworthy blur.

She popped two pieces of cheese into her mouth and ground them to dust with lantern jaws.

"I don't know that any of it is relevant to your story," she said. "Especially if it's a puff piece you're after."

I forced a laugh.

"Now that you've got me interested, don't leave me dangling."

She smiled. "One writer to another?"

"One writer to another."

"Oh," she sighed, "I suppose it's no biggie."

"In the first place," she told me, between mouthfuls of cheese, "no, Jedson College is not interested in attracting outsiders, period. It's a college, but in name and formal status only. What Jedson College really is—functionally—is a *holding pen*. A place for the privileged class to stash their children for four years before the boys enter Daddy's business and the girls marry the boys and turn into Suzy Homemaker and join the Junior League. The boys major in business or economics, the girls in art history and home economics. The gentleman's C is the common goal. Being too smart is frowned upon. Some of the brighter ones do go on to law school or medical school. But when they finish their training they return to the fold."

She sounded bitter, a wallflower describing last year's prom.

"The average household income of the families that send their kids here is over a hundred thousand dollars a year. Think of that, Alex. Everyone is rich. Did you see the harbor?"

I nodded.

"Those floating toys belong to students." She paused,

as if she still couldn't believe it. "The parking lot looks like the Monte Carlo Grand Prix. These kids wear cashmere and suede for horsing around."

One of her raw, coarse hands found the other and caressed it. She looked from wall to wall of the tiny room as if searching for hidden listening devices. I wondered what she was so nervous about. So Jedson was a school for rich kids. Stanford had started out that way too and might have ended up similarly stagnant if someone hadn't figured out that not letting in smart Jews and Asians and other people with funny names and high IQ's would lead to eventual academic entropy.

"There's no crime in being rich," I said.

"It's not just that. It's the utter mindlessness that goes along with it. I was at Madison during the sixties. There was a sense of social awareness. Activism. We were working to end the war. Now it's the anti-nukes movement. The university can be a greenhouse for the conscience. Here, nothing grows."

I envisioned her fifteen years back, dressed in khakis and sweatshirt, marching and mouthing slogans. Radicalism had fought a losing battle with survival, eroded by too much of nothing. But she could still take an occasional hit of nostalgia . . .

"It's especially hard on the faculty," she was saying. "Not the Old Guard. The Young Turks—they actually call themselves that. They come here because of the job crunch, with their typical academic idealism and liberal views and last two, maybe three years. It's intellectually stultifying— not to mention the frustration of earning fifteen thousand dollars a year when the students' wardrobes cost more than that."

"You sound as if you have first-hand knowledge."

"I do. There was—a man. A good friend of mine. He came here to teach philosophy. He was brilliant, a Princeton graduate, a genuine scholar. It ate him up. He talked to me about it, told me what it was like to stand up in front of a class and lecture on Kierkegaard and Sartre and see thirty pairs of vacant blue eyes staring back. *Ubermensch U.* he called it. He left last year."

She looked pained. I changed the subject.

"You mentioned the Old Guard. Who are they?"

"Jedson graduates who actually develop an interest in something other than making money. They go on to earn advanced degrees in humanities—something totally useless like history or sociology or literature—and then come crawling back here to teach. Jedson takes care of its own."

"I'd imagine they find it easier to relate to the students, coming from the same background."

They must. They stay on. Most of them are older—there haven't been too many returning scholars lately. The Old Guard may be shrinking. Some are quite decent, really. I get the feeling they were always outcasts—the misfits. Even the privileged castes have those, I suppose."

The look on her face bespoke firsthand experience with the pain of social rejection. She may have sensed she was in danger of crossing the boundary from social commentary to psychological striptease, for she drew back, put on her glasses and smiled sourly.

"How's that for public relations?"

"For someone new you're certainly got a handle on the place."

"Some of it I've seen for myself. Some I learned."

"From your friend the scholar?"

"Yes." She stopped and picked up an oversized imitation leather handbag. It didn't take her long to find what she was looking for.

"This is Lee," she said, and handed me a snapshot of herself and a man several inches shorter than she. The man was balding, with tufts of thick, dark, curling hair over each ear, a bushy dark mustache and rimless round spectacles. He wore a faded blue work shirt and jeans and high-laced hiking boots. Margaret Dopplemeier was dressed in a serape that accentuated her size, baggy cords and flat sandals. She had her arm around him, and looked maternal and childishly dependent at the same time. "He's in New Mexico now, working on his book. In solitude, he says."

I gave her back the photo.

"Writers often need that."

"Yes. We've gone round and round about that." She put her keepsake back, made a move toward the cheese and then retracted her hand, as if she'd suddenly lost her appetite.

I let a silent moment pass, then performed a lateral arabesque away from her personal life.

"What you're saying is fascinating, Margaret. Jedson is set up with all the enrollment it needs—it's a self-perpetuating system."

The word "system" can be a psychological catalyst for anyone who's flirted with the Left. It got her going again.

"Absolutely. The percentage of students whose parents are also Jedson graduates is unbelievably high. I'll bet that the two thousand students come from no more than five to seven hundred families. The same surnames keep cropping up when I compile lists. That's why when you called it a family before I was taken aback. I wondered how much you knew."

"Nothing until I came here."

"Yes. I've said too much, haven't I?"

"In a closed system," I persisted, "publicity is the last thing the establishment wants."

"Of course. Jedson is an anachronism. It survives the twentieth century by staying small and keeping out of the headlines. My instructions were to wine you, dine you, see that you took a nice little stroll around the campus, then escort you off the grounds with little or nothing to write about. The Trustees of Jedson don't want exposure in the *Los Angeles Times*. They don't want issues like affirmative action or equal opportunity enrollment to rear their ugly heads."

"I appreciate your honesty, Margaret."

For a moment I thought she was going to cry.

"Don't make it sound as if I'm some kind of saint. I'm not and I know it. My talking to you was spineless. Deceitful. The people here aren't evil, I have no right to expose them. They've been good to me. But I get so weary of putting up a front, of attending quaint little teas with women who can talk all day about china patterns and place settings—they give a class here in place settings, do you believe that?"

She looked at her hands as if unable to envision them holding anything as delicate as china.

"My job is pretense, Alex. I'm a glorified mailing service. But I'll not leave," she insisted, debating an unseen adversary. "Not yet. Not at this point in my life. I wake up and see the lake. I have my books and a good stereo. I can pick fresh blackberries not far from here. I eat them in the morning with cream.''

I said nothing.

"Will you betray me?" she asked.

"Of course not, Margaret."

"Then go. Forget about including Jedson in your story. There's nothing here for an outsider."

"I can't."

She sat straight in her chair.

"Why not?" There was terror and anger in her voice, something decidedly menacing in her eyes. I could understand her lover's flight to solitude. I was certain the mental deadness of Jedson's student body wasn't the only thing he'd been escaping.

I had nothing to offer her that would keep our lines of communication open, other than the truth and the chance to be a coconspirator. I took a deep breath and told her the real reason for my visit.

When I was through she wore the same possessive-dependent look I'd seen in her photograph. I wanted to back away, but my chair was inches from the door.

"It's funny," she said, "I should feel exploited, used. But I don't. You have an honest face. Even your lies sound righteous."

"I'm no more righteous than you are. I simply want to get some facts. Help me."

"I was a member of SDS, you know. The police were pigs to me in those days."

"These aren't those days, I'm not a policeman, and we're not talking about abstract theory and the polemics of revolution. This is triple murder, Margaret, child abuse, maybe more. Not political assassinations. Innocent people hacked into bloody gobbets, mashed into human garbage. Children run down on lonely canyon roads."

She shuddered, turned away, ran an unpolished fingernail along the top of a tooth, then faced me again.

"And you think one of them—a Jedsonite—was responsible for all of that?" The very idea was delicious to her.

"I think two of them had some involvement in it."

"Why are you doing this? You say you're a psychiatrist."

"Psychologist."

"Whatever. What's in it for you?"

"Nothing. Nothing you'd believe."

"Try me."

"I want to see justice done. It's been eating at me."

"I believe you," she said softly.

She was gone for twenty minutes and when she returned it was with an armful of oversized volumes bound in dark blue Morocco leather.

"These are the yearbooks, if your estimates of their ages are correct. I'm going to leave you with them and search for the alumni files. Lock yourself in when I'm gone and don't answer the door. I'll knock three times, then twice. That will be our signal."

"Roger."

"Ha." She laughed, and for the first time looked almost attractive.

Timothy Kruger had lied about being a poor boy at Jedson. His family had donated a couple of buildings and even a casual reading of the book made it obvious the Krugers were Very Important. The part about his athletic prowess, though, was true. He'd lettered in track, baseball and Greco-Roman wrestling. In his yearbook pictures he resembled the man I'd spoken to days before. There were shots of him jumping hurdles, throwing the javelin, and later on, in a section on drama, in the roles of Hamlet and Petruchio. The impression I got was that of a big man on campus. I wondered how he'd ended up at La Casa de los Niños operating under a phony credential.

L. Willard Towle's photo showed him to have been a Tab Hunter-type blond in his youth. Notations under his name mentioned presidency of the Pre-Med Club and the Biology Honor Society, as well as captain of the crew team. There was also an asterisk that led to a footnote advising the reader to turn to the last page of the book. I obeyed the instructions and came to a black-bordered photograph—the same picture I'd seen in Towle's office, of his wife and son against a backdrop of lake and mountains. There was an inscription beneath the photo:

In Memoriam
Lilah Hutchison Towle
1930–1951

Lionel Willard Towle, Jr.
1949–1951

Under the inscription were four lines of verse.

How swiftly doth the night move
To dash our hopes and dim our dreams;
But even in the darkest night
The ray of peace yet beams.

It was signed "S."

I was rereading the poem when Margaret Dopplemeier's coded knock sounded on the door. I slid open the latch and she came in holding a manila envelope. She locked the door, went behind her desk, opened the packet and shook out two three-by-five index cards.

"These are straight out of the sacred alumni file." She glanced at one and handed it to me. "Here's your doctor."

Towle's name was at the top, written out in elegant script. There were several entries under it, in different hands and different colors of ink. Most of them took the form of abbreviations and numeric codes.

"Can you explain it to me?"

She came around and sat down next to me, took the card and studied it.

"There's nothing mysterious about any of it. The abbreviations are meant to save space. The five digits after the name are the alumnus code, for mailing, filing, that kind of thing. After that you've got the number 3, which means he's the third member of his family to attend Jedson. The *med* is self-explanatory—it's an occupation code, and the *F:med* means medicine is also the family's primary business. If it were shipping, it would say *shp*, banking, *bnk*, and so on. *B:51* is the year he received his bachelor's degree. *M: J,148793* indicates that he married another Jedson student and her alumnus code is cross-referenced. Here's something interesting—there's a small *d* in parentheses after the wife's code, which means she's deceased, and the date of death is 6/17/51—she died when he was still a student here. Did you know that?"

"I did. Would there be any way of finding out more about that?"

She thought for a moment.

"We could check the local papers for that week, for an obituary or funeral notice."

"What about the student paper?"

"The *Spartan* is a rag," she said scornfully, "but I suppose it would cover something like that. Back issues are stored in the library, on the other side of campus. We can go there later. Do you think it's relevant?"

She was flushed, girlish, given over totally to our little intrigue.

"It just could be, Margaret. I want to know everything I can about these people."

"Van der Graaf," she said.

"What's that?"

"Professor Van der Graaf, from the history department. He's the oldest of the Old Guard, been around Jedson longer than anyone I know of. On top of that he's a great gossip. I sat next to him at a garden party and the sweet old thing told me all sorts of tidbits—who was sleeping with whom, faculty dirt and the like."

"They let him get away with it?"

"He's close to ninety, rolling in family money, unmarried with no heirs. They're just waiting for him to croak and leave it all to their college. He's been emeritus from way back. Keeps an office on campus, sequesters himself there pretending to write books. I wouldn't be surprised if he sleeps there. He knows more about Jedson than anybody."

"Do you think he'd talk to me?"

"If he was in the right mood. In fact I thought of him when you told me over the phone that you wanted to find out about illustrious alumni. But I figured it was too risky leaving him alone with a reporter. You never know what he's going to do or say."

She giggled, enjoying the old man's ability to rebel from a position of power.

"Of course now that I know what you want," she continued, "he'd be perfect. You'd need some kind of story about why you wanted to talk about Towle, but I don't imagine that would be very difficult for someone as artful as you."

"How about this: I'm a reporter for *Medical World*

News. Call me Bill Roberts. Dr. Towle's been elected
President of the Academy of Pediatrics and I'm doing a
background story on him.''

"Sounds good. I'll call him now."

She reached for the phone and I took another look at
Towle's alumnus card. The only information she hadn't
covered was a column of dated entries under the heading
$—donations to Jedson, I assumed. They averaged ten
thousand dollars a year. Towle was a faithful son.

"Professor Van der Graaf," she was saying, "this is
Margaret Dopplemeier from Public Relations. I've been
fine, thank you, and yourself? Very good—oh, I'm sure
we can work that out, Professor." She covered the receiver with her hand and winked at me, mouthing the
words 'good mood.' "I didn't know you liked pizza,
Professor. No. No, I don't like anchovies either. Yes, I do
like Duesenbergs. I know you do . . . Yes, I know. The
rain was coming down in sheets, Professor. Yes, I would.
Yes, when the weather clears up. With the top down. I'll
bring the pizza."

She flirted with Van der Graaf for five more minutes
and finally broached the subject of my visit. She listened,
gave me the okay sign with thumb and forefinger and went
back to flirting. I picked up Kruger's card.

He was the fifth member of his family to attend Jedson
and his degree was listed as having been granted five years
previously. There was no mention of current position—the
family was recorded as being active in *stl, shp,* and *rl-est.*
No mention of matrimony was present, nor had he donated
money to the school. There was however an interesting
cross-reference. Under *REL-F:* it said Towle. Finally, the
three letters DLT were written in large, block characters at
the bottom of the card.

Margaret got off the phone.

"He'll see you. As long as I come along, and quote:
Give me a brisk massage, young lady. You'll be prolong-
ing the years of a living fossil, unquote. The old lecher,''
she added affectionately.

I asked her about Towle's name on Kruger's card.

"*REL-F*—related family. Apparently your two subjects
are cousins of some sort."

"Why isn't that listed on Towle's card as well?"

"The heading was probably added after he graduated. Rather than go back and mark each card they simply used it on the new ones. *DLT*, though, is more interesting. He's been deleted from the file."

"Why's that?"

"I don't know. It doesn't say. It never would. Some transgression. With his family background it had to be something big. Something that made the school want to wash its hands of him." She looked up at me. "This is getting interesting, isn't it?"

"Very."

She put the cards back in the envelope and locked it in her desk.

"I'll take you to Van der Graaf now."

22

A GILDED CAGE of an elevator took us to the fifth floor of a domed building on the west side of the campus. It relaxed its jaws and let us out into a silent rotunda, wainscoted in marble and veneered with dust. The ceiling was concave plaster upon which a now-faded mural of cherubs blowing bugles had been painted: we were inside the shell of the dome. The walls were stone and gave off an odor of rotting paper. A stationary diamond-paned window separated two oak doors. One was labeled MAP ROOM and looked as if it hadn't been opened in generations. The other was blank.

Margaret knocked on the unadorned door and, when no answer was forthcoming, pushed it open. The room it revealed was highceilinged and spacious, with cathedral windows that afforded a view of the harbor. Every free inch of wall space was taken up by bookshelves crammed haphazardly with ragged volumes. Those books that hadn't found a resting place in the shelves sat in precariously balanced stacks on the floor. In the center of the room was a trestle table piled high with manuscripts and still more books. A globe on a wheeled stand and an ancient claw-footed desk were pushed in the corner. A McDonald's take-out box and a couple of crumpled, greasy napkins sat atop the desk.

"Professor?" said Margaret. To me: "I wonder where he's gone."

"Peek-a-boo!" The sound came from somewhere behind the trestle table.

Margaret jumped and her purse flew out of her hands. The contents spilled on the floor.

234

A gnarled head peeked around the curled edges of a pile of yellowed paper.

"Sorry to startle you, dear." The head came into view, thrown back in silent laughter.

"Professor," said Margaret, "shame on you." She bent to retrieve the scattered debris.

He came out from behind the table looking sheepish. Until that point I'd thought he was sitting. But when the head didn't rise in my sight I realized he'd been standing all along.

He was four feet and a few inches tall. His body was of conventional size but it was bent at the waist, the spine twisted in an S, the deformed back burdened with a hump the size of a tightly packed knapsack. His head seemed too large for his frame, a wrinkled egg topped by a fringe of wispy white hair. When he moved he resembled a drowsy scorpion.

He wore an expression of mock contrition but the twinkle in the rheumy blue eyes said far more than did the downturned, lipless mouth.

"Can I help you, dear?" His voice was dry and cultured.

Margaret gathered the last personal effects from the floor and put them in her purse.

"No, thank you, Professor. I've got it all." She caught her breath and tried to look composed.

"Will you still come with me on our pizza picnic?"

"Only if you behave yourself."

He put his hands together, as if in prayer.

"I promise, dear," he said.

"All right. Professor, this is Bill Roberts, the journalist I spoke to you about. Bill, Professor Garth Van der Graaf."

"Hello, Professor."

He looked up at me from under sleepy lids.

"You don't look like Clark Kent," he said.

"I beg your pardon."

"Aren't newspaper reporters supposed to look like Clark Kent?"

"I wasn't aware of that specific union regulation."

"I was interviewed by a reporter after the War—the big one. Number two—pardon the scatological entendre. He wanted to know what place the war would have in history. *He* looked like Clark Kent." He ran one hand over his liver-spotted scalp. "Don't you have a pair of glasses or something, young man?"

"I'm sorry, but my eyes are quite healthy."

He turned his back to me and walked to one of the bookshelves. There was queer, reptilian grace to his movements, the stunted body seeming to travel sideways while actually moving forward. He climbed slowly up a footstool, reached up and grabbed a leatherbound volume, climbed down and returned.

"Look," he said, opening the book which I now saw was a looseleaf binder containing a collection of comic books. "This is who I mean." A shaky finger pointed to a picture of the Daily Planet's star reporter entering a phone booth. "Clark Kent. *That*'s a reporter."

"I'm sure Mr. Roberts knows who Clark Kent is, Professor."

"Then let him come back when he looks more like him and I'll talk to him," the old man snapped.

Margaret and I exchanged helpless looks. She started to say something and Van der Graaf threw back his head and let out an arid cackle.

"April Fool!" He laughed lustily at his own wit, the merriment dissolving into a phlegmy fit of coughing.

"Oh, Professor!" Margaret scolded.

They went at each other again, verbally jousting. I began to suspect that their relationship was well-established. I stood on the sidelines feeling like an unwilling spectator at a freak show.

"Admit it, dear," he was saying, "I had you fooled!" He stamped his foot with glee. "You thought I'd gone totally senile!"

"You're no more senile than I," she replied. "You're simply a naughty boy!"

My hopes of getting reliable information from the shrunken hunchback were diminishing by the moment. I cleared my throat.

They stopped and stared at me. A bubble of saliva had collected in the corner of Van der Graaf's puckered mouth. His hands vibrated with a faint palsy. Margaret towered over him, legs akimbo.

"Now I want you to cooperate with Mr. Roberts," she said sternly.

Van der Graaf gave me a dirty look.

"Oh, all right," he whined. "But only if you drive me around the lake in my Doosie."

"I said I would."

"I have a thirty-seven Duesenberg," he explained to me. "Magnificent chariot. Four hundred snorting stallions under a gleaming ruby bonnet. Chromium pipes. Consumes petroleum with ravenous abandon. I can no longer drive it. Maggie, here, is a large wench. Under my tutelage she could handle it. But she refuses."

"Professor Van der Graaf, there was a good reason why I turned you down. It was raining and I didn't want to get behind the wheel of a car worth two hundred thousand dollars in hazardous weather."

"Pshaw. I took that baby from here to Sonoma in forty-four. It thrives on meteorological adversity."

"All right. I'll drive you. Tomorrow, if I get a good report on your behavior from Mr. Roberts."

"I'm the professor. I do the grading."

She ignored him.

"I have to go to the library, Mr. Roberts. Can you find your way back to my office?"

"Certainly."

"I'll see you when you're through, then. Good-bye, Professor."

"Tomorrow at one. Rain or shine," he called after her.

When the door had closed he invited me to sit.

"I'll stand, myself. Can't find a chair that fits me. When I was a boy Father called in carpenters and woodcarvers, trying to come up with some way to seat me comfortably. To no avail. They did produce some fascinating abstract sculpture, however." He laughed, and held on to the trestle table for support. "I've stood most of my life. In the end it probably was beneficial. I've got legs like pig iron. My circulation's as good as that of a man half my age."

I sat in a leather armchair. We were at eye level.

"That Maggie," he said. "Such a sad girl. I flirt with her, try to cheer her up. She seems so lonely most of the time." He rummaged among the papers and pulled out a flask.

"Irish Whiskey. You'll find two glasses in the top right drawer of the desk. Kindly retrieve them and give them to me."

I found the glasses, which looked none too clean. Van der Graaf filled them each with an inch of whiskey, without spilling a drop.

"Here."

I watched him sip his drink and followed suit.

"Do you think she could be a virgin? Is such a thing possible in this day and age?" He approached the question as if it were an epistemological puzzle.

"I really couldn't say, Professor. I only just met her an hour ago."

"I can't conceive of it, virginity in a woman her age. Yet the notion of those milkmaid's thighs wrapped around a pair of rutting buttocks is equally preposterous." He drank more whiskey, contemplated Margaret Dopplemeier's sex life in silence, and stared off into space.

Finally he said: "You're a patient young man. A rare quality."

I nodded.

"I figure you'll come around when you're ready, Professor."

"Yes, I do confess to a fair amount of childish behavior. It's a perquisite of my age and station. Do you know how long it's been since I taught a class or wrote a scholarly paper?"

"Quite a while, I imagine."

"Over two decades. Since then I've been up here engaged in long solitary stretches of allegedly deep thought—actually I loaf. And yet, I'm an honored Professor Emeritus. Don't you think it's an absurd system that tolerates such nonsense?"

"Perhaps there's a feeling that you've earned the right to retirement with honor."

"Bah!" He waved his hand. "That sounds too much like death. Retirement with honor and maggots gnawing at one's toes. I'll confess to you, young man, that I never earned anything. I wrote sixty-seven papers in learned journals, all but five utter garbage. I coedited three books that no one ever read, and, in general, pursued a life of a spoiled wastrel. It's been wonderful."

He finished his whiskey and put the glass down on the table with a thump.

"They keep me around here because I've got millions of dollars in a tax-free trust fund set up for me by Father and they hope I'll bequeath it all to them." He smiled crook-edly. "I may or may not. Perhaps I should will it all to some Negro organization, or something equally outrageous. A group fighting for the rights of lesbians, perhaps. Is there such a cabal?"

"I'm sure there must be."

"Yes. In California, no doubt. Speaking of which, you want to know about Willie Towle from Los Angeles, do you?"

I repeated the story about *Medical World News*.

"All right," he sighed, "if you insist, I'll try to help you. God knows why anyone would be interested in Willie Towle, for a duller boy never set foot on this campus. When I found out he became a physician, I was amazed. I never thought him intellectually capable of anything quite that advanced. Of course the family is firmly rooted in medicine—one of the Towles was Grant's personal sur-geon during the Civil War—there's a morsel for your article—and I imagine getting Willie admitted to medical school was no particular challenge."

"He's turned out to be quite a successful doctor."

"That *doesn't* surprise me. There are different types of success. One requires a combination of personality traits that Willie did indeed possess: perseverance, lack of imag-ination, innate conservatism. Of course, a good, straight body and a conventionally attractive face don't hurt, ei-ther. I'll wager he hasn't climbed the ranks by virtue of being a profound scientific thinker or innovative researcher. His strengths are of a more mundane nature, are they not?"

"He has a reputation as a fine doctor," I insisted. "His patients have only good things to say about him."

"Tells them exactly what they want to hear, no doubt. Willie was always good at that. Very popular, president of this and that. He was my student in a course on European civilization, and he was a charmer. Yes, Professor, no, Professor. Always there to hold out my chair for me—Lord, how I detested that. Not to mention the fact that I rarely sat." He grimaced at the recollection. "Yes, there was a certain banal charm there. People like that in their doctors. I believe it's called bedside manner. Of course his essay exams were most telling, revealing his true sub-stance. Predictable, accurate but not illuminating, grammatical without being literate.'' He paused. ''This isn't the kind of information you were expecting, is it?''

I smiled. ''Not exactly.''

''You can't print this, can you?'' He seemed disappointed.

''No. I'm afraid the article is meant to be laudatory.''

''Hale and hearty blah-blah stuff—in the vernacular, bullshit, eh? How boring. Doesn't it bore you to have to write such drivel?''

''At times. It pays the bills.''

''Yes. How arrogant of me not to take that into consideration. I've never had to pay bills. My bankers do that for me. I've always had far more money than I know what to do with. It leads one to incredible ignorance. It's a common fault of the indolent rich. We're unbelievably ignorant. And inbred. It brings about psychological as well as physical aberrations.'' He smiled, reached around with one arm, and tapped his hunch. ''This entire campus is a haven for the offspring of the indolent, ignorant, inbred rich. Including your Doctor Willie Towle. He descends from one of the most rarefied environments you will ever find. Did you know that?''

''Being a doctor's son?''

''No, no.'' He dismissed me as if I were an especially stupid pupil. ''He's one of the Two Hundred—you haven't heard of them?''

''No.''

''Go into the bottom drawer of my desk and pull out the old map of Seattle.''

I did what I was told. The map was folded under several back issues of *Playboy*.

''Give it to me,'' he said impatiently. He opened it and spread it on the table. ''Look here.''

I stood over him. His finger pointed to a spot at the north end of the Sound. To a tiny island shaped like a diamond.

''Brindamoor Island. Three square miles of innately unappealing terrain upon which are situated two hundred mansions and estates to rival any found in the United States. Josiah Jedson built his first home there—a Gothic monstrosity, it was—and others of his ilk mimicked him. I have cousins who reside there—most of us are related in one way or the other—though Father built *our* home on the mainland, in Windermere.''

"It's barely noticeable."

The island was a speck in the Pacific.

"And meant to be that way, my boy. In many of the older maps the island isn't even labeled. Of course there's no land access. The ferry makes one round-trip from the harbor when the weather and tides permit. It's not unusual for a week or two to elapse without the trip being completed. Some of the residents own private airplanes and have landing strips on their properties. Most are content to remain in splendid isolation."

"And Dr. Towle grew up there?"

"He most certainly did. I believe the ancestral digs have been sold. He was an only son and when he moved to California there seemed no reason to hold on to it—most of the homes are far larger than homes have a right to be. Architectural dinosaurs. Frightfully expensive to maintain—even the Two Hundred have to budget nowadays. Not all had ancestors as clever as Father."

He patted his midriff in self-congratulation.

"Do you feel growing up in that kind of isolation had any effect on Dr. Towle?"

"Now you sound like a psychologist, young man."

I smiled.

"In answer to your question: most certainly. The children of the Two Hundred were an insufferably snobbish lot—and to merit that designation at Jedson College requires extraordinary chauvinism. They were clannish, self-centered, spoiled, and not overly bright. Many had deformed siblings with chronic physical or mental problems—my remark about inbreeding was meant in all seriousness—and seemed to have been left callous and indifferent by the experience, rather than the opposite."

"You're using the past tense. Don't they exist today?"

"There are amazingly few young ones left. They get a taste of the outside world and are reluctant to return to Brindamoor—it really is quite bleak, despite the indoor tennis courts and one pathetic excuse for a country club."

To stay in character I had to defend Towle.

"Professor, I don't know Doctor Towle well, but he's very well spoken of. I've met him and he seems to be a forceful man, of strong character. Isn't it possible that growing up in the type of environment you describe Brindamoor to be could increase one's individuality?"

The old man looked at me with contempt.

"Rubbish! I understand you have to pretty up his image, but you'll get nothing but the truth from me. There wasn't an individual in the bunch from Brindamoor. Young man, solitude is the nectar of individuality. Our Willie Towle had no taste for it."

"Why do you say that?"

"I cannot recall ever seeing him alone. He palled around with two other dullards from the island. The three of them pranced around like little dictators. The Three Heads of State they were called behind their backs—pretentious, puffed-up boys. Willie, Stu and Eddy."

"Stu and Eddy?"

"Yes, yes, that's what I said. Stuart Hickle and Edwin Hayden."

At the mention of those names I gave an involuntary start. I struggled to neutralize my expression, hoping the old man hadn't noticed the reaction. Happily, he appeared oblivious, as he lectured in that parched voice:

" . . . and Hickle was a sickly, pimple-faced rotter with a spooky disposition, not a word out of him that wasn't censored by the other two. Hayden was a mean-spirited little sneak. I caught him cheating on an exam and he attempted to bribe me out of failing him by offering to procure for me an Indian prostitute of supposedly exotic talents—can you imagine such gall, as if I were unable to fend for myself in affairs of lust! Of course I failed him and wrote a sharp letter to his parents. Got no reply—no doubt they never read it, off on some European jaunt. Do you know what became of him?" he ended rhetorically.

"No," I lied.

"He's now a judge—in Los Angeles. In fact I believe all three of them, the glorious Heads, moved to Los Angeles. Hickle's some kind of chemist—wanted to be a doctor, just like Willie, and I believe he actually did begin medical school. But he was too stupid to pull through."

"A judge," he repeated. "What does that say about our judicial system?"

The information was pouring in fast and, like a pauper suddenly discovering a sizeable inheritance, I wasn't sure how to deal with it. I wanted to shed my cover and wring every last bit of information out of the old man, but there was the case—and my promises to Margaret—to think about.

"I'm a nasty old bugger, am I not?" cackled Van der Graaf.

"You seem very perceptive, Professor."

"Oh, do I?" He smiled craftily. "Any other tidbits I can toss your way?"

"I know Dr. Towle lost his wife and child several years back. What can you tell me about that?"

He stared at me, then refilled his glass and sipped. "All part of your story?"

"All part of fleshing out the portrait," I said. It sounded feeble.

"Ah, yes, fleshing it out. Of course. Well, it was a tragedy, no two ways about it, and your doctor was rather young to be dealing with it. He was married during his sophomore year to a lovely girl from a good Portland family. Lovely, but outside his circle—the Two Hundred tended to marry each other. The engagement came as a bit of surprise. Six months later the girl gave birth to a son and that mystery was cleared up.

"For a while the trio seemed to be breaking up—Hickle and Hayden slinked off by themselves as Willie attended to the duties of a married man. Then the wife and child were killed and the Heads were reunited. I suppose it's natural that a man will seek the comfort of friends in the wake of such a loss."

"How did it happen?"

He peered into his glass and downed the last few drops.

"The girl—the mother—was taking the child to the hospital. He'd woken up with the croup or some such ailment. The nearest emergency facility was at the Children's Orthopedic Hospital, at the University. It was in the early morning hours, still dark. Her car went over the Evergreen Bridge and plunged into the lake. It was daybreak before it was found."

"Where was Dr. Towle?"

"Studying. Burning the midnight oil. Of course this caused him to be guilt-stricken, absolutely wretched. No doubt he blamed himself for not having been there and been drowned himself. You know the type of self-flagellation embraced by the bereaved."

"A tragic affair."

"Oh yes. She was a lovely girl."

"Dr. Towle keeps her picture in his office."

"A sentimentalist, is he?"

"I suppose." I drank some whiskey. "After the tragedy he began seeing more of his friends?"

"Yes. Though as I hear you use the term I realize something. In my concept of friendship there is implied a bond of affection, some degree of mutual admiration. Those three always looked so grim when they were together—they didn't seem to enjoy each other's company. I never knew what the link between them was, but it did exist. Willie went away to medical school and Stuart tagged along. Edwin Hayden attended law school at the same university. They settled in the same city. No doubt you'll be contacting the other two in order to obtain *laudatory* quotes for your article. If there is an article."

I struggled to remain calm.

"What do you mean?"

"Oh, I think you know what I mean, my boy. I'm not going to ask you to present identification confirming you're who you say you are—it wouldn't prove a thing anyway—because you seem like a pleasant, intelligent young man and how many visitors to whom I can blab do you think I receive? Enough said."

"I appreciate that, Professor."

"And well you should. I trust you have your reasons for wanting to ask me about Willie. Undoubtedly they're boring and I've no wish to know them. Have I been helpful?"

"You've been more than helpful." I filled our glasses and we shared another drink, no conversation passing between us.

"Would you be willing to be a bit more helpful?" I asked.

"That depends."

"Dr. Towle has a nephew. Timothy Kruger. I wonder if there's anything you could tell me about him."

Van der Graaf raised his drink to his lips with trembling hands. His face clouded.

"Kruger." He said the name as if it were an epithet.

"Yes."

"Cousin. Distant cousin, not nephew."

"Cousin, then."

"Kruger. An old family. Prussians, every one of them. Power brokers. A powerful family." His mellifluousness was gone and he spat out the words with mechanical intonation. "Prussians."

He took a few steps. The arachnid stagger ceased abruptly and he let his hands drop to his sides.

"This must be a police matter," he said.

"Why do you say that?"

His face blackened with anger and he raised one fist in the air, a prophet of doom.

"Don't trifle with me, young man! If it has something to do with Timothy Kruger there's little else it could be!"

"It is part of a criminal investigation. I can't go into details."

"Oh, can't you? I've wagged my tongue at you without demanding to know your true intentions. A moment ago I judged them to be boring. Now I've changed my mind."

"What is it about the Kruger name that scares you so much, Professor?"

"Evil," he said. "Evil frightens me. You say your questions are part of a criminal investigation. How do I know what side you're on?"

"I'm working with the police. But I'm not a policeman."

"I won't tolerate riddles! Either be truthful or be gone!"

I considered the choice.

"Margaret Dopplemeier," I said. "I don't want her to lose her job because of anything I tell you."

"Maggie?" he snorted. "Don't worry about her, I've no intention of letting on the fact that she led you to me. She's a sad girl, needs intrigue to spice up her life. I've spoken enough to her to know that she clings longingly to the Conspiracy Theory of Life. Dangle one before her— she'll go for it like a trout for a lure. Kennedy assassinations, Unidentified Flying Objects, cancer, tooth decay—all the result of a grand collusion of anonymous demons. No doubt you recognized that and exploited it."

He made it sound Machiavellian. I didn't dispute it.

"No," he said. "I've no interest in crushing Maggie. She's been a friend. Apart from that, my loyalties to this institution are far from blind. I detest certain aspects of this place—my true home, if you will."

"Such as the Krugers?"

"Such as the environment that allows Krugers and their ilk to flourish."

He tottered, the too-large head lolling on its misshapen base.

"The choice is yours, young man. Put up or shut up."

I put up.

"Nothing in your story surprises me," he said. "I didn't know of Stuart Hickle's death nor of his sexual proclivities, but neither are shocking. He was a bad poet, Dr. Delaware, very bad—and nothing is beyond a bad poet."

I recalled the verse at the bottom of Lilah Towle's yearbook obituary. It was clear who "S" was.

"When you mentioned Timothy I became alarmed, because I didn't know if you were in the employ of the Krugers. The badge you showed me is well and fine, but such trinkets are easily counterfeited."

"Call Detective Delano Hardy at West Los Angeles Police Division. He'll tell you what side I'm on." I hoped he wouldn't take me up on it—who knew how Hardy would react?

He looked at me thoughtfully. "No, that won't be necessary. You're a dreadful liar. I believe I can intuitively tell when you're telling the truth."

"Thank you."

"You're welcome. A compliment was intended."

"Tell me about Timothy Kruger," I said.

He stood blinking, gnomelike, a concoction of a Hollywood special-effects lab.

"The first thing I'd like to emphasize is that the evil of the Krugers has nothing to do with wealth. They would be evil paupers—I imagine they were, at one time. If that sounds defensive, it is."

"I understand."

"The very wealthy are not evil, Bolshevist propaganda to the contrary. They are a harmless lot—overly-sheltered, reticent, destined for extinction." He took a step backward as if retreating from his own prediction.

I waited.

"Timothy Kruger," he finally said, "is a murderer, plain and simple. The fact that he was never arrested, tried or convicted does nothing to diminish his guilt in my eyes. The story goes back seven—no, eight years. There was a student here, a farm boy from Idaho. Sharp as a tack, built like Adonis. His name was Saxon. Jeffrey Saxon. He came here to study, the first of his family to finish high school, dreaming of becoming a writer.

"He was accepted on an athletic scholarship—crew, baseball, football, wrestling—and managed to excel in all of those while maintaining an A average. He majored in history and I was his faculty advisor, though by that time I wasn't teaching any more. We had many chats, up here in this room. The boy was a pleasure to converse with. He had an enthusiasm for life, a thirst for knowledge."

A tear collected in the corner of one drooping, blue eye.

"Excuse me." The old man pulled out a linen handkerchief and dabbed his cheek. "Dusty in here, must get the custodial staff to clean." He sipped his whiskey and when he spoke his voice was enfeebled by memories.

"Jeffrey Saxon had the curious, searching nature of a true scholar, Dr. Delaware. I recall the first time he came up here and saw all the books. Like a child let loose in a toy store. I lent him my finest antiquarian volumes—everything from the London edition of Josephus' *Chronicles* to anthropologic treatises. He devoured them. 'For God's sake, Professor,' he'd say, 'it would take several lifetimes to learn even a fraction of what there is to know'—that's the mark of an intellectual, in my view, becoming cognizant of one's own insignificance in relation to the accumulated mass of human knowledge.

"The others, of course, thought him a rube, a hick. They made fun of his clothes, his manner, his lack of sophistication. He spoke to me about it—I'd become a kind of surrogate grandfather I suppose—and I reassured him that he was meant for more noble company than what Jedson had to offer. In fact I'd encouraged him to put in for a transfer to an Eastern school—Yale, Princeton—where he could achieve significant intellectual growth. With his grades and a letter from me, he might have made it. But he never got a chance.

"He became attached to a young lady, one of the Two Hundred, pretty enough, but vapid. This in itself, was no error, as the heart and the gonads must be satisfied. The mistake was in choosing a female already coveted by another."

"By Tim Kruger?"

Van der Graaf nodded painfully.

"This is difficult for me, Doctor. It brings back so much."

"If it's too difficult for you, Professor, I can leave now and come back some other time."

"No, no. That would serve no purpose." He took a deep breath. "It comes down to a smarmy soap opera of a tale. Jeffrey and Kruger were interested in the same girl, they had words in public. Tempers flared, but it seemed to pass. Jeffrey visited me and vented his spleen. I played amateur psychologist—professors so often are required to provide emotional support to their students and I confess I did a fine job of it. I urged him to forget the girl, knowing her type, understanding full well that Jeffrey would be the loser in any battle of wills. The young of Jedson are homing pigeons, as predictable as their ancestors, reverting to type. The girl was meant to mate with one of her own. There were better things, finer things, awaiting Jeffrey, an entire lifetime of opportunity and adventure.

"He wouldn't listen. He was like a knight of old, imbued with the nobility of his mission. Conquer the Black Jouster, rescue the fair maiden. Total rubbish—but he was an innocent. *An innocent.*"

Van der Graaf paused, out of breath. His face had turned a sickly greenish shade of pale and I feared for his health.

"Perhaps we should stop for the moment," I suggested. "I can return tomorrow."

"Absolutely not! I'll not be left here in solitary confinement with a poisonous lump lodged in my craw!" He cleared his throat. "I'll be on with it—you sit there and pay close attention."

"All right, Professor."

"Now then, where was I—ah, Jeffrey as a White Knight. Foolish boy. The enmity between him and Timothy Kruger continued and festered. Jeffrey was ostracized by all the others—Kruger was a campus luminary, socially established. I became Jeffrey's sole source of support. Our conversations changed. No longer were they cerebral exchanges. Now I was conducting psychotherapy on a full-time basis—an activity with which I was most uncomfortable, but I felt I couldn't abandon the boy. I was all he had.

"It culminated in a wrestling match. Both the boys were Greco-Roman wrestlers. They agreed to meet, late at night, in the empty gymnasium, just the two of them for a grudge match. I'm no wrestler myself, for obvious reasons, but I do know that the sport is highly structured, replete with regulations, the criteria for victory clearly drawn. Jeffrey liked it for that reason—he was highly self-disciplined for one so young. He walked into that gym alive and left on a stretcher, neck and spine snapped, alive in only the most vegetative sense of the word. Three days later he died.''

''And his death was ruled an accident,'' I said softly.

''That was the official story. Kruger said the two of them had gotten involved in a complicated series of holds and in the ensuing tangle of torsos, arms and legs, Jeffrey had been injured. And who could dispute it—accidents do occur in wrestling matches. At worst it seemed a case of two immature men behaving in an irresponsible manner. But to those of us who knew Timothy, who understood the depth of the rivalry between them, that was far from a satisfactory explanation. The college was eager to hush it up, the police all too happy to oblige—why go up against the Kruger millions when there are hundreds of poor people committing crimes?

''I attended Jeffrey's funeral—flew to Idaho. Before I left I ran into Timothy on campus. Looking back I see he must have sought me out.'' Van der Graaf's mouth tightened, the wrinkles deepening as if controlled by some internal drawstring. ''He approached me near the Founder's statue. 'I hear you're traveling, Professor,' he said. 'Yes,' I replied, 'I'm flying to Boise tonight.' 'To attend the last rites for your young charge?' he asked. There was a look of utter innocence on his face, feigned innocence—he was an actor, for God's sake, he could manipulate his features at will.

'' 'What's it to you?' I replied. He bent to the ground, picked up a dry oak twig and sporting an arrogant smirk—the same smirk one can see in photographs of Nazi concentration camp guards tormenting their victims—snapped the twig between his fingers, and let it drop to the ground. Then he laughed.

''I've never in my life been so close to commiting murder, Doctor Delaware. Had I been younger, stronger, properly armed, I would have done it. As it was, I simply stood there, for once in my life at a loss for words. 'Have a nice trip,' he said, and, still smirking, backed away. My heart pounded so, I was assaulted with a spell of dizziness, but fought to maintain my equilibrium. When he was out of eyesight I broke down and sobbed.''

A long moment passed between us.

When he appeared sufficiently composed I asked him:

"Does Margaret know about this? About Kruger?"

He nodded.

"I've spoken of it to her. She's my friend."

So the awkward publicist was more spider than fly after all. The insight cheered me for some reason.

"One more thing—the girl. The one they were fighting over. What became of her?"

"What do you expect?" He sneered, some of the old vitriol returning to his voice. "She shunned Kruger—most of the others did. They were afraid of him. She attended Jedson for three more undistinguished years, married an investment banker and moved to Spokane. No doubt she's a proper hausfrau, shuttling the kiddies to school, brunching at the club, boffing the delivery boy."

"The spoils of battle," I said.

He shook his head. "Such a waste."

I looked at my watch. I'd been up in the dome for a little over an hour, but it seemed longer. Van der Graaf had unloaded a truckful of sewage during that time, but he was a historian, and that's what they're trained to do. I felt tired and tense, and I longed for fresh air.

"Professor," I said. "I don't know how to thank you."

"Putting the information to good use would be a step in the right direction." The blue eyes shone like twin gaslights. "Snap some twigs of your own."

"I'll do my best." I got up.

"I trust you can see yourself out."

I did.

When I was halfway across the rotunda I heard him cry out: "Remind Maggie of our pizza picnic!"

His words echoed against the smooth, cold stone.

23

AMONG CERTAIN PRIMITIVE TRIBES, there exists the belief that when one vanquishes an enemy it is not enough to destroy all evidence of corporeal life: the soul must be vanquished as well. That belief is at the root of the various forms of cannibalism that have been known to exist—and still exist—in many regions of the world. You are what you eat. Devour your victim's heart, and you encompass his very being. Grind his penis to dust and swallow the dust, and you've co-opted his manhood.

I thought of Timothy Kruger—of the boy he'd killed and how he'd assumed the identity of a struggling scholarship student when describing himself to me—and visions of lip-smacking, bone-crunching savagery intruded upon the idyllic verdancy of the Jedson campus. I was still struggling to erase those visions when I climbed the marble steps of Crespi Hall.

Margaret Dopplemeier responded to my coded knock with a "Wait one second!" and an open door. She let me in and locked the door.

"Did you find Van der Graaf helpful?" she asked airily.

"He told me everything. About Jeffrey Saxon and Tim Kruger and the fact that you were his confidante."

She blushed.

"You can't expect me to feel guilty for deceiving you when you did the same to me," she said.

"I don't," I assured her, "I just wanted you to know that he trusted me and told me everything. I know you couldn't until he did."

"I'm glad you understand," she said primly.

"Thank you for leading me to him."

"It was my pleasure, Alex. Just put the information to good use."

It was the second time in ten minutes that I'd received that mandate. Add to that a similar order from Raquel Ochoa and it made for a heavy load.

"I will. Do you have the clipping?"

"Here." She handed me the photocopy. The death of Lilah Towle and "Little Willie" had made the front page, sharing space with a report on fraternity hijinks and a reprint of an Associated Press report on the dangers of "mariwuana reefers." I started to read but the copy was blurred and barely legible. Margaret saw me straining.

"The original was rubbed out."

"It's okay." I skimmed the article long enough to see that it was consistent with Van der Graaf's recollection.

"Here's another story, several days later—about the funeral. This one's better."

I took it from her and examined it. By now the Towle affair was on page six, a social register item. The account of the ceremony was maudlin and full of dropped names. A photograph at the bottom caught my eye.

Towle led the mourners procession, haggard and grim, hands folded in front of him. To one side was a younger, still toadlike Edwin Hayden. To the other, slightly to the rear, was a towering figure. There was no mistaking the identity of the mourner.

The kinky hair was black, the face bloated and shiny. The heavy framed eyeglasses I'd seen a few days before were replaced by gold-rimmed, round spectacles resting low on the meaty nose.

It was the Reverend Augustus McCaffrey in younger days.

I folded both papers and slipped them in my jacket pocket.

"Call Van der Graaf,' I said.

"He's an old man. Don't you think you've questioned him enou—"

"Just call him," I cut her off. "If you don't I'll run back there myself."

She winced at my abruptness, but dialed the phone.

When the connection was made she said, "Sorry to bother you, Professor. It's *him* again." She listened, shot

me an unhappy look and handed me the receiver, holding
it at arm's length.

"Thank you," I said sweetly. Into the phone: "Professor, I need to ask you about another student. It's important."

"Go on. I've only Miss November of 1973 occupying
my attention. Who is it?"

"Augustus McCaffrey—was he a friend of Towle, too?"
There was silence on the other end of the line and then
the sound of laughter.

"Oh, dear me! That's a laugh! Gus McCaffrey, a Jedson
student! And him touched by the tar brush!" He laughed
some more and it was a while before he caught his breath.
"Mary Mother of God, no, man. He was no *student*
here!"

"I've got a photograph in front of me showing him at
the Towle funeral—"

"Be that as it may, he was no student. Gus McCaffrey
was—I believe they call themselves maintenance engineers
today—Gus was a janitor. He swept the dormitories, took
out the trash, that kind of thing."

"What was he doing at the funeral? It looks like he's
right behind Towle, ready to catch him if he falls."

"No surprise. He was originally an employee of the
Hickle family—they had one of the largest homes on
Brindamoor. Family retainers can grow quite close to their
masters—I believe Stuart brought him over to Jedson when
he began college here. He did eventually attain some kind
of rank within the custodial staff—supervising janitor or
something similar. Leaving Brindamoor may very well
have been an excellent opportunity for him. What's big
Gus doing today?"

"He's a minister—the head of that children's home I
told you about."

"I see. Taking out the Lord's trash, so to speak."

"So to speak. Can you tell me anything about him."

"I honestly can't, I'm afraid. I had no contact with the
nonacademic employees—there's a tendency to pretend
they're invisible that's acquired over time. He was a big
brute of a fellow, that I do recall. Slovenly, seemed quite
strong, may very well have been bright—your information
certainly points in that direction, and I'm no social Dar-

winist with a need to dispute it. But that is really all I can tell you. I'm sorry."

"Don't be. One last thing—where can I get a map of Brindamoor Island?"

"There's none that I know of outside the County Hall of Records—wait, a student of mine did an undergraduate thesis on the history of the place, complete with residential map. I don't have a copy but I believe it would be stored in the library, in the thesis section. The students' name was—let me think—Church? No, it was something else of a clerical nature—Chaplain. Gretchen Chaplain. Look under C, you should find it."

"Thanks again, Professor. Good-bye."

"Good-bye."

Margaret Dopplemeier sat at her desk, glaring at me.

"I'm sorry for being rude," I said. "It was important."

"All right," she said. "I just thought you could have been a little more polite in view of what I've done for you." The possessive look slithered into her eyes like a python into a lagoon.

"You're right. I should have. I won't trouble you further." I stood up. "Thanks so much for everything." I held out my hand, and when she reluctantly extended hers, I took it. "You've really made a big difference."

"That's good to know. How long will you be staying?"

Gently I broke the handclasp.

"Not long." I backed away, smiled at her, finally got my hand on the knob and pushed. "All the best, Margaret. Enjoy your blackberries."

She started to say something, then thought better of it. I left her standing behind her desk, a circle of pink tongue-tip visible in the corner of her unattractive mouth, searching for a taste of something.

The library was properly austere and very respectably stocked with books and journals for a college the size of Jedson. The main room was a marble cathedral draped in heavy red velvet and lit by oversized windows placed ten feet apart. It was filled with oak reading tables, green-shaded lamps, leather chairs. All that was missing were people to read the august volumes that papered the walls.

The librarian was an effete young man with close-cropped

hair and a pencil mustache. His shirt was red plaid, his tie a yellow knit. He sat behind his reference table reading a recent copy of *Artforum*. When I asked him where the thesis section was, he looked up with the astonished expression of a hermit observing the penetration of his lair.

"There," he said, languidly, and pointed to a spot at the south end of the room.

There was an oak card catalog and I found Gretchen Chaplain's thesis listed in it. The title of her magnum opus had been *Brindamoor Island: Its History and Geography*.

Theses by Frederick Chalmers and O. Winston Chastain were present, but Gretchen's rightful place between them was unfilled. I checked and doublechecked the Library of Congress number but that was a fruitless ritual: The Brindamoor study was gone.

I went back to Plaid Shirt and had to clear my throat twice before he tore himself away from a piece on Billy Al Bengston.

"Yes?"

"I'm looking for a specific thesis and can't seem to find it."

"Have you checked the card file to make sure it's listed?"

"The card's there but the thesis isn't."

"How unfortunate. I would guess it's been checked out."

"Could you check for me, please?"

He sighed and took too long to raise himself out of his chair. "What's the author's name?"

I gave him all the necessary information and he went behind the checkout counter with an injured look. I followed him.

"Brindamoor Island—dreary place. Why would you want to know about *that*?"

"I'm a visiting professor from UCLA and it's part of my research. I didn't know an explanation was necessary."

"Oh, it's not," he said, quickly, and buried his nose in a stack of cards. He lifted out a portion of the cards and shuffled them like a Vegas pro. "Here," he said, "that thesis was checked out six months ago—my, it's overdue, isn't it?"

I took the card. Scant attention had been paid to Gretch-

en's masterpiece. Prior to its last withdrawal a half year
ago, the last time it had been checked out was in 1954, by
Gretchen herself. Probably wanted to show it to her kids—
Mummy was once quite a scholar, little ones . . .

"Sometimes we get behind on checking on overdue
notices. I'll get right on this, Professor. Who checked it
out last?"

I looked at the signature and told him. As the name left
my mouth my brain processed the information. By the
time the two words had dissolved I knew my mission
wouldn't be complete without a trip to the island.

24

THE FERRY to Brindamoor Island made its morning trip at seven-thirty.

When the wake-up call from the desk came in at six it found me showered, shaved and tensely bright-eyed. The rain had started again shortly after midnight, pounding the glass walls of the suite. It had roused me for a dreamlike instant during which I was certain I'd heard the sound of cavalry hooves stampeding down the corridor, and had gone back to sleep anyway. Now it continued to come down, the city below awash and out of focus, as if viewed from inside a dirty aquarium.

I dressed in heavy slacks, leather jacket, wool turtle-neck, and took along the only raincoat I had: an unlined poplin doublebreasted affair that was fine for Southern California but of uncertain utility in the present surroundings. I caught a quick breakfast of smoked salmon, bagels, juice and coffee and made it to the docks at ten after seven.

I was among the first to queue up at the entrance to the auto bay. The line moved and I drove down a ramp into the womb of the ferry behind a VW bus with Save the Whale stickers on the rear bumper. I obeyed the gesticula-tions of a crewman dressed in dayglo orange overalls and parked two inches from the slick, white wall of the bay. An ascent of two flights brought me on deck. I walked past a gift shop, tobacconist and snack bar, all closed, and a blackened room furnished wall to wall with video games. A waiter played Pac Man in solitude, devouring dots with brow-furrowing concentration.

I found a seat with a view at the stern, folded my

raincoat across my lap and settled back for the one-hour ride.

The ship was virtually empty. My few fellow passengers were young and dressed for work: hired help from the mainland commuting to their assigned posts at the manors of Brindamoor. The return trip, no doubt, would be filled with commuters of another class: lawyers, bankers, other financial types, on their way to downtown offices and paneled boardrooms.

The ocean pitched and rolled, frothing in response to the surface winds that drag-raced along its surface. There were smaller craft at sea, mostly fishing boats, tugs and scows, and they danced in command, curtsying and dipping. For all the ferry moved it might have been a toy model on a shelf.

A group of six young men in their late teens came aboard and sat down ten feet away. Blond, bearded in varying degrees of shagginess, dressed in rumpled khakis and dirt-grayed jeans, they passed around a thermos full of something that wasn't coffee, joked, smoked, put their feet up on chairs and emitted a collective guffaw that sounded like a beery laugh track. One of them noticed me and held up the thermos.

"Swig, my man?" he offered.

I smiled and shook my head.

He shrugged, turned away and the party started up again.

The ferry's horn sounded, the rumble of its engines reverberating through the floorboards, and we started to move.

Halfway through the trip I walked over to where the six young drinkers sat, now slumped. Three of them slept, snoring open-mouthed, one was reading an obscene comic book, and two, including the one who'd offered me the drink, sat smoking, hypnotized by the glowing ends of their cigarettes.

"Excuse me."

The two smokers looked up. The reader paid no attention.

"Yeah?" The generous one smiled. He was missing half of his front teeth: bad oral hygiene or a quick temper. "Sorry, man, we got no more Campbell's soup." He picked up the thermos and shook it. "Ain't that right, Dougie?"

His companion, a fat boy with drooping mustaches and muttonchop sideburns, laughed and nodded his head.

"Yeah, no more soup. Chicken noodle. Ninety proof."

From where I was standing the whole bunch of them smelled like a distillery.

"That's all right. I appreciate the offer. I was just wondering if you could give me some information about Brindamoor."

Both boys looked puzzled, as if they'd never thought of themselves as having any information to give.

"What do you want to know? Place is a drag," said Generous.

"Fuckin-A." Fat Boy nodded assent.

"I'm trying to find a certain house on the island, can't seem to get hold of a map."

"That's 'cause there ain't any. People there like to hide from the rest of the world. They got private cops ready to roust you for spittin' the wrong way. Me 'n' Doug and the rest of these jokers go over to do groundswork on the golf course, pickin' up crap and litter and stuff. Finish the day and head straight back for the boat, man. We want to keep our jobs, we stick to that—exactly."

"Yeah," said the fat one. "No shootin' for the local beaver, no partyin'. Workin' people been doin' it for years and years—my dad worked Brindamoor before he got in the union, and I'm just doin' it until he gets me in. Then, fuck those hermits. He told me they had a song for it, back in those days: Heft and tote, then float on the boat." He laughed and slapped his buddy on the back.

"What you interested in findin'?" Generous lit another cigarette and placed it in the snaggled gap where his upper incisors should have been.

"The Hickle house."

"You related to them?" Doug asked. His eyes were the color of the sea, bloodshot and suddenly dull with worry, wondering if I was someone who could turn his words against him.

"No. I'm an architect. Just doing a little sightseeing. I was told the Hickle house would be of interest. Supposed to be the biggest one on the island."

"Man," he said, "they're all big. You could fit my whole fuckin' neighborhood in one of them."

"Architect, huh?" Generous's face brightened with interest. "How much school it take to do that?"

"Five years of college."

"Forget it," the fat one kidded him. "You're an airhead, Harm. You got to learn how to read and write first."

"Fuck you!" said his friend, good-naturedly. To me: "I worked construction last summer. Architecture's probly pretty interestin'."

"It is. I do mostly private houses. Always looking for new ideas."

"Yeah, hey, right. Gotta keep it interestin'."

"Aw, man," chided Dougie. "We don't do nothing interestin'. Clean up goddam garbage—hell, man, there's fun going on there at that club, 'cause last week Matt 'n' me found a couple of used rubbers out by hole number eleven—and we're missin, it, Harm."

"I don't need those people for my fun," said the generous one. "You want to know about houses, mister, let's ask Ray." He turned and leaned across one sleeping boy to elbow the one with the comic book, who'd kept his nose buried in his reading and hadn't looked up once. When he did, his face had the glazed look of someone very stupid or very stoned.

"Huh?"

"Ray, you dumbshit, man wants to know about the Hickle house."

The boy blinked, uncomprehending.

"Ray's been droppin' too much acid out in the woods. Just can't seem to shake himself out of it." Harm grinned, his tonsils visible. "C'mon, man, where's the Hickle place?"

"Hickle," Ray said. "My old man used to work there— spooky place he said. Weird. I think it's on Charlemagne. The old man used to—"

"All right, man." Harm shoved Ray's head down and he returned to his comic book. "They got strange names for streets on the island, Mister. Charlemagne, Alexander, Suleiman."

Conquerors. The little joke of the very rich was evidently lost on those who were its intended butt.

"Charlemagne is an inland road. You go just past the

main drag, past the market, a quarter mile—look hard because the street signs are usually covered by trees—and turn, lemme see, turn right, that's Charlemagne. After that you'd best ask around.''

"Much obliged.'' I reached in and pulled out my wallet. "Here's for your trouble,'' I said, taking out a five.

Harm held out his hand—in protest, not collection. "Forget it, mister. We didn't do nothin'.''

Doug, the fat boy, gave him an angry look and grunted.

"Up yours, Dougie,'' said the boy with the missing teeth. "We didn't do nothin' for the man's money.'' Despite his unkempt hair and the war zone of a mouth, he had intelligence and a certain dignity. He was the kind of kid I wouldn't mind having at my side when the going got rough.

"Let me buy you a round, then.''

"Nah,'' said Harm. "We can't drink no more, mister. Got to hit the course in half an hour. Be slick as snot on a day like this. Bubble Butt here, drink any more, he could fall and bounce down and crush the rest of us.''

"Fuck you, Harm,'' said Doug, without heart.

I put the money back. "Thanks much.''

"Think nothin' of it. You build some houses that don't need union help, you want reliable construction muscle, remember Harmon Lundquist. I'm in the book.''

"I will.''

Ten minutes before the boat reached shore the island emerged from behind a dressing screen of rain and fog, an oblong, squat, gray chunk of rock. Except for the coiffure of trees that covered most of its outer edges, it could have been Alcatraz.

I went down to the auto bay, got behind the wheel of the Nova and was ready when the man in orange waved us down the ramp. The scene outside might have been lifted off the streets of London. There were enough black top-coats, black umbrellas, and black hats to fill Piccadilly. Pink hands held briefcases and the morning's *Wall Street Journal*. Eyes stared straight ahead. Lips set grimly. When the gate at the foot of the gangway opened they moved in procession, each man in his place, every shiny black shoe rising and falling in response to an unseen drummer. A squadron of perfect gentlemen. A gentleman's brigade . . .

Just beyond Brindamoor Harbor was a small town square built around an enormous towering elm and rimmed with shops: a bank with smoked glass windows, a brokerage house, three or four expensive looking clothiers with conservatively dressed, faceless mannequins in their windows, a grocer, a butcher, a dry cleaner's that also housed the local post office, a book store, two restaurants—one French, the other Italian—a gift shop, and a jewelers. All the stores were closed, the streets empty and, except for a flock of pigeons convening under the elm, devoid of life.

I followed Harm's directions and found Charlemagne Lane with no trouble. A thousand yards out of the square the road narrowed and darkened, shadowed by walls of fern, devil ivy and shrub maple. The green was broken by an occasional gate—wrought iron or redwood, the former usually backed by steel plating. There were no mailboxes on the road, no public display of names. The estates seemed to be spaced several acres apart. A few times I caught a glimpse of the properties behind the gates: lots of rolling lawns, sloping drives paved with brick and stone, the houses imposing and grand—Tudor, Regency, Colonial —the driveways stabling Rolls Royces, Mercedes and Cadillac limousines, as well as their more utilitarian four-wheeled cousins—stationwagons paneled with phony wood, Volvos, compacts. Once or twice I saw gardeners laboring in the rain, their power mowers sputtering and belching.

The road continued for another half-mile, the properties growing larger, the houses set back further from the gates. It came to an abrupt halt at a thicket of cypress. There was no gate, no visible means of entry, just the forestlike growth of thirty-foot trees, and for a moment I thought I'd been misled.

I put on my raincoat, pulled up the collar and got out. The ground was thick with pine needles and wet leaves. I walked to the thicket and peered through the branches. Twenty feet ahead, almost totally hidden by the overgrowth of tangled limbs and dripping vegetation, was a short stone pathway leading to a wooden gate. The trees had been planted to block the entry; from the size of them they were at least twenty years old. Discounting the possibility that someone had taken the trouble to transplant a score of full grown cypress to the site, I decided it had been a long time since the normal human business of living had taken place here.

I pushed my way to the gate and tried it. Nailed shut. I took a good look at it—two slabs of tongued-and-grooved redwood hinged to brick posts. The posts connected to chain link fencing piled high with thorny spirals. No sign of electricity or barbed wire. I found a foothold on a wet rock, slipped a couple of times and finally managed to scale the gate.

I landed on another world. Acres of wasteland spread before me; what had once been a formal lawn was now a swamp of weeds, dead grass and broken rock. The ground had sunk in several places, creating pools of water that stagnated and provided oases for the mosquitoes and gnats that hovered overhead. Once-noble trees had been reduced to jagged stumps and felled, rotten hulls crawling with fungus. Rusted auto parts, old tires and discarded cans and bottles were scattered throughout what was now a sodden trash dump. Rain fell on metal and made a hollow, clanging sound.

I walked up a pathway paved in herringbone brick, choked with weeds and covered by slimy moss. In the places where the roots had pushed through, the bricks stuck out of the ground like loose teeth in a broken jaw. I kicked aside a drowned field mouse and slogged toward the former residence of the Hickle clan.

The house was massive, a three-story structure of hand-hewn stone that had blackened with age. I couldn't imagine it as ever being beautiful but doubtless it had once been grand: a brooding, slate-roofed mansion trimmed with gingerbread, festooned with eaves and gables and girdled by wide stone porches. There was rusted wrought-iron furniture on the front porch, a nine-foot-high cathedral door and a weather vane at the highest peak in the shape of a witch riding a broomstick. The old crone twirled in the wind, safely above the desolation.

I climbed the stairs to the front entry. Weeds had grown clear up to the door, which was nailed shut. The windows were similarly boarded and bolted tight. In spite of its size—perhaps because of it—the house seemed pathetic, a forgotten dowager, abandoned to the point where she no longer cared how she looked and sentenced to a fate of decaying in silence.

I forced my way through a makeshift barrier of rotting boards that had been stacked in front of the porte-cochere. The house was at least a hundred and fifty feet long and it took me a while to check each window on the ground floor: All were sealed.

The rear property was another three acres of swamp. A four-car garage, designed as a miniature of the house, was inaccessible—nailed and fastened. A fifty-foot swimming pool was empty save for several inches of muddy water in which floated a host of organic debris. The remains of a grape arbor and trellised rose garden were evident only as a jumble of peeling wood and cracked stone supporting a bird's nest of lifeless twigs. Stone benches and statues slanted and pitched on broken bases, Pompeii in the wake of Vesuvius.

The rain began to come down harder and colder. I put my hands in the pocket of my raincoat, by now soaked through, and looked for shelter. It would take tools—hammer and crowbar—to get into the house or the garage, and there were no large trees that could be trusted not to topple at any moment. I was out in the open like a bum caught in a blitz.

I saw a flash of light and braced myself for an electric storm. None came and the light flashed again. The heavy downpour made it difficult to see but the third time the light appeared I was able to draw a bead on it and walk in its direction. Several squishy footsteps later I could see it had come from a glass greenhouse at the rear of the estate, just beyond the bombed-out arbor. The panes were opaque with dirt, some of which ran in brown trickles, but they appeared intact. I ran toward it, following the light that flickered, danced, disappeared, then flickered again.

The door to the greenhouse was closed but it opened silently to the prompting of my hand. Inside it was warm, steamy and sour with the aroma of decomposition. Waist-high wooden tables ran along both sides of the glass room; between them was a walkway floored with woodchips, peat, mulch and topsoil. A collection of tools—pitchforks, rakes, spades, hoes—stood in one corner.

Upon the tables were pots of gorgeously flowering plants: orchids, bromeliads, blue hydrangea, begonias of every hue, scarlet and white impatiens—all in full bloom and spilling abundantly from their terra-cotta houses. A wooden beam into which metal hooks had been embedded was suspended above the tables. Hanging from the hooks were fuchsias dripping purple, ferns, spider plants, creeping charlies, more begonias. It was the Garden of Eden in the Great Void.

The room was dim, and it reverberated with the sound of the rain assaulting the glass roof. The light that had drawn me appeared again, brighter and closer. I made out a shape at the other end of the greenhouse, a figure in yellow slicker and hood holding a flashlight. The figure shone the flashlight on plants, picking up a leaf here, a flower there, examining the soil, pinching off a dry branch, setting aside a ripe blossom.

"Hello," I said.

The figure whirled and the flashlight beam washed over my face. I squinted in the glare and brought my hand up to shield my eyes.

The figure came closer.

"Who are you?" demanded a voice, high and scared.

"Alex Delaware."

The beam lowered. I started to take a step.

"Stay right there!"

I put my foot down.

The hood was pulled back. The face it revealed was round, pale, flat, utterly Asian, female but not feminine. The eyes were two razor cuts in the parchment skin, the mouth an unsmiling hyphen.

"Hello, Mrs. Hickle."

"How do you know me—what do you want?" There was toughness diluted by fear in the voice, the toughness of the successful fugitive who knows vigilance must never cease.

"I just thought I'd pay you a visit."

"I don't want visitors. I don't know you."

"Don't you? Alex Delaware—doesn't the name mean anything to you?"

She didn't bother to lie, just said nothing.

"It was my office darling Stuart chose for his last big scene—or maybe it was chosen for him."

"I don't know what you're talking about. I don't want your company." Her English was clipped and slightly accented.

"Why don't you call the butler and have me ejected?"

Her jaws worked; white fingers tightened around the flashlight.

"You refuse to leave?"

"It's wet and cold outside. I'd appreciate the chance to dry off."

"Then you'll go?"

"Then I stay and we talk awhile. About your late husband and some of his good buddies."

"Stuart's dead. There's nothing to talk about."

"I think there's plenty. Lots of questions."

She put down the flashlight and folded her arms in front of her. There was defiance in the gesture. Any trace of fear had faded and her demeanor was one of irritation at being disturbed. It puzzled me—she was a lone woman accosted by a stranger in a deserted place but there was no panic.

"Last chance," she said.

"I'm not interested in blowing your cover. Just let me—"

She clicked her tongue against the roof of her mouth.

A large shadow materialized into something living and breathing.

I saw what it was and my bowels went weak.

"This is Otto. He doesn't like strangers."

He was the largest dog I'd ever seen, a Great Dane the size of a healthy pony, colored like a Dalmatian—white dappled with gray-black splotches. One ear was partially shredded. His maws were black and wet with saliva, hanging loose in that half-smile, half-snarl so characteristic of attack dogs, revealing pearly-white fangs and a tongue the size of a hot-water bag. His eyes were piggy and too small for his head. They reflected orange pinpoints of light as they scanned me.

I must have moved, because his ears perked. He panted and looked up at his mistress. She cooed at him. He panted faster and gave her hand a fast swipe with the pink slab of tongue.

"Hi there, big fella," I said. The words came out strangled. His jaws opened wider in a growling yawn.

I backed away and the dog arched his neck forward. He was a muscular beast, from head to quivering haunch.

"Now maybe I don't want you to go," said Kim Hickle.

I backed away further. Otto exhaled and made a sound that came from deep in his belly.

"I told you I won't give you away."

"So you say."

I took two more steps backward. Baby steps. Playing a deranged version of Simon Says. The dog moved closer.

"I just wanted to be alone," she said. "Nobody to bother me. Me and Otto." She looked lovingly at the great brute. "You found out. You bother me. How did you find me?"

"You left your name in a library file at Jedson College."

She frowned, bothered by her carelessness.

"So you hunted me."

"No. It was an accident, finding the card. It's not you I'm after."

She clicked her tongue again and Otto came a few feet closer. His malevolent leer loomed larger. I could smell him, rank and eager.

"First you, now others will follow. Asking questions. Blaming me, saying I'm bad. I'm not bad. I'm a good woman, good for children. I was a good wife to a sick man, not a sick woman."

"I know," I soothed. "It wasn't your fault."

Another click. The dog moved within springing distance. She had him controlled, like a radio-operated toy. Start, Otto. Stop, Otto. Kill, Otto . . .

"No. Not my fault."

I stepped back. Otto followed me, stalking, one paw scraping the ground, the shorthairs rising.

"I'll go," I said. "We don't have to talk. It's not that important. You deserve your privacy." I was rambling, stalling for time, my eyes on the tools in the corner. Mentally, I measured the distance to the pitchfork, covertly rehearsing the move I might have to make.

"I gave you a chance. You didn't take it. Now it's too late."

She clicked twice and the dog sprang, coming at me in a blur of snarling darkness. I saw the forepaws raised in the air, the wet, hungry, gnashing mouth, the orange eyes zeroed on their target, all in a fraction of a second. Still within that second, I feinted to the right, sank to my knees and lunged for the pitchfork. My fingers closed around wood and I snatched it and jabbed upward.

He came down on me, a ton of coiled monster, crushing the breath from my chest, the paws and teeth scraping and snapping. Something went through cloth, then leather, then skin. Pain took hold of my arm from elbow to shoulder, piercing and sickening. The handle of the pitchfork slipped from my grasp. I shielded my face with one sleeve, as Otto nuzzled at me with his wet nose, trying to get those buzz-saw jaws around my neck. I twisted away, reached out blindly for the pitchfork, got hold of it, lost it and found it again. I landed a knuckle punch on the crown of his skull. It was like pummeling armor plate. He reared up on his hind legs, roaring with rage and bore down. I turned the pitchfork prong-upwards. He lunged, throwing his full weight down on me. My legs bent and my back hit the dirt. The air went out of me and I fought for consciousness, swallowed up in churning fur and struggling to keep the fork between us.

Then he whinnied shrilly; at the same time I felt the pitchfork hit bone, scrape and slide as I twisted the handle, full of hate. The prongs went into him like a warm knife into butter.

We embraced, the dog's tongue on my ear, his mouth slavering, open in agony, an inch from carving out a chunk of my face. I put all of my strength behind the pitchfork, pushing and twisting, vaguely aware of the sound of a woman screaming. He cried out like a puppy. The prongs went in a final inch and then could sink no deeper. His eyes opened wide with injured pride, blinked spasmodically, then closed. The huge body shuddered convulsively atop me. A tide of blood shot out of his mouth, splashing across my nose, lips and chin. I gagged on the warm, salty muck. Life passed out of him and I struggled to roll free.

The whole thing had taken less than half a minute.

Kim Hickle looked at the dead dog, then at me, and made a run for the door. I pulled myself to standing position, yanked the pitchfork out of the barrel chest and blocked her way.

"Get back," I gasped. I moved the pitchfork and droplets of gore flew through the air. She froze.

The greenhouse was silent. The rain had stopped. The silence was broken by a low, rumbling noise: bubbles of gas escaping from the big dog's corpse. A mound of feces followed, running down the limp legs and mingling with the mulch.

She watched it and started to cry. Then she went limp and sat on the floor with the hopeless, stuporous look of a refugee.

I jammed the pitchfork into the ground and used it to lean on. It took me a full minute to catch my breath, another two or three to check for damages.

The raincoat was ruined, torn and blood-soaked. With some effort I got it off and let it fall to the ground. One arm of the leather jacket was shredded. I slipped out of it, too, and rolled up the sleeve of the turtleneck. I inspected my bicep. The layers of clothing had prevented it from being worse but it wasn't pretty: three puncture wounds that had already begun to swell, surrounded by a maze of abrasions. The arm felt stiff and sore. I bent it and nothing felt broken. The same went for my ribs and my other limbs, although my entire body floated just above agony. I stretched carefully, using a limbering routine I'd learned from Jaroslav. It made me feel a little better.

"Did Otto have his shots?" I asked.

She didn't answer. I repeated the question, punctuating it with a grasp of the pitchfork handle.

"Yes. I have the papers."

"I want to see them."

"It's true. You can believe me."

"You just tried to get that monster to rip out my throat. Right now your credibility isn't high."

She looked at the dead animal and went into a meditative sway. She seemed to be one who was used to waiting. I was in no mood for a battle of endurance.

"You've got two choices, Mrs. Hickle. One, cooperate

and I'll leave you to your little *Walden*. Or, you can make it hard for me and I'll see that your story makes page one of the *L.A. Times* Metro section. Think of it: Molester's widow finds refuge in abandoned homesite. Poetic, isn't it? Ten to one the wire services pick it up.''

"What do you want from me?"

"Answers to questions. I've no reason—or desire—to hurt you.''

"You're really the one whose office Stuart—died in?''

"Yes. Who else were you expecting?''

"No one," she said too quickly.

"Towle? Hayden? McCaffrey?''

At the mention of each name her face registered pain sequentially, as if her bones were being broken in stages.

"I'm not with them. But I want to know more about them.''

She raised herself to a squat, stood, and picked up the bloodied raincoat. Carefully she placed it over the dog's still form.

"I'll talk to you," she said.

25

THERE WAS an entrance to the four-car garage that had eluded me: At ground level, hidden behind an untrimmed blue spruce, was a window covered with chicken-coop wire mesh. She kneeled, played with a couple of strategic strands and the mesh came loose. A push, a wriggle and she was inside. I followed. I was much larger and it wasn't easy. My injured arm brushed against the pane and I had to hold my breath to stop from crying out as I squeezed through.

A half-jump brought me to a narrow room that had originally been a root cellar. It was damp and dark, the walls lined with shallow wooden shelving, the floor of poured concrete painted red. There was a wooden shutter above the window, held in place by an eye and hook. She unfastened it and it slammed shut. There was a second of darkness during which I braced myself for something devious. Instead came the pleasing pungence of kerosene, reminiscent of teenage love by the light of the campfire, and smoky illumination. She tilted the slats of the shutter so that additional light came in but visibility from the outside was obscured.

My eyes adjusted to the light and the details came into focus: A thin pallet and bedroll lay on the floor. The kerosene lamp, a hot plate, a can of Sterno and a packet of plastic utensils shared space on a rickety wooden table that had been painted and repainted so many times it looked like soft sculpture. There was a utility sink in one corner and above it a rack holding an empty jam jar, a toothbrush, toothpowder, safety razor and a bar of laundry soap. Most of the remaining floor space was taken up by wooden milk cartons of a type I hadn't seen since child-hood. The boxes had tube-shaped hand holes on two sides and bore the imprint of "Farmer Del's Dairy, Tacoma, Wash—Our Butter Is Best, Put It to the Test." Below the slogan was a picture of a bored-looking heifer and a phone number with a two-letter prefix. She'd stacked the cartons three-high in places. The contents of some of them were visible—packets of freeze-dried food, canned goods, paper towels, folded clothing. Three pairs of shoes, all rubber-soled and sturdy, were lined up neatly against the wall. There were metal hooks hammered into a raw wood support beam. She hung her slicker on one of them and sat down on a straight-backed chair of unfinished pine. I settled myself on an overturned milk carton.

We looked at each other.

In the absence of competing stimuli the pain in my arm took over. I winced, and she saw it.

She got up, soaked a paper towel in warm water, came over and swabbed the wound. She poked around in one of the boxes and found sterile gauze, adhesive tape and hydrogen peroxide. Tending to me like Florence Nightingale, she bandaged the arm. The craziness of the situation wasn't lost on me—minutes ago she'd tried to kill me, now she clucked maternally and smoothed down the tape. I stayed karate-wary, expecting her to revert at any moment to murderous rage, to dig her fingers into the inflamed flesh and take advantage of the blinding pain to jab me in the eye.

But when she was finished she returned to her seat.

"The papers," I reminded her.

More poking around. But quick. She knew exactly where everything was. A sheaf of papers bound with a thick rubber band found its way into my hand. There were veterinarian's bills, rabies vaccination records, Kennel Club registration—the dog's full name had been Otto Klaus Von Schulderheis out of Stuttgart-Munsch and Sigourn-Daffodil. Quaint. There were also diplomas from two obedience schools in L.A. and a certificate stating that Otto had been trained as an attack dog for defensive purposes only. I handed the papers back to her.

"Thank you," she said.

We sat across from one another, pleasant as school

chums. I took a good look at her and tried to work up some genuine animosity. What I saw was a sad-looking Oriental woman in her forties, her hair chopped China-doll short, sallow, frail, homely in baggy work clothes and shabby as a churchmouse. She sat, hands in lap, docile. The hatred wouldn't come.

"How long have you been living here?"

"Six months. Since Stuart's death."

"Why live like this—why not open up the house?"

"I thought this would be better for hiding. All I want is to be alone."

She didn't make much of a Garbo.

"Hiding from whom?"

She looked at the floor.

"Come on. I won't hurt you."

"The others. The other sick ones."

"Names."

"The ones you mentioned and others." She spit out a half-dozen other names I didn't recognize.

"Let's be specific. By sick you mean child molesters—all those men are child molesters?"

"Yes, yes. I didn't know it. Stuart told me later, when he was in prison. They volunteered at a children's home, took the kids to their houses. Did sick things with them."

"And at your school, too."

"No! That was only Stuart. The others never came to the school. Only at the children's home."

"La Casa de los Niños. Your husband was a member of the Gentleman's Brigade."

"Yes. He told me he was doing it to help children. His friends recruited him, he said. The judge, the doctor, the others. I thought it was so nice of him—we didn't have children of our own—I was proud of him. I never knew what he was really doing—just like I didn't know about what he did at the school."

I said nothing.

"I know what you're thinking—what they all thought. That I knew all along. How could I not know what my own husband was doing in my own house? You blame me as much as you blame Stuart. I tell you, I didn't know!"

Her arms went out beseechingly, the hands saffron talons. I noticed that the nails had been gnawed to the quick. There was a desperate, feral look on her face.

"I did not know," she repeated, turning it into a self-punishing mantra. "I did not know. He was my husband but I did not know!"

She was in need of absolution but I didn't feel like a father confessor. I stayed tight-lipped and observed her with forced detachment.

"You must understand the kind of marriage Stuart and I had to see how he could have been doing all of those things without my knowledge."

My silence said Convince me.

She bowed her head and began.

"We met in Seoul," she said, "shortly after the war. My father had been a professor of linguistics. Our family was prosperous, but we had ties to the socialists and the KCIA killed them all. They went on rampages after the war, murdering intellectuals, anyone who wasn't a blind slave to the regime. Everything we owned was confiscated or destroyed. I was hidden, given to friends the day before KCIA thugs broke into the house and slit the throats of everyone—family, servants, even the animals. Things got worse, the government clamped down harder. The family that took me in grew frightened and I was turned out to the street. I was fifteen years old, but very small, very skinny, looking twelve. I begged, ate scraps. I—I sold myself. I had to. To survive."

She stopped, looked past me, gathered her strength and continued.

"When Stuart found me I was feverish, infested with lice and venereal disease, covered with sores. It was at night. I was huddled under newspapers in an alley at the back of a café where the GI's went to eat and drink and find bar girls. I knew it was good to wait in such places because Americans threw away enough food to feed entire families. I was so sick I could barely move, but I waited for hours, forcing myself to stay awake so the cats wouldn't get my dinner first. The restaurant closed shortly after midnight. The soldiers came out, loud, drunk, staggering through the alley. Then Stuart, by himself, sober. Later I found out he never drank alcohol. I tried to keep quiet but my pain made me cry out. He heard, came over, so big, a giant in uniform, bending over me saying 'Don't worry, little girl.' He picked me up in his arms and took me to his apartment. He had lots of money, enough to rent his own place off base. The GI's were on R and R, celebrating, making lots of unwanted babies. Stuart had nothing to do with those kinds of things. He used his place to write poetry. To fiddle with his cameras. To be alone.''

She seemed to lose track of time and space, and staring absently at the dark wooden walls.

"He took you to his place," I prompted.

"For five weeks he nursed me. He brought doctors, bought medicine. Fed me, bathed me, sat at my bedside reading comic books—I loved American comic books because my father had always brought them home to me from his travels. Little Orphan Annie. Terry and the Pirates. Dagwood. Blondie. He read them all to me, in a soft, gentle voice. He was different from any man I'd ever met. Thin, quiet, like a teacher, with those eyeglasses that made his eyes look so big, like a big bird.

"By the sixth week I was well. He came into bed and made love to me. I know now it was part of the sickness—he must have thought I was a child, that must have excited him. But I felt like a woman. Over the years as I became a woman, when I was clearly no longer a child, he lost interest in me. He used to like to dress me up in little girl's things—I'm small, I could fit into them. But when I grew up, saw the world outside, I would have nothing to do with that. I asserted myself and he withdrew. Maybe that was when he started to act out his sickness. Maybe,'' she said in a wounded voice, "it was my fault. For not satisfying him.''

"No. He was a troubled man. You don't have to bear that responsibility," I said, not with total sincerity. I didn't want it all to deteriorate into a wet session of self-recrimination.

"I don't know. Even now it seems so unreal. The papers, the stories about him. About us. He was such a kind man, gentle, quiet.''

I'd heard similar pictures painted of other child molesters. Often they were exceptionally mild-mannered men, with a natural ability to gain rapport with their young victims. But of course it had to be that way: kids won't flock to an unshaven ogre in a soiled trenchcoat. They *will* be drawn to Uncle Wally who's so much nicer than mean old Mom and Dad and all the other grownups who don't *understand*. To Uncle Wally with his magic tricks and neat collection of baseball cards and really terrific toys at his house and mopeds and video recorders, and cameras and neat, weird books . . .

"You must understand how much I loved him," she was saying. "He saved my life. He was American. He was rich. He said he loved me too. 'My little geisha' he called me. I'd laugh and tell him 'No, I'm Korean, you silly. The Japanese are pigs!' He'd smile and call me his little geisha again.

"We lived together in Seoul for four months. I waited for him to get off-base on leave, cooked for him, cleaned, brought him his slippers. Was his wife. When his discharge papers came, he told me he was taking me back to the states. I was in heaven. Of course his family—there was only a mother and some elderly aunts—would have nothing to do with me. Stuart didn't care. He had money of his own, trust funds from his father. We traveled together to Los Angeles. He said he'd gone to school there—he did go to medical school, but flunked out. He took a job as a medical technician. He didn't need to work, it was a job that didn't pay much, but he liked it, said it kept him busy. He liked the machines—the meters and the test tubes—he was always a tinkerer. Gave me his entire paycheck, as if it was petty cash, told me to spend it on myself.

"We lived together that way for three years. I wanted marriage, but couldn't ask. It took me a while to get used to American ways, to women not being just property, to having rights. I pushed it when I wanted children. Stuart was indifferent to the idea, but he went along with it. We married. I tried to get pregnant but couldn't. I saw doctors, at UCLA, Stanford, Mayo. They all said there was too much scarring. I'd been so sick in Korea, it shouldn't have surprised me, but I didn't want to believe it. Looking back now, I know it was a good thing we did not have any little ones. At the time, after I finally accepted it, I became depressed. Very withdrawn, not eating. Eventually Stuart couldn't ignore it any longer. He suggested I go to school. If I loved children I could work with them, become a teacher. He may have had his own motives, but he seemed concerned for me—whenever I was sick or low he was at his best.

"I enrolled in junior college, then college, and learned so much. I was a good student," she recalled, smiling. "Very motivated. For the first time I was out in the world, with other people—until then I'd *been* Stuart's little geisha. Now I began to think for myself. At the same time he drifted away from me. There was no anger, no resentment that he put into words. He simply spent more time with his cameras and his bird books—he used to like to read books and magazines on nature, though he never hiked or walked. An armchair bird lover. An armchair man.

"We became two distant cousins living in the same house. Neither of us cared, we were busy. I studied every spare moment, by now I knew I wanted to go beyond the bachelor's and get a credential in early childhood. We went our own ways. There were weeks when we never saw each other. There was no communication, no marriage. But no divorce either—what would have been the point? There were no fights. It was live and let live. My new friends, my college friends, told me I was liberated, I should be happy to have a husband who didn't bother me. When I became lonely I went deeper into my studies.

"I finished the credential and they gave me field placements at local preschools. I liked working with the little ones but I thought I could run a better school than those I had seen. I told Stuart, he said sure, anything to keep me happy, out of his way. We bought a big house in Brentwood—there always seemed to be money for anything—and I started Kim's Korner. It was a wonderful place, a wonderful time. I finally stopped mourning not having children of my own. Then he—"

She stopped, covered her face with her hands and rocked back and forth.

I got up and put a hand on her shoulder.

"Please don't do that. It's not right. I tried to have Otto kill you." She lifted her face, dry and unlined. "Do you understand that? I wanted him to *kill* you. Now you are being kind and understanding. It makes me feel worse."

I removed the hand and sat back down.

"Why the need for Otto, why the fear?"

"I thought you were sent by the ones who killed Stuart."

"The official verdict was that he killed himself."

She shook her head.

"No. He didn't commit suicide. They said he was depressed. It was a lie. Of course when he was first arrested, he was very low. Humiliated and guilty. But he bounced out of it. That was Stuart's way. He could block out reality as easily as exposing a roll of film. Poof, and the image is gone. The day before he was arraigned we spoke on the phone. He was in high spirits. To hear him talk, the arrest was the best thing that ever happened to him—to us. He'd been ill, now he would get help. We'd start all over again, as soon as he got out of the hospital. I could even get another school, in another city. He suggested Seattle and talked of our reclaiming the family mansion—that was how I got the idea to come here.

"I knew it would never happen. By then I'd decided to leave him. But I went along with the fantasies, saying, yes, dear, certainly, Stuart. Later we had other conversations and it was the same thing. Life was going to be better than ever. He was not talking like a man about to blow his brains out."

"It's not that simple. People often kill themselves right after an upswing in mood. The suicide season is spring, you know."

"Perhaps. But I know Stuart and I know he didn't kill himself. He was too shallow to let something like the arrest bother him for a long time. He could deny anything. He denied me for all those years, denied our marriage— that's why he could do those things without my knowing about them. We were strangers."

"But you know him well enough to be sure he didn't commit suicide."

"Yes," she insisted. "That story about the false phone call to you, the picked locks. That kind of scheming isn't—wasn't Stuart. For all his sickness he was naïve, almost simple. He wasn't a planner."

"It took planning to get those children down in the cellar."

"You don't have to believe me. I don't care. He's done his damage. Now he's dead. And I'm in a cellar of my own."

Her smile was pitiful.

The lamp sputtered. She got up to adjust the wick and add more kerosene. When she sat back down I asked her: "Who killed him and why?"

"The others. His so-called friends. So he wouldn't expose them. And he would have. During our last visits he'd hint around. Say things like, 'I'm not the only sick one, Kimmy' or 'Things aren't what they seem with the Gentlemen.' I knew he wanted me to ask him, to help him spill it out. But I didn't. I was still in shock over losing the school, wrapped in my own shame. I didn't want to hear about more perversions. I cut him off, changed the subject. But after he died it came back to me and I put it all together."

"Did he mention anyone by name as being sick?"

"No. But what else could he have meant? They'd come to pick him up, parking their big soft cars in the driveway, dressed in those sport jackets with the Casa insignia. When he'd leave with them he'd be excited. His hands trembling. He'd come back in the early hours of the morning, exhausted. Or the next day. Isn't it obvious what they were doing?"

"You haven't told anyone of your suspicions?"

"Who would believe me? Those men are powerful—doctors, lawyers, executives, that horrid little Judge Hayden. I wouldn't stand a chance, the wife of a molester. To the public I'm as guilty as Stuart. And there's no evidence—look what they did to him to shut him up. I had to run."

"Did Stuart ever mention knowing McCaffrey from Washington?"

"No. Did he?"

"Yes. What about a child named Cary Nemeth. Did his name come up?"

"No."

"Elena Gutierrez? Morton Handler—Doctor Morton Handler?"

"No."

"Maurice Bruno?"

She shook her head. "No. Who are these people?"

"Victims."

"Violated like the others?"

"The ultimate violation. Dead. Murdered."

"Oh my God." She put her hands to her face.

Telling her story had made her sweat. Strands of black hair stuck to her forehead. "So it continues," she said mournfully.

"That's why I'm here. To put an end to it. What else can you tell me that would help?"

"Nothing. I've told you everything. They killed him. They're evil men, hiding their ugly secret under a cloak of respectability. I ran to escape them."

I looked around the dingy room.

"How long can you continue this way?"

"Forever, if no one gives me away. The island is secluded, this property is hidden. When I have to go to the mainland to shop I dress like a cleaning maid. No one notices me. I stockpile as much as possible to avoid making too many trips. The last one was over a month ago. I live simply. The flowers are my one extravagance. I planted them from seed packets and bulbs. They occupy my time, with watering, feeding, pruning, re-potting. The days go by quickly."

"How safe can you be—Towle and Hayden have roots here."

"I know. But their families haven't lived here for a generation. I checked. I even went by their old homes. There are new faces, new names. There's no reason for them to look for me here. Not unless you give them one."

"I won't."

"On my next trip I'll buy a gun. I'll be prepared for them if they come. I'll escape and go somewhere else. I'm used to it. The memory of Seoul returns in my dreams. It keeps me watchful. I'm sorry to hear about the other murders, but I don't want to know about them. There's nothing that I can do."

I got up and she helped me on with my jacket.

"The funny thing is," she said, "this estate probably belongs to me. As does the Brentwood property and the rest of the Hickle fortune. I'm Stuart's sole heir—we wrote our wills several years ago. He never discussed finances with me so I don't know how much he left, but it has to be considerable. There were bearer bonds, other pieces of real estate all up and down the coast. In theory I'm a rich woman. Do I look it?"

"There's no way to get in touch with the executors of his will?"

"The executor is a partner in Edwin Hayden's law firm. For all I know he's one of *them*. I can do without wealth when all it means is a fancy funeral."

She used her chair to climb out of the window. I followed her. We walked in the direction of the big, black house.

"You worked with the children from my school. How are they doing?"

"Very well. The prognosis is good. They're amazingly resilient."

"That's good."

A few steps later:

"And the parents—did they hate me?"

"Some. Others were surprisingly loyal and defended you. It created a schism in the group. They worked it out."

"I'm glad. I think about them often."

She accompanied me to the edge of the swamp that fronted the mansion.

"I'll let you go the rest of the way by yourself. How does the arm feel?"

"Stiff, but nothing serious. I'll survive."

I held out my hand and she took it.

"Good luck," she said.

"Same to you."

I walked through weeds and mud, chilled and tired. When I turned around to look she was gone.

I stayed in the ferry's dining room drinking coffee for much of the return trip to the mainland, going over what I'd learned. When I got back to the hotel I called Milo at the station, was told he wasn't there and tried his home number. Rick Silverman answered.

"Hi, Alex. There's static. Is this long distance?"

"It is. Seattle. Is Milo back yet?"

"No. I expect him tomorrow. He went to Mexico on a supposed vacation but it sounds like work to me."

"It is. He's looking into the background of a guy named McCaffrey."

"I know. The minister with the children's home. He said you turned him on to it."

"I may have sparked his interest but when I spoke to him about it he brushed me off. Did he mention what led him to make the trip?"

"Let me see—I recall his saying he phoned the police down there—it's some small town, I forget the name—and they jerked him around. They implied they had something juicy for him but that he'd have to come up with some bucks to get it. It surprised me—I thought cops cooperated with each other—but he said that's the way they always are."

"That's it?"

"That's it. He invited me to come along but it didn't work out well with my schedule—I had a twenty-four-hour shift coming up and it would have required too much trading with the other guys."

"Have you heard from him since he left?"

"Just a postcard from the airport at Guadalajara. An old peasant pulling a burro next to a Saguaro cactus that looked plastic. Very classy stuff. He wrote 'Wish you were here' on it."

I laughed.

"If he does call, tell him to give me a ring. I've got some more information for him."

"Will do. Anything specific?"

"No. Just have him call."

"Okay."

"Thanks. Look forward to meeting you some day, Rick."

"Likewise. Maybe when he gets back and wraps things up."

"Sounds good."

I got out of my clothes and examined the arm. There was some oozing, but nothing bad. Kim Hickle had done a good patchup job. I did a half-hour of limbering exercises and a bit of karate, then soaked in a hot bath for forty-five minutes while reading the throwaway guide to Seattle the hotel had furnished.

I called Robin, got no answer, dressed and went for dinner. I remembered a place from my previous visit, a cedar-paneled room overlooking Lake Union, where they barbecued salmon over alder wood. I found it, using my memory and a map, arrived early enough to get a table with a view, and proceeded to put away a large salad with Roquefort, a beautiful coral-colored chinook filet, potatoes, beans, a basket of hot cornbread and two Coors. I topped it off with homemade blackberry ice cream and coffee and, with a full belly, watched the sun go down over the lake.

I browsed a couple of bookstores in the University District, found nothing exciting or uplifting, and drove back to the hotel. There was an Oriental imports shop in the lobby, still open. I went in, bought a green cloisonné necklace for Robin and rode the elevator back up to my room. At nine I called her again. This time she answered.

"Alex! I was hoping it was you."

"How are you, doll? I called you a couple of hours ago."

"I went out for dinner. By my lonesome. Ate an omelette in a corner of the Cafe Pelican all by myself. Isn't that a pathetic image?"

"I supped alone, too, my lady."

"How sad. Come home soon, Alex. I miss you."

"I miss you too."

"Was the trip productive?"

"Very." I filled her in on the details, careful to exclude my encounter with Otto.

"You're really on to something. Don't you feel strange, uncovering all those secrets?"

"Not really, but I'm not looking at it from the outside."

"I am, and believe me, it's freaky, Alex. I'll just be glad when Milo gets back and he can take over."

"Yes. How are things going with you?"

"Nothing nearly as exciting. One thing new. This morning I got a call from the head of a new feminist group—it's a kind of a women's chamber of commerce. I fixed this woman's banjo, she came down to pick it up and we got to talking. This was a couple of months ago. Anyway, she called and invited me to give a lecture to their group next week. The topic's something like The Female Artisan in Contemporary Society subtitle Creativity Meets the Business World."

"That's fantastic. I'll be sure to be there listening if they let me in."

"Don't you dare! I'm scared enough as it is. Alex, I've never given a speech before—I'm absolutely petrified."

"Don't worry. You know what you're talking about, you're bright and articulate, they'll love you."

"So you say."

"So I say. Listen, if you're really nervous I'll do a little hypnosis with you. To help you relax. It'll be a piece of cake."

"You think hypnosis will help?"

"Sure. With your imagination and creativity you'll be a terrific subject."

"I've heard you talk about it, how you used to do it with patients, but I never thought of asking you to do it with me."

"Usually, darling, we find other ways to occupy our time together."

"Hypnosis," she said. "Now I've got something else to worry about."

"Don't worry. It's harmless."

"Totally?"

"Yes. Totally, in your case. The only time you run into a problem is when the subject has major emotional conflicts or deep-seated problems. In those cases hypnosis can dredge up primal memories. You get a stress reaction, some terror. But even that can be helpful. The trained psychotherapist uses the anxiety constructively, to help the patient work it through."

"And that couldn't happen to me?"

"Certainly not. I guarantee it. You're the most normal person I've ever met."

"Ha. You've been retired too long!"

"I challenge you to come up with one single symptom of psychopathology."

"How about extreme horniness, hearing your voice and wanting to be able to touch you and grab you and put you in me?"

"Hmmm. Sounds serious."

"Then come on back and do something about it, Doctor."

"I'll be back tomorrow. Treatment will commence immediately."

"What time?"

"The plane lands at ten—a half-hour after that."

"Damn, I forgot—I have to go to Santa Barbara tomorrow morning. My aunt's sick, in the ICU at Cottage Hospital. It's a family thing, I have to be there. If you came in earlier we could have breakfast before I leave."

"I'm taking the earliest flight, hon."

"I suppose I could postpone it, show up later."

"Visit your aunt. We'll have dinner."

"It might be a late dinner."

"Drive straight to my place and we'll take it from there."

"All right. I'll try to make it by eight."

"That's great. Speedy recovery to your aunt. I love you."

"Love you too. Take care."

26

SOMETHING BOTHERED ME the next morning. The troubled feeling persisted during the ride to Sea-Tac and up the ramp to the plane. I couldn't get a handle on what is was that lurked in a bottom drawer of my mind, that lingered through the serving of the plastic food, the forced smiles of the flight attendants, the copilot's bad jokes. The harder I tried to bring it to the forefront of my consciousness the further back it sank. I felt the impatience and frustration of a child encountering a Chinese finger puzzle for the first time. So I decided to just ride with it, sit back and wait and see if it came to me on its own.

It wasn't until shortly before landing that it did. What had stuck in my head was last night's conversation with Robin. She'd asked me about the dangers of hypnosis and I'd given her a speech about it being harmless unless the experience stirred up latent conflicts. *Dredged up primal memories* had been my exact words. Dredge up primal memories and the reaction is often terror . . .

I was stuffed with tension as the landing wheels touched down. Once free, I jogged through and out of the airport, picked up the Seville in the overnight lot, paid a considerable ransom to get it out the gate and headed east on Century Boulevard. Caltrans, in its infinite wisdom, had chosen to set up construction in the middle of the road during the morning rush in and out of LAX and, caught in a jam, I cooked in the Cadillac for the mile to the San Diego Freeway on-ramp. I took the freeway north, connected to Santa Monica West, and exited just before Pacific Coast Highway. A drive down Ocean and a few turns brought me to the Palisades and the place where Morton Handler and Elena Gutierrez had lost their lives.

The door to Bonita Quinn's apartment was open. I heard cursing from within and entered. A man was standing in the front room kicking the floral sofa and muttering under his breath. He was in his forties, curly-haired, flabby and putty-colored with discouraged eyes and a steel-wool goatee separating his first chin from his second. He wore black slacks and a light blue nylon shirt that clung to every tuck and roll of his gelatinous torso. One hand held a cigarette and flicked ashes onto the carpet. The other groped for treasure behind a meaty ear. He kicked the couch again, looked up, saw me and waved the smoking hand around the tiny room.

"Okay, you can get to work."

"Doing what?"

"Loading this shit outta here—aren't you the mover—" he looked at me again, this time with sharpened eyes. "No, you don't look like a mover. Excuse me." He threw back his shoulders. "What can I do for you?"

"I'm looking for Bonita Quinn and her daughter."

"You and me both."

"She's gone?"

"Three friggin' days. With who know how many rent checks. I've got tenants complaining their calls weren't answered, repairs that haven't been done. I call her, no answer. So I come down here myself and find she's been gone for three days, left all this junk, hightailed it. I never had a good feeling about her. You do someone a favor, you get shafted. Happens every time."

He inhaled his cigarette, coughed and sucked again. There was yellow around the irises of his eyes; gray, unhealthy flesh pouched the wary orbs. He looked like a man recuperating from a coronary or just about to have one.

"What are you, collection agency?"

"I'm one of her daughter's doctors."

"Oh yeah? Don't tell me about doctors. It's one of you that got me into this in the first place."

"Towle?"

His eyebrows rose. "Yeah? You from his office? Cause if you are, I got plenty—"

"No. I just know him."

"Then you know he's a nag. Gets into stuff he has no business getting into. My wife hears me say this, she'll kill me. She loves the guy. Says he's terrific with the kids, so who am I to argue, right? What kind of doctor are you, anyway?"

"Psychologist."

"The kid had problems, huh? Wouldn't surprise me. She looked a little iffy, if you know what I mean." He held out his hand, tilted it like the wing of a glider.

"You said Dr. Towle got you into the mess with Bonita Quinn?"

"That's right. I met the guy once or twice, maybe. I don't know him from Adam. One day he calls me out of the clear blue and asks me if I could give a job to a patient of his. He heard there was an opening for a manager in this place, and could I help this lady out. I say does this person have experience—we're talking multiple units here, not some duplex. He says no, but she can learn, she's got a kid, needs the money. I say, listen, Doc, this particular building is singles-oriented, the job's not right for someone with a kid. The manager's place is too small." He looked at me scowling. "Would you stick a kid in a hole like this?"

"No."

"Me neither. You don't have to be a doctor to see it's not fit. I tell Towle this. I explain it to him. I say, Doc, this job is meant for a single person. Usually I get a student from UCLA to do it—they don't need a lot of space. I've got other buildings, I tell him. In Van Nuys, a couple in Canoga Park, more family-oriented. Let me call my man in the Valley, have him check it out, I'll see if I can help this person.

"Towle says, no, it has to be this building. The kid's already enrolled in school in this neighborhood, to move her would be traumatic, he's a doctor, he knows this to be a fact. I say, but Doc, you can't have kids making noise in a place like this. The tenants are mostly singles, some like to sleep late. He says I guarantee you this kid is well-behaved, she makes no noise. I think to myself this kid makes no noise, there's gotta be something wrong with her—now *you* show up and it makes sense.

"I try to put him off, but he presses me. He's a nag. My wife loves him, she'll kill me if I get him pissed off, so I say okay. He makes an appointment for me to meet this lady, shows up with the Quinn broad and the kid. I was surprised. I gave it a little thought the night before, figured he was humping this broad, that's why the Albert Schweitzer routine. I expected something classy, with curves. One of those aspiring actress types, you know what I mean? He's older, but he's a classy-looking guy, right? So in he walks with her and the kid and they look like a pair outta the Dust Bowl, real hicks. The mother is scared outta her skull, she's smoking more than me, which is a feat—the kid's, like I told you, a little iffy, just stares into space, though I'll grant you she's quiet. Didn't make a sound. I had my doubts she could handle the job, but what could I do, I already committed myself. I hired her. She did okay. She was a hard worker, but she learned very slowly. No complaints about the kid, though. Anyway, she stays for a few months, then she flies the coop leaving me with this junk and she's probably got five grand worth of rent checks, I have to go back and trace 'em and have the tenants put stops on 'em and write new ones. I gotta clean this place, hire someone new. Let me tell you, no more Mister Nice Guy for Marty. For doctors or anyone else."

He folded his arms over his chest.

"You have no idea where she went?" I asked.

"I did, would I be standing here jawing with you?"

He went into the bedroom. It was as bleak as I remembered it.

"Look at this. How can people raise kids like this? I got three, each has his own room, they got TV's, bookshelves, Pac Mans, all that stuff. How can a kid's mind grow in a place like this?"

"If you hear from her or find out where she is, would you please call me?" I took out an old business card, crossed out the number and wrote my home phone number on it.

He glanced at it, and put it in his pocket. Running one finger along the top of the dresser he came up with a digit cloaked with dust kittys. He flung the dust away. "Yecch. I hate dirt. I like things to be clean, know what I mean? My apartments are always clean—I pay extra for the best cleaning service. It's important tenants should feel healthy in a place."

"You'll call me?"

"Sure, sure. You do the same for me, too, okay? I wouldn't mind finding Miss Bonita, get my checks back, give her a piece of my mind." He fished in his pocket, pulled out an alligator billfold and from it produced a pearl-gray business card that said M and M Properties, Commercial and Residential, Marduk I. Minassian, President, followed by a Century City address.

"Thanks, Mr. Minassian."

"Marty."

He continued probing and inspecting, opening drawers and shaking his head, bending to look under the bed Bonita Quinn had shared with her daughter. He found something under there, stood up, looked at it and tossed it in a metal wastebasket where it landed with a clang.

"What a mess."

I looked in the basket, saw what he had discarded, and pulled it out.

It was the shrunken head Melody had shown me the day we'd spent together at the beach. I held it in my palm and the rhinestone eyes glared back, glossy and evil. Most of the synthetic hair had come loose but a few black strands stuck out of the top of the snarling face.

"That's junk," said Minassian. "It's dirty. Throw it away."

I closed my hand over the child's keepsake, more sure than ever that the hypothesis I'd developed on the plane was right. And that I had to move fast. I put the shrunken head in my pocket, smiled at Minassian, and left.

"Hey!" he called after me. And then he muttered something that sounded like "Crazy doctors!"

I retraced my route, got back on the freeway and headed East, driving like a demon and hoping the Highway Patrol wouldn't spot me. I had my L.A.P.D. consultant badge in my pocket but I doubted it would help. Even police consultants aren't supposed to weave in and out of traffic going eighty miles an hour.

I was lucky. Traffic was light, the guardians of the asphalt were nowhere to be seen, and I made it to the

Silver Lake exit just before one. Five minutes later I was walking up the steps to the Gutierrez home. The orange and yellow poppies drooped, thirsty. The porch was empty. It creaked as I stepped onto it.

I knocked on the door. Cruz Gutierrez answered, knitting needles and bright pink yarn in her hands. She didn't seem surprised to see me.

"*Sí, señor?*"

"I need your help, señora."

"No *hablo inglés.*"

"Please. I know you understand enough to help."

The dark, round face was impassive.

"Señora, the life of a child is at stake." That was optimism speaking. "*Una niña.* Seven years old—*siete años.* She's in danger. She could be killed. *Muerta*—like Elena."

I let that sink in. Liver spotted hands tightened around the blue needles. She looked away.

"Like the other child—the Nemeth boy. Elena's student. He didn't die in an accident, did he? Elena knew that. She died because of that knowledge."

She put her hand on the door and started to close it. I blocked it with the heel of my palm.

"I feel for your loss, señora, but if Elena's death is to take on meaning, it can be through preventing more killing. Through stopping the deaths of others. Please."

Her hands started shaking. The needles rattled like chopsticks in the grasp of a spastic. She dropped them and the ball of yarn. I bent and retrieved them.

"Here."

She took them, held them to her bosom.

"Come in, please," she said, in English that was barely accented.

I was too edgy to want to sit but when she motioned me to the green velvet sofa I settled in it. She sat across from me as if awaiting sentence.

"First," I said, "you must understand that darkening Elena's memory is the last thing I want to do. If other lives were not at stake I wouldn't be here at all."

"I understand," she said.

"The money—is it here?"

She nodded, got up, left the room and came back minutes later with a cigar box.

"Take." She gave me the box as if it held something alive and dangerous.

The bills were in large denominations—twenties, fifties, hundreds—neatly rolled and held together by thick rubber bands. I made a cursory count. There was at least fifty thousand dollars in the box, probably a good deal more.

"Take it," I said.

"No, no. I don't want. Black money."

"Just keep it here, until I come back for it. Does anyone else know about it—either of your sons?"

"No." She shook her head adamantly. "Rafael know he take it and buy the dope. No. Only me."

"How long have you had it here?"

"Elena, she bring it over the day before she was killed." The mother's eyes filled with tears. "I say, what is this, where you get this. She say, can't tell you, Mama. Jus' keep it for me. I come back for it. She never come back." She pulled a lace-trimmed handkerchief from up her sleeve and dabbed at her eyes.

"Please. Take it back. Hide it again."

"Only a little while, señor, okay? Black money. Bad eye. *Mal ojo.*"

"I'll come back for it if that's what you want."

She took the box, disappeared again, and returned shortly.

"You're sure Rafael didn't know?"

"I sure. He know, it would all be gone."

That made sense. Junkies weren't known for being able to hold on to their nickels and dimes, let alone a small fortune.

"Another question, señora. Raquel told me that Elena had in her possession certain tapes—recorded tapes. Of music, and of relaxation exercises given to her by Dr. Handler. When I went through her things I found no such tapes. Do you know anything about that?"

"I don' know. This is the truth."

"Has anyone been through those boxes before I got here?"

"No. Only Rafael an' Antonio, they look for books, things to read. The *policía* take boxes first. Nothin' else."

"Where are your sons, now?"

She stood up, suddenly agitated.

"Don' hurt. They good boys. They don' know nothin'."

"I won't. I just want to talk to them."

She looked to one side, at the wall covered with family portraits. At her three children, young, innocent and smiling; the boys with short hair, slicked and parted, and open-necked white shirts; the girl in a frilly blouse between them. At the graduation picture: Elena in mortarboard and gown, wearing a look of eagerness and confidence, ready to take on the world with her brains and her charm and her looks. At the somber-tinted photo of her long-dead husband, stiff and solemn in starched collar and gray serge suit, a workingman unaccustomed to the fuss and fiddling that went with having one's countenance recorded for posterity.

She looked at the pictures and her lips moved, almost imperceptibly. Like a general surveying a smoldering battlefield, she conducted a silent body count.

"Andy working," she said, and gave me the address of a garage on Figueroa.

"And Rafael?"

"Rafael I don' know. He say he go look for work."

She and I both knew where he was. But I'd opened enough wounds for one day, so I kept my mouth shut, except to thank her.

I found him after a half-hour's cruising up and down Sunset and in and out of several side streets. He was walking south on Alvarado, if you could call the stumbling, self-absorbed lurch that propelled him headfirst, feet following, a walk. He stayed close to buildings, veering toward the street when people or objects got in his way, quickly returning to the shadow of awnings. It was close to eighty but he wore a long-sleeved flannel shirt hanging loose over khakis and buttoned to the neck. On his feet were high-topped sneakers; the laces on one of them had come loose. He looked even thinner than I remembered.

I drove slowly, staying in the right lane, out of his field of vision, and keeping pace with him. Once he passed a group of middle-aged men, merchants. They pointed at him behind his back, shook their heads and frowned. He was oblivious to them, cut off from the external world. He

pointed with his face, like a setter homing in on a scent.
His nose ran continuously and he wiped it with his sleeve.
His eyes shifted from side to side as his body kept moving.
He ran his tongue over his lips, slapped his thin thighs in a
steady tattoo, pursed his lips as if in song, bobbed his head
up and down. He was making a concentrated effort at
looking cool but he fooled no one. Like a drunk working
hard at coming across sober his mannerisms were exagger-
ated, unnatural and lacking spontaneity. They produced
the opposite effect: He appeared to be a hungry jackal on
the prowl, desperate, gnawed upon from within and hurting all over. His skin was glossy with sweat, pale and
ghostly. People got out of his way as he boogied toward
them.

I sped up and drove two blocks before pulling to the
curb and parking near an alley behind a three-story building that housed a Latin grocery on the ground floor and
apartments on the upper two.

A quick look shot backward confirmed that he was still
coming.

I got out of the car and ducked into the alley, which
stunk of rotting produce and urine. Empty and broken
wine bottles littered the pavement. A hundred feet away
was a loading dock, unattended, its steel doors closed and
bolted. A dozen vehicles were illegally parked on both
sides; exit from the alley was blocked by a half-ton pickup
left perpendicular to the walls. Somewhere off in the
distance a mariachi band played "Cielito Lindo." A cat
screeched. Horns honked out on the boulevard. A baby
cried.

I peeked my head out and retracted it. He was half a
block away. I got ready for him. When he began crossing
the alley I said in a stage whisper: "Hey, man. I got what
you need."

That stopped him. He looked at me with great love,
thinking he'd found salvation. It threw him off when I
grabbed him by his scrawny arm and pulled him into the
alley. I dragged him several feet until we'd found cover
behind an old Chevy with peeling paint and two flat tires. I
slammed him against the wall. His hands went up protec-
tively. I pushed them down and pinioned both of them

with one of my own. He struggled but he had no strength. It was like tussling with a toddler.

"Whadyou want, man?"

"Answers, Rafael. Remember me? I visited you a few days ago. With Raquel."

"Hey, yeah, sure," he said, but there was only confusion in the watery hazel eyes. Snot ran down one nostril and into his mouth. He let it sit there a while before reaching up with his tongue and trying to flick it away. "Yeah, I remember, man. With Raquel, sure, man." He looked up and down the alley.

"You remember, then, that I'm investigating your sister's murder."

"Oh, yeah, sure. Elena. Bad stuff, man." He said it without feeling. His sister had been sliced up and all he could think of was that he needed a packet of white powder that could be transformed into his own special type of milk. I'd read dozens of tomes on addiction, but it was there, in that alley, that the true power of the needle became clear to me.

"She had tapes, Rafael. Where are they?"

"Hey, man, I don' know shit about tapes." He struggled to break loose. I slammed him against the wall again. "Oh, man, I'm hurting, just let me go fix myself up and then I talk to you about tapes. Okay, man?"

"No. I want to know now, Rafael. Where are the tapes?"

"I don' know, man, I told you that!" He was whining like a three-year-old, snotfaced and growing more frantic with each passing second.

"I think you do and I want to know."

He bounced in my grasp, clattering like a sack of loose bones.

"Lemme go, motherfucker!" he gasped.

"Your sister was murdered, Rafael. Turned into hamburger. I saw pictures of what she looked like. Whoever did it to her took their time. It hurt her. And you're willing to deal with them."

"I don' know what you're talkin' about, man."

More struggling, another slam against the wall. He sagged this time, closed his eyes and for a moment I thought I'd knocked him out. But he opened them, licked his lips and gave a dry, hacking cough.

"You were off the stuff, Rafael. Then you started shooting up again. Right after Elena's death. Where'd you get the dough? How much did you sell her out for?"

"I don' know nothin'." He shook spastically. "Lemme go. I don' know nothin'."

"Your own sister," I said. "And you sold out to her murderers for the price of a fix."

"*Puleeze*, mister. Lemme go."

"Not until you talk. I don't have time to waste time with you. I want to know where those tapes are. You don't tell me soon I'll take you home with me, tie you up and let you go cold turkey in the corner. Imagine that—think how bad you hurt now, Rafael. Think how much worse it's going to get."

He crumpled.

"I gave them to some dude," he stuttered.

"For how much?"

"Not money, man. Stuff. He gave me stuff. Enough for a week's fixing. Good stuff. Now lemme go. I gotta appointment."

"Who was the guy?"

"Just some dude. Anglo. Like you."

"What did he look like?"

"I don' know, man, I can't think straight."

"The corner, Rafael. Tied up."

"Twenny-five, six. Short. Built good, solid. Real straight-lookin'. Light hair, over the forehead, okay?"

He'd described Tim Kruger.

"Why did he say he wanted the tapes?"

"He dint say, man, I dint ask. He had good stuff, you unnerstand?"

"Didn't you wonder? Your sister was dead and you didn't wonder why some stranger would give you smack for her tapes?"

"Hey, man, I dint wonder, I don' wonder. I don' think. I just go flyin'. I gotta go flyin' now. I'm hurtin', man. Lemme go."

"Did your brother know about this?"

"No! He kill me, man. You hurt me, but he *kill* me, you unnerstand? Don' tell him!"

"What was on the tapes, Rafael?"

"I dunno. I don' listen, man!"

On principle I refused to believe him.

"The corner. Tied up. Bone dry."

"Jus' some kid talkin', man, I swear that's it. I dint hear the whole thing, but when he offered me the stuff for them I took a listen before I gave them to the dude. Some kid talkin' to my sister. She's listenin' and sayin' tell me more and he's talkin'."

"About what?"

"I don' know man. It started to get heavy, the kid's cryin', Elena's cryin', I switched it off. I don' wanna know."

"What were they crying about, Rafael?"

"I don' know, man, something about how somebody hurt the kid, Elena's askin' him if they hurt him, he's sayin' yes, she's cryin', then the kid's cryin', too."

"What else?"

"That's it."

I throttled him just hard enough to rattle his teeth.

"You wan' me to make somethin' up, I can do it, man, but that's all I know!"

He cried out, snuffling and sucking for air.

I held him at arm's length, then let go. He looked at me unbelievingly, slithered against the wall, found a space between the Chevy and a rusted Dodge van. Staring at me, he wiped his nose, passed between the two cars and made a run for freedom.

I drove to a gas station at Virgil and Sunset, filled up, and used the pay phone to call La Casa de los Niños. The receptionist with the upbeat voice answered. Slipping into a drawl I asked her for Kruger.

"Mr. Kruger isn't in, today, sir. He'll be in tomorrow."

"Oh yeah, that's right! He told me he'd be off the day I got in."

"Would you care to leave a message, sir?"

"Heck no. I'm an old friend from school. Tim and I go way back. I just blew in on a business trip—I'm selling tool and die, Becker Machine Works, San Antonio, Texas— and I was supposed to look old Tim up. He gave me his number at home but I must have lost it. Do you have it?"

"I'm sorry, sir, we're not supposed to give out personal information."

"I can dig that. But like I say, Tim and me are tight. Why don't you call him at home, tell him old Jeff Saxon's on the line, ready to drop in but stuck without the address."

A clatter of ringing phones sounded in the background.

"One moment, sir."

When she returned I asked her:

"You call him yet, ma'am?"

"No—I—it's rather busy right now, Mr . . . .."

"Saxon. Jeff Saxon. You call old Tim and tell him old Jeff Saxon's in town to see him, I guarantee you he'll be—"

"Why don't I just give you the number?" She recited seven digits, the first two of which signified a beach cities location.

"Thank you much, I believe Tim told me he lived near the beach—that far from the airport?"

"Mr. Kruger lives in Santa Monica. It's about a twenty-minute ride."

"Hey, that's not bad—maybe I'll just drop in on him, kind of a surprise, what do you think?"

"Sir, I have to—"

"You wouldn't happen to have the address? I tell you, it's been one hell of a day, what with the airline losing my sample case and I've got two meetings tomorrow. I think I packed the address book in the suitcase, but now I can't be sure and—"

"Here's the address, sir."

"Thank you much, ma'am. You've been very helpful. And you have a nice voice."

"Thank you, sir."

"You free tonight?"

"I'm sorry, sir, no."

"Fellow's gotta try, right?"

"Yes, sir. Good-bye, sir."

I'd been driving north for a good five minutes before I heard the buzzing. I realized, then, that the sound had been with me since I'd pulled out of the gas station. The rearview mirror revealed a motorcycle several lengths back, bouncing in the distance like a fly on a hot windshield.

The driver twisted the handle accelerator and the fly grew like a monster in a Japanese horror flick.

He was two lengths behind, and gaining. As he approached I got a look at him, jeans, boots, black leather jacket, black helmet with full-face tinted sun visor that completely masked his features.

He rode my tail for several blocks. I changed lanes. Instead of passing, he hung back, allowing a Ford full of nuns to come between us. A half mile past Lexington the nuns turned off. I steered sharply toward the curb and came to a sudden stop in front of a Pup 'n Taco. The motorcycle sped by. I waited until he'd disappeared, told myself I was being paranoid, and got out of the Seville. I looked for him, didn't see him, bought a Coke, got behind the wheel and reentered the boulevard.

I'd turned east on Temple headed for the Hollywood Freeway when I heard him again. Verifying his presence in the mirror caused me to miss the on ramp, and I stayed on Temple, dipping under the bridge created by the overpass. The motorcycle stayed with me. I gave the Seville gas and ran a red light. He maintained his position, buzzing and spitting. The next intersection was filled with pedestrians and I had to stop.

I kept a watch on him through the side mirror. He rolled toward me, three feet away, now two, approaching on the driver's side. One hand went inside the leather jacket. A young mother wheeled a small child in a stroller, passing directly in front of my bumper. The child wailed, the mother chewed gum, heavy-legged, moving oh so slowly. Something metallic came into the hand in the mirror. The motorcycle was just behind me, almost flush with the driver's window. I saw the gun now, an ugly little snub-nosed affair, easy to conceal in a large palm. I raced my engine. The gum-chewing young matron wasn't impressed. She seemed to move in slow motion, indolently working her jaws, the child now screaming at the top of his lungs. The light remained red but its catercornered cousin had turned amber. The longest light in the history of traffic engineering . . . how long could an amber light last?

The snout of the revolver pressed against the glass, directly in line with my left temple. A black hole miles long wrapped in a concentric halo of silver. The mother still dragged her heavy body lazily across the intersection, her heel in line with my right front tire, unaware that the man in the green Cadillac was going to be blown away any second. The finger on the trigger blanched. The mother stepped clear by an inch. I twisted the steering wheel to the left, pressed down hard on the accelerator and shot diagonally across the intersection into the path of the ongoing traffic. I gunned the engine, laid a long patch of rubber, heard a Delphic chorus of curses, shouts, honking horns and squealing brakes, and shot up the first side street, narrowly missing a head-on collision with a Water and Power van coming from the opposite direction.

The street was narrow and winding, and pocked with potholes. The Seville was no sports car and I had to fight its slack steering system to maintain speed and control around the turns. I climbed, bounced down hard, and swooped steeply down a hill. A boulevard stop at the bottom was clear. I sped through. Three blocks of level turf at seventy miles an hour and the buzz was back, growing louder. The motorcycle, so much easier to maneuver, was catching up fast.

The road came to an end at a cracked masonry wall. Left or right? Decisions, decisions, with the adrenaline shooting through every corpuscle, the buzz now a roar, my hands sweaty, slipping off the wheel. I looked in the mirror, saw one hand come off the bars and aim the gun at my tires. I chose left and floored the Seville, putting my body into it. The road rose, scaling empty streets, higher, spiraling into the smog, a roller coaster of a street planned by a berserk engineer. The motorcyclist kept riding up on my rear, raking his gun hand off the bars whenever he could, striving for steady aim . . .

I swerved continuously, dancing out of his sights, but the narrowness of the street gave me little leeway. I knew I had to avoid slipping unconsciously into a regular rhythm— back and forth, back and forth, a gasoline-fueled metronome —for to do so would be to offer an easy target. I drove erratically, crazily, jerking the wheel, slowing down, speeding up, careening against the curb, losing a hubcap that spun off like a chromium Frisbee. It was a direct assault on my axle and I didn't know how long it could last.

We continued to climb. A view of Sunset below ap-

peared around a corner. We were back in Echo Park, on
the south side of the boulevard. The road hit its peak. A
shot whizzed by so close that the Seville's windows vibrated. I swerved and a second shot went far afield.

The terrain changed as the altitude rose, thinning from
residential blocks of frame houses to progressively emptier
stretches of dusty lots, with here and there a decrepit
shack. No more telephone poles, no cars, no signs of
human habitation . . . perfect for an afternoon killing.

We began to race downhill and I saw with horror that I
was heading full-speed into a dead end, mere yards from
slamming into a pile of dirt at the mouth of an empty
construction site. There was no escape—the road terminated at the site and was additionally blocked by piles of
cinder block, stacks of drywall, lumber and more mounds
of excavated dirt. A goddam *box canyon*. If the impact of
smashing nose-first into the dirt didn't kill me, I'd be
imbedded, tires spinning hopelessly, as immobile as pars-
ley in aspic, a perfect, passive target . . .

The man on the motorcycle must have harbored similar
thoughts in that same instant, for he engaged in a quick
series of confident actions. He removed his gun hand from
the bars, slowed, and came around to the left, ready to be
at my side when my escape came to an end.

I made the only move left for me: I jammed on the
brakes. The Seville convulsed, skidded violently, spun and
rocked on its bearings, threatening to capsize. I needed the
skid to continue, so I steered away from it. The car spun
like a rotor blade.

Then a sudden impact threw me across the seat.

My front end had gone out of control and collided with
the cycle as it came out of a spin with full torque behind it.
The lighter vehicle bounced off the car, caromed and
sailed through the air in a wide arc over the hill of earth. I
watched as man and machine parted ways, the cycle climbing, stuntlike, falling, its rider thrown loose, flying higher,
a scarecrow cut free from its stake, then falling too, landing unseen.

The Seville stopped spinning and its engine died. I
pulled myself up. My sore arm had been knocked against
the passenger door panel and it hummed with pain. No
sign of movement came from the site. I got out quietly,

crouched behind the car and waited there as my head cleared and my breathing slowed. Still nothing. I spied a two-by-four several feet away, snatched it, hefted it like a stave and circled the mound of dirt, staying low to the ground. Creeping onto the site I saw that a partial foundation had been laid—a right angle of concrete from which corrugated steel rods protruded like flowerless stalks. The remains of the motorcycle were visible immediately, a rubbish heap of seared metal and shattered windshield.

It took several more minutes of poking amid the rubble to find the body. It had landed in a ditch at the junction of the two cement arms, a spot where the earth was etched with caterpillar tread marks, next to a broken fiberglass shower stall and half-concealed by molding sheets of insulation.

The opaque helmet was still in place but it had offered no protection from the steel rod that stuck out through a large, jagged hole in the rider's throat. The shaft extended just below the Adam's apple; it had created a good-sized exit wound coming through. Blood seeped from the hole, turning muddy in the dirt. The trachea was visible, still pink, but deflated, leaking fluid. A fleck of gore tipped the rod.

I knelt and undid the helmet strap, and tried to pull off the headpiece. The neck had bent unnaturally upon being pierced and it proved a difficult task. As I struggled I felt steel scrape against vertebrae, cartilage and gristle. My belly quaked with nausea. I heaved and turned away to vomit in the dirt.

With a bitter taste in my mouth and eyes brimming with tears, breathing hard and loud, I returned to the grisly chore. The helmet finally came loose and the bare skull flopped to the ground. I stared down into the lifeless, bearded face of Jim Halstead, the coach at La Casa de Los Niños. His lips were drawn back in death, cast in a permanent sneer. The force of landing after his final free fall had snapped his jaws down upon his tongue, and the severed tip rested on the hairy chin like some fleshy, parasitic grub. His eyes were open and rolled backward, the whites flooded with blood. He cried crimson tears.

I looked away from him and saw the sun hit something shiny several feet to the right. I walked to it, found the gun

and examined it—a chrome-plated .38. I took it and tucked
it in the waistband of my trousers.

The ground at my feet radiated heat and the stench of
something burning. Congealed tar. Toxic waste. Bio-un-
degradable garbage. Polyvinyl vegetation. A bluejay had
landed on Halstead's face. It pecked at his eyes.

I found a dusty drop cloth peppered with specks of dried
cement. The bird fled at my approach. I covered the body
with the cloth, weighted down the corners with large
stones and left him that way.

27

THE ADDRESS the receptionist had given me for Tim Kruger matched the oversized steel numbers on the face of a bone-white highrise on Ocean, just a mile or so from where the Handler-Gutierrez murders had taken place.

The entry hall was a crypt of marble floors and mirrors, furnished with a single white cotton sofa and two rubber plants in wicker canisters. The upper half of one wall was given over to rows of alphabetically arranged brass mailboxes. It didn't take long to locate Kruger's apartment on the twelfth floor. I took a short silent ride on an elevator padded with gray batting and exited into a corridor floored in royal-blue plush and papered with grasscloth.

Kruger's place was located in the northwest corner of the building. I knocked on the royal-blue door.

He opened it, dressed in jogging shorts and a Casa de los Niños T-shirt, shiny with perspiration and smelling as if he'd been exercising. He saw me, stifled his surprise and said, "Hello, Doctor" in a stagey voice. Then he noticed the gun in my hand and the stolid face turned ugly.

"What the—"

"Just get in," I said.

He backed into the apartment and I followed. It was a small place, low ceilings sprayed with plaster cottage cheese and starred with glitter. The walls and carpet were beige. There was little furniture and what there was looked rented. A wall of glass offering a panoramic view of Santa Monica Bay saved it from being a cell. There was no artwork on the walls, except for a single, framed wrestling poster from Hungary. A tiny convenience kitchen was off on one side, a foyer to the other.

Athletic equipment filled a good portion of the living room—snow skis and boots, a pair of waxed wooden oars, several sets of tennis rackets, running shoes, a mountaineer's backpack, a football, a basketball, a bow and quiver of arrows. A beige-painted brick mantel was topped by a dozen trophies.

"You're an active boy, Tim."

"What the hell do you want?" The yellow-brown eyes moved around like pachinko balls.

"Where's the little girl—Melody Quinn?"

"I don't know what you're talking about. Put that thing away."

"You know damn well where she is. You and your fellow murderers abducted her three days ago because she's a witness to your dirty work. Have you killed her too?"

"I'm no killer. I don't know any kid named Quinn. You're crazy."

"No killer? Jeffrey Saxon might not agree."

His mouth dropped open, then shut abruptly.

"You left a trail, Tim. Pretty arrogant to think no one would find it."

"Who the hell are you, anyway?"

"I'm who I said I was. A better question is who are *you?* A rich boy who can't seem to stay out of trouble? A guy who enjoys snapping twigs at hunchbacks and waiting for the tears? Or just an amateur actor whose best bit is an impression of Jack the Ripper?"

"Don't try to pin that on me!" He rolled his hands into fists.

"Hands up." I waved the gun.

He obeyed very slowly, straightening his thick, brown arms and lifting them above his head. It drew my attention upward, and away from his feet. That enabled him to make his move.

The kick came at me like a boomerang, catching the underside of my wrist and numbing the fingers. The gun flew from my grasp and landed on the carpet with a thud. We both leaped for it and ended in a tangle on the floor, punching, kicking, gouging. I was oblivious to pain and seething with fury. I wanted to destroy him.

He was an iron man. It was like fighting an outboard

motor I clawed at his abdomen, but couldn't find an inch of extra flesh. I elbowed him in the ribs. It knocked him backward, but he rebounded as if on springs and landed a punch to the jaw that threw me off-balance long enough for him to get me in a headlock, then hold me skillfully at bay so that my arms were ineffective.

He grunted and increased the pressure. My head felt ready to burst. My vision blurred. I struck at him help-lessly. With a strange kind of delicacy he danced out of reach, squeezing me tighter. Then he started pulling my head back. A little more and I knew my neck would snap. I experienced a sudden kinship with Jeffrey Saxon, drew upon a reserve of strength and brought my heel down hard on his instep. He cried out and reflexively let go, then tried to renew the lock, but it was too late. I landed a kick that snapped his head to the side and followed it with a series of rapid straightarm punches to the lower belly. When he doubled over I chopped down on the place where his head joined his neck He sank to his knees, but I didn't take any chances—he was strong and skilled. Another kick to the face. Now he was down. I placed one foot under the bridge of his nose. One quick forward motion and splinters of bone would lobotomize him. It turned out to be an unnecessary precaution. He was out.

I found a coil of thick nylon rope in the mountaineer's pack and trussed him as he lay on his abdomen, feet drawn up behind him, bound and secured to another piece of rope that similarly raised his arms. I checked the knots, drew them tight and dragged him clear of any weapon. I re-trieved the .38, kept it in one hand, went into his kitchen and soaked a towel in cold water.

When several minutes of slapping him with the towel elicited no more than a half-conscious groan, I made an-other trip to the kitchen, pulled a Dutch oven out of a dish drainer, filled it with water and dumped the contents on his head. That brought him around.

"Oh, Jesus," he moaned. He tried those first struggles that all prisoners attempt, gnashed his teeth, finally real-ized his predicament and sank back down, gasping.

I prodded the back of one leg with the muzzle of the .38.

"You like sports, Tim. That's fortunate because they'll let you exercise in prison. Without exercise the time can go very slowly. But I'm going to ask you questions and if you don't give me satisfactory answers I'm going to maim you, bit by bit. First I'll shoot you right here.'' I pressed cold steel into warm flesh. ''After that your leg might be good for getting you on the john. Then I'll do the same to the other leg. From there to fingers, wrists, elbows. You'll do your time as a vegetable, Tim.''

I listened to myself talk, hearing a stranger. To this day I don't know if I would have followed through on the threat. I never had to find out.

''What do you want?'' His speech came out in spurts, constricted with fear and hampered by the uncomfortable position.

''Where's Melody Quinn?''

''At La Casa.''

''Where at La Casa?''

''The storage rooms. Near the forest.''

''Those cinder block buildings—the ones you avoided discussing when you gave me the tour?''

''Uh-huh. Yes.''

''Which one? There were four.''

''The last one—furthest from the front.''

A spreading stain darkened the carpet at my feet. He'd wet himself.

''Jesus,'' he said.

''Let's keep going, Tim. You're doing fine.''

He nodded, seemingly eager for praise.

''Is she still alive?''

''Yes. As far as I know. Cousin Will—Doctor Towle wanted to keep her alive. Gus and the judge agreed. I don't know for how long.''

''What about her mother?''

He closed his eyes and said nothing.

''Talk, Tim, or your leg goes.''

''She's dead. The guy they sent to get the kid and her did it. They buried her in the Meadow.''

I remembered the stretch of field at the north side of La Casa. *We're planning to plant a vegetable garden this summer* he'd told me . . .

''Who is he?''

''Some crazy guy. A gimp—kind of paralyzed on one side. Gus called him Earl.''

It wasn't the name I expected but the description was right.

"Why'd he do it?"

"Leave as few loose ends as possible."

"On McCaffrey's orders?"

He was silent. I exerted pressure on the gun. His thigh quivered.

"Yeah. On his orders. Earl doesn't operate on his own."

"Where is this Earl character now?"

More hesitation. Without thinking I flicked the tip of the .38 over his kneecap. His eyes widened with surprise and hurt. Tears ran out of them.

"Oh, God!"

"Don't get religious. Just talk."

"He's gone—dead. Gus had Halstead rip him off. After they buried the woman. He was filling the grave and Halstead hit him with the shovel, pushed him in with her and covered them both with dirt. He and Gus were laughing about it later. Halstead said when he hit Earl on the head it gave off a hollow sound. They used to talk like that, behind the guy's back—call him the gimp, damaged goods . . ."

"Mean guy, that Halstead."

"Yeah. He is." Kruger's visage brightened, eager to please. "He's after you too. You were snooping around. Gus didn't know how much the kid told you. I'm tipping you off, man, watch your—"

"Thanks, pal, but Halstead's no threat anymore. To anyone."

He looked up at me. I answered the unspoken question with a quick nod.

"Jesus," he said, broken.

I didn't give him time to reflect.

"Why'd you kill Handler and Gutierrez?"

"I told you, I *didn't*. That was Halstead and Earl. Gus told 'em to make it look like a sex thing. Halstead told me later Earl was a natural for the job—carved 'em up like he enjoyed it. Really went to town on the teacher. Halstead held her and Earl used the knife."

Two men, maybe three, Melody had said.

"You were there, too, Tim."

"No. Yeah. I—I drove them there. With the headlights

out. It was a dark night, no moon, no stars. I circled the
parking lot, then figured I might get noticed, so I drove
around in the Palisades and came back. They still weren't
through—I remember wondering what was taking them so
long. I left again, drove around some more, came back
and they were just coming out. They wore black, like
demons. I could see the blood, even against the black.
They smelled of blood. It was all over them, dark, like the
clothing, but a different texture—you know, shiny. Wet."

Dark men. Two, maybe three.

He stopped.

"That's not the end of the story, Tim."

"That's it. They undressed in the car, stuffed the knife
in a duffel bag. We burned it in one of the canyons—the
clothes, bag, everything. Dumped whatever was left off
the Malibu pier." He paused again, out of breath. "I
didn't kill anybody."

"Did they say anything in the car?"

"Halstead was stone silent. It bothered me, how freaked-
out he looked, because he's a mean one—that story about
getting a knife pulled on him by a kid is bullshit. He was
kicked out of Manual Arts for beating up a couple of
students pretty badly. Before that he was booted out of the
marines. He loved violence. But whatever happened in
that apartment got to him—he was silent, man."

"How about Earl?"

"Earl was—different—like he *dug* it, you know? He
was licking his lips and rocking back and forth like an
autistic kid. Jabbering, saying 'Sonofabitch' over and over.
Weird. Crazy. Finally Halstead told him to shut the fuck
up and he yelled something back—in Spanish. The guy
spoke a lot in Spanish. Halstead yelled back and I thought
the two of them were going to tear each other up right
there. It was like driving around with two caged beasts. I
calmed them down, used Gus's name—that always worked
for Earl. I couldn't wait to get away from them that night.
Prototypical psychopaths, both of them."

"Save the scholarly stuff and tell me how you killed
Bruno."

He looked at me with renewed fear.

"You know everything, don't you."

"What I don't you're going to fill in." I waved the gun in the air. *"Bruno."*

"We—they did that the night after doing the doctor and the teacher. Halstead didn't want Earl along but Gus insisted. Said two men on the job was better. I had the feeling he played them off against each other. I wasn't there at all. Halstead drove and did the killing. He used a baseball bat from the athletic supplies bin. I was there when he came back and told Gus about it. They found the salesman eating dinner, beat him to death right there at the table. Earl ate the rest of the meal."

Two murders pinned on two dead men. Very neat. It stunk and I told him so.

"That's the way it was. I'm not saying I'm totally innocent. I knew what they were going to do when I drove them to the shrink's place. I gave them the key. But I didn't do any of the killing."

"How'd you get the key?"

"Cousin Will gave it to me. I don't know where he got it."

"All right. We've talked about who. Now tell me why all the butchery."

"I assumed you knew—"

"Don't assume a goddam thing."

"Okay, okay. It's the Brigade. It's a cover for child molesters. The shrink and the girl found out and they were blackmailing him. Stupid of them to think they could get away with it."

I remembered the pictures Milo'd shown me that first day. They'd paid far too high a price for their stupidity.

I chased the bloody images from my mind and returned to Kruger.

"Are all the Gentlemen perverts?"

"No. Only about a quarter. The rest are straight-arrows. It makes it easier to conceal, sneaking the perverts in among them."

"And the kids never talk?"

"Not until—we pick the ones that the pervs take home with care, mostly those who can't talk back. Retarded, or they don't know English, severely c.p. Gus likes orphans because they don't have family ties, no one looks out for them."

"Was Rodney one of the chosen ones?"

"Uh-huh."

"Did his fear of the doctor have something to do with that?"

"Yeah. One of the weirdos got a little rough with him. A surgeon. Gus warns them to go easy. He doesn't want the kids actually *hurt*—spoiled merchandise isn't worth as much. But it doesn't always work out. Those guys aren't normal, you know."

"I know." Anger and disgust made it hard to see straight. Kicking his head in would have been primally satisfying, but it was a pleasure I was going to have to deny myself . . .

"I'm not one of them," he was insisting, sounding almost as if he'd convinced himself. "I think it's disgusting, actually."

I bent down and grabbed him by the throat.

"You went along with it, asshole!"

His face purpled, the butterscotch eyes bulging. I let go of his head. It dropped to the floor. He landed on his nose and it started to bleed. He writhed in confinement.

"Don't say it. You were just following orders."

"You don't understand!" he sobbed. Real tears mixed with the mustache of blood on his upper lip creating a momentary illusion of harelip. But for his degree in drama I might have been impressed. "Gus took me in when the rest of them—my so-called friends and family, everyone—blackballed me for the Saxon thing. You can think what you want but that wasn't murder. It was—an accident. Saxon was no innocent victim. He wanted to kill *me*—that's the truth."

"He's in no position to state his case."

"Shit! No one believed me. Except Gus. He knew what it could be like at that place. They all thought I was a washout—shame of the family and all that crap. He gave me responsibility. And I lived up to his expectations—I showed my stuff, showed you don't need a degree. Everything was perfect, I ran La Casa as smooth as—"

"You're a terrific stormtrooper, Tim. Right now I want answers."

"Ask," he said weakly.

"How long has the Brigade been a cover for child molesters?"

"From the beginning."

"Just like in Mexico?"

"Just like. Down there, to hear him tell it—the police knew all about it. All he had to do was grease a few palms. They let him bring in rich businessmen from Acapulco—Japanese, lots of Arabs—to play with the kids. The place was called Father Augustino's Christian Home—whatever that is in Spanish. It went good for a long time until a new police commissioner, some religious nut, took over and didn't like it. Gus claims the guy ripped him off for thousands in payoff then double-crossed him and shut the place down anyway. He moved up here and set up camp. Brought Crazy Earl with him."

"Earl was his boy in Mexico?"

"Yup. I figure he did the shitwork. Followed Gus like a lap dog. The guy spoke Spanish like a beaner—I mean the accent was fine but what he said was gibberish—we're talking brain damage, man. A robot with the screws loose."

"McCaffrey had him killed anyway."

Kruger gave the closest approximation to a shrug the ropes would allow.

"You have to know Gus. He's cold. Loves power. Get in his way and you're done. Those suckers didn't have a chance."

"How did he get set up so fast in L.A.?"

"Connections."

"Cousin Willie?"

He hesitated. I prodded him with the .38.

"Him. Judge Hayden. Some others. One seemed to lead to another. Each one knew at least one other closet sicko. Amazing how many of those guys there are. Cousin Will was a surprise to me, 'cause I knew him really well. Always seemed such a priss, holier than thou. My folks held him up as an example to follow—fine, upstanding Cousin Doctor." He laughed hoarsely. "And the guy's a kiddy boffer." More laughter. "Though I can't say I actually saw him take a kid home—I set up the schedules and I never set him up with anything. All I *know* he did was patch injured kids up whenever we called. Still, he must

be as sick as the rest, why else would he be kissing up to
Gus?"

I ignored the question and asked one of my own.

"How long was the blackmail going on?"

"A few months. Like I told you we screened the kids,
to make sure they wouldn't talk. One time we blew it.
There was this one boy, an orphan, just perfect. Everyone
thought he was mute. Jesus, he never talked to *us*. We had
speech and hearing tests—the government pays for all of
that—and everything came back no speech. We were sure,
and we were wrong. The kid talked all right. He told the
teacher plenty. She freaked out and reported it to Cousin
Will—he was the kid's pediatrician. She didn't know he
was involved in it himself. He told Gus."

And Gus had him killed. Cary Nemeth.

"Then what?"

"I—do we have to talk about it?"

"We goddamn as hell do! How did it happen?"

"They ran him down with a truck. They took him out of
bed in the middle of the night, must have been close to
midnight. Nothing's out there at that hour. Put him on the
road, walking. In his pajamas. I remember the pajamas.
Yellow, with baseballs and mitts all over. I—I could have
tried to stop it but it wouldn't have made a difference. The
kid knew, he had to go. Simple as that. They would have
done it later and probably me, too. It was wrong to do that
to a little kid. Cold-blooded. I started to say something.
Gus squeezed my arm. Told me to shut up. I wanted to
scream. The kid was walking on the road, all alone,
half-asleep, like he was dreaming. I kept quiet. Halstead
got into the truck, drove it a ways down the road. I could
hear him revving it up, from around the bend. He came
back speeding, headlights on high beam. Hit the kid from
behind—he never knew what happened, he was half-asleep."

He stopped talking, panting, and closed his eyes.

"Gus talked about doing the teacher right then and there
but he decided to wait, see if she'd told anyone else. He
had Halstead follow her. He staked out her place. She
wasn't there. Just her roommate. Halstead wanted to kid-
nap *her*, beat it out of *her*, see if she knew anything. Then
he saw the teacher come back with some guy—it was
Handler—to pick up her stuff. Like she was moving in

with him. Halstead reported it back to Gus. Now it was getting complicated. They kept watching the two of them and finally saw them meet with Bruno. We knew Bruno—he'd volunteered at La Casa, seemed like a great guy. Very outgoing. The kids loved him. It was clear, at that point, that he'd been a spy. Now it was three mouths that had to be closed.

"The calls came a few days later. It was Bruno, disguising his voice, but we knew it was him. Saying he had tapes of the Nemeth kid telling all. He even played a few seconds over the phone. They were amateurs; they didn't know Gus had them from day one, right in the crosshairs. It was pathetic."

Pathetic *was* the word for the scenario: Take one nice girl. Elena Gutierrez, up from the barrio, attractive, vibrant. A little materialistic, but warm-hearted. A gifted teacher. Depressed about her job, burned out, she seeks help, enters therapy with Morton Handler, M.D., psychopath cum psychiatrist. Ends up going to bed with Handler but continues to tell him her problems—one major one being the kid who never talked before who's suddenly opening up and telling her terrible things about strange men doing bad things to him. He opens up to Miss Gutierrez because she's warm and understanding. A real talent for drawing them out, Raquel Ochoa had said. A talent for working with the ones who didn't respond to anyone else. A talent that cost Elena her life. Because what was human tragedy to her smelled profitable to Morton Handler. Nasty things in high places—what could be juicier?

Of course Handler thinks these things but he keeps them to himself. After all, maybe the kid is making it all up. Maybe Elena is overreacting—you know women, especially Latin women—so he tells her to keep listening, emphasizes what a good job she's doing, what a source of support she is for the child. Bides his time.

Shouldn't I report this to someone? she asks him. Wait, dear, be cautious, until you know more. But the child is crying out for help, the bad men are still coming for him . . . Elena takes it upon herself to call Cary's doctor. And thus signs his death warrant.

When Elena hears of the child's death, she suspects the awful truth; she falls apart. Handler shoves tranquilizers down her throat, calms her down. All the while his psychopathic mind is going click click click, because now he *knows* there's money to be made.

Enter Maurice Bruno: fellow psychopath, former patient, new buddy. A real smoothie. Handler recruits him and offers him a cut of the yield if he infiltrates the Gentleman's Brigade and finds out as much as he can. Names, places, dates. Elena wants to call the police. Handler quiets her down with more pills and more talk. The police are ineffectual, my darling. They won't do anything about it. I know from experience. Slowly, gradually, he gets her to go along with the blackmail scheme. This is the real way to punish them, he assures her. Hit them where it hurts. She listens, so unsure, so confused. Something seems so wrong about profiting from the death of a helpless little boy, but then again, nothing will bring him back, and Morton seems to know what he's talking about. He's very persuasive and besides, there's that Datsun 280ZX she's always wanted, and those outfits she saw last week at Neiman-Marcus. She could never afford them on what the damned school pays her. And who the hell ever did anything for her, anyway. *Look out for number one* Morton always says, and maybe he's got a point there . . .

"Earl and Halstead looked for the tapes," Kruger was saying, "after they tied them up. They tortured them to get them to tell where they kept them but neither of them talked. Halstead complained to Gus that he could have gotten it out of them but Earl went to work too fast with the knife. Handler passed out when he cut his throat, the girl freaked out totally, screaming, they had to jam something in her mouth. She choked, then Earl finished her, played with her."

"But you finally found the tapes, didn't you, Timmy?"

"Yes. She'd kept them at her mother's. I got them from her junkie brother. Used smack as a bribe."

"Tell me more."

"That's it. They tried to put the squeeze on Gus. He paid them once or twice—big amounts 'cause I saw large rolls of bills—but it was just to give them false confidence. They never had a chance from the start. We never got the money back, but I don't think it mattered. It was a drop in the bucket. Besides, money doesn't seem to turn

Gus on. He lives simply, eats cheap. There's big bucks rolling in every day. From the government—state and federal. Private donations. Not to mention the thousands the pervs pay him for their jollies. He stashes some away but I've never seen him do anything extravagant. It's power he's after, not bread.''

"Where are the tapes?"

"I gave them to Gus."

"Come on."

"I gave them to him. He sent me on an errand and I delivered."

"That's a strong-looking knee. Pity to pulverize it to bone meal." I stepped on the back of his leg and bore down. It forced his head up, had to hurt.

"Stop! Okay. I made a copy. I had to. For leverage. What if Gus wanted me out of the way one day? I mean I was his golden boy now but you could never know, right?"

"Where are they?"

"In my bedroom. Taped to the bottom of the mattress."

"Don't go away." I released my foot.

He gnashed his teeth like a netted shark.

I found three unmarked cassettes where he said they'd be, pocketed them and returned.

"Tell me some names. Of the molesters in the Brigade."

He recited like a kid delivering his confirmation speech. Automatic. Nervous. Overly rehearsed.

"Any more?"

"Isn't that enough?"

He had a point. He'd mentioned a well-known film director, a deputy D.A., a political biggie—a behind-the-scenes man who managed to stay in front—corporate attorneys. Doctors. Bankers. Real estate honchos. Men whose names usually got in print when they donated something or won an award for humanitarian service. Men whose names on a campaign endorsement roster brought in votes. Ned Biondi would have enough to turn L.A. society on its ear for quite some time.

"You're not going to forget all of this when the police ask you about it, are you, Tim?"

"No! Why should I? Maybe cooperating can buy me out?"

"You're not getting out. Accept it. But at least," I

added, "you won't end up fertilizing McCaffrey's vegetable patch."

He considered that. It must have been hard to count his blessings with the ropes biting into his wrists and ankles.

"Listen," he said, "I've helped you. Help me make a deal. I'll cooperate—I didn't kill anyone."

The power he attributed to me was fictitious. I used it anyway.

"I'll do what I can," I said magnanimously, "but a lot of it's up to you. If the Quinn kid gets out of this healthy, I'll go to bat for you. If not, you're down the toilet."

"Then get going, for God's sake! Get her out of there! I don't give her more than a day. Will put Gus off but it won't be for long. She'll have an accident. They'll never find the body. It's just a matter of time. Gus is sure she saw too much."

"Tell me what I need to get her out of there safely."

He looked away.

"I lied about where she is. It's not the furthest building, it's the one just before it. With the blue door. Metal door. There's a key in the pocket of my tan pants. Hanging in the closet in my room."

I left him, fished it out and came back dangling the key.

"You're batting a thousand, Tim."

"I'm being straight with you. Just help *me*."

"Is anyone with her?"

"No. There's no need. Will has her on sedatives. Mostly she's out of it or sleeping. They send in someone to feed her, clean her up. She's strapped to the bed. The room's solid, concrete block. Only one way in—through the door. There's a single skylight window they keep open. Close it, anyone inside suffocates in forty-eight hours."

"Could Will Towle get into La Casa without arousing suspicion?"

"Sure. Like I told you, he's on twenty-four-call for when the Gentlemen get too rough on the kids. Most of the time it's nothing serious—scrapes, lacerations. Sometimes the kids freak out, he gives them Valium or Mellaril, or a quick dose of Thorazine. Yeah, he could show up any time."

"Good. You're going to call him, Tim. You're going to tell him he needs to make just such an emergency call. I want him entering La Casa a half-hour after dark—let's say seven-thirty. Make sure he's on time. And alone. Make it sound convincing.''

"I could be more convincing if I could move around a little bit."

"Work with what you've got. I have faith in you. Use your dramatic training. You were pretty good as Bill Roberts."

"How'd you kn—"

"I didn't. Now I do. It was an educated guess. You're a trained actor, you were a natural for the part. Did your role include killing Hickle, too?"

"Ancient history," he said. "Yeah, I made the call. Setting it up in your office was Hayden's idea of a joke. He's a mean little mother. Sick sense of humor. But like I told you before, I didn't *kill* anybody. For the Hickle thing I wasn't even there. That was all Hayden and Cousin Will. They—and Gus—decided to shut him up—same old story, I guess. Hickle was a member of the Brigade, one of the originals. But he free-lanced with the kids at his wife's school.

"I remember after he got busted, the three of them were talking about it. Gus was ranting. 'Damned stupid shithead!' he was yelling, 'I furnish that fool with enough hairless pussy to keep him smiling for the rest of his life and he goes and does a dumbshit thing like this!' The way I figured it Hickle'd always been regarded as weak and stupid, easily influenced. They bet that once he started confessing the school stuff he'd open his yap and bring it all down around them. They had to put him away.

"The way they did it was for Hayden to call him and tell him he had good news. Hickle'd asked Hayden to pull strings downtown with the D.A., which just goes to show you how stupid he was. I mean at that time Hickle was page one. Just knowing him was the kiss of death. But he called Hayden, asked him anyway. Hayden faked it like he was going to try to help. Couple days later he called him, said yeah, there was good news, he could help. They met at Hayden's house, very hush-hush, no one around. From what I gather Will slipped something in his tea—the guy didn't drink booze. Something you could time precisely and that wore off, so traces were hard to find unless you were looking for something specifically. Will fixed the dosage—he's good at that. When Hickle was out they moved him to your place. Hayden picked the lock—he's good with his hands, does magic shows for the kids at La Casa. Dresses up like a clown—Blimbo the Clown—and does magic tricks.''

"Forget magic. Go on about Hickle."

''That's it. They got him up there, faked the suicide. I don't know who pulled the trigger. I wasn't there. The only reason I know anything about it is I did the Bill Roberts bit and a few days later Gus told me what it was all about. He was in one of those dark moods when he talks like a megalomaniac. 'Don't think your cousin the doctor is all that noble, my boy,' he was saying. 'I can fry his ass and the asses of lots of noble men with one phone call.' He gets that way—anti-rich, after he thinks back to how he was poor and all us rich folk mistreated him. That night, after they killed Hickle, we were sitting in his office. He was drinking gin and he started to reminisce about how he used to work for Mr. Hickle—Hickle's father—from the time he was a little kid. He was an orphan and some agency basically sold him to the Hickles, like a slave. He said old Hickle had been a monster. Vicious temper, liked to kick the help around. He told me how he took it, kept his eyes open, learned all the nasty family secrets—like Stuart's kinks, other stuff—saved it all up and used it to get off Brindamoor, to get the job at Jedson. I remember him smiling at me, half-drunk, looking crazy. 'I learned early,' he said, 'that knowledge is power.' Then he talked about Earl, how the guy was damaged goods, but would do anything for him. 'He'd eat my shit and call it caviar,' he said. 'That's power.' ''

Kruger had arched his back, picking his head up, stiff-necked, as he talked. Now exhausted, he sank back down.

"I guess," he said, "he's getting back at all of us."

He lay in the ochre stain of dried urine, pitiful.

"Anything else you want to tell me, Tim?"

"I can't think of anything. You ask, I'll tell."

I saw the tension travel up and down his bound limbs like a handcar on a twisted track and kept my distance.

There was a phone on the floor several feet away. I brought it near, stayed away from his arms and laid the speaker near his mouth. Holding the gun to his brow I punched in Towle's office number and stepped back.

"Make it good."

He did. I would have been convinced. I hoped Towle was. He signaled me the conversation was through by moving his eyes back and forth. I hung up and had him make a second call, to the security desk at La Casa to set up the doctor's visit.

"How was that?" he asked when he was through.

"Rave review."

Oddly enough that seemed to please him.

"Tell me, Tim, how are your sinuses?"

The question didn't throw him. "Great," he blurted out, "I'm never sick." He said it with the bravado of the habitual athlete who believes exercise and firm muscles are guarantees of immortality.

"Good. Then this shouldn't bother you." I crammed a towel into his mouth while he made enraged, muffled noises through the terrycloth.

Carefully I dragged him to the bedroom, emptied the closet of anything that resembled a tool or weapon and shoved him inside, molding him to the confines of the tiny space.

"*If* I get out of La Casa with the kid and myself in good shape I'll tell the police where to find you. If I don't, you'll probably suffocate. Anything else you want to tell me?"

A shake of the head. Beseeching eyes. I closed the door and moved a heavy dresser in front of it. I replaced the gun in my waistband, closed all the windows in the apartment, drew the bedroom curtains and shut the bedroom door, blocking it with two chairs stood on end. I cut his phone line with a kitchen knife, drew the drapes so that the view of the ocean was erased and gave the place a final once-over. Satisfied, I walked out the door, slamming it tight.

28

THE SEVILLE was running, but shakily, as a result of the grand prix with Halstead. It was also too conspicuous for my purposes. I left it in a lot in Westwood Village, walked two blocks to a Budget Rent-A-Car and picked up a dark brown Japanese compact—one of those square little boxes of molded plastic papered with an allegedly metal shell. It took fifteen minutes to putt-putt through the traffic from one end of the village to the other. I pulled into the Bullocks garage, locked the gun in the glove compartment, locked the car and went shopping.

I bought a pair of jeans, thick socks, crepe-soled shoes, navy blue turtleneck and a windbreaker of the same dark hue. Everything in the store was tagged with plastic alarm clips and it took the salesgirl several minutes to liberate the garments after she'd taken my money.

"Wonderful world," I muttered.

"You think this is bad, we have the expensive stuff—leather, furs—under lock and key. Otherwise they just waltz right out with it."

We shared righteous sighs and, after being informed I was likely to be under surveillance, I decided not to change in the store's dressing room.

It was just past six and dark by the time I was back on the street. Time enough to grab a steak sandwich, Greek salad, vanilla ice cream and lots of black coffee and watch the starless sky from the vantage point of a front table in a mom-and-pop eatery on West Pico. At six-thirty I paid the tab and went into the restaurant's men's room to change. While slipping into my new duds I noticed a piece of folded paper on the floor. I picked it up. It was the copy of

the Lilah Towle accident story given to me by Margaret
Dopplemeier. I tried to read it again, with not much
greater success. I was able to make out something about
the Coast Guard and high tides, but that was it. I put it
back in the jacket pocket, straightened up and got ready to
head for Malibu.

There was a pay phone at the back of the café, and I
used it to call the West L.A. station. I thought of leaving a
convoluted message for Milo, then thought better of it and
asked for Delano Hardy. After being kept waiting for five
minutes I was finally told he was out on a call. I left the
convoluted message for him, paid the check, and headed
for Malibu.

It was slow going but I'd constructed my schedule with
that in mind. I reached Rambla Pacifica just before seven,
and the county sign announcing La Casa de los Niños at
ten after. The sky was empty and dark, like a drop down
an endless well. A coyote howled from a distant gully.
Nightbirds and bats flittered and squeaked. I switched off
my headlights and navigated the next mile and a half by
sense of touch. It wasn't all that difficult, but the little car
resonated at every crack and bump in the road, and transmitted the shock waves directly through my skeletal system.

I came to a stop a half-mile before the La Casa turnoff.
It was seven-fifteen. There were no other vehicles on the
road. Praying it stayed that way, I swung the car perpendicular to the road and blocked both lanes: rear wheels
facing the ravine that bordered the highway, front tires
nosing the thick brush to the west. I sat in the darkened
compartment, gun in hand, waiting.

At twenty-three after seven I heard the sound of an
approaching engine. A minute later the Lincoln's square
headlights came into view a quarter-mile up the road. I
jumped out of the car, ran for cover in the brush and
crouched, holding my breath.

He saw the empty car late and had to screech to a stop.
He left his motor running, the lights on, and walked into
the beam, cursing. The white hair gleamed silver. He wore
a charcoal double-breasted blazer over a white open-necked
shirt, along with black flannel pants and black-and-white
golf shoes with tassles. Not a crease, not a wrinkle.

He ran a hand alongside the flank of the little car,

touched the hood, grunted, and leaned through the open driver's door.

It was then that I sprang silently on crepe and put the gun in the small of his back.

As a matter of taste and principle I hate firearms. My father loved them, collected them. First there were the Lugers he brought home as World War II mementos. Then the deer rifles, the shotguns, automatic pistols picked up in pawn shops, an old rusted Colt .45, nasty-looking Italian pistols with long snouts and engraved butts, blue steel .22's. Lovingly polished and displayed in the den, behind the glass of a cherrywood case. Most of them loaded, the old man toying with them while watching TV. Calling me over to show off the details of construction, the niceties of ornamentation; talk of chamber velocity, core, bore, muzzle, grip. The smell of machine oil. The odor of burnt matches that permeated his hands. As a small child I'd have nightmares of the guns leaving their perches, like pets slipping out of their cages, taking on instincts of their own, barking and snarling . . .

One time he had a fight with my mother, a loud and nasty one. In anger he went to the case and snatched at the first thing he put his hands on—a Luger: Teutonically efficient. He pointed it at her. I could see it now: she screaming "Harry!"; he realizing what he was doing; horrified, dropping the gun as if it were a venomous sea creature; reaching out to her, stuttering apologies. He never did it again, but the memory changed him, them—and me, five years old, standing, blanket in hand, half-hidden by the door, watching. Since then I've hated guns. But at that moment I loved the feel of the .38 as it dented Towle's blazer.

"Get in the car," I whispered. "Sit behind the wheel and don't move or I'll blow your guts out."

He obeyed. Quickly I ran to the passenger side and in beside him.

"You," he said.

"Start the engine." I put the gun in his side, rougher than I had to be.

The little car coughed to life.

"Pull it to the side of the road, so that the driver's door is right up against that rock. Then turn off the engine and throw the key out the window.'' He did as he was told, the noble profile steady.

I got out and ordered him to do likewise. The way I'd had him park, the exit from the driver's side was blocked by forty feet of granite. He slid out the passenger's side and stood motionless and stoic at the edge of the empty road.

''Hands up.''

He gave me a superior look and complied.

''This is outrageous,'' he said.

''Use one hand to remove your car keys. Toss them *gently* on the ground over there.'' I pointed to a spot fifteen feet away. Keeping the gun trained on him, I scooped them up.

''Walk to your car, get in on the driver's side. Put both hands on the wheel where I can see them.''

I followed him to the Lincoln. I got in the back, right behind him, and placed the tip of the gun in the hollow at the base of his skull.

''You know your anatomy,'' I said softly. ''One bullet to the medulla oblongata and the lights go out forever.''

He said nothing.

''You've done a fine job of mucking up your life and the lives of plenty of others. Now it's coming down on you. What I'm offering you is a chance for partial redemption. Save a life for once, instead of destroying it.''

''I've saved many lives in my day. I'm a physician.''

''I know, you're a saintly healer. Where were you when it came to saving Cary Nemeth?''

A dry, croaking sound came from deep inside of him. But he maintained his composure.

''You know everything, I suppose.''

''Just about. Cousin Tim can be talkative when the circumstances are right.'' I gave him a few examples of what I knew. He was unmoved, stoic, hands melded to the wheel, a white-haired mannikin set up for display.

''You knew my name before we met,'' I said, ''from the Hickle thing. When I called you invited me to the office. To see how much Melody had told me. It didn't make sense to me then, a busy pediatrician taking the time to sit and chat face-to-face. Anything we spoke about could have been discussed over the phone. You wanted to sound me out. Then you tried to block me.''

"You had a reputation as a persistent young man," he said. "Things were piling up."

"Things? Don't you mean bodies?"

"There's no need to be melodramatic." He talked like a Disneyland android: flat, without inflection, devoid of self-doubt.

"I'm not trying to be. It's just that multiple murder still gets to me. The Nemeth boy. Handler. Elena Gutierrez. Morry Bruno. Now, Bonita Quinn and good old Ronnie Lee.''

At the mention of the last name he gave a small, but noticeable start.

"Ronnie Lee's death bother you, in particular?"

"I'm not familiar with that name. That's all."

"Ronnie Lee Quinn. Bonita's ex. Melody's father. *R.L.* A blond fellow, tall, crazy-looking, with a bad left side. Hemiparesis. With McCaffrey's southern accent it may have sounded like he was calling him Earl."

"Ah," he said, pleased that things made sense once again, "Earl. Disgusting fellow. Unwashed. I remember meeting him once or twice."

"Piss-poor protoplasm, right?"

"If you will."

"He was one of McCaffrey's bad guys from Mexico, brought back to do a dirty job or two. Probably wanted to see his kid, so McCaffrey found her and Bonita for him. Then it dawned on him how she could fit in. She was a bright one, Bonita, wasn't she? Probably thought you were Santa Claus when you got her the job managing Minassian's building.''

"She was appreciative," said Towle.

"You were doing her a big favor. You set her up so you could have access to Handler's apartment. She's the manager, she gets a master key. Then the next time she's in the office for Melody's checkup, she 'loses' her purse. It's easy to do, the lady's a scatterbrain. She didn't *have it together*. That's what your office girl told me. Always losing things. Meanwhile you lift the key and McCaffrey's monsters can get in whenever they want—look for tapes, do a little slashing and hacking. No sweat off poor Bonita's back, except when she becomes expendable and ends up as food for next season's zucchini crop. A dull woman. More piss-poor protoplasm.''

''It wasn't supposed to happen that way. That wasn't in the plan.''

''You know how it is, the best-laid plans and all that.''

''You're a sarcastic young man. I hope you aren't that way with your patients.''

''Ronnie Lee finishes off Bonita—he may have done it because McCaffrey told him to, or perhaps it was just settling an old score. But now McCaffrey has to get rid of Ronnie Lee, too, because fiend that he is, even he may balk at watching his own daughter die.''

''You're very bright, Alex,'' he said. ''But the sarcasm really is an unattractive trait.''

''Thanks for the advice. I know you're an expert on bedside manner.''

''As a matter of fact, I am. I pride myself on it. Obtain early rapport with the child and family no matter how disparate your background may be from theirs. That's the first step in delivering good care. It's what I instruct the first-year students when I proctor the pediatric section of Introduction to Clinical Medicine.''

''Fascinating.''

''The students give me excellent ratings on my teaching. I'm an excellent teacher.''

I exerted forward pressure with the .38. His silver hair parted but he didn't flinch. I smelled his hair tonic, cloves and lime.

''Start the car and pull it to the side of the road. Just behind that giant eucalyptus.''

The Lincoln rumbled and rolled, then stopped.

''Turn off the engine.''

''Don't be rude,'' he said. ''There's no need to try to intimidate me.''

''Turn it off, Will.''

''*Doctor* Towle.''

''Doctor Towle.''

The engine quieted.

''Is it necessary to keep that thing at the back of my head?''

''I'll ask the questions.''

"It seems needless—superfluous. This isn't some cheap Western movie."

"It's worse. The blood is real and nobody gets up and walks away when the smoke clears."

"More melodrama. Mellow drama. Strange phrase."

"Stop playing around," I said angrily.

"Playing? Are we playing? I thought only children played. Jump rope, Hopscotch." His voice rose in pitch.

"Grownups play too," I said. "Nasty games."

"Games. Games help the child maintain ego integrity. I read that somewhere—Erikson? Piaget?"

Either Kruger wasn't the only actor in the family or something was happening that I hadn't been prepared for . . .

"Anna Freud," I whispered.

"Yes. Anna. Fine woman. Would have loved to meet her, but both of us so busy . . . Pity . . . The ego must maintain integrity. At all costs." He was silent for a minute, then: "These seats need cleaning. I see spots on the leather. They make a good leather cleaner now . . . I saw it at the car wash."

"Melody Quinn," I said, trying to reel him back in. "We need to save her."

"Melody. Pretty girl. A pretty girl is like a melody. Pretty little child. Almost familiar . . ."

I talked to him but he kept fading away. Minute by minute he regressed, the rambling growing progressively more incoherent and out of context, so that at his worse, he was emitting word salad. He seemed to be suffering, the aristocratic face crowded with pain. Every few minutes he repeated the phrase, "The ego must maintain integrity," as if it was a catechism.

I needed him to get into La Casa but in his present state he was useless. I started to panic. His hands remained on the steering wheel but they trembled.

"Pills," he said.

"Where?"

"Pocket . . ."

"Go ahead," I said, not without suspicion, "reach in and get them. The pills and nothing else. Don't take too many."

"No . . . two pills . . . recommended dosage . . . never

more . . . nevermore . . . quoth the raven . . . nevermore . . .''

''Get them.''

I kept the gun trained on him. He lowered one hand and drew out a vial not unlike the one that had held Melody's Ritalin. Carefully he shook out two white tablets, closed the vial and put it down.

''Water?'' he asked, childlike.

''Take them dry.''

''I shall . . . nuisance.''

He swallowed the pills.

Kruger had been right. He *was* good at adjusting dosages. Within twelve minutes on my watch he was looking and sounding much better. I thought of the strain he underwent each day maintaining himself in the public eye. No doubt talking about the murders had hastened the deterioration.

''Silly of me to miss . . . the afternoon dose. Never forget.''

I observed him with morbid fascination, watching the changes in his speech and behavior as the psychoactive chemicals took hold of his central nervous system, making note of the gradually increasing attention span, the diminishing non sequiturs, the restoration of adult conversational patterns. It was like peering into a microscope and watching a primitive organism mitose into something far more complex.

When the drug was still in its initial stage he said:

''I've done many . . . bad things. Gus had me do bad things. Very wrong for a . . . man of my stature. For someone of my breeding.''

I let it pass.

Eventually he was lucid. Alert, seemingly undamaged.

''What is it, Thorazine?'' I asked him.

''A variant. I've managed my own pharmacologic care for some time now. Tried a number of the phenothiazines . . . Thorazine was good but it made me too drowsy. Couldn't have that while conducting physicals . . . Wouldn't want to drop a baby. No, nothing like that. Dreadful, drop an infant. This is a new agent, far superior to the others. Experimental. Sent to me by the manufacturer. Just write away for samples, use M.D. after the name, no need to justify or explain. They're more than happy to oblige . . . I have a healthy supply. Must take the afternoon dose, though, or everything gets confused—that's what happened, isn't it?''

"Yes. How long does it take for kick in?''

"In a man my size twenty to twenty-five minutes— remarkable, isn't it? Pop, down the hatch, wait, and the picture tube regains clarity. Life is so much more bearable. Things hurt so much less. Even now I feel it working, like muddy waters turning crystalline. Where were we?''

"We were talking about the nasty games McCaffrey's perverts play with little children.''

"I'm not one of those,'' he said quickly.

"I know. But you helped those perverts molest hundreds of children, gave time and money to McCaffrey, set up Handler and Gutierrez and Hickle. You overdosed Melody Quinn to keep her mouth shut. Why?''

"It's all over, isn't it?'' he asked, sounding relieved.

"Yes.''

"They'll take away my license to practice medicine.''

"Definitely. Don't you think that's best?''

"I suppose so,'' he said reluctantly. "I still feel there's plenty left in me, plenty of good work to be done.''

"You'll have your chance,'' I reassured him, realizing that the pills were less than perfect. "They'll send you some place for the rest of your life where you'll experience little in the way of stress. No paperwork, no billing, none of the hassles of medical practice. No Gus McCaffrey telling you what to do, how to run your life. Just you—and you'll look and feel fine because they'll let you continue to take your pills—and help other people. People in need of help. You're a healer, you'll be able to help them.''

"I'll be able to help,'' he repeated.

"Absolutely.''

"One human being to another. Unencumbered.''

"Yes.''

"I have a good bedside manner. When I'm well. When I'm not well things get confused and things hurt—even ideas hurt, thoughts can be painful. I'm not at my best, when that happens. But when I'm functioning well I can't be beat for helping people.''

"I know that, Doctor. I know your reputation."

McCaffrey had spoken to me of an innate drive toward altruism. I knew whose buttons he'd been pushing with that one.

"I'm beholden to Gus," he said, "not due to any unusual sexual proclivity. That's his link with the others—with Stuart and Eddy. Since we'd been boys I'd known of their—strange ways. We all grew up in an isolated place, a strange place. We were cultivated, like orchids. Private lessons for this and that, having to look appropriate, act appropriately. Sometimes I wonder if that refined atmosphere didn't do us more harm than good. Look how we turned out, I, with my spells—I know there are labels for it these days, but I prefer to avoid them—Stuart and Eddy with their strange sexual habits.

"They started fooling with each other one summer, when we were nine or ten. Then with other children. Smaller children, much smaller. I didn't think much of it except to know that I wasn't interested in it. The way we were raised, right or wrong didn't seem as relevant as—appropriate and inappropriate. 'That's not appropriate, Willie,' Father would say. I imagine had Stuart or Eddy's fathers caught them with the little ones, that would have been their description of the entire affair: *Inappropriate.* Like using the wrong fork at dinner."

His description of coming of age on Brindamoor was strikingly like the one Van der Graaf had given me. At that moment he seemed akin to the fancy goldfish in the tank at Oomasa: beautiful, showy, cultivated by mutation and centuries of inbreeding, raised in a protected environment. But ultimately stunted and unadaptable to the realities of life.

"In that sense, the sexual one," he said, "I was quite normal. I married, fathered a child, a son. I performed quite adequately. Stuart and Eddy continued as my chums, going about their perverted ways. It was live and let live. They never mentioned my—spells. I let them be. Stuart was really a fine fellow, not overly bright, but well-meaning. It was a pity he had to . . . Except for that one kink, he was a good boy. Eddy was, is different. A sense of humor but a mean one. A nasty streak runs through him. He is habitually caustic and sarcastic—that's why I'm sensitive to that type of thing. Perhaps it's because of his size . . ."

"Your tie to McCaffrey," I prompted.

"Small men often get that way. You're—I can't see you now, but I recall you as being medium-sized. Is that correct?"

"I'm five-eleven," I said wearily.

"That's medium-sized. I've always been large. Father was large. It's just as Mendel predicted—long peas, short peas—fascinating field, genetics, isn't it?"

"Doctor—"

"I've wondered about the genetic impact on many traits. Intellect, for example. The liberal dogma would have us believe that environment makes the largest contribution to intelligence. It's an egalitarian premise, but reality doesn't bear it out. Long peas, short peas. Smart parents, smart children. Stupid parents, stupid children. I, myself, am a heterozygote. Father was brilliant. Mother was an Irish beauty, but very simple. She lived in a world where that combination served to create the perfect hostess. Father's showpiece."

"Your tie to McCaffrey," I said sharply.

"My tie? Oh nothing more serious than life and death."

He laughed. It was the first time I'd heard his laugh and I hoped it would be the last. It was a vacant discordant note, a blatant musical error screamng out in the middle of a symphony.

"I lived with Lilah and Willie Junior on the third floor of the Jedson dormitory. Stuart and Eddy shared a room on the first. As a married student I was given larger quarters—really a nice little apartment, when you got down to it. Two bedrooms, bath, living room, small kitchen. But no library, no study, so I did my reading at the kitchen table. Lilah had made it a cheerful place—bunting, trim, curtains, womanly types of things. Willie Junior was a little over two at the time, I remember. It was my senior year. I'd been having trouble with some of the premedical courses—physics, organic chemistry. I've never been a brilliant person. However, if I apply myself and keep my attention span steady I can do quite well. I desperately wanted to get into medical school on my own merits. My father and his father before him were doctors, all had been brilliant students. The joke, behind my back, was that I'd inherited my mother's brains as well as her looks—they didn't think I heard but I did. I wanted so much to show them that I could succeed on my own merits, not because I was Adolf Towle's son.

"The night it happened Willie Junior had been feeling poorly, unable to sleep. He'd been screaming and crying out, Lilah was frazzled. I ignored her requests for help, plunging myself into my studies, trying to shut out everything else. I had to bring my science grades up. It was imperative. The more anxious I got, the less able I was to pay attention. I tried to deal with it by embracing a kind of tunnel vision.

"Lilah had always been patient with me, but that night she became furious, started to come unglued. I looked up, saw her coming at me, her hands—she had tiny hands, a delicate woman—rolled up into fists, mouth open—I suppose she was screaming—eyes full of hatred. She seemed to me a bird of prey, about to swoop down and pick at my bones. I pushed her away with my arm. She fell, tumbling back, hit her head on the corner of a bureau—a hideous piece, an antique her mother had given her—and lay there, simply lay there.

"I can see the whole thing clearly now, as if it had just happened yesterday. Lilah lies there, motionless. I rise out of my chair, dreamlike, everything is swaying, everything is confusing. A small shape coming at me from the right, like a mouse, a rat. I swat it away. But it's not a rat, no, no. It's Willie Junior, coming back at me, crying for his mother, hitting me. Only dimly aware of his presence I strike out at him again, catch him on the side of his head. Too hard. He falls, lands, lies still. Unmoving. A large bruise masks the side of his face . . . My wife, my child, dead at my hands. I prepare to find my razor, cut my wrists, be done with it.

"Then Gus's voice is at my back. He stands in the doorway, huge, obese, sweaty, in work clothes, broom in hand. The janitor, cleaning the dormitories at night. I smell him—ammonia, body odor, cleaning fluids. He's heard the noise and has come to check. He looks at me, a long hard look, then at the bodies. He kneels over them, feels for a pulse. 'They're dead,' he tells me in a flat voice. For a second I think he's smiling and I'm ready to pounce on him, to attempt a third murder. Then the smile becomes a frown. He's thinking. 'Sit down,' he commands me. I'm not used to being ordered around by one of his class but I'm weak and sick with grief, my knees are buckling, everything's unraveling . . . I turn away from Lilah and Willie Junior, sit, put my face in my hands. Start to cry. I begin to grow more confused . . . A spell is coming on. Everything is starting to hurt. I have no pills, not like I'll have years later, when I'm a doctor. Now I'm merely a premedical student, powerless, hurting.

"Gus makes a telephone call. Minutes later my friends Stuart and Eddy appear in the room, like characters walking onstage in the midst of a dreadful play . . . The three of them talk among themselves, sometimes looking at me, muttering. Stuart comes to me first. He places a hand on my shoulder. 'We know it was an accident, Will,' he says. 'We know it wasn't your fault.' I start to argue with him but the words stick in my throat . . . The spells make it so hard to talk, so painful . . . I shake my head. Stuart comforts me, tells me everything will be all right. They will take care of everything. He rejoins Gus and Eddy.

"They wrap the bodies in a blanket, tell me not to leave the room. At the last moment they decide Stuart should stay with me. Gus and Eddy leave with the bodies. Stuart gives me coffee. I cry. I cry myself to sleep. Later that evening they return and tell me the story I'm to report to the police. They rehearse me, such good friends. I do a fine job. They tell me so. I feel some sense of relief at that. At least there is something I'm good at. Play-acting. That's what a bedside manner is, after all. Give the audience what it clamors for . . . My first audience is made up of the police. Then an officer of the Coast Guard—a family friend. They've found Lilah's car. Her body is macerated and bloated, I needn't identify it if it's too much of an ordeal. Scraps of Willie Junior's clothing have been found clinging to her hands. His body has drifted away. The tides, explains the officer. They'll continue to search . . . I break down and ready myself for the next show, the well-wishers, the press . . ."

The tides, I thought, the Coast Guard. Something there . . .

"Several months later I'm accepted at the medical school," Towle was saying. "I move to Los Angeles. Stuart comes with me, though we both know he'll never be able to finish. Eddy goes to law school in Los Angeles. The Heads are reunited—that's what they called us. The Three Heads of State.

"We go about our new lives, there is never a mention of the favor they've done for me. Of that night. However they are far more open than ever before about their sexual perversions, leaving nasty photographs where I can see them, not bothering to hide or conceal anything. They know I'm powerless to say a thing, even should I find a ten-year-old in my bed. A rotten mutual interdependence now binds us.

"Gus has disappeared. Years later, when I'm a doctor, on my way to prominence, the bedside manner fully developed, he appears at my office after the patients have all gone home. Further fattened, well-dressed, no longer a janitor. Now, he jokes, he's a man of God. He shows me the mail-order divinity degree. And he's come to ask a few favors from me. To *cash in some old IOU's* is the way he puts it. I paid him that evening and I've been paying him, in one way or another, ever since."

"It's time to stop paying," I said. "Let's not sacrifice Melody Quinn to him."

"The child is doomed, as things stand. I urged Gus to put it off. Her accident. Told him it was by no means evident that she'd seen or heard anything. But he won't be delayed much longer. What's one more life to a man like that?" He paused. "Does she really pose a danger to him?"

"Not really. She sat at the window and saw shadows of men." One of whom she'd recognized as her father—she didn't know him but she had a picture. On the day I hypnotized her, right after the session, she went into a spontaneous discussion of him. She showed me the picture and a trinket he'd given her. When she had the night terrors I should have figured it out. I thought the hypnosis hadn't evoked anything in her. It had. It had brought back memories of her father, of seeing him lurking outside her window, entering Handler's place. She knew something bad had happened in the apartment. She knew her daddy had done something terrible. She suppressed it. And it came back in her sleep.

It had started coming together for me when I'd seen the clue she'd left behind when Ronnie Lee had come by and abducted her and her mother. A shrunken head, precious until now, a symbol of Daddy. For her to have abandoned it meant she'd kissed him off, had come to grips with the fact that Daddy was a bad man, come back not to visit, but to hurt. Perhaps she'd watched him manhandle Bonita, or maybe it was the rough, uncaring way he'd spoken to her. Whatever it had been, the child had known.

Looking back it seemed so logical, but at the time the associations had been remote.

"It's ironic," Towle was saying. "I prescribed Ritalin to control her behavior and it was that same prescription that caused her insomnia, that led her to be awake at the wrong time."

"Ironic," I said. "Now let's go in there and get her out. You're going to help me. When it's over I'll see to it that you're cared for properly."

He didn't say anything. Simply sat straight in the seat, working hard at looking noble.

"Are you requesting my help?"

"I am, Doctor."

"Request granted."

29

I LAY on the floor of the Lincoln, covered by a blanket.

"My gun is pointed at your spine," I told him. "I don't expect any trouble but we haven't known each other long enough for trust to be worth much."

"I understand," he said. "I'm not offended."

He drove to the La Casa access road, turned left and steered smoothly and slowly to the chain link barrier. He identified himself to the voice on the squawk box and was let in. A brief stop at the guardhouse, an exchange of pleasantries, plenty of "Doctor, Sirs" from the guard and we were in.

He drove to the far end of the parking lot.

"Park away from the light," I whispered.

The car came to a halt.

"It's clear now," he said.

I crawled from under the blanket, got out of the car and motioned him to follow. We walked up the path, side by side. Counselors passed us in pairs, greeted him with deference and moved on. I tried to look like his associate.

La Casa was peaceful at night. Camp songs filtered through the trees. "A Hundred Bottles of Beer." "Oh Susanna." Children's voices. An off-key guitar. Microphoned adult commands. Mosquitoes and moths vied for space around mushroom lights imbedded in the foliage at our feet. The sweet smell of jasmine and oleander in the air. An occasional whiff of brine from the ocean, so close but unseen. To the right the open gray-green expanse of the Meadow. A pleasant enough graveyard . . . The Grove, dark as fudge, a piney refuge . . .

We passed the pool, taking care not to slip on the wet

cement. Towle moved like an old warrior heading into his
last battle, chin up, arms at his side, marching. I kept
the .38 within easy reach.

We made it to the bunkers unnoticed.

"That one," I said. "With the blue door."

Down the ramp. A hard twist of the key and we were in.

The building was divided into two rooms. The one in
the front was empty except for a single folding chair
pushed under an aluminum bridge table. The walls were of
unpainted block and smelled of mildew. The floors were
cold slab concrete, as was the ceiling. A square black
wound of skylight marked the ceiling's center. The only
light came from a single, unadorned bulb.

She was in the back, on an army cot, covered with a
coarse olive drab blanket and restrained with leather straps
across her ankles and chest. Her arms were pinioned under
the blanket. She breathed slowly, mouth open, sleeping,
head to one side, her pale, tear-streaked skin translucent in
the semidarkness. Wisps of hair hung loosely around her
face. Tiny, vulnerable, lost.

At the foot of the cot was a plastic tray holding an
uneaten, congealed fried egg, limp french fries, shriveled
brown-tipped lettuce and an open wax container of milk.

"Untie her." I pointed the gun.

Towle bent over her, working in the dimness to unfasten
the straps.

"What do you have her on?"

"Valium, high dose. Thorazine on top of that."

Dr. Towle's magic elixir.

He got the restraints loose and peeled back the blanket.
She was wearing dirty jeans and a red-and-white striped
T-shirt with Snoopy on the front. He lifted the shirt and
palpated her abdomen, took her pulse, felt her forehead:
played doctor.

"She looks thin, but otherwise healthy," he pronounced.

"Wrap her back up. Can you carry her?"

"Certainly," he replied, miffed that I could doubt his
strength.

"All right then, let's go."

He gathered her up in his arms, looking for all the world

like the Great White Father. The child let out a sigh, a shudder, and clung to him.

"Keep her totally covered once we get outside."

I began a half-turn. A soft, musical voice at my back drawled:

"Don't move, Doctor Delaware, or you'll lose your fucking head."

I stood still.

"Put the young one down, Will. Take his gun."

Towle looked at me blankly. I shrugged. He placed Melody on the cot gently and covered her. I handed him the .38.

"Against the wall with your hands up, Doctor. Search him, Will."

Towle patted me down.

"Turn around."

McCaffrey stood there grinning, filling the opening between the two rooms, a .357 magnum in one hand, a Polaroid camera in the other. He wore an iridescent lime-green jumpsuit decorated with a score of snap-pockets and buckles, and matching lime patent leather shoes. In the dim light his complexion reflected greenly as well.

"Task, tsk, Willie. What mischief are we up to tonight?"

The great physician hung his head and shuffled nervously.

"Not feeling loquacious tonight, Willie? That's all right. We'll talk later." The colorless eyes narrowed. "Right now there's business to attend to."

"Is this your idea of altruism?" I looked at Melody's limp form.

"Shut up!" he snapped. To Towle: "Remove the child's clothing."

"Gus—I—why?"

"Just do as I say, Willie."

"No more, Gus," Towle pleaded. "We've done enough."

"No, you idiot. We haven't done enough at all. This smartass here has the potential to cause us—you *and* me— lots of trouble. I made plans to eliminate him, but apparently I'll have to do the job myself."

"Plans," I sneered. "Halstead's rotting in a vacant lot with a spike in his throat. He was a bumbler, like all of your slaves."

McCaffrey pursed his thick lips.

"I'm warning you," he said.

"That's your specialty, isn't it?" I continued, playing for time. I saw his massive silhouette shift as he tried to keep me in his sights. But the darkness made it difficult as did Towle's body, which had gotten between us as he fidgeted under his master's glare. "You have a knack for finding bumblers and losers, emotional cripples, misfits. The same knack flies have for locating shit. You zero in on their open wounds, sink your fangs into them, suck them dry."

"How literary," he replied in a lilting voice, obviously fighting to maintain control. We were in close quarters and impulsiveness could prove hazardous.

"Her clothes, Will," he said. "Take them all off."

"Gus—"

"Do it, you sniveling piece of turd!"

Towle raised his arm in front of his face like a child warding off a blow. When none was forthcoming he moved toward the child.

"You're a doctor," I said. "A respected physician. Don't listen to him—"

Fast, faster than I thought possible, McCaffrey stepped forward in the clearing Towle had created. He slashed with one elephantine sleeve and raked the side of my head with his gun. I fell to the floor, my face exploding with pain, hands protecting myself from further assault, blood running between my fingers.

"Now you stay there, sir, and keep your fucking mouth shut."

Towle removed Melody's T-shirt. Her chest was concave and white, the ribs twin grilles of gray-blue shadow.

"Now the pants. The panties. Everything."

"Why are we doing this, Gus?" Towle wanted to know. To my ears, which were far from perfect, one being ripped and bloody, the other filled with watery echoes, his speech sounded slurred. I wondered if stress could break through the biochemical barrier he'd erected around his damaged mind.

"Why?" McCaffrey laughed. "You're not used to seeing this type of thing firsthand, are you, Willie? You've had a sanitized role up until now, enjoying the luxury of distance. Well, no matter, I'll explain it to you."

He raised an eyebrow at Towle contemptuously, looked down at me and laughed again. The sound reverberated painfully in my injured skull. The blood continued to run down my face. My head felt mushy, loose on its stalk. I began to grow nauseated and dizzy, and the floor rose up at me. Terror gripped me as I wondered if he'd hit me hard enough to cause brain damage. I knew what a subdural hematoma could do to the fragile gray jelly that made life worth living . . . Crazily, fighting for strength and clarity, I pictured my brain in an anatomist's tray, pinioned and splayed, and tried to localize the site of the injury. The gun had smashed against my left side—the dominant hemisphere, for I am right-handed . . . that was bad. The dominant side controlled logical processes: reasoning, analysis, deduction—the stuff to which I'd grown addicted over thirty-three years. I thought about losing all of that, of fading into dimness and confusion, then remembered two-year-old Willie Junior, struck down in much the same way. He'd lost it all . . . which might have been merciful. For had he survived, the damage would have been great. Left side/right side . . . the tides . . .

"We're going to put on a little stage play, Willie," McCaffrey lectured. "I'll be the producer and director. You'll be my assistant, helping me with the props." He swung the camera in an arc. "The stars of the show will be little Melody and our friend Doctor Alex Delaware. The name of the play will be—'Death of a Shrink,' subtitled 'Caught in the Act.' A morality play."

"Gus—"

"The plot is as follows: Doctor Delaware, our erstwhile villain, is well-known as a caring, sensitive child psychologist. However, unbeknownst to his colleagues and his patients, his choice of profession did not arise out of any great sense of—altruism. No, Doctor Delaware has chosen to become a kiddy shrink to be closer to the kiddies. To be able to fondle and abuse their genitals. In short, a deviate, an opportunist, the lowest of the low. An evil and gravely sick man." He paused to look down on me, chuckling, breathing hard. Despite the chill, he was sweating, his glasses sliding low on his nose. The top of his kinky head was a halo of moisture. I looked at the .38 in Towle's hand, and measured the distance between it and the spot where I lay. McCaffrey saw me, shook his head, and mouthed the word *no*, showing me his teeth.

"With these same depraved motivations in mind, Doctor Delaware applies for membership in the Gentleman's Brigade. He visits La Casa. We show him around. We screen him and our tests reveal him to be unsuitable for inclusion into our honorable fraternity. We reject him. Furious and frustrated at being denied a lifetime supply of hairless pussy and tiny little pricks, he simmers."

He stopped the narration and made loud slurping noises. Melody stirred in her sleep.

"He simmers," he repeated. "Stews in his own juices. Finally, at the height of his sick rage, he breaks into La Casa one night and roams the grounds until he finds a victim. A poor orphan girl, defenseless, alone in her dormitory because she is sick in bed with the flu. The madman loses control. Rapes her, virtually tears her apart—the autopsy will show uncommon savagery, Will. Takes pictures of the ghastly deed. A hideous crime. As the child cries out, screaming for her life, we—you and me, Will—happen to be passing by. We rush to her aid, but it is too late. The child has succumbed.

"We take in the carnage before us with horror and disgust. Delaware, discovered, rises up against us, gun in hand. Heroically we wrestle him to the ground, struggle for the weapon and in the process the murderer is fatally wounded. The good guys win, and there is peace in the valley."

"Amen," I said.

He ignored me.

"Not bad, eh, Will?"

"Gus, it won't work." Towle stepped between us again. "He knows everything—the teacher and the Nemeth boy—"

"Quiet. It will work. The past is the best predictor of the future. We have succeeded before, we will continue to triumph."

"Gus—"

"Silence! I'm not asking you, I'm telling you. Strip her!"

I propped myself on my elbows and spoke through aching, swollen jaws, struggling to make sense out of what I was saying even as I told it.

"How about another script? This one's called The Big Lie. It's about a man who thinks he's murdered his wife and child and sells out his entire life to a blackmailer."

"Shut up." McCaffrey advanced on me. Towle blocked his way, aiming the .38 at the half-acre of green-clad fat. It was a Mexican standoff.

"I want to hear what he has to say, Gus. Things are confusing me. Things hurt. I want him to explain . . ."

"Think," I said, talking as fast as the pain allowed. "Did you ever check Willie Junior's body for signs of life? No. *He* did. *He* told you your boy was dead. That you'd killed him. But was the body ever found? Did you ever actually see the body?"

Towle's face tightened with concentration. He was slipping, losing his grip on reality, digging his nails in, fighting to hold on.

"I—I don't know. Willie was dead. They told me. The tides . . ."

"Maybe. But think: It was a golden opportunity. Lilah's death wouldn't have brought a charge greater than involuntary manslaughter. Domestic violence wasn't even taken seriously in those days. With the lawyers your family would have hired, you might have gotten off with probation. But two deaths—especially with one a child—would have been impossible to brush off. He needed you to believe Junior was dead to be able to hook you."

"Will," said McCaffrey, threateningly.

"I don't know—such a long time . . ."

"Think! Did you hit him hard enough to kill him? Maybe not. Use your brain. It's a good one. You remembered before."

"I used to have a good brain," he muttered.

"You still do! Remember. You hit little Willie on the side of the head. What side?"

"Don't know—"

"Will, it's all lies. He's trying to poison your mind." McCaffrey looked for a way to silence me. But Towle's gun rose and nudged the spot where a normal person would have had a heart.

"What side, Doctor?" I demanded.

"I'm right-handed," he answered, as if discovering the fact for the first time. "I use my right hand. I hit him with my right hand . . . I see it . . . He's coming at me from his bedroom. Crying for Mommy. Coming from the right, throwing himself at me. I—hit him—on his right side. The right side."

The pain in my head turned the act of talking into torture, but I bore down.

"Yes. Exactly. Think! What if McCaffrey hoaxed you— you didn't *kill* Willie. You injured him, but he survived. What kind of damage, what kind of symptoms, could be caused by trauma to the right hemisphere in a developing child?"

"Right hemisphere cerebral damage—the right brain controls the left side," he recited. " Right brain damage causes left-side dysfunction."

"Perfect," I urged him on. "A severe blow to the right brain could bring about left-side hemiparesis. *A bad left side.*"

"Earl . . ."

"Yes. The body was never found because the child never died. McCaffrey felt his pulse, found one, saw you in shock over what you'd done and exploited your guilt. He wrapped up both bodies, with a little help from your buddies. Lilah was put behind the wheel of the car and dumped off the Evergreen Bridge. McCaffrey took the child. Probably got him some kind of medical help, but not the best, because a reputable doctor would have had to report the incident to the police. After the funeral he disappeared. Those were *your* words. He disappeared because he had to. He had the child with him. He took him to Mexico, who knows where, renamed him, changed him from your son into the kind of person someone raised by a monster would turn out to be. He made him his *robot.*"

"Earl . . . Willie Junior." Towle's brows knitted.

"Ridiculous! Out of the way, Will! I order it!"

"It's the truth," I said through the pounding in my head. "Tonight, before you took your pills, you said Melody looked vaguely familiar. Turn carefully—don't let *him* out of your sight—and take a look at her. Tell me why."

Towle backed away, kept the gun on McCaffrey, took a short look at Melody, and then a longer one.

"She looks," he said, softly, "like Lilah."

"Her grandmother."

"I couldn't know—"

Of course he couldn't. The Quinns were poor, illiterate, the dregs of society. Piss-poor protoplasm. His views on the genetic superiority of the upper class would have prevented him from even fantasizing a connection between them and his bloodline. Now his defenses were down and the insights were hitting his consciousness like drops of acid—each point of contact raising psychic wounds. His son a murderer, a man conditioned to be a night-hunting beast. Dead. His daughter-in-law, intellectually limited, a helpless, pathetic creature. Dead. His granddaughter, the child on whom he'd plied his trade and medicated into stupor. Alive. But not for long.

"He wants to murder her. To tear her apart. You heard him. The autopsy will show *uncommon savagery.*"

Towle turned on the man in green.

"Gus—" he sobbed.

"Now, now, Will," said McCaffrey soothingly. Then he blew Towle away with the .357. The bullet entered his abdomen and exited through his back in a fine spray of blood, skin and cashmere. He slammed backward, landing at the side of the cot. The report of the big gun echoed through the concrete room. A thunderstorm. The child awoke and began screaming.

McCaffrey pointed the gun at her, reflexively. I threw myself at him and kicked his wrist, knocking the gun loose. It sailed backward, into the front room. He howled, rabid. I kicked him again, in the shin. His leg felt like a side of beef. He backed into the front room, wanting the gun. I went after him. He lunged, his bulk rolling. I used both hands to hit him in the lower back. My fists sank into his softness. He barely budged. His hand was inches from the magnum. I kicked it away, then used my foot to smash his ribs with little effect. He was too damned big and too damned tall to be able to get a facial punch in. I went for his legs and thighs, and tripped him.

He came crashing down, a felled redwood, taking me with him. Snarling, cursing, drooling, he rolled on top of me and got his hands around my throat. He panted his sour breath on me, the lumpy face crimson, the fish eyes swallowed by fleshy folds, squeezing. I fought to get out from under him but couldn't move. I experienced the panic of the sudden paralytic. He squeezed tighter. I pushed up helplessly.

His face darkened. With effort, I thought. Crimson to maroon to red-black, then a splash of color. The kinky hair exploding. The blood bright and fresh, pouring out of his nose, his ears, his mouth. The eyes opening wide, blinking furiously. A look of great insult on the grotesque face. Gargling noises from the jowl-wrapped gullet. Needles and triangles of broken glass raining down upon us. His inert carcass a shield from the rain.

The skylight was an open wound now. A face peered down. Black, serious. Delano Hardy. Something else black: the nose of a rifle.

"Hold on, Consultant," he said. "We're coming to get you."

"Your face looks uglier than mine," Milo said when he'd pulled McCaffrey off of me.

"Yeah," I said, struggling to articulate through a mouth that felt as if I'd sucked on razor blades, "but mine will look better in a couple of days."

He grinned.

"The kid seems okay," said Hardy from the back room. He came out with Melody in his arms. She was shivering. "Scared but unharmed, as the papers say."

Milo helped me to my feet. I walked to her and stroked her hair.

"It's going to be all right, sweetheart." Funny how clichés seem to find their niche during rough times.

"Alex," she said. She smiled. "You look funny."

I squeezed her hand and she closed her eyes. Sweet dreams.

In the ambulance Milo kicked his shoes off and sat, yoga style, by the side of my stretcher.

"My hero," I said. It came out *Mmm mirrow*.

"This one's going to be good for a *long* time, pal. Free use of the Caddy on demand, cash loans with no interest, gratis therapy."

"In other words," I fought to enunciate through swollen jaws, "business as usual."

He laughed, patted my arm and told me to shut up. The ambulance attendant agreed.

"The man may need wires," he said. "He shouldn't talk."

I started to protest.

"Shh!" said the attendant.

A half-mile later Milo looked at me and shook his head.

"You are one lucky turkey, friend. I got into town an hour and a half ago and got Rick's note to call you. I call your place. Robin was there, sans you, worried. You had a dinner date at seven, but no you. She says it's not like compulsive old you to be late, please could I do something. She also filled me in on your jaunts—you've been a busy little bee in my absence, haven't you? I call in to the station—on a vacation day, I might add—and get this schitzy message about Kruger written in Del Hardy's fine cursive scrawl; also something about he's going to La Casa. I went to Kruger's, got through your barricade, found him trussed, scared shitless. He was a wreck, spilled his guts without being asked—amazing what a little sensory deprivation will do, huh? I beep Del, catch him in his car on Pacific Coast Highway—which is still full of traffic at this hour, what with producers and starlets going home— make believe it's code three and siren it all the way along the side of the road. The pros take over and the rest is goddamn history."

"I didn't want a full-scale raid." I forced out the words, in agony. "Didn't want anything to happen to the kid—"

"Please shut up, sir," said the attendant.

"Shush," said Milo, gently. "You did a great job. Thanks. Okay? Don't do it again. Turkey."

The ambulance came to a halt at Santa Monica Hospital's Emergency Room. I knew the place because I'd given a series of lectures to the staff on the psychological aspects of trauma in children. There'd be no lecture tonight.

"You okay?" Milo asked.

"Um-hmm."

"Okay. I'll let the white coats take over. Gotta go and arrest a judge."

30

ROBIN TOOK one look at me, jaws wired shut, eyes black-ened, and burst into tears. She hugged me, fussed over me and sat by my side feeding me soup and soda. That lasted for a day. Then she got in touch with her anger and let me have it for being so crazy to put my life on the line. I was in no position to defend myself. She tried not speaking to me for six hours, then relented and things started to get back to normal.

When I could talk I called Raquel Ochoa.

"Hi," she said. "You sound funny."

I told her the story, keeping it brief because of the pain.

She said nothing for a moment, then softly:

"There *were* monsters."

"Yes."

The silence between us was uncomfortable.

"You're a man of principle," she said, finally.

"Thank you."

"Alex—that evening—us. I don't regret it. It got me thinking. Made me realize I have to go out and find something—someone—for myself."

"Don't settle for less than the best."

"I—thanks. Take care of yourself. Mend fast."

"I'll work on it. Good-bye."

"Good-bye."

My next call was to Ned Biondi, who rushed over that afternoon and interviewed me until the nurses kicked him out. I read his stories for days. He had it all down—McCaffrey's Mexico days, the Hickle murder, the Gentle-man's Brigade, the suicide of Edwin Hayden the night he was arrested. The judge had shot himself in the mouth while dressing to go to the station with Milo. It seemed fitting in light of what he'd done to Hickle, and Biondi didn't miss the chance to wax philosophical.

I phoned Olivia Brickerman and asked her to take care of Melody. Two days later she found an older, childless couple up in Bakersfield, people she knew and trusted, with lots of patience and five acres for running. Nearby was a gifted child psychologist, a woman I'd known from graduate school, with experience in stress and bereavement. To them would be entrusted the task of helping the little girl piece her life together.

Six weeks after the fall of La Casa de los Niños, Robin and I met Milo and Rick Silverman for dinner at a quiet, elegant seafood place in Bel Air.

My friend's amour turned out to be a guy who could have walked out of a cigarette ad—six feet tall, broadshouldered, narrow-hipped, masculine, handsome face overlaid with just a touch of crag, head of tight bronze curls, matching bristle mustache. He wore a tailored black silk suit, black-and-white striped shirt and a black knit tie.

"Lucky Milo," Robin whispered as they joined our table.

Next to him, Milo looked baggier than ever, though he'd tried to spruce himself up, his hair slicked down like that of a kid in church.

Milo made the introductions. We ordered drinks and got acquainted. Rick was quiet and reserved, with nervous, surgical hands that had to be holding something—a glass, a fork, a stirrer. He and Milo exchanged loving glances. Once I saw them touch hands, for just a second. As the evening progressed he opened up and talked about his work, about what he liked and didn't like about being a doctor. The food came. The others had lobster and steak. I had to content myself with soufflé. We chatted, the evening went well.

After the dishes had been cleared away, before the pastry cart and the brandy, Rick's beeper went off. He excused himself and went to the phone.

"If you gentlemen don't mind, I'll make a stop in the ladies' room." Robin patted her mouth with her napkin and rose. I followed her sway until she disappeared.

Milo and I looked at each other. He picked a piece of fish off his tie.

"Hello, friend," I said.

"Hello."

"He's a nice guy, Rick. I like him."

"I want this one to last. It's hard, the way we live."

"You look happy."

"We are. Different in lots of ways, but we also have a lot in common. He's getting a Porsche 928," he said with a laugh.

"Congratulations. You're a good-lifer now."

"All comes to he who waits."

I motioned the waiter over and we ordered fresh drinks. When they came I said: "Milo, there's something I've been wanting to talk to you about. About the case."

He took a long swallow of scotch.

"What about?"

"Hayden."

His face grew grave.

"You're my shrink—so that this conversation is confidential?"

"Better than that. I'm your friend."

"Okay," he sighed. "Ask what I know you're going to ask."

"The suicide. It doesn't make sense on two grounds. First, the kind of guy he was. I got the same picture from everyone. An arrogant, nasty, sarcastic little bastard. Loved himself. Not a trace of self-doubt. That kind don't kill themselves. They search for ways to shift the blame to others, they weasel out of things. Second, you're a pro. How could you get so sloppy as to let him do it?"

"The story I told Internal Affairs was that he was a judge. I treated him with deference. I let him get dressed. In his study. They bought it."

"Tell me about it. Please."

He looked around the restaurant. The tables nearby were empty. Rick and Robin were still gone. He gulped down the rest of his drink.

"I went for him right after I left you. Must have been after ten by then. He lived in one of those huge English Tudor palaces in Hancock Park. Old money. Big lawn.

Bentley in the driveway. Topiary. A doorbell out of a Karloff flick.

"He answered the door, a little wimp of a guy, maybe five-four. Strange eyes. Spooky. He was wearing a silk dressing gown, holding a brandy in one hand. I told him what I'd come for. It didn't faze him.

"He was very proper, distant, as if what I was there for had nothing to do with him. I followed him inside the house. Lots of family portrait. Moldings around the ceilings, chandeliers—I want you to get the flavor of this. Lord of the Manor. Led me to his study in the back. The requisite oak panels, wall-to-wall leather-covered books, the kind people collect but never read. A fireplace with two porcelain greyhounds, carved desk, blah blah blah.

"I pat him down, find a .22, take it. 'It's for protection at night, officer,' he tells me. 'You never know who'll come knocking at your door.' He's laughing, Alex, I swear I couldn't believe it. The guy's life is crashing down around him, he's going to hit the front page as a kiddy-diddler and he's laughing.

"I read him his rights, go into the spiel, he looks bored. Sits down at his desk, like I'm there for a favor. Then he starts talking to me. Laughing in my face. 'How amusing,' he says, 'that they send you, the *faggot cop*, after me in a case like this. You of all people should understand.' He goes on like that for a while, smirking, implying, then coming right out and saying it. That we're birds of a feather. Partners in crime. Perverts. I'm standing there listening to this and getting hotter and hotter. He laughs some more and I see that's what he wants, to stay in control of the situation. So I cool down, smile back. Whistle. He starts telling me the things they did to the kids, like it's supposed to arouse me. Like we're buddies at a stag party. My stomach is turning and he's putting us in the same boat.

"As he talks, he comes into focus, psychological focus. It's like I can see behind the spooky eyes, into his brain. And all I see is dark and bad. Nothing good in there. Nothing good can come from this guy. He's a washout. I'm judging the judge. I'm prophesying. Meanwhile he's going on about the parties they used to have with the kids, how much he's going to miss them."

He stopped and cleared his throat. Took my drink and finished it.

"I'm still looking through him, into his future. And I know what's going to happen. I look around that big room. I know the kind of money behind this guy. He'll get a Not Guilty by Reason, they'll cart him off to some country club. Eventually he'll buy his way out and start all over again. So I make a decision. Right there on the spot.

"I walk around behind him, grab his scrawny little head and tilt it back. I take out the .22 and jam it in his mouth. He's struggling, but he's an old wimp. It's like holding down an insect, a goddamn bug. I position him—I've seen enough forensic reports to know what it should look like. I say 'Nighty-night, Your Honor,' and pull the trigger. The rest you know. Okay?"

"Okay."

"Now how about another drink? I'm thirsty as hell."

About the Author

With over two million copies of his best-selling novels in print, translations into numerous foreign languages, and receipt of both the Edgar and the Anthony awards, Jonathan Kellerman has received wide acclaim as a contemporary master of the psychological thriller.

Born in New York City in 1949, he grew up in Los Angeles, graduated from UCLA, and received a Ph.D. in clinical psychology from the University of Southern California, where he is currently clinical associate professor of pediatrics in the School of Medicine. Prior to earning his doctorate Kellerman worked as a cartoonist, illustrator, editor, teacher, and musician. During the course of his career as a psychologist, he cofounded and directed the Psychosocial Program at Children's Hospital of Los Angeles, headed a psychological consulting firm, conducted research in behavioral medicine, and acquired a national reputation as an authority on childhood stress.

In addition to *When the Bough Breaks*, *Blood Test*, (both available in Signet editions), and *Over the Edge*, Dr. Kellerman has written two nonfiction books and well over one hundred scholarly articles, chapters, reviews, and abstracts in the field of psychology. His short fiction and essays have appeared in *Alfred Hitchcock's Mystery Magazine*, *Los Angeles Magazine*, the *Los Angeles Times*, and *Newsweek*.

He lives in Southern California with his wife, novelist Faye Kellerman, and their three children, and is currently at work on a major crime novel.

IN THE HALL OF HATE

Someone—something—was lurking in a pool of darkness. He could feel its evil flow down in a vaporous cloud, sweeping over him and chilling his mind. A movement. A shape—a dark shape —emerged from the blackness and stopped just before him. A repulsive smell of unclean human staleness assailed his nostrils, almost causing him to vomit. He slowly looked up, searching the length of the figure towering over him, and when he reached its head, a face came floating down at him. The face of a dirty drooling demon who bore the features of a man the world had despised. . . .

It was then that he screamed. . . .

THE SPEAR

There is no escape from its cutting edge!

"CHILLING, EERIE . . . A FIRST-RATE THRILLER!"—Publishers Weekly

Big Bestsellers from SIGNET

- [ ] LAIR by James Herbert. (#E8650—$2.25)*
- [ ] FLUKE by James Herbert. (#J8394—$1.95)*
- [ ] THE FOG by James Herbert. (#J9193—$1.95)
- [ ] THE RATS by James Herbert. (#E8770—$1.75)
- [ ] THE SURVIVOR by James Herbert. (#J8369—$1.95)
- [ ] THE DOUBLE-CROSS CIRCUIT by Michael Dorland. (#J9065—$1.95)
- [ ] THE MOSSAD by Dennis Eisenberg, Uri Dan and Eli Landau. (#E8883—$2.50)*
- [ ] THE NIGHT LETTER by Paul Spike. (#E8947—$2.50)*
- [ ] EYE OF THE NEEDLE by Ken Follett. (#E8746—$2.95)
- [ ] TWINS by Bari Wood and Jack Geasland. (#E9094—$2.75)
- [ ] THE KILLING GIFT by Bari Wood. (#J7350—$1.95)
- [ ] LABYRINTH by Eric MacKenzie-Lamb. (#E9062—$2.25)*
- [ ] RITTER'S GOLD by Frank N. Hawkins, Jr. (#J9067—$1.95)*
- [ ] THE ENIGMA by Michael Barak. (#J8920—$1.95)*
- [ ] GOING ALL THE WAY by Susan Hufford. (#E9014—$2.25)*

* Price slightly higher in Canada

THE SPEAR

BY

JAMES HERBERT

A SIGNET BOOK

NEW AMERICAN LIBRARY

TIMES MIRROR

The author and publisher wish to thank Hugh Trevor-Roper and
Weidenfeld & Nicolson Ltd and Hermann Rauschning and
Eyre & Spottiswoode (Publishers) Ltd (as successors to
Thornton Butterworth Ltd) for their kind permission to quote
from *Hitler's Table Talk* and *Hitler Speaks* respectively.

SIGNET, SIGNET CLASSICS, MENTOR, PLUME AND MERIDIAN BOOKS
are published by The New American Library, Inc.,
1633 Broadway, New York, New York 10019

First Signet Printing, February, 1980

1   2   3   4   5   6   7   8   9

PRINTED IN THE UNITED STATES OF AMERICA

A deathly cry! I rushed in:
Klingsor, laughing, was vanishing from there,
having stolen the holy Spear.

—RICHARD WAGNER
Parsifal

For myself, I have the most intimate familiarity with Wagner's mental processes. At every stage in my life I come back to him. Only a new nobility can introduce the new civilization for us. If we strip "Parsifal" of every poetic element, we learn from it that selection and renewal are possible only amid the continuous tension of a lasting struggle. A world-wide process of segregation is going on before our eyes. Those who see in struggle the meaning of life, gradually mount the steps of a new nobility. Those who are in search of peace and order through dependence, sink, whatever their origin, to the inert masses. The masses, however, are doomed to decay and self-destruction. In our world-revolutionary turning-point the masses are the sum total of the sinking civilization and its dying representatives. We must allow them to die with their kings, like Amfortas.

—ADOLF HITLER

You realize now what anxieties I have. The world regards Adolf Hitler as a strong-man—and that's how his name must go down in history. The greater German Reich will stretch from the Urals to the North Sea after the war. That will be the Führer's greatest achievement. He's the greatest man who ever lived and without him it would never have been possible. So what does it matter that he should be ill now, when his work is almost complete.

—HEINRICH HIMMLER

33 A.D.

. . . So the soldiers came and broke the legs of the first, and of the other who had been crucified with him; but when they came to Jesus and saw that he was already dead, they did not break his legs. But one of the soldiers pierced his side with a spear, and at once there came out blood and water. . . .

JOHN: 19:32

23rd May, 1945

Sergeant-Major Edwin Austin almost smiled in pity for the pathetic figure who sat huddled on the couch, with a blanket wrapped around his trembling body. Almost, but not quite, for they said this innocuous little man had caused the deaths of millions in the vicious war that had just ended. His persecution of the Jews in his own country, then in other captured territories, had horrified the world, and even now, more atrocities were coming to light. Could this be the man who had instigated such evil, this timid creature wearing only shirt, pants, and socks beneath the army blanket? Was he really the person he claimed to be? Without the moustache, weak chin and bloated neck unshaven, without the military uniform, without the arrogance of his kind, it was difficult to tell. When he'd been captured, the German had been wearing a black eyepatch and a uniform with all the insignia removed. He'd claimed to be a member of the Secret Field Police, but under interrogation had announced a different—a more sinister—identity.

When he'd torn off the eyepatch and donned a pair of rimless spectacles, the likeness was evident, despite his bearing, his nervous affability.

Colonel Murphy, the chief of intelligence on Montgomery's staff, had accepted the German's claimed identity, so why should he, a mere sergeant-major, doubt it? They had insisted the prisoner be watched every moment of the day; that's how seriously they were treating the matter.

The sergeant had already lost one prisoner who'd been put in his charge: SS General Pruetzmann had crushed a cyanide capsule between his teeth. He'd make no mistakes with this one.

Through the German's interpreter, the sergeant informed him the couch was to be his bed, and he was to undress and lie down. The prisoner began to protest but became silent when he saw the resolution on the Englishman's face. He unwrapped the blanket from his shoulders and began to take off his underpants.

It was at that moment that Colonel Murphy, followed by another uniformed officer, entered the room. The intelligence chief brusquely introduced his companion as Captain Wells, an army doctor, then ordered the German to strip completely.

The sergeant knew what was about to happen, for a small vial had been found hidden in the lining of the prisoner's jacket two days before and they suspected he had another secreted somewhere on his person. They were taking no chances with a prisoner of this importance.

They began to search him, running their fingers through the hair on his head and pubic regions; they examined his ears and the cracks between each toe; they spread his buttocks and checked his anal passage. Nothing was found but there was still one area unsearched, and this was the most obvious hiding place. The doctor ordered the prisoner to open his mouth.

Captain Wells saw the black vial immediately, between a gap in the German's teeth on the right-hand side of his lower jaw, and with a shout of alarm thrust his fingers into the open mouth. But the German was too quick. He wrenched his head to one side. biting down hard on the medic's fingers as he did so. Colonel Murphy and Sergeant-Major Austin leapt forward and threw the struggling prisoner to the floor, the doctor holding him by the throat, squeezing with both hands, trying to force him to spit the capsule out. It was too late, though; the vial had been cracked and the poison was already finding its way

[4]

into the man's system. His death was inevitable but still they fought to prevent it.

Colonel Murphy told the sergeant to find a needle and cotton as quickly as possible, and valuable minutes were lost as the interrogation center was turned upside down in the search for such trivial articles. The doctor kept his pressure on the prisoner's throat, but the death spasms were already beginning. The sergeant soon returned and it was the steady hands of the intelligence chief that had to thread the needle and cotton. While Sergeant Austin forced the dying man's mouth open, the colonel grasped the slippery tongue and pierced it with the needle; by pulling on the thread they were able to hold the tongue out from the mouth, preventing it from blocking the throat. For fifteen minutes they used emetics, a stomach-pump and every method of artificial respiration. It was no use; the three men had prevented the cyanide from killing with its usual swiftness, but they had only delayed death.

The prisoner's body contorted into one last spasm of agony, his face hideous in its torment, then his body slumped into stillness.

Two days later, Sergeant-Major Austin wrapped the corpse in army blankets, wound camouflage netting tied with telephone wire around it, and buried the body in an unmarked grave near Lüneburg. The final resting place of Reichsführer SS Heinrich Himmler was never recorded.

ONE

The struggle for world domination will be fought entirely between us, between German and Jew. All else is façade and illusion. Behind England stands Israel, and behind France, and behind the United States. Even when we have driven the Jew out of Germany, he remains our world enemy.

—ADOLF HITLER

Harry Steadman locked the door of his gray Celica and glanced around the wide, grass-middled square. The majority of other parking spaces were filled, forming a many-colored machine fringe around the green lawns. Most of the square's working inhabitants of solicitors and accountants had arrived and were already easing their mental gears into the Monday morning pace. He'd noticed the couple sitting in their Cortina when he had driven toward his allocated parking space and would have paid them no mind had not the man's eyes snapped to attention on seeing Steadman; the forced casualness as the eyes glanced away again had not deceived the investigator. The man had recognized him, but Steadman had not recognized the man. Nor his female companion.

Both appeared to be in deep conversation as he looked across the roof of his car toward them. It was a small thing, for there was nothing unusual about clients waiting in their cars until their appointment with solicitor, accountant—or even private investigator—in Gray's Inn Square, but Steadman felt an unease he hadn't experienced for a long time. A throwback from the time he'd lived with unease for weeks, sometimes months, on end. And it had been triggered off just by the meeting of eyes.

He crossed the smooth roadway and entered the gloomy interior of the red-brick terraced building that contained his small agency, along with three company accountants' offices. It was a prime position for an inquiry agency, in the midst of the legal "ghetto," Lincoln's Inn and Bloomsbury on the doorstep, the law courts and the Old Bailey ten minutes away. The address gave respectability to a profession that was often looked upon as seedy, even sordid. Harry Steadman, along with his partner, Maggie Wyeth, had worked long and hard to establish an agency of high repute, beginning with the principle that no case, provided there were no illegalities involved, was too big or too small. Fortunately, over the past two years, because of their growing reputation, most of their cases were for big companies, involving anything from industrial espionage to fraud or embezzlement within a company, though they still handled matrimonial inquiries, traced missing persons, and carried out the service of legal process, delivering writs or warnings of prosecution to debtors. Their staff consisted of three: a retired police officer named Blake, whom they naturally called Sexton; a young trainee detective, Steve, who would leave them soon to set up on his own; and Sue, their receptionist/typist and general runaround—twenty-nine, plump, unmarried, and an absolute godsend.

Steadman ignored the small and generally unreliable lift and climbed the three flights of stairs to the agency, his breathing becoming sharper and his strides less agile as he neared the top. At thirty-eight, his condition could be described as "fair but wearing."

The clatter of Sue's typing met him in the hallway, and

her smile greeted him when he pushed open the office door.

"Hello, Sue," he said, returning her smile.

"Morning, Mr. Steadman. Good trip?"

"Good enough. One more week should cover it."

Steadman had spent the previous week in the north, setting up a complete security system for a manufacturer of electrical goods. The company's innovations in refining communications systems had a nasty habit of being "innovated" by a rival company just weeks ahead of their own; coincidence was one thing, but almost identical patents over a period of eighteen months stretched credibility too far.

"Is Maggie in yet?" Steadman asked, taking the letters Sue slid toward him.

"Yes, she's got someone with her at the moment. I'll let her know you're back as soon as she's free."

"Fine. I'll have to leave again about eleven so we'll need to talk soon." He headed toward his office, waving a hand toward Steve, who was frowning over a booklet outlining the laws of evidence and procedure.

"Stick with it, Steve," Steadman grinned. "In ten years it will all be crystal clear."

Steve smiled weakly back.

Steadman paused in the doorway of his office. "Is Sexton around?" he asked Sue. "I may need him this week to help find me some good security people." As an ex-policeman, his employee still had good connections with the force and knew who was soon to retire, or sick of the job and considering leaving. These men usually made excellent security staff.

"He's process server for Collins and Tullis this morning," Sue replied.

"Okay, I'll ring him from Salford if I miss him." Before he could close the door, Sue stopped him by waving a piece of paper in her hand.

"This gentleman wants to see you this morning, Mr. Steadman," she said apologetically.

"Oh, come on, Sue. You know I won't have time,"

Steadman said in an exasperated tone. "Can't he see Maggie?"

"I tried to get him to, but he insisted on seeing you. He rang last week and wanted to get in touch with you up north when I told him you were away. I didn't let him know where you were, of course, but he said it was very important that he saw you personally the moment you got back. He wouldn't even *talk* to Mrs. Wyeth."

Steadman walked back to the reception desk and took the folded piece of paper from the girl's fleshy hand. His stomach muscles tightened when he unfolded the paper and read the message. His earlier unease had been instinctively correct.

"Dark hair, dark complexion? In his early thirties?" he asked, still looking at the handwritten message.

"Yes," Sue replied, puzzled by her employer's reaction. "Goldblatt, he said his name was. I can put him off when he arrives, if you like. He did make it sound important, though, so I thought you might just fit him in before you went back to Salford."

"No, it's all right, Sue. He's already downstairs sitting in his car. I'll give him ten minutes."

As Steadman went into his office Sue stared across at Steve, who had been watching the brief exchange with interest. He shrugged his shoulders and turned his attention back to the intricacies of the law.

Steadman sat at his desk and reread the message on the piece of paper. "Zwi sends his regards" was all it said, but it stirred up memories of emotions and actions governed by a passionate vengeance. "Zwi Zamir," he said softly, then screwed the paper into a tight ball on his desk. He swiveled his chair and gazed at the gray autumn sky outside his window, the image of Zwi Zamir, ex-director of Mossad Aliyah Beth, the Israeli secret service, clear in his mind.

Ten minutes later, Sue buzzed him on the intercom. "Mr. Goldblatt for you, Mr. Steadman."

With a weary sigh, Steadman said, "Send him in."

He reached forward and picked up the crinkled ball of

[10]

paper still lying on his desk and tossed it into the waste-bin, just as the door opened and Sue ushered in the man he had spotted earlier in the car. Goldblatt was alone, his companion presumably still waiting below.

"Mr. Goldblatt," Steadman acknowledged, standing and stretching his hand forward across the desk.

Goldblatt shook it, his grip hard and dry. He was a short, stocky man, his hair black and crinkly, cut short, his features not as dark as Steadman had first thought. It must have been the darkness of the car deepening the man's natural swarthiness.

"David Goldblatt, Mr. Steadman. Thank you for seeing me." There was barely a trace of accent, except for a slight American inflection on certain words. His eyes searched Steadman's as though looking for some sign of recognition, not personal; perhaps a recognition of shared beliefs.

Steadman's eyes remained cold.

"I'll bring you some coffee." Sue's words interrupted the awkward silence. She closed the door, nervous of the coldness she felt emanating from her employer. He seemed angry at this little Jewish man.

"You saw the note?" Goldblatt asked, taking the seat the investigator had indicated.

Steadman nodded, sitting himself and lounging back in his chair to study the other man. "How is Zwi?"

Goldblatt smiled across at him. "He's well. He retired from the service, you know. He's chairman of a big construction company now. It's owned by the Israeli confederation of trade unions, so his interests are still for the good of our country—as are the interests of all of us. They used to be yours too, even though you're not a Jew."

Steadman dropped his gaze. "Things change," he said.

There was a silence between them. Goldblatt broke it by saying softly, "We need your help again."

"Forget it," Steadman snapped. "I told you, things change. Mossad changed. Ideals were replaced by vengeance."

"Only by revenge can we achieve our ideals!" Goldblatt's voice was angry now. "We have to avenge the persecution of our people. There must be retaliation for every Israeli man, woman, and child killed by terrorists! Only then can they respect our strength. Only then will they realize we will never be beaten. You know that!"

"And I know you've murdered innocent people." Steadman's anger matched the Jew's, but his voice was quieter, more steady.

"Innocent people? And the massacre at Lod Airport? Munich? Entebbe? Every time the PFLP or PLO guerrillas strike, innocent people are murdered."

"Does that give you cause to act in the same way?"

"We have made mistakes, Mr. Steadman. But they *were* mistakes, not deliberate acts of aggression against innocent bystanders! We have never hijacked a plane, nor planted bombs in crowded airports. How can you compare us with these animals?"

Steadman's voice had lost its anger now. "I don't, Mr. Goldblatt," he said wearily. "But I'd had enough of the Institute. I had to get out or be tainted by what we were doing. As you said, we made mistakes."

A gentle tapping at the door brought a brief halt to their exchange. Sue entered bearing a tray containing two cups of coffee. She smiled nervously at Goldblatt and placed the coffee and sugar on the table between them. The two men were quiet until she'd left the room again. Goldblatt sipped his coffee and, as an afterthought, added sugar. Steadman ignored his.

"I'm sorry, Mr. Steadman," Goldblatt began again. "I did not come here to argue with you. Israeli feelings run high, but then you understand that. Mossad needs your help again, and so far I have only succeeded in making you angry. Please accept my apology."

"Accept mine too, Mr. Goldblatt. I meant no disrespect to you, or your cause, but Zwi Zamir must have explained why I left the Israeli intelligence organization."

Goldblatt nodded. "Yes, he did. He also said you probably would not help us. But you did before; you left the

[12]

British Army to join us. Perhaps you will find that sympathy for our cause once again."

"No, I don't think so. I had a stronger reason then."

"Lilla Kanaan?"

Her name, after so many years, still caused the old grief to flood through him, its intensity almost causing a panic within him. He said nothing.

"Listen to me first, then if you still will not help us, so be it. We'll find other ways."

Goldblatt took Steadman's silence as approval for him to go on. "Everyone is well aware of the escalation of terrorism throughout the world. At first, we Israelis defended our country from the inside but, as you well know, we were forced to fight our war beyond our own boundaries. We did not wish it, but we had no choice . . ."

—Steadman's thoughts were racing back to that blood-filled night, Tuesday, 30 May, 1972. Lod International Airport. He and Lilla had been waiting for the flight that would take him back to England, his assignment in the Middle East over—his orders now to return to his regiment. Gunshots had startled them from the sadness of parting, and exploding grenades had made him hurl Lilla to the floor and push her beneath a row of seats. When he saw the three Japanese with their Kalachnikov carbines and laden with hand grenades, he covered her body with his, pulling a discarded suitcase in front of them as feeble protection against the hail of bullets and shrapnel. People were screaming, running in terror from the lethal fire; others threw themselves to the floor, too frightened to move, praying they would be spared. Steadman had looked up to see if there was any way to reach the gunmen and he had seen a grenade explode in the hand of one of the Japanese, tearing off the terrorist's head.

A second died as he carelessly strayed into his companion's line of fire. The third then seemed to lose his nerve and had begun to run; Steadman saw him disappear under a crush of border police and civilian police officers.

He pulled Lilla to him and they had sat there stunned

at the violence and the carnage it had caused. The wailing began and the hall came alive with the dying.

Twenty-eight people had been slaughtered, most of them innocent Puerto Rican pilgrims, and seventy had been wounded. The surviving terrorist, Kozo Okamoto, later confessed he was a member of the Japanese Red Army and had been trained for the suicide mission by the Black September group.

Three months later, Steadman had returned to Israel and the Central Institute for Information and Espionage, no longer as an advisor on loan from British military intelligence, but as a member of the organization . . .

". . . It was not long before we realized we were not fighting just one terrorist group but many." Steadman's attention was drawn back to Goldblatt. "In Ireland, the IRA; in Spain, the Basque; in South America, the Tupamaros; in Turkey, the Turkish Liberation Army; in Japan, the Red Army; in West Germany, the Baader-Meinhof. All are now aiding and abetting each other, a terrorist alliance brought about by the Russian KGB. They have even narrowed the split between the Arab factions, the PLFP and PLO. But the people we least expected to give succor to our enemies were the British."

Steadman raised his eyebrows in surprise. "The British? How are we helping such people?" he asked.

"By supplying them with arms—new, advanced weapons. Training the terrorists to use them effectively."

"Nonsense. Sure, the Middle East and Iran are big customers of the British government itself, but it doesn't deal with terrorist groups. Nor does it allow private armament companies to. Licenses are strictly controlled."

Goldblatt smiled without humor. "Come now, Mr. Steadman. As an ex-military man and as one who has negotiated the sale of arms to Israel yourself, you know just how far the arms business can be 'strictly controlled.' " He drew out the last two words scornfully. "It's no longer just Russian weapons we find in the hands of our assassins. There are certain highly sophisticated weapons we have traced back to your country."

"They may have been paid for and passed on by another source."

"Having worked for Israeli intelligence yourself, do you doubt our efficiency in these matters?"

Steadman had to shake his head, for he knew Israel had one of the most respected and feared intelligence organizations in the world. On his return to that country he had joined Mossad, which was responsible for external intelligence, and he soon appreciated the strength of Shin Beth, which was responsible for internal security and counterespionage. No, he didn't doubt their efficiency.

"We know for certain that the PLO bought direct from a British company. Unfortunately, our source of information died under interrogation so we have no proof, no first-person confession."

Steadman also knew how ruthless Israeli interrogations could be and shuddered inwardly.

"What do you know of Edward Gant?" the Mossad agent asked.

"Gant? You think he's the supplier?"

Goldblatt nodded.

"He's not one of the big dealers, but his weapons are of the sophisticated kind. Did your informant tell you it was him?"

"No, our informant didn't know. We believed him."

I'll bet you did, Steadman thought. Torture has a way of making people want to be honest. "So what makes you think he's your man?" he said.

"Let's just say several roads lead back to him. Now, what do you know of him?"

"Not much—he keeps out of the limelight. I know he's wealthy, respectable, and, as I said, deals in the sale of arms on a small scale. He seems to move in high circles."

"Appeared on the scene in the United States around the late fifties," Goldblatt continued. "His record shows he was an emigrant from Canada. He married a wealthy American widow and began his activity in the armaments field, his innovations in light weaponry outstanding at that time. His wife's connections and money helped him approach top-ranking army personnel as well as the odd senator here and there, and he soon became a steady supplier to the US forces. He seemed to have some influence himself at the time, even though he was new to the country, and he was by no means a *poor* immigrant. He came to England in 1963 after his wife's death and opened up a weapons development plant here, warding off any state control when he became successful. He's now a considerable force in the industry and, like many arms dealers, has kept away from publicity—until recently, that is.

"By all accounts he is a remarkable man, hardly looking his age, extremely fit, shrewd, and quite ruthless in business. Three weeks ago, one of our agents investigating Edward Gant's activities in this country disappeared. We have not heard from him since."

The last words were made to sound as though they were part of the arms dealer's biography. Steadman leaned forward across the desk. "You want me to find your man," he said as a statement.

Goldblatt nodded.

"And if I can dig up some evidence against Gant at the same time, that would be useful."

"Yes. Very."

"And what would you do with that evidence?"

"Turn it over to your government, of course."

Steadman sat back in his chair and stared coldly into the Mossad agent's eyes. "Good-bye, Mr. Goldblatt."

The Israeli sighed deeply. "Do you have no feelings for us any more?"

"None."

"What changed you? What turned you against us?"

"Zwi Zamir knows. I'm sure he told you."

"Did Lilla's death mean nothing to you?"

Steadman's hands clenched into fists on the desk top. "It meant everything to me," he said evenly.

"And would her brother's death mean anything?"

Puzzlement showed in the investigator's eyes. "What do you mean?"

[16]

"Her brother, Baruch, was the agent sent to contact Gant."

Baruch. Young. Anxious to serve his country. Even more so after the death of Lilla. They'd used him, just as they'd used his sister. Just as they used up the lives of so many of their young.

"I had no idea he'd joined the Institute."

"Our country needs such fine young men to survive, Mr. Steadman. Baruch Kanaan was conscripted into the Air Force and flew helicopter missions into enemy territory, giving support to GHQ assault groups on the ground, covering their retreat from Arab strongholds. I understand you, yourself, were recipient of such cover on several occasions when you were with us."

Steadman nodded and thought of the nightmare raids into Beirut, the hasty retreats through hostile streets, silenced Parabellums, hot from use, burning their hands. The welcoming sound of rotor blades, the huge dragonflies dropping from the night sky with guns blazing to disrupt enemy pursuit. Grenades and spikes dropped into the roads to thwart enemy vehicles. It all seemed a long time ago.

"Baruch eventually became a member of the GHQ, himself," Goldblatt continued, and allowed himself a brief smile. "He walked to Petra twice."

Steadman raised his eyebrows. The GHQ was a secret paramilitary outfit of the Israeli Defense Forces, its members specially chosen officers or sergeants from other units, an ability to fight in small groups against heavy odds an essential requirement. One of the initiation rites into the unit was a voluntary trip by foot from the Israeli border, across a stretch of the Jordanian desert to the abandoned city of Petra, only cunning and endurance keeping the lone traveler out of the hands of the prowling Bedouin battalion guarding the area. Some initiates declined to take the trip and these were considered unfit for future highly dangerous or solitary missions, while many others who accepted the challenge were never seen again. "He must be very special," the investigator said.

"Very special," the Israeli agreed. "It was not long before he became an agent for Mossad. He speaks French, German, and his English is particularly good. He is cool and resourceful under pressure, and quite ruthless where our enemies are concerned. He also has an excellent knowledge of the armaments market, much of it learned from you, I gather."

"Baruch liked to know everything about everything."

"You were a good teacher. Baruch Kanaan was chosen for this mission because of these qualities and because his face was unknown to our enemies. He hoped to contact you, by the way, to enlist your help. We forebade it. We did not want to involve you in any way, but now I am afraid we have little choice."

"What was his cover?"

"He contacted Gant as a representative of our government. He was to buy arms for us."

"And?"

"He made the contact and reported back that Gant was interested. Then we heard no more from him. We learned he had checked out of his hotel and left no forwarding address. Baruch left no message for us, nor did he try to contact any of our 'safe' houses. He just disappeared."

"Three weeks ago."

"Yes."

"And you've heard nothing since?"

"Nothing."

It was Steadman's turn to sigh. "Just how did you expect me to find him?"

"You could approach Gant in the same way, as a buyer for a Middle East power. You would not have to reveal your employer's identity at first—not until negotiations were under way."

"But Baruch let Gant know he was working for Israel."

"Yes. A mistake, we think."

Steadman smiled wryly. "Some mistake. If Gant is supplying arms to Arab terrorists, he may have some sympathy for their cause."

[18]

"It is not unusual for an arms dealer to supply both sides in a war."

"No. It can be an embarrassment sometimes, though."

"An embarrassed arms dealer? An amusing thought." Goldblatt's smile was cynical. "However, our point was this: If Gant showed any reluctance to deal with us, that would at least give some indication our information was correct."

"Indicate, but hardly prove."

"No. But that would only have been our first step. Surveillance, inquiries, bribery here and there, would have confirmed the rest. Proof would have followed."

"And if it hadn't? If you couldn't get the proof to hand to my government, what then? Eliminate Gant?"

"Probably." There was no hesitation.

"But you can't fight your war in this country." Steadman's anger was rising again.

"We have no choice."

"I have. I won't help you."

"We are not asking you to take any risks, Mr. Steadman. We merely want you to get close to Gant, to find out if Baruch saw him again. If not, then trace Baruch's movements from the last time he contacted us. That's all we ask: a straightforward investigator's commission. No involvement with Mossad."

"Why don't you go to the police?"

"That could prove rather embarrassing. Besides, we have no faith in the cooperation of foreign governments in Israeli affairs. You remember how France let the assassin Abu Daoud go free after arresting him in Paris in 1977? The French were worried that their sale of 200 Mirage jets to Egypt would fall through because of it. No, justice is governed by self-interest in all countries. I think your government would not be too concerned with the whereabouts of one missing Israeli spy."

"Then why not use another private investigator? Why me?"

"Because of your connections. You were with the military, you dealt in arms. You negotiated deals for arms for

Israel in the past, and there is no reason why you should not be believed as a freelance now. You have the perfect cover; and you also know Baruch. You are suited for the job in every way."

"Except one."

"And that is?"

"I'm not interested."

"Not even for Baruch's sake?"

"No."

There was disgust in Goldblatt's eyes now. "Will nothing I say persuade you?"

"Nothing. Find another agency, or do your own dirty work."

The Mossad agent stood and looked coldly down at Steadman. "You've lost your beliefs," he said.

"No, they're just different now." Steadman sat back in his chair, his face expressionless. "I hope you find Baruch."

With a shake of his head, Goldblatt turned and walked to the door. He stood there as if to say something further, then walked out, closing the door quietly behind him.

Steadman sighed deeply and drummed his fingers on the desk top. The past never wants to let go, he mused. He wondered about Lilla's younger brother, Baruch: always smiling, so easily excited, yet so intense when conversation turned to the political struggles of his nation. Had he been sacrificed now like his sister, all in the cause of his country's fight for freedom? The gentle tap at the door was a welcome relief from his brooding thoughts.

"Hello, Harry. That sounded heavy." Maggie Wyeth's head peered around the door.

He grinned. "Listening at keyholes again?"

Maggie entered the room and perched herself on the corner of his desk. Forty, elegant, she was attractive in the special way older women can be. A certain firmness in her lips and jawline gave her a slightly intimidating aura, and Steadman had frequently seen this turned to good use in many of the cases they had handled. Her husband had owned the agency and Maggie had helped run it, until a

[20]

heart attack had killed him five years before. She had continued to run the business, having learned much from her late husband, but the prejudices of clients against a woman handling their affairs were difficult to overcome. Although it was not unusual for a woman to be a private investigator, she soon realized the agency needed a masculine influence and image, so "feelers" were put out for the right man. Steadman had just returned to England, having resigned from Mossad, and a mutual acquaintance had brought the two together. They were cautious of each other at first, but a reciprocal respect had soon grown between them. They had both lost something, but they were determined not to wallow in self-pity. They recognized the need in each other.

After a three-month trial, Steadman bought himself in as a full partner and the agency's client list had steadily begun to grow again. It was inevitable their relationship should develop beyond that of a business partnership, but their affair was brief, both realizing they could only offer each other a shallow comfort. There was genuine fondness between them, but love was something they'd used up on others. It had lasted for three months, then, by mutual consent, they'd reverted to their business relationship, although a strong bond of friendship had grown between them.

Steadman glanced appreciatively at the smooth line of Maggie's thigh and felt some of the tension drain from him. They hadn't seen each other for a week and both found it good to be in contact again.

"Who was he?" Maggie asked.

"A voice from the past, you could say," Steadman replied casually.

"From Israel?"

"Yes."

"Mossad?" She knew of Steadman's past associations.

He nodded.

"Do they want you to work for them again?"

"In a way. They wanted to commission the agency to find a man."

"He wouldn't speak to me last week when you were away."

"I have special connections, it seems."

"But you didn't take the job on?"

"No. I want nothing to do with them."

"But if it was just a straightforward case we could have handled it. We're not that busy that we can turn down work."

Steadman frowned. "With Mossad it's never that straightforward. We don't need it."

"We could have discussed it first." Maggie's tone was soft, but he recognized the firmness behind it. "We could have given it to Sexton, or I could have handled it."

"I told you, Maggie, they wanted me. Let's drop it, eh?"

This time Maggie recognized the firmness in *his* tone.

"Sorry, Harry. It's the businesswoman in me. I hate to let one get away."

"Okay." He smiled and patted her thigh. "Now, what's been happening?"

"Well, we've still got a few cases on the go, nothing that Sexton and Steve can't handle, though. Sexton has a couple of writs to serve this week, although we'll probably let Steve have a go at one of them—he can run faster than Sexton. I'm in court giving evidence tomorrow and Thursday, and a client I've just seen this morning wants to investigate pilfering in his chain of hardware stores. He's losing several hundred a week and suspects it's an organized ring working in his shops."

"Is he losing stock or money from the till?"

"Oh, it's straight from the till. We'll check receipt books and till rolls in the evening and if we find too many 'No Sale' marks we'll try some test purchases."

Steadman nodded. Test purchases were an easy way of checking the honesty of suspect shop salesmen.

"You'll check on regular tradesmen to the shop, too?"

"Naturally. There might just be conspiracy involved. It shouldn't take too long to find the culprits, but after that,

[22]

we're pretty clear for work. That's why I was interested in your visitor."

"Oh, come on, Maggie. You know what happens when we begin to slack off. People go missing, couples want a divorce after twenty years of marriage, debtors do a bunk, blackmailers start blackmailing—we're up to our ears in it again. And they're just the little cases. We've always our main diet of company jobs: industrial espionage, embezzlement, security."

Maggie laughed aloud. "It's my insecurity showing. There's no reason why things should suddenly go bad for us—not now."

"Right. Look, I've got to get back up to Salford and there's a few things to tidy up before I go."

Maggie stood. "Is it going well?"

"The usual problem of old Joe retiring soon so why can't we put him in charge of security? Fortunately, they're seeing it my way and I want Sexton to select some good men and send them up to see me this week. Then it's just a matter of setting up systems and hiring and training the security."

"All right, Harry, I'll let you get on. I'll give you a ring if anything important crops up while you're away." She gave him an affectionate smile and walked to the door. "Maggie," he called after her. She turned, the door half open. "Forget about our Israeli friend," he said.

"Forgotten." She blew him a kiss, then left the office.

Sue looked up from her typewriter as Maggie approached.

Maggie's voice was low when she said, "Sue, did Harry's visitor leave an address where he could be contacted?"

TWO

. . . it is the tragedy of the elite to have to participate in acts of violence for the glory of the Fatherland.

—HEINRICH HIMMLER

The world can only be ruled by fear.

—ADOLF HITLER

Steadman threw his suitcase on the floor and slumped onto the bed. The night drive from Salford had been long and wearing, but he'd wanted to be home on Sunday evening. That way, he could be in the office the following day after a good night's sleep. His client had insisted he stay over for the weekend as his guest, after the long hours he'd put in during the week. Steadman had accepted gladly, for there were still a few loose ends to be tied up before he returned to London and these would be more easily concluded with his client in a congenial and relaxed mood.

Steadman was pleased with the way things had gone. Over the past two weeks he'd thoroughly screened all of the company's employees and had found nothing amiss; but from now on, every member of the firm would possess a works pass, numerically marked and containing a photograph of the employee stamped over with the company name. A daily report would be submitted by security on

[24]

any unusual happenings during the day or any early or late visits to the company by employees (even if the reports were negative they would still be submitted). All documents would be classified, the more important of which would receive special markings and closer attention. A better system of flood lighting was already being installed, and in future no windows or doors would be left in shadows; even the roof was to be illuminated. All locks and safe combinations had been changed, and ground-floor windows had been fitted with thin but sturdy bars. Steadman had been in favor of a silent alarm system so that the security guards and police could be alerted of illegal entry without actually warning the trespasser; he wanted the intruder to be caught, not merely frightened away. His client had wanted clanging bells and sirens at first, to show the power of his alarm system to would-be thieves so that they would be deterred from ever attempting a break-in again, but he had given way to Steadman's argument that the best deterrent to them, and any other villains who might have their eyes on the plant, was for them to be caught and made an example of. Steadman had also argued against the manufacturer's request for guard dogs; correctly trained dogs were expensive and required handlers. He also had a personal abhorrence of any animal being trained to attack a man. Besides which they could easily be drugged.

He had spent the weekend coaxing a higher salary for the chief of security out of the manufacturer, for Sexton had provided Steadman with the ideal man for the job. A soon-to-retire police officer, the man needed more persuading to move from London up to Salford, and only a good wage and financial help in moving would do it. The manufacturer argued that there were plenty of suitable men locally, but Steadman had not been totally happy with any he'd interviewed; they would be fine as guards, but were not sufficiently qualified in the key role of chief of security. The client finally succumbed to Steadman's wishes and the investigator pressed home his advantage by persuading him to employ his own maintenance men and even his own window cleaners rather than use outside tradesmen. It was a smaller issue, but as far as Steadman was concerned, of vital importance if strict security were to be maintained, so he was particularly pleased at the outcome and had allowed himself to relax for the rest of the weekend.

He flexed his shoulder blades against the softness of the bed and eased his shoes off with his toes. He had enjoyed the last two weeks' work even though they had been arduous and frustrating at times. If his client stuck to the agreed plan for security, then the plant should become thiefproof and, hopefully, spyproof, which would be good for the agency's reputation and could lead on to similar commissions from other companies. Steadman had set up four such security systems in the past, with variations for the particular needs of each individual company, and it had proved to be highly lucrative work. It beat the hell out of runaway debtors or stay-away husbands.

He briefly considered ringing Maggie to let her know he was back, but on glancing at his watch and seeing it was well after eleven, he dismissed the thought. He had spoken to her a few times during the week and there had been no crises at the office, so there was little point in disturbing her at such a late hour. Tomorrow morning would be time enough to catch up on any news.

Steadman stretched his limbs but resisted the urge to let himself sink into sleep. He was hungry and a stiff drink would do wonders for his metabolism. The investigator rolled off the bed and padded over to the window. He peered into the darkness, seeing little of the small church grounds opposite, a dark reflection of himself in the glass obscuring the view.

Steadman lived in a small terraced house in a quiet mews off Knightsbridge. It had cost a small fortune, but the cul-de-sac was central and its peaceful position in the thriving city was something to be relished. The tiny park that surrounded the church across the narrow road made an ideal spot to relax over the Sunday papers during the summer months; even the occasional gravestones, gray and white with age and bird droppings, gave the grounds a peaceful stability. A few benches were scattered at random in the grounds and his neighbors all seemed to have their allocated spot, their dogs their allocated trees. The money Steadman had acquired through working for Mossad, and the commissions he had received on negotiating arms deals for the Israelis, had been enough to pay for the house as well as buy himself into Maggie's business, and now his earnings came purely from the agency. It gave him a comfortable life and a busy one which, he reflected, was the most one could expect. You had more, once, he told himself, and you foolishly expected it to last. Foolishly, because danger was all around you both then, but you still thought it couldn't touch you. It had though, and it had killed Lilla. So never expect too much again. That way, you'll never be disappointed. He closed the curtains on his dark, brooding image.

He went downstairs, his stockinged feet silent on the heavy carpets, and along the short hallway to the tiny kitchen, where he poured himself a large vodka with a small tonic. Deciding it was too late to eat out, he took a pizza from the fridge, unwrapped it, and put it into the oven. His cleaning lady, who came in twice a week, had thoughtfully stocked up his food supply during his absence, but he rarely cooked elaborate meals for himself—women friends could be relied on for that.

Steadman padded back down the hallway to the front door and retrieved the week's mail that was lying there. He took the letters and his drink into the living room and settled into the armchair. He sipped at his vodka and tonic, then began to open the envelopes on his lap. The only bills he paid any attention to were the red ones; the others he crumpled and dropped on the floor. A letter from an ex-girlfriend made him groan aloud. She had grown tired of being an ex- just as quickly as she had of being current and now thought it would be "super" if they got together again. That letter, too, soon lay crumpled at his feet. An invitation to a security exhibition followed by a series of lectures on the subject interested him and he placed this one with the final demands resting on the arm of his chair. The rest were advertising circulars and these found their rightful place on the floor.

He ate his supper at the breakfast bar in his kitchen, the cool voice and records of a late-night DJ keeping him company. A hot shower and another large vodka eased the remaining stiffness from his muscles and left him pleasantly drowsy. He fell naked into his bed and was asleep within seconds.

The hammering woke him with a start. He lay on his back staring up into the darkness, wondering what had dragged him from his slumber with such suddenness. Then the banging came again. It came from downstairs—his front door. Who the hell could want him at this time of night? And why not use the doorbell? But this was hammering, not knocking. With a curse, he leapt from the bed and pulled back the curtains, pressing his face close to the glass of the window in order to see directly below. The banging stopped almost immediately.

Steadman blinked his eyes as he tried to see into the gloom. He thought he saw movement in the shadows below, but couldn't be sure. As he turned from the window, about to find his discarded trousers and dash downstairs, he thought he saw a black shape scurry across the narrow road into the darkness of the churchyard opposite. Again, he couldn't be sure, nothing was distinct in the poor light.

As he pulled on his trousers, he snatched a quick look at the luminous digital clock by his bedside. 2:23. If someone was playing a joke, he'd kill them. He ran down the stairs, angry now, but when he reached the hallway, he halted. Something made him hesitate. He stared at the door, for some reason reluctant to open it. There was a stillness in the air. A chill. And he could hear a strange muffled sound coming from the other side of the door.

He moved slowly along the hallway, his breathing held in check, his footsteps quiet and deliberate. He pressed his ear against the wood and listened.

Something was scraping itself against the door and he

[28]

thought he heard a low murmuring. The sound wasn't human; it was like the whimpering of an animal in pain. He considered going back for his gun which was locked away upstairs, but dismissed the thought as being over-dramatic. A sudden thump against the door made him draw away.

Then he realized how ridiculously he was behaving, standing there in the dark like an old woman, afraid to open the front door. He reached for the latch and swung the door inward with a jerk.

A figure stood spread-eagled in the doorway, arms outstretched, holding onto the doorframe. The head hung down and a dark liquid seemed to be drooling from its mouth. The figure seemed strangely slumped, for the knees were bent as if giving no support to the body. A low moaning noise came from it, occasionally rising to the animal-like whimper Steadman had heard from the other side of the door; but the noise had a strange gurgling to it, as though blood were running down the person's throat.

Steadman could see nothing beyond the feebly twisting body except blackness. He reached for the hallway light switch and flicked it down, blinking his eyes rapidly against the sudden light. When he finally focused them, he saw that the figure in the doorway was that of a woman. And there was something familiar about the slumped head.

"Maggie." The name came from Steadman's lips in a whisper. He reached forward and raised her head; blood ran from her mouth onto his hand. Her eyes were glazed and red-rimmed but he thought he saw a flicker of recognition there.

"Maggie, what's happened to you?" He moved forward to take her in his arms. For some reason her arms remained stretched outward, as though unwilling to let go of the doorframe. Her head moved and she tried to speak, but the blood in her throat choked her words.

"Oh God, Maggie! Who did this?" He pulled her forward, wanting to carry her to the sofa in the living room, but a weak scream came from her.

"Maggie, let go of the door. Let me take you in," he pleaded.

She tried to speak again and her head slumped forward as she lost consciousness. This time Steadman tugged a little more firmly, but still she clung to the doorframe. Then he noticed the trails of blood running down from her arms. He pushed his head past her shoulder and his eyes widened in horror as he saw the nail protruding from the back of her hand.

He grabbed her to support her weight and saw her other hand also had been nailed to the doorframe. "Maggie, Maggie," he said over and over again, holding her close, lifting her to prevent her hands from tearing. He called out, hoping a neighbor would hear, but no lights came on from the other houses. It was the dead of night; they were either in deep sleep or just didn't want to hear. He made up his mind quickly, sensing he had no time to lose. Someone would come eventually if he kept shouting, but by then it might be too late.

He eased Maggie's body down as gently as he could, then ran into the kitchen and threw open a cupboard where he kept his work tools. He found a hammer and raced back down the hallway, his heart pounding, his fear rising. Her torn clothes were covered in blood, most of which seemed to have come from her mouth. Steadman eased himself past her and with one arm around her body, pushed the forked end of the hammer underneath the nailhead with his free hand. He tried to pull the nail out without using the back of her hand as a lever, but it was deeply embedded. He had to let her go and use both hands. Maggie's body slumped again and he pulled at the hammer with all his strength, a cry of relief escaping him as he finally wrenched the bloody nail clear. He tried to catch her as her body fell sideways, prevented from falling completely to the ground by the nail in her other hand. Steadman let her go and again gave all his energy to yanking out the other nail. It was embedded deep into her hand and he had to push the hammer's fork into the skin to gain a grip. It made him nauseous to do so but he knew he had no choice; he had to get her free as quickly as possible.

The three-inch nail loosened, then came out smoothly and clinked into the road. Steadman dropped the hammer and carried the still figure into the house, gently laying it on the sofa in his living room. He snapped on the light, then knelt beside her, wondering if there was anything he could do before he called an ambulance. Her head lolled to one side and her open, unseeing eyes told him the worst. Frantically, he ripped open her jacket and placed his hand over her heart. He couldn't trust his trembling hand to give him an answer so he put his ear to her breast and listened. There was no heartbeat.

He cried out her name again and took her head in his hands, looking at her still face, pleading with her to be alive. Her mouth had dropped open and he saw it was thick with blood. Perhaps she was choking, perhaps if he laid her with her head down. Then his muscles froze as he stared into the blood-filled cavity. He fought against the sudden upheaval in his stomach and, as steadily as possible, rested her head back against the arm of the sofa.

He knew that she was dead. But he wondered why her tongue had been ripped out.

THREE

This time our sacred soil will not be spared. But I am not afraid of this. We shall clench our teeth and go on fighting. Germany will emerge from those ruins lovelier and greater than any country in the world has ever been.

—ADOLF HITLER

Steadman sat at Maggie's desk and covered his face with trembling hands. There were no tears in him, just a great weariness, a feeling of hopelessness. He thought he had banished violence as savage as this from his life once and for all, but now it had searched him out again like an old enemy who refused a truce. Why Maggie? Who could have done this to her?

The police, summoned by a neighbor in the mews who was not quite brave enough to answer Steadman's call for help, but alarmed enough to call in the law, had burst into the investigator's house, finding him cradling the dead body of his partner in his arms, his bare chest soaked in her blood. They had regarded him warily, listening gravely to his story, but ready to pounce at the slightest indication of aggression.

An ambulance had taken away the mutilated body, and the hours that followed were filled with questions, questions, questions. Who was the dead person? What had

[32]

been her relationship to him? Had they quarreled? Was the business going well? Were they lovers? Describe exactly what had happened. Again. Again. What had their quarrel been about? Had there *never* been disagreements in their partnership? What had their *latest* conflict been over? What cases were they currently working on? When was the last time he'd seen her before tonight? Describe again what had happened. What time had he woken? Why hadn't he phoned for the police? Was she alive when he had found her? Start at the beginning again.

His temper had flared then subsided. He was still in shock, and the questions—the situation—seemed unreal. The small house appeared to be filled with moving figures, hostile, disbelieving faces. Their attitude toward him seemed to change imperceptibly as the hours wore on and answers he gave them matched answers he'd given earlier. They allowed him to shower and dress, then two detectives accompanied him to the agency in Gray's Inn Square where all three searched through recent files, looking for any clue in recent cases that might shed some light on the gruesome murder. One of the questions uppermost in their minds was why Maggie Wyeth's murderer should crucify her to her partner's front door. Could their agency have helped convict someone in the past, and now this lunatic was taking his revenge? Other policemen were going over Maggie's Highgate home with a fine-tooth comb at the same time, looking for such evidence, but they, like the two detectives with Steadman, found no leads.

Business hours were approaching when they finally left Steadman alone in Maggie's office, his mind weary with fatigue and his senses still dulled by shock. They asked him to come to New Scotland Yard to make a statement later on in the day, and warned him not to say too much to the press at this stage of the investigation, which they felt sure would soon be on to him. And they warned him not to leave the city without telling them of his destination first.

Sue found him there when she arrived for work. The door to Maggie's office was open and, still in her coat and shaking the rain from her umbrella, Sue put her head around the door, expecting to see Maggie. She looked at Steadman's disheveled figure in bewilderment.

"Oh, I thought it was Mrs. Wyeth. Would you . . ."

"Come in, Sue." Steadman cut off her words, barely glancing at the girl.

Sue was puzzled, then concerned, as she entered the room and drew nearer to the investigator. His eyes had an unfocused look to them.

"Are you all right, Mr. Steadman? You look . . ."

"What case did Maggie have on last week, Sue?" His eyes now became clearer and fastened on the secretary's.

The question—and its intensity—surprised her. "Er, it should be in her book. She was in court twice—er, Tuesday and Thursday, I think—and she investigated some suspected pilfering in the Myer's chain store. That was about it, I think. It's in the book." She pointed toward the red diary lying on the desk in front of Steadman.

"Yes, I've been through it," he said, picking up the diary and flicking through the pages again. "Was there anything nasty going on with this pilfering business?"

"No. No, I don't think so. Mrs. Wyeth had only just started on the investigation. But she should be in soon, she'll be able to tell . . ."

"Sue." She stopped at his quiet tone. "Mrs. Wyeth won't be coming in."

Sue stood in the center of the room, the dripping umbrella still in her hand creating a pool of rainwater on the wood floor, her face suddenly pale. The look on Steadman's face told her she was about to hear something terrible, but she couldn't find the words to prompt him.

Steadman decided not to tell her until he'd learned as much as possible about Maggie's activities during the last week or so, for he knew the shock to his secretary would prevent further questioning. "Try and think, Sue. Was Maggie involved in anything else while I was away?"

She shook her head, then froze. "Well, there was another case, but . . ."

Steadman waited, but the girl seemed reluctant to go on. "You've got to tell me, Sue. It could be important."

"She wanted to tell you herself when you got back. She asked me not to say anything."

"Please tell me, Sue." There was frustration in Steadman's voice.

"The man . . . the man who came to see you last week. Mr. Goldblatt? I think Mrs. Wyeth was working on something for him."

"Christ!" The girl jumped as Steadman's fist hit the desk. "I told her I didn't want to handle that!" he shouted.

"She . . . she said we weren't busy, that we could easily fit it in. It was only tracing a missing person." Sue felt uncomfortable for she felt a strong loyalty toward both her employers.

"I'm sure Mrs. Wyeth will explain . . ."

"She won't, though. She's dead!" The investigator regretted his anger immediately as Sue's face broke into lines of distress. He stood up and walked around the desk to her. "I'm sorry, I shouldn't have told you like that." He put two hands on her shoulders and guided her toward a chair.

"How did it happen?" she asked as she searched for a handkerchief in her pocket. "She was fine on Thursday morning after court. There didn't seem to be anything wrong at all."

"Was that the last time you saw her?" His voice was gentle now.

"Yes, Thursday morning." She dabbed at her eyes with the handkerchief. "She told me she would be out that afternoon and probably most of Friday. What happened, Mr. Steadman? How did she die?"

Steadman hesitated, but realized the newspapers would carry the story even if the more grisly details were left out. "She was murdered. Last night. That's why I have to know her movements last week."

"Murdered? But who . . . ?"

"We don't know, Sue. The police will probably want to question you later today."

Steadman tried to comfort the girl as her shoulders shook with sudden grief.

"When did Mrs. Wyeth see Goldblatt?" he asked after her sobs had become more controlled.

"On the same day you did. She arranged to see him at his hotel that afternoon."

"Which hotel, Sue? Have you got the name?"

She nodded. "It's in my pad. I'll get it for you." Sue rose from the chair, still holding the crumpled handkerchief to her nose.

"Who would do it, Mr. Steadman? Who would murder her?"

Steadman could give her no answer. He doubted if he even wanted to find out. Somehow he knew it would lead to even more death.

The hotel was in northwest London, close to Belsize Park, a modern motor motel, the kind favored by businessmen who spent only a week or so in town, then moved on to other parts of the country. It was central to London and anonymous—ideal for members of organizations such as Mossad.

Steadman paid the cabbie and strode purposefully through the swinging doors into the hotel's reception area. He had left Sue in the capable hands of Sexton. The older detective had arrived with Steve just as Sue had been finding Goldblatt's address for him, and Steadman had explained to all three exactly what had happened to Maggie. There had been more hysterics from Sue, and Steve had gone deathly white, but Sexton had taken it all in his stride. He had been stunned, of that there was no doubt, but experience and acceptance of the ills of the world had enabled him to cast emotion to one side for the moment, for he was needed to calm the others. The retired policeman had wanted to accompany Steadman to the Mossad agent's hotel, but his employer had insisted he stay behind and do his best, under the circumstances, to carry on the

[36]

business as normal. His firmness would also be needed to keep the press at bay. Sexton had accepted his role without argument.

The hotel receptionist eyed Steadman coolly. The investigator realized his appearance was unkempt, the stubble of an unshaven chin, the open-necked shirt, and the signs of a sleepless night apparent in his face, making him an unwelcome guest; but he was in no mood for offended hotel receptionists.

"You have a Mr. Goldblatt staying here. What room is he in?"

The authority in Steadman's voice allowed no dissent from the man behind the desk. The receptionist quickly ran a finger down the guest list.

"Room 314, sir. Third floor. I'll give Mr. Goldblatt a call and let him know you're here. What name shall I say?"

"Don't bother," Steadman told him as he turned away and walked toward the lifts.

"Just a minute, sir," the receptionist called out, but the lift doors were already opening, disgorging a group of businessmen, and Steadman had stepped in behind them. The receptionist hastily picked up the phone and dialed a number.

The lift reached the third floor and the doors opened smoothly. Steadman stepped into the carpeted corridor and looked for room numbers. A door farther down opened and the Mossad agent's figure appeared. He raised an arm in surprise toward Steadman.

The detective walked toward him, his eyes fixed firmly on the Israeli's. The Mossad agent was still in shirtsleeves and clearly had not expected a visitor so early in the morning.

"I'm pleased you have come, Mr. . . ." His voice wavered as he recognized the look in Steadman's eyes. It reminded him of his old instructor's look when one of Goldblatt's companions had shot a fellow trainee in the throat with a machine gun through carelessness; the veteran instructor had beaten his pupil to a pulp for wasting a badly needed Israeli life. That same cold look was now in Steadman's eyes.

He felt strangely powerless to prevent Steadman from striking him, for the look held him rigid. The blow sent him reeling back into the room. He rolled over on his back and came to his knees, but Steadman's foot sent him over again. Goldblatt sprawled on his back, then felt himself lifted by his shirtfront. "Steadman, don't . . ." he cried out, but his words were cut off by a vicious slap in the face. His head shot to one side, then to the other, as Steadman brought his hand sharply back.

"You used her, you bastard!" Steadman shouted down into the agent's face. "You used Lilla and you used me. Now you've killed Maggie, too!"

"Steadman, what are you saying?"

"Maggie!" Steadman screamed. "You killed her!"

The Israeli agent was thrown to the floor again and Steadman raised his fist to bring it down into the upturned face.

"Enough, Steadman. Please do not move!" The command came from the bedroom doorway.

Steadman swung his head around and saw the woman standing there, a small but long-barreled Beretta in her hand and aimed at his chest. He recognized her as the woman he had seen with Goldblatt in the car the week before.

"Please don't make me shoot you," she pleaded, her eyes nervously glancing at Goldblatt. Steadman knew she meant it, for the gunfire would make little noise: it was Mossad's custom to use bullets carrying light powder loadings to reduce their blast. The only problem for them would be the disposal of his corpse, but with the help of others that could be arranged without too much difficulty. He stepped away from the recumbent Mossad agent and toward the woman, ready to pounce at her slightest distraction.

Her long black hair falling to her shoulders and her dark skin gave her a seductive attractiveness. The man's

[38]

bathrobe she wore—obviously Goldblatt's—somehow heightened that attractiveness.

"It's all right, Hannah," Goldblatt said hastily, wiping blood from the corner of his mouth. "Don't shoot him. Yet."

The Israeli staggered to his feet and went to the door, looking into the hallway before he closed it. No one had been disturbed. He walked back to Steadman, keeping behind him. He ran skillful, searching hands down the investigator's body, then straightened when satisfied there were no concealed weapons. He walked around to the woman called Hannah and took the gun from her hand, keeping it pointed at Steadman.

"Now, explain. Why did you do this?" he said.

"Don't you know what you've done?" Steadman asked angrily.

Goldblatt shook his head. "Please explain."

"You used my partner to find your missing agent, didn't you?"

"She came to us."

"But I refused to work for you!"

"That was your choice, not hers. She wanted to take the job on. She said you could be persuaded once you saw it was just another routine commission."

"Routine? With Mossad?" Steadman shook his head in disgust.

"What has happened to your partner, Mr. Steadman?" It was the woman who spoke.

Steadman's eyes shifted to her. "She was murdered last night. I found her nailed to my door. Her tongue had been torn out." He said the words coldly, stifling the emotion he felt.

The woman closed her eyes and seemed to sway. Goldblatt reached out a hand to steady her, but he was too experienced to let the gun drift away from the investigator's direction.

"Why was this done to her?" he said to Steadman.

"You tell me," came the bitter reply.

"But did they leave no message? Have they not contacted you?"

"They? Who would *they* be, Goldblatt?"

"It must have been Gant."

"Why should he have done this to Maggie?"

"Perhaps she got too close, found out too much."

"But why do that to her?"

"As a warning, Mr. Steadman."

"To me? But I wanted nothing to do with it!"

"Gant must know of your past association with Mossad." The Israeli lowered his eyes briefly. "Your partner must have told him."

The realization hit Steadman hard. Maggie must have been frightened or tortured into disclosing that information. He clenched his fist and would have leapt at Goldblatt at that moment, gun or no gun, had not the woman suddenly burst into tears.

"That poor woman. Oh God, forgive us!" She slumped down onto one of the room's armchairs. Goldblatt lowered the gun.

"You see the evil of these people, Mr. Steadman? You see what they will do to achieve their ends?"

"And what about you bastards? What do you do to achieve yours?"

"Not this. We do not make war on innocents."

"But they get killed anyway."

Goldblatt walked over to the room's other armchair and sat, no longer caring if the investigator attacked him again.

"Forgive us, Mr. Steadman. We did not think they would harm a British citizen," he said.

The anger had drained from Steadman. He had known people like these Mossad agents. They were mostly decent, dedicated people; their one common fault—to him—was their fanaticism toward Israel's cause.

He walked to the window and looked down on the busy street below. The drizzle had stopped and already fumes from the traffic were filling the air. "Tell me exactly what happened when she contacted you," he said quietly.

Goldblatt glanced at Hannah and an agreement seemed to pass between them. "She came here to the hotel and we told her of Baruch's disappearance," Goldblatt said. "We were doubtful of using your agency after our meeting, Mr. Steadman, but Mrs. Wyeth convinced us you would see reason once the case was under-way. And she thought perhaps you would not even have to know of it if Baruch could be found quickly. She said you were busy in the north."

"But I'd have seen the books eventually," said Steadman.

"By then—hopefully—it wouldn't have mattered."

Goldblatt paused, but Steadman's expression urged him on. "We told her of Baruch's contact with Edward Gant and how he had disappeared shortly after. She said she could start by making inquiries at Gant's London office to see if Baruch had visited him that day. A commissionaire, a receptionist—anyone in the building might recognize him if we could provide her with a photograph. It would be somewhere to start, anyway. She said she would check out the staff at the hotel where he had been staying. They might have seen something on that day and a few pound notes here and there would probably help them remember. She left after we had given her a thorough description of Baruch and an agenda of his activities since he'd been in this country. We told her as much as we could but, of course, not everything. Within twenty-four hours we had a photograph of Baruch—it was flown over from Israel—and this we gave to her on Wednesday. Since then, we have heard nothing."

"Just how much did you tell her, Goldblatt?"

"We told her Baruch's mission was to make an arms deal with Gant."

"And not that Gant is on your assassination list!"

"But he is not! We are merely investigating his dealings with terrorists."

"My God," Steadman scoffed, "I could almost believe you."

"Mr. Steadman." It was Hannah who spoke now. "We

did not realize the danger to your friend. We were desperate. It is not easy for our agents to operate in this country and we had used up all our resources to find Baruch. We thought her neutrality would protect her."

"You were wrong!"

"Yes, we know that now. But doesn't this murder make you want to help us?"

"Help you?" Steadman shook his head in wonder. "If—and I mean *if*—Maggie was killed by Gant, then the whole point of nailing her to my door was to serve as a warning for me to keep my nose out. And it worked!"

"But surely you will avenge her death?" Goldblatt was on his feet. "Surely you will help us now?"

"Oh no. I've had my share of bloodletting in the name of revenge. Those days are over for me."

The two Israeli agents stared at him in disbelief. "You will let him get away with this murder?" Goldblatt said. "What has happened to you, Steadman? How can a man be this way?"

"In this country we have a police force to find murderers," Steadman told him evenly.

"You will tell the police of us?" The gun in Goldblatt's hand was raised toward the investigator again.

"I'll tell them everything I know." Steadman saw the knuckles on the hand whiten.

"David. It would be wrong." Hannah reached up and placed a gentle hand on Goldblatt's arm. After a few seconds' hesitation, the gun was lowered again.

"You are right," Goldblatt said. "Go then, Steadman. You are wrong about us, but we will never convince you of that now. I have pity for you."

Steadman stood in silence, a tight smile on his face. It was ironic, he thought. A battle was going on inside him. These people didn't understand that he *wanted* to help them. Old fires had been rekindled, Maggie's death had stirred up feelings he had thought of as long buried; and now the struggle was to quench those fires, to remember the tragedies these feelings had led to in the past.

"You would do well not to mock us, Mr. Steadman."

Goldblatt had mistaken the meaning behind the investigator's smile. His voice was menacing and his grip on the gun was rigid.

With a sigh, Steadman walked from the room. "Go to hell," he said mildly as he closed the door.

FOUR

It is becoming more and more obvious that a rift in public opinion is gradually widening, each individual going to the Right or Left as it suits them.

We shall have friends who will help us in all the enemy countries.

—ADOLF HITLER

Pope was waiting for Steadman when he returned to his house. The investigator had decided not to go back to the agency; he needed sleep and time to think.

He was surprised there were no reporters loitering as he pushed the key into the latch and twisted. A crucifixion in a London street was just the story to whet their ghoulish appetites. He went straight to the kitchen, poured himself a large vodka, and carried it through to the living room. He had taken off his jacket and slumped into an armchair before he noticed the overcoated figure sitting on the sofa.

"Good morning, Mr. Steadman. May I call you Harry?" The voice was gruff but contained a mixture of politeness and amusement. The man looked powerful, but in a gross way—the muscles had long been covered by layers of fat.

"My name is Nigel Pope." The big man leaned forward

[44]

with effort and proffered an open wallet toward Stead-man. "British intelligence," he said, almost apologetically.

Steadman barely glanced at the plastic-covered identity card in its frame of leather, wondering how they had got on to Mossad so quickly.

The wallet was flicked shut and returned to an inside breast pocket of the man's suit. "I let myself in, I hope you don't mind."

Steadman settled resignedly back in his chair and sipped his vodka. "What has my partner's death got to do with security?"

Pope gave the investigator a reproving look. "What has Israeli intelligence got to do with Mrs. Wyeth's death?"

"How did you find out about that?"

"Why didn't you tell the police about your agency's connections with Mossad?" Pope countered.

"We don't have any connections with them! I only found out this morning that Maggie had accepted a commission from Mossad! I was going to tell the police that."

"A man named Goldblatt came to your office and saw you, in particular, a week ago. We know he is a Mossad agent."

"He wanted me to trace a missing agent, Baruch Kanaan. I turned the job down."

"Harry, let me tell you what we know of you. Perhaps that way we can avoid unnecessary time-wasting between us." Pope rose and stood with his back to the mantel, closed his eyes for a few moments, and then proceeded as though giving a lecture. "You were born in Chichester in 1940 and had a perfectly normal childhood until your father died when you were thirteen. Your mother took in another man a year later, whom she subsequently married. But you didn't like him and he didn't much like you. You left home at fifteen, much to your mother's distress, and, lying about your age, worked in restaurants around London. You joined the Army in 1956—perhaps the Suez crisis aroused the fighting man in you—as a junior soldier, and were trained in the Junior Infantrymen's Company in Bassingbourn. You were soon transferred into a Junior Leader's Regiment when it was realized you had some potential as an NCO but, although you later reached the rank of captain, there was something of a—what shall I say—'rebel' would be too romantic, 'oddball' not quite correct. Let's just say team spirit was not one of your finer points." Pope smiled and wagged a finger at Steadman. "Er, yes. Ironically enough, at the age of nineteen you were diverted into the Corps of Royal Military Police—I believe the British Army enjoys ironies, don't you?—and you became more disciplined. You spent some time in Germany and Hong Kong and, while you were there, your mother died after a long illness." He looked at the investigator as if for affirmation.

Steadman nodded, wondering how long it had taken the fat man to memorize all this.

"Let's see, that would be in 1959?"

"'60," Steadman corrected him.

"Oh, yes, you were twenty then. Four years of service behind you. In '62 you married a German girl, but that lasted barely two years. It seemed she didn't like army life. Fortunately, there were no children. In '65 you joined the intelligence corps and there, I think, you found your niche. Leastways, you seemed contented enough for a few years. You were loaned to Israeli intelligence in 1970, more as a means of keeping an eye on their activities than anything else, I shouldn't wonder, and you were with them for quite some time."

"Two years," Steadman informed the fat man needlessly.

"Yes, two years. Just about. It was while you were there that you formed an attachment with one of their operatives, a young lady by the name of Lilla Kanaan—the sister of this missing Mossad agent, Baruch."

Attachment? The word was hardly adequate for a relationship that had run as deep as theirs.

"Correct so far, eh?" Pope inquired, a smile of satisfaction on his broad face. There was no answer from the investigator and the fat man went on. "Well, we know you were very close. You more or less moved into her apartment in Tel Aviv, in fact. You spent a lot of time with her and her family, who lived in Anabta, and they became the family you had been denied. I think Israeli intelligence probably tried to persuade you to leave British intelligence long before you witnessed the massacre at Lod Airport." He looked questioningly at Steadman, but still received no response. He shrugged his huge shoulders, then went on, "You were on your way back to England, recalled to London. Whether or not it was already on your mind to return to Israel I don't know, but it seems the incident at Lod was the turning point for you. Within a few months, you had bought yourself out of the Army and were back in Israel as a member of Mossad, and in time to become part of the new 'revenge squad' set up by Golda Meir at the encouragement of Major-General Zwi Zamir. The killing of their athletes at the Munich Olympics had set the final seal of approval on this new outward-going organization within Israeli intelligence, and they knew your background would help them in taking their war outside the boundaries of their own country.

"You were not easily accepted by your Jewish colleagues, but your part in the attack on the Palestine Liberation Organization's quarters in Beirut in April '73 overcame their qualms, and you more than proved your physical abilities in the training camp at Caesarea."

"You and your friend Lilla became part of the squad known as Heth. Your role was to set up a cover in other countries which would help the rest of the group to operate as a whole. You set up communications, rented apartments, arranged hotel reservations, provided hire cars, and supplied any information concerning the local area your group was to operate in. As an Englishman, your cover was ideal, and Lilla easily passed as a European. You worked together as man and wife.

"We're fairly certain of three killings you were involved in. Abdel Hamid Shibi and Abdel Hadi Nakaa, two known PLO terrorists who were living in Rome, were blown to pieces in their Mercedes. The same happened to

Mohammad Boudia, a key organizer of Black September; he was blown up in his Renault in Paris.

"Oh, I don't say you actually carried out the killings yourself, but you and your woman friend certainly smoothed the way for Aleph, the assassins of your little liquidation group. There are other 'incidents' we're not too sure of, but it seems it was a busy year for you."

Pope sat down again, as though his bulk had suddenly become too heavy for his legs. He looked thoughtfully at Steadman, then continued: "Apart from these missions, you were also involved in certain arms deals for the Israelis, working from Brussels and using your old army connections for contacts. You were, indeed, valuable to the Institute—as the Central Institute for Information and Espionage is known—and to the Israeli Army itself. No wonder they were sad to see you go."

Still Steadman was silent. He wasn't surprised that British intelligence had this information—he was impressed more by Pope's memory than knowledge—but he was growing increasingly apprehensive as to the purpose of the fat man's visit.

"It was in August that, for you, tragedy struck. Mossad was suffering from a loss of morale due to the killing of an innocent man in Lillehammer, Norway, and the capture by the authorities there of the group involved. Lilla Kanaan and yourself were not part of that misguided mission. You were both exhausted by now and your nerves needed rest. The Israelis thought they had finally located the man behind the Munich massacre, Ali Hassan Salemeh, but in fact the man they killed turned out to be a harmless waiter. In a way, it was unfortunate you hadn't been included in the mission because you might have been safely tucked away in a Norwegian prison at that time. An explosion in your Brussels apartment injured you and killed the girl."

The memory no longer caused Steadman's hands to shake uncontrollably, but it still seemed to drain him of any strength.

Pope quickly went on: "When you had recovered—

your health, that is—it seems you went on the rampage. At least, you appeared to be everywhere at once: Paris, Rome, Oslo, as well as Benghazi and Beirut, and in all these places violence occurred prior to your departure. Even the Yom Kippur war in October of that year hardly seemed to contain your energies. But then in January '74 it all stopped."

Pope sat back in his chair and entwined his fingers across his huge paunch. He regarded Steadman quizzically. "Why *did* you leave Mossad at that point, Harry?"

"I thought you knew all the answers," came the reply.

"Not all, Harry. We have two conjectures: One, that you were suddenly sick of all the violence around you; two, that you didn't wash your hands of Mossad at all."

Steadman raised his eyebrows.

"No, you see, we think perhaps it was meant to look that way, severing all ties with Israel, returning to England and joining Mrs. Wyeth's inquiry agency. Perhaps it was all a new cover for you."

"For nearly five years?" said Steadman incredulously.

" 'Sleeper' agents are valuable assets to any espionage organization. Adopt a role, carry on as a normal member of a community for as long as five, ten, fifteen years even, until the occasion to be used comes along. It's far from rare in these uneasy times."

Steadman laughed aloud, but he felt little humor in the situation. "Why here? There's no hostilities between Britain and Israel," he said.

"No, there's no open aggression. But Israel knows it has to spread its net, it has to fight its country's battles in other countries. With worldwide terrorism as it is now, the Israelis have to meet it on neutral territory. They can't afford to sit back and wait for it to hit their own country! Do you think I might have a cup of tea?"

Steadman was taken aback by the sudden innocuous request.

"Tea might do you some good too, Harry. It really is awfully early to be drinking vodka, you know," Pope said reprovingly.

Steadman placed his glass on the carpet and rose from his seat. Bemused, he walked through to the kitchen.

"What use to Mossad would I be in this country?" he called back down the hallway as he waited for the kettle to boil. Pope's massive body appeared in the small hallway, almost blocking it completely. He leaned his bulk against a wall.

"Oh, keeping an eye on the scene," he said casually. "Maybe keeping an eye on the arms dealings, who's trading with whom, that sort of thing. Perhaps doing a little trading yourself."

"Why would I need a cover for that?"

"Convenience? It's not unusual for a buyer to remain anonymous to the seller in such matters. You would be the link, the go-between."

Steadman poured boiling water into the teapot and stirred it vigorously.

"Or maybe you were merely here to observe any terrorist activities," Pope suggested. "London, with its great foreign student population, makes a wonderful hive for such groups. Milk but no sugar for me, Harry. And do have one yourself. You look all in."

Steadman poured two cups and carried them down the hallway. Pope backed into the living room before him.

"It's awfully cold in here." Pope took his seat again, shuddering inside his huge overcoat.

"I've been away," Steadman said and added, "as you probably know." He went back into the kitchen and flicked down the switch that operated the central heating. "It'll take a while to warm up," he said, returning to the living room. He sat facing the fat man once again. "Do you really believe that?" he asked Pope. "That I'm still with the Institute, I mean."

Pope gulped his tea and watched Steadman over the rim of his cup. After a few moments' hesitation, he said, "Actually, no, I don't. But that's just a personal judgment, neither here nor there. As a matter of fact, I rather admire the Israelis' cause, so it wouldn't matter that much to me anyway. However, we are not going to allow the

[50]

wars of other nations to be fought in our country. We've kept a close eye on you, Harry, ever since your return to England, and nothing you've done has given us grounds for suspicion of any sort. Until last week, that is."

"Look, that was the first contact I've had with Mossad for nearly five years!"

"Drink your tea, Harry, it'll get cold."

Steadman drank until the cup was empty, then he put it aside. "Okay, Pope," he said abruptly. "My partner—who was also a close friend—has been murdered. I've been interrogated by the police for most of the night, I've had to organize the office and now I'm beat. I just want to lie down and sleep. So let's get to the point. What do you want from me?"

"Why, Harry, you left out your visit to Mr. Goldblatt this morning," Pope said smoothly.

Steadman groaned aloud. "I wanted to beat his brains in! For getting Maggie killed!"

"Of course, Harry."

"I told him I wasn't interested last week. He hired Maggie in spite of that."

"Yes, we know. I spoke to your staff this morning myself after you'd left. Your secretary told me you practically threw our Mr. Goldblatt out of your office last week. It could have been an act, but I don't see that there would have been much point to it. I told you, Harry, I believe you—personally."

"Then what the hell do you want?"

"Some help from you," the big man said mildly.

"From me? How can I help you?"

"Well, you want to find your partner's murderer, don't you?"

"No, I bloody don't!"

Pope looked at Steadman in surprise. "Dear me, Harry! You don't really mean that."

"Listen to me, Pope. I've seen enough killing for revenge to last me a lifetime. I've had enough. It's all burned out of me. Can you understand that?"

"But Mrs. Wyeth was an innocent bystander. Surely you can't let her death go unaccounted for?"

"Can't I?"

"I think you're trying to convince yourself you can. But it won't work, Harry, I can assure you. You've had five years to get over your last bout of bloodletting, five years for that passion inside you to simmer. It's still there, make no mistake."

"You're wrong."

Pope smiled coldly. "It makes no difference. You're still going to help us." Steadman shook his head, but the big man held up a hand. "Just hear me out first," he said to the investigator. "You said Goldblatt only wanted you to find out what had happened to their missing agent, Baruch Kanaan. Correct?"

Steadman nodded.

"And did they tell you his mission in England?"

"He was to contact an arms dealer to place an order for weapons," Steadman said tiredly.

"The arms dealer was Edward Gant."

"Yes. How did you know?"

"Gant is a man we've been watching for a very long time now. Unfortunately, he's influential, and not a man to intimidate."

"The Israelis think he's supplying weapons to terrorists, as well as training them."

"Oh, he is. Has been for some years."

"You know that? And you've done nothing about it?"

"Nothing we could do. Never been caught red-handed."

"You couldn't have warned him not to?"

Pope scoffed. "He would have laughed in our faces, Harry. He's a very unusual man, our Mr. Gant. The outrage last night is a mark of his manic confidence."

"You *know* he killed Maggie?"

"No proof. We've put the lid on this murder for now, Harry. You won't be bothered by police or reporters for the moment."

"But how . . ."

"It needed to be done—just for now. Publicity is the last thing we want at the moment. Apart from finding the missing agent, did Goldblatt want you to do any other investigating?"

"He wanted me to dig up any evidence on Gant that I could."

"What sort of evidence?"

"His dealings with terrorists."

"Nothing else?"

Steadman shrugged his shoulders. "Anything I could get on him, I suppose."

Pope took a deep breath, then quickly let the air escape. "I don't think our friend Goldblatt has been entirely honest with you, Harry," he said. "True, the Israelis would like to provide proof to the British government of Gant's clandestine dealings, but their interest goes beyond that." The big man paused and drained the last of his cold tea. He placed the cup and saucer at his feet and dabbed at his moist lips with a neatly folded handkerchief from his overcoat pocket.

"Are you aware of the growing revival of Nazism throughout the world, Harry? Perhaps not, because it goes under many different names and guises. You may imagine such fanaticism could never become a threat again after the last World War, but you'd be wrong. It's a cancer spreading throughout the world, a parasite feeding on political unrest, poverty—and terrorist activity. Do you know, for example, that an extreme right-wing group from Belgium known as the Flemish New Order is fighting with the UDA in Ireland? They are not alone. You'll find other right-wing groups encouraging wars and becoming involved in them in many countries, supplying money, *supplying arms*."

Steadman looked sharply at Pope. "Gant?"

"In this country, and in America, we have several such organizations—the National Front here and the National Socialist Party in America being the more obvious. But lurking beneath these, and well in the shadows, are the more sinister factions such as Column 88, and these Hit-

lerite movements are growing, many joining in the common cause. I hardly need tell you of these organizations'
detestation for everything Jewish. We believe Gant is at
the head of one of the most powerful, but shadowy, Nazi
organizations, right here in Britain. The Thule Gesellschaft."

"That's why Mossad's interested in Gant? Not because
he deals with terrorists?"

"Oh no, no. Both. One goes with the other."

"But why this story about Baruch?"

"Because it's true. They wanted to hire you to find
him—anything else was incidental. But Baruch's purpose
was not to find proof of Gant's dealings with Arab terrorists, but to find out more of this Thule Society, this Thule
Gesellschaft. It would seem he found out too much."

"As did Maggie."

"Yes, we think so. Only this kind of fanaticism could
breed such killers as these. She must have unearthed
something they weren't prepared to let become common
knowledge."

The investigator's shoulders slumped. "My God, in this
day and age . . ." he said wearily.

"Especially in this day and age."

"But why didn't Goldblatt tell me the whole story?
Why would he let me walk into a setup like that without
warning?"

"I should imagine he thought it safer for you not to
know. He wanted to hire you for a fairly routine investigation job, not to get you involved in this Hitlerite movement."

"It didn't protect Maggie."

"No, they underestimated the fanatical dedication of
this group. I suppose they thought using her was even
safer than your becoming involved. It's all very regrettable."

"Regrettable? What do you intend to do about it?"

"What do you intend to do, Harry?"

"Me? You're security. It's up to you to do something."

"We will. With your help!"

[54]

"Sorry. I want nothing to do with it."

"Did I offer you a choice, Harry?" Pope's tone was pleasant, but there was a sinister intent to the words. "We could get you in so many ways. Suspicion of spying for Israel would do for a start. Coupled with suspicion of murder, of course."

"Murder? You can't . . ."

"We can, Harry, and make no mistake—we will." All hint of pleasantness was suddenly gone. "We'd have to let you go eventually on those counts, of course, but then we'd ruin your business in this country for you, and in most other countries as well. Law forces of the world like to cooperate nowadays, Harry. It's in all our interests."

"Bastard!"

With an effort, the fat man leaned forward, elbows on knees, and the pleasantness came back to his features. "Look," he said, his voice gentle, "I know you're just stubborn enough to resist, even if you bankrupted yourself. But take a good look at yourself. Inside, I mean. You want your partner's killers to pay, don't you? You can't ignore that old feeling inside you. You've suppressed it for years, but you can never lose it. You fought for Israel because you didn't like the way it was being oppressed. You fought because you hated to see the innocent hurt. You'll help us not because we'll force you to, but because you'll want to. You haven't lost that aggressiveness, Harry, you've just kept it smothered for some time."

And Steadman realized the fat man was right; the urge to strike back was still in him. He wanted this man Gant to pay for Maggie's death just as he had wanted the Arab terrorists to pay for Lilla's. Maybe Pope's blackmail played some part in it, but he realized the old anger in him was the deciding factor. "But why me?" he asked. "You must have plenty more qualified."

"None of our chaps fit in as nicely as you, Harry. You're a link, you see. A link between Mossad, Edward Gant—and now us. It gives us an advantage."

"How can I help anyway? Gant knows who I am," he said.

Pope settled back in his chair once again. "Yes, he knows who you are, but that doesn't matter. He'll play out the game."

"Game? This is just a game?" Steadman said incredulously.

"To someone like Gant everything is a game. He enjoys subterfuge, enjoys testing his cunning against others."

"And what's to stop him from giving me the same treatment as Maggie?"

"Nothing. Except we'll be keeping an eye on you."

"That fills me with confidence."

Pope gave a small laugh. "Well, you see, if he does make a move against you, we'll have him for that, won't we?"

The fat man laughed once again at the expression on Steadman's face, his stomach quivering with enjoyment. "No, no Harry. I don't think even our Mr. Gant can risk another murder so soon. Look, we need you because there's something in the wind. Something's about to happen and we don't know what. You'll be just a small part of this. Any information you come up with will just fit into a larger picture."

"I feel like the sacrificial goat."

"Nonsense. I told you, you'll be under surveillance all the time—we won't let any harm come to you. We want you to go back to your Mr. Goldblatt and tell him you've changed your mind. You want Mrs. Wyeth's murderers to be punished. He'll believe you because he needs you. You'll contact Gant on the grounds that you have a client who wishes to buy Gant's particular kind of weapons."

"And if he refuses to deal with me?"

"He won't. He's an arms dealer and it would be too unprofessional not to enter discussions at least with a prospective client. He'll be curious about you too; I told you, he is an arrogant man.

"Get close to him. He'll invite you to his private testing-grounds—it's his usual custom—and that's what we

[56]

want to know about. Find out as much about the place as possible and what's going on there. That's all you need to do."

"That's all?"

Pope pushed himself to his feet, his weight making the movement an effort. "Yes," he said. "For the moment. Oh, you might find time to read this." Pope reached for a green-covered file that had been lying unnoticed by Steadman on the sideboard. He handed it to the investigator. "Not much in there, I'm afraid, mostly recent stuff. Something of a mystery, our Mr. Gant, but the file will provide you with some information on the man, mainly his recent dealings with the Arabs. Don't lose it, will you?"

Steadman regarded him with suspicion. None of it made sense. It just didn't add up.

"I'll see myself out, Harry. You get some rest now," Pope said, walking to the door. His parting questions gave the investigator even more cause for puzzlement.

"Just a small thing, Harry," the big man said. "Have you ever heard of the Heilige Lance?"

FIVE

It is not arms that decide, but the man behind them—always.

—ADOLF HITLER

Only the loyal in blood can be loyal in spirit.

—HEINRICH HIMMLER

Steadman slouched low in the passenger seat of the Jaguar and flexed his shoulder muscles against its soft back. He let his head loll slightly to one side and gazed up into the clear blue sky. It was one of those bright winter days, the air crisp and cold, hinting at the chill months to come, but invigorating with its keen-edged freshness.

As the car sped through country roads and busy towns, he reflected on Pope's last words to him. He had shaken his head—no, he'd never heard of the Heilige Lance, but what had that got to do with this Gant affair? The big man told him not to worry about it, it was just that the arms dealer seemed to have an interest in the Heilige Lance, which was in fact, an ancient spearhead and he, Pope, had merely wondered if Steadman had any knowledge of the relic. With a wave of his hand as if to dismiss the subject, Pope had left Steadman with an even greater feeling of unease. Yet he felt a familiar excitement running through him, an old excitement that had been lying dormant for so many years. Now that he had no choice but to be involved, his reluctance had vanished, and increased adrenaline had sharpened his senses in the way it had years before when he had been a Mossad agent. Steadman appeared to be relaxed, but his thoughts and reflexes had become acute.

David Goldblatt and his companion, Hannah, had seemed relieved but not that surprised at his return, for it had been beyond their comprehension that he could walk away from the bizarre murder of his friend and business partner. The new Israelis no longer believed in turning the other cheek; in fact, they considered it cowardice and not humility to do so, and Steadman's past record showed him to be far from cowardly. His fire had been rekindled just as a cold blast would stir dying embers. His prior rejection of them had been due to shock and his passion had now overcome that shock. They understood. They needed him.

Peppercorn, a solicitor who had handled arms contracts for Steadman in the past, had arranged the meeting between him and Gant, and it was the solicitor's Jaguar in which they were traveling now. An arms exhibition was being held by the ministry of defense at their military range in Aldershot, and Edward Gant, along with other private arms companies, would be present with his own weapons display. It was there that Gant and Steadman would meet.

"It was surprisingly smooth, you know." Peppercorn's words broke into Steadman's thoughts. The investigator allowed his head to incline toward the solicitor.

"What was that?" he asked.

"Getting you the pass for the exhibition. Usually takes a while with these ministry people, wanting to know who you are, what you've got your eye on, what country it's for. That sort of thing. They got you cleared in no time at all. Have you been pulling strings with your old military chums behind my back?"

"Old connections never die, Martin," Steadman said. He guessed Pope had smoothed the way.

"Very opportune, really. Not an easy man to get hold of, this Gant. Better for you too, to meet him on neutral ground among his competitors. Should help your bargaining power psychologically." He pulled out to overtake a heavy goods vehicle, then gently eased back into the stream of traffic. "Why Gant's outfit in particular, Harry? Looking for something special?"

"Very special." Steadman straightened from his slouched position, knowing they would soon be at their destination.

"Well, Gant deals in specialties, all right. For Israel, is it?"

Steadman gave the solicitor a sharp look.

"Sorry, Harry. Shouldn't have asked at this stage," Peppercorn grinned. "I'll bet items like Swingfires and Blowpipes are on your shopping list though."

It was an easy enough assumption for the solicitor to make, for not only did Gant deal specifically in these kinds of wire-controlled and hand-launched missiles, but Israel had suffered heavy losses when their tanks and jets had been attacked by such weapons in the 1973 conflict with the Egyptians. The Russian Strella shoulder-launched, infrared-seeking antiaircraft missile, for instance, had wreaked havoc on their air force, and if Steadman was representing the Israelis as Peppercorn more than suspected, then they would naturally regard such weapons as a priority for themselves.

"You'll know soon enough, Martin, when the deal is under way," Steadman lied. The investigator hated to use his acquaintance in this way, but the deal had to look fairly legitimate so both parties could play out their deceptions without too much embarrassment. It was a game often utilized by politically opposite governments when superficial detente was not allowed to be harmed by private knowledge on both sides—undercurrents too dangerous to be acknowledged, but nevertheless secretly acted upon. He and Gant would play out the game until either one had reached the moment to strike. Steadman prayed the advantage would be his.

The car swung off the road and halted before tall, wire-mesh gates. An army sergeant stepped from an office built to one side of the gates and peered into the car. The two men showed their passes and the soldier gave a signal for the gates to be opened. The car swept through, making toward Long Valley where the solicitor knew they would find Gant.

Steadman mentally identified the various military vehicles they passed along the route: Chieftain and Scorpion tanks; Chieftain Bridge Layers; Spartan carriers; AT105 carriers; Fox armored cars; Shorland SB301 troop carriers. Overhead, Gazelle helicopters hovered, occasionally swooping low. He was pleased he still had some knowledge of army hardware, but knew the progress made in other areas would leave him completely bemused. Computers were used to wage wars nowadays: microwave systems to detect the enemy, lasers to beam in on them, missiles to destroy. And the enemy had its own systems to counter every phase of an attack. The human brain could no longer react swiftly enough to cope in complex electronic warfare; computers had become the generals.

Muffled sounds of explosions came to their ears as they passed through a wooded area, which had warning signs of a quarry at intervals on their left.

"The Army showing off its Chobham Armor, shouldn't wonder," Peppercorn said.

Steadman nodded. The tank armor had been a British breakthrough which provided three times greater protection than conventional steel armor. It had regenerated the life of the tank throughout the world, for missiles had all but made the vulnerable vehicle obsolete; the new armor—a honeycomb of materials such as steel, ceramics, and aluminum—added little to the weight or the cost of the tank. He could imagine the smug smiles on the faces of the British in the deep quarry below as their armor was blasted with rockets and mortar shells for the benefit of their prospective foreign buyers.

The car soon arrived at a huge area filled with exhibition stands proudly displaying military hardware, ranging from laser rangefinders to barbed tape, from the multirole MRCA combat aircraft to a set of webbing, from an AR18 rifle to pralidoxime mesylate counter-nerve gas tablets.

Peppercorn drove the Jaguar into the allocated parking area and the two men stepped out. The noon sun was high and harsh in the sky, feebly trying to warm the autumn air but succeeding only in stealing the dampness from it. The solicitor reached back inside the car and pulled out an overcoat which he quickly donned.

"Deceptive, this weather," he muttered. "Catch a cold without knowing it."

Steadman smiled. If Peppercorn knew the true nature of the man they were about to meet, his blood would run even colder.

They trudged across the field and past a long stand where foreign officers, diplomats, and civil servants sat on wooden chairs, observing the antics of Strikers, Spartans, Scimitars, and Scorpions as they paraded before them. As they walked, Peppercorn asked, "Tell me, Harry, why Gant in particular? There are plenty of other dealers who sell similar weapons, and as far as I know, Gant has never dealt with the Israelis before." He smiled at Steadman and added, "Assuming your client is from Israel, of course. The contracts I've been involved in personally as far as Gant is concerned have been for Iran and some of the African states. To my knowledge, he's never been interested in selling to Israel."

"Gant manufactures a wider range of more specialized items than most," Steadman answered, "from missiles to antiterrorist devices. My client requires both and thinks he'll get a better deal by buying from the same source." A little too pat, Steadman thought, but the solicitor seemed satisfied.

Peppercorn was too professional to press for the identity of Steadman's client any further, for that would soon be made clear the moment negotiations began; and

[62]

besides, Steadman had virtually confirmed his suspicions in his last statement. Who else would he be buying for—the Arabs? Hardly, with his past associations.

"Ah, there he is," Peppercorn said, pointing ahead.

The investigator's gaze followed the pointing finger and he saw a group of men gathered around a green-uniformed figure demonstrating a shoulder rocket launcher. The uniform was unfamiliar to Steadman and he assumed it was merely worn by Gant's demonstrators to give individuality to his company.

"Which one is Gant?" he asked Peppercorn.

"The tall one in the middle. The one talking to the girl."

Steadman had not noticed the girl in his eagerness to catch sight of the arms dealer, but now he briefly wondered what connections she could possibly have with someone like Gant. His eyes quickly flicked to the man beside her.

Gant was tall, even taller than Steadman, towering over the assembled group, who must have been foreign buyers, judging by their dark-skinned features. His body was thin and seemed stiff, as though having little flexibility. The assumption was wrong, for as Gant turned to answer a question from one of the group, his body swiveled with a controlled grace. It was a small movement, but Steadman was a professional observer and the action revealed the man's hidden suppleness. As they advanced, Gant's attention became focused on them. He stood without moving for several moments and Steadman could feel himself being scrutinized with cold efficiency. He returned the stare and suddenly a chill ran through him. It was inexplicable, but he felt as though he were being drawn into a spider's web; and the man before him was well aware of the thought.

The visual link was broken when Gant turned to his prospective clients and excused himself. He broke away from the group and came forward to meet Steadman and the solicitor. Their eyes locked again and Steadman was only vaguely aware of the man in military uniform who followed the arms dealer.

Gant stopped two yards away from them so they had to keep walking to meet him. Steadman saw his eyes were light gray and he thought he detected a mocking amusement in them. The tall man's face was long and angular, high cheekbones and hollowed cheeks giving it a slightly cadaverous appearance; his nose was strong with a firm bridge, and his high forehead, with short light brown hair swept back from it, held few wrinkles. He seemed younger than his years and emanated a strength that belied his gaunt frame. Only his neck gave an indication of the ravage the years had taken. It was long, therefore not easy to disguise with collar and tie, and its hollowed and wrinkled flesh caused a faint revulsion in Steadman.

"Good morning, Peppercorn," Gant said, his eyes not leaving Steadman's. "And this is Mr. Steadman?" He raised a hand toward the investigator and once again Steadman noticed the amusement flicker in his eyes.

Reluctantly, Steadman grasped the proffered hand and returned the hardness of Gant's grip. The investigator loosened his hold, but the arms dealer held it firm and he was forced to resume his own pressure. There were no secrets between them as they stood that way for several seconds. Gant seemed to see into him and mocked what he saw; Steadman returned the unspoken challenge and even allowed his own glint of amusement to show. He noticed there were many tiny scars around the arms dealer's cheeks and mouth, only visible at such close range, and he briefly wondered what kind of accident would cause such a proliferation.

His hand was abruptly released and the investigator was uncertain if he hadn't imagined the whole exchange.

"This is Major Brannigan," Gant said, inclining his body toward the soldier who had followed him. The major leaned forward and gave a swift handshake to Steadman and Peppercorn. He was a few inches shorter than Gant, and Steadman judged him to be in his early forties.

[64]

Whereas he had detected the mockery in the arms dealer's eyes, Brannigan's showed an unrelenting hardness.

"And this is Miss Holly Miles, who is taking advantage of her distant relationship to my late wife," Gant said, stepping aside to allow a view of the girl who had followed both men and had been hidden by their tall figures.

"Louise Gant and my mother were cousins—of sorts," she smiled apologetically and Steadman was surprised to hear her American accent, but then he remembered Gant's wife had come from the United States. He nodded at her and she acknowledged with a broader smile, flicking her long yellow hair to one side and behind an ear with delicate fingers. He noticed the Pentax draped around her neck.

"Pictures? Here?" he said quizzically.

"I'm a free-lance writer," she explained with a grin. "I'm doing a feature on arms dealers for one of the Sunday magazines."

"She used her flimsy connections with my family to persuade the magazine to give her the commission," Gant interrupted, but his mocking tones now had more amusement in them than malice. Nevertheless there was a disquieting quality to his voice, a rasping sibilance that was slight, but seemed to create unease in the people around him. "Major Brannigan is keeping an eye on her, making sure she doesn't photograph the wrong things."

Brannigan did not seem in the least amused.

"Now, Mr. Steadman," Gant said, his voice suddenly becoming brusque. "Peppercorn tells me you have a client who is in the market for certain types of weapons which I have a reputation for producing rather well."

"That's right," Steadman answered, his attention now diverted back to the arms dealer.

"May we establish from the start who your client is?"

"I'm afraid that will have to wait until I'm satisfied you can meet all our requirements," Steadman countered.

"Very well, that's not unusual. Can you tell me specifically what you are looking for?"

"There's quite a list. I have our broad order for you here." Steadman produced an envelope containing a detailed list, compiled by himself and Goldblatt, of armaments and defensive equipment that Israel would logically need but was, at the moment, obtained from other sources. It had a bias toward the type of weapons produced in Gant's factories. He handed it to the arms dealer. "I believe you manufacture most of these items."

Gant scrutinized the list, nodding occasionally. "Yes, most of these are in our range," he said, and Steadman suddenly found it difficult to believe it was all a charade. The arms dealer appeared to be perfectly sincere. "I have a few other items, in fact, that you might also be interested in. Our new laser sniper rifle, for example, accurate up to a distance of half a mile. Our submachine gun, similar to the Ingram but far more accurate, made with many plastic components and very cheaply mass-produced." The mockery seemed to return to Gant's eyes then, and he said, "I also have certain kinds of missiles, small and convenient to launch, but with enough power to bring down a jumbo jet."

There seemed to be some special significance to the words, for Gant said them slowly and deliberately, his gaze fixed steadily on Steadman and throwing out some kind of challenge.

"Sounds interesting," he said, and was suddenly aware that the exchange had not gone unnoticed among the other members of the small group. There was a tenseness in their silence. Even the girl had a puzzled expression on her face.

"You think your client could have a use for such a weapon?" Gant asked, raising his eyebrows.

"Possibly. It would depend on the price," Steadman answered.

"Of course. Would you like to see it?"

"Yes, I would."

"Difficult to demonstrate, of course." Gant gave a small laugh and Steadman smiled back agreeably. "But I think we can show you its range and power. Why don't you ring me at my office tomorrow and we'll fix something. Peppercorn has the number."

"That would be fine."

"In the meantime, I'll go through your list and work out some figures for you. I take it your client isn't too frightened of figures, is he?" Again the mocking tones.

"It takes more than that," said Steadman, still smiling.

"Yes, I'm sure. You must excuse me now. I'm afraid our visitors from Latin American are rather demanding today," he gestured toward the gathering he had just left, "and I think they're in a buying mood. And you, too, Miss Miles, will have to forgive my rudeness. I'm afraid business transactions of this nature might embarrass your magazine. If not, perhaps our government, if they saw it in print. Why not take the time to tell Mr. Steadman the nature of your article on armament sales and show him some of the nasty weapons you've discovered here today. He may have a view on the subject."

With one last glance at Steadman, he turned and walked back to his group of impatient foreign buyers.

"Er, yes. I'm afraid I have certain duties to perform, too," Major Brannigan suddenly said. "I'll have to take your camera with me, though. I'm sure you've got enough shots for today, anyway." He held a hand out, and with a shrug the girl lifted the Pentax from her neck and gave it to the major. "Thank you," Brannigan said. "I'll send it down to the sergeant on the gate and you can collect it when you leave." With that, he strode briskly away.

"Well, that was short and sweet," said Peppercorn turning to Steadman and the girl. "I think Gant will show you some things that'll surprise you, Harry."

"I don't doubt it," the investigator said wryly.

"Now then, Miss Miles," the solicitor said, turning on the charm. "It's very rare to find such blue-denimed beauty at these functions. Makes a welcome change from khaki. Why don't we all wander down to the big top and have a little drink?"

The girl glanced at Steadman and he said, "I could use one."

"Okay, so could I. Lead on."

Once inside the large tent, Peppercorn threw himself in quest of drinks into the crowd that pressed itself to the bar, leaving Steadman and the American journalist alone.

"Are you really a distant relative of Gant's?" Steadman asked her, finding her face an agreeable distraction from the tension before.

She laughed. "Well, let's say my mother was a distant cousin to Mr. Gant's late wife. I'm surprised he still allowed me to interview him, though. These arms dealers are usually shy people."

"Yes, publicity is one thing they don't need. I'm surprised he did."

"It took a long, long time, I can tell you. Then suddenly, last week, right out of the blue, he agreed."

"What changed his mind?" Steadman asked, puzzled.

"I've no idea. Perhaps his wife's memory stirred his conscience; he had little enough to do with her relatives when she was alive."

"Do you know what she died of."

"Yes. She was killed in a car crash."

"Have you found out much about him. He seems a very private man."

"He is. But I've spent some days with him and he's let me photograph most of what I want. He suddenly seems to want to exploit his name—well maybe not quite his name, but the new weapons he's producing, at least." She frowned and bit the nail on the small finger of her right hand. "I don't know, it's as if he's suddenly emerging from his dark shell, and actively seeking publicity."

The idea somehow worried Steadman. Why should a man like Edward Gant, whose business transactions had always been kept in the shadows, suddenly emerge into the public eye? It made little sense.

He decided to change the subject. "How long have you been in England?" he asked.

"Oh, about six months now. I used to roam the world before that, writing stories, taking pictures to go with

[68]

them. I used to work for a syndicate, but now I prefer to find my own commissions. It makes me feel more free to come and go as I like."

Peppercorn returned at that moment, carrying a Campari for the girl, vodka for Steadman, and a gin drowned in tonic for himself, all precariously held in two hands.

"Look, Harry," he said urgently. "I've just bumped into a couple of people I know. It could lead to a nice little bit of business for me so I've rather selfishly arranged to have a spot of lunch with them. I hope you don't mind?"

Steadman shook his head, taking the Campari and vodka from his friend's outstretched fingers. "Don't worry about it."

"I could meet you back here afterward and take you back to town?" the solicitor said anxiously.

"It's okay. I'll catch a train."

"I could give you a lift," said the girl.

"Ah, there you are, all settled." Peppercorn grinned with satisfaction.

"Fine," said Steadman, taking a swallow of his drink. The vodka scorched his throat, but it felt good.

"Right, must get back to them, Harry," said the solicitor. "I'll get my secretary to give you Gant's telephone number." He was already moving away. "Let me know how you get on and when you want me to do my bit. 'Bye for now, er, Miss Miles. Hope to see you again."

The girl chuckled at the solicitor's retreating figure as it backed into a black-skinned dignitary who eyed him with wide-eyed alarm.

"Thanks for the lift," Steadman said as her attention returned to him.

"I have to report back to the magazine, anyway. They'll want to know my progress." She looked directly into Steadman's eyes. "Tell me about yourself. Have you always been involved in the sale of weapons?"

"No, not always. I've spent a good portion of my life in the Army."

Holly raised her eyebrows. "You don't look the military type," she said.

Steadman grinned, presuming the girl meant it as a compliment.

"What made you leave?" she asked, sipping at the Campari.

"Oh, I decided I'd had enough of the British Army. There were other things to do."

"Like buying and selling arms?"

"Among other things. I eventually joined an inquiry agency."

"An inquiry agency? You're a gumshoe?"

Steadman laughed. "It's a long time since I've been called that."

Holly laughed with him. "Sorry. You don't look like Sam Spade either."

"Not many of us do. As a matter of fact, my partner . . ." He suddenly broke off and Holly saw the pain in his eyes.

"Is something wrong?" she asked.

Steadman took a large swallow of vodka, then answered, "I was going to say my partner is a woman. She's dead now."

"I'm sorry, Harry."

He shrugged.

"Was it recent?" she asked, then was puzzled by the strange smile on his face and the hardness in his eyes.

"Very," he replied. "Let's drop it, eh? Tell me more about your article. Any startling discoveries about Gent?" The question was put lightly, but Holly sensed its seriousness.

"Oh, I haven't got that close. Everything I've seen, everything he's told me, all seems studied, as though he's only revealing a top layer. I get the feeling there're plenty more layers underneath. Usually, when you do this kind of in-depth study of a person, you find out certain things by accident—a slip of the tongue, or maybe they get carried away with their own reminiscences. But Edward

Gant's information has been guarded all along. I just can't get under the surface."

"You've been to his home?"

"The one near Guildford, yes. I spent two days there and he's invited me back again. It's a small mansion in about six or seven acres of grounds; very quiet, very private."

"Does he have another place?"

"Well, it seems so. When I was there he seemed to have a constant stream of visitors—some were important people, too—and I did hear them making arrangements for some kind of get-together in his home on the West Coast. Gant was deliberately vague when I asked him about it, though, but he did say it was a testing ground for some of his more powerful weapons."

"Do you know exactly where it is?"

"No. I asked directly, but he told me that in the arms business, and especially with innovatory weapons, testing sites were strictly private and their locations, as far as possible, kept secret. He clammed up after that."

"These visitors. You said some were important."

"You're kind of curious, aren't you? I guess that goes with the job, huh?"

"I guess it does," Steadman said. "Really, it's just that I want to know as much about Gant as possible so I can make sure I get a good deal for my clients. It might help to know his connections, that's all."

"Okay. 'Nough said. A couple of them were politicians—minor ones, I may add. The others I recognized as industrialists and a few of your City guys. I can't put names to their faces, though."

"Never mind. Would you like another?" Steadman pointed to the girl's empty glass.

"Er, no. I think I'd like to get back to town now. Are you ready to leave?"

Steadman drained his glass, then nodded. As he took Holly's arm and guided her through the crowded tent, the morning's displays over, the preliminary discussions having taken place, he caught sight of Major Brannigan listening politely to a foreign visitor. The major caught his eye, but gave no acknowledgement.

Steadman and the girl left the tent and the major's eyes followed them until they had disappeared from view.

Holly led the investigator toward her car, a bright yellow Mini. They climbed in and Holly snapped on her seat belt. The car threaded its way through the other parked vehicles and turned into the graveled roadway. It picked up speed and they left the display area with its businesslike stands and array of sophisticated machinery of death.

"Tell me, Harry," Holly said. "Do you ever get a conscience about the weapons you buy?"

"Occasionally," he replied, "but greed generally manages to overcome it."

She looked at him quickly, surprised at his rancor.

"I'm sorry," she apologized. "I didn't mean to sound high-minded."

He studied her profile for a few moments, then said, "I'm sorry, too. I didn't mean to snap. It's really a question of whom you're buying for. There are certain countries and groups I would have nothing to do with, while there are others I have every sympathy for. Of course, dealers aren't supposed to have sympathy for any particular cause, it should be strictly business, but there are laws governing just who they can sell to."

"And do you have a sympathy for the cause of the people you are negotiating for?"

"I used to," was all he would say.

The road was winding through the wooded area now and the ground on either side was thick with fallen leaves. Steadman turned to the girl again and could not help glancing down at her body, her long legs bent to accommodate the slightly cramped space of the Mini. Her wrists were slender, yet handled the wheel firmly, and there was a quiet strength about her that had not been apparent on first sight. She suddenly turned her head toward him, feeling his gaze on her, and for a brief moment something passed between them. Her attention went back to the road and he wondered if he had only imagined the understanding in her look.

He, too, turned his head back toward the road, and it was at that moment that the tank roared from the trees on their left.

SIX

Brutality is respected. *Brutality and physical strength. The plain man in the street respects nothing but brutal strength and ruthlessness—women, too, for that matter, women and children. The people need wholesome fear. They want to fear something. They want someone to frighten them and make them shudderingly submissive. Haven't you seen everywhere that after boxing matches, th beaten ones are the first to join the party s new members? Why babble about brutality and be indignant about tortures? The masses want that. They need something that will give them a thrill of horror.*

—ADOLF HITLER

The girl saw the Chieftain emerging from the trees a fraction of a second later than Steadman. Instinctively, her foot jammed down on the accelerator and the little car surged forward in an effort to escape the fifty-two tons of crushing metal.

Steadman automatically pushed himself away from his side of the car, thankful that he wasn't restricted by a seatbelt, and taking care not to crowd the girl. Their lives

[74]

depended on her reaction. The tank loomed larger in his window-framed vision until it filled the rectangular shape completely, and the investigator clenched his teeth against the anticipated impact. But the blackness left the window nearest to him and he knew there might just be a chance to squeeze by the cumbersome monster.

The Chieftain had been too close, though, and it smashed into the back of the Mini, slewing the car around, mercifully pushing rather than crushing. The screaming of tearing metal and shattered glass filled their ears as the girl fought to control the car's spin. It slid across the road and spun into a tree, almost facing the way they had just come.

Again it was Steadman's side which took the brunt of the crash, but he had steadied himself by pushing one hand against the dashboard and the other around the back of the driver's seat. His head snapped back with the impact, but the car's buckled metal failed to touch him.

He reached for the girl, whose head hung low on her chest. She still clutched the steering wheel, her seatbelt preventing her from being tossed around. He took her chin, and her head came up and turned toward him. With relief, he saw she had not been hurt, but was stunned by the impact. Her eyes were wide and looked questioningly at him.

"Bloody fools!" Steadman shouted, the anger in him now rising over the shock. He looked through the windshield at the green goliath completely blocking the road in front of them. "Why didn't they check to see if the road was clear before they tried to cross!" He was about to push the passenger door of the Mini open when the tank began moving backward, the pin-jointed links of its tracks spitting up gravel from the roadway. The movement puzzled Steadman into immobility for a moment, then he saw the tank stop. Its far-side track gripped the road and began to go forward once again, the near-side tract rotating at a slower pace. The Chieftain was turning toward them.

"Holly, I think . . ." he began to say, but the tank's

objective became frighteningly clear. "He's going to ram us again!"

The girl's face was horror-struck and Steadman knew he would never have time to release her from the seatbelt and get her out of the car before the tank crushed it to pieces.

"Drive!" he screamed at her. "Into the trees!"

Fortunately, the engine was still running, for she had dipped the clutch as she had braked, and her feet still had both pedals pressed to the floor. Her eyes suddenly seemed to focus as she realized the further danger, and she reacted to Steadman's command. Pushing the gear lever into first, she gunned the engine and the car leapt forward. Steadman prayed the back wheel hadn't been damaged in the crash, then once again clenched his teeth as the tank loomed up ahead of them.

It seemed there would be no escaping the mountain of metal this time as it rushed toward them, completely blocking their path, but Holly wrenched the wheel hard to her left and the Mini passed beneath the long 120mm gun of the Chieftain, scraping its side against the front of the tank's right-hand tracks. Metal clanged and buckled once more as the car was knocked to one side, but Holly managed to control the sideways deflection and the car skidded into the trees, its wheels tearing at the damp earth and leaves to maintain a grip. She turned the wheel to the right to avoid a tree which was directly in their path, but it was too late, and again Steadman's side of the car took a vicious blow against its metalwork.

The Mini stopped and Holly declutched to prevent the engine from stalling. Steadman glanced back through the rear window and saw that the Chieftain was swiftly turning toward them.

"For Christ's sake, move it!" Steadman knew that even if the girl got clear, his door was jammed up against the side of the tree which would mean he'd have to try and scramble out on her side. The odds weren't promising.

The girl must have realized the same, and he was thankful for her courage in staying with him. The car

[76]

moved forward a few inches, then sank back into the grooves it had dug for itself. Once again, the tank completely filled Steadman's view from the rear window and seemed poised to overwhelm them.

Then the car lurched forward, the wheels spinning but gaining a small grip, enough to draw them from the crushing belly of the Chieftain. It gathered speed as the wheels found firmer ground and Steadman saw the tank hit the tree they had skidded into, tilting it as though it were on a swivel, then coming on, chasing them as an armadillo would chase a millipede.

The car's speed was limited, for Holly had to steer a careful path through the trees and undergrowth, whereas the tank had only to avoid the stoutest trees, the other less firm trees and undergrowth easily succumbing to its massive weight. Steadman urged the girl on, his eyes constantly switching from the path ahead to the tank behind. He was shocked at the audacity of the attack, at Gant's— it *had* to be Gant behind it—arrogant confidence that he could get away with two outrageous murders within just a few days. First Maggie, now him. And the girl. Three murders.

Holly's eyes were narrowed in concentration as she struggled to keep the car under control on the slippery surface of leaves, and he saw that although there was fear in her there was no panic.

The Mini suddenly bumped over a fallen branch hidden by leaves and it rose into the air, throwing the passengers forward and up. Holly's seatbelt and her grip on the wheel checked her movement, but Steadman was tossed toward the windshield. His arm struck the window first and fortunately the glass held. His head hit the roof of the car and he was thrown back into his seat, dazed but still conscious.

The car spun around as it landed and this time Holly lost control completely. It bounced off a tree and came to rest sideways onto the advancing tank. Steadman saw that the ground sloped down into a dip on his side of the car. The engine had stalled and for a few valuable seconds Holly was too numbed by the sudden jolt to move. Steadman shook the haze from his head and looked at the girl. Beyond her profile he saw the Chieftain looming larger and larger. Holly quickly looked to her right and saw that the tank was only a few yards from them and she desperately reached forward for the keys in the ignition. She twisted them viciously and depressed the accelerator to the floor. The engine roared and the car lurched forward and stalled again; in her haste she had left it still in gear. The tank was only a yard away.

Steadman knew they wouldn't make it and was reaching for the release on the girl's seatbelt in a vain attempt to pull her from the car on his side, when the Chieftain tank ploughed into them.

The noise of crunching metal, the rumbling of the tank's engines, and Holly's scream combined into a terrifying sound. The car on her side rose into the air and Steadman was thrown back against the passenger door. The world outside the small windows spun around crazily as the car was pushed completely over, first onto its side, then onto its back. The trees and the sky began to spin even faster as the Mini rolled over the brink of the dip it had come to rest on. Steadman threw one arm around the back of his seat and pushed the other against the dashboard in an attempt to wedge himself as the car rolled over and over down the slope. The dip had saved their lives for that moment, for if the car hadn't plunged into it, then it would have been crushed completely under the massive bulk of the tank.

For those few nauseating seconds as the car rolled down, Steadman lost his senses. He still managed to keep his grip on the seat and the dashboard through sheer reaction, only losing that hold when the car crashed to a halt on its back. He found himself lying bundled on the upturned roof of the car when he opened his eyes. He wasn't sure if he had blacked out or his mind had just gone blank for a few moments, but instinct told him he had no time to lose. From his curled-up position inside the overturned Mini, he could see back up the slope, and

[78]

the tank poised at the top, a huge metallic predator making ready to plunge for the kill.

He pulled himself around on the buckled metal and saw Holly hanging upside down, her head and shoulders against the roof, her lower body still trapped by the seatbelt. Her eyes were closed, but when he called her name, they opened and looked toward him.

"Jesus Christ!" she said.

He scrambled into a better position to reach her, barely registering the fact that no sudden pain bespoke broken bones. He pressed the button to release her, taking her weight with his arm. She slid to the roof which was now the floor.

"We've got to get out!" he told her urgently. "The tank'll be coming down after us." He reached past her and tried to push open the driver's door. It opened two inches then jammed solidly into the hard earth.

He quickly turned around and tried the door on his side and it opened easily. He pushed it wide and to his horror saw the Chieftain had begun its descent. This time, the Mini would be squashed flat under the impact. Steadman reached back for the girl and yanked her toward him, heedless of any harm she might have suffered in the crash. She gasped at his roughness, but threw herself forward, realizing their danger. They scrambled from the car together and the tank towered above them, its speed increased by the angle of the slope.

Holly tried to scramble to one side, but Steadman knew it was already too late. The sheer width of the tank allowed them no room for escape—they would be crushed by either of its two-foot-wide set of tracks. He grabbed her arm and threw her upward toward the onrushing monster. She screamed in fright, not understanding his motives. He pushed her down hard into the earth, throwing a protective arm over her head, holding her there, trying to make them both as flat as possible.

Everything went black as the Chieftain rumbled over them, and Steadman pressed his face close to Holly's, exerting pressure on her with his arm to make sure she didn't try to rise in panic. The underbelly of the tank was only inches from their bodies and the smell of diesel fumes and oil was overpowering. The investigator prayed that the angle of the slope would not alter before the vehicle had passed completely over them, for if it did, the tank's rear end would become lower as the main body righted its angle, and their bodies would be scraped into the earth.

They felt the tank shudder as it ploughed into the Mini, and the screech of grinding metal threw fresh terror into them.

"Try to move upward!" he screamed at her over the noise. "Keep moving up, but keep low!"

They inched forward as the tank sped over them, for any distance they gained could save their lives. He saw the rectangle of daylight ahead and realized the angle was narrowing; the shuddering tank was beginning to level. He closed his eyes and stopped moving forward, knowing there was nothing they could do to save themselves now. He pressed himself close to Holly, holding her head against his, his lips against her cheek.

The noise of the car being crushed rose to a crescendo and suddenly he felt all movement around them shudder to a halt. The tank's engine still roared on, but the clanking links of its tracks had ceased to move. The small car's tough little body had halted the tank's progress momentarily and Steadman realized they had been granted a few seconds' grace.

"Quick, move!" he yelled at the girl, and began to pull her up with him. With relief, he felt her body begin to worm its way up; she hadn't frozen.

The Chieftain's engine began to whine and suddenly it lurched forward again, demolishing the yellow car completely. But they were clear. Steadman reached safety first, then dragged the girl after him just as the tank's rear dropped and almost brushed the soil of the slope.

Holly fell against him and they stood drawing in deep breaths, their bodies heaving. Steadman looked back at the tank and could see nothing of the flattened Mini. The

Chieftain was motionless and, irrationally, Steadman had the feeling the battle vehicle was a living thing, a mechanical beast that had somehow come to life to destroy them. It seemed to be watching them.

The tracks began to clank into life once again, but this time they had changed direction. The tank was coming back for them.

"Run!" he shouted, pushing the girl forward but keeping a grip on her arm in case she should fall. The slope would have been too treacherous to have attempted to climb, so they ran along the side of it, stumbling once and rolling down into the gully created by the dip. Steadman pulled the girl to her feet and looked into her face anxiously and again he felt an understanding pass between them. The Chieftain had turned its huge bulk toward them and now it made its destructive way along the gully, picking up speed as it came. They fled from it.

Leafless branches tore at their clothes and skin as they stumbled through the undergrowth, their throats raw with the effort of breathing. The gully took on a gentle slope and soon they were free of the dip, running toward an area of dense bracken and bramble. Steadman glanced back over his shoulder and saw they were out of the tank's vision.

"In there," he gasped, pointing at the thick canopy, and they plunged into the bracken, wading deep, ignoring the stings of resisting bramble. They heard the rumbling of the tank behind them as it cleared the rise, and Steadman pulled the girl to the ground, the foliage closing around them. He lost sight of the tank but could still hear its engine. They tried to control their breathing as though the mechanical dinosaur might hear and seek them out.

"Why?" Holly whispered, desperation in her voice. "Why are they trying to kill us?"

Steadman put a finger to her lips and shook his head. The Chieftain's engine seemed to be getting louder and they could hear the crashing of broken undergrowth. The investigator raised his head slightly to catch sight of the approaching vehicle and nearly cried out when he saw it was heading straight toward them. It was as if it could sense their presence.

They ran again, away from their relentless pursuer, lost in the woodland, not knowing in which direction lay the road. Bursting free of the bracken, they discovered the ground was rising slightly, but they couldn't see what lay beyond the incline. Their muscles were aching now, their bodies bruised. Steadman dragged the girl forward, knowing she could not carry on much farther. Her legs were dragging and she leaned heavily against him. They heard a muffled explosion and something vaguely registered in Steadman's head.

He put one arm around Holly's waist and helped her up, pulling her toward the incline. The tank, now relatively unimpeded by trees, was gaining on them. They staggered on and finally reached the top of the gentle slope. The ground dropped away dramatically into a vast quarry.

"It's the explosives testing ground," said Steadman, realizing now why the muffled explosion moments earlier had registered in his mind. Deep below, they could see the long slabs of concrete, shelters for observers in the man-made valley, as they witnessed the damage caused by rockets, mortars, and shell fire. Battered skeletal frames of army vehicles lay scattered around the gray plain, victims of weapons turned against them to demonstrate their destroyers' deadliness. As they watched, they saw a rocket leave the muzzle of a launcher held on a soldier's shoulder and strike what must have been a sheet of Chobham armor three hundred yards away; the rocket exploded on impact but the metal sheet appeared to remain undented.

"We're trapped!" the girl cried and seemed to be about to sink to her knees in despair.

Steadman held her steady and pointed toward a clump of gorse that ran along the rim of the huge pit. "In there!" he yelled at her. "We may be able to hide from them!"

They stumbled toward the gorse patch and threw themselves into it, keeping as far away from the cliff edge as possible. They buried themselves in the waist-high spiky bushes, but Steadman forced them on, crawling on hands and knees until they were in the center of the patch. They lay there panting and the investigator put an arm around the frightened girl's shoulders, pulling her toward him. He felt her trembling against his chest and tightened his grip on her. Her confusion was adding to her fear.

He decided he had to risk seeing if the men—or man—in the tank had observed their desperate run for cover. The rumble of the Chieftain was close and their position too vulnerable if their location was known.

He raised his head above the gorse and was dismayed when he saw the close proximity of the armored vehicle. And it was headed straight toward them, increasing speed as it came, knowing where they were as if by instinct. He dragged the girl up and she screamed when she saw the approaching tank. She began to move away but he held her tight, to prevent her from backing toward the quarry's edge. He pulled her through the gorse, running to their left in a desperate attempt to dodge their uncanny and unerring pursuer; but a stout root, hidden from his view, tripped him and they both went down in a heap, the winter foliage cruelly ripping at their faces and hands. Holly lay slumped against him, unwilling or unable to move any more, giving in to their relentless hunter, too exhausted, too despairing to go on.

The tank was above them, the long phallic muzzle of its gun barrel passing over their heads like an antenna sensing their presence. In one last hopeless gesture of defiance, Steadman picked up the girl bodily, and with all the strength he could gather, leapt to one side, afraid to go under the tank again in case it stopped above them to grind its tracks backward and forward until their bodies had been crushed into the ground.

He almost made it, but the right-hand track caught his shoulder and he went down. The girl was clear, thrown forward by his rush, and she saw his body fall beneath the tank's wheels. Fortunately for Steadman, he had fallen into the angled space between the upper and lower wheels of the Chieftain, and it was enough to save the investigator from being dragged beneath the vehicle: he kept rolling, pushing himself away from the deadly moving links. He was inches clear, then suddenly found his movement checked. The back of his jacket was caught beneath the grinding track. He tried desperately to prevent his weight from being pulled back under, and his hands reached out to clutch roots—anything to hold on to.

Holly clamped her hands around his wrists and pulled with all her strength, her eyes tightly closed against the effort. Steadman felt his jacket tear, then suddenly he was free and moving forward into her arms. They clutched at each other as the tank lumbered by.

Steadman twisted his head, ready to pull the girl up and begin running again.

His eyes widened when he saw the Chieftain had not decreased its speed, but was trundling onward toward the quarry's edge only feet away. The tracks spun in free air and screeched when the huge vehicle tilted forward, the edge of the cliff breaking away under its weight. The tank gave Steadman a view of its metal underbelly before sliding forward, the bare tracks now spinning in the air. Then it was gone, careering down toward the gray plain two hundred feet below.

Steadman scrambled forward, carefully avoiding the freshly broken earth at the cliff's edge, and was in time to see the Chieftain bounce off the limestone wall of the cliff and turn over, its gun pointing toward the sky. It bounced again, and again, then the tank seemed to disintegrate. Its tracks tore loose, and ran as streamers behind the main body; its gun caught against the rock face as the tank turned over, and the turret was ripped from the hull. The fuel tank must have been punctured, for suddenly a bright flame flowered from the body and the blast of the explosion swept back up against the cliff face and hot air seared Steadman's face. A large, more powerful explosion joined the first almost immediately, and he realized the Chieftain had been carrying live ammunition.

The Chieftain reached the bottom of the quarry in many separate pieces.

Steadman blinked his eyes, moistening them against the scorching heat of the blast, and he saw figures emerging from behind concrete shelters. They were too far away for him to see their expressions, their faces just white blobs, but their shock was apparent in their stance.

He pushed himself away from the edge and scrambled back through the rough gorse toward the sobbing girl.

SEVEN

> *But then it is the curse of the great to have to walk over corpses.*
>
> —HEINRICH HIMMLER

> *Terrorism is absolutely indispensable in every case of the founding of new power.*
>
> —ADOLF HITLER

Steadman drew back the covers of the bed and gazed down at Holly's golden body. The tips of her breasts were pink and alive, protruding from their soft mounds, erect and excited. His eyes followed the curve of her waist and reached the rise of her hip, then traveled inward along the triangle that dipped into her smooth thighs. Her stomach was flat and had a firmness that told of muscles developed just beneath the skin; her whole body had that firmness to it, soft to look at and to touch, but conditioned to a surprising toughness.

"Please," she said, looking up at him, "just hold me."

He was aware of his hardness as her eyes searched his body too, and he slid in beside her, pulling the sheets up to their shoulders, encircling an arm around her waist, drawing her to him. They stayed that way, their bodies pressed together, enjoying each other's warmth, relaxing into one another.

The girl had surprised Steadman earlier that day. Army

vehicles had arrived at the top of the quarry within seconds of the tank's descent and questions had been fired at them mercilessly. Holly had recovered from her tear-shedding and remained calm at the barrage, whereas Steadman had soon lost his temper and flayed the curious officers with his tongue. They had been taken into the Aldershot HQ and the questioning had continued. Why had they wandered off the road toward the quarry? Hadn't they seen the warning signs? Why should a Chieftain chase them? Hadn't they just driven into the woods into the path of the tank? What had made the Chieftain plunge into the quarry? Had they spoken to the crew at any time?

All through the interrogation, the girl had answered quietly and firmly, showing no sign of the ordeal she had been through, apart from the physical aspect—her clothes were torn in places and scratches showed on her hands and face. Then she had turned the interview about, demanding to know why there was not stronger security on the site, and why they were being treated like offenders when it was *they* who would be suing the British Army.

The lieutenant-colonel in charge of the questioning was taken aback by the sudden onslaught and Steadman had smiled at his confusion. The arrival of Major Brannigan, who vouched for their identities, had brought the hasty inquisition to a close. Reserved apologies and assurances were given that the matter would be fully investigated—fully implying that they were most definitely still under suspicion.

Major Brannigan had organized a limousine to take them back into London, and after they had picked up Holly's Pentax from the Long Valley guard post, Steadman suggested she return with him to his house for a nerve-steadying drink and to clean herself up after her ordeal. She readily agreed, for at the moment she was living and working out of an address in north London and she felt she could not face the trip across the busy town just yet.

She was quiet on the trip back to London, and the

moment of closeness their mutual danger had brought about seemed to have been lost. But when he had settled her in an armchair in his living room, and before she had even sipped the brandy he had offered her, the tears broke through and she had buried her head into his shoulder. He'd held her and tried to soothe her, knowing it was merely the relief of having survived the nightmare, the fear having gone.

After a while, her trembling had stopped, and again he forced the brandy on her, urging her to drink. He saw the tension begin to drain away. He drank with her, for she was not alone in having been shaken by the experience. The worst moment for him had been when the tracks of the Chieftain had tried to drag him back by his jacket and crush him. He remembered her hands clutching his wrists, her closed eyes and the effort on her face as she had struggled to pull him toward her. The brandy warmed them both, their senses acute and vulnerable after the shock, and as they looked into each other's eyes, the understanding—the intangible closeness—returned.

Steadman wasn't surprised when she asked him to take her to bed and, somehow, both knew the prime purpose was not to make love, but to share physically this closeness they were both feeling. For Steadman it was a feeling he hadn't experienced for a long, long time; not since Lilla. Strangely, the memory of her gave him no sense of guilt. He had felt it and rejected it when he had made love to other women—even Maggie—but now, when his emotions were beginning to run deep, the guilt hadn't even appeared. Who was she, this Holly Miles? And why were they reacting so strangely toward each other?

He led her upstairs and watched her undress. She had showered and reappeared, her hair now darkly wet and clinging. Her legs were long and the curve of her calves graceful, her thighs swelling just enough to give them shape. Her shoulders were wide for a girl, but only noticeably so when they were compared to her slim hips. Her breasts were full, and firm with youth.

She had climbed into bed, water from her hair dampening the pillow, and resting on one elbow, had watched him undress. His body was still lean and well muscled enough to be pleasing; he felt no self-consciousness under her gaze. He caught her look of concern when she saw the old scars scattered across his back, but she made no comment. He showered, then returned to the bedroom, finding a peacefulness in her he wanted to share.

Now he held her close, and for a fleeting second as her eyes opened, he thought he glimpsed something. Not fear, not confusion, but anguish. It was gone in a moment, yet he knew it wasn't imagined.

"Why did they try to kill us, Harry?" she asked, drawing slightly away so she could see more of his face. "Why would the men in the tank want to do that?"

"I don't know, Holly," he lied. "You make enemies in this business. Maybe someone was trying to get at me. We don't know that there was a complete crew in the tank."

"Hijack a tank just to kill you?"

Steadman shrugged. "Like I said—you make enemies."

"Unless whoever it was was trying to kill me."

Steadman looked at her sharply. "Kill you? Why should anyone want to do that?"

"I don't know. I just felt the menace there. Didn't you feel it? It was somehow—evil. As if the tank were a living thing."

She had experienced it too. It had been uncanny.

Her body shivered and he drew her close again.

"Put it out of your mind for now," he told her. "They'll find the bodies—or body—in the tank and maybe their identities will tell us why they were trying to kill us."

She pressed against him. "There's more, isn't there? You're not telling me everything."

He suddenly felt the overwhelming desire to tell her all—about Maggie, Mossad, British intelligence, this man Edward Gant. He wanted to confide. After all these years of introversion, he now felt the need to talk to someone, maybe not to share in the problems he faced, but at least to know of them. But something held him back.

Was it years of discretion as a private detective, as a Mossad agent, as a member of military intelligence? Had years of never trusting anyone been ingrained into his character? He felt he knew the girl so well, yet common sense told him she was still a stranger. Maybe it was that which held him back.

"Yes," he said to her, "there is more, but it's better that you're not involved."

She was silent for a while, then said, "Who are you really, Harry? Why are you involved in weapons? Can't you tell me that?"

"I've told you who I am."

"You've told me what you are."

He grinned at her. "What I am is who I am."

She shook her head. "No, that's too easy. It doesn't explain anything. Why do you deal in armaments, Harry?"

"If it wasn't me, it'd be somebody else," came the stock reply.

"You're still evading."

His hand touched her cheek. "Give it time, Holly," he said quietly. "We've been thrown together by mutual danger. Tomorrow our feelings could be different. So let's be patient, eh?"

She nodded and silently reached behind his neck to touch his damp hair. "You feel it too, then?" she asked.

He smiled back, then kissed her softly. "I feel it," he said.

"Then let it happen."

She kissed him fiercely and quietened nerves became alive again, this time responding to a far different sensation than fear. His hand swept down her back and found her buttocks. Pulling her tight against him, he grew erect once more against the softness of her stomach.

He heard her sigh as their bodies filled each other's, their skin joining, its coolness turning to heat. His fingers fondled the sensitive base of her spine, and her long fingers reached down to touch him in the same place, then traveled farther to the back of his legs. He could feel her stretching against him and suddenly her legs parted and his thigh filled the gap. He ran his hand down the smoothness of her skin and pulled her leg up slightly so that it rested over his own; then he caressed the back of her leg from the top to the sensitive area behind her knee.

Holly reached up again, laying her hand flatly against his back, exerting pressure so that his lips bore down hard against hers. The softness of her mouth aroused him further and her teeth bit down gently on his probing tongue. He felt her hand reach around to his chest and their bodies parted slightly to give it access. She touched him easily at first, then squeezed the firm skin of his chest hard, not to hurt, but to excite. Her fingers slid down toward his stomach and the muscles there quivered at her touch. He pushed himself toward her searching hand, demanding to be touched at his most sensitive area. Her fingers ignored his demands and passed that point, reaching below and encircling his testicles. She squeezed them and he groaned aloud at the warmth of the touch.

His own hand swept back upward, never losing contact with her body, heightening her sensations as it journeyed toward her breasts. He covered a breast with his hand and moved his fingers gently to find her nipple, stroking it delicately, controlling the passion he felt.

They paused in their movements for a moment and kissed softly, both afraid to talk of love for it was too soon, but allowing their kiss to express feelings that ran deep, feelings that surprised them both. Only then did they allow their passions to rise uncontrolled.

He reached down, still keeping his fingers against her skin, tantalizing her with the direction his hand was taking. Over her stomach, staying there briefly to explore and awaken, then down into her hair, stroking and kneading, firm enough to reach deeper nerve cells, but soft enough to excite rather than fulfill. She could wait no longer and grabbed his wrist, forcing his hand lower, down between her thighs, into the aroused wetness there.

Her moan of pleasure mingled with his, for the sensation of probing her sweet dampness was almost as great as the exhilaration she felt at his touch. His fingers entered her, careful not to hurt, but she pushed against him and her wildness incited him further. His touch was hard now and her motion was rapid. Her whole body squirmed as she reached for his penis, reluctant to lose the excitement of his hand, but eager for something more fulfilling, more satisfying.

She turned onto her back and he rose above her, kissing her face and neck, her closed eyes. Her smile was inward, but she suddenly put an arm around his neck to pull his cheek against hers, to let him know she was sharing their pleasure, not retreating into her own. Her other hand was gently insistent, drawing him into her. He paused, then advanced slowly so there would be no pain, no sharpness; he sank further, pausing again when she gasped. But pain meant little to her now and she urged him on, pushing upward with her hips to help him complete his journey.

His weight bore down on her and their mutual desire became exquisitely intolerable. It was no time to linger, no time to tease; that could come later when they were used to each other. Now they needed to climb and reach their peak, to find release for screaming sensations. He thrust into her and she met and countered his movements with equal force, her fingers crooked and pressing into his skin, her knees raised slightly, her thighs squeezing against him.

She surprised him by reaching down between their bodies, her hand desperately feeling underneath him, finding the area between his legs and pulling upward as though to force him further into her. His passion grew even more and he felt the nerve-tingling tension begin its ascent, all the senses in his body drawn to that one region as though through a vortex. The same was happening to Holly. Her mouth was open, lips drawn back from her teeth. Her eyes were tightly shut and short gasps escaped her as she twisted her head against the pillow. Her muscles stiffened and juices inside her began to flow as though being squeezed through tiny apertures, faster, faster, until they burst through and flowed freely.

And Steadman's juices flowed to mingle with Holly's at the same time.

Even as the sensations subsided they still murmured their delight, Steadman resting against her, unwilling to relinquish the physical closeness. Holly kissed his neck, slowly stroking his back with gentle fingertips, happy at what had passed, but confused at the strength of her feelings for him. She was giving too much too soon.

She was unaware that the same confusion was running through Steadman. When he finally withdrew and lay by her side, they regarded each other with curious eyes.

"What's happening to us?" she asked, and she seemed nervous.

He put a finger to her lips. "It's too uncertain to say."

Holly seemed about to speak again, then changed her mind. She pulled her head away, but not before Steadman had seen the troubled look on her face. He turned her head back toward him and kissed her lips. "Don't worry about it, eh?"

Her eyes were misted and damp as she pulled his head down and kissed his lips.

"I don't want to be involved with you," she said.

"What are you afraid of, Holly? Are you really that scared of giving yourself to someone?"

"You don't understand . . ."

Her words were cut off by the insistent ringing of the telephone downstairs. She suddenly felt Steadman's whole body go rigid and a distant look came into his eyes.

"Harry, what's wrong?"

There was no recognition when he looked at her; his mind had traveled back to another time, in another country. The phone had rung there too, in their apartment in Brussels, when he and Lilla had just finished making love. It was to be the last time for them.

Lilla had urged him to ignore the ringing, had clung to him, demanding more, more love. Laughing, he'd smothered her face with a pillow, telling her the call might be important, perhaps a new mission. He was becoming too used to the inactivity, getting to like it. All the more rea-

son to let it ring, she had called after him as he leapt
away from her and went through to the living room.

The pillow had sailed through the air after him and
struck the side of the open door, her pretended anger
making him smile as he headed toward the phone. As he
picked up the receiver he saw she had followed him and
was standing in the doorway, a mischievous grin on her
face, one hand cupping her breast, the other reaching between her legs, as if to say if he wouldn't stay to please
her, she would amuse herself.

He turned his eyes away from the provocative sight and
said hello into the mouthpiece.

A voice, in French, asked if it was Monsieur Clement
speaking, and he had answered yes—Clement was the
name he used at that time.

He knew immediately what the high-pitched whine
from the earpiece meant, for the Israelis had used the
same device against the Chief PLO representative in
France, Dr. Mahmoud Hamshari. The sound was an electronic signal transmitted through the telephone to trigger
off a bomb hidden somewhere in the apartment, probably
near the phone itself.

As he dived toward Lilla he knew he was already too
late.

The sudden searing flash which lit up the horror on her
face told him there was no escape.

Not for Lilla. But he had survived.

They told him later it must have been the angle of his
body as he had dived for Lilla. Shrapnel had imbedded itself in his feet and legs, but the rest of his body had been
spared from the worst of the blast. A miracle they had
called it, but for him there was no mercy in his salvation.
He had no desire to live if Lilla was to die.

It had taken her three days to do so, this young, once
vivacious Israeli, her face torn away and her body lacer-
ated and burned. Three hideously pain-filled days. Never
fully conscious, but her shredded lips constantly moving
in her agony.

Steadman had prayed for her death, had begged the

doctors to end the torture for her; but their job was to preserve life no matter how shattered or painful, and they paid no mind to his entreaties, finally sedating him against his own pain and anguish.

When he had finally recovered and she was long dead, there had been a blackness in him that had taken many other deaths to purge.

Now, in circumstances so similar to that time before, the telephone was ringing, calling to him, reminding him, telling him the past was always present.

"Harry?" Her hand shook his shoulder. "What is it? You look so pale."

His eyes snapped back into focus and he looked down into the anxious face of Holly.

"Aren't you going to answer it? It keeps ringing," she said.

He eased himself from the bed without a word, and picked up a bathrobe lying over the back of a chair. He moved as though automated, but the concern in Holly's voice finally sank through.

"Stay there," he ordered, and she saw the somnambulic quality of his movements change to one of alertness. He shrugged on the robe and disappeared through the doorway. She heard his footsteps padding lightly down the stairs.

Steadman reached the living room and quickly glanced around, ignoring the shrilling phone for the moment. Nothing seemed out of place, but he quickly checked on the few places where a bomb could have been concealed, carefully lifting the settee and armchair to check beneath, peering behind the books on their shelves, examining the back of the television to see if it had been tampered with. Reasonably satisfied that everything was in order, he turned his attention to the telephone itself, the caller's persistence arousing his suspicions even more. There was nothing underneath the small coffee table it rested on, but he knew the telephone itself could contain a bomb. He picked it up to feel its weight: it seemed normal enough. He took the gamble and lifted the receiver to his ear.

"Steadman, is that you?"

With a sigh of relief, he recognized Pope's voice.

"For Christ's sake. Steadman, answer!"

"It's me," he said quietly.

There was a pause at the other end, then Pope said gruffly, "It took you long enough to answer."

"How did you know I was here?" Steadman countered.

"It's my business to know," came the curt reply. The tone changed as the fat man relaxed. "I heard what happened to you down at Long Valley. Tell me your end of it."

Steadman told him flatly, without emotion, as though making a report to a client. He mentioned the invitation from Gant to arrange a further meeting.

"Good," said Pope. "Do so. Who's this girl, this, er, Holly Miles?"

"She's a writer—free-lance. She's doing an article on the arms trade for one of the Sundays."

"And Gant's obliging her?"

"It seems so."

"Hm. Peculiar. Not like him to want publicity."

"Maybe he wants to come out of the shadows." Steadman whirled as he felt a presence in the room. Holly stood in the doorway, his shirt covering her small body seductively. She smiled at him and he relaxed. Pope's voice drew his attention back to their conversation.

"You say this tank was definitely chasing you," he was saying.

"Yes, it was trying to ram us."

"You're sure it wasn't just a runaway?"

"Look, we've been through all this with the military. The bloody thing wrecked the car, then tried to squash us flat when we ran for it! It chased us for at least five minutes."

"Yes, yes. Very strange."

Steadman's impatience grew. "Is that all you can say? We know it was strange, but you and I . . ." He cut off his words, remembering Holly was still in the doorway. "Look, who was in the tank? Were they working for him?" He was careful not to mention Gant's name.

There was a long silence on the other end of the line.

"Pope? Did you hear me?"

"Er, yes, dear boy," came the reply eventually. "The tank was a complete wreck, of course, by the time it reached the bottom of the quarry. Its fuel tank exploded, you know, then its ammo."

"I know that. Were the bodies badly burned?"

"That's just it, Harry." Again, Pope paused, as though considering his words. "There were no bodies. The tank was empty."

"But that's impossible! They must have escaped or been destroyed completely." There was alarm in Steadman's voice and a chilling sensation in the pit of his stomach.

"No chance of escape. And there would have been some trace of human bodies, no matter how bad the damage. No, Harry. The tank was empty. There was no one driving it."

Steadman stared at the receiver, unable to believe the words. Then he turned toward Holly and she saw the confusion in his eyes.

EIGHT

The eternal life granted by the Grail is only for the truly pure and noble!

—ADOLF HITLER

And many of them that sleep in the dust of the earth shall awake, some to everlasting life, and some to shame and everlasting contempt.

—DANIEL 12:2

Smith shivered and tightened his scarf, silently cursing the coldness of the night. It was morbid, too, sitting in the churchyard in the dark, ancient gravestones scattered around, black and weathered, some tilting at odd angles suggesting their occupants had become restless. He wondered briefly if he should risk lighting a cigarette, but decided against it. Although the bench on which he sat was well hidden in the darkness, there was just a chance that the cigarette's glow would be seen from the small road opposite. It wouldn't do to have any passerby getting curious about someone sitting in a graveyard in the dead of night smoking a fag. Not that there *were* any passersby at this time of bloody night!

He glanced at his watch, the luminous dial telling him he still had two hours to go before he came off shift. Two more hours in this stinking burial ground, he grumbled to himself. Two more hours of watching the stinking house opposite! And for what? They wouldn't be stupid enough to try anything like the other night. God, what kind of bastards would nail a woman to a door? He wondered if there were any other eyes watching the house. The police, maybe? It was strange they hadn't made more of the business, it wasn't the normal everyday kind of murder. And they'd managed to keep it out of the news, too. That must have taken some doing. Probably didn't want to encourage any similar types of crime. Unusual murders were always followed by other unusual murders. All the nuts around read about the first, got a kick out of it, and tried it out themselves. Same with bomb freaks.

What kind of man was this Steadman? He'd heard the detective was reluctant to help them at first, but the killing of his partner had persuaded him. Goldblatt had been furious at the investigator's previous refusal, even though he, Smith, had told the Mossad chief it would probably be so. He had kept an eye on Steadman over the years, it was part of his job as a "sleeper" in the country, and he had seen how the agency had begun to flourish, how Steadman had settled down to live a relatively peaceful existence in England. The man had left wars and violence behind. Why should he become involved again? The brutal murder of Mrs. Wyeth was the answer to that!

How *he* would like to be free of the organization. Joseph Solomon Smith, aged fifty-eight, jeweler in Walthamstow. Known as Solly to his friends. *Schmuck* to his wife, Sadie. Solly had fled to England along with thousands of other Jewish refugees just before the outbreak of the last World War, when Hitler's purge of Germany's and Austria's Jewish population was in full swing. It had been either flee or be interned in those days, not many realizing it was actually flee or die. The mass name-changing that had taken place as the refugees had arrived in England and gone through the far from friendly formalities of entering the country had been almost comical. The group in front of him had told the official their family name was Harris, for they had heard the people in front of them use the name. It sounded English. If the officials receiving the immigrants had been surprised at the amount of Harrises, Kanes, and Golds among the arrivals, they'd given no indication of it. Perhaps they understood the stigma attached to names ending with "berg," or "stein," or "baum," the danger such names threatened in the world at that terrible time. Perhaps they couldn't have cared less; there were too many to check.

He had chosen Smith because he knew it was indisputably British and he'd heard one of the customs officers call his companion by that name. It was a safe name. In fact, he'd nearly wet himself at the official's suspicious look and feared he'd been too blatant with his choice. However, the moment had passed, and with a resigned smile the man had cleared him.

Many of his compatriots had reclaimed their original names when the threat had died years later, but he had found no need to go to that trouble. Smith suited him fine.

He had escaped from Germany alone, his parents, two brothers, and one sister having been rounded up by Hitler's thugs on the very eve of their departure from the country. He would have been taken with them, but he was young, and young men, when about to leave a place forever, often have bittersweet good-byes to say, undying love to pledge. His farewell had taken most of the night and the girl had used his body as though there would never be any other for her.

He watched in horror from the shadows as the SS dragged his screaming family from their house, and he shrank back deeper into those shadows. He'd wept at his own cowardice then, and had wept with that same shame for many years after. Even the sight of his father falling into the gutter, his white beard now black in the moonlight—black because it was matted with blood—and the old man's screams as the rifle butts battered his frail body into unconsciousness, had not overcome his own terror. The brutality had only increased it. He had sunk to a squatting position, pressing himself hard against the rough wall, afraid to run lest the Gestapo hear his footsteps, stifling sobs with both hands against his mouth, unable to look away from the dreadful scene and unable to help his family. Even when his younger brother had been kicked senseless when he tried to go to the aid of his aged father. Even when his mother had been dragged by her hair into the waiting van. Even when his sister's young body had been bared and pawed by the uniformed thugs. Even when his older brother had been shot through the throat as he'd tried to escape. The terror had only been compounded.

The nightmares had finally ceased twenty years later, the horror gradually diminishing through repetition. The shame, too, had become numbed, for his spirit had grown weary of it and now kept it contained in a remote part of him. But the memory remained. And two faces burned within that memory: the faces of those who had caused the holocaust, the evil countenances of the two men responsible for the genocide, the decimation of his race, the murder of his family. Adolf Hitler and his henchman, Heinrich Himmler!

Their faces haunted him still because they were the cause of his terror, the source of his shame. And because he was aware their evil could so easily rise again.

After the war, when he learned the rest of his family had died in Auschwitz, he had tried to join the remnants of his race in Palestine, desperate to atone for his cowardice, yearning to take part in the rebirth of his nation. But the new Israelis now had a different way of thinking. For them, the centuries of oppression were over. They had returned to their home country and there they would either be free or perish fighting for that freedom. No longer would they accept persecution.

Defiance had to be tempered with cunning if they were to survive. They were a small nation in a small country; the world stood outside their boundaries, a giant wolf outside the door. The Israelis would never trust another nation again: they would work with them, they would trade with them, they would even encourage social intercourse.

But they would never trust another race, another country.

Because they were surrounded by enemies on all sides, their strength would have to reach beyond their own boundaries so they would always be forewarned of enemy action against them, enabling them to strike from behind when necessary.

They had persuaded Smith to remain in England, to build an identity there, to become British. And to be ready.

He had worked in a small jeweler's in the Hatton Garden area of London at first, for that had been the family business, a trade he had been taught by his father. His claim against the German government for the restoration of his family's wealth had taken years to materialize, for there were many others like him claiming compensation for losses they had suffered under the Nazi regime, and each claim had to be carefully checked. Very few received compensation from the then impoverished country, but Smith was lucky enough to receive a small settlement. This, plus the marriage to Sadie, which brought in some extra capital, enabled him to set up his own shop in Walthamstow.

Another source of income which Sadie never knew about were the regular amounts of money he received from the Shin Beth. The payments were small, but the work he carried out for his country was minimal and irregular. When he was younger, he had become impatient with the menial tasks they asked of him, but they had begged him to wait, to stay calm and serve his nation in the way they asked. His day would come.

It hadn't, though, and gradually the fires in him dimmed and almost burned out. He carried out the minor tasks asked of him with a sense of resigned duty and no passion. One of his "duties" had been to keep an eye on the man Harry Steadman when he had returned to England from Israel and joined an inquiry agency. Smith had done this by employing the agency to check on the background of his one and only employee, an innocent little countryman of his, whom he knew to be completely trustworthy, but who provided a good excuse for making contact with the investigator. The ex-policeman, Blake, had carried out the investigation, providing Smith with a clean bill of health for his shop assistant, but complimenting the jeweler on his wisdom in checking out his staff. One could never be too careful where goods of such value were involved. Smith had cultivated a friendship with the ex-policeman and engaged him privately in other concocted matters to do with his business. In that way, he was able to hear of the agency's progress and catch odd bits of information relating to Harry Steadman without becoming directly involved himself. He had skillfully avoided having his curiosity about the investigator become overt in any way, and most of the information had been volunteered by Blake without direct questioning. After all, they were good friends, they and their wives sometimes dined out together or visited the theater. Hadn't he, Smith, introduced his friend into his own golf club at Chingford? If the very-British ex-policeman ever wondered about the beginnings of his friendship with the very-Jewish dealer in precious stones, then he would put it down to an obvious desire for the jeweler to have some connections with the law.

Smith blew on his hands to try and warm them, then pushed them deep into the pockets of his overcoat. I'm becoming too old for this sort of thing, he told himself. Surveillance in this kind of weather was no good for a man of his health. His heart wasn't as strong as it used to be, his constitution no longer robust. It seemed a waste of time, anyway. Surely Steadman wouldn't be touched in his own home? Why was he so important to Israeli intelligence? Smith cursed the secrecy his employers maintained. Why couldn't their own people be informed of what was going on? And what do I tell Sadie, who knows nothing of Mossad and my little jobs for them, when she asks what kind of business deals keep me out till the early hours of the morning? The woman is becoming tiresome. Becoming? She always was. You got a loose woman, she'll tell me. Chance would be a fine thing, I'll tell her. You got . . . His body stiffened as something caught his eye.

Did I see something? he asked himself. Or was it my imagination? The street lighting is bad there over the road. Was it something moving?

Smith peered into the darkness, his eyes narrowed and his breath held. There it was again, a movement among the shadows.

He rose to his feet, his limbs stiff with cold, and bent his body forward as though it would help him see more clearly. He thought he saw movement again, but it somehow seemed unreal, his imagination playing tricks on him. The air around him was still, no wind to cause the stirring of tree branches which might create mysteriously moving shadows.

He moved forward, careful to make no sound, his breathing now thin and uneven. He had a number to call if anything suspicious occurred, but the nearest phone booth was two streets away. How stupid of them! If anything were to happen it would all be over by the time he reached the phone booth and they got here. But then, he had been told nothing had been expected to happen; he was only being used as an extra precaution.

He silently cursed the men who employed him, the silly little Jewish boys playing cloak-and-dagger. Then he forced himself to relax. It's probably nothing at all. I've been in the dark too long—and in creepy surroundings at that. My eyes are tired and small wonder! My God, what time is it now? The luminous dial told him it was 1:35 A.M.

The jeweler stood and stared at the terraced house for a few seconds more and was about to return to his bench when he noticed something odd. His mind couldn't register just what that oddness was for a few moments, and then he focused his vision on the door of the house. There was a long, dark shadow at one side. It may just have been a shadow cast by the half-moon against the door's frame, but then he realized the moon was on the other side; the shadow—if there had been one caused by the frame on that side—should have been cast on the left and not the right. He moved forward for a closer look, keeping to the hard earth and grass of the churchyard so his footsteps would not be heard. He pushed his way through the sparse shrubbery at the perimeter and peered over the iron fence. Only then did he see that the front door to Steadman's house was partially open.

What to do now? Phone his contact or investigate further? If Steadman were sleeping—and he undoubtedly was—he could be in serious danger. But what could he, an old man, do to help the detective? Warn him, at least.

Perhaps it was the memory of having done nothing so many years before, or perhaps it was just the thought of its being a false alarm and his looking foolish in the eyes of the young Israelis who employed him. He decided to investigate further before calling in help.

He reached the gateless exit to the churchyard and stealthily crossed the road, welcoming the concealing shadows on that side. The jeweler, one hand on the wall as if to steady himself, moved along toward Steadman's house. He reached the open door and hesitated.

All the muscles in his aging body had become tense, making his movements awkward and stiff. He felt a strange fear, as though someone—something—was waiting for him inside that house. Something that compelled him to enter.

He tried to break the spell, tried to tell himself he was being a foolish old man. He should try to get away, now, while there was still time. But there was something in there he had to see. Something there waiting just for him.

He pushed the door open further, his fingers trembling. His breathing had become heavier and he tried to suppress small whimpers escaping from his throat. Even then, he tried to turn and run, but his body—or was it his mind?—refused to obey. The door swung open and the hallway was a black, ominous tunnel.

Smith stepped over the threshold and felt his way along the passage, his eyes becoming more accustomed to the darkness. He stopped when he thought he heard breathing. Breathing that wasn't his own. But no other sounds came as he listened, although he felt that the beating of his own heart would surely drown out any other noise. He moved on and suddenly stumbled against the base of the stairway.

His hands took his weight, holding onto the high stairs for support, one knee resting on a lower step, and he grunted with the sudden jarring. Then he felt its presence.

His gaze traveled up the stairway, step by step, until it reached the bend. It was darker just there, a black hole in the general gloom, but there was someone—something— lurking in that pool of darkness. His whole body began to shake now, for he felt its evil; it seemed to emanate from that dark area, to flow down the stairs in a vaporous cloud, sweeping over him and chilling his mind.

A movement. A shape began to descend the stairs.

Smith moaned and tried to break away, but his limbs were locked rigid, paralyzed by a fear that was even greater than on the night of his family's abduction in Berlin. His eyes widened as the dark shape emerged from the total blackness of the bend in the stairs, and his mouth opened to form a scream as the figure became more discernible. And yet, the image still wasn't clear. It was just a black shape against the overall darkness of the hallway; but his mind saw more than his eyes. It came closer and stopped just before him. He tried to pull his hands away, for they were almost touching the shadow, but he found they would not obey him. The smell of decay pervaded the air, assailing his nostrils and almost causing him to vomit. He slowly looked up, searching the length of the figure towering over him and when he reached its head, a face came floating down at him as though the shape was bending.

"Oh, dear God." Smith's moan rose to a wail. "You! Oh God, it can't be!"

It was then he screamed.

The scream hadn't roused Steadman, for he'd been awake minutes before. He had lain there in the dark, unsure of what had dragged him from his deep slumber. He listened for any noises, and none came. He had become aware of the iciness of the room. It was a still coldness, penetrating the blankets of his bed, and not the normal chill of autumn. It was as though the temperature of the room had taken an abrupt downward plunge. He was aware of being very much alone.

Steadman had taken Holly home to her flat earlier that evening, both of them shaken by the revelation that the Chieftain tank which had tried to crush them that day had been empty. They were halfway to Holly's flat when the thought struck Steadman of how it could have been managed, and he had difficulty in keeping his sudden theory from the girl. There was no point in involving her. it would have meant telling her everything; better it remain a mystery to her.

He ran the idea through his mind as he drove and it seemed to fit; at least, there were no *other* possible explanations. Gant dealt in sophisticated armaments, the advanced technology of his weapons renowned and respected. It would not have been impossible for him to rig up remote-control-operated machinery inside the tank, a mechanical driver which would obey instructions from afar. But from where? The operator had to be able to see them to send the Chieftain on their track. He had to be in close visual proximity. Weight was added to his theory when he realized how: helicopters had been buzzing over the testing grounds all morning. They had been too busy trying to escape the tank to be aware of any helicopter hovering above them, but that must have been the answer! How else could their hiding places have been found so easily? The searching eyes had been above them! For a moment his theory floundered: whoever had been guiding the tank from the helicopter must have seen the quarry and would have taken avoiding action. But then he had been close to the quarry's edge; maybe the controller had not been quick enough to change the Chieftain's direction, maybe his eagerness to crush the detective had distracted his judgment. It had to be the answer! Steadman relaxed a little: he liked his mysteries to have some solution.

He had kissed Holly good-bye in his car when they reached her home, neither invited inside nor wanting to be. They were both curious about each other, both disturbed by the strength of their feelings; but both had had enough for one day. It was time for them to be alone, to lick their wounds and digest the events of the day. An unease showed in her eyes as she promised to see him soon. Then she was gone.

Steadman had driven to the agency, luckily catching Sexton and their young trainee, Steve, before they left for the night. He briefed them on two specific jobs they were to carry out during the following few days—current assignments would have to be slotted in somehow even if it meant spreading their load onto another agency. After warning them their investigations would require the utmost caution, he returned to his home in the back streets of Knightsbridge.

He made coffee, then settled down to reread the file on Edward Gant. Five cigarettes and three cups of coffee later he lay the document down by his feet, rubbing his eyes in weariness, his mind buzzing with unformed thoughts. There was still a smell about the whole business he didn't like. Why should British intelligence, with all their resources, use him to get at Gant? Pope's explanation that he was a link with all the parties concerned didn't quite ring true. He was even more certain he was being set up as the sacrificial goat, the bait to draw out the tiger. Mossad's use of him seemed more genuine, but just as ruthless. Their resources in England were limited and he was in a good position to find their missing agent. But was that all there was to it? They had admitted they wanted to nail Gant, but then why not just eliminate him? They'd done so with their enemies in the past, so why balk at it this time? There was much more to it than either intelligence organization was letting on, and that was why he was taking out extra insurance. Sexton's task was to find out more about Gant, hearsay matters that might not be entered in official documents; young Steve's task was to keep an eye on the hotel near Belsize Park, to follow the movements of Goldblatt and Hannah. Steadman had decided not to tell the two men any more than they would need to know, but he warned them there would be danger involved. Steve's eyes had lit up at the idea and Sexton had accepted it with a weary grin. If it had something to do with Mrs. Wyeth's death, then they were only too pleased to put in as many extra hours as it would take to help find the murderer or murderers. And that *was* what it was all about, wasn't it?

He had nodded and both men had resisted asking further questions. Before Steadman left the office, Sexton had promised to begin his investigation of the arms dealer the following morning when he had sorted out their current jobs, and Steve was already on the phone to Goldblatt's hotel, booking a room for an indefinite period beginning the following day. It would work out expensively for the agency, but Steadman was determined to recoup any losses from both Mossad and British intelligence, whatever the outcome. He prayed he would still be around to forward the bills himself.

He had prepared a simple meal for himself, then phoned Holly, dialing the number she had given him earlier. He had been disappointed when there was no reply. She hadn't relaxed even after their lovemaking that afternoon, and who could blame her after what she'd been through? He replaced the receiver with a shrug. Perhaps she was in a dead sleep. Or visiting friends. What did he really know about her anyway? He had climbed the stairs, thrown off his clothes, and slumped wearily into bed. But first he had made sure all the doors were locked.

He lay there listening, his breath held. The coldness of the room made him shudder. What had made him wake so abruptly? Light from the street filtered through the open curtains, but was no match for the room's darker shadows and gave little comfort. No sounds came to his ears, yet the tension inside him mounted. His impulse was to leap from the bed and draw out the revolver he kept in the top of his wardrobe, but something held his body in check. Somehow he knew there was someone downstairs. The atmosphere seemed heavy with menace and he trusted his instincts too much to ignore the feeling. Then he sensed that the stairs leading to the bedroom were being mounted. The approach was slow, deliberate, its only physical warning a breathing sound, a sound which grew louder and more urgent as it drew nearer. The smell drifted under the door then. It was vile, choking, the smell of defecation and . . . he struggled to remember where he had experienced it before. It came to him. Years ago, when one of Israel's border towns had been heavily mortared by their enemy, he had helped clear the rubble and search for bodies. A family had hidden in the cellar of their house, a cellar specially dug for such emergencies, and the building had collapsed around them, burying them alive. It had taken days to find them, and when they had, the flesh had decomposed. This was the same smell, only far stronger, more putrid: the stink of long-rotted flesh.

Steadman forced himself to sit upright, using every ounce of willpower he had. He felt his strength was being inexplicably drained away, drawn from his body, leaving him lifeless. He had to reach the gun. He moved as though deep beneath the ocean, pressure all around him, his breathing harsh and quickened. He staggered and fell to the side of the bed, forcing himself up again, moving toward the wardrobe, his naked body bent, walking like an arthritic old man. His eyes never left the door to the bedroom, even though he was moving toward the wardrobe. He was afraid to look away. He thanked God it was locked. But then he had locked the front door downstairs.

A sudden bump stopped him. The sound had come from outside. Everything had become still.

He thought he heard a moan, then words, but he

couldn't understand them. The scream snapped him into action.

It was as though a spell had been broken; the heaviness was gone, the fear overcome for the moment. Steadman jerked open the wardrobe door, reached up for the metal case containing his .38, pulled open the lid, and snatched the gun out. He was thankful his old habit of always keeping it loaded was still with him. He leapt toward the bedroom door and fumbled with the key, the screams from downstairs still ringing in his ears.

The sounds stopped as he pulled open the door.

He jumped into the bend of the stairs, sure of his footing even in the dark, the gun held before him, the hammer ready to cock. He saw a dark shape lying at the bottom of the stairs and for a moment he thought he saw another shape moving away from it along the hallway, toward the open door. It could have been a trick of light, though, or imagination, for it seemed to have no form and was gone in an instant.

Steadman descended the stairs, moving cautiously, his senses alive and jumping. In the darkness, he could just make out the shape of a man lying at the foot of the stairs, his eyes white and staring. He leapt over the figure and ran to the open front door, quickly looking into the street beyond, oblivious of his own nakedness. The street was empty, although it would have been easy for someone to disappear into the churchyard opposite.

He slammed the door shut and flicked on the hall light all in one movement. Still keeping the gun poised before him, he quickly checked the living room and then the kitchen, ignoring for the moment the still figure on the floor. Only when all the downstairs lights were on and he was sure no one was lurking in any of the rooms did he return to the collapsed body.

The man's eyes stared at the ceiling, the eyelids pulled back revealing their whites, the pupils dilating under the sudden glare. His lips were moving, but Steadman could hardly hear the words; they were soft and rambling.

Spittle bubbled at the side of the man's mouth. His body was stiff and the investigator could see he was in a catatonic state. He had the look of someone who had seen a creature from hell.

NINE

The hierarchical organization and the initiation through symbolic rites, that is to say without bothering the brains but by working on the imagination through magic and the symbols of a cult—all this is the dangerous element that I have taken over. Don't you see that our party must be of this character?

An Order, that is what it had to be—an Order, the hierarchical Order of a secular priesthood.

—ADOLF HITLER

Steadman brought his car to a halt outside the large wrought-iron gates and waited for the guard to step from his hut on the other side. The two Alsatians accompanying the guard looked menacingly toward him.

"Mr. Steadman?" the guard called out and the investigator nodded.

"Identification?" There was neither belief nor disbelief in the guard's voice; it was all a matter of routine.

Steadman was forced to leave the car and walk over to the gate, pulling his license from his wallet as he did so.

The guard, dressed in green tuniclike overalls, took the license from him and said, "Won't keep you a moment, sir." He disappeared into the tiny hut, leaving the dogs glaring through the bars at the investigator. Steadman glared back but decided he couldn't outstare them. He walked back to his car and leaned on the hood, hands in his pockets. He wondered if the Mossad agent had come out of shock yet.

As he'd crouched over the trembling form the night before, he had been puzzled by the absolute terror on the man's face. What had put that look there? And why had he broken into his house? Steadman had tried to shake the man into awareness, but the eyes never lost their glaze and the lips never stopped their burbling. He had tried to catch the words, but they were incoherent. He quickly searched the shaking body and found no weapons. His driving license revealed the man to be Joseph Solomon Smith and it was then that Steadman remembered him; Smith's features had altered so drastically in his horrified state that the investigator hadn't been able to recognize him, but the name had jolted his memory. Smith had come to the agency some time ago and had become one of its smaller clients. He was—what was it?—a jeweler. That's right, he'd wanted the background of one of his staff checked, a job Sexton had handled. There had been a few minor assignments for him over the last couple of years, but Steadman had had no call to see the jeweler again after the initial visit. It was only his particular ability to remember names, places, and events that helped him recall the man at all. The obvious connection soon hit him. Smith, despite his English-sounding surname, was Jewish. It didn't take much to realize he was a hireling— or perhaps even an agent—of Mossad. Steadman shook his head in disgust. That was why the little jeweler had come to the agency in the first place, to keep an eye on him for the Institute. Sexton had been Smith's contact. How much had the ex-policeman told the jeweler over the years? There wasn't much to tell, anyway, and Steadman was confident that his employee would have committed no serious indiscretions. But to use an old man like this, even for just a routine and periodic check! Look at him now. If the little Jew's heart didn't give way under the strain, then he would be fortunate.

It was the sudden draft rather than any sound which had caused Steadman to throw himself against the wall and point the .38 toward the slowly opening front door. Whoever was entering had silently used a key and was now stealthily pushing the door to one side. It suddenly opened all the way, still quietly but very swiftly. Two men stood on either side in crouched positions, their bodies partially hidden, and two revolvers were leveled at Steadman's naked figure.

"Don't shoot, Steadman!" a voice commanded and the investigator's finger froze on the trigger. "MI5," the voice came again, low but urgent. An open wallet was tossed down the hallway, coming to a halt against the head of the prostrate jeweler. Without taking his eyes off the two men, Steadman reached forward for the wallet. He quickly checked the credentials framed inside the wallet and then stood up, waving for the two men to enter.

They did, the second man closing the door quietly behind them.

"What the hell's been going on?" the first asked, staring down at Smith.

"Let me get something on," said Steadman, suddenly aware of his nakedness.

"Leave the gun," the first man ordered as the detective turned to climb the stairs.

"Go fuck yourself," Steadman said over his shoulder as he climbed.

The two MI5 agents looked at each other and the second shrugged his shoulders.

When Steadman returned, his heavy gun tucked into the deep pocket of his bathrobe, the two men were kneeling over the little Jew.

"What's been going on, Steadman?" the first man asked again, rising. "What's happened to him?" There seemed to be some disgust in his tone as he pointed down at the figure lying on the floor.

"You tell me," Steadman replied, irritated by the

agent's abrupt manner. "I heard a noise, then a scream. I came down to find him lying at the bottom of the stairs." Had he heard a noise at first? He was already casting aside the unreasoning fear he had felt while lying in his bed.

"Did you see anyone? Did anyone get out the back way?" the second agent asked as he searched through Smith's pockets.

"No, it's still locked. I thought I saw someone going out of the front door, though. It was just a shadow, I couldn't make much out in the dark."

The two agents regarded him with puzzled expressions. "No one came out; we'd have seen 'em," the first said.

"But I'm sure . . ." Steadman's voice trailed off.

"He's an old man," the MI5 agent said. "He's been sitting out there in the cold, in the churchyard over the road, for hours. Maybe it was too much for him. He came over to see you and collapsed on the stairs."

"How do you know he was over there? And why should he come over to see me at this time of night?"

"He was there watching you. And we were watching him. Your Mossad friends seem to want to keep an eye on you. They must be bloody desperate to use old men like him, though."

"But why were you there?" Steadman asked.

"To keep an eye on you, of course. Compliments of Mr. Pope. As to why the old man came over—who knows? Maybe he thought he saw something."

"How did he get in? The door was locked."

"Same way as us, Mr. Steadman." The agent held a Yale key aloft. "I'm afraid we had it made during your absence. It was for your own protection," he added by way of an apology, then looked back at the figure huddled on the floor. "He's probably got a key on him somewhere, or maybe he picked the lock. We'll find out later."

Steadman shook his head resignedly. "What do we do about him?" he said, kneeling once again by the old man whose body was still shaking. "He needs to go to a hospital."

"We'll get him to one. Don't mention any of this to your Mossad friends or they'll want to know how MI5 got involved. They've got to think you're working on your own."

"Aren't I?" Steadman asked caustically.

The two agents ignored the question. "As far as you're concerned, you never saw this man tonight. Let them worry about his disappearance."

They had carried the old man out, assuring Steadman that one of them would maintain the vigil outside the house through the night. Steadman made sure the door was locked, then poured himself a stiff drink. He spent the rest of the night dozing fitfully in an armchair, the .38 near at hand on a coffee table. The next morning, after shaving, showering, and eating, he had rung Holly. Again, there had been no answer, and although a little concerned, he told himself she was a working girl and was probably at the magazine which had commissioned her current feature. Besides, she had nothing to do with this business, so why should she be in any danger? Yesterday's incident with the tank was because of him and nothing to do with any involvement on her part. Later, he had rung Edward Gant's company, using the number supplied by Peppercorn, and had been told the arms dealer would like him to visit his home that day where their business might be better dealt with. With some trepidation, Steadman had agreed and had been given instructions on how to get there. He had rung Pope immediately after and the fat man had been delighted with the invitation. "Do be careful, dear boy," had been his only hint at the risk Steadman was running. They had briefly discussed the incident of the night before and Pope had questioned the investigator on exactly what he had seen. Steadman detected a keen interest in the large man's voice and had almost told him of his own uncanny feelings about the incident, but in the cold light of day, it all seemed very much a part of his own imagination.

After a quick call to his office and checking with Sue that everything was in order as far as their clients were concerned, he set out in his car toward Guildford, a nervousness in him, and yet an excitement. Maybe Pope was right—he had only smothered the flames inside him, the fire not completely put out.

The guard came back to the gate and held Steadman's license through the bars. The investigator took it and climbed back into his car.

The gates were opened and he drove through, the Alsatians silent, but their eyes never leaving him. The gravel road curved through a small cluster of trees, then the house loomed up before him. It was a large house but by no means as grand as Steadman had expected, for Gant was, reportedly, a wealthy man. He remembered that this was not the arms dealer's only property; hadn't Holly mentioned a place on the West Coast?

The grounds appeared to be perfectly normal for an English country house, and showed little evidence of the nature of the man's business. But surely there must be a testing range somewhere on the estate, otherwise why would Gant have invited him there? Why indeed? he asked himself. There were several other cars parked outside the house and a BMW was just pulling away. The two men inside glanced around at Steadman, then quickly turned their heads, the passenger looking through the window on his side so only the back of his head was visible. But in the brief instant before, Steadman had recognized him; he was a Tory MP, well-known for his right-wing views and the brilliant but inflammatory speeches he made in support of those views. He seemed appropriate company for Gant, Steadman thought wryly as he parked beside a silver Mercedes. His door was already being pulled open by a man wearing a dark suit as he turned off the ignition.

"Mr. Gant is in the house waiting for you, sir," the man said. "Can I take your briefcase?"

"I don't have one," said Steadman, climbing from the car.

"Follow me then, sir." The man's voice and movements

were brisk, and his words were more like an order than an invitation. Steadman followed him.

"Won't keep you a moment, sir," the dark-suited man said, leaving him standing in a wide, gloomy hallway, and disappearing into one of the high-doored rooms leading off from it. Steadman began to wander down the hallway, studying the gilt-framed portraits hanging on either side, portraits of men he'd never heard of but all dressed military style, when the door opened again and Gant stepped into the hall.

"Ah, Mr. Steadman. Glad you could come," the arms dealer said, smiling.

Steadman's eyes widened in shock, but he quickly recovered and strode toward Gant. The arms dealer did not offer his hand and his eyes glittered with some inner amusement.

"Did I . . . surprise you?" he said. "It is a shock at first, but you'll soon get used to it."

Steadman found it hard to take his eyes away from the large square sticking plaster, punctured by two small holes, which covered the area where Gant's nose had been only the day before. He cleared his throat and said, "Sorry, I didn't mean to . . ."

"No need for apologies," Gant raised a hand as if to ward off the sentiment. "This happened many years ago. Fortunately my nasal passages function quite normally. It is unsightly at first, I know, but it's very uncomfortable wearing an artificial nose all the time. When I'm at home, I like to dispense with such vanities. Now, do come in, there are some people I'd like you to meet."

The room was large, the ceiling high, the furniture tastefully traditional. The four people in the room, two seated, two standing, looked toward Steadman as he entered and their conversations stopped. He was surprised to see that one of the men was Major Brannigan, this time out of uniform but still looking very much the military type, open hostility on his face. The other faces showed interest—perhaps curiosity would have been more accurate. Steadman felt uncomfortable under their gaze.

One of the seated occupants was a woman and Steadman found his eyes drawn toward her, to be held by her own deep gaze. She had extraordinary beauty. Her hair was dark and lush, cascading down to her shoulders, her skin smooth and sallow in an exotic way; her nose was strong but well-formed and her lips full, half-smiling, slightly arrogant. It was her eyes that mesmerized him, though, for they were dark, almost black from this distance, and seemed to draw him into her. And there was a shining expectancy about them that puzzled yet attracted him.

"Let me introduce everybody." Gant's words broke the contact and Steadman swiftly took in the other two members of the group. The man seated next to the woman was aged and wizened, his skin full of deep creases and his eyes set back in shadows cast by a prominent forehead and brows. His wispy white hair was long, straggling over his ears, and his body seemed frail, ready to crumble at the slightest pressure. He held a thin, black cane before him, his gnarled yellow hands resting on its metal top.

The other man was much younger, probably in his early thirties. His short hair was sleeked back, cut in an old-fashioned style, his face pale and unblemished, the sneer on his lips part of his features rather than an assumed expression. He wore a suit of darkest gray, elegantly cut and accentuating the slimness of his body. His eyes, though showing curiosity, were heavy-lidded, giving that curiosity a disdainful insolence.

"Kristina, this is Harry Steadman," Gant said, presenting the investigator to the seated woman. Her lips widened into a full smile as she rose and walked toward him, a hand outstretched.

He took the hand and was surprised at its firmness.

"I'm very pleased to see you, Harry." Her voice had a sensual huskiness to it. She was tall, at least five-nine, and wore a deep green velvet suit, the jacket thrust open by high breasts beneath a beige blouse. He recognized the same amusement in her look that he had noticed in Gant's the day before, and his feeling of taking part in a charade heightened. He smiled back, the hardness in his eyes causing her a brief moment of unease.

"Dr. Franz Scheuer," said Gant, indicating the old man still seated. Steadman nodded, making no attempt to go over. There was no reaction from the old man.

"Felix Köhner," Gant looked toward the slim young man who raised a hand in acknowledgement, "and of course, you've already met Major Brannigan."

The soldier glared at Steadman.

Nice to be among friends, the investigator told himself, and the thought helped him keep the amused defiance in his own eyes.

"Mr. Steadman is here for preliminary discussions in arranging an arms contract for an overseas client," Gant said, leading the detective toward an armchair and indicating that he should sit. "Would you like a drink, Mr. Steadman? Sherry? Martini? Something stronger for a man like you, I suspect." That same mocking tone to his voice.

Steadman noticed that the man who had ushered him into the house was poised at a large cabinet containing an array of drinks.

"Vodka would be fine," he said. Steadman was aware he was under scrutiny while the other glasses around the room were being replenished. The old man leaned forward and whispered something to the woman and she hid a smile behind her hand.

"Now then, Mr. Steadman," said Gant, placing himself with his back toward the huge fireplace, "can you tell us now who this mysterious client of yours is? Or must I make wild guesses?"

"No need to," Steadman replied. "I'm working for the Israelis."

If Gant was surprised at the investigator's frankness, he hid it well. "I see. You know I've never made any arrangements with the Jews before, don't you?" The word "Jews" seemed to carry all kinds of insinuations.

"I was aware of it. I wondered why."

"Because they've never approached me before," Gant

said, and laughed aloud. "Until a few weeks ago, that is."

Steadman raised his eyebrows in surprise.

"Yes, a young Jew approached me with a request for arms. I told him I was sure something could be arranged, but unfortunately . . ." he smiled down at Steadman ". . . he never returned. I wonder why he suddenly lost interest?"

Bastard, Steadman thought, tired of the cat-and-mouse game. "I wouldn't know, Mr. Gant. What was his name, this . . . Israeli?"

"Oh, Kanaan, something like that. Something very Jewish. It's not important now, is it?" His voice was taunting.

Steadman grinned, wanting to smash the glass in the arms dealer's disfigured face. "Not to me," he said. "I'd like to inspect some of your weapons."

"Naturally. I've studied your list and I think I can accommodate you on all counts. Felix will show you the more moderate weapons we keep here, then perhaps you would like to visit our other testing grounds for further demonstrations of our more powerful weapons."

"And where is that?" Steadman asked mildly.

Gant chuckled. "All in good time, Mr. Steadman. Our Wewelsburg is not for your eyes yet."

Heads turned sharply toward Gant, and Steadman saw the surprise—or alarm—in their eyes.

"I'm sorry. Your . . . ?" he prompted.

But Gant only laughed again. "Never mind, Mr. Steadman. All in good time. Felix, will you go through the list and tell our guest of the weapons we can provide his clients with? These are weapons developed only by my company, Mr. Steadman, weapons far superior to any of those of our competitors—government or otherwise."

For the next hour, he was lectured by the man called Felix Köhner, who, as his name implied, was a German, while the others silently looked on as though studying him. Only Gant sometimes spoke, expounding on the merits of certain weapons mentioned. Steadman felt his every movement was being watched, his every question analyzed and filed in their minds. It was unnerving, yet the sense of challenge appealed to him. He felt a brooding malevolence emanating from the group, almost a force, and the old man with the shadowed eyes was at its center.

Even Kristina's beauty seemed to conceal something corrupt, yet he found it difficult to keep his eyes from straying in her direction. She returned his looks with meaningful smiles and twice he caught a look of annoyance on Brannigan's face at those smiles. Was there something between them? What was a major in the British Army doing in such company anyway? What were his ties with Gant? Come to that, what had a member of Parliament to do with the arms dealer? He had been told Gant had influential friends, but he had not realized they were in government.

Later, he was taken by Köhner and Brannigan through to the rear of the house, where he was surprised to find a firing range and a long brick building in which many kinds of weapons and their machinery were housed. A Gazelle helicopter rested lifelessly on a circular launching pad a hundred yards from the house, and Steadman wondered if the same machine had been used to guide the Chieftain the day before. Thoughts of danger were cast aside for the moment as he became absorbed in the new weapons demonstrated to him by green-uniformed teams. Most of the demonstrations were in principle only—it was hardly practical for the effects to be shown, but the effects *could* be shown on film and in the next two hours, the lethality of the weapons was projected on screen for his benefit.

It was early evening by the time the demonstrations were completed, and Steadman was weary of the deadly machinery, the sharpness of Köhner's voice, and the open hostility of Major Brannigan. They returned to the house to find Gant waiting for them, the usual mocking smile on his face.

"Do you like what you've seen, Mr. Steadman? Will your friends be interested?" he asked.

"Yes, I think so," said Steadman, playing the game.

"But it's all pretty soft stuff so far. There are bigger items on my list. When do I get to see them in action?"

"We have, as I've already mentioned, more suitable testing grounds for the weapons you have in mind. Today we wanted to whet your appetite. We've done that, haven't we?"

"Yes, you've done that. Where are these testing grounds?"

Gant laughed aloud and turned to the woman, Kristina. *"Unser Parsifal ist neugierig—und ungeduldig."*

She gave the arms dealer a sharp look and quickly covered it with a smile at Steadman. "Would you like to see some other demonstrations, Harry?"

He was puzzled. Gant's relish in the game he was playing was obviously not shared by his companions. That had been the second remark of Gant's that had made them nervous. Why had he spoken in German? And why had he called him Parsifal? "Yes, I'd like to see more," he answered.

"And so you shall," said Gant taking him by the shoulder. "Instantly. Please come with me, Mr. Steadman." The flattened face made his grin seem all the more sinister.

"Edward! Is this the way?"

All eyes turned toward the old man who was now on his feet, his cane supporting him. His voice was thickly accented and had a strength which belied his feeble frame.

Gant's eyes were cold as he appraised Dr. Scheuer. *"Bezweifelst du jetzt die Wörter des Propheten? Alles bewahrheitet sich doch?"*

The old man returned the cold stare. *"Dazu zwingen Sie es,"* he said with suppressed anger.

Now Steadman knew the game was drawing to a close, the pretense coming to an end. And he had achieved nothing apart from putting his head inside the lion's mouth. He tensed, waiting for the right moment to make a break. The advantage was all theirs, but he felt disinclined to wait for them to make their final move. The arms dealer's grip on his shoulder tightened.

"Please come with me, Mr. Steadman." All humor had gone from his eyes as they bore into Steadman's. "I promise you what I have to show you will be of great interest."

The moment, for the investigator, had gone. Curiosity had replaced resistance. It could also be a chance to buy more time. He nodded and followed the arms dealer from the room, Major Brannigan and Köhner falling in close behind as an undisguised escort.

Gant led the way into the hall and up a broad staircase. They turned into a long corridor and marched its length to a room at the far end. Gant pushed open the door and motioned Steadman to go through. With some trepidation, he did so.

The sight confronting him wrenched at his gut, dragging it down and his spirits with it. The two slumped figures tied to chairs in the center of the room were barely recognizable, their faces distorted by swelling and covered in blood. He went to them, knowing instinctively who they were, but lifting the sagging heads to make sure. The woman first, then the man.

David Goldblatt and Hannah.

TEN

*Follow Hitler! He will dance, but it is I
who have called the tune!*

*I have initiated him into the "Secret Doc-
trine," opened his centers in vision and given
him the means to communicate with the
Powers.*

*Do not mourn for me: I shall have
influenced history more than any other German.*

—DIETRICH ECKART

*Thule members were the people to whom
Hitler first turned and who first allied themselves with Hitler.*

—RUDOLF VON SEBOTTENDORFF

*The legend of Thule is as old as the Ger-
manic race.*

—LOUIS PAUWELS AND JACQUES BERGIER

"What should we do, Mr. Blake? Shall we follow them or
go in?" Steve looked toward the ex-policeman, trying to
discern his features in the darkness of the Cortina's interior.

Sexton shivered, wanting to be on the move, but his

training curbed his impatience. "No, boy. We'll just wait a bit longer and see what happens."

The car was parked off the road and invisible in the darkness to anyone emerging from the gates farther down. Steve had spent half the day within sight of the entrance to the house and his boredom was hard to contain. His only break had been his hasty dash to the nearest phone booth to contact Sexton and let him know what had happened and why he was there. The older man had arrived shortly after dusk and found Steve lurking in the undergrowth not far from the spot where they were now parked. He'd had to drive slowly along the quiet stretch of road twice before the apprentice detective had emerged from the trees; he had felt pleased the boy was so cautious.

"Do you think Mr. Steadman's all right?" Steve asked, blowing into his hands to create some warmth. "Maybe he was in one of those cars that left."

"I dunno, Steve. There's something very funny going on. I just wish Harry had taken me into his confidence." Very funny indeed, Sexton thought. All starting with Mrs. Wyeth's terrible murder. Was this man Gant connected with that? Sexton had spent the best part of the day probing the few old friends he still had in Special Branch, but they couldn't tell him much about Gant. A bit of an enigma all around, it seemed. Quietly supplying arms to governments abroad—and our own—for years, then suddenly coming to the fore, becoming one of the most important dealers in the country. His dubious association with the Arabs had worried them at first and they'd taken great pains to investigate his background, only to find he was vouched for by men of considerable power and influence. There were certain details they could give Sexton, but nothing that would reveal any deeper insight into the man. The phone call from Steve had sent him racing through town and down into the country, where the boy had explained his reason for being there in greater detail.

Steve had taken a room as instructed in the same hotel as Goldblatt and his woman friend. Unable to get a room on the same floor as the two Israelis, he had spent most of his time in the reception area reading newspapers and magazines, situated close to the lifts and stairway so that neither Goldblatt nor the woman would be able to leave without his seeing them. It was a busy hotel and people—mostly businessmen, it seemed—were coming and going all day. But Steve had had trouble keeping the newspaper he was holding from shaking violently when the lift doors had opened and the two Israelis had emerged with three men pressed close to their sides, hemming them in, forming a tight group. He had seen the other three enter the lobby fifteen minutes earlier and disregarded them as they had waited for the lift; they looked like normal businessmen to him. But now, because of the nervousness on the faces of the two Israelis, the woman in particular looking quite agitated, and the rigidity of the tightly packed group, they took on an altogether more sinister aspect. He watched them walk to the reception desk, one of the men breaking off from the group, leading the woman with a hand on her arm toward the swinging doors. With the other two on either side of him, the Israeli asked for his bill, informing the clerk he was checking out and that his luggage would be collected later that day.

Steve was both nervous and excited. To him, this was real detective work, the kind he had read about. There was obviously something dangerous going on—you didn't have to be a supersleuth to see that—but what to do about it? He didn't have time to ring the office or Steadman at his home, for the men would soon be leaving the hotel and he might lose them. He had to move fast. His Mini was parked in the hotel's underground garage; if he were to follow them, he had better be ready. He folded the newspaper with trembling hands, making a great effort to look outwardly calm. Then he strolled nonchalantly toward the swinging doors and out into the open. He saw the man who had left first with the woman sitting in a car opposite, a gray Daimler, and he gulped anxiously; he hoped his Mini would be able to keep up with it. When he was out of sight of the vehicle, he dashed down the ramp leading to the underground parking area and jumped into his little car. He dropped the keys once and then tried to use his front door key in the ignition by mistake before he finally gunned the engine into life, and he emerged just in time to see the other three men climbing into the Daimler. Hands were taken from pockets and he realized that the two strangers must have been holding guns inside their overcoats. His bowels felt loose at the thought.

The car moved slowly out of the forecourt and nosed its way into the stream of main road traffic, Steve following and checking his mileage indicator before he, too, eased into the flow. He would have to charge for mileage, of course, and Sexton insisted on accurate figures and no rounding off. The Daimler was easy to follow through London, but once they were past the busy roads of the southern suburbs, the pace increased, and Steve broke into a sweat trying to keep the fast-moving car in sight. He managed to, though, more than once due to opportune traffic lights halting the Daimler's progress, and it was with relief that he saw the car turn off the road to stop outside a pair of ornate wrought-iron gates. He drove by slowly, glancing quickly to his right as he drew level with the opening gates, and just having time to see the guard and two vicious-looking Alsatian dogs. He parked his car farther down the road and around a bend where it couldn't be seen from the gates, then he crept back through the trees on that side of the road. A high wall enclosed the property, the only break being the iron gate itself. He settled down behind a tree when he was opposite the gate and wondered what his next course of action should be. The words of his tutor came to him. "When in doubt," old Sexton would say, "sit and wait for something to happen. Remember, you're an observer, not a partaker in the action."

So he settled down to wait, checking the time and making a note of the morning's events in his notebook. He felt pleased with himself, but soon the cold dampness in the air and the increasing boredom of the observation began to depress him. He had just made up his mind to find a pub and have a beer and a sandwich—after all, he was entitled to have lunch—when a familiar car slowed down and pulled over into the gate's entrance. It was Harry Steadman's gray Celica! He almost called out, but ducked down when he saw the guard emerge from his wooden hut on the other side of the gates. Steve watched as the detective left his car and walked over to the guard, passing something through the bars. The temptation again to call out when Steadman strolled back and rested against the hood of the Celica was overpowering and he had a hand cupped to his mouth ready to shout when the guard was back at the gate. He stilled his voice and swore under his breath. There was nothing he could do.

Dismally, he watched the car drive into the grounds and disappear down a road leading into a clump of trees. Only a few moments later, a BMW emerged from the drive and stopped before the gates for them to be swung open. He thought he recognized the passenger as the car swept into the road, but he couldn't quite place the face. Steve waited another twenty minutes before he made up his mind. He would have to get in touch with Sexton—he would know what to do.

He found the phone booth a few miles farther down the road and fortunately the ex-policeman was still at the agency. Steve returned to his lonely vigil, happy in the knowledge that Sexton would soon join him and glowing with the praise that had been bestowed upon him. An hour or so later, Sexton's Cortina had slowly driven by, but he had waited until he was sure it really was the ex-policeman before he'd run farther down through the undergrowth and stood by the roadside waiting for the car to pass again.

"Do you think Mr. Steadman's in trouble," he asked Sexton for the third time. "He's been in there a long time."

The old man pondered over the question again. Finally,

he said, "Let's give it another hour. Then we'll go and find out."

"Have you heard of the Thule Gesellschaft, Mr. Steadman?" Gant stood over the investigator, his hands tucked neatly into his jacket pockets, his body straight, the smile on his face now arrogant rather than mocking.

Steadman tried to clear his thoughts. He wasn't tied, but the .38 Webley, pressed into his neck by Major Brannigan, bound him to the chair more securely than any ropes. He saw the hate in Goldblatt's eyes as the Israeli glared at the arms dealer. Hannah's body was still slumped, held to the chair by restraining ropes. Goldblatt had recovered consciousness minutes before and had groaned aloud when he saw Steadman, utter despair filling his face. He had tried to speak, but a vicious slap from Köhner had quickly silenced him.

Flickering shadows, cast by a blazing fire, played on the room's high ceiling, creating sinister patterns which were never still. The room itself was large and lit only by the red flames and a single corner lamp. The only furniture was the straight-back chairs on which Steadman, the woman, the old man, and the two Israelis sat, and a long table at the far end. Gant, Brannigan, and Köhner stood over them all; their very stance seemed threatening.

"The Thule Gesellschaft, Mr. Steadman. The Thule Society. Surely, in your years in military intelligence and with the Israelis you learned something of our organization?"

Steadman tried to clear the clouding fear from his mind. There was a coldness around him—a coldness that shouldn't have been, for the fire was fierce, its flames high. The chill made his limbs tremble and he consciously fought to keep them still. He vaguely remembered mention of the Thules in the many lectures on the Second World War he'd had to attend as part of his training in intelligence. They were some kind of occult society which had come into prominence just before the war but had faded since.

"Ah, I see you have heard of us." There was some satisfaction in Gant's voice. "But obviously, our part in the events leading to the last war has not been emphasized to you enough." He looked around at the assembled group. "It seems our knight needs some education if he is to know his enemy."

Köhner, standing over the Mossad agent, chuckled and looked at Steadman with contempt. "I think our *knight* will soon shit himself," he said.

Gant joined in the laughter but the remark, if anything, helped steady the investigator's nerves. His fear gave way to anger and Steadman had learned a long time ago to control that anger and channel it into a single-minded strength. And curiosity helped too. Why had they referred to him as a knight? Just what *was* his part in this whole bizarre affair?

"I'm sure you've heard, read—perhaps studied—the allegations that Adolf Hitler was involved in black magic, satanic rites and such like, in his rise to power, haven't you, Mr. Steadman?" Gant raised his eyebrows and waited for a reply, his flat face even more repulsive now that it was bathed in a red glow from the fire, almost shadowless because of the absence of any prominent feature.

"I've heard the theories," Steadman answered, "but nothing's ever been proved conclusively."

"Not proved? Hah! The refusal of men to accept such things is astounding! Keep such things away in the shadows, don't examine them too closely, don't bring them into the light. We might find it's true; then what? We might decide we like the joys such worship brings." His sarcasm bit through the air. "And that might mean the rejection of everything we've achieved since the Dark Ages. And look at those achievements: poverty, starvation, continual wars! What has happened to our spiritual quest? We believe we are advancing, that mankind, aided by science, is moving further away from his primitive beginnings; but just the reverse is happening, Mr. Steadman. We are moving further away from our spiritual—our ethereal—beginnings! That was our sin, don't you see! Our Original Sin! Mankind's bestiality! His lust for the physical. And Hitler's great crime against mankind—in the eyes of mankind—was trying to lead us away from that evolvement, back to the spiritual. That's why he was rejected, that's why he had to die. *They killed your Christ for the same reason!*"

Steadman shuddered at the madness in Gant's eyes. He had seen that same madness in the eyes of fanatics all over the world—that same blind reasoning, that same passion for a belief that was based on perverted logic. And he knew the hypnotic effect it had on others, men who looked to a leader because of their own inadequacies, who yearned for someone to give a greater meaning to their own existence. He looked around the room and saw that yearning on their faces, their eyes shining with the emotion that the words had instilled. Only Goldblatt's eyes were filled with loathing.

"Hitler tried to purify his race from the breeds that had infiltrated it, mingled with it, and brought it down to their own animal level, away from its natural Germanic heritage. That he failed meant a step backward in man's natural evolution—I might say reversion, for Thulists believe we need to *return* to our beginnings, not progress away from them. Hitler's plans for the Master Race were based on *völkish occultism*, and it was there the Thulists were able to help and guide him, for we were the roots of National Socialism! Even in those early days, our emblem was the swastika with a curved sword and a wreath. A Thulist even designed the Nazi flag for Hitler! A swastika on a white circle against a red background, a symbol of the movement's ideology: the white its nationalism, the red its social ideal—and the swastika itself the struggle for victory of Aryan man." Gant turned away from the group, his hands tucked deep into his jacket pockets, and walked toward the huge fireplace. He gazed into the flames for a few moments, then spun around to face them again. "Do you know the meaning of the swastika, Mr. Steadman?" he said harshly.

With the blaze behind him, Gant's body was thrown into silhouette, the outline tinged red. Without waiting for a reply he said, "It's a symbol of the sun, light, life itself; and for thousands of years, among many races, it's been used as such. The Buddhists believe it to be an accumulation of luck signs possessing ten thousand virtues. For the Thulists—and for Hitler—it was a symbolic link with our own esoteric prehistory, when we were not as we are now, but energy patterns existing on the lost island of Thule. Ethereal shadows, Mr. Steadman. You might call them spirits."

Steadman shivered again. The temperature of the room had dropped even more—or was it only his imagination? The air seemed charged and the arms dealer's silhouette had grown more dense, blacker.

"Signs, symbols, rituals—all are used by occultists to evoke power, just as the Eucharist and the Mass are used in the church to evoke power. Whether that power is used for good or bad is up to whoever calls on it. Think of how the Catholic Church had abused its use over recent centuries, the crimes committed in God's name. But there is a direct way to tap evil forces and Hitler was advanced enough spiritually to know the Christian Good was evil, the Christian Evil was good! His reading of Nietzsche, the man who claimed God was dead, had convinced him of this. Hitler sought to draw from those evil powers and to do this he used the knowledge he had been given by men like Dietrich Eckart, the Thule propagandist, a dedicated satanist; Karl Haushofer, the astrologer, who later persuaded Hess to defect to England; Heilscher, the spiritual teacher to many of the Nazis. Even Wagner played his part in Hitler's spiritual ascension. Men like the Englishman, Houston Stewart Chamberlain, who had written the *Foundations of the Nineteenth Century*, the inspiration of the Third Reich, while possessed by demons. And Friedrich Nietzsche, who had announced that the time was right for the Übermensch—the Superman, the elite of the race. They had helped form Hitler's ideologies. But it was the magicians who initiated him into the practices that would enable him to draw on the forces he needed to reach total power.

"And one of those practices was the reversal of magic symbols. As the Black Mass is a reversal of the Holy Mass in order to evoke powers of evil—the ceremony performed by an unfrocked priest, feasting rather than fasting takes place as a preparation, lust replaces chastity, the altar is the body of a naked woman, preferably a prostitute, the Crucifix is reversed and broken, and the host becomes a black turnip which is consecrated in the whore's vagina—so symbols are reversed to do the same. The swastika, as a solar symbol, spins clockwise to attract the Powers of Light, the trailing arms indicating the direction of the spin. Hitler ordered that *his* swastika be reversed, to spin anticlockwise, to attract the Powers of Darkness! And the whole world was witness to his meteoric rise!"

Gant was still speaking in low tones, but the words were hissed, sibilant, as they carried round the room. His audience was rapt and Steadman considered tackling Brannigan, who stood behind him, but the pressure from the gun on his neck never ceased for a moment. He glanced over at Goldblatt and flinched at the desperation on the man's face.

"But Hitler rejected all occult societies, didn't he?" he suddenly shouted at the arms dealer. "He banned them from the party."

All heads swung toward Steadman as though he had suddenly roused them from a dream. A thin laugh came from Gant as he moved away from the fire and approached the investigator, his steps slow and deliberate. He stopped before Steadman, hands still inside his jacket pockets. One hand suddenly snaked out and grabbed the investigator's hair, forcing his head back, and he brought his own forward so that his flat face was only inches away.

"He did not reject *us*, Mr. Steadman," he said, his voice tight. "In the end, *we* rejected *him*." He pulled

Steadman's head forward again, released it, then slapped him viciously. The investigator tried to heave himself from the chair, but the restraining arm of Brannigan encircled his neck and the gun pressed even deeper into his skin.

"I wouldn't do that, Steadman," the major warned. "Just sit quietly, will you?"

Steadman allowed himself to relax back into the chair and his neck was released. Gant smiled, then turned away, returning to the fireplace as though it were a stage for his oratory.

"When Adolf Hitler's ideals were still unformed—perhaps that is a bad word—'unchanneled' might be better, the Thule Society and the German Order Walvater of the Holy Grail were practicing Nordic freemasonry, to counter the Orthodox Jewish freemasonry which was slowly strangling the German economy in the years after the First World War. We were strongly opposed to the Republican government in Berlin at that time because of their sinister alliance with the rabble of the land: Jews, Slavs, Marxists. These—these degenerates—were gradually seizing control of the state and industry, crippling the country with their demands and their greedy conniving ways, and had created a situation that is not too unlike the situation in Britain today. You would agree with the similarity, wouldn't you Mr. Steadman?"

Gant waited for a reply, but when none was forthcoming his voice suddenly shrieked through the stillness of the room. *"You would agree?"*

"The comparison's a little extreme," Steadman said blandly.

"You think so, do you?" There was malicious sarcasm in Gant's voice now. "You think the elected government still rules this country? You think management still runs industry? You think the pure Anglo-Saxon still owns the country? Look around you, Mr. Steadman, with your eyes open. Not just at this country, but throughout the world. It's happening everywhere, just as it happened in Germany so many years ago: *The upsurgence of the lower races!* The African states, the Arabs—look how fast they're growing. Latin American. China. Japan. *Russia!* And, of course, Israel.

"The comparison is too extreme, you say. Let me assure you, today the threat is even greater!"

Steadman knew there was no point in arguing. Men like Gant were too obsessed with their own bigotry to see reason.

"The Aryan people needed a strong leader then, just as they need one now. Hitler knew this and he saw we could help him be that leader. We were already creating the climate of feeling against the Jewish–Bolshevik infiltration. We, the Thules, and the members of the German Order Walvater, had already formed a new party within our own—the Deutsche Arbeiterpartei, later to become known as the National Socialist German Workers Party. The Nazi Party."

Gant paused as if for effect, and Steadman wondered if his audience was going to break into applause. They didn't, but there was a luster in both Köhner's and Kristina's eyes. The old man sat rocklike, unmoving, his eyes hidden beneath deep shadows. Steadman's attention was drawn back to the arms dealer as he went on.

"Hitler, who was still in the Army at that time, had been selected by his commanding officer for a course in political instruction and one of his duties was to attend meetings such as ours. It wasn't too long before he had joined us in our cause! And it was with us that men like Eckart and Guthbertlet initiated him into the study of Teutonic mysticism. It was with us he found his destiny.

"After years of struggle, after persecution and bloodshed, we conquered the enemy within our own country. In 1933, Hitler was made chancellor of Germany—a great day for the Thules! And a tragic day for Hitler. For it was then he turned against us. He endeavored to purge Germany of all mystical societies, and on the surface, we suffered with the rest. To the world it appeared he had rejected such cults, but in fact he had found a new source of power. A symbol. A weapon that had been wielded by glorious conquerors of the past! And he set in motion his plans to obtain it."

ELEVEN

This modern (British) Empire shows all the marks of decay and inexorable breakdown because there is nowhere in it the courage of firm leadership. If you no longer have the strength to give orders to rule by means of force, and are too humane to give orders, then it's time to resign. Britain will yet regret her softness. It will cost her her Empire.

For England, the First World War was a pyrrhic victory.

To maintain their Empire, they need a strong continental power at their side. Only Germany can be this power.

—ADOLF HITLER

One thing is certain—Hitler has the spirit of the prophet.

—HERMANN RAUSCHNING

"Hitler did not reject occultism, as you seem to believe, Mr. Steadman. Even the historians who dismiss such ideas as cheap fantasy cannot explain the many indications of Hitler's deep faith in all things occult. The Russians, when they finally overran Berlin, found a thousand corpses of Tibetan monks, all wearing the Nazi uniform—but without any insignia. Every one had committed suicide. Why would Hitler have such men drafted into his army and why should they have finally killed themselves? Why the bizarre experiments carried out on the degenerates of his concentration camps? The deep-freezing of living bodies; the scattering of the ashes from the gas ovens across the land; the thousands of severed skulls the Allies found when they invaded. Hitler held up experiments on the V2 rocket—the weapon that could have won the war for Germany—because he believed they might disintegrate an etheric structure he believed encircled the earth. Were these the acts of a man who had rejected occultism? The SS symbol of the Schutzstaffeln was derived from the ancient Sig rune; the black uniform itself, with its black cap and necromantic death's head insignia—would a man who no longer believed in the black arts place such importance on regalia of this kind? Even British intelligence made use of an occult department as a countermeasure to the Nazi Occult Bureau."

Although Gant's face was in darkness, Steadman could feel his eyes boring into him. "You said Hitler had found a source of power. Some kind of symbol." He remembered Pope's mention of an ancient spearhead. "Would it have been the Heilige Lance?"

"Why yes, Mr. Steadman." There was a malicious satisfaction in Gant's smile. "The spear that was believed to be the weapon that pierced the side of Christ as he died on the cross. The Spear of Longinus the Centurion. Adolf Hitler found the spearhead in Vienna's Hofburg Museum when he was little more than a vagrant in the city, and he made an extensive search into its history. Even at that time his head was filled with the past glories of the German people —and the glories yet to come. He also had visions of other battles, those fought in another dimension, mystical wars between the forces of God and the forces of the Devil.

"Richard Wagner portrayed these conflicts in many of his finest works and Hitler believed Wagner was the true prophet of his race! It was in *Parsifal*, Wagner's last and most inspired opera, that Hitler discovered the true significance of the Holy Grail, the search for mankind's spiritual fulfillment. The kings, the emperors—the tyrants—who had claimed the holy relic throughout the centuries also knew its secret. It had caused Christ's blood to flow into the ground, to replenish, regenerate the very earth. Its spiritual powers were regarded as the symbolic manifestation of the constant cosmic struggle. It was a symbol of the conflicting powers, and only the bearer could choose which it represented. Hitler's knowledge of both history and mysticism made him realize that he had found the link between earthly and spiritual forces. That link, in its material form, was the Spear of Longinus, for it was the weapon, in the hands of a Roman soldier, that had spilled Christ's very spirit into the ground. Hitler vowed he would one day possess the weapon. That day came when he annexed Austria.

"Churchill himself ordered the true facts to be kept secret from the public. The Nuremberg Trials did not even try to explain why such 'atrocities' took place. The world had been frightened enough without bringing demonic significance to its attention. Oh no, Mr. Steadman, the Führer did not give up his beliefs; far from it. He banned such secret societies because he believed them to be a threat to his own occult power. But the Thule Group continued. We had already become integrated into the SS thanks to the vision of another man, a man far greater than the failure who deigned to be Führer! The man who never gave up even when his beloved country had been betrayed by Hitler. I mean, of course, the Reichsführer, Heinrich Himmler!"

Steadman almost laughed aloud, but he knew Gant was deadly serious. The arms dealer's hands were held clasped together before him, almost in a gesture of prayer.

"Himmler knew the power of the spear. He had pleaded with his Führer to allow him to take it from Vienna to his Wewelsburg, his shrine of the new Holy Order. But Hitler refused. He had other plans for the sacred relic. The spear, along with all the other regalia of the Hofburg Treasure House, would be removed legally—not plundered—and taken to St. Katherine's Church, Nuremberg, where it would remain until he had attained world dominance. *He failed because he ignored Himmler.*"

Gant was silent now, his shoulders heaving slightly as though he were finding it difficult to breathe. Vapor escaped from his mouth and Steadman realized just how cold the room had become. Unnaturally cold. The fire roared behind the arms dealer, yet no heat seemed to come from it. Gant would never have been able to stand so close otherwise. The arms dealer approached Steadman once again and the investigator tensed, knowing he would not accept another slap without some resistance. But Gant returned his hands to his pockets and stood over Steadman, his attitude menacing.

"But that is the past, Mr. Steadman," he said. "Let us concern ourselves with the present. As you see—" he nodded toward Goldblatt and Hannah "—your two colleagues are of no use to you now. But we would like to know more about you, about your feeble plans to destroy our organization. I'm afraid your friends are not very good talkers. I wonder if your other Mossad associate is?"

"My other associate?" Steadman was perplexed. "Wait. You mean Baruch Kanaan. You have him . . ."

"No, Mr. Steadman." Gant spat out the words. "I mean your colleague, Holly Miles."

"Holly? No, you've got it wrong! She's got nothing to do with Mossad."

"Really? I must say, she had a perfect cover. Even her credentials checked out. It seems she really is some distant relative of my late wife. But then Mossad is known for its thoroughness. As for the other one—this Baruch—I think he regrets the day he ever visited my Wewelsburg."

"He's alive?"

Gant grinned maliciously. "Almost," he said.

Steadman wondered what "almost" meant. "Look, the girl—Holly—she has nothing to do with all this. She really is a journalist."

"Of course."

"No, I mean it. I don't belong to Mossad either. I finished with the Institute years ago. They hired me for a job, that's all, to find their missing agent, Baruch Kanaan."

"I haven't got time for all this, Mr. Steadman," Gant said with an air of weariness. "Köhner will find out all we need to know from you when we're gone. We have more important things to attend to, you see. I'll give your love to Miss Miles. I shall enjoy speaking to her."

"Where is she, Gant? What have you done with her?" Steadman began to rise, but Brannigan pressed a heavy hand down on his shoulder. "For Christ's sake, Brannigan, why are you involved with this madman? You're in the bloody British Army!"

Gant's hand cracked across his face again, snapping it to one side and drawing blood from the corner of his mouth.

"Please don't be so impolite, Mr. Steadman." Gant said quietly. "I am not mad. It's the leaders of this country who are mad, allowing it to sink to these depths."

"But your sympathies were with the Germans, weren't they," Steadman said through his clenched teeth. "You kept saying we—we helped Hitler, we, the Thules."

"I am a German, Mr. Steadman. And a loyal friend to Heinrich Himmler. But we never hated the British. We wanted them as allies. We even admired the British aristocracy, for their views were much in line with ours. Unfortunately, your country chose to condemn us. The ironic part is that many see their error now—not just in this country but in others, too. They've witnessed the rise of the lower races and are suffering because of it! It isn't too late, though. Powerful men are behind us now that the climate is right for the counterrevolution. It will be slow at first, but various 'happenings' will cause its escalation. And these 'happenings' will be engineered by us, the Thule Gesellschaft. Our first major strike will be tomorrow, which is why we have to leave you in the hands of Mr. Köhner. He rather enjoys gathering information from people, you know. He especially enjoyed his conversation with your partner, Mrs. Wyeth."

Steadman ignored the restraining hand on his shoulder and the gun at his neck. His hands found Gant's throat and he began to squeeze with all his strength, the blind fury in him overcoming any fear. His head spun wildly as the gun barrel glanced off his skull, but still he clung to the arms dealer, still he tried to choke the life from him. Gant's fingers clenched around Steadman's wrists and tried to pull his hands away, but incredibly strong though the arms dealer's grip was, Steadman's hate was stronger. Only another blow from the gun barrel weakened his hold. The weapon struck yet again and he slowly sank to his knees, grasping at his victim's body as he went down. Gant's knee sent him keeling over onto the floor. He tried to rise, dazed and hurt, succeeding only in getting his knees under him, his hands flat against the floor. Brannigan stepped forward and kicked his ribs viciously, sending him rolling over onto his back. He tried to clear his head and open his eyes. Through the spinning haze, he saw the withered face of the old man peering down at him, the eyes still hidden inside the two dark caverns. A shriek made him twist his head and though the room tilted and turned, he could see it was Goldblatt who was screaming, straining at his ropes, his hands tied to the arms of the chair, like claws, pointing toward the tall figure of Gant as though wanting to tear him to shreds.

"You bastards," he was screaming. "You're still Gestapo filth! You're still the animals you always were. Assassins. You were called the Society of Assassins! And that's all you are!"

Everything took on a dreamlike quality as his vision slowly began to fade. He saw Köhner draw something from his inside pocket, saw it gleam redly in the light from the fire, saw Gant slowly nod his head, saw Goldblatt's head pulled back by the hair, saw the knife's blade sweep across the exposed neck as if in slow motion, saw the blood spurt out in a great flood, turning the Israeli's shirt a deep crimson, soaking the floor at his feet. He saw the body stiffen, then go into a spasmodic twitching dance.

And he felt the terrible coldness enveloping him as he lost consciousness.

TWELVE

A great deal of potentially useful information can be extracted from suspects. Even if suspicion of their treasonable activities proves to be unfounded they can often be persuaded to give the SD information that will lead to other suspects. Such information is usually given under duress, threat, or promise of release.

—HEINRICH HIMMLER

"Bloody hell, a helicopter!" Steve looked anxiously at the older detective, then ducked his head toward the windshield so he could see the red taillight of the helicopter as it rose above the treetops and into the air. "It's come from the house, I'm sure!"

Blake squinted into the night. "It must be Gant's own private helicopter. Now I wonder where he's off to?"

"If he's in it. I can't see it too well in the dark, but it looks big enough to carry four or five people. D'you think Mr. Steadman's there?"

"God knows. It doesn't make me feel any easier, though. I think we're going to have to do something soon."

Steve nodded in agreement. He was cold, tired, and bored. Cramped, too. Sexton hadn't let him leave the car to exercise his stiff limbs. "What do we do? Drive up to the gate and demand to see him? Or shall we get the police?"

"Get the police? What for? As far as we know, everything's in order. The governor's doing a bit of business with the arms merchant. What could we tell the police?"

"Sorry. Just feeling a bit twitchy, that's all."

"All right, son, I feel the same. Harry's been in there a long time. I think the first thing we'll do is get nearer the gates, see if anything . . ."

"Hold it!" Steve's hand closed over his arm in the dark. "Something's happening. Look, headlights!"

Bright beams of light swung into view, shining through the gates and lighting up the dense forest opposite. Their movement stopped for a few seconds, the vehicle presumably waiting for the gates to be opened. Then they were in motion again, swinging away from the two hidden men, moving off down the road toward the west. They had just made out the shape of a large truck before it had turned fully away from them. They watched the taillights disappear down the road and were aware of the helicopter's drone fading into the distance.

"Looks like an exodus," mused Sexton.

"What, Mr. Blake?"

"Nothing. Come on, let's have a closer look."

They left the Cortina and crept as quietly as possible through the undergrowth toward the entrance to the grounds. When they were opposite and still well hidden, they waited, shivering against the chill night air.

Steadman brought a hand up to the back of his head, wincing at the sudden sharp pain. He was still lying on the floor where he had fallen, the hazy red shadows dancing on the ceiling confusing him for a few seconds. His head began to clear slowly, but when he tried to raise himself on one elbow, the room spun crazily and he sank back, both hands covering his eyes. Hearing movements, he lowered his hands again and blinked. Still not rising, he swung his head around, careful not to move too fast. He saw the hunched figure of a man—the same man who had shown him into the house that afternoon—dragging something along the floor, something that left a dark, liquid trail behind. It hit him suddenly, the memory tearing into his numbed brain. He tried to rise again, turning himself over onto his side, pushing against the floor with his hands, and this time he was partially successful. He was able to support himself with an elbow and get a clear view of the room. Dimly, in the background of his awareness, he heard the fading sounds of what could only have been a helicopter.

"You bastard!" he yelled, seeing Köhner at the far end of the room standing by the long table. He tried to stagger to his feet, but it was too soon and he fell to the floor again.

"Ah, Steadman. So glad you are awake again." Köhner walked toward him, hands behind his back, a pleasant smile on his face. The man who had been dragging Goldblatt's bloodied body along the floor continued his journey after a curious glance at Steadman. When he reached a far corner of the room, he bundled the body up and pushed it as close to the wall as possible until it was just a black shape in the shadows. Köhner stopped just before Steadman and the investigator stared at the immaculately polished shoes, their highlights hued red in the glow from the fire. The room was no longer so cold, but now Steadman shivered with the rage building up inside him. What kind of man would kill as cold-bloodedly as this one had?

"We are just a small group now, Steadman. You and me, Craven—" he indicated toward the small man who was now wiping blood from his hands with a handkerchief "—and a few guards. The others have all gone to the Wewelsburg. A big day tomorrow, you know. Many preparations to make." A shoe playfully tapped Steadman in the ribs. "So, for tonight, you're all mine." Still smiling, Köhner raised his foot to Steadman's shoulder and pushed him down onto his back again. Then he walked away.

Questions crowded the detective's mind. What was the "Wewelsburg" and why had Gant and the others gone there? What was going to happen tomorrow? Was Gant completely mad, with all his talk of Hitler and this spear? If he was, it was a dangerous madness. But just how dangerous? Were they just a small group of fanatics or were they widespread? Pope had said Gant had influential friends, powerful men. My God—the man he'd seen drive away in the BMW that afternoon, the MP. Was he one of them? And Holly. Why had they taken her? Did they really believe she was a Mossad agent? What would they do to her? Why had they left him with this murderer, Köhner?

His mind stopped churning when he saw his captor standing behind Hannah, his hands resting on her shoulders, fingers kneading the flesh. She was still tied to the chair, but she was conscious. Her eyes were staring at the bundle lying in the corner.

"Come along now, Steadman," Köhner said, the smile, so pleasant, so sinister, still on his face. "Come and join us here." He picked up the empty chair next to Hannah, the chair which had been occupied by Goldblatt, and moved it to a position facing her, a little distance away. "Bring him over, Craven."

The small man ran forward, drawing a gun from inside his jacket. Without a word, he grabbed Steadman just above the elbow and yanked him to his feet. With a hard push, he sent the investigator staggering down the room toward the empty chair. Steadman stumbled and fell, but a prod in his back from Craven's gun encouraged him to rise again. He stood in front of the chair, swaying slightly, and was roughly pulled down into it. He looked across at Hannah and there was sadness in her eyes. Regret.

"I'm so sorry . . ." she began to say, but Köhner lashed out with his hand, stopping her words abruptly.

"Shut up, you Jew bitch! You'll talk, but you'll talk to me—not him!"

"Let her be, Köhner," Steadman said wearily. "She's only a woman, she . . ."

Köhner's hand lashed out and again it was the woman he struck. She cried out this time and the regret in her eyes was replaced by fear.

Köhner smiled sweetly at Steadman. "You see, she is the one to be hurt, not you. You are going to tell me what we need to know, because if you don't it will be the woman who will suffer." He pulled Hannah's jacket apart, then ripped open her blouse. "It's incredible how sensitive certain areas of the body are, you know, the erogenous zones, in particular. Ironic, isn't it, how parts that can give so much pleasure can also give so much pain." He reached inside his jacket and once again withdrew the wicked-looking blade from a sheaf worn like a shoulder holster. Steadman saw the knife was double-edged and still bore the bloodstains of its previous victim. He prepared to launch himself forward as the blade descended toward Hannah's exposed stomach, but Köhner glanced toward him and hesitated.

"Better tie him, I think, Craven," he said. "This may be too much for the poor man."

The cold metal of the gun barrel was placed against Steadman's temple and Craven's rough hand grabbed his shirt and jacket collar, sharp fingernails raking the back of his neck. "Don't worry, sir, he won't move while I've got him like this."

Satisfied, Köhner knelt before Hannah and once again directed the knife toward her bare flesh. His other hand reached for the waistband of her skirt and tugged at the material, inserting the blade into the gap, then ripping, tearing the skirt down its middle until the two sides flapped open and hung loosely by her sides. He repeated the process with her panties and tights, then snipped open her bra as he rose again. Now her body was completely exposed to him.

Steadman averted his eyes, feeling her shame, wanting to strike out, but forcing himself to wait for the right moment.

There were tears in Hannah's eyes and she closed them so she would not have to see the three faces before her. Their cause was lost now: David had been murdered and Baruch was probably dead too. Steadman would be killed even though he was an innocent in the whole affair. But they'd had no choice; *they'd had to use him.*

Köhner left them and walked to the end of the room toward the table. He picked up something, and as he returned Steadman was puzzled at the object's familiar appearance. "A simple hairdryer, Steadman. It doesn't take sophisticated instruments to hurt someone—anything handy will do. This is one of my specialties, actually." He plugged it into a socket by the door, unwinding the long lead as he rose. Köhner flicked the switch with a thumb and the machine whirred into life. He switched it off again, satisfied, and took up a position behind Hannah.

He grabbed her under the chin and held her head against his body in a vicelike grip. "The ears, first, I think. It'll do terrible damage to her eardrums. Bad enough when it's cold air, but when it really warms up . . ."

"There's nothing to tell, Köhner. For God's sake! They hired me to find their missing agent and that was it! That's all I can tell you!" Steadman's hands gripped the sides of the chair, his knuckles white. The hold on his collar tightened.

"Oh, come now," Köhner said, shaking his head. The dryer was switched on again and air was sucked into its fan and thrown out in a quickly heated stream. "You can't expect me to believe that, Steadman. You're much more involved. Mr. Gant expects quick answers, that's why he left you to me. Pity he was too busy to watch: I think he'd have enjoyed my skill. He has in the past." He tested the heat by blowing air against his own cheek. "Ah, yes. Nicely warming up. It's of the more powerful variety, of course—the type used by hairdressers—so it gets a little hotter than usual. Although that isn't really necessary. An ordinary hairdryer is just as good—it takes a little longer, that's all. Let me see, the breasts after the ears. No, perhaps not. I think she'll be too far gone by that time to feel anything there. Maybe the eyes. Yes, the eyes will be good, even with the lids closed."

"Köhner!"

"And finally, the vagina. That will kill her, of course, Steadman." The whining machine was pushed against Hannah's ear and she tried to struggle away from it. She screamed as the hot air blasted its way down her ear canal and reached the eardrum.

"Please, stop! I'll tell you everything I know!" Steadman pleaded.

Köhner looked disappointed. He took the dryer away from Hannah's ear but left the motor running. She moaned and tried to twist her head from his grasp, but he was too strong for her. "Well?" he said.

"It's true what I said about being hired by Mossad to find Baruch Kanaan. I did belong to Israeli intelligence, but that was years ago. I'd left them."

"Why would you do that?"

"I—I was sick of the bloodshed. The Arabs killed someone . . . someone close to me. I went on the rampage after, killing, killing—until I was sick of it!"

"How traumatic."

"It's true, fuck you! I'd had too much of it! Too much killing. Too much revenge."

"And you left them."

"Yes. I wanted nothing to do with them any more. But they had someone watching me all the time, an old man who'd lived in this country since the war."

"The jeweler."

"Yes." Steadman stared at Köhner. "Yes, how did you know?"

"It doesn't matter how I know. The old man's dead now—he didn't survive his visit to you last night." Then he added with a grin, "Something frightened him to death."

There was so much happening that Steadman didn't understand. He shook his head and went on: "They came to me a couple of weeks ago, Goldblatt and this woman, Hannah. I refused to help them find their missing agent, but my partner agreed to without my knowing."

"Yes, Mrs. Wyeth. I had an interesting chat with her.

Unfortunately—for her—she couldn't really tell me much. Mr. Gant was right: she really didn't know anything."

"You . . . you were the one . . ."

"Keep talking, Steadman. No questions, just answers, please."

Craven made the gun's presence known even more strongly when he felt the investigator tense again. Steadman was nearing the breaking point, he told himself. Perhaps they should have tied him after all. Pity he was talking to soon, though; he'd have liked to have seen the woman squirm more. She had a beautifully ripe body, the cut clothes accentuating its sensuality; it would be good to see it writhe, see those smooth thighs open wider with agony. Pity to kill her. Maybe Köhner would let him use her first. If he didn't . . . well, he would be the one who had to dispose of the body. Plenty of time then . . .

The dryer was moving toward Hannah's head again and Steadman quickly resumed talking. "After Mag . . . my partner . . . was killed, a man named Pope came to see me. He was from British intelligence and knew Mossad was operating here. He's also investigating Edward Gant."

Hannah stopped twisting her head and stared across at the investigator, her eyes wide. "Steadman, don't . . ."

Köhner clamped his hand over her mouth and snarled, "Don't interrupt, you Jew whore. It's getting very interesting. Go on, Steadman."

Köhner suddenly yelped in pain as Hannah bit deep into his hand, her teeth drawing blood. He dropped the dryer and reached for the knife again, all in one reaction.

Steadman screamed "No!" as the blade plunged deep into the flesh of Hannah's stomach and Craven, whose eyes had been watching the exposed parts of her body, froze at the suddenness of it all. The knife, still embedded, was traveling upward in a straight line toward her chin when Steadman grabbed the gun barrel and pushed it aside.

The investigator was on his feet, the hand at his neck having no effect on his enraged strength, the chair crashing over behind him. He still held on to the gun and realized the little man hadn't even released the safety clip. Twisting his body, he brought his leg up and Craven was lifted into the air, his scream piercing the air.

Steadman whirled, forgetting about the injured man for the moment, knowing his agony would keep him out of action for a while. He flew at Köhner, hands outstretched, grabbing for the knife that was now raised against him, its blade red with blood. He was lucky enough to find the knuckles clasped around the knife's handle and he pushed the weapon away as both men went over, dragging the chair holding Hannah with them. They went down in a heap. Steadman pushing the knife hand to the floor, while Köhner kicked and struggled beneath him, grabbing at the investigator's hair and trying to pull his head back. Hannah, still tied securely to the chair, rolled onto her side, the blood flowing from the long rent stretching from her lower stomach to her breastbone, creating a dark viscous puddle on the wood floor.

As Köhner pulled at his assailant's hair, he managed to bring a knee up and bring it hard against Steadman's hip, the blow sending the investigator to one side, Köhner rolling with him. The knife came up from the floor and he almost managed to wrench himself from the investigator's grip. But Steadman knew if the knife hand got free again, Köhner had the speed and experience to kill him easily. Both men were on their sides and Köhner used his strength to carry his body through with the roll so that he gained the advantage of having Steadman beneath him. He let go of the investigator's hair to add strength to the hand pressing the knife toward Steadman. The pointed tip pushed against Steadman's cheek, pressing the skin inward until the flesh broke and a trickle of blood emerged. Steadman had both his hands around Köhner's and he tried to hold the straining blade away, but he felt it slowly sinking into his cheek, millimeter by millimeter, eager to burst through into the cavern of his mouth. Köhner's eyes were above him, staring down, a gleam of triumph and blood-lust in them. He felt no pain; only the relentless force of the cold metal.

He slowly turned his head, feeling the skin tear as the steel blade sliced a shallow red-lined path across his cheek.

He used his whole body to try and squirm away from Köhner and felt his opponent moving with him, endeavoring to keep him pinned. The knife edge was grating against bone now and he knew his head would move no further; metal and bone were locked together. With a roar he changed his direction and heaved upward, using all his strength against the other man's weight. Köhner resisted but the movement was too sudden; he was forced backward. When he knew he had reached the point of overbalance and the knife had been pushed clear of Steadman's cheek, he allowed himself to be carried with the momentum, skillfully using his weight and strength to his own advantage. His intention was to continue the roll, using pressure only when the movement would put him on top again. But Steadman still retained enough cunning in hand-to-hand combat to break away at the right moment. He hadn't wanted to release the hands holding the knife, but he had guessed Köhner's reason for withdrawing the pressure. He twisted away from his surprised antagonist and kept rolling, knowing the weapon would be following, striking toward his exposed back.

He felt rather than heard it thud into the floor behind, and swiftly rose to a crouching position while the knife was tugged free. He turned to face his antagonist, hands held poised before him.

Köhner had also risen and both men were silent as they watched one another, each waiting for the other to make the first move. Steadman stared into Köhner's eyes, the blade still in the periphery of his vision but not in focus; the eyes would tell him what the man would do. He could hear Craven groaning and writhing on the floor to his left, and he knew he would have to move fast if he were to avoid having two opponents again: Köhner was enough on his own. Köhner's eyes widened slightly before he lunged, but it was enough to give the investigator warning. He threw himself to one side, ducking low, and the blade went on past his shoulder. Their bodies made contact and Köhner staggered, spinning around, but managing to control his movements so that he was balanced and ready to lunge again. Steadman wasn't there though; he was racing toward the black object lying in the center of the room. Köhner followed, confident that the knife would be deeply embedded in the investigator's back before he had time to use the gun.

Steadman realized the same. He stooped and reached for the back of the overturned chair he'd been held captive in only minutes before, and hearing the footsteps behind, he swung his body around, bringing the chair up as he did so. It crashed against Köhner's shoulder causing him to stumble to one side, and before he could recover fully, the chair was on its return journey, this time aimed at his head. He ducked instinctively and Steadman was momentarily thrown off balance. He recovered quickly enough to swing the chair up again, this time as a shield against Köhner's oncoming rush. It struck Köhner's body and Steadman pushed, the knife waving in the air in a vain attempt to reach him. Steadman exerted all his force and kept pushing, moving the other man backward. Köhner resisted, hopelessly caught up between the legs of the chair, unable to thrust it aside. He took the only course available; he dropped to the floor, pulling the chair with him but lifting it so it sailed over his head. It still left him at a disadvantage, for he was flat on his back, and he struck out at Steadman's legs with the knife as he lay there.

The investigator drew in his breath as the knife's razor-sharp edge slid along his shin-bone, only its angle preventing it from cutting deeply. He tried to leap clear of the thrashing blade as he staggered over Köhner's recumbent figure and fell heavily against the chair which had crashed into the floor just beyond the fallen man's head.

Steadman found himself lying on his stomach, the chair leaning against him and, for the briefest second, he looked into the face of Hannah, who was still trapped in her chair in the center of the big room. Her eyes were pleading and her lips moved as her life oozed from her. She was looking directly at him. He staggered to his feet, bringing the chair up so it cracked against the advancing Köhner's chin, sending the German reeling back. Köhner raised a hand, reaching for his eyes as if to wipe the dizziness from them. Steadman was on him, relishing his sudden advantage, reaching for the arm clutching the weapon with both hands and bringing it down sharply against his rising knee in an effort to break it. He didn't succeed, but at least the knife flew from Köhner's grasp, clattering uselessly against the bare floorboards.

The investigator used his elbow against the other man's ribs, still holding the now limp arm outstretched with one hand. Steadman heard Köhner gasp, but his satisfaction was short-lived as his opponent twisted and managed to encircle the investigator's neck with his other arm, squeezing hard to cut off his air. Steadman leaned forward and jerked Köhner off the floor, bending almost double so the other man tumbled over his shoulders onto the floor before him.

Lithe as a cat, Köhner was up again and turning to face him. But Steadman's rage at this creature who could destroy lives without remorse, and with an ease that said he was a master of it, drove him on relentlessly. He plunged into the murderer, his fists striking the man's face, sending him staggering back toward the low-burning fire. Fear began to show in Köhner's eyes as Steadman bore down on him. He knew the investigator's rage had made him unstoppable; only a weapon would have any effect. He looked around, desperate for a means of escape or a weapon within reach and saw there was nothing. The knife had disappeared into the shadows, Craven's gun was on the other side of the room. But Craven was beginning to rise now. He was on his knees, his shoulders hunched, his hands still pressed between his legs. But he was beginning to rise! If he would only reach for the gun!

Köhner was about to call out to the kneeling man when

another blow sent him reeling. "Wait, I can help you! Don't . . ." Steadman paid no heed to the words. The same hatred he had felt when Lilla had been so mercilessly killed had once again taken over.

Köhner recognized the hate and put up his hands to ward Steadman off, but they were easily knocked aside. He backed away until he could feel the heat behind him. The fire! Oh God, he was backing into the fire! He tried to make a break to one side, but Steadman grabbed his collar and struck him again, a hard, stinging blow that covered his vision with a blinding light. He fell, his arms flailing, instinctively trying to grab the sides of the fireplace. His hands made no contact and he screamed as he fell into the small, dancing flames. As the heat burned his coat and scorched his body, he pleaded with the investigator to pull him out.

Steadman raised a foot and planted it squarely on the burning man's chest, holding him there, his loathing rejecting any mercy. Köhner screamed again and again, twisting his body, trying to wriggle free while Steadman held him, no expression on his face. It was only when Köhner's hair began to burn that the investigator reached forward, grabbing him by the lapels of his jacket, and pulled him clear. Köhner's screams echoed around the room as Steadman tore the jacket from him, much of the shirt coming away with it, and threw it toward the fireplace. The investigator beat out the smaller flames on the man's clothing with his hands, not even wincing at the sight of the scorched flesh. Köhner's singed hair hung in blackened clumps on the back of his head and his teeth chattered as though he was freezing.

Craven's cry of alarm warned Steadman and he turned just in time to see the little man crawling rapidly toward the gun lying on the floor. The investigator sprang forward, racing toward the scrambling man, who looked up in fear at the sound of his approach. It was that moment of hesitation that lost Craven his chance. He was half up, no longer crawling, reaching down for the gun, when it was kicked from under his grasp. He saw it scudding away into the shadows and felt terror as a hand fell onto his exposed neck. Another hand grabbed the back of his trousers, and then he was being propelled forward, his own rush toward the gun now working against him. He was powerless in the grip that held him and the floor-boards sped beneath his feet as he tried to keep his balance. They were gathering momentum, heading toward the table at the far end of the room, toward the twisting body of Köhner. He tried to sink to the floor when he realized Steadman's intention, but the grip was too strong, the pace too fast. He felt himself lifted, skidding across the table's surface—and then beyond.

He felt the glass break around him, yet did not hear the sound. The ground rushed toward him and, mercifully, he felt nothing as his head broke open against it.

Steadman stood with his hands resting against the tabletop, breathing in deep lungfuls of the cold night air as it gushed through the shattered window, his shoulders heaving with the exertion. The fury was still in him, hardly dissipated by the violence he had just committed; but it was a cold fury now, his mind working almost dispassionately. He knew the disgust for himself would come later, would torment him with the knowledge that he was little better than the men he had acted against. For the moment, though, those feelings would be held in abeyance—there was so much more to do.

He pushed himself away from the table and crossed the room, ignoring Köhner, who lay on his stomach, moaning softly, parts of his clothes still smoldering. Steadman knelt beside Hannah and grimaced at the sight of the terrible wound the knife had inflicted. The floor around her was awash with blood and he turned his eyes away from the long gash when he saw glistening organs beginning to protrude from the opening. He thought she was dead, but as he began to untie her bonds, her eyelids fluttered, then opened. Her lips moved as she tried to speak.

"Don't talk," he told her. "I'm going to get you to a hospital." He knew the words were without meaning, for there was no chance she would live.

Hannah knew it too. "Steadman," she said, her voice faint, as though she were calling back to him from a distance as her life seeped away. He leaned down toward her, putting his ear close to her mouth to listen. It was difficult to make out the words, but she kept repeating them as though making sure he understood. "The . . . spear . . . for . . . Israel, Steadman . . . you must . . . for Israel . . . get . . ."

Her voice trailed off as Hannah sank into her death. Steadman drew away from her, closing her eyes with his fingers and arranging her clothing to cover her nakedness and the awful gaping wound. He touched a hand to her cheek, then rose to his feet. He looked toward Köhner, his eyes cold.

The burned man was on his hands and knees, moving toward the door. He turned his head at the sound of Steadman's approach and his eyes widened in fear when he saw the expression on the investigator's face.

Steadman pulled him to his feet and pushed him onto the table. Köhner screamed as his scorched back made contact with the tabletop.

"You're going to tell me some things, Köhner," Steadman said, shaking him by his shoulders. "You're going to tell me what will happen tomorrow." He brought Köhner's face close to his own and said, "You're going to tell me where Holly Miles and Baruch Kanaan are being held."

Köhner tried to pull himself away, but his injuries—and his fright—had weakened him. "I can't tell you anything, Steadman. Please, you've got to get me to a hospital."

"Not until you've told me all I want to know, Köhner."

"No, they'll kill me!"

"*I'll* kill you."

"Please, listen. There's nothing you . . ."

"Where has Gant gone to?"

"I can't tell you!"

Steadman slammed him back down onto the table. He placed his elbow under Köhner's chin, pushing it up, ignoring his feeble efforts to pull away. He grabbed the German's right hand and held it by the wrist with one hand, then with the other he took hold of one of the fingers. The smallest. He pulled it back swiftly and it snapped.

He closed his mind to Köhner's scream and fought his own revulsion. He had to fight them on their own level, evil for evil. For Holly's sake. For Baruch's. He would not let them be taken as Lilla had been taken.

"Tell me, Köhner. Where have they gone? Where are they holding the girl?"

Tears ran down the sides of Köhner's face and Steadman was afraid the man might pass out. It said much for his toughness that he hadn't.

"The Wewelsburg! They've gone there! Please don't!"

The Wewelsburg. That name again. Steadman took hold of another finger. "What *is* the Wewelsburg, Köhner?" he asked, beginning to apply pressure again.

"Don't! It's a house—an estate. It belongs to Gant."

"Where?"

"On the coast. North Devon. Please don't hurt me again . . ."

"*Where exactly?*"

"Near a place called Hartlands. Farther on!" Köhner tried to squirm away and the investigator pressed down harder with his elbow. "The girl is there, Steadman. She's all right, she's alive!" The words were meant to appease him.

The West Coast. Holly had said Gant had a place on the West Coast. Was that his Wewelsburg? "Okay. Now tell me what Gant is up to. What's happening tomorrow?"

"I can't. I can't tell you."

It was only footsteps on the stairs that prevented another of Köhner's fingers from being broken.

THIRTEEN

We must interpret "Parsifal" in a totally different way to the general conception . . . It is not the Christian-Schopenhauerist religion of compassion that is acclaimed, but pure, noble blood, in the protection and glorification of whose purity the brotherhood of the initiated have come together.

—ADOLF HITLER

The two guards, both armed with a general-purpose machine gun and rifle similar to the NATO FN, but of Gant's own manufacture and considerably lighter because of it, raced up the stairs to the room where the prisoner was being held. They were veteran mercenaries who had finally found a binding allegiance—as had all the soldiers in Edward Gant's private army. It was a small army, no more than fifty carefully chosen soldiers, a guard really—a *corps d'élite*. Some were mercenaries who fought battles for others, their loyalty only bought with money; others were taken from the crack SAS regiments, chosen because of their special skills and aptitudes by Major Brannigan and steered into Gant's organization. Their common bond was their extreme right-wing views and a dislike for the world in general. They admired strength and craved strong leadership: Gant provided them with that leadership. Officially, they were merely employees of

Gant's weapon factory, testing the weapons in practical ways and acting as security for the plant. They wore dark green overalls which somehow succeeded in having a military air without actually being uniforms. There were no insignia, no badges of rank; but each man knew his position and who his superiors were. They enjoyed their secret military ceremonies which took place only on the arms dealer's vast North Devon estate, even grateful for the harsh discipline imposed on them there, and disliked their dealings with the various factions who visited the estate to learn how to use the many weapons they were buying from Gant. They sneered at the groups of Arabs, Africans, Japanese, and Irish they had to teach, *wanting to turn the weapons on them,* but patiently went through the exercises, demonstrating, explaining, because they knew it helped the cause of world disunity. These groups of fanatics would help create the world unrest which would succor their own movement. They had learned to obey their orders without question, the fate of their comrades who had failed to do so ever-present in their minds. Hanging may have been abolished in England, but Edward Gant worked to his own laws. They had no title, but sometimes, when they were very drunk and only when they were safely inside the estate's boundaries, they laughingly gave themselves a name. They called themselves the Soldiers of the Fourth Reich.

These two, McGough and Blair, had been left behind with the guard on the gate, the three others of their unit returning to the estate by truck that night. The rumor was that a special operation was planned for the next day, but as yet no briefing had been given and speculation on their part was strictly forbidden. They had regretted being left behind, though did not question it. Nor did they question Gant's particular instructions.

They rounded the bend in the wide stairs and stopped abruptly, aiming their guns at the two figures that had appeared on the landing above them. One of the figures was Köhner, his face contorted with pain and his blackened shirt hanging loosely around him; the other man standing immediately behind Köhner was the prisoner, the private investigator who had been shown through the weapons store at the back of the house that afternoon.

"Don't move!" Blair commanded and resumed his ascent of the stairs, McGough following close behind.

Steadman did not hesitate. There was no time to search for the fallen gun in the room he and Köhner had just left, so he used the nearest thing at hand to stop the progress of the two men below: Felix Köhner. He shoved the injured man hard, sending him careering down the stairs, his arms flailing wildly. Köhner's body struck McGough and Blair with a force that sent all three tumbling backward until they landed in a tangled heap at the bend. Steadman descended the stairs three at a time and was able to kick the gun from one of the soldier's hands before it could be aimed at him. The other man was scrambling toward his gun which had clattered farther down the stairs, and Steadman hooked a foot beneath him, sending the soldier well beyond the fallen weapon.

The investigator lifted the dazed Köhner to his feet and said. "Come on, I still need you." He pushed him forward and turned to the soldier who was beginning to rise. Steadman's knee hit him full in the face and the soldier slammed back against the wall, then slid to the floor. The investigator pulled Köhner away from the bannister and raced him down the stairs past the disorientated second man lying at the bottom. He dragged Köhner down the hall toward the doorway, knowing only speed would prevent a bullet in his back. If he had tried for one of the guns himself, the men would have been on him before he'd had a chance even to aim it; past experience told him, when outnumbered, keep on the move. He reached the front door and yanked it open, pushing Köhner ahead of him into the night.

On the stairs, McGough had reached his weapon and was automatically sighting it on Steadman's back below, when he caught sight of Blair's upturned face. It was white and the lips were clenched, but it shook hastily.

McGough lowered the gun and stared regretfully at the front door as it slammed shut.

Steadman was relieved to find no guards outside and his car still waiting. He hurried the dazed Köhner over to it and yanked open the passenger door, pushing the injured man into the seat. He ran around the front of the car, reaching in his trousers' pocket for the keys, then jumped into the driver's seat, hauling the weakened Köhner back as he tried to scramble out.

"I told you I need you, Köhner. You're going to get me through the gate."

He gunned the engine, expecting the door of the house to be flung open at any moment and the two guards to run out, machine guns blazing. But his luck held: there was no movement from the house. They still must have been stunned. The Celica spewed up gravel as it roared away from the building toward the main gate. Steadman switched on high beams to blind the guard and his dogs, knowing he would have to be through those gates within seconds, for the two soldiers would soon ring the hut from the house—if they hadn't already done so.

As the car sped around the curve in the long drive, the guard, standing before the solid gate with the menacing Alsatians, was frozen in the headlights. The investigator brought the car to a halt ten yards away from him and the guard raised an arm up to his brow to cut out the blinding glare. The dogs strained at their leash.

"Who's there?" the guard called out. "Turn those bloody lights out so I can see you."

"Tell him to let us through, Köhner," Steadman said quietly.

Köhner shook his head, his injured hand clasped to his stomach. His smoke-dirtied face was streaked with tears. "Go to hell," he managed to gasp.

The guard began advancing on the car, a hand reaching inside his tunic for a gun he kept hidden away from usual visitors to the house. The dogs were excited, instinctively catching the mood of the situation. The guard's arm was at full stretch as he tried to hold them back and he had to dig his heels into the gravel to prevent himself from being dragged forward too fast. The growls of the dogs became barks and then howls as they struggled to break free.

Steadman moved fast. He reached across the injured man and hooked his finger around the door catch, pushing the door open. Then he shoved Köhner out of the car.

Köhner rolled onto his back, screamed, and tried to rise. It was too much for the Alsatians. They broke away from the guard and pounded toward the rising man. They leapt on him, teeth slashing, sensing their victim was injured and easy prey.

The confused guard was hurrying forward, his gun aimed at the frenzied group, the car's lights still dazzling his vision. Steadman depressed the accelerator and the car shot forward, striking the guard, knocking him over the hood and into the gravel. Hitting the brakes immediately, Steadman leapt from the car, snatched the revolver from the stunned guard's grasp, and reached for the key to the gate which hung on a chain from the man's belt. It was a huge key and Steadman's shaking hands fumbled at the clasp securing it to the chain for several precious seconds before it was free. He could hear Köhner's screams and the blood-chilling snarls of the dogs on the other side of the car as he fumbled. The guard, whose legs felt numb and lifeless from the blow they had received, raised himself onto his elbows and tried to grab at the gun. Steadman pushed the man's head back onto the driveway with a force that put him completely out of action.

The investigator finally yanked the key free and ran to the gate, keeping a wary eye over his shoulder in the direction of the dogs, who by now were wild with bloodlust. He inserted the key and twisted, then swung the gates wide. As he returned to the car, holding a hand up against the headlights' glare, he knew he could not just leave Köhner to the mercy of the Alsatians. He stepped out of the beam of light, the gun raised before him, and blinked his eyes rapidly to get them used to the sudden darkness again. The screams had stopped and the snarls were less wild as the dogs pulled and tugged at the inert

body. One of the Alsatians sensed his approach and
turned its eyes towards him. Its growl was deep-throated
and full of warning. The other looked up too, its mouth
bloody and drooling pink foam. Steadman saw their
muscles tense as they readied themselves to spring at him.
He raised the gun and fired two rounds into each body as
they leapt, taking a step back as one of the dogs slumped
against his legs.

He quickly glanced at the unmoving body of Köhner,
then walked around to the other side of the car and
climbed in. He drove through the open gateway onto the
main road.

Steadman was forced to jam on his brakes once again
as he began his turn. Two figures had emerged from the
woodland on the opposite side of the road and were frantically waving their arms at him.

"Sexton! Steve! What the hell are you doing here?"
Steadman wound down his window and looked at his two
employees with amazement.

Sexton jerked a thumb at his companion. "Goldblatt
and a woman were picked up by three men. Steve followed 'em here. Are you all right, Harry?" he asked, suddenly noticing the fresh blood on Steadman's cheek.

The investigator ignored the question. "I've got to get
to a phone."

"There's one about a mile and a half down the road,
Mr. Steadman," Steve said, excited by the action.

"Okay. Jump in, both of you. There'll be men coming
from the house any minute."

The two men hurried around to the passenger side of
the car, Steve nimbly climbing past the front seat into the
back, and Sexton slumping his cold-stiffened frame beside
Steadman.

"It's back that way, Mr. Steadman." Steve pointed. The
investigator quickly reversed, the rear of the car almost
entering the grounds again, then spun the wheel to the
right as it screeched forward. Sexton just had time to see
a dark figure sitting in the driveway rubbing the back of

his head. He turned to face Steadman as the car gathered speed along the road.

"What's been happening, Harry? We were a bit worried."

"It's Gant. He's a madman. He had Goldblatt and the woman killed. And Maggie." There was a weariness in Steadman's voice.

"Christ! What do we do? Get the police?"

"Not yet. I'm going to call a man named Pope. He works for intelligence—MI5. He'll have to sort it out."

"But what about this Gant? He'll get away."

"Already gone," Steadman replied grimly.

"The helicopter. We saw a helicopter leave and a truck drove out shortly after."

Steadman dimly remembered the sound of rotor blades as he'd recovered consciousness back in the house. "Yes, that would be it. I saw one earlier in the afternoon. He's gone to somewhere he calls his 'Wewelsburg.' Somewhere in North Devon."

"He's got an estate there where he tests weapons," Sexton said. "I found that out this morning. A lot of the country around that area is used by the military for testing."

Steadman nodded. "He's got something planned for tomorrow—I've no idea what. It sounds important to him and his crazy organization, though."

"What's he up to?"

"He imagines himself as the new Hitler—only stronger. I told you—he's completely mad. Where's this bloody phone, Steve?" There were street lights now, and houses lined the roadside.

"Not far. Just up here a bit on the left."

"What happened back at the house, Harry?" Sexton asked. "How did you get away?"

"Gant left me behind—with his special inquisitor. Fortunately for me, neither he nor the few remaining guards were too efficient. I had a lot of luck on my side, though." He pulled over to the telephone booth. "Wait here," he told the two men as he left the car, its engine still running. "Keep an eye on the way we've come. They may decide to look for me." Sexton and Steve turned their attention to the rear window.

The pips indicating someone had lifted the receiver at the other end began almost as soon as Steadman had finished dialing the memorized number, and he pushed the coin into its slot. A voice said, "Pope," and the investigator breathed a sigh of relief.

"Pope," he said. "Thank God you're there."

"Steadman? I've been waiting for your call. Been rather anxious, actually. Now, have you found out any more on Gant?"

There was a hint of relief in Pope's voice, but it was hardly comforting to Steadman. "I found out plenty, but it's all so incredible. You were right. Gant is the head of an organization called the Thule Gesellschaft." Steadman quickly told him what had happened at the house and Pope listened patiently, occasionally interrupting with a pertinent question. "But why did he leave you in the hands of this man Köhner?" he asked when Steadman explained Gant's departure from the house.

"To get information from me, to find out what I knew and who else was involved. Gant has a big operation to mount and he had no time personally to waste on me."

"Operation? What sort of operation?" Pope's voice had a keen edge to it.

"I don't know. He's gone to his North Devon estate—somewhere near Hartlands—to carry it out. Do you know anything that's going to happen sometime tomorrow, Pope? Anything in that area?"

There was a long silence at the other end, then Pope said, "There is something, but . . ." Another silence. "No, it can't be that, it's nothing to do with that area. Unless . . . Oh God, he wouldn't try to do anything like that."

"What, Pope? Remember, he's a madman. He'd do anything to further his crazy cause."

"Not over the phone, Harry—I'll tell you later. We'll have to move in. We know this estate—a large part of his weapon-testing takes place there, so it's usually under some sort of surveillance by us."

"There's another thing. He's got the girl there. Holly Miles. He thinks she's working for Mossad."

"The journalist? *Is* she working for Mossad?"

"I was going to ask you the same question."

"I've no idea, dear boy. Rather confusing, isn't it?"

"What about Major Brannigan and the MP I saw down here? What will you do about them?"

"They'll be hauled in when we have Gant. It's all very delicate, though."

"The murders of Maggie, Goldblatt, and Hannah—and maybe Baruch Kanaan—are all very *indelicate*, Pope," Steadman said angrily.

"Of course, Harry. They'll be accounted for, don't worry. Now listen, can you get to Hartlands?"

"Are you crazy? Why the hell should I go there? It's up to you now."

Pips began, informing them that their allocated time was up, and Steadman fiercely pushed another coin into the slot.

"Harry, are you still there?"

"I'm here."

"I need you to go there, Harry. You know Special Branch has to make the arrests—I haven't that power as MI5. You're the only man who knows the full story, and if I order a large force into the estate, I need some verification. Your personal evidence will save a lot of unnecessary official wrangles. Please believe me, I need you there if only to convince my superiors."

"Why can't I just come over to your HQ now?"

"It's easier this way. It's pointless for you to come back to London when you're already on the way to the west. I want you on the spot, Harry. Do you feel up to it?"

"I'll manage."

"Good man. There's a town called Bideford not far from Hartlands. Find yourself a hotel and book in. We'll find you there easily enough by checking around."

"Will you involve the local police?"

"They'll be informed but not involved. Too many people in high places involved for this to be made public, I'm afraid."

"Listen, Pope, if you're going to protect . . ."

"Please, Harry, there's no time for discussion now. I've got a lot to do and you have a long journey ahead of you. I'll have to have any calls from Gant's estate in Guildford intercepted for a start. If any of those guards warn Gant before I can get a squad down . . ."

"Christ, Pope . . ."

"Please, Harry. There's no time. Remember, the girl's in danger. I'll see you tomorrow."

The receiver at the other end was put down and Steadman stared blankly at the burring earpiece. He slammed down the phone and left the booth.

His two companions looked at him anxiously as he threw himself back into the driver's seat. He ran his hands over his face as though to wipe away the fatigue.

"What now, Harry?" Sexton prompted gently.

"I'll take you back to your cars, then I've got a trip to make. To Devon."

"Are we coming with you, Mr. Steadman?" Steve asked eagerly.

"No, I don't want either of you involved in this thing."

"We work for you, Harry," said Sexton. "If you're involved, we're involved. Besides, we thought a lot of Mrs. Wyeth."

Steadman smiled at them. "There's one thing you can do, but I'll tell you what on the way back to your cars. Tell me, though, have either of you heard of something or someone called 'Parsifal.' When I was in the house, Gant said something in German to his friends. He said, 'Our Parsifal is inquisitive and impatient.' He was referring to me and obviously didn't know I understand a little German, thanks to my ex-wife. Have either of you heard the name before?"

Sexton shook his head, but Steve leaned forward toward the front seats, his eyes gleaming.

"There is a Parsi*val*, Mr. Steadman. He was one of the

Teutonic knights. Wagner wrote an opera about him, but he changed the spelling to 'Parsifal' for some reason. It was all about the Holy Grail and the sacred spear that was stolen from the king, Amfortas, the Keeper of the Grail."

The two men twisted their bodies to stare at his excited face, lit by a nearby streetlight.

"A sacred spear?" Steadman said quietly.

Steve suddenly became embarrassed under their scrutiny. "I'm a bit of an opera freak—that's how I know the story. I think *Parsifal* was one of Wagner's greatest. He was . . ."

Steadman interrupted him. "You say this spear was stolen?"

"Yes, by Klingsor, the evil magician. It was Parsifal who had to get it back . . ."

"What's all this got to do with Gant, Harry?" Sexton asked impatiently. "Aren't we wasting time?"

Steadman silenced him with a raised hand. "Tell me the whole story of this *Parsifal*, Steve," he said. "Try to remember every detail. It could be the key to this whole bloody business."

Steve looked in bewilderment at the investigator, took a deep breath, then began.

═══ FOURTEEN ═══

But are we to allow the masses to go their way, or should we stop them? Shall we form simply a select company of the really initiated? An Order, the brotherhood of Templars, round the holy grail of pure blood?
—ADOLF HITLER

Steadman relaxed onto the bed and reached for the cigarettes on the small side table. He lit one and drew in a deep breath, watching the smoke swirl in the air as he exhaled. He felt rested now and his mind was beginning to think more clearly. He winced when he crossed his ankles, then drew up a trouser leg to examine the knife wound inflicted by Köhner the previous night. It wasn't deep, but it was irritatingly painful. Fortunately the hotel receptionist hadn't noticed the torn trousers from behind the desk. After reading the investigator's London address as he filled in the card, she had merely accepted Steadman's somewhat disheveled appearance as a result of his long drive. In fact, Steadman had broken his journey.

It was just outside Andover that events had caught up with him. He had been forced to stop the car as tiredness overwhelmed him, and a feeling of remorse had had a lot to do with that tiredness. Even the thought of the danger Holly—and Baruch, if he really was still alive—was in could not spur him on. In his present condition, he knew he could not help anyone. Slumping against the steering wheel, he cursed himself for having become involved with such violence, for having broken his vow to himself and Lilla that never again would he become part of such things. It wasn't his fault, he knew. He'd been reluctantly drawn into it; yet he'd used their own kind of violence against them. And it had been perpetrated with a coldness that now disturbed him. Pope had been right at their first meeting. His aggressiveness *had* only been smothered; it was still there waiting to be unleashed.

He felt no pity for Köhner or the little man, Craven— they had deserved to die—but he felt concern for his own actions. He had recovered enough energy after a while to find a motel and there he'd spent the night, surprisingly falling into a deep and dreamless sleep. The following morning, after a shower, then a half-eaten breakfast, and covering the gash in his cheek with a Band-Aid obtained from the curious but sympathetic motel receptionist, he had resumed his journey, feeling better for the rest, his mind clear again. The guilt was still there but, he thought cynically, he would wallow in it when matters had been put right. The remainder of his journey had been more relaxed and it had given him time to sort out his thoughts. By the time he reached Bideford he had a new resolve. Before, his purpose had been to protect Holly, to let Pope deal with Gant and whatever he was up to; but now he had decided to take care of the arms dealer himself. After all, wasn't that the reason for his involvement in the whole bizarre affair—the final confrontation between himself and Edward Gant?

The blood on the knife wound had hardened, forming a natural healing seal. He slid his trouser leg back down and rested the injured limb; he could bandage it later. He looked at his watch, impatient for Pope's call. Had he missed him because of his unplanned late arrival at the hotel? No, Pope would keep checking all the hotels until he showed. What was keeping him, though?

It was strange how it all made a crazy kind of sense: Hitler, the Spear of Longinus, Gant's referring to him,

Steadman, as Parsifal. But what was the Wewelsburg? More symbolism, ancient beliefs? Steve had told him about Wagner's opera, and the significance had begun to sink into Steadman's confused brain. It was the reason for his involvement, why it had to be played out to the end. It was the fulfillment of the legend, but this time with a different ending, and that ending would be the omen of their success.

The ringing of the bedside phone startled him from his thoughts. He picked up the receiver.

"Oh, Mr. Steadman? Two gentlemen in reception to see you. A Mr. Griggs and a Mr. Booth. Acquaintances of a Mr. Pope."

"I'll be right down," he replied and put down the phone.

He stubbed out the cigarette in an ashtray and swung his legs off the bed, groaning at the stiffness of his bruised ribs and limbs, then donned his jacket and left the room.

Mr. Griggs and Mr. Booth were sitting in the lounge area, a small coffee table between them, an empty chair awaiting his arrival. He recognized them as the MI5 agents who had taken the collapsed jeweler from his house two nights before. They jumped up at his approach and one said, "Glad you made it okay, Mr. Steadman. I'm Griggs, by the way."

Steadman nodded and took the provided easy chair. "Where's Pope?" he said bluntly.

"Up at the estate. We moved in early this morning without much trouble." Steadman could not be bothered to register surprise.

"Is the girl all right?"

The second man, Booth, spoke up. "Fine, sir, a bit confused, though." He grinned at the investigator.

"And you've got Gant?" Steadman didn't grin back.

"Yes, Mr. Pope's still interrogating him," said Griggs. "He's refusing to say anything, even though he knows the game's up. I think the sight of you should unsettle him, though."

"What about Major Brannigan and the others?"

"Quiet as mice. The whole operation was extremely smooth. Hardly any resistance at all."

"Have you found out what they had planned for today?"

"Not yet," said Booth, "but we think we know already."

"Can you tell me?" Steadman looked directly at Griggs, who seemed to be the senior of the two.

"Afraid not, Mr. Steadman. Not yet, anyway. I'm sure Mr. Pope will fill you in on the details, though. In fact, er, I think they're rather anxious to see you out there. Special Branch have cooperated rather well, but they'll be relieved to have some hard evidence to substantiate the allegations against Gant. What we've found is highly suspicious, but not enough to warrant any arrests to be made. It's your evidence that will hang Gant and his friends."

"But what about the dead bodies of the two Mossad agents at Guildford? That's pretty damning evidence."

"He denies any knowledge of them."

Steadman laughed humorlessly. "They died in his house," he said. "Does he deny that?"

"He says he left Guildford early yesterday evening, and you were still there at that time!"

"And I probably killed them."

"And Köhner. When we told him the man called Köhner was dead, he said you must have been responsible."

Steadman shook his head, a thin smile on his face.

"We'll soon break him, Mr. Steadman. We've got too much against him and his organization now. But they do need your help at the estate. The SB boys are hopping up and down with frustration and demanding to see you personally."

"Okay, let's go then," the investigator said, rising to his feet. "I'd like to make a phone call first."

"Oh, you can do that from the house," Griggs said as the two men rose with him. "It really is important that you get there right away. Booth and I just have to check in with the local police to put them in the picture—it's all a bit much for country coppers—so I'll tell you how to get to Gant's estate and you can go on ahead. Mr. Pope will be waiting for you."

And so the game continues, Steadman thought grimly.

Ten minutes later, he was in the Celica driving along the A39 toward Hartlands. It was a cold day, the clouds hanging dark and heavy against the horizon, but Steadman kept his side window open, wanting to feel the cool air on his face. His mind was clear and resolute.

He turned right when he reached Hartlands, and the banks of the narrow roadway rose up sharply on either side, blocking the view to the surrounding fields. Then the road swung to the left, suddenly widening, and an ancient church confronted him. It was a gray stone building with a high, square-shaped tower that must have offered a fine view over the surrounding countryside. A grotesquely twisted tree stood beside the low stone wall which enclosed the churchyard, reaching toward the building like a withered and gnarled claw. Then it was gone, the road dipping suddenly, and he saw the sea less than a mile ahead. The road leveled once more, and again the steep banks of undergrowth restricted his vision.

There was no sign at the entrance to the estate, but Steadman knew from the directions he had been given that this was the right place. He stopped before the open gates, feeling very much alone.

His hesitation was brief. He pushed the gear stick into first and sped through the wide opening, changing up and gathering speed, as though his pace would override too many doubts. The road was well laid and straight, and he saw the huge white mansion in the distance, surrounded by open fields fringed with deeply wooded areas. The brooding metal-gray sea lay beyond the house, a dark backdrop that seemed to threaten him as ominously as the building he was approaching. The stillness of it all added to his unease. There were many cars parked in the forecourt of the mansion, but no people anywhere. He slowed the car, delaying his arrival at the house, his resolve giving way to trepidation. He could turn back now, swing the car around and race back to the gates before they had a chance to lock them. But where would that leave Holly? And Baruch? He was their only chance.

A rainspot came through the open window and touched his cheek as the threatened drizzle began to soak the ground. His speed was less than ten mph now, and the huge house loomed up before him, giving him the feeling that the black windows were eyes staring. Watching. Waiting for him.

He saw the main door open and a rotund figure step out onto the low terrace that ran the length of the house. A hand was raised in salutation, but Steadman failed to respond to Pope's greeting. He stopped the car, switched off the engine, took a deep breath, and climbed out.

═══ FIFTEEN ═══

*One day ceremonies of thanksgiving will be
sung to Fascism and National Socialism for
having preserved Europe from a repetition of
the triumph of the Underworld.*

*That's a danger that especially threatens
England. The Conservatives would face a
terrible ordeal if the proletarian masses were
to seize power.*

Fanaticism is a matter of climate.

—ADOLF HITLER

The interior of the huge house was clinically clean; it
resembled an expensive sanatorium. Pope had stepped
aside wordlessly, indicating that Steadman should go
ahead of him through the polished wood doors. Once inside, Pope closed the doors almost ceremoniously, then
turned to face the investigator.

"I'm glad you arrived safely," he said. "We were rather
concerned this morning when we couldn't locate you at
any of the hotels in town. It was a relief when we went
through the list again later on."

"I broke my journey," Steadman replied, then added
by way of explanation, "Events kind of caught up with
me."

The hallway they stood in was wide and long, almost a room in itself. An occasional gilt-framed picture broke up the blinding whiteness of the walls.

"It's very quiet," Steadman commented.

Pope smiled, two cheeks suddenly blooming like rosy apples at each end on the smile. "Everything's under control, Harry. Things have worked out rather well."

"No trouble?"

"None at all."

And the operation? Did you find out what it was?"

"Oh yes. Come along with me and you'll hear all about it." The large man took Steadman's elbow and gently propelled him toward one of the doors leading off from the main hallway. He knocked, pushed open the door, and once again invited the investigator to enter before him.

Steadman stopped just inside the room and stared into Edward Gant's mocking eyes, too weary of the game to fake surprise.

"It's good to see you again, Mr. Steadman. Unbelievably good." Gant's artificial but perfectly natural-looking nose was back in its place, disguising his disfigurement. He looked around the room, and the sight of Major Brannigan, Kristina, and the old man, Dr. Scheuer, gave him a feeling of *déjà vu*; it was like their first meeting in Guildford all over again. But there were some new faces present this time—new, yet familiar. All eyes were on him, and all eyes revealed a strange curiosity, a discerning interest in him.

He swung around as he heard the door close behind him and looked straight into the face of the still-smiling Pope. The intelligence man was leaning against the door, both hands behind his broad back and clasped around the handle, as though his huge bulk was an extra barrier for the investigator to break through should he decide to run. The smile wavered slightly under Steadman's steady gaze and Pope was relieved when the investigator turned back to face Gant.

"So, he's in it with you," he said to Gant, not having to point at the fat man behind him.

"Yes, Mr. Steadman. Mr. Pope has been enormously helpful to the cause—as you have."

"Me? I've done nothing to help you, Gant—or your crackpot organization."

"Ah, but you have." Gant walked to a high-backed easy chair and sat facing Steadman, his hands curling around the arms of the chair like talons. "We have many men like Pope among the Thulists, men in positions of power who see the hopeless plight this nation is in—indeed, the world is in. Make no mistake, Mr. Steadman, we are not a tiny 'crackpot' organization existing in this country alone. Our society has a network spread throughout the world, the United States providing us with some extremely powerful members, one of whom will join us later tonight. We have money, influence, and, most important, an ideal.

"An ideal to conquer the world?"

"No, Mr. Steadman. To govern it. Look at the men in this room," Gant said, his arm sweeping outward. "I'm sure you recognize most of them. Ian Talgholm, financial advisor to the chancellor himself—some call him the inner Cabinet's secret member; Morgan Henry and Sir James Oakes—industrialists well known for their nationalistic pride, envied and feared by the Jewish money grabbers because of their wealth and power; General Calderwood, a soldier who will eventually govern all the armed forces of this country—he is but a representative of many other high-ranking military men who support our society; and last, but hardly least, Lord Ewing, fast becoming the most vital and powerful man in today's media.

"And these are just a few of our Order, Mr. Steadman. The rest will be joining us later today and this evening. Our special council of thirteen, I, myself, being the thirteenth and principal member."

"Just who are the others, Gant?"

"Ah, you're really interested. Excellent. Well, you, of all people, have the right to know. After all, without you, the omens would not have been in our favor." Gant chuckled, but it was obvious that not everyone in the room shared his humor. Steadman saw several members of the "Order" give the arms dealer uncertain looks. One of them— Talgholm, the financier—spoke up.

"Look, Edward, do you think this is necessary?" he said, irritation in his voice. "We've gone along with you on most of this, but he could have been highly dangerous to the whole project. Why tell him any more?"

"Because," Gant snapped back, "my dear Ian, because he has played a key part. Because there is no danger from him, nor has there ever been."

"But the risk last night, letting him go free . . ."

"There was no risk, everything was planned. But he had to come here of his own initiative. *It had to be his choice!*"

The financier looked around at his companions as though appealing for support, but they avoided his eyes. He shrugged his shoulders and said, "Very well, there's nothing he can do now, anyway."

"Thank you, Ian," Gant said icily, then proceeded to list the names of the absent members of the Order, one of whom was the racialist member of Parliament Steadman had seen leaving the arms dealer's estate at Guildford the day before; the others were important men in their fields—and their fields were greatly diversified.

"We are but the nucleus," Gant explained, "the governing body, so to speak. We make quite a powerful group, wouldn't you agree?"

Steadman nodded, but his mind was concentrated on making a quick count of the names. "You said there were thirteen in the Order and you've mentioned, including yourself, only twelve. Who is the thirteenth member, Dr. Scheuer or Major Brannigan?"

"Why, neither, Mr. Steadman. They, although extremely important, are only tools. Men like our Major Brannigan and the unfortunate and unstable Mr. Köhner—it was his unreliability, by the way, that prompted us to leave you in his hands, a calculated test for you, if you like—these men merely implement our plans. As for the esteemed Dr. Scheuer," he smiled benignly at the wrinkled old man, "he is our medium, the one who brings our thirteenth member to us. He is the physical voice of our Leader."

Even as Gant said the name, Steadman knew who the thirteenth member of the Order—the Teutonic Order of the Holy Knights—was. They had rejected Hitler because he'd failed them and switched their allegiance to the SS Reichsführer, founder of the Nazi Occult Bureau, who had encouraged and sustained the Thule group.

Gant was smiling as he spoke, his eyes radiating a passion felt by everyone in the room. "He will be with us tonight. Dr. Scheuer will bring him to us. And you will meet him, Mr. Steadman. You will meet our Führer, Heinrich Himmler, before you die."

Gant spoke to the investigator for over an hour, laying out his plans for the new Order before him, treating him almost as a confidant, or perhaps a guest to be dazzled by his host's genius. The others had added their own comments, reluctant at first, then swept along by the arms dealer's fervor, realizing Steadman could do them no harm, for he was already a dead man. They needed an outsider they could boast to, impress with the magnitude of their schemes. And Steadman listened, sometimes goading, sometimes visibly astonished by their thoroughness, at the far-reaching effects their fanatical plans would make on the governance of the country. By intricate and brilliantly devious routes, it all arrived at one simple but major conflict: Right against Left. It would be the only choice for the people of Britain. No in-betweens, no fence-sitting. The public would be forced to choose. Civil war would be balanced in favor of the Right, for the majority would be the wealthy, those whose sympathy lay toward nationalistic pride; and the middle classes who had suffered so much between the elite of the country and the working classes, would choose to join them rather than be ruled by the economy-wrecking socialists. The choice would be made easy for them. New leaders would emerge and their ideals would be uncompromising, just as Hitler's had been in the 1930s. Edward Gant had been in the shadows for many years, emerging from those shadows, a new figure to the public, but already powerful enough to repel any attacks from those already in power. Steadman saw how their inner Cabinet—their Order—had been carefully chosen, comprising men already in key positions, all waiting for the right moment to throw off their disguises and unite publicly, and so unite the masses to them. Timing was of the essence, and events to further their cause were manipulated at *exactly* the right time.

Steadman prodded and they eagerly reacted. He drew information from them in a way that made them feel they were merely obliging a doomed man's last wishes to know the reason for his impending death; and their fanaticism, calm though it was, made them try to convert him to their cause and accept his sacrificial role. And all the while, the woman smiled, and the old man gazed at him from shadowed pits.

The Thule Society's next move was imminent. Other actions had already been implemented over the past years, insignificant in themselves, but creating a pattern vital to their cause, subconsciously affecting the climate of the free world's feelings. The worldwide terrorist attacks, the emergence of the neurotic African nations, the ever-present threat of Russia, détente merely used as a cover while they took a further step toward controlling the Western world, the gradual breaking-down of the world's economic structure, the Middle Eastern countries' sudden strength and bold demands because of their ownership of two-thirds of the world's oil: all these shifts in the world's power balance were creating fear and mistrust on a universal scale which could easily be exploited by those who sought to create a new regime where only the pure-blooded races would rule. Thulists in many countries had contributed to the unrest, working behind the scenes, encouraging, advising, building the strength of their own enemies to the point where other nations would be forced to take action to break that strength lest its greedy eyes look toward them.

Gant, and many like him, secretly sold arms to terrorists not just for profit, but to encourage them on their road to self-destruction. The more outrages they committed, the more they were reviled and feared. And fear was the perfect tool for the new Reich, for fear created revolution.

A strategic move was to be made in the early hours of the following morning—1:55 A.M. to be exact—when the American secretary of state would be flying in to Britain for talks with the prime minister and foreign secretary before journeying on to a neutral country in a new bid for peace—reconciliation between the Arab countries and Israel. The world knew that this was the culminative peace talk, all others—particularly Egypt's, which had begun the fresh moves toward peace in '77—having led up to this point, both frustrated nations poised for a war that would decide the ultimate victory for either side. But the American statesman's jet would never touch down in England, for the Thulists wanted no such peace between Arab and Jew. The aircraft would be blown to pieces while still over the Atlantic.

No one would know just who had been to blame, although the suspicions and accusations would lean more toward the Arabs than the Israelis, for the PLFP and the PLO had the worst reputation for such atrocities. The responsibility would hardly matter, though; civilized counstand by and watch. Of course, certain evidence would be allowed to attempt mutual annihilation, the world would stand by and watch. Of course, certain evidence would be "discovered" among the floating wreckage of the aircraft which would suggest it had been destroyed by a missile of probable Russian make. It was well-known that the Russians supplied their Middle East friends with such weapons.

The fact that the missile had been produced by Edward Gant's munitions factory and launched from the shores of North Devon would never be discovered; antiradar devices would insure its flight path was not traced. Ironically, the RAF had a radar tracking station not far away at Hartlands Point, but they would never suspect the missile had been launched from their own area.

At that point, Steadman's probing had been brought to an abrupt halt, for there had been new arrivals at the estate—other members of the Order, Steadman assumed—and details of the operation had to be discussed with them. The assassination of the American secretary of state was just one of a series of major catastrophes, Gant had explained to the investigator; there were more to follow in rapid succession, each escalating to the next, until world hysteria reached breaking-point. Anarchy by the left wing had to be nurtured until it could be smashed, and terrorism encouraged until it could no longer be tolerated by the masses.

The door was opened for Steadman and he found the two bogus MI5 men who had come to the hotel in Bideford waiting outside. Neither of them spoke as they led him away, and Steadman felt little inclined to acknowledge their previous meeting; his mind was too busy absorbing all he had learned.

They took him upstairs and along a stark white corridor, then pushed him into a room, locking the door behind him.

Holly was sitting on a bed facing him, her face white as the walls around them.

"Harry?" she said, not believing what she saw. Then she was on her feet and rushing toward him. "What's happening, Harry? Why are they keeping me here?"

She raised a hand toward his injured cheek, concern in her eyes, but he held her at arm's length, looking down into her frightened face, unsure, not believing in anything any more. She smiled up at him, her pleasure at seeing him undisguised. It faded as she looked into his cold eyes, and suddenly her mouth quivered as though the toughness had finally been knocked out of her.

"Harry, you're not with them . . . ?"

"Do you work for the Institute?" he asked harshly.

"The Institute?"

"Come on, Holly, don't lie to me. You're a Mossad agent. You've been playing me along, like all the others."

"No, Harry." She pulled away from him, angry now and defiance beginning to show through the tears. "They've been asking me the same thing. What the hell's going on, Harry? Why do you all think I'm working with the Israelis?"

Her anger seemed genuine and he wavered for a moment. Could he trust anyone? They hadn't reached the end yet; the final act had not been played out. Was Holly part of that?

"Okay," he said softly, placing his hands on her upper arms. "Okay. Just tell me what's happened to you, nice and slow. And tell me who you really are, Holly, it's important that I know."

He led her back to the bed and gently pushed her down, then sat by her side.

She looked at him, hurt and confusion showing on her face. But was it all an act? "You know who and what I am, Harry. I told you, I'm a free-lance writer and photographer. I came here to do a feature on Edward Gant, using my family connections with his late wife. That's all there is to it, why should I lie to you?"

He ignored the question. "And you've never heard of David Goldblatt and Hannah Rosen? You've never heard of Baruch Kanaan? You're not a member of Israeli intelligence?" She shook her head vehemently, and then another thought struck him. "Or British intelligence?"

"No, for God's sake, no! What have I got into, Harry? What have *you* got to do with all this? The other day at Long Valley, the tank—why were they trying to kill you? Who are they and who are you?"

He told her then, not because he believed her, but because if she was with Mossad, then she already knew most of it, and if she wasn't . . . Well, what did it matter? But he didn't tell her everything. Just in case.

When he informed her of the plan to assassinate the US secretary of state at 1:55 that coming morning, she just sat there, a stunned expression on her face. Then she said, "So that was why they locked me up."

He looked at her quizzically.

"The missile launcher," she said. "I found it. They caught me taking photographs of it. I thought it was just another part of Gant's testing ground—the whole estate's riddled with testing ranges." She flicked her blonde hair away from her face. "No wonder they got so mad." She almost managed a smile.

"Where was it, Holly? Where did you find it?"

"Oh, it's toward the shoreline," she pointed vaguely in the direction of the sea. "I'd slipped my guard—Gant wouldn't allow me to wander around free, naturally enough, even though he was anxious I do this article on him—and I pretended I was going to take a nap. It was late afternoon and we'd been trudging around most of the day, so I guess my guide believed me when I told him I was tired. Anyway, he escorted me up here, then disappeared for a while. I sneaked out and started exploring the areas he's taken care to keep me away from. This is a strange house, Harry. Did you know the back half is completely different from the front, as though the section we're in now is just a facade?"

He shook his head but remained silent.

"Well, I'd been taken in completely opposite directions before, toward the weapons plant about half a mile away, but this time I headed around the back. I was surprised it was so easy, but I guess with Gant away they'd all relaxed a little. Anyway, I got to the back of the house and took a peek in some rear windows on the way. The interior's like a castle back there, very old, dark wood and heraldic symbols, you know? There was no way in, though; all the doors were locked. I heard guards coming—did you know he's got his own private army here?—so I took off away from the house, toward the cliff tops.

"I hid behind an old outhouse for a while, waiting for the guards to disappear. It was a little way off from the main house, but was locked and the windows boarded up, so I didn't get a look inside to see what it was used for.

When the coast was clear, I took off again, staying away from the road leading to the beach, not looking for anything in particular, but curious enough to keep a lookout for something peculiar. Well, I found something peculiar, all right, but I found it by accident. I'd ducked into some undergrowth about fifty yards or so from the cliff edge because one of their patrol Range Rovers was heading in my direction—they keep regular patrols all over the estate—and I nearly fell into a huge hole the undergrowth had been disguising. It was about twenty feet wide and had camouflage netting spread over it. I could see through the netting, and the hole looked natural enough except the sides had been smoothed with concrete all the way down, and there was a circular staircase running around the edge. I looked into it and saw it was about forty feet deep and light was coming in from one side below. It was the shaft of a cave, you see, the cave leading up I assume, at an angle from the beach—I could hear the sea down there. The tide wouldn't get into it because the bottom of the well was much higher than the beach. And there, at the bottom of the shaft, was the missile mounted on its launching pad. It wasn't very big, but it looked kind of lethal."

"They must keep the shaft camouflaged because of all the low-flying military aircraft around these parts," said Steadman.

"I guess so. Anyway, it was too good to miss. I started clicking away with the Pentax and I became too engrossed in what I was doing. Two guards snuck up on me and all but threw me into the hole. They brought me back here and confiscated my camera. Then the grilling began."

She put a tentative hand out toward him and rested it on his arm, unsure of his reaction. He let it stay there. "They asked me about you, Harry: what I knew about you, who you were working for, were we working together. Then they started in on me about Mossad. I told them the same as I told you: I'm a free-lance journalist trying to make some bread. *They* didn't believe me, either."

She stared earnestly into Steadman's eyes. "Didn't the other day mean anything to you? Weren't your feelings the same as mine?"

He looked away from her, confused.

"God, you're like a stranger," she said, anger returning.

"Holly," he began, trying to come to terms with his doubts, wanting to believe in her. "So much has happened in the last few days, I swear to God I don't know who I can trust. Those men downstairs with Gant—Christ, they're high-level people. And Pope. He's with British intelligence! Even one of my own clients has been spying on me since I left Mossad. How can I trust anybody?"

She drew his hand toward her and at that point he wanted to give in, to hold her, to believe. But another part of him held back.

"Okay, Harry," she said, no longer angry. "Don't trust me, be as suspicious as hell. But what it all boils down to is that we—just you, if you like—are in big trouble and have to get out. Now, does anyone else know you're here?"

He shook his head, still doubting.

"That's kind of dumb, but okay, we're on our own. So, let's think of a way." She tried to smile. "Like the movies, huh?"

"Some movie," he said, extricating his hand and moving away from the bed and toward the curtainless window. She watched him peering down into the grounds below.

"There's a guard out there all the time," she said, "and the window can't be opened—I've tried. You'd break a leg jumping, anyway, and the guard would put a bullet through you before you even reached the ground."

The guard was looking up at him, face expressionless, but his pose menacing. Steadman looked back at Holly. She seemed calm enough now. Did she have reason to be or was it just a natural facet of her character?

"Any ideas?" she asked, conscious of his gaze.

"We wait," he said. "Gant wants me to meet someone later tonight."

He grinned without humor at her surprise and suddenly felt she had been telling the truth. But still he remained withdrawn. He could be wrong.

Major Brannigan's face was flushed with a brooding sulkiness as he tapped lightly on the door. He wanted to rap hard at the wood with his fist, for he knew she would be laughing inwardly at his mood. He wanted to throw open the door and slap away the smirk she would have on her face. He held his anger in check, however, for he was both afraid and in desperate need of her.

Kristina's voice came to him from inside the room: "Who is it?"

"It's me—Andrew," he said, leaning close to the wood, his voice already losing its rancor. "May I come in?"

"It's open, Andrew."

He entered and closed the door quickly behind him. He hesitated before approaching, the mere sight of her filling him with the usual desire—*and shame for being in bondage to such a creature.*

She was sitting before a mirror, deftly tucking strands of damp hair beneath a towel worn around her head. The long, white bathrobe she wore was parted around one thigh, and he could not help but stare at the smooth skin, wanting to touch its softness, stroke it, to reach for her and hold her close.

She knew his look, and knew his desire—and laughed at him.

He looked down at her, resisting the temptation to reach out for her elegant neck, the neck he had caressed with his lips so many times, wanting to choke the life from it now, but knowing his hands would never have the strength. They would squeeze until the knuckles were white, until her eyes showed panic, fear, laughter, gone from them; then his grip would loosen and his hands would reach down, across the smooth flesh, down until they cupped her hard-nippled breasts—for her very fear would have aroused her, made her want him as much as he wanted her. That was the kind of perverse creature Kristina was. And her fear would have aroused him—*that was the kind of perverse creature he was.* He would sink to his knees and beg forgiveness, his hands still clutching her breasts as though afraid to let go. And Kristina would sink down beside him and they would make love in their unnatural way.

"No, Andrew," she said, reading his mind. She turned from him and resumed tucking away the damp strands of hair, watching the reflection of his clenched fists in the mirror, smiling at the conflict of desires he was going through.

"Please, Kristina, I . . ." He fell to his knees and pushed his cheek against the roughness of the bathrobe, a hand resting on her exposed thigh, fingers spreading and moving inward toward the even softer flesh on the inside of her leg.

She snatched his hand away and drew the bathrobe over her nakedness. "You know what has to be done later," she said scornfully. "We've no time for this."

"Why?" Brannigan said, almost wearily. "Why does it have to be you?"

Her eyes flashed angrily. "You know why. He has to be debased."

"As I was? As I am now?"

"This is different, Andrew. It's nothing to do . . ." She stopped abruptly, but he completed the sentence for her.

"Blackmail? No need to blackmail him as you did me?"

"It began as blackmail, Andrew. But you believe in our cause now, don't you? You've told me so many times that you do, and you've done so much for us."

"Of course. But why Steadman? For God's sake, Kristina . . ."

"God? What has He got to do with this?"

Brannigan was silent.

"Dr. Scheuer says the legend has to be refuted," Kristina said impatiently.

"And Gant believes all this nonsense."

"Nonsense? You can say that after all you've seen?"

"I . . . I don't understand all of it, Kristina. I don't understand how these . . . things happen." His voice was pleading. "You said you loved me. Was that also just for the cause?"

She dropped a hand to the back of his head and stroked his hair. Her voice softened. "Of course not. You know how much I think of you." The major could not see her smile at her own reflection in the mirror. "I have to do this, Andrew. Our Parsifal has to be"—her smile was filled with malice—"corrupted."

Without force, she pushed Brannigan away, then tilted his head up so she could look into his eyes. "Now go away and check that everything's secure for tonight. This is the beginning, Andrew, and nothing must go wrong." Kristina kissed his lips, holding herself back from his passion, restraining him with a gentle hand. "I must rest," she said. "Tonight is important to us all."

Major Brannigan rose clumsily and, with a last penetrating look at Kristina, left the room. He walked toward the right wing of the house and entered a room next door to the one in which Steadman and Holly Miles were being held. A green-uniformed man wearing headphones, seated next to a tape recorder, looked up and acknowledged him with a respectful nod.

"Anything?" Brannigan asked.

The man shook his head. "They've been quiet for some time now. He asked her direct if she worked for Mossad when he first went in and she denied it. Looks like she really is clean."

"Unless she suspects the room is bugged. What else did Steadman have to say?"

"He told her quite a bit—about Mr. Gant and the organization, about tonight's op—but he doesn't know the whole story himself."

Brannigan nodded briskly and turned to leave. "Keep listening till he's taken out of there. I still don't think that woman is what she seems. If anything does slip out, let me know immediately."

"Very good, sir." The eavesdropper saluted and Brannigan left the room, making his way toward the main stairway and the front entrance. A check on the guards, posted at various spots around the estate's boundaries, then a visit to the missile site to make sure everything was set for tonight's—or more accurately, tomorrow morning's—launching. Things would be moving at last and they'd begin to see some fruition of their dream. The society had remained in the shadows for so many years, but the time was coming for the strong leaders to emerge. *They* would rule, and the military would no longer be the puppets of weak men. No longer would the country's defenses be whittled away by the weaklings in government. No longer would the leftists be allowed to dominate. That kind of destructive freedom was to end in England. It had to if the nation was to survive. Of course, the identity of their true leader would never be revealed, for it would be abhorrent to the people who had so misguidedly fought against his great ideals in the last World War. And they would never allow themselves to be ruled by someone they thought had perished so many years before.

Dusk fell and the white house was silent. The drizzle had ceased, but it seemed all life, animal and human, was still sheltering from its dampness. Only the roar from the ocean could be heard, the sound of cruel Atlantic waves breaking on the rocky beaches, their thunderous crashes drifting up the cliff faces and rolling over the grassy slopes.

The night slowly closed in around the house and its whiteness turned gray, the windows black and impenetrable. A cold wind stirred the grass in spreading ripples and disturbed the tree branches, dislodging the final stubborn leaves.

The darkness became solid, and a heaviness, despite the just-fallen rain, seemed to hang in the air. It was as if the very night was waiting, and time was a creeping thing.

SIXTEEN

But the day will come when we shall make a pact with these new men in England, France, America. We shall make it when they fall in line with the vast process of the reordering of the world, and voluntarily play their part in it. There will not be much left then of the clichés of nationalism, and precious little among us Germans. Instead there will be an understanding between the various language elements of the one good ruling race.

—ADOLF HITLER

"Come along, Harry, separate rooms for you two, dear boy."

Pope's gross figure stood in the doorway, a grin on his face and a gun in his hand. When he saw the investigator was a safe distance away from him and not lurking near the door, he returned the gun to his jacket pocket. He always felt ridiculous holding the "Baby" Parabellum .25 in his immense hand anyway, but it was a convenient and unobtrusive size for his pocket.

Steadman swung his legs off the bed, his hand squeezing Holly's as he stood, his eyes warning her to keep quiet.

"Where are you taking me?" he asked Pope.

"Mr. Gant felt that now that you've been assured of Miss Miles' well-being, you should be kept apart just in case you should get up to any mischief." Griggs and Booth leered from their position behind the fat man.

Steadman walked toward the trio crowded in the doorway and Pope stood aside to let him through.

"Harry, don't go with them!" Holly suddenly shouted, leaping from the bed.

Pope turned his huge bulk toward her and held up a hand to keep her at bay. "He has no choice in the matter, my dear. Now go back to where you were *and keep quiet!*"

Holly glared at him defiantly. "What are you bastards going to do with him?"

"Nothing, dear lady, absolutely nothing." The smoothness had returned to Pope's voice. "Until midnight, that is. In fact, it should be rather pleasant for him until then." One of the men in the doorway chuckled aloud, but there was no amusement in the fat man's eyes. "Now, move!" he ordered Steadman.

With a last backward glance at Holly, the investigator stepped into the hallway and began to follow Griggs and Booth, with Pope close behind.

She looked scared, Steadman mused. Genuinely scared for him. Was she really innocent in all this or was it merely an elaborate ploy to get him to talk to her, to make sure he knew only what *they* wanted him to know? And to make sure he was completely alone?

He was led up a flight of stairs onto the next floor, taken along another corridor and finally shown into a room that was infinitely more comfortable than the one he had just left. The decor was still stark, but a fire blazed in the grate, throwing a warm glow around the walls. A small lamp gave the room an intimate atmosphere and a long pin-buttoned couch stood at right angles to the fire. A four-poster bed dominated half the large room and its soft, inviting quilt reminded Steadman how tired he was. It had been a day full of tension. He fought against the tiredness that suddenly dragged him down.

Turning to the big man, he said bitterly, "Why, Pope? Why did someone like you get involved in all this?"

The fat man laughed hollowly, then motioned his two henchmen to leave the room. When he and Steadman were alone, he said, "I've always been *involved*, Harry. The British Secret Service was never much *before* the last war, and after . . . just a shambles, a complete bloody shambles."

Pope crossed the room and gazed into the fire, one pudgy hand resting on the mantel above. "You were in military intelligence," he said, his face lit by the flames, "so you must have been aware of the general incompetence that was rife throughout the whole of the British Secret Service."

Steadman nodded unconsciously, remembering the frustration he had felt over the apparent idiocy of many of his superiors. At the time, he had forgiven their seemingly senseless directives on the assumption that there was some deeply hidden motive behind them, and when he had often later discovered the motive was just as senseless as the directive, he'd almost given up in despair. That was why the Shin Beth had been so attractive to him. Israeli intelligence had been, and probably still was, the most respected intelligence organization in the world, the British equivalent paling in comparison. However, some sense of loyalty forced the investigator to refute Pope's damning statement.

"But it's changed now—the dross has been cleared out, the 'old school tie' network doesn't work any more."

"Hah!" Pope faced him, amusement and scorn turning him into a jovial gargoyle. "I *am* part of the 'old school tie' network, dear boy. Only *I* do not choose to socialize—ideologically, of course—with my peers at the ministry. Even after the outrageous attempts by the SIS to protect traitors like Philby in the sixties, the 'old boy' network was allowed to go on ruling the roost. Even when Burgess and Maclean defected and it was evident Kim Philby had tipped them off, they went on protecting him—*and were allowed to*. God, it was no wonder the

CIA lost all confidence in us after that debacle—after all, they suffered as much as us through our incompetence. Cooperation between our two organizations has been slight, to say the least, after the sixties. The exposé of spy rings such as Lonsdale's, and the internment of men like Vassal, far from gaining our security service glory has, in fact, cast serious doubts on our reliability in matters of state secrecy. And these are only our publicized defections! You'd be amazed at the disasters that have been swept under the carpet in the interest of national confidence in the department! You can't blame the bloody Americans for not collaborating with us any more!"

Steadman sank down onto the couch. Before he could speak, Pope had continued his tirade against his own organization. "And when the change comes in this country, dear boy, I'll be directing the new broom as far as my own department is concerned. No more kid-glove treatment for suspect aliens, no more foreign trawlers in our waters. Family connections will mean nothing in the organization. Chinless wonders and nancy boys will be flushed out. Our 'gray' people will be made to earn their keep."

"You're as insane as Gant," Steadman said quietly.

"Insane? Am I ranting, Harry? Am I raving? Do I really sound as though I'm mad?"

Steadman had to admit, he didn't. "But what you're talking about—what you're all talking about—is revolution. That's impossible in England."

"What we're talking about is *counter*-revolution. The revolution is already taking place. We intend to oppose it."

"What's to stop your kind of power from becoming corrupt?"

Our one ideal, Harry. Don't you see, we are a Holy Order? The thirteen men who will ultimately control the country will not be ordinary men. We'll use the corruption around us, we'll fight fire with fire . . ."

"And not get burned yourselves?"

"Our spiritual leader will see we don't."

"Himmler? A man who's been dead for over thirty years? How can a corpse help you, Pope?"

The fat man merely smiled. "You must rest now, tonight will not be an easy one for you." He walked to a large oak bureau to one side of the room, on which stood a tray containing a dark bottle and one glass. He brought the tray over to Steadman and placed it at his feet. "Brandy," he announced. "I'm sure you need it." He straightened his huge frame, grunting at the effort. "Compliments of Mr. Gant. Now, would you like some food, Harry? I'm sure you must be starving."

Steadman shook his head. The hollowness in his stomach couldn't be filled by food. The brandy might help, though.

"I'll leave you to rest." Pope walked to the door and for a brief moment the investigator considered attacking him, smashing the brandy bottle over that obese head. His muscles tensed and he reached down for the neck of the bottle.

"I shouldn't, dear boy," Pope warned with a pleasant smile. "Griggs and Booth are just outside; you wouldn't get very far. There is no escape for you, don't you see? You've almost served your purpose, so why not relax and enjoy your final hours?" Before the fat man disappeared through the door he gave Steadman a meaningful look. "Thank you, Harry, thank you for all your cooperation." Then, with a deep-throated chuckle, he was gone.

Steadman stared at the closed door for some time before he picked up the brandy. He uncorked the bottle and poured the dark brown liquid into the glass. He raised the glass to his lips, and just before he sipped he wondered if the drink could be drugged. But what would be the point? He was captive here, no chance of escape. Would they need him in a drugged state for whatever was to happen later that night? He doubted it; they had enough strong-arm men to keep him passive. He took the tiniest of sips and rolled the fiery liquid around his mouth. He longed to swallow, knowing the brandy would do him good, but the faintest bitter taste held his throat muscles in check. Was it only his imagination or was there really a strange taint to the drink? Because of his danger his senses were acute; but was their sensitivity exaggerating the ordinary bitterness of the spirits?

He spat the liquid into the fire and the sudden flare-up made him jump back. The interior of his mouth burned with the thin coating of brandy left there, and he ran his tongue around it to dilute its strength. He looked longingly at the remaining contents of the glass and asked himself what they would try to drug him with—*if* they were trying to drug him—and his mind ran through the legend, the mythical story of the Holy Grail which had inspired Wagner's *Parsifal*. The mystical opera he insisted be performed only at Bayreuth, the spiritual capital of the Germanic peoples. The opera Hitler had believed was the divine ideology of the Aryan race!

Young Steve had told Steadman the basic story of the opera, which was a dramatization of Wolfram von Eschenbach's thirteenth-century Grail romance, and the investigator had begun to understand why Gant—perverse though it was—had referred to him as "his Parsifal." The central theme of the opera was the struggle between the Grail knights and their adversaries over the possession of the Holy Spear—*the Spear of Longinus which had pierced the side of Christ.*

The spear had been stolen from the knights by Klingsor, a castrated evil magician who embodied paganism. In the act of stealing the spear, Klingsor used the weapon to deal Amfortas, the leader of the knights, a wound that would never heal. In the hands of Klingsor, the spear had become an evocator of black powers, which only a completely guileless knight could overcome.

In Gant's devious—or was it desperate?—reasoning, he had seen himself as Klingsor, for Gant believed more in the powers of evil than in good, despising—as had Hitler—the Christian rituals connected with the myth, and in the arms dealer's strange mind, Steadman had become his Parsifal, the "guileless" knight who would have to be thwarted if the legend's meaning was to be revoked. Parsifal had become a battle-weary soldier, a man whose mother had died grief-stricken when he had left her while still a boy. Although Steadman had always believed in the cause he had fought for, he would hardly have ascribed any deeply noble instincts to his own character, yet Gant had cast him in the romantic role of defender of the Good. Was it desperation on the arms dealer's part, a need to create an omen where none existed, a megalomaniac's desire to symbolize his own destiny? Perhaps Gant felt time was running out for him, the moment to launch his offensive was at hand, and someone was needed quickly to reenact the final scene of Good against Evil, with the outcome this time heavily weighted on the side of Evil. A charade, a false ceremony for the benefit of the New Order! Steadman found it difficult to smile at the foolishness of it all. This was why he had been drawn into the elaborate game. Unwittingly, David Goldblatt had provided them with their symbolic knight, a single man to be foiled, then destroyed as an omen of their future success. Gant must have been filled with elation when Maggie, under torture, had revealed she had been sent by Mossad, but only as second choice to her partner, Steadman, an ex-soldier, an ex-Mossad agent. An untainted Englishman.

It would have been easy for Pope to have gained access to the file kept by military intelligence on his, Steadman's, past activities, and they had probably gloated on how his background could be compared—albeit loosely—to the mythical Parsifal's. From then on, it had just been a matter of drawing him in. Maggie's vile murder had been committed in order to tear him from the state of passivity he had built up over the last few years; the visit from Pope when he had declined to go against them despite his partner's cruel death; the meeting with Gant at the armaments exhibition to assess his worth as an opponent; and

the subsequent test when the tank had tried to crush him
(had Holly's life been as expendable as Köhner's, or was
this real proof of her innocence in the deadly game?); the
revelations at Guildford to insure his further involvement,
and the next test of his worth against the sadistic Köhner,
knowing if he escaped, he would contact Pope, who
would send him off on the last part of the charade without
risk to their plans; and his being lured to Gant's North
Devon Estate, the "*Wewelsburg*."

And now the final act was drawing near and one last
test remained; but they wanted him to fail this one, so
that his degradation would refute the outcome of the
original legend. In the thirteenth-century poem adapted
by Wagner for his opera, a woman, Kundry by name,
had tried to seduce Parsifal and degrade him as she
had so many other knights. How these ancient stan-
dards of honor and chastity could compare with today's, Steadman was at a loss to know, but nothing was
sane in this whole bizarre plot. Gant and his followers
would derive their own meaning from his sexual "down-
fall." Anger boiled up in him and he threw the contents
of the glass into the fire, enjoying the searing throwback
of heat as the fire flared greedily, almost as though it were
an emanation of his own rage. But they had made one
small mistake in their elaborate scheme: Köhner had
known about the Israeli agent, Smith; he had told Steadman the man had died. How could he have known unless
he had been told by the bogus MI5 agents, Griggs and
Booth? And that implicated Pope. It was enough for
Steadman to have taken precautions before allowing himself to be drawn finally and irrevocably into the spider's
web. But had those precautions been enough? He looked
at his watch and cursed. Where were they? What the hell
were they waiting for? Were *they* part of the game too?

He leapt up and strode briskly to the window. It, too,
was locked, and he looked out into the dark night, seeing
little but his own reflection in the glass. He had lost track
of time standing there, when the sound of a key turning in

the lock made him look toward the door. The handle turned and the door opened slowly.

He was almost relieved when she slipped into the room; relieved it wasn't Holly.

SEVENTEEN

And I shall not shrink from using abnormal men, adventurers from love of the trade. There are countless men of this sort, useless in respectable life, but invaluable for this work.

—ADOLF HITLER

Holly decided it was time to make her move. She knew her people would be reluctant to close in, but her absence would force them to do so. That might be too late, though.

She had been genuinely astounded when she had "stumbled" on the hidden missile site. She was aware that Gant and his lunatic followers had some pretty twisted plans in mind, but had not realized those plans could involve such overt armed aggression. Even though it was known to her organization that Gant encouraged terrorist activities and supplied these various factions with arms— for a price—it was thought his own methods of undermining world peace were more subtle, more insidious. She had been stupid to get caught taking "snaps" of the site, but they were still unsure of her. After all, if she *was* a free-lance journalist and photographer as she claimed, then it would be perfectly natural for her curiosity to be aroused at such a discovery. Many journalists had been anxious to write a feature on "Edward Gant, Twentieth-

Century Arms Dealer," over the past decade, so it was not unnatural that she had been so persistent. The fact that Gant had now begun to seek publicity and that her story of connection with his late wife's family in the States had checked out had led to her privileged position. Some privileged position, she reflected wryly.

Gant had invited her to his closely guarded estate the day before, promising her an "exclusive" that would be the envy of the journalistic world. A car had arrived at Holly's flat in the early hours of the morning, with the arms dealer's invitation, and had whisked her away before she had time to inform her own people. She was sure they were keeping tabs on her, though.

When she learned from Harry the purpose of the missile, she had been astounded at the flagrant cunning of Gant's plan. There would be no tracing those who launched the rocket, though both Israelis and the Arabs would obviously be suspected. But the Israelis would *know* the Arabs were the perpetrators, and the Arabs would *know* the Israelis were the perpetrators. It would unsettle all the negotiations for peace between the two nations, and lead to another full-scale war, which, in all likelihood, the Israelis would not win this time.

Holly had guessed the room was bugged—why else would they send Harry in to her?—and had had to deny any knowledge of Gant's secret organization. However, she hadn't lied about Mossad. She had wanted to hold him, tell him he wasn't alone in all this, that others knew of the arms dealer's intent. Harry had looked so grim, his mistrust undisguised, and she had wanted to blurt out the truth, to tell him of her government's suspicions and anxiety over this, the most powerful Hitlerite group since the war. They knew its tentacles spread into high places, British intelligence not the least of those places, and that they had to tread carefully and secretively in this country where the actual nest existed and thrived, for it was not just a threat to Britain but to world equilibrium in general.

The investigator's sudden appearance on the scene had mystified them at first and Holly still hadn't figured out why he was so important to Gant. Her brief, though unexpectedly emotional, acquaintance with Harry had revealed nothing of any significance apart from the fact he had once been a Mossad agent. So why was he so important to Gant and why had he been allowed to get so close? And why, Holly asked herself, had he become so important to her?

Holly rose from the one easy chair in the room and moved toward the door. She pressed her ear against the wood and listened. No sound came from the other side. Even if they thought she wasn't involved, Holly doubted that they would leave her unwatched. She tried the door handle, twisting it to and fro.

"Leave it, lady," a voice commanded from the other side. "You're not going anywhere." Holly looked around the room, searching for an idea more than an object. But it was the object that gave her the idea.

Kristina closed the door and smiled across the room at Steadman.

He had to admit she was beautiful, her long, dark hair framing her pale face like a black sea flowing around an ice drift. The deep red of her full lips could have been an imprint of blood on the snow, a curving stain that was as cold as the ice around. Only her eyes were alien in the frozen landscape of her face, for they were alive, deep, and glowing, as though containing some inner amusement. Yet, there was an excitement in them too, and he felt it had to do with desire.

Her skirt was of the darkest umber, velvet in texture, and ending well below the knee where high and slim-heeled boots clung to her calves and ankles, flowing with the shape of her lower legs as the skirt flowed with the shape of her thighs. A brown shirt, two tones lighter than the skirt, open to a point below the cleft of her breasts, completed the picture of aggressive sexuality and, despite himself, he felt the opening pangs of desire. He caught the sudden flick of her eyes toward the brandy bottle and his passion was immediately stemmed.

"I wanted to see you, Harry," Kristina said before advancing on him.

"Why?" he asked bluntly.

She stopped before him. "To talk to you. Perhaps to help you escape."

For a moment he was too stunned to speak. "You'd help me escape from here?"

"I'd help you escape from the fate Edward Gant has in store for you."

The sudden hope drained from Steadman and he asked, "How?"

"By persuading Edward to let you in, by convincing him you could be useful to us." She was close to him now, having imperceptibly drawn nearer as they spoke. He looked down at her, interest more than contempt in his eyes.

"How could I be useful to your Thulists?" he asked.

"You're a resourceful man; you've done well to survive so far. You know much about Israeli intelligence, a natural enemy to our movement, and any information you could give us would be invaluable. Your past record shows you are a ruthless man, and ruthlessness is something this country will need in the years ahead."

"But wouldn't I have to believe in Nazism?" Steadman asked scornfully.

"You'd come to believe in time. Not all our members are convinced of our ideals, we're aware of that. They seek power for power's sake, not for race advancement, but for personal gain. Eventually, they'll see it our way."

"And you think Gant would trust me?"

"You'd have to convince him you could be trusted. I could help you do that."

"How?"

"If I trusted you I could influence his judgment. I have in the past." She placed a hand on his shoulder and, inexplicably, a shudder ran through him.

"But why should you believe me?" he said.

"If we were lovers . . ." he almost laughed aloud as she said the words. ". . . I'd know."

"And Major Brannigan. Isn't he your lover?"

She smiled indulgently at Steadman. "You're very observant. Andrew is a weak man. He doesn't have your qualities, your strength."

"But I bet you helped draw him into all this."

"It's not important now, Harry." She closed the gap between them and pressed her body against his. The contact was at once strongly repulsive yet intoxicating. Had the tiny amount of tampered-with brandy he'd allowed into his mouth begun to have some effect? Or was it her eyes? They had a peculiar mesmeric quality and he felt a tiredness overcoming him. He tried to flood any other thoughts from his mind, filling his head with the Parsifal legend, reminding himself of Gant's malignity. Yet when he looked down at the beautiful face before him, it was difficult to imagine any reasonable motive behind the seduction. It would hardly be humiliating to succumb to such a woman, and he had certainly not taken any knightly vows of celibacy. Her dark eyes gazed back at him, unblinking, drawing him down, his head bending toward her, his lips reaching. It was almost as though he was being hypnotized, she exerting a stronger will over his . . .

It was then he realized exactly what was happening: she was drawing his strength, sapping his will. Her power was not in her body, but in her mind. It drank in his will, drew him into a mental whirlpool, her deep eyes sucking him in, drowning him. Her hand took his and placed it on her breast, holding it there, making him feel her firmness, the nipple hard and thrusting. Their thighs pressed close, his body stirring, no longer unwilling, oblivious to the legend, subject now only to physical need. Their lips were almost touching, only minimal resistance preventing him from crushing his against hers. But it was the physical stirring in her that suddenly froze his movement, that tore through the overwhelming net of carnality she had cast over him. For her own desire had manifested itself against his lower body, a protuberance that pushed against her clothes, and deemed to match his.

With a cry of rage he pushed her away, driving his fist hard into her face. She screamed with the shock and sudden pain, falling to the floor, and he knew why they'd sent *her* to seduce him. Why he would have been humbled before them, and more importantly, himself, if he had succumbed. The door flew open and Pope stood there, others behind him with guns drawn. There was anger in Pope's eyes as he looked at Steadman, then down at Kristina, who lay propped up with one hand against the floor, the other clutching an already swelling face.

Kristina spat at Steadman. "You bastard!" she screamed, and her voice had become guttural. "You lousy bastard!"

Disgustedly, and before Pope's musclemen could rush him, Steadman took a step forward and aimed a vicious kick at the hermaphrodite lying prone on the floor.

It took two minutes for Pope's men to knock him senseless, but as Steadman sank into unconsciousness, he took relish in the sobs of pain coming from the creature lying only a few feet from him.

Holly Miles stood on the bed and reached up toward the lightbulb, a pillowcase cover draped over one hand to prevent her fingers being burned by the hot glass. With a deft twist, the lightbulb was free of its socket and the room plunged into darkness. She stood still for a few seconds, allowing her eyes to adjust to dense blackness, the hand clutching the lightbulb becoming warm with the heat. The full moon outside suddenly broke free from smothering clouds and she was grateful for the increased visibility, although it might work against her in a few moments. She stepped off the bed and moved silently toward the thin bar of light that shone beneath the door from the hallway. Once again, Holly listened with her ear pressed against the woodwork, praying she would not hear sounds of muffled conversation, indicating there was more than one guard outside; she didn't think she could tackle two of them. Reasonably satisfied, she tapped lightly on the door with her fingernails.

"Hey," she called softly. "Open up. I want to see Gant."

There was no reply and this time she rapped harder, using her knuckles.

"Hey, you! I've got something to tell Gant. It's important."

Still no answer, and she began to wonder if there *was* still someone out there. "Can you hear me?" she demanded to know, thumping the door angrily.

"Keep it down, lady," came the surly reply.

"Ah, the zombie speaks," she said, loud enough for the guard to hear. "Listen to me, I've got to see Gant."

"Mr. Gant's busy."

"No, look, I've got information for him. I warn you, it's important."

"Go fuck yourself," came the lazy reply.

"Cretin!" she said, and gave the door a powerful kick.

"Cut it out, lady, I'm telling you!" There was menace in his voice now.

She kicked it again.

"I'm warning you, I've got orders to keep you quiet," Holly heard the disembodied voice say, and she smiled grimly. She kicked at the door again.

"You'd better let me see him, moron. You'll regret it if you don't."

There was a brief silence as though the guard was pondering, then his voice came through the woodwork again. "What have you got to tell Mr. Gant?"

"That's between me and him."

"Oh no. There's a meeting going on tonight and I'm not interrupting it just for you."

"Then let me see whoever's in charge of you—your commanding officer." She used the description of rank scornfully, refusing to accept that these mercenaries were genuine soldiers. Perhaps if he went to find his superior she would have a chance to work on the door. It was a slim chance, but slim was better than none at all.

"Major Brannigan's busy."

Yes, probably supervising the missile launch, Holly told

herself. "Okay, your captain or sergeant, or whatever," she shouted back.

"Leave it out, lady. There's enough going on tonight without you causing problems."

She swore furiously and began to pummel at the door. My God, what if she really *had* some vital information for Gant? This cluck would still carry out his orders and keep her imprisoned here, no matter what.

"Cut it out!" the guard shouted. "I'm telling you, I'll come in there and sort you out!"

She nodded to herself and increased the rain of blows on the door.

"Right!" she heard him say. "You've asked for it!"

The rattle of a key entering the lock was music to her ears. She flew across the room, diving on the bed and rolling over it onto the floor beyond. She crouched there, praying for a cloud to snuff out the moon's brightness. The door opened, slamming back against the wall, the guard's way of insuring she wasn't lurking behind it. Light flooded in from the hallway, and she heard him curse and the light switch being flicked.

Holly knew if he was professional he would immediately step back into the hallway and to one side, to make his silhouette less vulnerable, so she had to act first.

Without showing herself, she hurled the still-warm lightbulb into the corner of the room to the left of the guard. The glass popped and shattered, the noise resembling the blast of a small firearm. The guard whirled toward the sound, his single-hand submachine gun aimed at the corner.

Holly was like a banshee streaking from the shadows and it was already too late for the guard as he turned to meet her rush. She hurled herself at him, twisting her body as she leapt, so that her back and one shoulder struck him just below chest level. He cried out in alarm, falling backward, striking the door frame as he went down, the shock of the blow causing him to lose his grip on the submachine gun. They sprawled halfway out into the hall, and Holly, lithe as a cat, rolled to a crouching position, her eyes already searching the long corridor for other guards. With relief, she realized it was empty.

The guard's gun was lying back through the door, bathed in light from the hall, and she scrambled toward it. A hand grabbed her ankle and tripped her, sending her flat.

The guard, still stunned and wincing at the numbing pain between his shoulder blades, had seen her intent and was quick enough to snatch at her leg. He pulled her toward him and that was his second mistake.

His first had been to underestimate her because she was a woman. His second was to clutch at one lethal appendage while allowing the other to remain free. Her other foot shot out and struck him just below the chin, snapping his head back so it struck the hard wood of the door frame once more. The foot struck again with deadly skill as his head bounced back, smashing his nose and hastening his already speedy flight into unconsciousness.

Holly sprang to her feet, the guard's hand falling limply away from her ankle. She cleared the curtain of blonde hair that screened her vision with a toss of her head and peeped back into the hallway, listening for the sound of approaching footsteps. Satisfied that their struggles had not aroused anybody's attention, she reached down for the unconscious guard's ankles and dragged him away from the doorway and farther into the room. Flicking his eyelids up, she was careful to avoid the blood flowing from his broken nose, and guessed he would be out for quite some time. Nevertheless, she decided to bind him with bedsheets just to be safe. Within minutes it was done, and his inert body lay beneath the bed out of sight of anyone who should casually check on the room. It was probably an unnecessary precaution, for she knew her mere absence and the sight of the unguarded hallway would set off alarms throughout the estate, but she was a firm believer that in her business every little detail could sometimes help. Her one concession to the man's condition was to leave him ungagged; with his nose and throat clogged with blood, she knew he could easily choke if air from his mouth was cut off. She even positioned him on his side to help the flow of blood run onto the carpet rather than down his throat, feeling slightly foolish and knowing her past instructors would have cursed her vehemently for her unprofessionalism. But she was prepared to take the small risk of his coming to his senses and calling for help rather than let him die in such a defenseless manner.

Holly straightened, running her hands down her jeans, trying to wipe the bloody stickiness from them. She walked over to the submachine gun still lying near the doorway, light bouncing off its oily black surfaces, and noted it was similar to an Ingram. Small and compact, inaccurate over any great distance, but deadly effective at close quarters. She wondered if it had the same firing power of 1,200 rounds a minute as the Ingram. A small stock was hinged to the main body, providing a recoil buffer when pulled back and held against the upper arm. She picked it up, surprised because it was even lighter than the Ingram: Gant's private army was privileged with the finest equipment.

Once again she checked the hallway, listening for sounds, her senses keened to the atmosphere. All was quiet.

She closed the door, locking it with the key still protruding beneath the handle, and crept stealthily down the long corridor, keeping close to the wall, prepared to use the recessed doorways as cover should anyone suddenly appear. Holly made her way toward the back of the house, away from the main stairway, and toward the curiously castlelike older part.

The wind howled around the ancient church tower, the breeze cold, sweeping over the land from the sea, biting and tangy with salt. As the moonlight struggled through the thick, rolling clouds once again, a group of men was revealed crouching for shelter behind the parapet at the top of the tower. At all times, however, one man remained kneeling, his elbows resting against the cleft in the fortlike wall, night-sighted binoculars held to his eyes, watching the dim white house in the dip of the land almost a mile away.

"Still no movement, sir," he muttered, ducking his head below the parapet so his words were not whisked away by the wind. "Reckon they've settled down for the night."

The man he was speaking to half covered his watch with a hand so that the luminous dial could function. "Nearly half-eleven," he said to no one in particular. "The last helicopter arrived about ten, didn't it?"

Sexton, crouched next to him, nodded, and said, "Yes, about that time. Look, it must have been the last of 'em. Can't we move in now?"

"Sorry, we can't go in until we've been given the order from the commissioner." Detective Chief Inspector Burnett sympathized with the retired police officer, Blake, but there were bigger things at stake here than the safety of one man. He was acting under the directions of the commissioner *and* the home secretary. They were running the show—so if his orders were to wait, then wait he would.

"But what are you hanging on for?" Blake persisted. "For fuck's sake, he could be dead by now."

The chief inspector turned to him and said patiently, "Look, Mr. Blake, I can appreciate your concern, but this Steadman went in there of his own free will . . ."

"He said he had to. He had to play it out the way Gant wanted. He was worried about the girl, he didn't know if she was involved or not, whether she was safe or . . ."

"Holly Miles. Yes," Burnett said wearily, "we know all about her now."

"Why weren't we informed about her before, governor?" a voice came from close by.

"Mistrust, Andy. They played everything close to their chests. Christ, who would have thought Pope was dodgy?"

The detective sergeant shook his head in the dark. "How long have they known about him?"

"God knows. You can bet that's why the CIA were in on it, though—nobody knew who could really be trusted in MI5. If someone with Pope's rank could be part of Gant's group, then who else—upstairs *or* downstairs—could be involved? Aah," he waved a hand disgustedly, "makes you sick to think of it."

Sexton rose to his feet, his cramped position making his bones ache. The wind hit him instantly and he pulled the lapels of his overcoat up around his neck, tucking one point beneath the other to protect his chest. He looked over the edge and could clearly make out the ugly, twisted tree that stood by the roadside at the base of the old church. On the other side of the ancient stone building, groups of cars and Special Branch Land Rovers lay hidden from the road, all filled with cold, bored men, impatient for the action to start.

It had been a frustrating twenty-four hours for Sexton, and with every passing minute his concern for Steadman's safety grew. They had done what Harry had told them, he and Steve, continuing their vigil on the house at Guildford, waiting for the police to arrive, trying to keep awake through the night. All that had happened was that the guards had come and locked the gates, seemingly unconcerned with thoughts of escaping, gathering up the bodies of the man and the two dogs, loading them into a truck, and driving back up to the house. He and Steve waited beyond that time because Harry had said to wait a few hours, give this man Pope the chance to act—give him the benefit of the doubt.

Nothing had happened, though, and in the early hours of the morning, Sexton had felt sure nothing was going to happen. He had left poor Steve there—the boy had really acted well throughout all this—and driven back to town, straight to New Scotland Yard. It was fortunate he still had good contacts there, otherwise he would have had a difficult time convincing them his story was true. It sounded unlikely even to him as he related it, but eventually the police had been persuaded to make a few inquiries, strictly as a favor—and there were a few of them there who owed him a favor or two—about Pope. Special Branch had been contacted to see if they knew anything of the matter, then the whole thing had taken on a new pace.

When questions are asked by Scotland Yard about a member of MI5, the reaction is swift and tight. Sexton had soon found himself being interviewed by several obviously senior people, one of whom was an American. He told them all he knew, which wasn't much; but it seemed to be enough for them. Events took on a new impetus and a clampdown on internal security was immediate; only a select few seemed to know exactly what was going on.

Steve was brought in and a discreet guard placed around the Guildford house. The house was still under observation, untouched and unwarned. The men inside were probably feeling very smug.

There was much Sexton didn't understand and it was obvious the Special Branch officers he was now with were not fully in the picture either. But one thing was certain: the authorities—those at the very top—were aware something was afoot, otherwise action on such a grand scale would never have happened so promptly. It was as though Harry Steadman was the trigger that had set it off. And the American who had interviewed him earlier that day—did that mean the CIA were involved too? It seemed Harry had uncovered a hornet's nest.

He crouched down again, out of the stinging wind, cursing softly under his breath.

"We can't just sit here!" he shouted at no one in particular.

Burnett placed a hand on Sexton's arm and moved his head closer. "We've got to wait, Mr. Blake. It won't be much longer, I promise. The commissioner's coming down himself to direct operations. That's how important it is."

"Then why isn't he here now?" Sexton said angrily. "Why is he keeping us bloody waiting?"

"I don't know for sure. I think he's got to make arrangements at the other end. The word is that it's not just a bunch of terrorist fanatics we're bringing in, but some very high-placed bastards, men as rich and powerful as Gant himself, maybe even more so. If you ask me, the commissioner's consulting the PM himself on just how to handle the whole affair."

"It's wasting so much bloody time, though!"

"We'll be in there in a matter of minutes once we get the word. We're having a force of Marine commandos flown up from their base in Plymouth by RNAF helicopters. We know Gant's got his own private army, so if he resists there's going to be some bloody battle. Now I'm just as keen to get it over with as you—waiting makes me nervous—but there's nothing we can do until we get the order. So be patient and try not to worry about this Steadman. He hasn't done too bad so far, has he?"

Sexton turned his head away in frustration. No, Harry hadn't done bad so far. But how much longer would his luck last?

EIGHTEEN

He clipped him in such a way that he can never more give pleasure to any woman. But that meant suffering for many people.
—WOLFRAM VON ESCHENBACH

We are more valuable than the others who now, and always will, surpass us in numbers. We are more valuable because our blood enables us to invent more than others, to lead our people better than others. Let us clearly realize, the next decades signify a struggle leading to the extermination of the subhuman opponents in the whole world who fight Germany, the basic people of the Northern race, bearer of the culture of mankind.
—HEINRICH HIMMLER

Steadman's eyes slowly began to focus on the moving floor beneath him. His head still rang with the blows it had received.

He realized he was being hauled along a corridor, hands gripping him by the armpits and his feet dragging behind on the dark wood floor. He twisted his head to see where he was and recognized the voice that spoke; it belonged to Griggs.

"He's awake. Let him walk the rest of the way."

The investigator was hoisted to his feet and the somber face of Pope glared at him.

"I'm very glad you've rejoined us, Harry, though I think you'll wish you never had."

"Go screw yourself, Pope," Steadman replied, trying to shake the dizziness from his head. Griggs and Booth, on either side, prevented him from falling again.

"Ah, still the same arrogance. I could admire it if you weren't such a fool."

"You're the fool, Pope, to think all this is actually going to happen." Steadman managed to steady himself, but rough hands still gripped his upper arms.

A deep scoffing sound came from the fat man's throat. "Look at it this way, Harry," he said without smiling. "What's the alternative?"

He turned away, motioning his two men to bring the investigator along. Steadman was propelled forward and felt too groggy to resist. His curiosity was aroused by the long corridor's decorations. It was like being in a medieval castle, for the walls were dark gray stone, tapestries hanging in the spaces between doorways. The doors themselves were of intricately carved oak, the handles elaborately shaped wrought iron. His examination of the carving on the doors was perfunctory, but they seemed to be individual coats of arms, with an inscription or a title worked into each, and embellished with metal and what looked like precious stones.

They soon reached a point where the corridor opened out on one side and he realized they were now on a balcony overlooking a large, darkened hall. They stopped at the head of a broad stone stairway and Steadman's eyes widened in new alarm at the sight below him.

The huge room was decorated in the style of an ancient banqueting hall, with deep rich carpets, heavily brocaded curtains flanking the high windows; more tapestries adorned the walls. High, thick candles were placed symmetrically around the room, their color black, providing the only light apart from the fire that raged in the deep, man-sized cavity behind what appeared to be a dais. The design theme throughout was that of a golden spear.

In the center of the vast floor stood a huge round table, made as far as Steadman could tell, from solid oak, and around it were placed wooden high-backed chairs. He could see from those facing away from him that each had an inscribed silver plate on the back. Every chair—save for two—had an occupant; and the face of each occupant was turned toward him.

"Welcome to our Wewelsburg." It was Edward Gant's voice and Steadman's eyes darted around the table to trace the source. A figure began to rise and he saw it was Gant in a central position, his back to the curious dais. "Bring him down!" There was anger in the command.

Steadman was shoved brutally from behind, causing him to lose his balance and reach out for the stout bannister to one side of the stairway. It prevented the fall from being too serious, but still he tumbled down, losing his grip and rolling to the bottom. Footsteps behind, then he was again hauled to his feet. He shook the clutching hands off, forcing himself to stand alone.

"It would appear Kristina has failed in her task." Gant's voice was cold, the familiar mocking tones absent now.

"Did you really believe I could be corrupted by that . . . thing?" Steadman said harshly.

"Her power is in her mind, Mr. Steadman. Yes, I am surprised you resisted that. It seems she still has much to learn from her mystagogue, Dr. Scheuer." Gant made a motion with his hand, and a chair was brought from the shadows of the room to be placed three feet away from the round table. Steadman was shoved into it. A gap had opened up between the seated figures, offering him an unrestricted view of the arms dealer opposite. He had time to notice several uniformed guards situated at strategic points around the room, submachine guns held across their chests, before looking into the mad, glaring eyes of Edward Gant. The artificial nose was still affixed to the arms dealer's disfigured face, making him at least look human. He was dressed in a charcoal gray suit, his shirt white, though it looked yellowish in the suffused light, and his tie was black. The investigator was surprised Gant and his cohorts were not clad in robes or medieval costumes, such was the atmosphere in the dark baronial hall. Around the table, neatly placed before each member of the group, was a short ceremonial dagger and he noticed that those whose hands were placed on the table's surface wore curiously designed signet rings. The guests he had met earlier that day were among those seated, and others were familiar to him through the media. Dr. Scheuer was there, looking even older and more frail; Steadman felt his eyes boring into him even though he could not see them in their dark caverns. He was distracted as the vast bulk of Pope filled one of the unoccupied chairs.

"You are an honored person, Mr. Steadman." Gant's voice echoed around the stone walls, increasing its sibilance.

"Honored? To be part of this?"

"To be one of the few outsiders to visit the Wewelsburg."

"I'm overwhelmed."

"Don't mock us, Mr. Steadman!" Gant warned, his hand toying with the dagger before him. "Your death will be painful enough, but it can be made excruciating. The honor bestowed upon you is to see this, almost an exact replica o fthe Reichsführer's fortress, which he had built in Westphalia. A shrine devoted to the Teutonic knights. Only a select few, twelve in all, were allowed to visit Himmler's domain, all SS officers. There they meditated, remembered their Nordic origins. Each had his own room and that room was dedicated to great kings and emperors such as Otto the Great, Henry the Lion, Frederick Hohenstauffen, Philip of Swabia, and Conrad IV. The Reichsführer's own room was in honor of Henry I. Adolf Hitler's belonged to Frederick Barbarossa. But Hitler refused to visit the Wewelsburg! He turned his back on the forces that brought him to power. He would not even allow Himmler to bring the spear to its natural resting place! That is why the Führer failed, you see. Because at the end, he no longer possessed the Holy Spear—Heinrich Himmler had taken it for himself!"

Gant twisted in his chair and pointed toward the altar-like dais. "And we have possessed it ever since!"

Steadman saw the leather case resting on top of the dias and guessed at the object lying inside. So the Heilige Lance was here!

The arms dealer turned back to face Steadman across the table, but his eyes flicked upward to the balcony above.

"Come, Kristina, join us. You have failed, but then so did the original Kundra. It matters little now; the final achievement will be ours."

Steadman heard the footsteps on the stone stairway behind him and the man/woman came into view. Her face was swollen and bruised where he had struck her, and her beauty now seemed obscene. She scurried around the table, avoiding all the eyes that were on her, and sat in a chair placed behind Dr. Scheuer. The old man ignored her, still looking directly at Steadman.

The figure of Major Brannigan emerged from the shadows then, pure hatred in his eyes. He strode toward Steadman, a hand reaching for the revolver strapped at his side.

"Major!"

Brannigan halted at Gant's harsh command. "Wait outside for our latecomer, Major Brannigan, and take your guards with you. We have no need for them here."

"But what about Steadman? You know he's dangerous." The major's voice was resentful.

"I'm sure Griggs and Booth are capable of taking care of Mr. Steadman should he become . . . restless. Now go and wait by the helicopter pad. Our visitor should be here at any minute and I want him brought straight in."

Brannigan whirled and called for the soldiers around the room to fall in after him. They marched out, boots heavy on the solid floor.

"Forgive the major, Mr. Steadman," Gant said. "He's

insanely jealous over Kristina. Rather pathetic, don't you think, to be so concerned over such an aberration?"

The hermaphrodite's head snapped up and she looked balefully at Gant.

"Unfortunately," the arms dealer went on smoothly, "she is of the utmost importance to our cause. She will eventually take over from Dr. Scheuer, you see. Our poor doctor's health is failing and I'm afraid he has not much longer for this world. Somehow, I think he will prefer the next." Gant smiled warmly at the old man.

"Don't you think we should get on with the ceremony, Edward?" Sir James Oakes, the industrialist Steadman had been introduced to earlier that day, said from the far side of the table.

"I agree." It was Talgholm who spoke, and a few others murmured their approval. "Time's running out, Edward. The missile will soon be launched."

"Gentlemen, there is ample time. Our ally from overseas expressed a specific desire to be present tonight and we shall abide by his wish. You all know how necessary he is to us." Gant held up a hand, warding off any further protests, but when the voices still persisted he banged his fist down hard on the table. "Enough!" he shouted. "Have you forgotten what is to happen tonight? The atmosphere must not be disturbed for Dr. Scheuer!"

Their protests faded into silence and Gant smiled grimly. "There is too much tension in the air," he said by way of explanation to Steadman. "Our members are—shall we say—on edge?"

"They're as crazy as you, Gant," Steadman said evenly.

"Yes. And you are the only sane one here tonight." The mockery was back in the arms dealer's eyes. "I wonder if you will still be sane before you die?"

Steadman's brain was racing. What had happened to Sexton and Steve? Had they failed to convince the authorities? Were they *still* trying to? Or worse—had they been taken by Gant's men at Guildford? They were his only chance, but now it looked a very poor one.

"Okay, Gant," he said. "I'd like to hear more about

your organization. You say you're Thulists, but I thought such societies in Germany were wiped out after the last war."

"Only people are 'wiped out' in wars, not ideals. Some of us survived to further those ideals."

"You were in Germany during the war?"

"Oh yes." Gant chuckled, enjoying the puzzlement on the investigator's face. "I was not a common soldier, but I served the Reich in a more meaningful way. I've already told you how Hitler rejected us and how, because of the Führer's final foolishness, the power passed on to Reichsführer Heinrich Himmler. Thanks to plans carefully laid out long before the end of the war, Herr Himmler and I managed to escape the clutches of the Allies . . .

The four men hurried single file across the field, their feet sinking inches into the mud at each step, their breathing—particularly the third man's—labored and sharp. It was quiet in this part of the country, for the rumble of guns had been left far behind. But still they hurried, knowing they were near to freedom, near to Kiel where a boat would be waiting.

They had successfully evaded the clutches of the US Ninth Army, abandoning their armor-plated Mercedes early on in their hazardous journey for a less-conspicuous gray Volkswagen. The little car had taken them a great distance and they had kept to the smaller roads and away from the jammed autobahns, traveling only when it appeared safe to do so, hiding the vehicle in wooded areas off the road when not. But now they were on foot, for, in their haste, they had neglected to bring along extra cans of petrol. It may have been for the best, though; the roads were too dangerous and SS Colonel von Köhner felt they had pushed their luck far enough in that respect.

The third man in line suddenly stumbled and went down on one knee in the mud. Von Köhner took him by the elbow and gently helped him back to his feet, asking if he might carry the faded leather case for the

*Reichsführer. Himmler shook his head and they contin-
ued their traverse of the field, eyes wary for any other
signs of life.*

*Heinrich Himmler held the leather case containing the
ancient spearhead tightly against his chest, refusing to let
anyone else take possession, unwilling to let it out of his
grasp, even for one second. The others—Reichskriminaldirektor Mueller, Erik Gantzer, and SS Colonel von
Köhner—could carry the money and the valuables that
would buy their escape and insure their freedom. And of
course, the secret files, his beloved files kept through the
years—documents concerning not only the devious activities of his fellow countrymen, but men, influential men, of
other countries. Regretfully, they had taken only the most
important, those which could be used again at another
time; they would have needed ten trucks to bring all the
others along. His three loyal followers would manage
those between them but he, alone, would bear the holy
relic.*

*All four wore civilian clothing, Himmler, Mueller, and
von Köhner having discarded their uniforms at the beginning of the journey, Erik Gantzer a civilian anyway. A
strange and powerful man, this Gantzer, Himmler reflected, studying the tall figure ahead of him. His grandfather,
Otto Gantzer, had been apprenticed to the Royal Prussian
Arms Factory in Spandau, near Berlin, working there as a
master gunsmith for many years until he left to establish
his own business in the port of Rostok, which his son
Ernst, also a master gunsmith, had continued. The
business had prospered after the old man's death, Ernst
developing and diversifying the range of weapons he produced. His son, Erik Gantzer, after graduating from high
school, was apprenticed to the arms factories in Suhl and
Zella-Mehlis, following the family tradition, and eventually took over the whole Gantzer industry when the father
died. Spared from service in the Army because of his immense contribution to the war effort, Erik Gantzer had
played a great part in introducing the Führer himself into
the Thule Gesellschaft, the society in which Gantzer had*

become a key member. He had proved to be extremely useful, a brilliant young man with no conscience, who fought only for the future of the Aryan race. A man whose eventual disenchantment with the madman, Hitler, had led him to switch his allegiance to the Reichsführer himself. And now, even though their beloved country had been crushed, he would still serve him. It was his connections that would see they survived, his genius that would insure the furtherance of the cause! It was he who had devised the escape, planned the route, made the contacts, long before it was inevitable that Germany would lose. He had ignored the normal Nazi escape routes, had dissuaded Himmler from making deals with the Allies, had insisted all was not finished, that the new beginning would be better planned, that more guile, more subterfuge, would be used. Nothing was lost; only the moment delayed.

From Kiel, the boat would take them through the Kieler Bucht, traveling by night till they reached the rough waters of the Store Baelt, then on to Ebeltoft in Denmark, where they would journey overland to a small landing strip owned by a contact of Gantzer's. From there they would fly to Iceland and eventually, when world affairs had moved on to more important matters than the hunting down of elusive Nazis, they would go to Canada, then down into America, and finally, the ironic twist— back across the ocean to England. A bitter smile contorted Himmler's lips at the thought and, if he had had the breath, he would have laughed aloud. No South America for Heinrich Himmler! Let the Bormanns and the Mengeles go there!

He suddenly doubled over as pain wrenched at his gut and, once again, Colonel von Köhner was there to support him. Himmler waved him away, grateful for his concern but indicating he would be all right in a short while. Franz von Köhner: another good man! A true German, prepared to leave his wife and young baby son—as he himself had left his own family, not to mention sweet Hedwig, his mistress—for the good of the cause! It was von Köhner who

*had secretly replaced the real Heilige Lance with a skill-
fully made replica that Himmler himself had had made
even before the annexation of Austria. The fool Hitler
had never realized he possessed only a forgery painstak-
ingly reproduced with metal almost as ancient as the Spear
itself! He, Himmler, kept the original spearhead in the
Wewelsburg, his mighty fortress in Paperdorn, Westphalia,
dedicated to the Teutonic Knights; it was the natural resting place for the legendary relic.*

*Despite the pain, Himmler smiled grimly. Von Köhner
had served him well. And so had Heinz Hintzinger, the
corporal in the Feldpolizei who looked so incredibly like
him! When it had become an indisputable fact that Germany would lose the war, the hunt for doubles had almost
become a game among the Nazi generals and officials, so
many of them unwilling to face the wrath of the Allies.
Cowards, all of them! For Himmler, it was different. It
was his duty to survive! Now that the Führer had lost
his mind, someone had to carry on, to rise like the Phoe-
nix when the ashes had settled. He was that man.*

*Von Köhner had found many who resembled Himmler,
but all had been rejected for Hintzinger; this man was
prepared to die for his Reichsführer. His zeal for the Nazi
cause amounted to fanaticism and the Schutzstaffeln knew
how to use fanatics. He had been sent out under an escort
who believed him to be their real leader, thinly disguised,
and ready to admit he was no less than Heinrich Himmler
himself when caught. And ready to crush the cyanide capsule between his teeth when he was sure the officials believed his statement.*

*Himmler again sank to his knees. He had to rest, just
for a little while. The other three gathered around him, but
he waved them on. See if it was safe on the other side of
the field. Von Köhner could stay with him, help him on
when the pain in his belly had subsided.*

*Mueller and Gantzer turned away, concern on their
faces. They began to trot toward the screening hedge at
the far side of the field.*

Von Köhner squatted beside the Reichsführer and waited patiently.

He had been present when Himmler had received the message from Hitler's successor, Admiral Dönitz, dismissing the SS Reichsführer from the service of the Reich. How could they humble such a great man in that manner, a man who was prepared to fight on when others had given up? He had never looked impressive, this middle-aged man with his paunch, his narrow shoulders and curved back—too many hours hunched over paperwork—but what vision! What stature! The generals—traitors like SS General Wolf—already falling over each other to make deals with the enemy, to save their own necks, were not fit to lick his boots! The untermenschen would never defeat this man!

He wished the mystical masseur, Kerston, was here to ease his master's pain with those strange deft fingers that gave the Reichsführer such instant release. He wished he could provide a glass samovar containing a hot mixture of gentian and dandelion tea, for he knew how it soothed the Reichsführer's stomach pains . . .

The explosion shook the ground beneath their feet and mud and stones spattered their clothing. They looked in horror across the field to where two bodies lay, one still, the other writhing and screaming in agony.

They raced toward the two bodies, wondering which one was dead—Gantzer or Mueller? One of them must have trodden on a landmine or disturbed a concealed unexploded bomb; whoever had made the contact would be the dead one.

They reached the twisting body and realized only by the clothing that it was Erik Gantzer. His knees were hugged to his chest, his hands between them, clutching at his lower body. Von Köhner resisted the urge to vomit as he looked at the arms manufacturer's face—or lack of it. Blood spurted from a red hole in the center of his face, a loose piece of flesh hanging by a thin tendril, the remnants of his nose.

Himmler's stomach was not as strong as the SS

colonel's. He paled and bent over as the contents of his stomach spilled onto the muddy earth. As he looked down, he caught something that made him close his eyes tightly and wheel his body away. Two feet that must have been Mueller's, one still inside a boot, lay on the ground before him. The one in the boot was standing upright, the bloody stump facing up at him, splintered bone showing whitely against the red flesh. His vomit had covered it before he twisted away.

Himmler dropped the leather case containing the spear and fell to his hands and knees and retched, his whole body shuddering with the effort. He crawled, trying to get away from the grotesque sight of Mueller's dismembered feet, and when he finally found the strength to look up, he saw von Köhner's figure kneeling beside the twitching body of Gantzer, a Luger pointed at the injured man's temple.

Himmler staggered to his feet. Gantzer must not be shot. If there was a chance that he might live, no matter what pain he was in, he must be saved!

He pulled von Köhner's arm away just as the SS colonel's finger began to squeeze the trigger. The gun never fired, but when Himmler stared down at Erik Gantzer's body and the mass of blood that covered his face and groin area, he wondered if he, the Reichsführer, should not have been more merciful.

"But Himmler was captured. He was identified before he committed suicide."

Gant laughed and the sound echoed hollowly around the hall. "That was another man, a double. A good German, prepared to die for his Reichsführer. Of course, his family would have suffered if his courage had failed him at the last moment. Fortunately, that was not necessary."

"But he was examined, surely? They'd have had to be sure."

"Can you imagine the confusion that was taking place in Germany at that time, Mr. Steadman, with thousands—millions—fleeing? Have you any idea how many

Germans the Allies caught trying to escape and whom they thought to be Himmler, Goebbels, Göring, or Bormann? Or even Hitler himself? When they found one who confessed to being a Nazi leader and looked exactly like him with his disguise removed, do you really think they questioned the matter in any great detail? And when the chaos began finally to take on some order, it was too late: the body of the Reichsführer had been long buried in an unmarked grave. I promise you, the aftermath of such a war, with each nation fighting over territories like wolves over a dead carcass, is infinitely more complex than the planning of an enemy's defeat. With the removal of the obvious enemy, the allied nations became enemies to each other. It was not difficult for mistakes to be made."

"But where could a man like Himmler go? Surely he would have been recognized?"

"You forget just how insignificant our great leader looked. I mean this as no disrespect, for this was the wonderful dichotomy of the man. He was one of Germany's greatest heroes, yet his appearance was that of an ordinary man."

"I've read that he looked like a typical filing clerk," said Steadman pointedly.

"Exactly, Mr. Steadman," said Gant as though the slight had been a compliment. "A filing clerk with true Nordic blood."

"So his very insignificance allowed his escape?"

"It allowed him to exist in another country."

"Might I ask where? I take it that South America, the obvious place, was out of the question."

"Of course. We could have fled there, lived among the Nazi colony; but we would have been impotent. No, we needed a country where we could build again, not a place where we could sit in the sun and reminisce over the past glories of the fatherland."

"So where, Gant? Where did you choose?"

"Why, England, of course. What better place?"

Steadman looked incredulously at the smiling faces around him. "But that would have been impossible!"

"At the time, yes," said Gant. "Although we had many friends in Great Britain, even then—several were Thulists—many had been interned for the duration of the war because of their sympathies, and were never entirely trusted after.

"No, our first stop was Denmark. It hadn't been our intention, but we stayed hidden there for many months. I had been severely injured, you see. It was the Reichsführer who saved my life."

The arms dealer paused as though the memory was a precious thing. "We left Flensburg on 10th May 1945; Reichsführer Himmler, Colonel Franz von Köhner—the father of the inept fool you disposed of last night, Reichskriminaldirektor Ernest Mueller, and myself. Unfortunately. after making good progress toward Kiel, a bomb killed Mueller and almost killed me. It was only the Reichsführer's intervention that prevented von Köhner from putting a bullet through my brain. Herr Himmler insisted that I should be carried to our rendezvous point, where my wounds could be treated. He even sacrificed his sacred files for my life. They were buried, along with Mueller, in that very same field. Colonel von Köhner carried me, and the Reichsführer carried our valuables and our talisman, the one object he refused to leave behind: the Heilige Lance!

"I was almost dead by the time we reached our contact near Kiel but again Herr Himmler refused to allow me to die. They treated my wounds as best they could and then we went on by sea to Ebeltoft in Denmark. The journey was an extraordinary nightmare for me, Mr. Steadman, and I pleaded with the Reichsführer a hundred times to put me to death; he would not allow it, though. He saw that some day I would be the new leader, the Grand Master, in his place. His vision was far beyond human limitations.

"We stayed in an area far inland from Ebeltoft until I had recovered from my injuries; not fully, you understand, but enough to travel on. From there we were flown to Iceland and, a few years later, to Canada. Seven years passed before we dared enter the United States of America. Our contacts, both in America and England, had been renewed long before, and our movement was already beginning to thrive. We kept undercover, for obvious reasons, allowing the more vulgar nationalistic organizations to take all attention from us. Subterfuge and progressive infiltration has been our policy since the setback."

"You call the last World War a setback?"

"Yes, Mr. Steadman. Nothing more than that!" There was silence around the table as though each member was defying the investigator to refute Gant's statement. Steadman shrugged.

"So Himmler was alive all that time," he said.

Gant nodded solemnly. "Yes. Colonel von Köhner died in '51 while we were still in Canada. A stroke. Before he died he made us promise to find the young son he'd left behind in Germany, and to indoctrinate him into our cause. We readily agreed. The offspring of a man like Franz von Köhner would indeed be valuable to the society. Perhaps it was fortunate for the colonel that he never knew the incompetent his son was to become. The youth, Felix, readily joined us, for in Germany he had nothing. Von Köhner's wife had died shortly after the war and the boy was being raised by relatives. They allowed him to come to us, for they were poor, the war having stripped many such families of their wealth. Felix joined us in England when he was twenty-one."

"When . . . when did you . . . and Himmler come to this country?"

Gant smiled and the smile made Steadman shudder. "In 1963, Mr. Steadman. A historic date."

The others around the table voiced their agreement. "He was very ill by then. The stomach pains that had plagued him most of his life had finally broken his health, but even at that time, we did not realize how serious his condition was . . ."

Steadman was so stunned at the idea of the infamous mass murderer living in England that he missed the arms dealer's next few words. When he had recovered enough to listen again, Gant was talking of his marriage in America.

"Louise was an extremely rich American, from the Deep South. Our ideals matched, for the Southerners' intolerance toward race impurity was almost on a par with the Nazis'. She never really knew the true strength of our ambitions, and the real identity of our permanent, reclusive house guest was kept a secret from her. She suspected he was an ex-Nazi, I'm sure, for she knew I was, but I don't think it ever occurred to her she was housing one of the world's most 'notorious' men. She was an extraordinary woman who shared our ideals and demanded nothing physically from me. She lived only for the day when our ideals would find fruition, and I cannot tell you how much her wealth and contacts furthered our cause. It was tragic that a road accident should have taken her from us so early in our rising."

The whir of helicopter blades suddenly drew everyone's attention. "Ah, that sounds like the arrival of our twelfth member," Gant said.

"It's about time!" said Lord Ewing, the news magnate.

"The general has had a long journey," Gant reproached, and the man fell silent.

Astonished by the arms dealer's authority over such powerful men, Steadman looked around the table at each one in turn, then said, "How can you follow a man like this? An ex-Nazi, a man who helped one of the most evil men in history, a man who fought against us in the war. How cay you betray your country for someone like that?"

"Betray? You're the one who's a traitor, Steadman," said Talgholm. "You claim to be British, but you'd sit by while the country sinks. What kind of loyalty is that?"

"Look . . ." Steadman began.

"Shut up!" It was Ewing who shouted across the table, his face red, his eyes bulbous with rage. "We're sick of do-gooders like you. Live and let live, that's what you believe, don't you? Do you think *they'll* let us live once they've taken over? Your kind are almost as bad as them!"

"Let's get rid of him now, Edward," came another cry.

"Yes, we don't need him," Talgholm agreed. "The legend will still be fulfilled."

"Not yet!" Gant's voice was stern. "You know how it's to be done."

"We're running short . . ."

"There is time." The pronouncement was made quietly, but the assembled group became silent again.

"Tell me more, Gant," Steadman said with a calm he hardly felt. "How . . . where did Himmler live in this country?"

"Always in this area, Mr. Steadman. He was fascinated by the Arthurian legends. King Arthur's knights were based on the Teutonic Order, and their activities took place mainly in this part of the country. He was so overjoyed when I had the Wewelsburg built here for him.

"The Thule Gesellschaft was a wealthy organization by then. The arms industry I had set up, aided substantially by the money my dear late wife had left me, was thriving, and donations from our secret members were flooding in. We had recovered the files von Köhner had buried so many years before and they opened many . . ." he smiled and looked at the faces around the table ". . . so many doors for us."

Steadman began to realize how blackmail had played such an important part in the rebuilding of their movement.

"The Reichsführer, despite the pain he was in, was very happy in his final days," the arms dealer said softly. "He knew this time we would win."

"He died here?" Steadman asked, somehow—inexplicably—expecting a denial of the Reichsführer's death, for his presence felt so real.

"Yes, Mr. Steadman. In a sense. He was sixty-seven when cancer took his life. But even though his body failed him, his spirit did not. Almost a year after his death he sent someone to us." Gant turned to Dr. Scheuer seated next to him. "Dr. Scheuer was a spiritualist living in Austria. The Reichsführer chose the Herr Doktor to be his intermediary."

At that point, approaching footsteps were heard outside the hall. A door set back in the shadows against the wall opened and a broad-shouldered figure strode in briskly followed by Major Brannigan.

"Good evening, gentlemen." The voice was unmistakeably American, and when the man drew closer to the light, Steadman groaned inwardly as he recognized him. The assembly stood in deference as he took his place in the empty chair beside Dr. Scheuer.

"Is this the man?" He glowered across at Steadman.

"Yes, General, this is our Parsifal," Gant said smoothly "Mr. Steadman. I'm sure you recognize Major-General Cutbush, the US forces deputy commander."

They weren't crazy at all, Steadman realized. They really had the power and influence to dominate a nation's thinking. Over the years, by bribery, blackmail, or sheer mutual agreement on racial ideals, they'd built up an incredible force, a force strong enough to direct public motivation wavering between the two extremes toward their own aims. It was just the worship of the dead Himmler and all it entailed that was their madness, and he was puzzled at the necrophiliac devotion displayed by such men. What could instigate such an insanity? Suddenly, he was terrified.

"Okay, Edward, I said I'd go along with all this because *he* wanted it this way." The American's burly figure and grizzled features looked strange to Steadman, for he had been used to seeing pictures and film of him in full military uniform "But I don't like it one bit. It's too . . ." he searched for the word ". . . theatrical."

"I understand your feelings, General, but it would be unwise not to comply with *his* wishes now," said Gant.

"Maybe," the general said gruffly, "but I still don't like it. Brannigan!" The British major flinched to attention. "Shouldn't you be at the launching site?"

"We were just waiting for your arrival, sir. I'm on my

way now." Brannigan marched from the room, his back stiff and his stride determined.

"Goddamn fag," Cutbush muttered to no one in particular when the door closed. "Okay, let's get on."

Gant stood and made to move away from the table toward the dais, but Steadman's shout stopped him.

"For God's sake, General, you're a veteran of the Second World War. You fought against men like him!" The investigator's finger was pointing at Gant and the two guards on either side had stepped forward and clamped their hands on his shoulders to prevent him from rising from the chair.

The general looked across at him and his eyes narrowed. "Now you . . . shut . . . your . . . mouth, mister. Sure, I fought against him and his kind. That was my mistake. I was with Patton throughout the damn war and I saw how his ass was kicked around by the so-called free-thinking leaders of our country. We had long chats, the old war-horse and me, and I know the kind of man he was. He saw the Russian threat while everyone else was still messing with the Germans. He wanted to march right through Germany and straight on into Moscow itself! It was he who told me the legend of the spear—even though he was a pragmatist, he had a deep belief in such things— an' I was with him in a Nuremberg bunker when he thought he'd found it. We didn't know it then, but there'd been a switch. 'Blood and Guts' never could figure out why nothing had happened for him. Himmler had already vamoosed with it!

"Now I don't mind admitting it: General Patton was my God, an' if he said there was something in the legend, there sure as hell was! I saw what they did to Patton when they no longer needed him. You think the car smash that killed him after the war was an accident? And I see what they're trying to do to me because they think I'm not needed. Old 'Blood and Guts' became an embarrassment to them because of his aggressiveness, and they feel the same about my hard-line views. But unlike the general, I started making plans a long, long time ago and it was our good fortune . . ." he waved his hand around the table ". . . that Edward Gant brought us together. We all believe in the same thing, sonny, and we don't need any crap about who we were fightin' in the last fuckin' war!"

Steadman relaxed back into his chair and managed to stare insolently at Cutbush. "So they were putting you out to pasture."

"You fuckin' crud. I'll break . . ." Gant checked the general's rising figure with a hand on his shoulder. The general sat but glowered at the investigator. "I'm goin' to enjoy the next few minutes, jerk," he said.

Steadman returned the glare.

Gant nodded at Griggs and Booth, and Steadman felt his arms gripped tightly.

"The time has come, Parsifal," Gant said, walking toward the dais. He reached inside the leather case and turned with a long dark object in his hands. Steadman saw it was the spearhead, the holy relic whose legendary powers had caused the bloodshed of millions and the glory of a chosen few. There was no shine to the ancient black metal only a dull glow from the section of gold but the blade still tapered to a menacing point. Gant placed it on the table, its flattened blade pointed toward the investigator.

Steadman looked at the ancient relic and began to tremble inwardly. It was strange, but it felt as if a force were emanating from the cold metal, a force that was already piercing his heart. And then, he knew what was to be his fate—he was to die from a spear thrust. Gant would refute the Parsifal legend by using the weapon itself to kill his adversary.

He closed his eyes, but the image was still there in his mind: the evil tapering blade, the nail driven into an aperture in the blade, the small crosses engraved in the dark metal. He tried to force it from his thoughts but it stayed, a cold, dark object, a dead thing that somehow thrummed with energy. In his mind's eye he saw it was blood-stained.

"Can you feel its power, Parsifal?"

Steadman opened his eyes and now he saw the spearhead only as an aged piece of metal, lifeless and cold. He tore his eyes away and looked into the face of Gant, who was leaning forward over the spear.

"Do you know Wolfram von Eschenbach's legend of Parsifal?" The arms dealer's eyes seemed to glow in the darkness of the room. "The legend which inspired Wagner's mystical opera. Parsifal served the dying king Amfortas and sought to regain the Spear of Longinus, the holy symbol, for his master. As you sought to regain it for your masters—the Jews!"

"That's not true!" The hands on Steadman's arms tightened their grip. "They wanted me to find their missing agent, Baruch Kanaan. You know that!"

"Lies, Parsifal. Their agent came for the spear and when he failed, they sent you."

Why hadn't Goldblatt told him of the spear? Why hadn't he leveled with him from the start? The woman, Hannah, when she lay dying in his arms, had told him to find the spear. But why hadn't they told him at the very beginning? Did they assume that finding Baruch would lead them to the ancient weapon? Resentment rose up in Steadman. They had used him just as the Thulists were using him. He'd been manipulated by both sides, one side using him as a tool, a lever to uncover a viper's nest, the other using him as a player in a symbolic ritual.

"You were to kill me, just as the knight Parsifal killed Klingsor, who held the spear at his castle. Klingsor, the evil magician whose manhood was cut away by the fool king—as mine was taken from me. A sword took Klingsor's testicles from his body—an explosion took mine. The Reichsführer saved my life and when he saw the damage that was done to me, he *knew* I was Klingsor reincarnated! He knew I would be the future bearer of the Spear of Longinus."

Gant's shoulders were heaving with the mental stress he was going through. To Steadman, it seemed as though the man was possessed. Abruptly, the tone of the arms

dealer's voice changed, and he spoke as if he were revealing a long-kept secret to friends.

"The legend, you see, was neither a myth nor a
prophecy. It was a warning. Von Eschenbach was our
guide from the thirteenth century. He was warning us of
the disaster that could come if we allowed it. And he
warned us again at the appropriate time in this century
through Richard Wagner!"

"It's fantasy, Gant. Can't any of you see that?" There
was desperation in Steadman's voice now. "You're just
twisting everything to make it seem as if the story is coming true. I'm not your Parsifal and he's not your Klingsor.
The spear has no power. It's all in *his* mind!"

A rough hand was cupped over his mouth and his head
jerked back. He tried to twist away, but Griggs held him
firmly.

"No, it's not all in *my* mind, Mr. Steadman," Gant said
calmly. "We are led by another. Someone who knows you
now. Someone who sent a tank against you as a test.
Someone who visited you at your home just two nights
ago, but who was disturbed by the meddling old Jew.
Someone who wishes to meet you again." Gant chuckled.
"As it were, face to face."

There was silence in the vast room, the shadows flickering and weaving with the dancing candle flames. Gant
sat and the thirteen around the table put their hands on
its rough surface as though a signal had been given. Their
fingers touched and Steadman could see that their eyes
had closed and each man's face was creased in concentration. Nothing happened for a while, then suddenly he felt
his muscles weakening as if all strength was being drained
from them. His head was released and he felt rather than
saw the two MI5 men step back from their position
directly behind. He tried to rise but found he couldn't; an
invisible force seemed to be holding him there. He opened
his mouth to speak but no sound came. The sudden oppression in the room had become an increasing pressure,
weighing down on him like a physical force. He saw that
several members of the circle were sagging in their seats,

their heads lolling forward as though their energy was being sapped. Dr. Scheuer's head was resting almost on his chest.

A stillness had crept into the room. The candle flames seemed to be frozen solid, their light dimmed. It became cold. A terrible, cloying coldness that closed in and gripped the skin. An odor pervaded the air and the room became even darker, the chill more intense.

Steadman stared hard into the shadows behind Gant and Dr. Scheuer, for he thought he had seen something move, a dark shape against a black backcloth. From the balcony overlooking the hall, he had noticed steps set to one side of the room leading down to a door, the top half only, level with the floor. The black shape had seemed to emerge from that point. But now it had disappeared and he wondered if it had been merely a trick of the fading light.

A humming vibration reached his ears and his attention was drawn to the table's surface. Some of the Thulists' heads were sagging, almost resting on the table but still their fingers touched, trembling and grayish in the poor light. His eyes came to rest on the dark object lying opposite, and somehow he knew that was the source of the vibration. The ancient weapon lay unmoving, yet it seemed to throb with some inner life. He shook his head and the effort seemed almost too much; he felt giddy with fatigue. He knew the humming vibration was only in his own head, yet it seemed to come so definitely from the talisman. He became weaker and for a moment his eyes rolled in his head; he had to fight consciously to control them. He found himself looking across the table at the bowed head of the old man, Dr. Scheuer, the scant white hair hanging loosely around his hidden face.

Steadman stared, for it seemed all the energy in the room had been drawn into the old man. The others, those who could, were watching him too, their bodies swaying slightly. The investigator fought against the weariness, trying to build a wall in his mind against the will-devouring force. But he could not tear away his eyes from the bowed head of Dr. Scheuer.

As he looked, the white-haired figure began to straighten. The head came up, slowly, smoothly, taking long, long seconds for the eyes to meet Steadman's. And when they finally looked deep and penetratingly into his, the investigator's blood seemed to stop flowing, and the hair on his neck rose as though a cold hand had swept it upward, for he found himself staring at the hate-filled image of SS Reichsführer Heinrich Himmler.

═══ NINETEEN ═══

> *Though he had the mind of an ordinary clerk or schoolmaster he was dominated by another Himmler whose imagination was controlled by such phrases as "The preservation of the Germanic race justifies cruelty," or, "Unqualified obedience to the Führer." This other Himmler entered realms which transcended the merely human and entered into another world.*
>
> ——FELIX KERSTON

> *For us the end of this war will mean an open road to the East, the creation of the Germanic Reich in this way or that . . .*
>
> ——HEINRICH HIMMLER

Holly crept stealthily down the corridor using only the balls of her feet, measuring each step and gently easing her weight onto the solid floorboards. There was a tension in the house that had nothing to do with her own nervousness. The air was heavy with it.

She wondered about the strange building, half house, half castle. What was the purpose of such a place? She had found her way toward the back of the house, heading for the baronial-type rooms she had seen only from the outside. There had been only a blank wall at the end of the corridor leading from her room—it was too short to have run the length of the house—and she had been forced to retrace her steps to the staircase near the front of the house.

Guessing it might be a mistake to descend—bound to be more guards around—she had decided to go up onto the next level and make her way back from there. There had to be another way of getting to the rear of the house on the second floor. She moved silently up the stairs, holding the miniature machine gun ahead of her, wishing she had taken time to search the unconscious guard for the silencer that went with the deadly weapon. She knew that the Ingram MAC II, on which this weapon's design had been based, could be fitted with a lightweight sound suppressor which cut out even the light "plopping" noise silenced guns usually made. She would have to take her chances without it—if someone discovered her, she would shoot to kill and to hell with the noise.

She reached the tip of the stairs and paused. The house was deadly silent.

The long corridor running down the building's center lay ahead of her, two minor corridors ran to the left and right from her position at the top of the stairs. She had just begun her long walk down the central corridor when a door ahead opened.

Her reaction was fast. She ducked back into the left-hand corridor, prepared to run its length if the footsteps came her way. They didn't; she heard the footsteps receding into the distance. She stole a quick look around the corridor's corner and caught sight of the woman, the one they called Kristina. She was holding the side of her face as though she had been hurt and Holly caught a glimpse of her leaning against the wall momentarily for support. Holly held her breath, waiting for the footsteps to fade away. She was a strange one, this woman, Holly felt intuitively. She couldn't quite understand why, but was distinctly uneasy in her presence when Gant had introduced her. Not that she'd felt at home with the arms dealer himself.

She took another look and saw that the woman had vanished. Good. She'd definitely walked the length of the corridor, so maybe she was headed for the back of the house. There had to be a way through. Holly stole down the passageway.

There was a T-junction at the end and Holly debated with herself which way to go. She chose the right and at the end of it found a solid-looking oak door, its intricate carving suggesting it wasn't just the door to the broom closet. She tried the wrought-iron handle and discovered it was locked. Okay, the left-hand turn might have a similar door. It did, and this one was open.

It was like stepping into another world: the walls on either side of the dim passageway were of heavy gray stone and the doors along its length again were of delicately carved oak. The lights overhead were deliberately dim so their brightness would not jar against the medieval atmosphere. Holly moved forward, carefully closing the door leading from the new to the fake old behind her. If anything, the tension was even more acute in this part of the unusual house.

She crept forward, remembering to breathe again. Fainting from lack of oxygen wasn't going to help her any.

Holly stopped at one of the doors on her left and listened: no sounds came from within. She noticed a name was inscribed in the carving of the door and tried to decipher it in the poor light. It looked like Philip of . . . somewhere-or-other . . . Swabia? That was it. Where the hell was Swabia? She moved on to the next door which was even more difficult to read. Frederick Hohen . . . oh, what difference? She listened again, but still heard nothing. She gently tried the handle and found the door was unlocked. Pushing it open slowly and pointing the gun into the widening crack, she peered into the dark room. Deciding it really was empty, she pushed the door wide and was provided with a soft light from the hallway.

The room was furnished with antiques and smelled musty, unused. A four-poster bed dominated the floor space and a portrait of someone in ceremonial—or at least, ancient—garb hung over the mantel. Maybe that was Fred what's-his-name. Holly closed the door and went on to the next room. She was able to make out Henry I on this one and sheer instinct told her that this time the room was not empty. The question was: to look in or not to look in? Well, she decided ruefully, I'm not going to find Harry by not looking for him. She turned the handle as softly as she could.

The odor hit her nostrils immediately, vile and unclean; it was as if a malevolent spirit was rushing past her, fleeing through the opening she had created. It was a smell of dust, human sweat—and something else. Rank meat? No, it was indefinable. She pushed the door open further.

Holly saw the rows of books lining the walls first, then, as she cautiously stepped into the room, its other contents were revealed to her. It was a larger room than the one she had just peeked into, containing a long, solid-looking desk, two high-backed chairs, a carpet of richly woven design, the shelves running around the walls on three sides, holding volumes of books. In a break between the shelves to her left hung a picture—it looked like a portrait in the dim light—and again, the subject seemed to be wearing the clothing of centuries before. Old Henry, presumably. Opposite, on the wall to her right, another picture hung between two bookshelves, its enclosure almost shrinelike. It was a portrait also, but this time the clothing was not as ancient. The man in the picture wore a uniform. A black uniform.

She guessed the identity of the subject: the modern-day Nazis still worshiped their old heroes.

A sudden sound drew her attention toward the desk. Something had moved there, she was sure. She raised the machine gun, her hand trembling slightly. Above the desk, between the heavy drapes concealing the room's two high windows, hung their symbol—the white circle on a red background, the circle containing the evil black swastika. She felt exposed under its glare and suddenly sensed that the two portraits on either side were watching her. She quickly shrugged off the uncanny feeling.

Again she heard the noise, a slivering sound as if something had dragged along the floor. It came from behind the desk.

She wondered if she should turn and run, but quickly dismissed the thought. If someone was hiding from her, someone who'd seen she had a gun, they would raise the alarm as soon as she left the room. Whoever it was had to be temporarily put out of action. The decision made, she crept toward the desk.

It was a wide-top desk and its base was solid, a panel covering the center leg space. It was a pity, for Holly could not duck down to see if anyone was lurking behind. The smell seemed to hit her in waves now, but it was human staleness that dominated the general rancidity of the room.

The natural course of action would have been to move around the desk, rapidly but cautiously, ready to spring away from anybody crouched behind it; Holly believed in unpredictability, though. She smoothly swung her hip onto the desk and slid herself across its surface, ready to poke the machine gun into any inquiring face. As she peered over the edge she realized she had been mistaken: the noise hadn't come from beneath it, but beyond it.

What looked like a bundle of rags lay on the floor against the wall and, even in the gloomy light from the hallway, she could see two frightened eyes staring at her. The bedraggled figure seemed to be pushing itself away, trying to sink into the wall itself. That had been the sounds she had heard: the slivering of bare feet on the floor, as the figure had tried hopelessly to get away from whoever had entered the room.

Holly slid off the desk and knelt beside the quivering bundle and it was then she realized the figure was that of a man and that he was cruelly tied, a nooselike rope around his neck, biting into the flesh, making it raw: the rope stretched down behind his back to bound wrists and ankles. A shirt hung loosely around him, the front completely open and exposing a chest which bore the marks of severe beatings. His trousers were filthy and stiff with stains as though the man had soiled himself many times. He lay on his side, his neck craned around to see her, and she noticed his wrists and ankles were caked in dry blood caused by the tightness of the ropes. Fresh blood was seeping around the ropes binding his ankles, probably caused by his struggle to get away from her. His hair was completely white, yet, as she looked into his frightened eyes, she realized he was not an old man. His face was lined with strain, heavy dark circles surrounding his eyes, the lips cracked and sore. But even through that, and through the bruises and dried blood that marred his features, she could see he was young. His face had aged not because of years but because of shock. She'd seen the same kind of aging in released Vietnam prisoners—the ones who had been returned to their own country, but would probably never return to their own homes. Their minds had deteriorated beyond repair.

"Who are you?" she whispered.

The eyes only watched her in terror.

"Can't you speak? Can't you tell me who you are?"

Still the eyes watched her, but now a wariness had crept into them.

"Look, I'm a friend," Holly tried to reassure him. "I'm not with these people, I'm against them. Something's going to happen here tonight that I've got to prevent and time's running out. You've got to tell me who you are."

She reached forward to touch his shoulder and the figure tried desperately to move away. The sudden movement jerked the noose around his neck tighter and a gurgling noise came from his throat as he began to choke.

"Hey, take it easy," Holly whispered in alarm. She grabbed his wrists and pulled them upward to ease the pressure on the noose. He stopped twisting and kept his body still. Holly wondered if his mind was functioning normally again or sheer animal instinct had made him stop moving.

"Look, I'm going to untie these ropes, but before I do,

I want you to realize I'm not with the people who did this to you. I'm a friend, okay?" Holly placed the machine gun on the floor and reached for the ropes binding his wrists. The knots were difficult, obviously pulled tighter by the man's own efforts to free himself. She looked around for something sharp to cut them with. Rising, she scanned the desk-top and found what she had been searching for. The letter opener had a long point to it and could be pushed between the twists of rope to loosen the knots. She knelt beside the tensed figure again, placing her free hand on his upper arm. This time, he did not flinch.

"I'm going to get you free with this, so just try and relax. If you pull against the ropes they'll only get tighter."

Holly tossed her hair back over her shoulder and set to work on the knots.

It took several minutes, but eventually she pulled with her fingers, using the knife as a lever, and then his wrists were free, one length of rope hanging loose from his neck, the other from his still bound ankles.

Holly breathed a sigh of relief and relaxed onto her haunches. She examined her broken fingernails and shrugged. "I hate long nails, any . . ." The man pushed her back with a strength that belied his appearance. He grabbed the gun lying on the floor and pointed it at her, using two hands to hold the light weapon steady.

"Do not move," he hissed fiercely. The three words were thickly accented.

"Hey, I'm trying to help you," said Holly from her prone position. "We're on the same side—I think." She bit her lip when she saw him flick the safety catch off. "I was trying to help you," she said desperately.

"Who are you?" His eyes were burning, all fear from them now gone. "Why are you here?"

"My name's Holly Miles. I'm a free-lance writer." Better to tell him that, she thought. Better to find out more about him first. "I was doing a feature on Edward Gant as an arms dealer until I found out he was into something more sinister."

His eyes darted around the room, wild again.

"Can't you tell me your name?" she pleaded. "I promise you I've nothing to do with Gant."

His eyes came to rest on her again. "How do I know that?"

"I set you free, didn't I?"

He sagged back against the wall as though the sudden effort had drained him of any strength he had left. His bound feet slid out from beneath him and came to rest against Holly's denimed legs. He motioned at her with the gun and murmured, "Untie them."

She began to work at the knots again with the letter opener.

"Why would a journalist carry a gun like this?" he asked, indicating he still had his wits about him even in his weakened state.

Holly threw caution to the wind and told him everything, realizing she had to move fast, had to trust the man. She thought he showed some reaction when she mentioned Harry Steadman's name and that he was also being held a prisoner in the house, but he sat up in alarm when she told him of the proposed plan for the US secretary of state's jet.

"The missile site—where is it?" he asked, his feet free now. He tried to rise, but the circulation was still not flowing freely.

"At the back of the house, toward the cliffs." Holly moved closer to him and he waved her back with the gun's barrel.

"You've got to trust me," she cried out in frustration. "Someone might come along at any moment!"

He ran a hand across his face, wincing in pain as it touched the bruises. "I . . . I don't know. They've done so much to me. I cannot think."

"How long have they kept you here?"

"Years . . . years. No, it cannot be. I do not know."

"Let me help you," she said softly.

"They used me. They used my strength!" The man rolled his head in despair. "They left me in this room so *he* could take my strength."

"Who?" Holly urged. "Who took your strength?"

"Him . . . him . . ." He pointed the machine gun at the picture on the wall behind them. She saw his finger tighten on the trigger and for a moment she thought he would fire at the portrait.

"No, don't," she said quickly. "You'll bring the whole house down on us."

The hand holding the weapon dropped limply to his side and she exhaled in relief. "How did they take your strength?" she asked him.

"They . . . beat . . . me. Kept me tied . . . in here. That is how . . . he survives. He draws . . . power . . . from others. Used me."

Holly shook her head, not understanding. She glanced down at her wristwatch. 12:35. "Look, we have to get moving. You must trust me."

He nodded, knowing there was no choice. Some of his strength was returning, but he didn't know how long it would last. They had barely fed him, just given him enough to keep him alive. Had it been years? Or was it really only weeks? Time had become meaningless to him. He had been able to stand the beatings—for a while, anyway. It was the other things that had defeated him. The humiliation. The abuse of his body by the freak human, the one that was both man and woman. The base things they had made him do with the creature, taking away his manhood, shaming him . . . . Tears clouded his vision and his shaking hand wiped them from his eyes.

He had told them everything they wanted to know, for eventually they had reduced him to an animal state. The man, Köhner, how well he knew the most vulnerable parts of the body, where to apply pressure, where to insert a blade. Even worse were the nights alone in this room where *he* had visited him—the Jew hater—mocking him and existing parasitically on his spirit. Had it all been in his own mind? Had they finally driven him mad with their torture?

But even more terrible than that were the times they had taken him to the strange room below, beneath the great hall. To the room they called the crypt.

It was there that all previous horrors had been surpassed.

He felt the girl shaking him and he opened his eyes to look into her concerned face. He had to trust her; there was nothing else he could do.

"Will you help me?" she was saying. He nodded his head and she gently took the light machine gun from his loose grip.

"Tell me, then," she said. "Who are you? Tell me your name."

"Baruch Kanaan," he said. "My name is Baruch Kanaan."

The commissioner looked around the ring of tense faces. Operational HQ had become the interior of the church overlooking the Gant estate. The vicar, who had been roused from his peaceful evening by the fireside in his nearby house earlier that evening, was busy organizing relays of coffee for the bitterly cold men, and had even allowed the ancient church's heating system to be switched on to combat the icy cold. It was no match for the wind that had collected its chill from the ocean and sought to invade any opening in the old masonry it could find.

The commissioner knew his men were impatient for action; this was always the worst time for them, waiting and praying they'd come out of it all right. It bothered him too; he liked to get things over with. However, the years had taught him to be patient. So much harm could be done by rushing in at the wrong time. Sir Robert had been a great advocate of patience and the commissioner had learned well from him.

He caught sight of the man called Blake, the retired policeman who worked for Steadman's agency. Blake's face was anxious and he was looking at the commissioner as though deciding whether to approach him or not. The police chief beckoned him over and Blake bounded forward like a puppy to its master.

"We'll be going in at any moment, Mr. Blake, so please try not to worry."

"I'm sorry, sir, I don't mean to be an old woman, but Mr. Steadman has been in there for quite some time."

The commissioner nodded sympathetically. "I know that, but if we move in now we could upset some carefully laid plans."

"I don't understand, sir," said Sexton, puzzled.

"We're waiting for one last guest to arrive. The others—those we know about—have already been accounted for. Their movements have been watched for weeks and we're sure they're all down there with Edward Gant. They make a powerful group and we can't just barge in and arrest them purely on grounds of conspiracy. They have to be taken away and broken separately. I've spent most of the day with our American colleagues in Central Intelligence persuading the prime minister to let us do so."

Sexton caught his breath. This really was the big one.

"We've got a fair amount of evidence on this group, but much of it is circumstantial," the commissioner went on. "We need to catch them red-handed and then, as I say, break down their stories individually. Thanks to your employer, Harry Steadman, I don't think that will be too difficult. He seems to have triggered off quite a bit of action."

"But did you know what Harry—I mean Mr. Steadman—was getting into all this time? Did you know about this man Pope?"

The commissioner raised a hand as if to ward off Sexton's questions.

"We've known about Nigel Pope for some time; his intolerance toward his superiors and his own colleagues could hardly go unnoticed. But he was part of the pattern and we couldn't remove him without destroying the whole framework. It had to be allowed to fester so it could be lanced once and for all—at the right time. Harry Steadman is the instrument we are using for drawing the poison."

"You could have warned him . . ."

"No. Mr. Blake We didn't know his part in the whole business. He appeared out of the blue. For all we knew, he was one of them."

"But Mrs. Wyeth!"

The commissioner had the good grace to look down at his shoes. "I'm afraid we weren't aware of any involvement from your agency at that time. It was most unfortunate." He looked up again and gazed steadily into Sexton's eyes. "We were only really sure of Steadman's good intent when he sent us the warning through you last night."

Sexton shook his head wearily. "I don't pretend to understand all this, commissioner, but it seems to me no one was really bothered about Harry getting himself killed. He was getting kicked from all sides."

"Not at all, Mr. Blake," said the American who had just returned from the vicar's house where he had been using the telephone. "We just allowed him to wander around loose for a while until we could be sure of him."

"And even if he was straight, he might stir something up anyway. Is that right?"

The American smiled, his chubby face friendly but his eyes steely. "You got it, Mr. Blake. Let me say, though, we had someone watching out for him some of the time." He suddenly turned to the commissioner, his manner now brusque "We got the word from your man outside on the radio. Commissioner; I said I'd let you know. The last helicopter just landed. The general's in."

"Right, I'll give the order to move in immediately."

"Also, there's activity around the estate's perimeter. Gant's private army is keeping the area tightly sealed. I guess." The American frowned and looked at his watch. "I'd be happier if we really knew if this meeting tonight has anything to do with the secretary of state's arrival in the country."

"They'll be able to tell us that themselves."

"I wouldn't count on it."

The commissioner did not bother to reply. Instead he began issuing orders to the Special Branch officers around him. When his men were moving he turned back to the American. "I'll be going in immediately after the first assault. Will you be with me?"

"Sure," the American said, smiling pleasantly. "I wouldn't miss it."

"You'll have to stay here I'm afraid, Mr. Blake," the commissioner said, then he was gone, his officers jumping from his path. He disappeared through the church doorway. The American tucked his hands into his overcoat pockets and headed after the commissioner. Sexton caught his arm.

"You said someone was looking out for him some of the time. Who was it?"

The American grinned. "One of our agents. Girl by the name of Holly Miles. We poached her from our Domestic Operations Division when we discovered she was a distant relation of Edward Gant's late wife. She's in there with Steadman now."

Blake was left standing alone in the empty church.

═══ TWENTY ═══

I witnessed for the first time some of the rather strange practices resorted to by Himmler through his inclination toward mysticism. He assembled twelve of his most trusted SS leaders in a room next to the one in which von Fritsch was being questioned and ordered them all to concentrate their minds on exerting a suggestive influence over the general that would induce him to tell the truth. I happened to come into the room by accident, and to see these twelve SS leaders, all sunk in deep and silent contemplation, was indeed a remarkable sight.

—WALTER SCHELLENBERG

The Beast does not look what he is. He may even have a comic moustache.

—SOLOVIEV: *The Anti-Christ*

Steadman's muscles were locked rigid.

His mind tried desperately to deny the vision his eyes saw so clearly. Heinrich Himmler was dead! Even if he had not killed himself at the end of the war as the world believed, the arms dealer had said the Reichsführer had died of cancer at sixty-seven. Yet he was here in this room, his eyes burning with life!

Hypnosis, Steadman rationalized. It had to be hypnosis of some kind. It couldn't really be happening.

"*Ist das der lebendige Parsifal?*" It was a thin, piping voice, completely different from Dr. Scheuer's, and came from the apparition that had somehow superimposed itself over the old man's features.

"*Ja, mein Reichsführer, der ist unser Feind.*" It was Gant who spoke, his face shining in a strange ecstasy.

The men around the table were staring at the vision, some rapturously, others in fear. They all appeared unsteady, as though their energy had been drawn. One or two could barely lift their heads off the table. The figure of Kristina lay inert in her chair.

Gant spoke again, a deferential tone to his voice. "*Herr Reichsführer, darf ich ergebenst darum bitten, dass wir uns auf Englisch unterhalten? Viele Mitglieder unseres Ordens verstehen nicht unsere eigene Sprache.*"

"*Er versteht sie.*" The words were hissed and the apparition glowered at the investigator.

Steadman flinched. The vision was so real: the pudgy white face and small piglike eyes; the clipped moustache and hair cropped to a point well above the ears; the finely formed lips marred by a weak chin receding into a flabby neck. Was it just a dream? Would he wake soon?

The figure began to rise and it was stooped, still in the shape of Dr. Scheuer; its eyes never left Steadman's. It smiled evilly. "Do you feel weak, Parsifal?" The words were spoken in English. A snigger from the apparition rang around the room. "They feel it too. But they give me their strength willingly, while you resist."

The investigator tried to move his arms and found it impossible. It was all he could do to hold his head up. He tried to speak, to shout, to scream, but only a rasping sound came from his throat.

"It's useless to struggle," said Edward Gant as the macabre creature beside him chuckled. "You cannot resist his will. This is how the Reichsführer still lives, you see. He draws etheric energies from the living, and feeds upon them. Adolph Hitler could do this when he lived. Heinrich

Himmler learned the art, with the help of Dr. Scheuer, when he was dead."

"*Adolf. Ja, der liebe Adolf. Wo ist er doch jetzt? Nicht mit uns.*" The figure swayed and a hand rested against the tabletop. The head sank for a moment and the image of Himmler's face seemed to waver, become less distinct. Then the moment was gone and the head rose again, the small eyes piercing into Steadman's, transfixing him.

"It is time, Herr Gantzer. He must die now. His death will signify our beginning."

"Yes, Reichsführer. It has finally come." Gant reached forward for the ancient relic lying on the table's rough surface. "The spear that protects the Holy Grail, Reichsführer. Take it now and feel its potency. Let its force flow through you. *Use its power!*"

The figure took the Spear of Longinus from Gant and held it in both hands. The weapon quivered in the apparition's hands and Steadman sensed or saw—it was all the same now—the light emanating from it. A blueness seemed to glow from the worn metal and the light stretched and grew, traveling over the gnarled hands that were still those of the old man, up along the arms, spreading and enveloping the frail body.

The figure began to straighten and Steadman could hear a screaming sound tearing around the hall, screeching from corner to corner, an inhuman cry that told of unseen demons. The coldness of the room deepened, becoming so intense that Steadman felt ice stiffening against his skin. His limbs were trembling uncontrollably, his hands a shaking blur. He wanted to cry out against the screaming cacophony of the unseen things, but only frosty air escaped his lips. The sounds tore from wall to wall like birds trapped in a dark room, screeching across the round table, sometimes beneath it, the seated men shying away as though their flesh had been touched by something unholy. The strident pitch grew louder, higher, reaching a crescendo.

Steadman saw the figure was no longer stooped and frail; it stood erect, powerfully vibrant. The etheric glow encompassed the whole body and the spear was held in arms stretched rigid at chest level. The face of Himmler was directed toward the ceiling, the eyes closed but movement beneath the eyelids showed that the pupils were active. The lids began to open slowly and Steadman could just see the slits of white between them. Then the head began to lower and the screaming became even more shrill. The investigator pushed himself against the chair, trying to break free of the invisible bonds that held his body and mind. It was no use, his strength was no longer there.

He could not tear his eyes from the face of Himmler even though he managed to twist his head; no matter in which direction he turned, his eyes remained locked on the creature before him.

The face was directed at him, watching his vain struggle with a grin made vile both by its intent and the shiny wetness of the lips. The eyes were watching him, but the fully opened lids revealed only blank whiteness; the pupils were still turned inside the head. The figure laughed aloud and the laughter mingled with the undulating screams. Suddenly the pupils dropped into place and Steadman tried to close his own eyes against their glare.

He had to make himself move! He had to will himself to run!

The figure began to move, the spear held before it. Around the table it came, moving nearer to the investigator, the wicked point aimed low, ready to strike at his heart.

Gant was on his feet, his face covered with a sheen of excitement. This was the time! This was the time for Parsifal to die, not by the hands of Klingsor, but by the true Master—*the Antichrist*! And the Spear of Longinus would pierce the side of their adversary just as it had pierced the side of the Nazarene two thousand years before!

The figure raised the spear higher, but the point was still aimed at Steadman's heart. It was drawing near to him now, still walking slowly around the huge table, the eyes always on him, holding him there. And then the figure was looming over him, the blackened spearhead held in two hands, raised above the head, ready to strike deep into his heart.

He was aware that the screaming had reached fever pitch, and the air was being violently disturbed by the frenzied, unseen things. He was aware that he was going to die by the hand of this unclean, drooling demon who bore the features of a man the world had despised. And he was aware there was nothing he could do to save himself.

But as the ancient weapon quivered at its zenith, ready to plunge into his unprotected chest, the table's surface erupted in an explosion of flying splinters. The bullets embedded themselves in the old wood, then spattered into the soft body of the creature bearing the Spear of Longinus.

TWENTY-ONE

We shall never capitulate—no, never. We may be destroyed, but if we are, we shall drag a world with us—a world in flames.

> —ADOLF HITLER

I am a strong believer that, in the end, only good blood can achieve the greatest, most enduring things in the world.

> —HEINRICH HIMMLER

Jagged splinters from the oak table flew into Steadman's face and the shock galvanized him into action. His strength had returned and with it, old instincts. He threw himself to the floor and lay still, stunned by the piercing sounds around him: the screams of those hit by the deadly rain of bullets; the noise of the bullets themselves, thudding into the table, into bodies, ricocheting off stonework; the agonized gurgling of the old man, Dr. Scheuer, as his body was shredded, blood vomiting from his mouth in an explosive stream.

Steadman saw the old man still held the spear aloft in one hand, but it suddenly skidded from sight as his wrist was shattered. Dr. Scheuer fell to his knees, then slowly toppled forward, his head striking the floor inches from the investigator. For the first time, Steadman was able to see the old man's eyes, as they stared into his, wide but with no disturbing force emanating from them; just the inanimate stare of the dead, even though the body twitched and seemed alive.

The hail of bullets continued, spraying the hall at random, a lethal, indiscriminate strafing. Steadman twisted his head and felt a flicker of recognition when he saw the man with the gun on the balcony above. But it couldn't be; it was an old man up there, his hair white, his hate-filled face lined and aged. His mouth was open and he seemed to be shouting, but the investigator could not hear him over the barrage of sound. A figure appeared next to the disheveled man and Steadman called out her name as he realized it was Holly. He saw her try to snatch the light machine gun, but the white-haired man held her off with one hand, continuing his vengeful onslaught.

He saw her quickly scan the room, fear in her face, and when their eyes met, he knew that fear was for him. Her lips formed his name.

A wild bullet suddenly stung the side of his hand, close enough to burn, but not enough to tear the skin. Pushing himself forward with toes and knees, he dived beneath the heavy table, drawing his legs after him. There were other bodies crouched there.

He watched the carnage around the hall from his place of safety, saw the running legs, the overturned chairs that tangled and tripped them, the bodies that suddenly slumped into view as they were hit. Booth was crawling toward the table, gun in hand, but staring straight ahead. He almost made it.

As he reached the shadow of the table his head suddenly jerked up, a look of astonishment on his face. A line of bullets had raked across his back, snapping his spine. He tried to turn and fire back, but his body collapsed and he rolled over, the gun pointing at the ceiling, his finger curling around the trigger guard and squeezing it uselessly. He lay there looking into the blackness overhead and waited for the pain to begin.

Steadman began to crawl toward the other side of the table and saw there were at least three others crouched in the darkness. It was the hugeness of the shape before him that told him the identity of one of the cowering men.

There was just enough light for Pope to see it was Steadman moving toward him. The fat man wasn't afraid, only angry that everything had gone so terribly wrong. He had just had time to see it was their prisoner, the Israeli agent, who was causing such havoc, before he dived for cover. They should have killed him as soon as they had captured him. He cursed Gant for his sadism, the sadism he disguised as ritualistic symbolism. Major General Cutbush was dead—Pope had seen him rise then fall across the table, arms outstretched—and so were many of the others. Talgholm. Ewing, Oakes—he'd seen them go down. Others he could see writhing around the floor, curling themselves into tight balls to avoid being struck again. Griggs had been one of the first to be killed and Booth had not made it to cover, so he, Pope, was on his own. These others—those not dead or wounded—were not fighting men, didn't even carry arms. Where was Gant? What had happened to him? It was only seconds since the firing had begun, but every fragment of time stretched into a bloody eternity. They had been foolish not to have kept some guards in the room. It was Gant who refused to allow them full knowledge of the Order. Now they were paying the price.

Pope reached inside his jacket pocket for the small gun, his hand fumbling in its haste. There would at least be some revenge.

Steadman accelerated his movements when he saw the big man reaching for the weapon. Unfortunately, he was too restricted and, as Pope drew the gun and aimed it at his head, Steadman realized he wasn't going to make it. It was at that moment that another body hurled itself into the table's shelter and staggered between Steadman and the MI5 man. Pope's gun went off and the body in front of Steadman twitched violently but remained poised on hands and knees; the power of the small firearm was not enough to topple its victim even at that close range.

The investigator went barging on, keeping the injured

man between himself and Pope. His shoulder hit the man just below his ribs and Steadman shoved hard, pushing him against Pope. Pope pumped bullets into his dying fellow member, wanting him prone so he could get a clear aim at the investigator. It was no use; the body was pushed into him, knocking him backward.

He struggled to prevent himself from being ejected from the table's protective cover and, as the body finally fell to the floor, he grinned with relief, aiming the gun once more. Steadman had abruptly changed his tactics. As soon as the body he had been pushing had slumped to the floor, he had swiveled his body around in order to strike out with his feet. He lay with his back against the stone floor and kicked with all his strength.

Pope, despite his great weight, went tumbling out into the open, rolling once with the force of the thrust. There was a lull in the shooting from above and the big man had a moment to reach his knees and aim the gun at the figure beneath the table.

The firing began almost at once and bullets flew off the stone around Pope. He whirled, this time aiming upward at the balcony, but bullets tore into him before he even had a chance to pull the trigger. He keeled over backward and tiny explosions ripped his obese body.

It was then that Steadman saw the shadowy figure emerge from behind the altarlike structure which shielded the room's blazing fire. The movement was fleeting, and whoever it was had ducked into the shadows of the hall. Steadman realized that the machine-gun fire was now in short bursts rather than the continuous onslaught of before. The shape appeared again, then plunged down into the stairwell that led to the door set in the room's wall. Before it disappeared completely, Steadman had time to recognize the hawklike features of Edward Gant.

He pushed himself from the protective cover and ran, leaping over Pope's recumbent form, tripping once but rolling with the fall, jumping into the stairwell and crashing through the open doorway below.

Holly screeched Steadman's name and tried to grab the machine gun at the same time.

The Mossad agent seemed to realize who it was below and his finger suddenly released the trigger and he swayed backward. Only the screams and moans of the dying filled the air now, but the atmosphere was heavy with the smell of death.

Baruch stiffened as though recovering his senses and once again, he aimed the machine gun at the twisting bodies below.

"No," Holly implored. "Leave them—please!"

He stared at her with uncomprehending eyes.

"We've got to stop the missile from being launched." Holly held his head between her hands to keep him looking directly at her, desperately wanting him to understand. "The missile will be launched soon. We've got to stop them."

A sadness swept over the Israeli. He tore his head from her grasp and surveyed the carnage he had created. When he turned to look at her once again, there was a hardness in his eyes and she knew the sorrow had not been for those he had just killed.

"How . . . long . . ."

She guessed his meaning and glanced down at her watch. She groaned. "We're too late. There's only four minutes left."

He gripped her arm. "Where . . . is the site? Where is it?" His grip tightened.

"Near the cliffs. It's too late, though; we'd never make it."

"Helicopter. All day . . . I have heard . . . a helicopter landing and . . . taking off. If we can find it . . ."

"Can you fly helicopters?" she asked, hope rising in her.

He nodded, then clung to the balcony for support. "Get me to it, quickly," he whispered.

Holly gripped him around his back, her shoulder beneath him. "Give me the gun," she said, and he handed it to her without any reluctance.

They staggered down the stairs, almost stumbling once

but Holly's determined effort saving them. She averted her eyes from the terrible scene below and prayed that those still alive would not try to stop them. She hated to kill.

Once again Holly called out Steadman's name, but there was no answer. She had seen him leap into the stairwell at the side of the hall and knew he had been chasing somebody—why else would he have broken cover? She longed to go after him, but the stairwell would only lead to the lower level of the house, and not to the outside. Her priority was to prevent the US secretary of state's jet from being blown to pieces. She said a silent prayer for the investigator and ignored the awful wrenching feeling inside her.

"This way," she said to the Israeli, pointing the gun into the shadows. "I think there's a door over there. It's in the right direction, anyway."

The pilot and the two guards who had been patroling the exterior of the house glanced nervously at each other. They had heard gunfire inside and were making toward the back entrance when a different sound, much farther away, had attracted their attention.

"What's that?" one asked, skidding to a halt with the others. Instead of going on toward the back door, they rushed to the corner of the house and peered inland, toward the estate's easterly perimeter. They were filled with dismay at what they saw.

"Oh, fucking hell," one said in a low voice.

Four helicopters, powerful light beams descending from them, hovered in the distance. They began to fly along the estate's boundaries where Edward Gant's private army was deployed and dropping what looked like small bombs onto the soldiers below. The three men realized they were gas cannisters as white vapor erupted from the ground. Lights suddenly appeared on the road leading down to the estate as vehicles began moving in.

"It's the bloody Army!" the pilot exclaimed. "We're under attack from the bloody Army!"

Even as he spoke, one machine broke away from the

action and came racing toward the house. The others began to settle on the ground and the three men saw figures
begin to pour from them. Above the whirring of rotor
blades they heard the crackle of gunfire.

"I'm getting out!" the pilot suddenly announced, whirl-
ing around and racing back to the Gazelle.

The two soldiers glanced at each other, their faces
white in the moonlight. Without a word, they turned and
chased after the pilot. "Wait for us," one of them called
out, "we're coming with you!"

The pilot was already in his seat and had set the chop-
per's blades in motion, thankful that the aircraft's engine
was still warm from its previous flight. The two soldiers
had almost reached him when the door of the house behind them opened and Holly Miles and Baruch Kanaan
staggered through.

The brightness of the moon gave Holly a clear picture
of the two running soldiers and the small four-seater helicopter they were headed for. She and Baruch had the advantage; the men had their backs to them and the pilot
was too busy with his controls to notice them.

She freed herself from the Israeli and raised the light
machine gun.

"Hold it!" she shouted and the running soldiers halted
dead in their tracks. They turned and one went down on
his knee aiming his standard machine gun at the two figures in the doorway.

Regretfully, she squeezed the trigger and the fast-firing
machine gun spewed its lethal dosage at the soldier. As he
fell, his companion threw down his own gun and ran to
the right, screaming back at Holly not to shoot. She let
him go.

The pilot inside his cabin was frantically increasing his
engine's power to give him lift and the machine was trembling around him. Holly shouted, ordering him to cut his
motors, but he didn't hear her over the noise of the whirring blades. She bit her lip and said, "Shit," then raised
the gun in both hands and sighted it at arm's length. Only
when she was sure of her aim did she squeeze the trigger;

she did not want to damage any of the Gazelle's machinery.

The pilot toppled from his aircraft, the short burst killing him instantly. He hit the hard landing pad with a dull thud.

Holly stole a quick look at her wristwatch, but the moon suddenly vanished behind a heavy black cloud and she failed to see its hands.

"Come on," she said to Baruch and pulled him toward her. "We don't have much longer."

Baruch took a deep breath. then pushed himself away from her and stood erect. "I will be all right." The words were spoken singularly, but there was a certain strength behind them. He began to move toward the helicopter, his legs stiff, as though he were consciously willing them to bear his weight.

Holly caught up and the wind tore at their bodies as if to hold them back; she held onto his arm to keep him steady. The moon suddenly burst through again and she took advantage of the light to have another look at her watch.

She swore silently. They would never make it. There were only thirty seconds to go.

TWENTY-TWO

*The German conscience is clear because
the blame for everything sinister, contempt-
ible, criminal and horrible that happened in
Germany and the occupied countries between
1933 and 1945 rests on Himmler.*

—WILLI FRISCHAUER

Darkness enveloped Steadman like black liquid. He had
fallen through the doorway at the bottom of the stairwell and continued his descent, for there were more stairs
on the other side.

The stone steps had scraped painfully at his limbs as he
had tried in vain to halt his tumbling fall. He reached the
bottom with stunning force and lay there, gasping to fill
his lungs with air again.

He managed to push himself to a sitting position,
groaning softly at the effort. He blinked and tried to see
into the blackness ahead but the only light was coming
from the doorway above and behind him, and that was
very faint. He reached out and felt nothing before him,
then waved his hand from side to side. It came in contact
with a wall to his left.

The wall was damp and he could feel the velvety
smoothness of moss. He rose to one knee, leaning against
the wall for support, and drew in a deep breath. Jesus, it
was freezing. Cold like a tomb.

He stood, cautious of broken limbs. The plunge had numbed him and he could not be sure he hadn't damaged himself badly. His legs supported him and he could move his arms around, so all he had suffered was some nasty bruising.

Keeping one hand against the wall, he moved out at right angles to it and stretched his other hand outward. The fingertips touched another smooth surface and he guessed he was in a fairly narrow passageway. He knew what lay behind him, so the only way to go was forward. Dropping his right arm, he inched forward, using his left to feel his way. It was an eerie sensation; at any moment he expected his hand to come in contact with human flesh, Gant lurking there, waiting for him in the dark.

The only sound he heard was his own harsh breathing and he briefly wondered what was happening above.

His hand came in contact with a wall running across the one he was following. He ran his fingers along it and felt it dip forward again. He touched a rough surface; there was a door in front of him. Holding his breath, he felt around for a handle, hesitated, then gave it a twist.

The handle was stiff, rusted by the dampness of the underground passage, but with extra pressure, it gave. Steadman pushed the door open slightly, listening for any sounds before he entered. Then he opened it fully and stood to one side.

A wave of icy air hit him and he shivered against it. It had been cold enough in the narrow passageway, but it was even colder ahead. A faint aroma reached his nostrils and it was familiar to him. Just a waft of—what? Oil, spices? It was too slight to be certain.

There was a diffused light coming from a point in the blackness ahead and the investigator narrowed his eyes to make out some shape or form. The light was too soft, though; it was just a dull hue against a black backdrop. For some reason, Steadman felt it was beckoning, inviting him to come closer. He fought down the inclination to go back the way he had come; he had to find Edward Gant. And kill him.

He stepped through the doorway and crept stealthily toward the light source, each step measured and slow. He stretched out his hands on both sides as he walked and neither made any contact with the walls. He was either in a wider passage or in a room of some kind, perhaps an antechamber. He drew nearer to the hazy light and realized it was being diffused by something, and when he was close enough to touch, he reached out, his fingers brushing against coarse material. It was a curtain and the light shone through the tiny apertures in its rough texture. Once again, he stood and listened, controlling his breathing, but unable to still the pounding in his chest. A small voice inside told him not to look, to turn away and run from whatever lay in wait on the other side of that curtain, that some things were better left unseen. The voice persisted, but he succumbed to the compelling fascination that had taken hold of him. It was as if there were no choice; he dreaded what might be there, but there was no denying its lure. Steadman ran his fingers over the rough, mildewed material, searching for an opening.

He found it slightly to his right and maneuvered himself so his eyes would be directly before it when he parted the curtains. He drew them open and looked into the strange chamber beyond, his pupils shrinking against the unimpeded light.

It was a circular room, the walls of stone shiny with damp. Recesses containing small, black crucibles in which green flames glowed were placed at regular intervals around the room's perimeter. It was these tiny green flames that gave the room its peculiar light, and the color suggested that chemicals or herbs of some kind were being burned. It explained the aroma that drifted along the passageway. A stone platform ran around the wall's edges and another door lay directly opposite to where Steadman was standing, steps leading down from it to the chamber's lower level.

The floor area was large even though the ceiling was comparatively low and, because of its shape and the higher-level walk around the sides, it had the appearance of a miniature arena. Twelve four-foot-high pedestals stood around the circumference at well-ordered points like stone sentinels gazing silently toward the room's center. And there, at the center, stood a solitary, high-backed chair.

It was facing away from Steadman so he could not see whether it was occupied, but kneeling six or seven feet from it was the shadowy form of a woman. The long, black flowing hair identified her as Kristina and Steadman could see she was clutching something rising from between her thighs, like a huge phallus. As he watched, she crawled forward holding the object before her, and placed it on the stone floor two feet away from the high-backed chair. She crawled back to her original position and began to sway on her knees, her arms stiff by her sides.

Steadman knew by its shape it was the Spear of Longinus she had put down before the chair and, as he prepared himself to enter the chamber, a fresh feeling of unease swept through him. Sounds came from the hermaphrodite's lips, but they were unintelligible, a wailing incantation. He closed his mind to his misgivings, forcing himself to ignore his frenzied imagination, and began to slip through the curtain.

It was then he became aware that he wasn't alone in the antechamber.

A sound from behind. A rustle of material? A scraping of a foot against the floor? He couldn't be sure. But as he turned, his back now to the curtain, he heard breathing. It came in jerky rasping sighs, as though whoever it was could no longer control its rhythm; and as he listened, it became even more agitated, louder, the air sucked in greedily and exhaled in short gasps.

Steadman felt momentarily paralyzed, wanting to move away from the curtain, knowing the dim light shining through must show his body in rough silhouette. The rasping grew louder and he peered into the darkness, trying desperately to discern a shape. It was no use, he could see nothing. But he could feel the warm breath on his face; and the cold fingertips that reached out to touch his cheek.

He staggered back from sheer reaction and hardly felt the knife blade slice across his stomach, the tip barely penetrating the skin through his shirt. He went through the curtain and his assailant came after him, the ritual dagger slashing at the air between them. The investigator fell but kept his body moving, twisting to his right, aware there was a drop onto the chamber's floor behind him. The tall figure of Edward Gant lunged and missed again, overbalancing and falling to one knee.

They both crouched, facing each other, Gant's eyes wild with malice and Steadman's cold with hate.

"I still have you, Parsifal. I can still destroy you," Gant hissed.

"You can try, you crazy bastard," Steadman replied, rising immediately and aiming a foot at the arms dealer's face.

Gant avoided the blow and rose more slowly, the silver dagger pointing at the investigator's stomach. He inched forward, his manner even more menacing because of its deliberation. Steadman backed away.

"Stay, Parsifal. You can't run from fate." Gant smiled, his face evil in the soft green hue. "My soldiers will take care of the Jew and the slut. They won't get far."

"It's all over, Gant, don't you understand?" Steadman's attention was directed more at keeping the blade at a safe distance than his own words. "There's too many dead up there. Important men. How will you explain their disappearance?"

"Why should I have to?" The familiar mocking look had returned to Gant's eyes. "No one knows they were here. Our associations have been quite discreet."

"But you've lost the power behind your organization."

Gant sneered. "They were only the nucleus; there are others equally revered only too eager to take their place. All we have suffered is a setback."

"Another setback, Gant? Like the war?" The mockery now in the investigator's attitude had the desired effect.

Gant screamed with rage and leapt at his quarry, just as Steadman reached for the burning crucible in the recess he had been trying to reach. His hand encircled the hot metal and brought it from its resting place in one swoop, smashing it into the side of Gant's face as he advanced. The arms dealer screamed again, this time in pain, as the hot, burning oil poured into his face and down his neck. The dagger embedded itself in Steadman's arm and was jerked free again when the arms dealer staggered away.

Steadman cried out with the sudden tearing pain, but he had the satisfaction of knowing his assailant's wound was far greater. Gant had dropped the dagger and was slapping at his face, trying to dislodge the fiery oil that was sizzling into his skin. Small dots of fire were spattered over his jacket and shirt, but he ignored them for the greater pain in his face. Steadman saw oil had splashed onto Gant's nose and it was melting like wax, a pink stream flowing over his tortured lips. The investigator flinched as the naked bone and gristle beneath the artificial organ was exposed, but he felt no pity for the injured man.

Even in his agonized state, the arms dealer's virulent hatred for the investigator and the force he symbolized rose to the surface like a bubbling volcano. He had known great pain before, and had learned to keep one part of his mind secure from its distracting influence. With one eye only, the other seared by the oil, he searched for the fallen dagger. It was lying close to his left foot and he quickly stooped, screeching against the intense heat in his flesh.

Steadman saw his intention and stepped forward, his right arm outstretched, reaching for the weapon.

Gant was faster. He picked up the silver dagger and began to bring it up, the wicked point aimed at the stooped investigator's chest. Steadman grabbed at the wrist holding the knife and deflected its direction, using his own strength to continue the upward arc. The blade sank up to the hilt into a point just below Gant's breastbone. He stared disbelievingly at Steadman, his fingers still curled around the dagger's handle, the investigator's hand still gripped around his wrist, and there was a moment of absolute silence between them. One side of Gant's face was popping and blistering, a scorched eyelid covering one eye; the gaping wound where his nose had once been was weeping fresh blood. And then the arms dealer screamed and fell forward, his chest coming to rest against his knees, the dagger's hilt between them, his forehead touching the cold stone floor as though he were paying homage to the victor. Blood gurgled up from his throat and created a thick, red pool around his head, and he died in that position, his body refusing to topple onto its side, escaping gas from his abdomen taking any last shred of dignity from his dying.

Steadman stepped away to avoid the spreading pool and leaned against the wall, shock and weariness overcoming him. He looked down at the slumped body and felt no regret nor any gladness that the man was dead—only relief that it wasn't himself crouched there.

The throbbing in his arm reminded him of his wound. He touched a hand to his injured limb, flexing it at the elbow and wincing as the pain flared. It wasn't too bad, though; he could still lift his arm, so no muscles had been torn. He glanced back at the dead arms dealer. Was it all over? Had the death of Gant signified the end of the new Reich, or was the net too widely spread, already too powerful to falter just because its leader had been killed? There would be chaos upstairs, the injured and the dying screaming for attention, Gant's soldiers searching for Holly and the man she had been with—had it been Baruch? Perhaps they were already dead. The idea that Holly might have been shot filled him with a new desperation. He knew she had lied to him, that somehow she was deeply involved in the whole affair, and he was angered by the deception; but stronger feelings overrode that anger, feelings he had thought burned from him with the death of Lilla long ago.

He had to go back and find her even though it was probably hopeless. He turned toward the curtained doorway. It was finished down here. The arms dealer was dead, there was nothing left. It was over.

But the sudden stillness, the sudden thick, cloying odor, the sudden drop in the already cold room's temperature, told him it was not over. Not yet.

The presence seemed to be everywhere, filling the gloomy underground chamber, and it was a familiar thing to Steadman now. The same feeling of intense pressure, the awareness that something unseen had manifested itself. Unconsciously, the investigator had backed himself against the curved wall, his eyes darting from left to right, searching the chamber, trying to *see* the presence and not just perceive it. They came to rest on the figure in the center of the room.

The hermaphrodite was rigid, no longer swaying, no longer moaning. Kristina's lips were open wide as though mouthing a silent scream of agony; her eyes were tightly closed. She was still in a kneeling position before the high-backed chair, and the ancient spearhead lay on the stone floor where she had placed it. It seemed to quiver slightly, as though a current were running through its black metal, and Steadman felt rather than heard its vibration. He knew he had to take it from her, away from that dark room, away from the forces that were using its power . . . and he wondered at himself for believing such things.

Sounds seemed to be swirling around the circular chamber, soft voices that laughed and called, building to a crescendo as they had in the room above. The crucibles were burning black smoke and the wind swirled the smoke around the room, weaving dark patterns in the air, and Steadman imagined the shapes were lost spirits, twisting and writhing in a secret torment. Cold air brushed against his face, ruffling his hair, tearing at his clothes, seeming to beat against him, forcing him to raise an arm to protect his eyes, willing him to fall, to cower against the wall. Abruptly it ended, and silence returned to the underground chamber.

Only *the presence* remained.

The investigator forced himself away from the wall, dropping to the lower floor level, crouching for a moment. He retched at the overpowering stench, the terrible smell of corruption, and his body felt leaden, the weakness spreading through him, drugging his brain, dragging him down. He tried to rise and staggered against one of the small pillars set around the arena. He saw the metal plate on the stone pillar, bare of any inscription, and he suddenly knew the reason for the twelve pedestals facing the room's center: they would bear the ashes of the members of the new Teutonic Order as each member died. How he knew was no mystery to him; the presence had made him aware. It was telling him the truth of the spear's legend, the power the holy relic held, the power that could be used for good or evil. It taunted him, cursed him, reviled him. And it feared him.

The knowledge that he could be feared drove Steadman on. He stumbled across the room he now knew was a place of the dead—a crypt—feeling his energy draining from him, forcing himself onward to reach the spear, resisting the urge to lie down and rest, just for a moment, just for one sweet second.

He fell, and began to crawl, one hand before the other, one knee forward then the other, one hand, one knee, one hand one knee . . .

Kristina watched him, a tremor running through her body with a ferocity that made her shape blurred. Her mouth was still wide, and black smoke from the low flames in the crucibles entered her throat, descending into her lungs, filling her.

Steadman was near the spearhead, his hand reaching out, meeting a force that pushed his grasping fingers away. He looked up at Kristina and her eyes were straining against their sockets as she stared down at him, the pupils glazed yet strangely filled with life. Her body convulsed once, twice, became rigid again, her back arching but her gaze still on him. One more convulsion, this time even more violent, her hair crackling with the tension, her grimace stretching her lips and tearing them in several places. Then, with a long rattling exhalation of air, she fell backward, and life was drawn from her body.

Steadman closed his eyes and rested his head against the cold floor for a brief moment, wanting to stay there, to sleep and so take himself away from the malevolent force in the chamber. He resisted, knowing to succumb would mean his death. Forcing his eyes open again, he saw the slumped form of the hermaphrodite, her tortured face mercifully turned away from him. He twisted his head, not wanting to look at the miscreation, and his eyes fell on something far worse. He faced the husk sitting in the high-backed chair.

The rotted corpse wore the faded uniform of the Nazi Schutzstaffeln: the brown shirt and black tie, the tunic with three silver-thread leaves enclosed in an oak-leaf wreath on each lapel, the sword belt with ceremonial dagger attached, the cross belt passed beneath silver braiding on the right shoulder, the swastika armband on the sleeve, the breeches tucked into long jackboots. On its head was the silver-braided cap with the Death's Head emblem at its center. The whole uniform was covered in a fine layer of dust and hung loosely over the still form, as if the body had shriveled within it.

It sat upright as though locked in position, and Steadman's horrified gaze traveled up from the jackboots, across the body, to the shrunken head that stared sightlessly across the dark chamber. The flesh on its face was stretched taut, grayish cheekbones clearly showing through huge festering rents in the skin alive with tiny white moving shapes. The yellow skin at the throat sagged over the shirt collar, a shriveled sack resembling a balloon that had been punctured. The lower lip had been eaten away, revealing an uneven row of teeth stumps, and white, wispy hair clung sparsely to the upper lip. The face appeared chinless, as though the jawbone had receded back into the throat. One ear was missing completely, while all that remained of the other was a remnant of twisted, dried flesh. Thin strands of white hair hung from beneath the cap, whose peak fell low over the forehead, several sizes too big.

Peculiarly, pince-nez glasses were stuck firmly against the bridge of the nose as though permanently glued there, and one eye had escaped from its retaining socket and pressed against a lens. The tip of the nose was missing but the rest, although wrinkled and pitted, was intact. As Steadman watched, something black crawled from a nostril and scurried down the lower lip into the gaping mouth, disappearing from sight.

The investigator's stomach heaved and he could no longer control the bile that rose in his throat. It poured from him in pain-wracking convulsions, steam rising in the deeply cold air. He pushed himself away, away from his own sickness and away from the vile, stinking creature they had kept embalmed in the underground crypt.

He knew, without any doubt, whose mummified body it was: the Gestapo uniform, the pince-nez, the remnants of a moustache—their Reichsführer, Heinrich Himmler. The stupid, demented bastards had kept his body all these years!

He shook with the horror of it. They had continued to worship not just his memory, but his physical body as well, hiding it here, a corrupted husk of dried flesh, an abomination which they could idolize as though he were still there to lead them!

He looked at the skeletal hands resting on the cadaver's lap, withered and yellow, conscious that they had written the orders which had sent millions to their deaths: the hands of a clerk, the hands of a murderous butcher. And as he looked at them, the fingers began to move.

"Oh, sweet Jesus," he said as the head slowly swiveled around to look down at him.

TWENTY-THREE

And the devil that deceived them was cast into the lake of fire and brimstone, where the beast and the false prophet are, and shall be tormented day and night for ever and ever.
—THE REVELATION OF ST. JOHN
THE DIVINE 20:10

"Quickly. In which direction is . . . the launching site?" Baruch's voice was raised so it could be heard over the sound of the Gazelle's engine and the whirring blades overhead.

"It's too late, Baruch. There're less than twenty seconds left," Holly shouted. She sat next to the Israeli in the small cockpit, tugging at his arm to make him understand.

"Just point," he commanded, and she did so immediately.

"Toward the cliffs . . . there, you can just make it out in the moonlight . . . that bushy area!"

Baruch weakly moved the collective pitch lever upward and the helicopter began to lift; he pressed the foot pedals, changing the pitch of the tail rotor blades to swing the machine around so it faced the direction they wanted to go. It was a jerky ascent and the Israeli concentrated his mind on controlling the engine power with the twist-grip throttle, thinking only of flying, shutting the nightmare from his mind. The machinery around him, the smell, the noise, brought him back to the world of the normal and he adjusted the cyclic control stick to speed the helicopter toward the cliff tops.

Dark clouds scurried through the night, hiding the bright moon for long seconds, blacking out the land below them.

"I've lost it!" Holly cried, her head craned forward to look through the cockpit's plastic dome. "I can't see a bloody thing down there!"

Baruch felt himself spin and he knew he had hardly any strength left. "It . . . it must be somewhere . . . below us. I will keep to this area."

"It's no good Baruch. Even if we find it, what can we do? They'll be under cover down there. This gun won't stop them."

The Israeli was silent, his head beginning to loll down onto his chest. The helicopter began to weave dangerously close to the ground. Suddenly, the moon appeared again and the grassy slope below was bathed in its silvery light.

Holly gripped the Israeli's shoulder. "Over there! The small building—the outhouse! It's near there. Yes, I can see it, that circle of undergrowth. They've cleared the opening."

Baruch's head jerked up and he looked in the direction the girl was indicating. The helicopter veered toward the spot and Holly was thrown back against her seat. They reached the shaft within a matter of seconds and Baruch hovered the machine before it.

Without turning toward his companion he yelled, "Jump!"

Holly regarded him with astonishment. "What are you going . . . ?"

"Jump!" His voice had reached a screech and he shoved her roughly toward the door at her side. Then she realized his intention and knew it was the only way.

"Get out! Now!" Once more he pushed her, and this time she reached for the handle and threw the small side door open. She tumbled to the soft grass eight feet below and lay flat, unhurt but the wind knocked from her. She raised her head just in time to see the helicopter surge forward, hover for a brief second, then plummet down into the deep, brush-surrounded hole in the grassy slope.

Major Brannigan waited patiently for the second hand to reach the appointed time, his body and brain keen with the excitement of a military operation that would alter the course of history. He and his staff were tucked away in a small alcove set in the side of the deep circular shaft, a thin metal partition erected at the alcove's entrance to protect them from any back blast of the missile. The sound of crashing waves was driven up from the beach by the wind. along a winding tunnel, and the sea tang was strong in Brannigan's nostrils.

He quickly looked over the metal barrier's top to check visually that everything was in order. The stone staircase built around the shaft's circumference was free of personnel, the missile, bathed in a dim red light, was poised, waiting for its thrust into the sky. The surface-to-air missile stood only ten feet high and resembled the Soviet Goa in design. but it had been manufactured in Edward Gant's own weapons factory, and to his specifications.

"Broad Band Jamming in action?" he asked over his shoulder.

The technician seated at the control unit gave him a thumbs up and was immediately relieved that the major had his back to him. Such informal gestures were frowned upon by the stiff-backed officer. "All's fine, sir," the technician answered quickly. None of the nearby radar stations dotted along England's southwest coast would pick up the missile's flight path.

"Target on screen?"

"On screen and our beam locked in."

Brannigan grunted with satisfaction. Their missile would home in on the US secretary of state's jet like a needle drawn to a magnet. They knew the exact flight path and time schedule thanks to Cutbush. He looked up at the circular area of sky, the inconsistent moon a silver bright circle encompassed by the larger black circle of the shaft's entrance. He listened intently for a moment. He thought he had heard the whirring sound of rotor blades, but the crashing sea echoing up the long cave and swirling around the shaft's walls made it impossible to be sure. He glanced down at his watch. No time for pondering now. Only five seconds to go.

"Right," he said, crouching down.

The technician was intent on the dials in front of him, his finger poised over a particular button. He had his own timer and that alone would give him the signal to press the button and not an order from the major. Two of Gant's special militia stirred uncomfortably behind the technician; they didn't like their confinement with the missile, even though they had been assured there was no possible danger.

"Three. Two . . ." Brannigan's index finger ticked the seconds away on his knee. ". . . One. Let her go!"

The technician's finger stabbed at the button as Brannigan spoke and, on the other side of the metal screen, the surface-to-air missile roared into life, vapor pouring from its base and filling the sunken cavern with its flames.

Just as it began its ascent, Major Brannigan looked up through the gap between the top of the screen and roof of the alcove, and had time to frown and wonder what the huge object blocking out the round circle of moonlight was before the helicopter plunged down the shaft and met the missile on its way out.

There was not even time for the men inside the deep well to scream their terror as the explosion created a massive ball of fire which swept around the shaft, filling it completely, and searing their flesh and bones to charcoal.

Steadman stared at the obscenity in the chair and felt every hair on his body stiffen, a coldness running up his back and clamping itself against his neck. His skin crawled with revulsion and the urge to urinate was almost irresistible. He tried to push himself back, to get away from the decayed creature, but his strength was drained, there was no power in his muscles. Kristina's energy had been taken completely by this dead thing; she had not had the power to control its ravenous demands and now it was feeding off her psyche, had become a living entity. Now it was drawing on his, Steadman's spirit, sucking the life from him as it had sucked Kristina's.

The head leaned forward, and Steadman shuddered as tiny white crawling worms were dislodged from the cavities in its cheeks. He saw one shaking, skeletal hand reaching down, flesh flaking from the fingers, and he drew in his breath at the thought of being touched by it. But the hand was stretching down toward the stone floor and he realized it was reaching for the ancient spearhead lying near the jackbooted feet. Steadman knew, beyond all doubt, that if the monstrosity grasped the spear it would derive more strength from its strange power, and the weapon would once again be used against him, used to take his life.

With a cry of desperation, the investigator lunged forward and grabbed the spearhead just as the corpse's fingers curled around it. As he pulled the ancient weapon away, one of the creature's fingers fell to the floor, the rotted skin and brittle bones unable to resist the sudden movement.

Steadman drew the spear to him, clasping it to his chest in both hands. He felt new strength coursing through him and though the pressure still drugged his brain, he was able to fight against the sensation, was able to rise from the floor and stagger away from the moving carcass. He backed away, stumbling over the dead body of Kristina, losing his grip on the spearhead, feeling the weakness again, crawling after the talisman, gripping it tightly, turning to see the dead thing rising from the chair and walking toward him, one arm raised, mouth gaping open, willing him to return the spear, urging him to come back and be embraced.

Steadman screamed and staggered to his feet. He found the stairs on the opposite side of the chamber's curtained entrance and clambered up them, the weakness making his movements slow, his footsteps leaden. He reached the door and slammed against its rough surface, one hand scrabbling madly for the handle, sensing the figure was behind, mounting the stairs, reaching for him.

He pulled at the handle, but the door was locked. He half collapsed against it and, as he sank to his knees, he saw a rusted iron key projecting from the lock. He tried to twist the key, but it was jammed and his strength was useless. A shadow fell over him and he refused to turn around, too frightened to look into the corrupted face again, knowing the sight would paralyze him with its closeness. The foul smell swept over him, drawing his senses with its stench, and he wanted to close his eyes, to roll himself into a ball and hug himself tight.

Instead, he dropped the spear and used both hands to turn the key, praying to God the mechanism would be released. His hands and arms shook with the exertion, but he felt the lock give, slightly at first, only a half turn, and then completely. He swung the door open as a hand grasped his shoulder and he pulled himself away from the deathly grip, scooping up the ancient weapon as he stumbled through into the black passage beyond.

There was no light. Only the freshness of the air drew him on, for it had to come from aboveground, from the world of the living. He had no idea how long the passage was for he could see nothing ahead, only total darkness. Soft, tenuous material clung to his face and he thrashed wildly at the unseen cobwebs, smashing through them, revolted by their touch. His flesh crawled as tiny legs scurried across his cheek, and he slapped the spider away, shuddering at the sensation as its fragile body popped against his face. The floor was wet and he slipped, crashing painfully to his knees, his hand reaching out and scraping down a slimy wall. He turned his head as he rose and saw the corpse silhouetted in the doorway, a black shape growing larger as it moved forward. Then the door, urged by the breeze flowing along the passageway, slammed shut, and he knew the husk was in the darkness with him.

A sudden muffled sound came to his ears, the noise of

a distant explosion, and the earth beneath his feet seemed to tremble with its force. He slipped again before he had fully risen, and heard the metal of the spearhead clang against the wall, nearly falling from his grasp. He gained his feet and forced himself on, a sudden thought bringing him to an abrupt halt. He wasn't sure in which direction he was headed. In the panic-stricken moment of rising he had lost his bearings; for all he knew he was running straight back into the decomposed arms of the corpse. He held his breath and listened.

A shuffling noise to his left sent him scuttling away, once again using his hand as his only guide forward. The slowness of his actions taunted him, but he could not make his limbs move any faster. It was only his greater fear of what stalked him that made him progress at all. When he stumbled into the stone steps ahead, it was his own lethargy that prevented any serious injury. The freshness of the air drifting down seemed to confirm that the stone steps led outside. Steadman began to climb, his breath escaping in short, sharp sobs.

As he climbed, the effort became greater, as though the creature below were using a stronger force to prevent him from reaching the surface. He fell against the stairs, too tired to move, too exhausted to try, and the shock of clammy, cold fingers entwining themselves around his exposed ankle made him scream again, sending the blood pounding around his system, releasing the adrenaline that sent him crawling upward, tearing himself free from the loathsome grip.

The husk that had once been a living being followed.

The stairs ended abruptly and Steadman knew he had reached ground level. A thin silvery bar laying horizontally before him made him halt; then he realized it was moonlight—beautiful, silver moonlight—shining beneath a door. With an exclamation of hope, he rushed forward, crashing against the wooden structure in his haste. But this door, too, was locked. And this time, there was no key in the lock.

He looked around the room, searching for something

with which to pry open the door, but the silver bar sub-
denly vanished as clouds obscured the moon's rays. He
groaned with frustration and footsteps made him look
toward the stairway he had just emerged from. Even
though he could not see in the dark, he knew the corpse
was mounting the steps, was near the top, its head level
with the room's floor. He turned back to the door and
banged against it with the spearhead, striking out in anger, fear, dread. The sound of the metal against wood
brought him to his senses: he was holding the tool for his
escape in his own hands.

He felt again for the lock, then moved his hand to the
right, feeling for the gap where door joined frame. He
found it and inserted the spearhead's tip into the narrow
gap, pressing his whole body against the rest of the blade,
praying it wouldn't snap with the force. Fortunately the
wood was rotted and the lock none too strong.

The door flew inward with a sharp cracking sound and
fresh night air flew in as though to do battle with the
nauseating stench of the thing that was now on the top
step. Steadman rushed through the door and the cruel
wind whipped at his body, unbalancing him in his weakened state. He went down and, in a night of bizarre
sights, his eyes focused uncomprehendingly on yet another. In the darkness ahead, huge flames leapt into the
sky, flames that seemed to spring from the very earth. It
acted like a beacon to him, for it was light among total
darkness.

He clutched the spear to his chest as the corpse appeared in the doorway of the strange, vaultlike building,
the black uniform now blood-red in the glow from the
fire. Steadman sensed that this creature—this abomination—wanted not just him but the spear also. It needed
the spear to exist.

He lurched to his feet, the drugging sensation making
his head reel. He staggered toward the flames, the corpse
of the Reichsführer following, the wind tearing strips of
parchment skin from its body, revealing the bones beneath.

The grass beneath Steadman's feet was soft, sending new life into him as though the earth was trying to help him escape the unnatural thing. The fire was close and he swayed like a drunken man toward it, feeling its heat, welcoming its attack on the abnormal coldness behind him. His legs were in quicksand, but he forced them on, each step a single battle, each one taken, a new victory. He finally reached the brink of the pit, swaying dangerously before it, the heat singeing his hair and eyebrows, his skin reddening and beginning to scorch. He turned his back to the inferno and faced the advancing demon, knowing he could run no farther, that if he could, he would drag the thing down with him into the depths below, back to the hell it had risen from.

Then the creature was before him and he was gazing into one sightless eye, the pince-nez torn away by the wind, the eye that had rested against the lens hanging down onto the fleshless cheek. The mouth was open wide as though the creature was screaming at him, but no sounds came from the lipless gap. Loose skin hung in flaps, breaking away, flaking into swirling dust. The corpse of Heinrich Himmler raised its withered arms to take Steadman in its embrace, the skeletal hands reaching behind the investigator's neck to draw him forward, to touch its face to his. And Steadman was powerless to resist, mesmerized with horror, feebly trying to twist his head away as the skull came forward, a small cry of terror his only sound.

He felt his senses swimming, and though he turned his head, his eyes refused to look away from the terrible face. For a moment, he thought he saw the images of Edward Gant and Kristina in the hideous features, screaming out at him from their new-found torment. The skull seemed to grow larger, to fill his vision completely, the eaten-away features sharp in detail. He knew the creature wanted to drag him back to the crypt, to take his will and exist on it. The thing pulled at him and Steadman was powerless to resist.

The ravaged head suddenly burst apart in a hail of bullets, exploding into a fine powder, the remnants toppling from the corpse's body and rolling in the grass at its feet. Steadman drew back and felt his strength return, surging through his body till every nerve end tingled with the sensation of it. He saw Holly on her knees no more than four yards away, her arms stretched before her, the gun she held in both hands aimed at their swaying figures. He called out her name, the relief of seeing her alive almost too much for his battered emotions, and her face was a mask of fear and incomprehension.

Inexplicably, the headless corpse remained erect, the hands having dropped from Steadman's neck to its side. It stood like a statue, the howling wind whipping at its clothing and threatening to disintegrate the frail body completely. Lights in the distance distracted Steadman for an instant and the crackle of gunfire came faintly to his ears, telling him it really was all over for Edward Gant's macabre new Order. He saw figures scurrying around the house and heard shouted commands, the breaking of glass as they forced their way into the building. Other figures had broken off from the main body and were hurrying toward them, toward the blaze.

He felt the vibration running through the spearhead and looked down, the power from its black metal seeming to course along his arms, penetrating his bloodstream. Then he felt the weakness again, the dragging sensation of energy being drained from him, siphoned from his body by a magnetic force. He fought against the sensation, against the power from the spear. The headless figure before him reached out, the withered fingers grasping his wrists, and Steadman felt the strength in his arms begin to leave him, to flow from the spear into the body of the dead Reichsführer.

Steadman screamed in rage, pulling away from the corpse, twisting his arms to break the grip. He staggered and the corpse lurched forward, almost toppling onto him. The investigator turned his body, the heat from the fire burning into his face again, his eyes narrowing with its intensity. In a last desperate effort, and with the agonized cry of the near defeated, Steadman raised the ancient weapon and plunged it down at the figure's chest, aiming at the heart that had long ceased to beat. The spearhead sank deep, seeming to melt into the rotted flesh. The screech that tore into Steadman's mind was from a tormented creature, a piteous soul suffering the final torture.

Steadman pressed the spearhead in even deeper, pushing the body back toward the flames, ignoring the fresh screams that came from it, closing his mind to its beseeching, wailing cries. They were at the edge of the pit and he saw smoke rising from the black uniform as it began to smolder. The pain was too much; Steadman knew he would soon collapse with it. But then the body was over the edge, the jackbooted feet scrabbling against the shaft's side, falling away from him, a black shape disappearing into the inferno below, to be devoured by the fires. Consumed into nonexistence.

Steadman swayed on the brink, the full power of the spear now flowing through him. Something had made him cling to the holy weapon as the corpse had fallen away from it, something that had told him he was now the bearer of the ancient talisman, that he now held the key to revelations sought by those who yearned for power and glory. In the flames he saw a mighty battle taking place, a cosmic war between hierarchies of Light and Darkness, a mighty struggle between Good and Evil powers to control the destiny of mankind. It waged before him, a battle that was eternal, neither in the past nor in the future, but always in the present.

Holly screamed his name, seeing his body sway on the edge of the pit, knowing his skin was already being seared by the fire. She tried to reach him but found it impossible to move. She could only watch as he raised his arms above his head, holding something that had a tapering point, something wicked. A blue glow seemed to effuse from the object, an energy she could see clearly against the background of roaring yellow flames. It moved down his arms, flowing like incandescent water, encompassing his body, spreading to his lower limbs, and she saw his body quiver with some strange elation.

Holly called his name again and tried to crawl toward him in an attempt to drag him back from the fire. His body became rigid, and she wondered if he had heard her. She heard him shout as though in anger. He stretched his body back and with an effort that seemed to take all his strength, he hurled the object into the pit.

The flames swallowed the spear, and Steadman knew it would melt in the inferno. He prayed its powers would melt with it.

The fire suddenly lost its intensity, became cold, frozen yellow tentacles rising from the deep shaft, the wind scarcely influencing their straight path into the sky; and it was the chill that drove Steadman back from the edge, not the heat.

Holly ran to him and for a moment his eyes were strange, looking down at her as though he did not know her, as though he did not know the world she was in. Then recognition flooded back and he held her to him in a grip that threatened to crush her; but she held onto him, returning the pressure, loving him and feeling his love.

The blazing heat returned, pouring from the pit like an explosion, and they moved back, away from its scorching blast. He leaned against her, now feeling the pain in his blistered face, the wound in his arm. But it was welcome pain, for it was real. It was something he could understand.

They held each other close as the first of the soldiers reached them, watching the flames rise into the sky, and they were suddenly aware of the distant droning of an aircraft in the deep, night air. The Marine commando wondered why the disheveled couple's upturned faces were smiling.